Praise for the "delectable"*

The Chocolate Frog F

"A Joanna Carl mystery will be a winner. The trivia and vivid descriptions of the luscious confections are enough to make you hunger for more!"
—Roundtable Reviews

"Delicious."   —Cluesunlimited

"The descriptions of the chocolates are enough to make your mouth water, so be prepared. . . . Once again, I enjoyed each page of the book and am already looking forward to my next visit to Warner Pier, Michigan."
—Review Index

The Chocolate Bear Burglary

"Do not read *The Chocolate Bear Burglary* on an empty stomach because the luscious . . . descriptions of exotic chocolate will have you running out to buy gourmet sweets. . . . A delectable treat."   —*Midwest Book Review*

"[Carl] teases with descriptions of mouthwatering bonbons and truffles while she drops clues. . . . [Lee is] vulnerable and real, endearingly defective. . . . Fast-paced and sprinkled with humor. Strongly recommended."
—I Love a Mystery

The Chocolate Cat Caper

"A mouthwatering debut and a delicious new series! Feisty young heroine Lee McKinney is a delight in this chocolate treat. A real page-turner, and I got chocolate on every one! I can't wait for the next."   —Tamar Myers

"One will gain weight just from reading [this] . . . delicious . . . the beginning of what looks like a terrific new cozy series."   —*Midwest Book Review*

"Enjoyable . . . entertaining . . . a fast-paced whodunit with lots of suspects and plenty of surprises . . . satisfies a passion for anything chocolate. In the fine tradition of Diane Mott Davidson."   —*The Commercial Record*

JoAnna Carl's Chocoholic Mysteries

THE CHOCOLATE KIDNAPPING CLUE (short story)

THE CHOCOLATE CAT CAPER
THE CHOCOLATE BEAR BURGLARY
THE CHOCOLATE FROG FRAME-UP
THE CHOCOLATE PUPPY PUZZLE
THE CHOCOLATE MOUSE TRAP

NEW AMERICAN LIBRARY
Published by New American Library, a division of
Penguin Group (USA) Inc., 375 Hudson Street,
New York, New York 10014, USA
Penguin Group (Canada), 90 Eglinton Avenue East, Suite 700, Toronto,
Ontario M4P 2Y3, Canada (a division of Pearson Penguin Canada Inc.)
Penguin Books Ltd., 80 Strand, London WC2R 0RL, England
Penguin Ireland, 25 St. Stephen's Green, Dublin 2,
Ireland (a division of Penguin Books Ltd.)
Penguin Group (Australia), 250 Camberwell Road, Camberwell, Victoria 3124,
Australia (a division of Pearson Australia Group Pty. Ltd.)
Penguin Books India Pvt. Ltd., 11 Community Centre, Panchsheel Park,
New Delhi - 110 017, India
Penguin Group (NZ), cnr Airborne and Rosedale Roads, Albany,
Auckland 1310, New Zealand (a division of Pearson New Zealand Ltd.)
Penguin Books (South Africa) (Pty.) Ltd., 24 Sturdee Avenue,
Rosebank, Johannesburg 2196, South Africa

Penguin Books Ltd., Registered Offices: 80 Strand, London WC2R 0RL, England

Published by New American Library, a division of Penguin Group (USA) Inc. "The Chocolate Kidnapping Clue" was previously published in the Signet anthology *And the Dying Is Easy. The Chocolate Cat Caper, The Chocolate Bear Burglary,* and *The Chocolate Frog Frame-Up* were previously published in separate Signet editions.

First New American Library Printing (Omnibus), December 2005
10 9 8 7 6 5 4 3 2

Copyright © Eve K. Sandstrom, 2005
"The Chocolate Kidnapping Clue" copyright © Eve K. Sandstrom, 2001
The Chocolate Cat Caper copyright © Eve K. Sandstrom, 2002
The Chocolate Bear Burglary copyright © Eve K. Sandstrom, 2002
The Chocolate Frog Frame-Up copyright © Eve K. Sandstrom, 2003
All rights reserved

NEW AMERICAN LIBRARY and logo are trademarks of Penguin Group (USA) Inc.

LIBRARY OF CONGRESS CATALOGING-IN-PUBLICATION DATA:

Carl, JoAnna.
  Crime de cocoa : three chocoholic mysteries / by JoAnna Carl.
    p. cm.
  Contents: The chocolate cat caper—The chocolate bear burglary—The chocolate frog frame-up—The chocolate kidnapping clue (short story).
  ISBN 0-451-21694-6
  1. McKinney, Lee (Fictitious character)—Fiction. 2. Detective and mystery stories, American. 3. Women detectives—Michigan—Fiction. 4. Chocolate industry—Fiction. 5. Michigan—Fiction. I. Title.

PS3569.A51977A6 2005
813'.6—dc22   2005052221

Set in Palatino and Cooper Black
Designed by Eve L. Kirch

Printed in the United States of America

CRIME de COCOA

Chocoholic Mysteries

JoAnna Carl

NEW AMERICAN LIBRARY

Dedicated to the wonderful folks at Morgen Chocolate, Dallas, with thanks for explaining how to make fine bonbons, truffles, and molded chocolates and for allowing TenHuis Chocolade to copy their product line.

CONTENTS

The
Chocolate
Kidnapping
Clue

People think working in a resort town is like one long vacation. And it might be, if the tourists would only stay home.

I stood behind the counter of TenHuis Chocolade ("Handmade chocolates in the Dutch tradition") and hated the girl on the other side. I'd been working for my aunt and uncle, Nettie and Phil TenHuis, for only a week, and this girl had been in every day, apparently with the sole objective of ruining my life.

Her name, according to her credit card, was Alana Fairchild Hyden. She would have been pretty if she hadn't been so thin. She was about my age—which was sixteen that year—and she had dark hair and big brown eyes, which she emphasized with liner, mascara, and shadow until they dominated her face.

Alana Fairchild Hyden was about the only teenaged customer TenHuis Chocolade ever drew, since Aunt Nettie and Uncle Phil's candy wasn't the kind you'd eat in the movies. Oh, they had some inexpensive items, like a milk chocolate sailboat on a stick, but most of their stock was luxury chocolates and fancy dipped fruits. One bonbon cost as much as two Hershey bars.

But Alana Fairchild Hyden came in every day and bought half a pound of bonbons and truffles, a different assortment every day. She did this, I'd decided, to torture me. She got this smirk on her face, and she went through the whole display case, pointing.

"Now what's that one?"

Since I was new, I'd have to consult the list. "Creamy, European-style caramel in dark chocolate."

"How about the one behind it?"

I'd look at the list again. "Raspberry cream."

"No, the one with the yellow dot."

"Lemon canache."

"Yuk! How about the white chocolate with the little nutty things on top?"

That one I knew, because it was my favorite. "Amadeus," I said. Then I winced. She'd goaded me until I was nervous, and that was when my tongue twisted itself into knots and the wrong word came out. "I mean, Amaretto."

Of course, Alana Fairchild Hyden laughed. " 'Amadeus'! How funny! How about the one at the back of that row?"

Back to the list. "Frangelico."

"Frangelico? Just what the hell is that?"

"I'll ask." I turned toward the big window that overlooked the sparkling white room where middle-aged women in white aprons and hair nets produced the chocolates.

"Oh, never mind! You'd think people would train their employees. Give me four of the fudgy ones and four square ones with the white centers. Then I'll have eight of the dark chocolate balls. The rummy ones."

Seething, I put her chocolates—four double fudge and four Bailey's Irish Cream bonbons and eight Jamaican rum truffles—in a little white box with "TenHuis Chocolade" in the corner in classy type, and I tied the box with a blue ribbon. I ran her credit card through the imprinter, then pushed the receipt and the card across the counter.

"Here's your crevasse card." I tried to pretend I'd said it right, but Alana Fairchild Hyden laughed.

"You are such a sketch!" she said.

I tried to look blank. Pleasant would have been more than I could manage. She went out, still laughing, leaving the shop empty, except for the other clerk, Lindy Bradford, and me.

"What a bitch," Lindy said.

I felt crushed, as well as angry. Alana Fairchild Hyden completely destroyed my confidence. It's just a stupid sales clerk job, I told myself, and I can't do it right because I can't talk like a normal person.

"Don't worry about it, Lee," Lindy said. "She acts rude just to cover up her own inferiority complex."

I gulped hard and decided it was safe to talk. "Who is she?"

"Oh, she's one of the Hydens. They have that big house at the lake end of Orchard Street. Her grandfather made his money building airplanes. My mother says her mother is trying to spend every cent her grandfather ever made. They're summer people."

In the week I'd been working at TenHuis Chocolade, I'd discovered there were three social classes in Warner Pier—locals, summer people, and tourists. Locals either lived there year-round, or they owned businesses there and spent most of the year in the area. Summer people owned homes—what us Texans would call "cabins," but what these Michigan people called "cottages"—and spent several months there each year. Tourists came for periods ranging from a day to a month and rented rooms in the motels, inns, or bed and breakfasts.

So Alana Fairchild Hyden was a "summer person," not a "tourist." I sighed. "I guess she'll be in every day until I leave in August."

"Who knows?" Lindy reached into the showcase and straightened the Italian cherry creams. "I feel kinda sorry for her, I guess. She always comes in alone." She shot me a sidelong glance. "Hey, three of us are going into Holland to the late show tonight. Ask your uncle if you can come. We'll be home by twelve-thirty."

"Not tonight," I said. "But thanks." Luckily, three people came in right then. I couldn't tell if they were tourists or summer people, but I was glad for the distraction. Not that I didn't appreciate Lindy acting friendly. I just wasn't ready to be friendly back. While Lindy told the new customers that we didn't carry candy bars, I stood there miserably and wished I was on the beach. Alone. Without the bag lady I'd seen that morning.

The beach was the best place to cry. That's why I resented sharing it, especially with a bag lady.

The bag lady had scared me. She looked like a homeless old hag, the kind you might see under a bridge in a big city. I hadn't expected to run into someone like that on a Lake Michigan beach, down the road from Aunt Nettie and Uncle Phil's house.

I kept telling myself she was harmless. But I still resented her. As I said— the beach was the best place I had to cry, and I didn't want to meet anybody.

For one thing, I had always lived on the Texas plains. I was used to lots of sky, and Michigan's tall trees made me feel closed in and choked up. But from the beach I could see Lake Michigan stretching west to somewhere beyond the horizon, and it was easier to breathe.

But all I wanted to do down there was sit behind a clump of beach grass and let the tears roll. I had a lot to cry about that summer. I'd lost my family and my friends and been exiled to work in a chocolate factory.

My privacy had gone at the same time. Now I was living with my Aunt Nettie and Uncle Phil, and the walls of their house—which had been built in 1904—were too thin to hide sniffling. If I cried in bed at night, Aunt Nettie would creep upstairs to be sympathetic. If I declined her sympathy— after all, she was almost a stranger to me—they sat downstairs and talked about how unhappy I was. I could hear every word. Why couldn't they leave me alone?

Then there was my stupid speech problem. Every time I opened my mouth the wrong word came out. So the last thing I wanted to do was talk to some scary old lady. I wanted to be alone, and the beach had seemed to be the answer.

I'd pretended I was planning to go out for track and told Aunt Nettie and Uncle Phil I had to run a mile on the beach every morning. I didn't go to work in the chocolate shop until one, when Uncle Phil went in, so that worked.

I would get up when they were eating breakfast—7:00 A.M. or some horrible hour. About seven-thirty Aunt Nettie would head for the factory. Aunt Nettie was a solid, heavyset woman with fair hair and light blue eyes. She was a descendant of the Dutch who settled West Michigan before the Civil War, and she would have looked right at home in wooden shoes and a winged cap. She supervised making the chocolates.

Uncle Phil was of pure Dutch descent, too, but he was one of these thin Dutchmen with a turned-up nose, the kind Rembrandt used to paint. He had a big desk in the corner of their bedroom, and after breakfast he'd go in there to do paperwork.

I'd wash the dishes, because my mother had told me to be a good girl and help Aunt Nettie and Uncle Phil. And as miserable as I was at their house, I didn't want them to send me back to Texas. This whole thing was my mother and dad's fault, and I didn't want to see them any sooner than I had to.

By eight-fifteen every morning I'd tell Uncle Phil I was going to the beach, and every morning he'd say, "Watch the traffic on the curve." I'd walk a quarter of a mile down the Lake Shore Road, looking carefully both ways before I crossed the road near the blind curve, and I'd turn at the sign that said PUBLIC ACCESS and slip and slide down the sandy path to the beach thirty feet below. Later in the day, I had discovered, the beach could be crowded. But that early the shoreline was still cloaked by the heavy shade from the trees on top of the bank, and there was rarely anyone but me around.

From the public area you could walk on the beach for at least two miles either north or south. Of course, the public area was only about a hundred feet wide, so for most of those miles you were on private property. I didn't think anybody would complain as long as I stayed at the edge of the water and didn't go near the fancy houses on the bluff above, the ones with the expensive views and the major engineering systems of walls and terraces needed to keep the lake from washing the houses away.

Uncle Phil was always telling me that the beach was different when he was my age. In those days, he said, most of the houses were smaller, not so fancy. They were owned by teachers, carpenters, factory workers—people who were willing to rough it in simple little cottages for the summer. Now the area had been taken over by millionaires, I guess. Uncle Phil had pointed out the biggest house—from the beach it looked like three stories of glass boxed in by redwood decks—and said it belonged to the president of the Lally Corporation. When I didn't act impressed, he told me they owned the company that made my favorite tennis shoes. Cool.

Aunt Nettie and Uncle Phil lived in a house that had been built by my great-grandfather, who was Uncle Phil's grandfather. It was on the inland side of Lake Shore Drive, so we couldn't see the lake. In Warner Pier that meant we gained points with the "locals," but lost points with the "summer people." It was a complicated system.

When I got to the beach I usually walked a quarter of a mile south to my hidey-hole, a niche behind some beach grass in front of the Lally house, and I hid and waited for the tears to come. Instead, on that particular morning this bag lady had walked into my life.

I was sitting with my knees up against my chest and my face down on my knees, and I didn't see or hear her until she spoke.

"Young woman," she said. "Are you all right?"

I scrambled up. For a minute I was sure one of the Lally family had come down, discovered a trespasser, and called the cops. Then I thought the woman must be a trespasser herself.

She looked like a bag lady because she was carrying a big brown plastic trash bag. She wore a hat, the limp-brimmed kind that you can throw in the laundry, but this one hadn't been washed lately. She had on a poplin windbreaker and blue jeans. The face under the hat was weathered, and her eyes were that faded blue that makes people look blind. She was old. Probably at least ninety. (Or that's what I thought when I was sixteen. Later I found out she was in her late sixties that year.)

The old woman shook the bag at me. "Are you all right?"

"Yes," I said. Suddenly I was afraid. She looked so scary, and we were alone on the beach. I blurted a question out. "Do you live here?"

She looked sharply at me.

"Am I trashing?" I said. "I mean, am I trespassing?"

A strange smile passed over the woman's face, like a cloud racing past the sun. "I suppose we're both trespassing, but as long as we stay on the beach and don't build a fire, the Lallys aren't likely to complain. And I certainly hope you're not trashing. Getting rid of trash is my goal in life. I only wish it were the Lallys' goal."

She bent, picked up a beer car, and chucked it into her sack. Then she gestured in the direction of the big house high on the bank above us. I looked up, and I could see a young guy standing at the window. He was staring at us, not moving. "That son of theirs is staying there alone—judging from the alleged music that blares over the neighborhood and from the cars that block the road. His parties overflow onto the beach. I find amazing things."

She looked at me narrowly. "You're sure you're all right? I always wonder about girls I find outside the Lally house. But you look healthier than the skinny little dark one I saw last week." Her weathered face scrunched up into a dried apple.

I looked at my watch. "I'm fine," I said. "I don't have anything to do with the Lally house. But I'm going to be late to walk. I mean, to work. I mean, I've got to get hum. Home." I jumped over a clump of beach grass to get past her, and I headed up the beach at a trot. Which showed how scared I was. I'd never have called Uncle Phil and Aunt Nettie's house "home" normally.

I guess I was panting when I got back to the house, because Uncle Phil asked me if anything was wrong.

"No," I said. "But there was an odd woman on the beach. She looked like a bag lady."

Uncle Phil laughed. "You must have run into Inez Deacon. She'll think that's hilarious."

"Who is she?"

"She's a retired teacher. She lives in that little gray house right before the curve. She had heart surgery several years ago, so the doctors told her to walk several miles a day. She picks up trash as she walks."

I thought about that. "I guess that's a good thing to do. But she looks sort of scary. Don't tell her I said so!"

"I won't. I'll introduce you when I have a chance."

The next morning, however, I introduced myself. I'd been hiding out behind the beach grass again, and this time Mrs. Deacon scrunched on the sand, so I heard her coming. My Texas grandmother—my dad was a Texan—insisted on teaching me old-fashioned Southern manners, so I came out and introduced myself.

"I wondered if you weren't Phil's niece," she said. "They were excited about having you up for the summer."

"They're being awful nice to me."

"Are you meeting any young people, Lee?"

"Well, there's Lindy Bradford. She works in the store."

"I know Lindy. She's no intellectual giant, but she's a nice girl."

"She's really cute."

"Yes, Lindy is cute, and she has a bubbly personality. Of course, she'll never have your looks."

I was astonished. My "looks" consisted of long skinny legs, a flat chest, narrow shoulders, and eyes and mouth so pale they might as well not have existed. If I had a good feature, it was my hair—a light blond that didn't need "touching up."

I must have gaped, because Mrs. Deacon frowned. "Surely your parents have told you you're going to be a beautiful woman, Lee. They've been remiss if they haven't. You're going to have the sort of looks that attract attention, and you should be prepared to deal with the problems that brings."

After that I adored Mrs. Deacon. I began to look forward to running into her. We'd chat about the birds on the beach and about the interesting rocks that the lake waves uncovered. Sitting on a driftwood log and looking out at those waves, I was able to tell her that my parents were getting a divorce, and that when I went back to Texas I'd be leaving the little town where I'd always lived and moving to Dallas, where my mother had a new job in a travel agency. I'd have to go to a new school that was eight times bigger than my old one, and I'd have to make all new friends. Mrs. Deacon assured me I would be able to do it, and for practice she suggested I accept the next invitation I got from Lindy. Sometimes Mrs. Deacon and I talked so long I didn't have time to hide behind the grass and cry.

Work began to go better, too. Uncle Phil discovered I could add right, even if I couldn't talk straight, and he started allowing me to balance the cash register when we closed at 9:00 P.M. I learned to pronounce the shop's name as "TenIce," which wasn't quite the way Uncle Phil did it, but was closer than "Tin-Hahs," the way my Texas mouth wanted to shape the word. I memorized all the bonbons and truffles, and I could rattle them off without saying "model Pyrenees," instead of "mocca pyramid" or "Midol liquor," instead of "melon-flavored Midori liqueur."

Except when the customer was Alana Fairchild Hyden. I couldn't say a word to her without stumbling over my tongue. Lindy knew how she affected me, and she tried to wait on her, but Alana would refuse to select something until Lindy was busy. Then she'd ask me a lot of questions in a loud voice and laugh when I goofed.

The last time she came in, I almost cried. After she left Lindy shook a fist at the door. "I hate that girl!" she said.

I parroted the advice Mrs. Deacon had given me. "I try not to waste my time hating her," I said, though a little voice inside admitted that I did hate Alana. "How does she get the money for all this candy?"

"Oh, her family's got all the money in the world, I guess. Her mother's in Europe this summer. With a boyfriend."

"Then who's she staying with?"

"I think there's a housekeeper."

"How does she eat that much chocolate and stay so thin?"

Lindy shrugged. "I don't know. Bulimia?"

The thought of someone eating the beautiful chocolates Aunt Nettie and the ladies worked so hard to make and then vomiting them up—well, it was nauseating. That made me feel a little bit sorry for Alana for real, not just pretending. But I almost wished she'd fall off the balcony of her family's big house and break her neck.

So I felt guilty the next day when I heard she'd been kidnapped.

There are no secrets in a town of twenty-five hundred, even when it grows by ten thousand tourists and summer people. The police and the FBI might keep Alana's kidnapping out of the newspapers and off the television, but the Hydens' housekeeper told the man from the lawn service, and within an hour everybody up and down Peach Street knew.

The housekeeper hadn't missed Alana until about 8:00 A.M., when she got a phone call demanding ransom. She thought the call was a prank until she found Alana's bed empty and her sports car sitting at the foot of the drive with the door open, the headlights switched on and the battery dead.

"My brother says he saw Alana in the Dockster at 2:00 A.M.," Lindy told me excitedly. "It looks like they snatched her when she got home."

"I guess Alana won't get her chocolates today," I said.

Lindy and I were silent after that. In a way I felt a kinship with Alana. Her mother had shuffled her off to the big house in Warner Pier and ignored her for the summer while she went to Europe with a boyfriend. My mother had shuffled me off to an aunt and uncle in Michigan to work in a chocolate factory while she started a new job and got a divorce.

The difference was that the Hyden housekeeper obviously didn't care what happened to Alana, and my aunt and uncle did care what happened to me. They didn't let me hang out at a place with a reputation like the Dockster's until 2:00 A.M. They didn't let me run wild with an expensive sports car. When I cried at night, they worried about me, even if it annoyed me. Even my mother and my dad, I admitted, each called me once a week, even though I knew neither of them had any money for long-distance bills that summer.

And like all the TenHuis Chocolade employees, I was allowed two pieces of candy a day. I ate them, and I was not tempted to vomit them back up.

Aunt Nettie, Uncle Phil, and even my mother and dad came out looking pretty good next to Alana Fairchild Hyden's family.

I tried to express this the next morning, when I met Mrs. Deacon on the beach, right under the Lally house. "I do appreciate Aunt Nettie and Uncle Phil," I said. "But it's hard to tell them. It seems like nothing I say comes out right."

"So write them." She picked up the remains of a small, white box, then turned to me and gestured with it. "If you can't tell people something face-to-face, then write it out. That way you can work it over until it suits you."

"Maybe."

"They'd be thrilled."

We might have gone on, but someone yelled at us from above.

"Get out of here!"

I looked up and saw the Lally boy leaping down the stairs toward us. The morning was cool, but he wore no shirt or shoes, just a pair of jeans. He was taking the stairs two at a time. His long, greasy hair was flying in the wind, and he continued to shriek at us.

"Scram! Get lost, you bitches! Get off our beach!"

Mrs. Deacon stood her ground, and I couldn't leave her. She merely looked at the Lally boy until he got to a little railed deck at the top of the final flight of stairs that led down to the beach. He stopped there, still cussing at us. Mrs. Deacon kept looking at him with a politely attentive expression, and he gradually quit talking.

"Young man, I wanted to thank you for omitting your usual music last night," she said.

"Get out," he said again. This time his voice was a low growl.

Mrs. Deacon nodded regally. She stuffed the little white box she was still holding into her trash bag, then stooped and picked up a beer can, revealing a blue ribbon that was embedded in the sand under it. She added the beer can and the blue ribbon to her trash sack, then walked slowly in the direction of the public access area, stopping to pick up more refuse—a soft-drink can, a package that had once held bratwurst, one flip-flop, a pleated candy cup, a potato-chip sack. I picked up a few things as well, and we meandered up the beach. I pretended I didn't notice that the Lally boy was still on the deck, glaring after us.

"He sure is rude," I said.

Mrs. Deacon shook her head. "I hate to think of what he's done to that house." We trudged up the path to the road, separated, and went to our homes, watching carefully for traffic on the blind curve.

The next morning was wet, but I wrapped up in a sweatshirt and a rain jacket and headed for the beach as usual. I was just getting near the blind curve when I heard the roar of a car's engine. It was drawing closer, and it sounded as if it were gaining speed. The sound scared me. Ahead I saw Mrs. Deacon come to the end of her driveway. She looked toward the sound, and she stopped, too, waiting for the car to pass. I jumped into the bushes and got clean off the road. Both Mrs. Deacon and I were being careful to give the roaring car all the room it needed.

When the car came around the curve I saw that it was an old model, big and boxy and some dark color. It was gaining speed. I stood still, braving the possibility of poison ivy in the bar ditch, and waited for it to go by.

I will never forget what happened next. As the car drew near Mrs. Deacon, it swerved, ran up over the edge of the road, and came up into her drive.

It hit Mrs. Deacon a glancing blow. She went flying into the air, arms and legs lopped out like a rag doll.

I'm sure I screamed, but I must have stood still. The next thing I remember the car had gone past me. Then I was running, running toward Mrs. Deacon and shrieking. "Help! Help! Help! Oh, someone! Help!"

Mrs. Deacon was lying in her own shrubbery. I had the sense not to touch her, and I ran to the nearest house, a neat white frame house between Mrs. Deacon's and Uncle Phil's. The woman who lived there called the ambulance, then got Uncle Phil, and the three of us waited for the sheriff's deputies and the rescue truck. I knelt beside Mrs. Deacon. I put my hand over hers, and I sobbed.

"He did it on purpose," I said. "He did it on purpose."

Later, at the Holland hospital, I repeated that to the sheriff, and he nod-

ded seriously. "I'm afraid you're right," he said. "The tread marks show that
the car went right up into the driveway, and there's no sign he tried to put
on his brakes. If you could just describe the car . . ."

But I couldn't say much about it. It was a big, old car and a dark color. I
hadn't gotten a look at the driver.

Mrs. Deacon was still unconscious when the sheriff came and told us
that they'd found a big, old, dark-colored car in a ditch a mile up the Lake
Shore Drive. It had a dent in the right front fender. Unfortunately, it was a
car that had been reported stolen an hour before Mrs. Deacon was hit.

"First that kidnapping, and now this," the sheriff said. "I tell you, Phil,
maybe we have too many summer people and tourists around here. The
tracks and all—well, it does look as if he stole the car and deliberately ran
Mrs. Deacon down. But why would anybody want to do that?"

At 6:00 P.M. Mrs. Deacon's daughter got there from Detroit, and Uncle
Phil and Aunt Nettie made me go home with them. I took a shower and
got in bed, and for once I didn't object to Aunt Nettie coming in and talking to me after I got in bed. Mrs. Deacon was her friend, too. We grieved
together.

"Why?" I said. "Why on earth would anybody want to hurt Mrs. Deacon?"

Aunt Nettie repeated the refrain. "Why, why in the world should something like this happen?"

Then I heard Uncle Phil come in the kitchen door. He was muttering angrily, and Aunt Nettie hugged me and went down.

Of course, I could hear every word she and Uncle Phil said. "What on
earth are you grousing about, Phil?"

"I went over to check Inez's house, the way I told her daughter I would,
and some dogs had gotten in her trash. They tore open some of those bags
she collects. I'll have to go back in the morning and pick up the rest."

"Oh, Phil! And after what happened this morning."

After what happened this morning.

Somehow the words electrified me. What happened this morning was
that somebody tried to kill Mrs. Deacon—and they might well have suc-
ceeded. And none of us could think of any reason for anybody to want to
harm Mrs. Deacon.

But one person had threatened her. The Lally boy. I didn't even know his
name. But he had run down the stairs and screamed at her, ordering the two
of us off his family's bit of beach.

Mrs. Deacon and I had walked along that stretch of beach every morning for weeks, and he'd looked down at us from his three stories of glass,
and he'd glared, but he'd never so much as come outside before. What had
we done the day before that made him so angry? What had been different?
And did this have any link to a pack of dogs tearing up the trash sacks that
Mrs. Deacon filled on the beach?

Had Mrs. Deacon found something on the beach that had caused the Lally boy—or someone—to attack her?

Well, I'd been with her when the Lally boy came down and cussed at us. I didn't see anything odd. Just potato chip sacks, beer cans, boxes . . .

Oh, lordy! All of a sudden I remembered, and I sat straight up in bed. There had been one odd thing. Actually, two odd things. Maybe three.

But the idea seemed too fantastic. If I told the sheriff, he'd think I was crazy. He'd have to get a search warrant to check it out. And he'd never have the nerve. He'd have to have good evidence before he could search the Lally house.

If there was just a way to prove my suspicions were right.

I pictured the Lally house, with its entire lake side one big wall of glass. And I decided that anybody who lived in a glass house would have no secrets at night.

Downstairs Aunt Nettie and Uncle Phil had moved into their bedroom, and then Uncle Phil turned on the shower—the loud, old shower with the pipes that knocked. I slipped out of bed and into clothes—some black jeans, a navy sweatshirt, and a heavy jacket. I tied a black scarf on my head, took my tennis shoes in my hand, and walked softly down the stairs. The shower would cover any noise I made.

I crept out the kitchen door, put on my shoes, and started for the beach at a run. I wasn't going near the Lally house. I was simply going to look at it from below.

I was terrified of course. The trees. Those tall, scary Michigan trees were being tossed by the wind and might be hiding who knows what. I walked right down the middle of the Lake Shore Drive, staying as far as I could from the threat of bushes and trees one either side of the road. When I got to the access path, I slid down it.

The moon was nearly down to the western horizon and was behind a layer of clouds. Its reflection made a path on the water, but it was a faint path. The lake surf was fairly high. Lake Michigan surf never gets like the Pacific, of course. But that night the waves were coming in fast, one right on the heels of another, and they were noisy.

I told myself that was lucky. If the Lally boy was outside, he wouldn't be able to hear me. And it was too dark for him to see me. However, I found out that I couldn't see him either. The house was lighted from top to bottom—all three stories—but from the beach I was looking up at it, and all I could see was ceilings. I'd have to get closer.

I eyed the stairs that led up from the beach. Did I dare go up them? Then I really would be trespassing.

I stifled a laugh. Trespassing? If I was right, the Lally boy had tried to kill Mrs. Deacon. What was trespassing compared to that? I started up the stairs.

The first dozen steps led up to the deck on top of the wall, the wall that was the first line of defense against the lake's winter waves. After that the steps were stone, and they switched back and forth, crisscrossing the terraced hillside. The whole flight must have been sixty feet high.

Each floor of the house, including the basement, had a deck overlooking the lake. As my head came up even with the basement floor, I stopped and looked in. I saw nothing. Nobody. The house wasn't wide, and I could see into every room. The entire lowest level was empty. I tiptoed on up the stairs, to the deck that was outside the first floor, again stopping with my head just over floor level, so that I could see in, but hoping that my low profile would help keep me invisible from inside the brightly lighted room. And then I saw the Lally boy.

Two rooms opened off that deck, and he was in the left-hand one, a large L-shaped room with a dining table in the narrow section. Living-room furniture in the larger section was grouped around a big stone fireplace. A door opened in the back wall of the dining area, and I could see kitchen cabinets and appliances through it. The area was a mess, as Mrs. Deacon had predicted. The living room had been decorated in a heavily rustic style, with animal heads on the walls, chairs made out of sticks of wood, and furry throws on the floor and the couch. Now every surface was covered with beer cans, and take-out sacks and pizza boxes were tossed under the dining table.

My first impression of the Lally boy was that he must be crazy. He was walking up and down, gesturing wildly, his face furious, talking to himself. I couldn't hear him; the noise of the waves and the thick glass windows blocked the sound.

Then he turned around and strode across the room. He reached over the back of a long, off-white couch that faced the fireplace, and he yanked at something angrily.

The head of Alana Fairchild Hyden appeared. He was holding it up by the hair.

I nearly had a heart attack. For a minute it looked as if her head had been severed from her body. Then she threw up her hand, and I realized with relief that she was alive. She'd been lying on the couch, and the Lally boy had reached down, grasped her hair, and yanked her to a sitting position.

As I watched, he swung his other hand back and slapped her face. He slapped it again. Then he let go of the hair, and she fell out of sight again.

Well, he might not have decapitated her, but she sure was in danger. I'd done a report on violence against women for social studies. "Escarole," I said, barely breathing the word. "I mean, escalate. The violence is likely to escalate."

I needed to get help quick.

I started to edge down the stairs, but the Lally boy suddenly swung around, crossed to the window, and looked out at the lake. He was staring right at me.

I froze. Then he turned his back, and I decided that he hadn't seen me. He walked back to the couch, but this time he didn't hit Alana Fairchild Hyden again. He simply stood looking at her. Then he walked out of the living room. Within a second or two he appeared in the other room that faced the lake.

It was like watching TV with the sound turned off. I could see clearly as the Lally boy walked slowly into the room—it was a luxurious bedroom— and crossed to the bedside table. He opened a drawer and looked inside. Then he slowly reached inside and pulled out a pistol.

I was mesmerized. He sat on the edge of the bed, holding the pistol and staring at it. It was as if a balloon were flying in the air over his head, just like a cartoon. And the words in the balloon said, "Should I kill her?"

I will say that his face was bleak. He didn't want to kill her. Then his face hardened, and the balloon's words changed. "I've got to do it," the words said.

He laid the pistol on the bed, then crossed to a closet. He opened the door and began to toss boxes off the shelf. My dad had a pistol, and he kept the pistol one place and the clip another. Could the Lally boy's dad do the same thing? Could he be looking for ammunition?

Suddenly I was sure Alana was going to be dead within the next few minutes. Her only chance was to run. And she didn't know she was in immediate danger.

Luckily, the stairs led up to the end of the deck away from the bedroom, so I was able to tiptoe up without being seen and tiptoe across to the door to the living room. If it had been locked—but it wasn't. I opened it a foot— enough to let me in, but too little to make the sound of the waves louder inside the house. I ran lightly across the room.

"Alana! Alana!"

Alana didn't move. At first I thought she couldn't hear me because of the waves. But when I shook her, she still lolled on the couch limply. She was unconscious.

What could I do! She was skinny, true, but she was too heavy to carry. I needed to run for help. But I couldn't just leave her there to die.

The fur rug gave me the idea. I ran around the couch and yanked the cushions out from under Alana, then put them on top of her. I tried to leave her a little space for breathing. Then I draped the fur rug over the seat of the couch.

Did it look as if Alana was gone? I could only hope so.

I ran back to the door to the deck, slid the door open, and edged outside. I shut the door gently, then headed for the stairs to the beach.

Behind me, I heard a yell. I couldn't tell if the Lally boy had found Alana, or if he had seen me. I didn't stop to find out. I started racing down those terraced stairs. Back and forth, switching across the slope. I was afraid to go straight down, through the ivy and other plants, so I stuck to the steps. But I ran.

Behind me I heard the door open. The Lally boy was coming. Then I heard a terrific bang, and I knew he was shooting at me.

By then I was on the little deck at the bottom of the stairs. I fell flat, just as a second shot was fired. Then I slid backward down the final stairs to the sand. When I felt the sand under my toes, I stood up and began to run up the beach.

The trees and shrubs along the bank hid me, I deduced, and the Lally boy would have to run down all those stairs before he could see me. I meant to be long gone by the time he got to the bottom. I ran for home as fast as I could. But considering the sand I was running in, that wasn't too fast.

Still, I was more than halfway to the public access path when I heard the Lally boy yell behind me and knew he was at the bottom of the stairs. I ran on. He chased me. I could see the clump of trees that marked the path up to the road. I aimed for them, and I ran. I swung around the last driftwood log and went up that path, clawing the sand with my hands.

Suddenly I was out in the middle of the road, pounding toward Aunt Nettie and Uncle Phil's house. Behind me, I heard the Lally boy come out at the top of the path. His feet scrunched on the gravel of the parking area, and I hadn't reached the curve yet. I knew he'd be able to see me.

I ran to the edge of the road and cowered among the trees—those threatening Michigan trees that had frightened me so much. Now they looked like a fortress where I could hide. I hugged a tree, blessed the dark, and stood absolutely still.

But he had heard my footsteps. He knew which way I had gone. So, running and then walking, he came toward me. I didn't even breathe.

"Where are you, baby?" he said. "What's all this dumb stuff? Come on out, Alana."

Alana? He thought I was Alana? For the first time I remembered I had covered my hair with a black scarf. He had looked into the living room and been momentarily fooled by my ruse of hiding Alana under the couch cushions and the fur rug. Then, as I ran away from him, I had looked like Alana.

"Come on, babe. We're gonna make this work. We'll get the money. Come on."

Get the money? Alana was going to get the money?

So she'd been a party to her own kidnapping. Why wasn't I surprised?

The Lally boy came up even with me. "Alana? Come on, honey."

I huddled behind my tree, hiding my hands and face in it, exposing no part of me that wasn't dark.

He walked on. Now I was behind him. I still didn't move.

"Alana? Come on!" He sounded exasperated. He was at least thirty feet farther on, almost into the dangerous curve, the curve just before Mrs. Deacon's drive turned off the Lake Shore Drive.

"Dammit! Come out, you little bitch!"

I pictured him swinging his pistol around, looking everywhere for Alana. I just hoped he'd stay where I could hear him, so I'd know where he was.

He was still out in the middle of the road at the blind curve, muttering and calling for Alana, when Mrs. Deacon's daughter's car came around the curve, hit him, and knocked him into the same bush where her mother had landed that morning.

Again I ran to the neat white cottage next door, and again the woman who lived there called the sheriff, an ambulance and Uncle Phil.

"Call two ambulances," I told her. "Alana Fairchild Hyden is down at the Lally house, and I think she's been beaten up pretty bad."

I ran back to the Lally house—this time on the road. The front door was unlocked, luckily, and I was able to pull the couch cushions off Alana before she smothered. Then the door opened behind me, and I screamed.

It was Uncle Phil. I threw my arms around his neck. "Oh, Uncle Phil! I'm so glad it's you!"

The sheriff scolded me, but he didn't deny that the evidence that had made me suspect the Lally boy was involved in Alana Fairchild Hyden's kidnapping was too slight for him to have used as a basis for a search warrant. An empty candy box, a scrap of blue ribbon, and a screwed-up candy cup from the last box of candy Alana had bought were not much to go on. Especially when someone had stolen them from Mrs. Deacon's trash bag, and I was the only person who knew they existed.

Mrs. Deacon lived. She was in the hospital several weeks, but Uncle Phil let Lindy and me drive into Holland to see her.

Alana lived, too. She admitted she had connived at her own kidnapping. It was plain even to a nut like her mother that she had done it to get attention. Alana got a suspended sentence, and her mother promised to go into therapy with her. They sold the Warner Pier house, and they didn't come back there again.

The Lally boy—it turned out his name was Brian—died. His family hadn't known he was at the Lake Michigan house. He was supposed to be at an Outward Bound camp.

Mrs. Deacon came home from the hospital the day before I went back to Texas. I took her some candy, plus a casserole Aunt Nettie had made.

"Lee, you've had an exciting summer," she said. "And if you hadn't noticed the TenHuis box, the ribbon, and that little candy cup, I guess Alana Fairchild Hyden might be dead."

"TenHuis chocolate is not the kind of thing you usually take to the beach," I said. "So when somebody attacked you, then tore up your trash—well, it was just a simple reduction. Alimentary, my dear Mrs. Deacon."

The Chocolate Cat Caper

Chapter 1

"Every town has a crooked lawyer," I said. "But even crooks have the right to buy chocolate."

"Clementine Ripley isn't our town's crooked lawyer," Aunt Nettie said scornfully. "Clementine Ripley is just a crooked summer visitor. And I'd be a lot happier if she kept her crookedness elsewhere."

"We can't refuse her business."

"We can refuse if we're not going to get paid."

"Oh, I'll make sure we'll get our money before she gets her chocolate."

Aunt Nettie knotted her solid fists on her solid hips and stood solidly on her solid legs. Solid is definitely the word for Jeanette TenHuis. Even her thick hair, blond streaked with gray, with its natural curl firmly controlled by a food-service hairnet, looked substantial and dependable—hair that wouldn't stand for any nonsense. She is five-foot-four and may weigh 175, but she doesn't look fat. She looks like a granite statue hewn by a sculptor who got tired of chiseling all the excess stone off a big block, so he just whacked a little around the edges, then polished the whole thing smooth and shiny.

But if I compared Aunt Nettie to one of the delectable chocolates she makes, I'd say she was a Frangelico truffle (described in her sales material as, "Hazelnut interior with milk chocolate coating, sprinkled with nougat."). In other words, she's firm outside, but soft at the heart and has a slightly nutty flavor. When I left the guy I sometimes refer to as Rich Gottrocks and gave up my career as a trophy wife, all my other relatives told me how stupid I was. Aunt Nettie offered me room, board, and a job running the business side of her chocolate shop and factory while I studied for the CPA exam.

Of course, after a couple of days of working on her books, I saw she wasn't being merely philanthropic. My uncle's death eighteen months earlier had thrown her into a financial hole I hoped was temporary, and she needed a cheap manager. But I needed a place where nobody knew my ex-husband, a place to lie low and gather energy for a new attack on life. So we made a good pair.

Soft center or no, Aunt Nettie was quite capable of refusing to sell chocolates to Clementine Ripley, even if it cost her money. It was my job to keep her from doing that, so I spoke firmly. "Listen, Aunt Nettie, when you brought me back to Warner Pier, you said the business side of TenHuis Chocolade was my responsibility. And the business side can't stand for you to snub a two-thousand-dollar order. That would buy a bunch of all-natural ingredients. So load those chocolates up."

She rolled her round blue eyes, and I knew I'd won. "All right, Lee," she said. "But you'll have to deliver them. I won't speak civilly to Clementine Ripley."

"Sure."

"And you'll have to use your minivan. Because of the air-conditioning."

"I'll be glad to," I said. "Maybe I'll get a look inside that house."

"And make sure we get our money!"

"Cross my heart."

I watched while Aunt Nettie loaded six giant silver trays with handmade truffles and bonbons and with fruits dipped in chocolate coating for Clementine Ripley. Candies in dark chocolate, milk chocolate, white chocolate; strawberries and dried apricots half covered with dark chocolate; fresh raspberries mounted on disks of white chocolate and drizzled with milk chocolate—she arranged them into swirling designs of yummy. Each type of truffle or bonbon was decorated in a different way or came in a different shape. A dark chocolate pyramid was coffee-flavored. The white-chocolate-covered truffle with milk chocolate stripes was almond-flavored, its milk chocolate interior flavored with Amaretto. The oval bonbon, made of dark chocolate and decorated with a flower, had a cherry-flavored filling. This went on through sixteen different kinds of truffles and bonbons.

When I'd worked behind the counter as a teenager, I'd known them all. Now I could identify only a few, but that didn't matter. All were genuine luxury chocolates—no jellies or chewy caramels or hard centers—and every flavor could lift me into a state of ecstasy. Aunt Nettie's chocolates were guaranteed to wow the guests at the fund-raiser Clementine Ripley was sponsoring for the Great Lakes Animal Rescue League. It was a big event, or so the Warner Pier weekly had claimed. Guests were coming from Chicago and Detroit—all carrying big checks for the Rescue League.

I snagged an Amaretto truffle Aunt Nettie hadn't placed on a tray yet and bit into it, savoring every sweet, almond-flavored morsel. Every Ten-Huis Chocolade employee is allowed two free chocolates each working day—a perk I found more pleasant than a company car would have been.

When the first tray was completely filled, Aunt Nettie covered it with plastic wrap, and I picked it up and carried it toward the alley, where I had parked.

"Start the air-conditioning!" Aunt Nettie said.

"I will, I will! I'm not taking a chance on having a couple of thousand dollars' worth of chocolate melt all over my van."

Warner Pier's summer weather is usually balmy. People come here to get away from the heat elsewhere in the Midwest. Most Warner Pier folks don't bother to have air-conditioned cars, and many—including Aunt Nettie don't even have air-conditioned houses, though she keeps the chocolate shop and workroom chilly. But the lakeshore does have a few really hot muggy days each summer, and this happened to be one of them.

In Texas, we've all given up trying to live without air-conditioning and it's installed everywhere—in houses, offices, industrial plants, cars, trucks, and tractors. My used van had a Texas tag and enough Texas air-conditioning to keep chocolate from melting in any temperature the Great Lakes region was likely to hand out.

I went back and forth out the back door, sliding the trays onto the floor of the van, making sure each tray was wedged firmly. Aunt Nettie didn't get a lot of orders for trays already arranged, but when she did, she wanted them to look artistic. She always arranged them herself, without the help of any of the "hairnet ladies," who were also bustling around the workroom.

These chocolates looked gorgeous. Aunt Nettie carried the last tray out, and I put it in the floor of the front seat. Then I looked at the array and sighed. "They're almost too beautiful to eat."

Aunt Nettie gave a satisfied snort. "They'll eat them," she said. "Now I'll get the cats, and you can go."

While Aunt Nettie went to the storage room, I popped into the rest room off the break room and freshened up. I had to duck to see the top of my head in the mirror; I got a tall gene from both the Texas side and the Michigan Dutch side of my family, so I'm just a shade under six feet. I tucked my chocolate-brown shirt with the TenHuis Chocolade logo into my khaki slacks. I rebrushed my hair—whitish-blond like the Michigan side—and clipped it into a barrette on the back of my neck. Then I added the merest touch of mascara, tinted faintly green like my Texas hazel eyes. I wiped my mouth and put on a new coat of medium pink lipstick. It was nice to look like myself again. Mr. Gottrocks, whose name was actually Richard Godfrey, always liked me to wear bright red lipstick and big hair, but I'd left the glamour behind with my wedding ring.

As I came out Aunt Nettie was arranging the last of Clementine Ripley's special order of cat-shaped candies onto a smaller silver tray. I admired these, too. Each about three inches high, they were made of solid white chocolate, formed in a mold specially ordered from the Netherlands. They had been hand-detailed with milk chocolate glaze and colored chocolate, so that the blue eyes and the light brown markings of the cats mimicked the photo Clementine Ripley had provided of her Birman male, Champion Myanmar Chocolate Yonkers. To a non-cat-fancier like me, Yonkers looked as if a Siamese cat had decided to let his hair grow. He had immensely fluffy Persian-like fur, but had the delicate light brown paws, ears, nose, and tail of a Siamese.

Even to a non-cat-fancier, Yonkers was a beautiful creature, and his chocolate replicas looked scrumptious on their silver dish. "Gorgeous!" I said.

Aunt Nettie wrapped the dish with a huge sheet of food-service Saran, then picked up a small white box tied with blue ribbon from the table behind her. "Here are the samples," she said.

"Samples? For me?"

"No! For Clementine Ripley. I don't want my display ruined. So I packed a few extra chocolates for her to sample. I wrote her name on top."

I laughed. "Maybe you'd better send an extra cat, so she won't get into those either."

"There's a cat in there. Amaretto truffles are her favorite, though. She buys those every time she comes in. So I sent a half dozen. But I'd better get my money!"

"No check, no chocolate. I talked to her assistant—Ms. McCoy?—and she assured me she'd have the money ready."

"Good girl!"

I shook my finger at Aunt Nettie. "And unlike some other people—I'm sticking to it. Not a chocolate comes out of the van until I have that check."

Aunt Nettie smiled sheepishly. She's much too understanding and patient. A year earlier she had let Clementine Ripley have chocolates for her big benefit party on credit. But in the offhand way of the really rich, Ms. Ripley neglected to pass on the invoice in a timely manner to the person who paid her bills. It was several months before Aunt Nettie got her money. This year we weren't going to let that happen.

I'd insisted that Clementine Ripley use a credit card, but that hadn't worked either. Now I'd arranged to get a check when the chocolates were delivered.

I checked to be sure I had the invoice, slung my purse over my shoulder, and took the tray of cats to the van. I was settled behind the wheel when Aunt Nettie ran out, waving. "Wait! Take these."

I rolled down the window, letting out valuable air-conditioned air, and took what she handed me—a dispenser box containing a few pairs of plastic food-service gloves.

"In case any of the chocolates shift, use these to move them back in place."

"I'll drive slow and steady," I said. "And I'll try not to say anything stupid, either."

Aunt Nettie laughed. "You're not stupid, Lee," she said. Bless her heart. I hope she's right, but not everybody agrees with her. She waved as I drove off.

Nothing's very far away from anything else in Warner Pier. Clementine Ripley's overly dramatic showplace home on the cliff at Warner Point was only two miles from TenHuis Chocolade, located on Fifth Street between Peach and Pear Avenues.

I pulled out of the alley and very gently turned onto Peach Street, then followed that a block to Dock Street, the pride of Warner Pier. Dock Street has been turned into a real attraction—a mile of marinas, all crammed with boats and yachts in the summer. And dividing the street from the marinas is a mile-long park—a narrow series of green spaces, gazebos, and wooden walkways. Boaters can dock at a Warner Pier marina, then walk across the park to reach a business district filled with good restaurants, antique and gift shops, art galleries, trendy and expensive clothing stores—and the occasional specialty shop like TenHuis Chocolade. It's pretty neat, or so we Warner Pier merchants think. I followed Dock Street, driving slowly because of the chocolates and because of the tourists who roamed the streets, until I was out of the business district.

The older residential neighborhoods of Warner Pier were designed by Norman Rockwell in 1946. At least, my mother always claims she grew up on the cover of an old *Saturday Evening Post* magazine. The town looks as if it's under a glass dome. Just shake us, and it snows on the white Victorians, Craftsman bungalows, and modified Queen Anne cottages and on their lush, old-fashioned gardens.

Warner Pier lies along the Warner River, not far upstream from the spot where the river enters Lake Michigan. In the 1830s, settlers—some from the Netherlands and some from New England—saw a chance to make money by cutting down all the native timber. With those trees gone, the next generation planted replacements, but they concentrated on fruit trees, and Warner Pier became a center for production of "Michigan Gold," which was the early-day promoters' nickname for peaches. By 1870 Warner Pier had become a town of prosperous fruit growers and ship owners—solid citizens with enough money to build the substantial Victorian houses that today are being gentrified into summer homes or into bed-and-breakfast inns. Warner Pier is still a fruit-producing center, but today a lot of the area's "Michigan Gold" comes from tourists and summer residents.

I followed the curves of Dock Street to the showplace home of Clementine Ripley, one of Warner Pier's most famous summer visitors. Most summer people come for the beaches and Victorian ambiance, but Ms. Ripley seemed to have come seeking seclusion. Several years earlier she had acquired ten acres of prime property on top of a bluff overlooking the Warner River, right at the point where it entered Lake Michigan. She built a low stone house that appeared to be about two blocks long, with a tower slumped at one end. That tower was apparently based on an abstract idea of a lighthouse—or maybe planned as a squatty version of the Washington

Monument. It was known to boaters up and down the lake as "the sore thumb," because that's what it stuck out like.

The house might be highly visible from the lake, but it was not inviting. Signs warning boaters and swimmers to keep away were posted along the shore. Guards and a high brick wall kept Clementine Ripley private and protected from the land side.

Clementine might well need protection, and from more than prying eyes. Her office was in Chicago, but she had a national practice in criminal law. As one of the nation's toughest defense lawyers, she'd kept a series of high-profile clients out of prison on charges that ranged from fraud to murder. Not a few people—witnesses she'd shredded on the stand, prosecutors she'd made look like circus clowns, former clients and their victims, plus the tabloid press—had it in for Clementine Ripley. Even sainted Aunt Nettie, who loved everybody else in the world, didn't like her. She hadn't told me why, but her feelings seemed to be deeper than a payment problem.

So Clementine Ripley might need her guards, I told myself as I drove up to the metal security gate. The gate was probably eight feet high, and its grill seemed to snarl. I wouldn't have touched it on a bet; the thing looked as if it would carry thousands of volts of electricity. I stopped by the intercom mounted on a post and punched a button on its face, feeling as if I was about to order a hamburger and fries.

A disembodied voice answered, "Yes?"

"Lee McKinney, with a delivery from TenHuis Chocolade."

"Just follow the drive up to the house," the voice said.

The gate slid sideways, and I drove on in, almost frightened of what might happen once I was behind the brick wall and in the area controlled by Clementine Ripley.

There was nothing scary in there, of course, unless you find deep woods threatening. But the undergrowth in these particular woods was largely cleared out, and ahead I could see the long stone house, its tower leaning like a drunken troll. I drove on slowly—still remembering my fragile cargo—and I coasted around the circular drive and came to a halt in front of the wide flagstone steps.

On the steps was a hulking man—broad and tall. He had a shaved head and a thick upper lip that curled into a snarl. He wore a gray uniform, and the patch above his shirt pocket read GRAND VALLEY SECURITY SERVICE. He motioned for me to lower my window.

When he spoke, his voice surprised me by being a high-pitched squeak. "Ms. McKinney? I'll unload the delivery here."

I told myself not to say anything stupid. Then I took a deep breath and spoke. "Do you have my check?"

He spoke curtly. "Check? No, payment is handled by Ms. Ripley's personal assistant, Ms. McCoy."

"I told Ms. McCoy we had to have payment before we delivered the chocolates."

"It will be taken care of." The gray-uniformed man went to the back of the minivan.

I jumped out, leaving the motor running, and went after him. *Keep calm and speak carefully,* I thought.

"I can't allow the chocolates to be unloaded until we are paid."

Gray Uniform reached for the handle to the back door. "You'll be paid," he squeaked, but he still sounded curt.

I stepped between him and the door. I was taller, but that didn't give me any real edge, since he was broader. "I'm sure we will be paid, but I need the password today."

Rats! I'd done it. Said something stupid.

The security guard looked puzzled. "Password?"

"Payment," I said. There was nothing to do but go on. "I need payment. I explained to Ms. McCandy."

That ripped it. Now Gray Uniform was grinning, obviously amused. Darn! If I'm going to have a speech impediment, why can't I lisp? People recognize a lisp as a problem. This saying the wrong word business simply makes me sound like an idiot.

I tried again, speaking slowly and carefully. My insides were twisting up to match my tongue. "I can't unload the chocolates until I receipt the check. I mean, receive! Receive the check."

Gray Uniform's grin became patronizing, and he gave a clumsy wave, as if he were going to brush me out of the way. "Now listen, young lady . . ." Then his eyes widened, and he looked behind me, obviously surprised.

Could it be the famous Clementine Ripley? I whirled to see.

It wasn't. It was a tall man—at least two inches taller than I am. He had dark hair and was wearing navy-blue pants and a matching shirt. Sunglasses seemed to cover his face from hairline to upper lip.

"What's the problem, Hugh?" His voice boomed. Definitely a basso.

The guard squeaked in reply. "Joe! How did you get here?"

The mouth of the tall guy shaped into a sardonic grin. Somehow that grin seemed familiar. "I tied up at the boathouse and walked. Why? Have you got orders to run me off?"

"No, no!" Gray Uniform sputtered, but the newcomer cut off his excuses. "What's your problem here?"

Gray Uniform stumbled through an explanation, while the dark-haired man and I eyed each other warily. Or I think he eyed me behind his sunglasses. I kept trying to place him. Who was he? I was sure I'd met him, but I couldn't figure out where or when.

Gray Uniform's mouth began to run down, and the tall man scowled. "Sounds like Clemmie hasn't been paying her bills. Where's Marion?"

"Out on the terrace, but—"

The man's head turned toward me. "I'll take you around."

"Let me get the invoice." I opened the driver's door and retrieved my purse and the small box of sample chocolates Aunt Nettie had sent. I checked to see that I had my extra car keys; then I locked the door and slammed it.

The tall guy spoke again. "You left the motor running."

"Air-conditioning," I said. "I can't let the chocolates melt."

"Oh." He turned and led the way along a flagstone walk that circled the house. I tried to keep up.

"I do appreciate this," I said. "The security man seemed determined to unload the chocolates, and I promised my aunt—"

He stopped and turned toward me. "Your aunt? Are you Jeanette Ten-Huis's niece?"

"Lee McKinney." I put out my hand.

He took the hand. Then he took off the sunglasses and hung them on his shirt pocket.

I gave a gasp. "You're Joe Woodyard! I thought you looked familiar, but I didn't recognize you with clothes on."

I'd really done it this time. Joe's smile almost turned into a glare. I spoke quickly. "I used to hang out at Warner Pier bitch when you were a lifeguard." I decided to ignore turning "beach" into "bitch" and kept talking. "I always saw you looking down from that high chair."

"Yeah, Joe Lifeguard, lording it over the beach." He started walking again. I trailed him. "I remember you."

Joe Woodyard had been the head lifeguard at the Warner Pier beach the year I was sixteen, the year my parents divorced and I was packed off to work for Aunt Nettie and Uncle Phil in the chocolate shop. I'd made a few friends among the local girls who had summer jobs in the downtown businesses, and we'd spent our off hours at the beach, flirting with the Warner Pier guys (dating a summer visitor could ruin your rep) and drooling over Joe Woodyard. He'd been the best-looking guy in Warner Pier in those days—dark curly hair, dark brows, long lashes, and vivid blue eyes, not to mention great shoulders. He was three or four years older than we were, and he had an air of dangerous arrogance. To the sixteen-year-old mind he had been the epitome of cool, but intimidating.

He had been a sharp dresser, too. But now I recognized his matching shirt and slacks as "work clothes," the kind you buy at Kmart. And he wasn't as good-looking now. Or maybe he was good-looking in a different way. At twenty he'd been almost too handsome; now he looked tougher, more rugged, sadder—as if he'd had a few rocky nights and rough days.

Joe spoke again. "What are you doing back in Warner Pier?"

"Working for Aunt Nettie. I'm planning to commute to Grand Rapids and take the CPA review course. What are you doing now?"

Joe's smile twisted into its sardonic version, but before he could speak, a new voice sounded from in front of us. It was a deep, throaty voice, a voice with vibrato that could make a stone shudder—or at least sway a jury.

"Don't you know?" the voice said. "Joe is the former Mr. Clementine Ripley."

Chapter 2

I recognized her, of course. *Sixty Minutes*, the *Today* show, *Dallas Times-Herald*, *Time* magazine—Clementine Ripley and her photograph had been everywhere during the prominent cases she had worked on. After Thomas Montgomery's estranged wife was found beaten to death, for example, nobody had believed even the Montgomery millions could keep him off death row. But Clementine Ripley had done it. When rock star Shane Q. was accused of burning down his record producer's house, the evidence looked damning. But Clementine Ripley kept him out of jail. And the fee from either case—or from any of a dozen others she had handled—could have paid for the house in Warner Pier.

Clementine Ripley would have drawn attention even if her photo hadn't been plastered over the world's news media. She was an attractive woman, but there was nothing showy about her looks. She simply looked competent. If I'd had a small country that needed running, I'd have hired Clementine Ripley for the job on sight, never mind the references.

Then she came out of the house, down a step, and I was surprised to see that she wasn't very tall. She had a full figure—no skinny lightweight could look as reliable as Clementine Ripley looked—but she wasn't plump. She wore casual pants in light blue denim with a matching man-tailored shirt, but the embroidered trim showed that the outfit hadn't come off the rack at Penney's. Her hair was blond—bottled, but not brassy—her features symmetrical, her makeup subtle. Her skin was outstanding—fine-textured and smooth, but with lines around the eyes.

She was at least fifteen years older than Joe Woodyard, I realized.

"Meow." The comment made me jump guiltily, for my cattiness. Had Clementine Ripley read my mind?

Then Ms. Ripley emerged from behind a bush that had partially hidden her, and I saw that she was holding a cat, an enormous ball of white-and-minky-brown fur.

The cat spoke again. "Meow."

"Oh!" I said. "Is this Yonkers?"

Ms. Ripley caressed the cat with a gesture as sensuous as Aunt Nettie's chocolate cream. "Yes."

"He's beautiful!"

Champion Myanmar Chocolate Yonkers accepted my admiration as his due, and Ms. Ripley ignored it. She looked at Joe Woodyard. "Joe, are you going to introduce me to your attractive friend?"

She managed to make the last word almost objectionable, and I spoke quickly, before Joe could react. "I'm Lee McKinney, from TenHuis Chocolade. Mr. Woodyard showed me the way back here. I'm here to deliver your order."

Ms. Ripley's eyes narrowed like the cat's. "I'm sure that the security guard can help you unload the chocolates. You can go back the way you came."

She was beginning to unnerve me, and that always had a bad effect on my tongue. "I was told I could find your personal assailant here." Oops! I went back and tried the remark over. "I need to talk to your personal assistant."

The catlike eyes blinked twice, and Ms. Ripley called out. "Marion!" She looked into the room behind her. "Someone wants to talk to you!"

She turned around and put the cat inside the house, then slid a screen door shut, imprisoning him. Champion Yonkers immediately leaped onto the screen and climbed, using his claws as pitons and grumbling deep in his throat. The screen was speckled with enlarged holes; apparently the cat made this climb frequently. At any rate, both Joe Woodyard and Clementine Ripley ignored his stunt.

The real cat reminded me of the candy one. I lifted the white box and thrust it toward Ms. Ripley. "My aunt sent these."

She eyed the box suspiciously. "Your aunt?"

"Jeanette TenHuis. She's the chocolate expert. She wanted you to see one of the special order cats. She sent several Amaretto truffles as well."

I kept the chocolates extended, and Ms. Ripley took them. She slid the blue ribbon off the box, opened it, and pulled out the white chocolate cat. She smiled. It was impossible not to smile at the chocolate version of Champion Yonkers.

"Delightful!" She held the cat up for Joe Woodyard to see. "Isn't it lovely, Joe?" She sounded slightly sarcastic when she spoke to him.

"Just dandy," Joe said. "I need to talk to you. Where's Marion?"

"I'm coming," a woman's voice answered. "I was upstairs."

The woman who came toward us, sliding the door open only a few inches and making sure the cat didn't get out, was frankly middle-aged. Or maybe she was much the same age as Clementine Ripley, but not as well kept. Her hair had been allowed to stay its natural gray, and she didn't seem to be wearing makeup. She had on polyester pants and a loose, sloppy T-shirt. She was almost as tall as I am, and she was thin. Not slender, not svelte, not slim, but something close to skinny. Her skin had been weathered by the sun.

She stopped a few feet away from Clementine Ripley and stared at Joe Woodyard. "What's he doing here?" she said.

Ms. Ripley ignored her remark. "It's the chocolate delivery," she said. "This woman says she needs to talk to you."

Marion McCoy glared at me. "The security man could have called me to the door."

"I'm sorry to bother you," I said. "But you promised to have a check—"

She cut me off before I could finish the sentence. "Just come this way." Still glaring, she brushed past her employer.

"Wait a minute," Ms. Ripley said. She put her hand on Ms. McCoy's arm and stopped her, but she looked at me. "Did you say you were to receive a check?"

I nodded unhappily.

"But I thought I put the chocolates on my Visa card."

"I'll take care of it," Ms. McCoy said firmly.

"Please wait, Marion. Let this young woman answer me. Didn't I give you my credit card number?"

I glanced at Joe Woodyard, standing with his arms folded, and at Marion McCoy, who was glaring. I didn't want to have to answer that question.

"Have you stopped taking credit cards?" Ms. Ripley was insistent. "Someone asked for one when I called the order in."

"Oh, we still take them! It's just that—well, there was some discrepancy. The card was dejected." Oh, I'd done it again. "It was rejected," I said.

Ms. Ripley stood there deadpan, then gave her slow, catlike smile again. "Rejected?"

Joe Woodyard gave a barking laugh. "You're maxed out, Clem. Is that why you've gone back on our deal?"

Clementine Ripley turned on him, and now she looked like a cat who was ready to claw. I spoke quickly, before she could attack either of us. "There are a lot of possible explanations," I said. "We may have taken down the wrong number over the phone, for example. But Ms. McCoy assured me—"

"Yes, I'll write a check on the personal account," Marion McCoy said. She shook her employer's hand off her arm and moved toward me.

Ms. Ripley was back in control of herself, but her eyes were still narrow. "You do that, Marion," she said. "And we'll discuss this later." Then she reached into the little white box of chocolates, but she didn't offer to share. She pulled out the chocolate cat and took a bite. She chewed and swallowed, made a satisfied "ummm" sound, and popped the rest of it in her mouth. Then she slid the blue ribbon back around the box, effectively reserving the chocolates for herself.

"Here, Marion," she said. "Take these into the house, please. Just put them in my room. I'll eat them later."

Marion snatched the box ungraciously, then walked off without another word. I followed her. Behind me I heard Ms. Ripley speak. "So, Joe—why are you here?"

"I want my money," Joe said.

I didn't hear any more. I didn't want to. I didn't know just where Joe Woodyard and Clementine Ripley stood. Maybe they were in the middle of their divorce. Or maybe they were divorced already. Maybe Joe was asking for alimony. And maybe the credit card "dejection" meant Ms. Ripley had more serious money problems than a bill from TenHuis Chocolade.

I followed Ms. McCoy along the flagstone terrace, which overlooked a broad lawn dotted with trees trimmed carefully to avoid blocking the view of Lake Michigan. It wasn't as hot or muggy here on the lakeshore. The sky was blue, the clouds fluffy, a fresh breeze teased the water into rhythmic lines of whitecaps.

"This is beautiful," I said.

Ms. McCoy ignored me. She certainly wasn't friendly. She led me past a long row of windows, then through a French door and into a paneled office. I stood by while she dug a big flat checkbook out of a drawer in the walnut desk that centered the room. She took the invoice I handed her and wrote the check.

As she gave it to me, she glared. "There was no need to bother Ms. Ripley about this."

"I didn't intend to. Joe Woodyard happened to pop up as I arrived, and he told the security goon—I mean, he told the security guard that he'd take me out to the terrace to find you." I could feel myself blushing. Goon! Had I really said that? I went on quickly. "How do I get back to the drive where I left my van?"

Without a word Ms. McCoy led me across a hall, through a utility room, and out a door. We emerged behind some bushes, turned a corner, and were back on the circular drive. My minivan and the security guard— he did look and act like a goon—were right where I had left them. Another vehicle, a sporty vintage Mercedes convertible, had been parked behind me. Its driver—a tall man with a beautiful head of gray hair—got out, waved at Marion McCoy, and went up the steps to the front door.

I unlocked the van, and the security man and Ms. McCoy unloaded the chocolates, turning down my offer to help. The security man managed to tip one of the trays, of course, and all the chocolates slid to one side. I offered to rearrange them, but they again refused my offer. So I handed Ms. McCoy the food-service gloves and advised her to use them to rearrange the chocolates. Then I got in the van and drove away.

I met only one more crisis. When I got to the massive gate, I slowed, wondering how to open it. It slid back on its own, and I found myself hood to hood with a police car.

A pair of sunglasses and a head of dark hair sprinkled with gray poked out the window of the police car, and its driver called out, "I'll back up!"

He backed onto the street, and I drove out the drive. I waved as I passed him, to acknowledge his courtesy, and he gave me an answering wave and a friendly grin. If he was on official business, it didn't seem to be anything serious. In fact, his grin was the only genuine one I'd seen since I left Ten-Huis Chocolade.

"Whew!" I said aloud as I turned toward the Warner Pier business district. "What a bunch. Rude secretary. Officious security man. Family fight. Everybody at everybody else's throat." It would be nice to get back to the chocolate shop, where Aunt Nettie kept all her employees happy. And where I could absorb the news that Joe Woodyard, the guy the sixteen-year-old me had thought was so cool, was trying to squeeze money out of his ex-wife.

But as I turned onto Peach Avenue, I realized I hadn't seen the inside of the house. I refused to count the office and the utility room as a view of a showplace home.

When I came through the back door of TenHuis Chocolade, I could see Aunt Nettie standing at a stainless-steel worktable, using a big metal lattice to cut a sheet of lemon canache into diamond shapes. Canache—it rhymes with "panache"—is a thick filling, stout enough to stand up on its own, but not as solid as a jelly. Pieces of this are "enrobed," or covered with chocolate, and turned into a type of bonbon I think is actually more like a truffle.

Aunt Nettie was talking to a woman whose back was toward me. All I could see of her was shoulder-length brown hair.

Aunt Nettie beckoned. "Lee! See who's here!"

The woman turned around. "Lee!" She held her arms out.

I yelled at her, "Lindy Bradford! I mean, Lindy Herrera!"

We hugged each other enthusiastically and made good-to-see-you-again noises. Lindy had worked for TenHuis Chocolade the same summers I did. The two of us had lazed on the beach and ogled the local guys on our days off. I'd always thought Joe Woodyard was the coolest, but Lindy had had her eye on Tony Herrera even then.

Lindy still had a sweet dimpled face. She'd gained a little weight since high school, of course, but she looked great.

"Aunt Nettie says you have three kids now," I said.

"Right. And I hope you're ready to look at pictures!"

Everybody who comes into TenHuis Chocolade gets a sample, so Lindy picked a strawberry truffle ("White chocolate and strawberry interior coated with dark chocolate"). Then we went into the office, where I admired the pictures of three cute, dark-haired kids. Lindy had married Tony a year after we graduated from high school. I'd been working in Dallas and hadn't had the time or money to come for her wedding. Aunt Nettie hadn't been too optimistic about the marriage. Tony and Lindy were "too young," she had said. Tony had been working for his dad's catering business when they got married.

"Is Tony still working for his dad?"

"Oh, no! He hated that, you know. He went to school, became a machinist."

"Does he like that better?"

"He did—until he got laid off a month ago."

"Ouch! Has he found anything else?"

"They're supposed to call everybody back in the fall. For now he's doing what he can find—helping Handy Hans repair cottages, painting houses. He's been working with Joe Woodyard some."

"I guess it's reunion week," I said. "I ran into Joe out at the Ripley house."

"Joe! What was he doing there?" Linda leaned close. "He and the Ripper split up two years ago."

"I guess they had some business to discuss." I might be disappointed in Joe for trying to get money out of his ex, but I decided I didn't need to spread the word around Warner Pier. It would spread fast enough without my help. Warner Pier is a town that size.

"Tony says Joe's having some business problems," Lindy said.

"What does Joe do?"

"Well, he used to be a lawyer. But now he's restoring antique powerboats."

"Antique powerboats?"

"You know. Wooden speedboats and such."

"He quit practicing law to do that?"

Lindy shrugged. "His mom was mad as hops. She was real proud of her son the lawyer. But when Joe walked out on the Ripper, he dropped out of law, too. He bought the old Olson shop at the far end of Dock Street. It caused a lot of conversation in the local coffee klatches."

I laughed. "I guess so. When I was in Warner Pier Joe was definitely tagged as 'most likely to succeed.' "

"Oh, yeah, Joe's kept the town on its ear since he was state high school debate champ and state wrestling champ in the same year. Then he organized the student Habitat for Humanity chapter for Michigan. He won all kinds of scholarships. And apparently he did real well in law school, ran the—what do they call it?—law review."

I nodded. "That's quite an honor."

Lindy went on. "His mom was bragging about all the big law firms that offered him high-paying jobs, but he went with one of these outfits that help the poor. Legal Aid? That was in Detroit. Then he married big, and his mom started bragging again. But two years ago he left the Ripper and quit law completely."

"Money isn't everything."

Lindy rolled her eyes. "Wish I had enough of it to say that."

"Money." I opened my purse, produced the check, and leaned out into the workroom. "Tah-dah!" When Aunt Nettie looked around I waved the check.

She smiled sweetly. "Oh, good!"

I turned back to Lindy. "Mission accomplished. I delivered a huge order of chocolates to Clementine Ripley, and this is the check for them. But I didn't get to see the inside of the house."

"It's ugly as sin. I get to see it several times a year."

"How do you rate? Are you an Animal Rescue League supporter?"

"No, I'm a waitress! Tony quit his dad, but I've been working for him sometimes—Mike Herrera's Restaurant and Catering. We do all of Clementine Ripley's parties." Her dimples deepened, and her face lit up. "Do you really want to see the inside of the house?"

"Sure. But what excuse do I have to go back?"

"Waitress! You waited tables when you were in college, didn't you?"

"I did it more recently than that. When I walked out on Rich it was the only job I could get in a hurry. Rich nearly had a fit."

"Why?"

"He was telling all his friends I was out to take him financially. Then I showed up on the lunch shift at his favorite Mexican restaurant. Running my feet off. It made it sort of obvious that I hadn't taken a lot of his worldly goods with me. Waiting tables is hard work."

"Well, the Ripley parties are a snap. It's just circulating with a tray and picking up dirty napkins. And Papa Mike's been looking all over for an extra waitress for tonight. If you really want to see the inside of the house, I'll call him and see if he's found anybody."

I thought about it a second. "What do you wear?"

"Black slacks, white shirt. Mike will furnish the vest and tie."

"It might be easier to wait until the house is in *Architectural Digest*."

"Come on, Lee, do it!" Lindy said. "It'll give us a chance to talk without the kids underfoot."

I considered for a long moment before I spoke. "Sure. I'll do it. Call."

It wasn't until after Mike Herrera had agreed to take me on and after Lindy had gone home that Aunt Nettie heard about the plan. Her reaction amazed me. She looked horrified.

"Oh, no!"

"What's wrong?" I said. "It's just a chance to talk to Lindy."

"I just don't like the thought of you working for the woman who was responsible for your uncle's death!"

Chapter 3

I stared at Aunt Nettie. When Uncle Phil, my mother's brother, had died eighteen months earlier, that left Aunt Nettie as sole owner of TenHuis Chocolade—an expert on chocolate, but a little hazy on the business side. Uncle Phil had been killed by a drunk driver. But the guy had been tried and sentenced to jail, and this was the first time I'd heard that Clementine Ripley had anything to do with it.

"What do you mean, 'the woman who was responsible for Uncle Phil's death'?"

"That was the reason I didn't want to do all that chocolate!"

"But you had the chocolate cat mold."

"Oh, I ordered that two years ago, and it got here too late to use. When Clementine Ripley called the order in, it was your first day. I wasn't here, but I guess somebody told you about the cat mold."

"Yes, I asked one of the ladies, and she said the special mold was available. But what's this about Clementine Ripley's connection with the wreck that killed Uncle Phil?"

"She kept that terrible Troy Sheepshanks out of prison."

"Troy Sheepshanks? Wasn't that the driver?"

"Yes! He killed your uncle Phil. But it was the second time he'd been involved in a fatal accident. The first time he hired Clementine Ripley, and the district attorney wouldn't even file charges."

"Then the evidence must not have been good."

"It would have been good enough if Troy had had any other attorney. The district attorney was simply scared to face her in court. So he dropped the case."

"That's terrible. But . . ."

Aunt Nettie sat down in an office chair and pursed her lips. She looked as solid as ever, and she hadn't burst into tears. Only someone like me, who'd known her a long time, would have realized that she was extremely upset.

"Because Troy Sheepshanks was never charged in that first case, he got

his license back and was on the highway—drunk again—when he killed
Phil." She sat back and folded her arms across her solid bosom. One lonely
tear ran down her cheek. "I've always blamed Clementine Ripley as much
as I blamed Troy Sheepshanks. If she'd been responsible at all, she would
have seen that he shouldn't be driving. You don't know how often I've
longed to kill that woman."

I was sitting in an office chair that was on rollers. So I dug in my heels,
grabbed the end of the desk, and scooted across the floor until I was knee to
knee with Aunt Nettie. Not graceful, but I got there. "Why didn't you tell
me all this?"

She shrugged, sniffed, and shook her head silently.

"If I'd known, I'd never have urged you to fill that order for chocolates."

"No. You were right. We can't refuse to sell chocolates just because we
don't like the customers who want to buy them." Aunt Nettie sniffed again,
but this time she smiled. "I hate Hawaiian shirts, but I'm glad to sell chocolates to people who wear them."

"We could put up a sign on the door: 'Hawaiian shirts? No service.' "
That made her laugh, just a little, and I gave her a one-armed hug. "Listen,
I'll call Mr. Herrera and tell him I can't serve at the party after all."

"No! No! He's counting on you now."

I could have predicted that reaction, I guess. The Warner Pier business
community is not large, and the merchants help each other out. "I won't
make a habit of being backup help for Mike Herrera," I said. "But Mom
didn't tell me a thing about all these problems with Clementine Ripley."

"She probably didn't know. For the last few years your uncle and I
haven't had much contact with her. And you were having your own problems when Phil died."

That was true. Uncle Phil had died a month after I left Rich and when I
was hitting my lowest point financially. My mom is notorious for never saving a cent. She is totally immersed in her work as a travel agent, though that
has its good side. When Uncle Phil died, she was able to get us a standby
flight. If she hadn't, neither of us would have even been able to come to
Warner Pier for the funeral. But we had stayed only two days. Neither of us
had been any help to Aunt Nettie.

Aunt Nettie took a tissue from her pocket and blew her nose. "I guess
that's why I hate that big house of Clementine Ripley's so much. It's like a
memorial to the injustice of Phil's death."

"What does the house have to do with Uncle Phil's death?"

"The first time Troy was accused of drunk driving, the Sheepshankses
paid Clementine Ripley's fee by giving her that ten acres out on Warner
Point. The city had been trying to get hold of the property, but Ms. Ripley
ruined that."

We left the situation as it stood. Aunt Nettie didn't want either of us to have anything to do with Clementine Ripley, but I'd promised to help out one of Aunt Nettie's fellow Warner Pier merchants, and she wouldn't hear of my backing out.

I dashed to the bank to deposit the check for Ms. Ripley's chocolates, making it into the main lobby before three p.m., when the bank closed for the weekend. I could have deposited the check at the drive-through, which would be open Saturday, but I was trying to establish rapport with Barbara, the branch manager. Then I went out to the house, changed into black slacks and a white shirt, and pulled my hair into a knot at the back of my head. Not glamorous, and not really required by the health department, but I hate waitresses who look as if they're shedding hair into the onion dip. At four-thirty, I picked up Lindy at her house—Tony had taken the kids to the beach, so I didn't see them—and I headed the minivan toward Clementine Ripley's estate for the second time that day. And this time I planned to see the inside of the place.

We were allowed through the gate and directed around the house by a service drive. We parked in a gravel area beside a four-car garage, next to the Herrera Catering van. The van was brand-new and had a classy logo painted on the side.

"Looks as if your pa-in-law is doing well," I said.

"He's really thrown himself into the business since Tony's mother died four years ago," Lindy said. "He's become a workaholic. Though recently we've caught a few hints that he's got some new romantic interest."

"How does that hit Tony?"

"Not very well. Of course, we both want Mike to be happy. But he's so secretive. We don't know who he's seeing. It makes us feel . . . worried."

I had the sense to nod understandingly and keep quiet.

Lindy took a deep breath before she spoke again. "It sounds silly, but Tony's afraid he's dating an Anglo."

"So? Tony married one."

"I know. Maybe that's why he's trying so hard to hang on to his cultural heritage. Trying to teach the kids Spanish. Stuff like that." She smiled. "It all started when Papa Mike changed his name from Miguel."

The breeze had switched to the north, dropping the temperature and humidity from their earlier highs and promising a pleasant evening for Clementine Ripley's party. The terrace overlooking the lake faced west, so sun might be a problem on that side of the house, but the terrace on the river side was shaded by some big trees.

I greeted Mike Herrera. I barely remembered him from my teenage summers in Warner Pier; all I had was a vague recollection of a man with slicked-down hair and a little Latin mustache who was always cheerful. Now I saw that he'd changed his persona over the past twelve years, with a shave and a new hairstyle that turned him into a sort of heavyset Antonio

Banderas. It was a surprising transformation. The twenty-eight-year-old me noted that he was an attractive man, something the sixteen-year-old me had missed.

Mike Herrera had been the first Hispanic to own his own business in Warner Pier—most Mexican-Americans in the area pick fruit—and I knew Aunt Nettie thought a lot of him. I felt sure he didn't remember me at all, but he pretended that he did. Every successful caterer is a born glad-hander, and Mike Herrera had the act down pat.

He smiled broadly as he took my hand in both of his. "Lee. The little Texas lady who stayed with Jeanette and Phil and worked in their shop. Welcome back to beautiful Lake Michigan." His accent was very faint.

"This time I plan to stay through the winter, Mr. Herrera. Do you think a Texan can stand the snow?"

"You'll grow to love it, Lee. Brisk! Invigorating! And the summers—ah, yes. Life without air-conditioning. You know I grew up in Denton? But I'd never go back to Texas now that I've discovered this beautiful place." He gave my hand a final pat, and a subtle change came over his face. When he spoke again I recognized it; Mike Herrera had moved from Warner Pier booster to businessman.

"I can't do your paperwork today," he said. "But I'll be in the office to-morrow. Can you bring your Social Security number by?"

"Sure."

"Hokay." He nodded. "Have you ever tended bar?"

"A few times. I can manage highballs and martinis. If they get into any-thing more exotic . . ."

Herrera smiled. "If they want anything more exotic, you'll ask Jason to mix it." He led, I followed, and I was finally inside the house.

I could see why Lindy had described the interior as "ugly as sin," but some interior designer had been paid a bunch of money to make it that ugly. The walls were white and completely bare. The ceilings were white, too, and they soared. The floor was bare wood, with a finish so dark it al-most hit black. A stairway—dark wood risers with stark white balustrades—led to a balcony that loomed over the shortest side of the room. The south and west walls were lined with French windows, which showed off the views of the lake and the river. The windows were bare; no curtains, blinds, valances, or even lengths of fabric twisted around poles. If the room had a focal point—other than the views of river and lake—it was a severe stone fireplace at the narrow end. An unobtrusive area rug lay in front of that, and the fireplace faced a white leather couch—the kind you have trouble getting out of. All the other furniture was dark wood and looked spindly and uncomfortable.

I pictured the room in winter, with all that bare wood, no comfortable chairs, and nothing to block the view of icy river and lake outside. *Clemen-*

tine Ripley must have to keep the thermostat set on ninety degrees, I thought. The room was beautiful, in an austere way, but it was a visual deep freeze.

It was not a room I could imagine Joe Woodyard in.

A half dozen men, women, and teenagers in black pants and white shirts were bustling about, setting up tables and dressing them with white cloths and silver dishes. I spotted two silver trays of TenHuis chocolates.

Through a double door I could see a dining room—more dark wood and unadorned white walls. A man in a white undershirt was building a white linen nest for a steamboat round. I felt sure he'd put on a double-breasted jacket and a chef's hat before the guests arrived.

I hadn't ever waitressed at a party like this, true, but in my role as Mrs. Rich Gottrocks, I'd gone to hundreds of similar events. Boooorrring. At least I wouldn't have to make conversation this time.

The last person I expected to see was Clementine Ripley herself. She should have been upstairs soaking in the whirlpool or treating her beautiful complexion to a last-minute facial. But as Mike Herrera and I crossed toward the bar, she came in the terrace door, still wearing her casual denim outfit. Herrera nodded and smiled his caterer's smile.

"Hello, Mike," she said. "Everything looks fine."

"Thank you very much, Ms. Ripley. We wish to please in every way." Herrera would have moved on, but Ms. Ripley touched his arm, and he stopped politely, still smiling professionally.

Her voice was almost flirtatious. "Don't you approve of my home? Now that it's built? Isn't it better than an auditorium?"

"It is truly beautiful, Ms. Ripley."

She laughed. It wasn't a pleasant sound. Then she walked on.

Herrera moved on, too, but he muttered as he walked. He spoke in Spanish, but all Texas kids learn a few Spanish swear words in junior high. I was pretty sure I understood him. "Bitch," he said. "Bitch, bitch, bitch."

Herrera showed me to the built-in bar, which was about eight feet long. It was under the balcony and located between the kitchen and this big black-and-white whatever-it-was room—you couldn't call it a living room, certainly. A lifeless room, maybe?

Herrera introduced me to Jason, who was the head bartender. Around fifty, Jason had dark, dramatic eyes, but his hair was his most striking feature. He had a high forehead and a long tail of salt-and-pepper hair, which he wore just like I usually wore mine—in a clump at the back of his neck. The combination of bare forehead in front and long hair behind made him look as if his scalp had slipped backward. He smelled of some spicy cologne or aftershave. Jason asked me a few questions about my bartending experience, and while he talked, his hands kept busy arranging glasses. I went around the bar, knelt, and started handing him glasses from racks on the floor.

Herrera left us, and Jason leaned closer. "I saw the Ripper talking to Mike," he said. "What did she have to say?"

"Something about how she hoped he liked the house better than an auditorium. What did she mean by that?"

Jason rolled his eyes. "I'd better not say."

"Look," I said. "Is there something going on here that I need to know about?"

"I'd better shut up."

"Whatever you think," I said. Then I kept my mouth shut—a method I've found works like a charm when somebody says they don't want to tell you something. If you act as if you don't want to know—they'll tell you.

It took Jason thirty seconds to start talking again. "You know that Mike is mayor of Warner Pier?"

"No, Aunt Nettie never mentioned it."

"Warner Pier is too small a town to have a village idiot, you know. We all have to take turns."

I laughed. "So it's Mr. Herrera's turn to be mayor?"

"Yeah," Jason said. Or I think that's what he said. To a Texan, the Michigan "yeah" sounds a lot like the Dutch "ya." But they think I'm the one with an accent.

Jason was still talking. "Mike's been mayor for five years. Warner Point was one of the last bits of undeveloped land inside the city limits, and Mike had this great plan for it. He wanted to build a conference center that would attract business in the winter, as well as the summer."

"Get rid of the off-season slump?"

"It might have helped. A lot of us have to go on unemployment."

"But Clementine Ripley got the land instead?"

Jason nodded. "Oh, she'd owned the land for several years. She'd acted interested in selling it—Mike was about to propose a bond issue. Then all of a sudden she built this huge place. And she employs a grounds service, a housekeeping service, and a maintenance service—all out of Grand Rapids."

"Tough on Mr. Herrera's plan to increase year-round employment."

"If she just wouldn't keep rubbing it in."

Jason and I finished the glasses. Then he handed me a box knife, one of those gadgets that holds a razor blade, and told me to start opening cases of soft drinks and mixers. "This'll be a wine crowd," he said. "Maybe some beer. I don't think we'll have many requests for mixed drinks, but we'd better have several mixers out. Then you can slice the lemons and limes. Not too many. I'm going into the kitchen to chill wine."

I was kneeling on the floor, ripping open the first soft drink box, when I heard Marion McCoy's voice. "Here, kitty! Kitty, kitty, kitty!" I saw no sign of the cat, so I kept working with the box knife. Suddenly Ms. McCoy's face poked around the end of the bar.

"Oh!" I jumped up.

"Is that cat back there?" she said. Now I could see her dress. It was a basic black, and it hadn't come cheap, but it hung on her. She still looked weather-beaten and skinny, though she wasn't exactly flat-chested.

"No, Ms. McCoy. I haven't seen him."

She looked at me narrowly. "I know you—oh, you're the young woman from the TenHuis Chocolade. What are you doing here?"

I resisted the impulse to go into a detailed explanation. "Mr. Herrera needed an extra waitress."

"You're a waitress?"

"I was when I was in college. Now I'm an accountant. But all the Warner Pier merchants try to help each other out, and Mr. Herrera needed an extra set of hands. If I see the cat, I'll try to catch him."

"We wanted to shut him up in the office until he makes his appearance for the donors. He always jumps up on the tables and tries to get in the food."

I smiled, still determined, in my Texas way, to be friendly. But she was making me nervous. "I'll tell the others, and we'll try to keep him from sampling the bubbly—I mean, the buffet!"

Ms. McCoy sniffed, straightened up, and left. I heard, "Here, kitty, kitty," from the dining room.

I had the box open by then. So I stood up, leaned over, and took two two-liter bottles of Diet Coke out of their box.

"Here. Lemme hep you."

A handsome, gray-haired man came around the corner of the bar. He took the bottles out of my hands, put them on the counter, then turned back with his hands out, ready for more bottles.

"Thanks," I said. I opened another box and handed him two club sodas, and he lined them up neatly at the left end of the work counter.

All the time I was trying to figure out who he was. He wasn't with Herrera Catering; I'd figured that out from his blue knit sports shirt. All us worker bees were wearing black and white. But he did seem familiar—a lean face with a grin that made him look rakish and with serious glasses that made him look reliable. But his most eye-catching characteristic was a gorgeous head of gray hair . . .

"Oh!" I said. "You were in the Mercedes convertible."

He looked at me narrowly, then smiled. "And yew were in the van." He definitely had a Texas accent. I had tried hard to get rid of my Texas accent, but this man had evidently tried to emphasize his.

"Right," I said. "And I think you're a guest, not an employee of Herrera Catering, so maybe you'd better get out from behind the bar before I get in trouble."

"Ah don't want yew to git into trouble!" He moved around the end of the bar. "I was about to ask for a favor, and I thought if I did one first . . ." He grinned, and it was a grin nobody could resist.

I didn't even try. "I do appreciate the help, and I'll be happy to do you a favor. Anything that's legal."

He leaned over the bar and dropped his voice. "I know you're not open yet. But do you hev any bourbon back there?"

"Sure. On the rocks?" I looked around for ice and found none. "Actually, I don't have any rocks yet. But I can get some from the kitchen."

"Straight up will be fine. I kin git my own ice."

I found a bottle of bourbon—a very good brand—and used the tip of the box knife to break the seal. I found a shot glass, filled it, and poured it into an old-fashioned glass. Then I lifted my eyebrows and looked questioningly at the gray-haired gent. "Double?"

"Why not? I'm staying in Clementine's guest cottage, so I won't be driving, and I'm as dry as a west Texas toad frog." He stuck his hand over the bar in shaking position. "I'm a cosponsor of this wingding. Clementine Ripley is one of my clients. Duncan Ainsley."

"Oh, that's why you look famous!" Oh, God, I'd done it again. "I mean, I mean"—I was stammering—"I mean, familiar! You look familiar. I read an article about you in *Business Week*, Mr. Ainsley. I should have recognized you from your pictures."

Now he was the one who seemed surprised. "You read *Business Week*?" He kept holding my hand.

"I have a degree in accounting. Someday I'll take that CPA exam."

"Don't want to spend your whole life behind the bar? Good fer yew! And many thanks." He squeezed my hand, grinned again, and moved toward the kitchen.

Well, this might turn out to be an interesting party. Duncan Ainsley! Investments weren't my specialty, but the things I'd read about him sounded fascinating. Colorful Texan famous for his parties. Investment counselor to stars of stage and screen. And apparently to Clementine Ripley, too. No wonder she could afford the house at Warner Point.

Now I understood his accent. If Duncan Ainsley was operating out of Dallas or Houston, he'd try to sound like he'd been to Harvard. Since he was a Texan operating out of Chicago, he used his Texas talk to make himself stand out from the crowd of Harvard MBAs. The thought of Duncan Ainsley kept me pepped up while I sliced the lemons and limes, then put olives and cherries in little dishes on the bar.

In a minute I scented Jason's spicy cologne, and I looked up to see him walking toward me. Then there was a flash of white fluff, and Jason screeched as he was attacked by a giant ball of fur.

Champion Myanmar Chocolate Yonkers had jumped down, apparently from the balcony, and landed on Jason's shoulder, barely missing the long queue. Using Jason as a springboard, he bounced on over to the bar.

It was hilarious, but I tried not to laugh. Jason didn't look amused, for one thing, and for another, the cat was now reaching a languorous paw out toward the dish I had just filled with olives.

"Oh, no!" I said. "Those are not for cats. Even gorgeous champion chocolate cats." And I grabbed.

I guess Champion Yonkers didn't expect to be denied his little treat. Anyway, he didn't dodge in time, and I was able to scoop him up. He gave a low snarl, and he kicked, but I had him.

"Into the office with you, fella," I said. "If I only knew where it was."

I carried the enormous cat out from behind the bar and started looking. I assumed Ms. McCoy had meant the office I had visited earlier that day, somewhere at the east end of the house. So I went past the kitchen and into a hall that seemed to lead in the right direction. At least I'd get to see a few more rooms of the house.

Almost immediately I found myself in a covered corridor, maybe forty feet long, with windows on both sides and a room at the far end. A parabola? Pergola? I was a little hazy on the name of this architectural feature. I was beginning to figure out that the house wasn't really one big building. It was a series of little buildings strung together. I'd heard a couple of people call it "the village," and that name was close to the feel of the thing. The tower—the "sore thumb"—was a sort of village church steeple.

As I entered the room at the end of the passageway, I called out, "Ms. McCoy!" She didn't answer.

This was obviously not one of the public areas of the house. It was too pleasant and homey, with some comfortable-looking chairs and a couch covered in a nubby fabric in front of a rustic-looking fireplace. The color scheme was still severe, but it had texture. I could remember my Dallas decorator talking about "texture." Texture is good.

"Ms. McCoy?" Still no answer.

I was sure the office had been at this end of the house. I spotted a hall with doors on either side of it. I opened one and peeked through. "Ha!" It was the utility room I had gone through when Ms. McCoy showed me out. That meant that the room on the left should be the office.

I knocked at the door. No answer there, either. Champion Yonkers yowled and kicked.

"Sorry, Champ," I said. "I think this is where you're supposed to be." I opened the door and found myself facing the big walnut desk. Marion McCoy was sitting behind it. We both jumped.

"Oh!" I said. "Is this where you wanted the cat?"

"Yes! Give him to me."

I handed him over, and Ms. McCoy held him at arm's length, apparently trying to keep the cat hair off her basic black. But Yonkers saw prison on the horizon, and he wasn't happy. He yowled and kicked, and he managed to draw blood from her wrist.

"Ouch! Let me help you," I said. "Bad cat!" I quickly closed the door behind me, then looked around the room and spotted a box of tissues on an end table. I plucked one and held it out to her.

Ms. McCoy put Champion Yonkers down. He ran under the desk and knocked over a small wastebasket, then looked at us proudly.

"You're a naughty cat," I said. Ms. McCoy was pressing the tissue to her arm. "You should put something on that. Cat scratches can be dangerous."

"Yonk never roams through garbage cans," Ms. McCoy said. "Just the office trash."

I knelt and started scooping papers back into the wastebasket.

"I can take care of that," Ms. McCoy said. She was glaring now. I didn't understand why she should be mad. She certainly was acting oddly. "I'm sure you need to get back to the bar."

I was dismissed. I stood up. And as I did Champion Yonkers jumped out from under the desk. He capered about, knocking some wadded-up papers around like balls.

"You're a character," I told him as I edged toward the door. "And you were right, Ms. McCoy. He jumped down onto the barker—I mean the bartender—I guess from that balcony. The he tried to eat the olives."

"Jumping down like that is one of his favorite tricks. Thank you for bringing him back. You can go now."

"Certainly." But before I could open the door, something shot out across the floor and hit my foot. Champion Yonkers chased it, still capering around. I looked down, but Ms. McCoy moved casually, and her foot almost touched mine. Something crunched.

Startled, I looked around. "Did something break?"

"It's that cat," Ms. McCoy said easily. Her glare had softened into a watchful look. "I'll clean it up. Would you mind taking those two glasses on the coffee table back to the kitchen?"

I nodded. In a chair near the door, I saw a wad of plastic, and I recognized it as a pair of the plastic gloves used by food-service workers. "How did these get here?" I said. I scooped them up and stuck them in my pocket. Then I picked up two glasses from the coffee table. One smelled strongly of bourbon. "Sorry about the scratch," I said, and I left.

I went back through the sitting room and down the corridor or pergola or whatever—suddenly I remembered. "Peristyle," I said. "It's a peristyle."

Well, I was glad I hadn't tried to say *that* in front of Marion McCoy. It would probably have come out "parachute" or "percolator."

Why did the woman intimidate me so much? I wondered all the way down the peristyle, past the kitchen, and into the huge, cold reception room.

And there I stopped, because six people were looking in my direction in horror.

For a moment I wondered wildly just what I had done. Then I realized that they weren't looking at me. All six of them were staring at something over my head. And whatever it was, it was making a horrible choking sound.

I quickly took six steps forward and whirled to see what they were looking at, what the ghastly noise was.

I looked up just in time to see Clementine Ripley tumble over the balcony rail.

She hit the floor in front of the bar, landing all splayed out, like a bean-bag toy. She didn't move. But something brown and white rolled toward me and stopped at my feet.

It was a half-eaten Amaretto truffle.

CHOCOLATE CHAT

HEALTH

- Chocolate is only figuratively "to die for." Modern nutrition has found many health benefits in the luscious stuff. Chocolate contains antioxidants, a substance that protects cells. A 1.4-ounce piece of milk chocolate typically has four hundred milligrams of antioxidants. A piece of dark chocolate the same size has twice as many, but white chocolate—which contains cocoa butter only—contains none.

- Chocolate does contain caffeine. But even a dark chocolate bar contains from a tenth to a third of the caffeine found in one cup of coffee.

- But isn't chocolate fattening? Not in moderation. In Switzerland, where the annual consumption of chocolate is twice that of the United States, the obesity rate is half as high.

- While chocolate may not harm humans, it can be lethal to dogs and cats. Both the Cat Fancier's Association and the American Veterinary Medicine Association warn against allowing either species to have chocolate in any form.

Chapter 4

I reached down to pick up the Amaretto truffle, just on general principles of neatness. But before I could grab it, Mike Herrera stepped in front of me, blocking me like an opposing guard jumping in front of a top scorer. He didn't single me out, but shooed all of us into the kitchen.

The Warner Pier hospital closed several years ago, so the village relies on a team of volunteer EMTs, and someone called them pronto. While we waited, Jason, who turned out to be Herrera Catering's official first aider, did what he could. Of course, there was nothing anyone could do for Clementine Ripley. All of us who had seen her fall knew that. I felt sure she had been dead before she fell over the balcony rail. She certainly hadn't moved after she hit the floor.

The speculation in the kitchen was that she'd had a stroke. "My grandmother dropped over just the same way," Lindy said. "Got up to answer the phone and died before she could get into the living room." Everybody nodded wisely and muttered about Clementine Ripley's heart.

But the chef who'd been preparing the nest for the steamboat round laughed harshly and spoke under his breath. "What heart?" he said.

The paramedics arrived within ten minutes, and Jason came into the kitchen with the rest of us. He was shaking his head, and his aftershave was almost overpowered by sweat. "God, Mike," he said. "I was afraid to touch her much. The way she fell—her neck . . ."

"I do not think eet is of importance," Mr. Herrera said. Excitement had brought out his accent. "Eet's hokay."

Jason shook harder. "If Greg just wasn't on duty—"

"Everybody knows hee's an idiot," Herrera said.

Lindy and I were leaning against the sink. She snorted. "Oh, no! Not Greg Gossip!"

I spoke in an undertone. "Greg who?"

"Gregory Glossop," Lindy said. "You remember, Mr. Glossop at the Superette pharmacy? He's a creep."

"All I remember was that Aunt Nettie always insisted that her prescriptions be filled at Downtown Drugs."

"That's because Gregory Glossop is such a blabbermouth. I bought some prenatal caps in there the day I found out I was pregnant with little Tony, and the phone was ringing when I got home. My mom's club had already set a date for the baby shower."

"What's Mr. Glossop doing as a paramedic?"

She shrugged. "He took the training and all. I think he just hates to miss anything."

We stood silently, and in a minute I heard a loud voice coming from the cold room where Clementine Ripley was lying on the cold floor. It was a prissy, high-pitched tenor, and its owner had projection. The voice carried into every corner of the kitchen.

"Well! I'm willing to stake my reputation on it." The tenor's voice was filled with pleasure.

Lindy grimaced. "There he goes. Greg Gossip."

A deeper voice, a baritone, muttered, but I couldn't catch the words.

The tenor squawked again. "You're going to have to call in the state police!"

The baritone made soothing sounds, but the tenor didn't calm down.

"Well! I believe that piece of candy killed her!"

A piece of candy killed her? One particular piece? That was the most ridiculous thing I'd ever heard. What could a single chocolate do? Send her into some kind of diabetic fit? Or was it one piece too many—a chocolate last straw, as it were—and it laid down the final piece of plaque on a key artery, giving Clementine Ripley a heart attack? How could the guy—whoever he was—say a piece of candy could kill anybody?

While I was thinking all that, the lower voice rumbled again. Then the tenor answered, even higher than ever.

"Chief, this is cyanide poisoning! I can smell the scent of almonds."

Well, that did it. The tenor was claiming that one of my aunt's delicious chocolates had contained poison. I wasn't going to stand for it.

I walked to the kitchen door, pushed past Mike Herrera, crossed the dining room, and entered the room where Clementine Ripley had died.

"Of course, that chocolate smells like almonds," I said loudly. "It's an armadillo truffle!"

That stopped everybody in the room in their tracks. Two paramedics kneeling by Clementine Ripley swiveled their heads toward me, and two uniformed cops, both very young, swung around to see who this fool was. But I focused on the two men who were facing each other in the center of the room. They had to be the tenor and the baritone who had been arguing. They had also whipped their heads in my direction when I spoke up.

I walked closer to them before I said any more. "I mean, Amaretto. It's an Amaretto truffle," I said. "I work for TenHuis Chocolade. We furnished the chocolates for the party, and Nettie TenHuis sent an extra half dozen Amaretto truffles for Clementine Ripley personally."

Both men stared at me. The taller man seemed familiar, and in a moment I realized he was the man who had backed up his police car and let me out of Clementine Ripley's driveway that afternoon. Standing up, he looked like Abraham Lincoln with a shave and a buzz cut. His features hinted that he'd been in several fights over the years, but he didn't look tough or angry. In fact, he was peering over the top of a pair of half glasses, and the angle of his head gave an impish look to his soft brown eyes. He looked humorous, somehow, but dependable.

He spoke calmly, repeating the key word. "Amaretto?" I recognized the deep voice I had heard from the kitchen.

I nodded. "Yes. It's an almond-flavored liqueur. Aunt Nettie uses it in that particular chocolate."

The second man sputtered again. "Well! I don't care what flavor the chocolates were," he said. "I still think Ms. Ripley was killed by cyanide."

This man was several inches shorter than I am. He was chubby and almost completely bald, and he had light-colored eyelashes and eyebrows. The combination managed to give the impression that he had more skin than the rest of us. His pouty little mouth was pursed into a disagreeable little circle.

"It's not up to me to say how cyanide could have gotten into the candy," he said. "That will be up to law enforcement authorities. But I'd be derelict in my duty if I smelled that almond aroma and said nothing."

"We wouldn't want you to be derelict in your duty," the tall man said. He spoke deliberately. "And now, miss, I gather that you're Mrs. TenHuis's niece."

"Yes. I'm Lee McKinney."

"I'm Hogan Jones. I'm chief of police for Warner Pier. And I gather that you know something about the chocolates."

"I delivered them."

"Tell me about it."

I told him. About how Aunt Nettie had taken the bonbons, truffles, molded chocolate, and fruits from the workroom storage and loaded them onto the silver trays that Clementine Ripley had sent. And how she had prepared a small box with samples.

"Did you see her put the chocolates in that box?"

"No. She did it while I was combing my hair. But I'm sure someone saw her. There's nothing sneaky about Aunt Nettie. And she's very proud of the quality of her chocolates."

The tenor—he wore an EMT jacket—sniffed. "Well! She may be proud of her candies, but we all know she had a good reason not to like Clementine Ripley."

I turned on him. "I've only been back in Warner Pier a week, and I've already heard all kinds of bad things about Clementine Ripley. She was supposedly crooked. She beat the city out of this land and hurt the community economically. Plus, every news magazine in the country has had some story about how she kept some guilty clinic—I mean, client!—out of prison. Who did like her?"

"I used to."

The words came from behind me, near the French doors. I whirled toward the speaker.

It was Joe Woodyard. He was standing in one of the doorways that led out to the terrace.

I could have died on the spot. Not only had I been speaking ill of the dead—I'd been doing it at the top of my voice in front of the dead's ex-husband. I expected Joe to tear into me about the way I'd been talking about Clementine Ripley.

But he didn't pay any attention to me.

"Hi, Joe," the police chief said. "This is bad business. How'd you find out about it?"

"Hugh called me."

"Ah." The chief nodded.

Hugh? Wasn't that the security guard? I didn't ask the question. In fact, I stood as still as a rabbit with a coyote nosing around outside its hole. I didn't move. I didn't speak. I didn't do anything that might call anyone's attention to me.

Joe Woodyard walked around the three of us, zigzagged past the uniformed cops, and knelt beside Clementine Ripley's body. I couldn't see his face. He reached out and touched her hair gently. Then he stood up and turned toward the police chief. He looked pretty serious.

"I assume you'll do an autopsy."

Chief Jones nodded. "We'd have to, Joe. Unattended death. You have any objection?"

"It wouldn't matter if I did. I've been out of the picture for two years, remember?"

"How come you're here?"

"Clementine and I might not have been able to live together, but I didn't wish her any harm." Joe nodded toward me. "Like the lady says, Clementine was pretty short on friends. And she didn't have any family. Except maybe Marion. And Hugh said Marion took off for Holland right before somebody called the EMTs."

"We're looking for Ms. McCoy now," the chief said. "Joe, I'd appreciate it if you'd hang around awhile."

Joe nodded. He pulled a spindly Windsor chair away from the wall, moved it toward Clementine Ripley's body, and put it down several feet from her head. "I'll be here," he said. "I'll stay until they take her away."

He sat down in the chair, and though he didn't snap out a salute, bark out orders, or even sit up straight—actually, he leaned over with his elbows on his knees, clasped his hands, and stared at the floor— it was clear that he was standing guard over his ex-wife.

The EMTs brought in a sheet and laid it over Ms. Ripley. Gregory Glossop helped them, but he didn't say another word. The chief conferred quietly with his two uniformed officers. I made a quick retreat to the kitchen and slunk into my spot beside Lindy.

She leaned close and spoke in my ear. "What happened?"

I shook my head. I didn't want to describe either my stupidity or Joe Woodyard's behavior.

Why had Joe married Clementine Ripley? She was a lot older than he was. She was also a lot richer, and he'd been asking her for money earlier that day. The conventional opinion around Warner Pier would probably be that he married her for money—just as most of Rich's friends had thought I married him for his money—or to advance his career as an attorney. But somehow I thought Joe's relationship with Clementine had been more than that.

Whatever Clementine Ripley had been, she was definitely not a fool. She must have known that "everyone," whoever that is, would have thought she bought Joe as a boy toy, a plaything. I couldn't imagine a woman with the ego Clementine Ripley must have had allowing her friends to laugh at her over her choice of a husband. Unless Joe had fooled her completely, and his behavior now was another act. I'd never know. It was, I reminded myself, none of my business.

The catering crew huddled in the kitchen until we got the word that we could pack up and leave. Mike Herrera came in, smiled, and told us we were all wonderful employees, and he appreciated our calmness. The food, he said, was to be donated to the homeless shelter in Holland. He didn't explain who made that decision.

I didn't quarrel with that—obviously, the party was off—but it made me wonder about Marion McCoy. I couldn't believe she wasn't out there giving orders. If she'd gone to Holland—which was an odd thing to do right before a party—hadn't she taken a cell phone? Had anybody even told her that Ms. Ripley was dead?

And Duncan Ainsley? Where was he? If he was a house guest—he'd told me he was staying in "the guest cottage"—you'd think he'd show some concern over the death of his hostess.

All the Herrera Catering employees bustled around, putting the glasses, plates, and silverware back into their racks, wrapping rolls, refolding tablecloths, and stuffing napkins into sacks. I tried to help—I expected to be paid and wanted to earn my wages—but somebody had to explain everything about the routine to me.

When the new excitement began I was in the dining room concentrating on refolding tablecloths. The others on the crew were nudging each other and whispering before I caught the raised voices from the big room and realized something was going on.

"You've got to be wrong!" It sounded like a scream from a tortured animal. I had to listen to the second scream before I could identify the voice as coming from Marion McCoy.

"I only ran into Holland for a few minutes! Clementine can't be *dead*!"

A low rumble answered her. It could have been either the police chief or Joe Woodyard. But whatever was said didn't mollify Marion.

"No! No! It can't be true!"

Then I heard Greg Glossop's whiny tenor. "She may have been poisoned," he said. He sounded self-important.

"Poisoned!" Marion was still out of control. "That's impossible!"

Another voice tried to calm her. Was it Duncan Ainsley?

Then Marion again. "It must have been natural causes! No one would have wanted to hurt Clementine!"

That's not the way I'd heard it, of course. I kept folding, resisting the temptation to look around. But I admit I was listening hard.

"Nobody would have wanted to hurt Clementine." Marion said it more quietly. Then she gave a gasp. "Except—except you!"

Then I did look around. Marion was pointing at Joe Woodyard.

"Don't be silly, Marion," Joe answered her calmly. "I know you and I never got along, but Clem and I had settled our differences two years ago."

"Oh, is that true? Then why were you arguing with her just a few hours ago?"

"We didn't have an argument."

"Didn't you? You were here asking for money."

Joe didn't answer, and when I looked through the archway that separated the dining room from the living room, I saw that his face was like a thundercloud rolling in over the lake.

Marion McCoy evidently thought she was winning, and she pressed her advantage. "He was here, Chief Jones. And he did ask for money." She looked around, her face furious and excited, and her eyes rested on me.

"I can prove it, too," she said. "There was another witness. That woman from TenHuis Chocolade!"

She pointed at me, and everybody in the room turned in my direction. The chief, Joe, and Marion—all of them stared at me.

"Lee McKinney!" Marion McCoy said. "She can back me up. She heard every word Joe said!"

Chapter 5

I didn't do the first thing that occurred to me—turn and run out the kitchen door. I stood still, looking at everybody looking at me.

I'm not a fast thinker. If I hadn't become aware of this on my own over the years, I have plenty of friends and family who tell me about it. So I compensate. I don't act in a hurry. Rich used to yell at me over it. "Why are you just sitting there? Say something!" But I've found out from sad experience that, when I pop off and do or say the first thing that comes into my head, it usually lands me in a worse mess than I was in to begin with. As the old saying goes, it's better to keep quiet and be thought a fool than to say something and remove all doubt.

So after Marion McCoy yelled at me, I just stood there, and Marion, Joe Woodyard, Chief Jones, Duncan Ainsley, and two members of the Herrera Catering crew all stared at me.

Then Marion McCoy spoke again. "Well? You heard him, right? You heard Joe Woodyard demanding money from Clementine. If I heard him, you must have heard him, too. So tell the chief about it!"

After that, I knew what I wanted to do—the opposite of whatever Marion McCoy wanted me to do. So I picked up the tablecloth I'd been told to put away, and I matched up the right and left corners and shook it out, ready to fold again. Then I turned toward Marion McCoy, and I said, "I'm sorry, but if there's some sort of quarrel going on out here, it's none of my affair. I will be happy to answer any questions Chief Jones has for me, but for now I don't think I'll make any comment."

Marion McCoy looked as if she were going to explode. Joe Woodyard gave a barking laugh—just one *Ha!*—and Chief Jones looked over the top of his glasses and grinned.

Duncan Ainsley patted Marion's shoulder awkwardly. His hands were shaking. "Now, Marion," he said. "The chief will be taking statements from all the witnesses. Why don't you go back to your apartment? You prob'ly feel like the ragged end of a misspent life."

I had to admire the guy. He could keep up the colorful Texan act even when he seemed shook up himself. He escorted Marion past me, into the hall that led to the office where I'd taken the cat. He was all attention as he walked with her, patting her arm, very much the friend who was helping her cope with the death of her employer.

There was just one odd thing. Right before he led Marion McCoy past me, as he reached a point when only I could see him, he nodded and winked at me.

What did that mean?

Of course, an investment counselor—even a famous one—is basically a salesman. That sort of gesture, designed to build rapport, was second nature to a man like Duncan Ainsley. There was no way he could have a personal interest in me.

Not long after that Mike Herrera told Lindy and me that we were finished, and the police chief didn't seem to have any more interest in us, though he warned that we might have to make formal statements later. The phrase "after we know the cause of death" was left unsaid.

So Lindy and I left. I was surprised that there was no crowd outside the heavy security gate. I guess I'd lived in a big city too long; I'd expected a lot of reporters to be gathered there, but the street was empty. I reminded myself that Warner Pier is a long way from major news agencies. As for the expected guests, Clementine Ripley had died two hours before the benefit was scheduled to begin, so apparently somebody—maybe Mike Herrera—had known whom to call to announce that the party was canceled. The security guard—Hugh?—would have turned away any guests who showed up.

I will say, however, that as we drove back toward the main part of Warner Pier we saw an unusual number of people sitting on their screened-in porches; it was a warm evening, and maybe they didn't have air-conditioning. But they all seemed to be paying close attention to the vehicles driving by. Warner Pier wasn't ignoring Clementine Ripley's death, whatever had caused it.

Personally, I was betting on natural causes.

It wasn't dark yet—just after eight o'clock. TenHuis Chocolade would be open another hour. I dropped Lindy off at her house and declined her halfhearted invitation to come in. Tony came out to the car and we spoke briefly; I wouldn't have known him as the skinny kid who used to flirt with Lindy over a limeade at the Downtown Drugs soda fountain. He'd grown five or six inches and gained forty pounds in the ten years since I'd seen him.

I saw what Lindy meant about his trying to get in touch with his Hispanic heritage. When we'd been in high school, Tony had tried hard not to look Mexican, while his father had been definitely Latino. Now his father just looked like a dark-haired American, and Tony had grown a mustache and sideburns.

I drove back to the chocolate shop and parked in the alley. As soon as I walked inside, Aunt Nettie ran to meet me. "Lee! Are you all right?"

"Of course. What are you doing here? You were supposed to go home at four."

"I had to make sure you were okay. I went out to Clementine Ripley's house, but they wouldn't let me in. What happened?"

I told her the story, but I slurred over the chocolates and the accusations that Gregory Glossop had made about one of them containing cyanide. I told her he had suggested cyanide poisoning, but I didn't specifically say that he'd accused an Amaretto truffle of being responsible for her death.

As I finished, Aunt Nettie shook her head. "Terrible, terrible. Such a thing to happen. And that Gregory Gossip! He's terrible, too."

"Then you don't trust his opinion on the cause of death?"

"Of course not. Greg always wants things to be as bad as possible. Nobody would poison anybody in Warner Pier. It's just a little place!"

I was torn. Should I tell her the rest, prepare her for the worst? Or let well enough alone? Which cliché applied?

Before I could decide, the phone rang.

I answered. "TenHuis Chocolade."

"Oh! Are yew open?" The voice on the phone was startled, but it still sounded Texan.

I checked my watch. Eight-thirty. "We close in half an hour."

"Ah see. Is this Lee McKinney?"

"Yes." The accent made the caller's identity plain. "Is this Mr. Ainsley?"

He laughed. "Shore is. I guess it's impossible for me to hide up here in Michigan. But if I try to talk different, it's like putting a high-dollar saddle on a jackass."

Why on earth was he calling? I wondered, but I tried to be polite. "My Texas grandma would have said your accent sounds as nice as a cotton hat."

"I'd better watch you, young lady. A Texas gal can tell when I'm bullin'. But when I called I was expectin' an answerin' machine. Do y'all work round the clock?"

"The shop is open from ten a.m. until nine p.m. My aunt comes in at eight, since she's in charge of making the chocolates. I come in at noon and work until the place is closed and the cleanup finished. Why? Did you need chocolates tonight?"

Ainsley chuckled. "An emergency chocolate attack? No, I just wanted to tell you I'm sorry Ms. McPicky"—his voice was scornful—"tried to put you on the spot, and to tell you that you handled her as smart as a tree full of owls."

"Thank you, Mr. Ainsley." I assumed he was trying to explain the wink. "I know Ms. McCoy's really upset."

"She is, as we all are, so we have to make allowances. But she shouldn't have asked you to make a statement discrediting your friend."

"You mean Joe Woodyard? I really can't claim him as a friend. I was one of the girls who used to hang around on the beach when he was a lifeguard. That was twelve years ago. I doubt he even remembered me, except as a face in the crowd."

"Oh, then you're not seeing him—socially?"

"Oh, no! I hadn't thought of him in years. When we ran into each other this afternoon, it took me a few minutes to figure out who he was."

"I see. Well, in that case . . ." He paused for a moment, then spoke again. "Well, before I go back to Chicago I just wanted to assure you that you shouldn't be upset over Marion's actions, and to say you handled the situation as slick as a peeled onion."

"Thank you, Mr. Ainsley."

"Please call me Duncan."

Well, that was peculiar. What did it matter what a peon like Lee McKinney called a man like Duncan Ainsley? He wasn't coming on to me, was he? Back when I'd been a beauty queen, that had been known to happen. But now that I had gone in for the natural look . . . Ainsley mystified me.

"I appreciate your call," I said lamely. "Then you're leaving tonight?"

"The police asked me to stay overnight. It's kind of awkward, being a house guest when the hostess dies. It's not as if we were even close friends. Clementine just asked me to stay because I was a cosponsor for this event that didn't come off. But I'm assuming the police will let me go in the morning, after they get this druggist fellow's stupid ideas straightened out."

"Then you don't take the cyanide charge seriously?"

"Of course not! From what Marion said, I guess this man and Clementine had had some sort of disagreement earlier. But the thought of someone poisoning Clementine is plumb silly."

"I thought she had a lot of enemies."

"Well, yes. If a disgruntled client shot her—but to poison her in her own house? That's ridiculous. Anyway, I do want to keep on top of the situation. Could I call you again?"

The request surprised me, and I reacted with my usual aplomb. I gasped and said, "What for?"

Ainsley chuckled. "You're a bright young woman. Perhaps I might at least call on you for local knowledge as the situation develops?"

I was even more surprised at that idea. And right then another strange thing happened. I looked out into the shop—as I said, the office had glass windows that overlooked the workroom where the chocolates were made and the little retail shop—just as the street door opened.

Joe Woodyard walked in.

He looked through the several thicknesses of glass that separated us, and he glared at me.

I stood holding the phone, completely silent, until I heard Duncan Ainsley's voice again. "Lee? May I call you? For local background?"

Suddenly I was very nervous. "I'll be happy to help in any way I can," I said. "But I'm not really a yokel." And I hung up.

I stood there, feeling like a complete fool and staring at Joe Woodyard. This was all too strange. First a call from Duncan Ainsley. Then a visit from Joe Woodyard. I couldn't believe my personal magnetism was suddenly attracting all the men I'd met that day.

Like other Warner Pier retailers, Aunt Nettie hired the children of friends to deal with the summer trade, and now Joe was talking to the teenager behind the counter, a girl with brown hair tucked into a stringy ponytail. She was no dippier than I had been the summer I was sixteen and worked for TenHuis Chocolade for the first time. She gestured behind her while she spoke to Joe. Then she came to the door to the shop and beckoned to me. "You have a visitor."

I went to the counter.

Joe scowled. "I just wanted to talk to you about that scene out there. Marion has her reasons—"

Little Miss Teenage Counter Help was drinking in the whole conversation. I interrupted Joe. "Come on back."

I ignored the disappointed look on the teenager—I'd just met her the day before, and I couldn't remember her name. I decided the office was a little too close to the front counter, so I led Joe back to the break room. It's more like an old-fashioned dining room, since it's furnished with a heavy oak dining suite, including a tall china cupboard, which had belonged to Aunt Nettie's grandmother, and with several mismatched easy chairs. The floor may be easy-to-clean tile, and the only window may look out on an alley, but the room is bright and cheerful, and even decorated with several watercolors painted by local artists. Aunt Nettie and Uncle Phil used to eat dinner there a lot.

Joe Woodyard frowned. "I guess you and your aunt live here."

It wasn't such an odd thing to say. Nearly all the "downtown" businesses in Warner Pier have apartments upstairs, and some of the merchants do live over their shops.

"No," I said. "But Aunt Nettie's hours are so long she must feel as if she lives here. She comes to work before eight in the morning, and since Uncle Phil died she's been staying until closing a lot of the time." I turned to face Joe. "What did you want to talk to me about?"

"About what happened out at Warner Point." He frowned again. I was beginning to get impatient with Mr. Woodyard. Had he come down to the shop to bawl me out?

"Listen," he said. "I can handle the situation. Don't get any dumb ideas about helping me out. Just keep your mouth shut."

Actually, his remarks made me open my mouth. I was so astonished at what he had said that my jaw dropped like a drawbridge. I was so surprised that I didn't even get mad, at least right away.

"What do you mean?" I said.

"Just because we once knew each other, that doesn't mean you have to cover up for me or anything. Don't let anybody get the idea that we're friends."

What in the world was he talking about? Did he think that I'd refused to repeat his remarks to Chief Jones because I had a personal interest in him?

Suddenly I was furious. What a jerk!

Joe spoke again. "If Marion heard what I said to Clem, then you must have heard it, too. But you'll be better off if you just say no comment."

"What?"

"I had a legitimate reason for asking Clem for money. I simply don't want—"

By then I knew what I wanted to say, and I said it. "Stop! You keep *your* mouth shut!"

He obeyed so fast his jaws snapped, and I was the one who went on.

"What I said out there had nothing to do with you. If the chief asks me, I'll tell him exactly what I heard. I just didn't want Marion McCoy ordering me around. And frankly, I don't want you ordering me around, either."

"What do you mean? Ordering you around?"

"Why did you come by here to tell me how to handle the situation?"

"The situation? What are you talking about?"

"Chief Jones, of course."

"I don't care about him. Tell him any damn thing you want!"

"Then what are you talking about?"

"I'm trying to warn you about the tabloids."

"Tabloids? I'm not interested in the tabloids."

Joe laughed harshly. "About this time tomorrow you will be."

"What do you mean?"

"After the tabloid reporters hit town, ready to make big bucks from Clementine's death, then you'll care. When you've seen your life displayed for the grocery-store checkout line, you get sort of paranoid."

Maybe I looked surprised, because he laughed again.

"Oh, nobody reads them! Or admits it. But somehow all the people you thought were your friends know what was in the latest issue."

"Why would the tabloids be interested in Clementine Ripley? She was a lawyer, not a movie star."

"True, but she represented a lot of celebrities. When the word got out that we were married—God! It was awful. I was still with Legal Aid, but all of a sudden I couldn't get any work done. I didn't have a staff to insulate me from the reporters the way Clem did. Can you imagine trying to represent some woman whose ex-husband has been using his court-ordered visitation to beat their baby—and you have to do it with a dozen photographers swarming you every time you came out of the courtroom?"

"You may have had problems, but . . ."

Joe didn't hear me. "When we split and I started the boat business, it was worse. For about a month every time I dipped a brush in varnish or sawed a board, a strobe flashed."

"But . . ."

Joe smiled, but he didn't look amused. "I guess I deserved it. Obscure young lawyer walks out on famous wife, chucks law for manual labor," he said, as if quoting a headline. "Defense attorney's toy boy husband flees toy box."

"Stop!" I'd had enough. "Hush up!"

Joe shut up and glared.

I glared back. "Why am I getting this lecture? No reporters will be interested in me."

"Oh, yes, they will. You were a witness. You're involved."

"No, I'm not! And TenHuis Chocolade isn't, either."

"That's the spirit. Just remember that. No matter who calls you—*Time* magazine or the *National Enquirer*—just tell 'em they'll have to talk to the police."

I did my thinking-about-it act for thirty seconds. "Why do you think you need to tell me this? Do I seem that stupid?"

"No. I'm telling you because you're going to be getting a lot of pressure." He stopped and seemed to consider his next words. "And now I'd better get out of here before the correspondents arrive from Chicago, or you and your aunt are likely to get the full treatment."

"What do you mean?"

"Oh, the tabloids would love our getting together like this, in a quiet back room. Cinderella widower of famed lawyer has tête-à-tête with high school sweetheart."

"That's not true! You and I weren't sweethearts. We barely knew each other."

"The tabloids don't care. They take one little lie and hang a whole string of phony implications on it. Didn't my mom tell me you were in some beauty contest? They'll dig that up. Famed attorney killed by beauty queen's chocolates."

As Joe said the final, bitter word, I heard a loud gasp behind me. For a mad moment I thought the tabloid press had already arrived, and I swung around.

I was relieved for a second. The gasp had come from Aunt Nettie. Then I saw the look on her face.

"Chocolate? The chocolate killed Clementine Ripley? That's just not possible!"

I tried to soothe her. I explained that Gregory Glossop had picked up on the smell of almonds from the chocolates, but that the Amaretto flavoring was a more logical explanation for the aroma.

Joe lost some of his glare when he talked to Aunt Nettie. "Lee jumped right in and told the chief about the flavoring," he said. "Greg Glossop may be an idiot, but his opinion won't count. The medical examiner will be running scientific tests to ascertain the cause of death. And I hope to God it's natural causes."

He gestured. "Is that the alley door? Can I get out that way?"

"Wait," Aunt Nettie said. For the first time I realized that she was holding a TenHuis Chocolade box. "I've got something for you."

Joe took the box, looking perplexed. "Chocolates? Nettie, I don't think this is a good time . . ."

"It's just a sandwich," she said. "A chocolate box was all I had to put it in. A meat loaf sandwich and some carrot sticks. I'm sure you haven't eaten anything. I wish I had something worth giving you."

For a moment Joe stared at her blankly. Then he gave a mocking laugh. "Nettie, you just don't get it," he said. "We can't be friends right now! It will cause too much trouble. Lee, you explain it to her!"

That made me madder than anything else he'd said.

"I won't tell her a thing!" I said. "Aunt Nettie is Aunt Nettie, and if she wants to feed the whole world, it's all right with me."

"I give up," Joe said. "Is that the alley door?"

I opened it without a word, and he went out into the dark. "You two are going to be eaten alive," he said.

I resisted the temptation to slam the door after him. He hadn't even thanked Aunt Nettie for his meat loaf sandwich. But he took it with him.

Chapter 6

Aunt Nettie made me eat a meat loaf sandwich, too. I sat at a stainless-steel worktable in the back of the shop, and she talked to me while I ate.

As she talked she plucked bits of rum-flavored dark chocolate nougat—nougat is what the chocolate maker calls the filling of a truffle—from a plastic dish. This had been mixed earlier and set aside to get firm. Talking a mile a minute, she rolled each piece of nougat into a ball. She made five dozen while I ate my sandwich, her hands working as fast as her mouth. Now and then she stopped to weigh one, to make sure they were all uniform in size, but she didn't once have to start over. Then she took a mixing bowl and drew several cups of dark chocolate from the spigot on the big electric kettle, where a supply is always kept warm and melted. She rolled each nougat ball in the dark chocolate, creating a rum-flavored truffle to die for. And she did it all without looking at her hands. It was a darn impressive performance.

By the time I'd eaten, the counter girls had finished cleaning up the shop. I balanced the cash register, and Aunt Nettie and I went out to the house she and Uncle Phil had shared for thirty-nine of their forty years of marriage. During one year they'd lived in the Netherlands, learning the chocolate business.

I find the house both homey and spooky. It's on the south edge of Warner Pier on Lake Shore Drive. I guess that every town that borders Lake Michigan has a Lake Shore Drive.

We're on the inland side—in other words, we don't have a view of the lake. A lot of well-to-do people have built either summer cottages or year-round homes in the neighborhood, but Aunt Nettie's house is older than most. It was built by my great-grandfather—Uncle Phil's grandfather—in 1904. He was a carpenter in Grand Rapids who put it up as a summer cottage for his wife and kids. One of his sons, my grandfather, opened a gas station in Warner Pier in 1945, and he winterized the family cottage so that he and his family could live there year-round.

So my mother and Uncle Phil grew up in the house. It's a white two-story frame house, with odd bits sticking out here and there for a bathroom and a dining room and a screened porch, which were added on over the years. It's not luxurious; the bathroom has a claw-footed tub that was probably bought secondhand in 1910 and the kitchen sink was new in 1918. It has a "Michigan basement"—cement walls, but a sand floor—which I think must have been ideal for farm families needing a place to store apples and potatoes, but seems kind of odd in the twenty-first century. The decor is authentic country, not decorator "country," and features an accumulation of furniture old enough to be antique, but not valuable enough to be worth selling. As I said, it's homey.

I also find it spooky, because the area is heavily wooded. That makes it beautiful, I suppose, to anybody who wasn't born and raised on the Texas plains. I've read that people raised in wooded areas find plains threatening because the openness makes them feel exposed. But plains people like me find woods threatening because we feel as if some enemy might be hiding among all those trees. I've been spending time in Aunt Nettie's house since I was sixteen, and I'm still a little uneasy about the place.

But I was too tired to feel uneasy that night. I didn't even have nightmares, despite a few vivid presleep flashbacks of Clementine Ripley's body crashing over that railing and landing at my feet.

The next day started off routinely. It was Saturday, the busiest day of the week for a retail business in a resort community at the height of the tourist season.

I got up in time to have a cup of coffee with Aunt Nettie before she went to work at seven-thirty. After she left I turned on a cable news show and caught Duncan Ainsley commenting on the death of Clementine Ripley.

"I'm proud to say she was a friend, as well as a client," he said. "Her death is truly shocking." He seemed quite genuine.

The television newsman said the cause of death was not yet known.

"Well, it's gonna be natural causes," I told him firmly.

I flipped the TV off, washed a load of underwear, and tossed my dry cleaning into the van. I dressed in Warner Pier business casual—clean khaki shorts and chocolate-brown polo shirt with a TenHuis logo. At ten I fixed myself a bowl of local blueberries, lightly sugared, and followed them with bacon, eggs, and toast, a brunch that would last until my six p.m. dinner break. At eleven-thirty, I left. I stopped at the corner where the dry cleaner used to be, only to discover it was now a real estate office. So I left the dry cleaning in the van and went on to TenHuis Chocolade, ready to start my first shift as a supervisor. Which on a Saturday during the busy season was going to include helping out behind the counter—the reason I'd worn the company outfit.

Aunt Nettie, who believes that tourists want to watch chocolates being handmade even on Saturdays, was working with a limited crew—just three hairnet ladies—when I arrived. She kept rolling creamy white chocolate truffles in coconut ("Midori coconut truffles—very creamy all white chocolate truffles, flavored with melon and rolled in coconut.") as she reported on the morning. It had been routine, she said, except for lots of phone calls from her friends as Greg Glossop spread his opinion around town. We were both delighted that neither Chief Jones nor the tabloid press had shown up with questions.

"The longer we wait to hear from Chief Jones," I said, "the more I think Clementine Ripley had a stroke. Or maybe some kind of aneurysm." Aunt Nettie agreed.

Aunt Nettie took a lunch break at one, but worked until four-fifteen, so I was able to ask her some questions before I took over. One of the questions was the name of the counter girl with the stringy ponytail. Her name was Tracy. Her partner that afternoon was a plump girl of similar age, but with better hair, and her name was Stacy. So if I mixed them up, who could tell?

Aunt Nettie obviously wasn't confident about leaving me in charge, but Stacy and Tracy assured her they'd show me the ropes, and we shooed her and the ladies in hairnets out the door.

At four-thirty the phone rang. I didn't exactly jump to answer it, since I expected it to be another of Aunt Nettie's pals wanting to gossip. When I picked it up after the third ring, I was surprised to hear Aunt Nettie herself.

"Lee?" Her voice was all quavery.

"Aunt Nettie? What's wrong?"

"The house is all torn up. We've had a burglar!"

I didn't have to stop and think about that one. "Get out of the house!" I said. "He might still be there. I'll call the cops and be right there."

I called nine-one-one, left Tracy and Stacy on their own, and ran out the back door. I got to the house half a block behind the Warner Pier patrol car.

Aunt Nettie was standing in the drive beside her big Buick. I hugged her, and the two of us waited outside while the deputy checked the four rooms downstairs and the three upstairs. Nobody was there.

When we looked in the door, the house was a wreck. I started inside, ready to begin cleaning up, but I was stopped by the patrolman, a burly young guy whose uniform had been tailored to fit like a second skin. His name tag read CHERRY.

"Let me call in and see what the chief wants to do about this," he said. "He'll probably want photos at least. Maybe fingerprints."

I was surprised. I'd lived in Dallas too long. My mom's apartment there was burglarized, and the cops didn't bother to take fingerprints. She had to wait hours for an investigator to show up at all. I was glad to learn things were still different in a small town.

Aunt Nettie and I were sitting on the porch when another car pulled in, and Chief Jones unfolded his long legs and got out.

I hadn't expected to see him. "What are you doing here?" I said. "Do you do all the investigations?"

"Most of them. Warner Pier has a force of five, and that doesn't include a detective, so I have to do double duty." He looked over the top of his half glasses and grinned his folksy grin. "Besides, when a newcomer to town is involved in two emergency calls in two days, I'd better check it out. What's going on?"

"I don't understand it," Aunt Nettie said. She'd gotten over being frightened. Now she sounded miffed. "Usually Warner Pier burglars just hit the summer people."

"Guess these guys don't have any hometown spirit," the chief said. He opened the trunk of his car and revealed all sorts of esoteric equipment.

"Oh, you know what I mean," Aunt Nettie said. "It's so much easier to break into a house that's going to be empty for weeks or months. Even that doesn't happen so often since most people have alarm systems. And I don't even have anything worth stealing!"

"You've got a television set, haven't you?"

"Yes, but—"

"A VCR? A stereo?"

"No. Phil and I were at the shop so much that we don't have anything but a TV and a clock radio. All our furniture's old, and none of it's valuable. We don't have silver tea services or jewelry or fine art."

The chief sent Patrolman Cherry off to find out if any of the neighbors had seen anything, and he showed us where the burglar got in, which turned out to be a dining room window. It was an old casement that locked with a latch. Someone had smashed out a pane with a rock, then reached inside and opened the window. He found fingerprints on the window, of course, but I began to have a feeling they were going to belong to Aunt Nettie and me.

As soon as the police allowed us into the house, Aunt Nettie called Handy Hans Home Repair Service to come and fix the window, and then we looked around. I began to think Aunt Nettie's assessment of the situation was right—she and I apparently owned nothing that a burglar was interested in taking. At least I couldn't see any big gaps among our possessions. Things just seemed to be all messed up.

The sheets and towels, which Aunt Nettie kept in a cedar chest at the foot of her bed, had been dumped out onto the floor, and clothes were tossed on the floor of her bedroom downstairs and of mine upstairs. The living room furniture was turned over, but when we put it back in place, nothing seemed to be irreparably damaged. The sofa cushions and the pads in the seats of the rocking chairs had not been ripped open, and the magazines hadn't been shredded. The food stuffs were still in the kitchen cupboards. A couple of bottles of wine—Michigan wine, of course—were still on the shelf in the pantry.

"What about you, young lady?" the chief asked. "Your aunt said she doesn't own any electronic gadgets or jewelry. I hate to quote gossip, but the talk around Warner Pier—among the people who knew you when you worked here before—was that you were married to a wealthy man. Do you have any good jewelry? Diamond watches? What's missing?"

I really didn't want to answer. It's embarrassing to be twenty-eight years old and own nothing worth stealing.

"I don't have anything like that. When I divorced Rich, I left everything behind," I said. "I don't own anything but my clothes and the old van."

He frowned at me. "Nothing valuable?"

"Nothing."

I tried to sound firm, the way I had when I argued with my lawyer. But the chief kept staring at me, and I began to feel that I had to give him some explanation.

"Look," I said. "Money was in the middle of every argument Rich and I ever had. I was sick of it, so I refused a financial sentiment."

Darn, tongue-tied again. "I mean settlement! I refused a financial settlement."

Chief Jones looked unbelieving. "Didn't you at least take the dishes and furniture?"

"I guess you had to be there," I said.

That was all the explanation I could give anybody for what I did—leave a marriage after five years and wind up poorer than when I said, "I do." But a complete explanation would be a novel, and I didn't feel like writing one.

I called the shop to check on Tracy and Stacy. They were all agog over the emergency, but they said things were going okay. Aunt Nettie and I kept on straightening up. We still didn't find anything gone. Then I heard Aunt Nettie give a gasp.

"What did you find?" the chief said.

"I did have a hundred dollars in my underwear drawer," Aunt Nettie said. "Five twenties. They're gone."

Chief Jones duly noted the missing money.

"I guess the burglars were mad because they didn't find anything else," Aunt Nettie said. "Maybe that's why they messed everything up."

The chief shrugged.

"They could have messed things up a lot more," I said. "A sack of flour and a dozen eggs on the kitchen floor would have kept us busy twice as long as it's taken us to hang up all these clothes. Is this restraint typical of Warner Pier burglars and vandals?"

"I wouldn't say so. Your aunt's right when she says they usually hit the empty summer cottages and clean out the electronic gadgets and other stuff, things that are easy to pawn. Guns—they'll take those. Sometimes they go for antiques. Of course, lots of people are like Mrs. TenHuis and keep a little money in the house, and if a burglar finds it, it's gone." He began to gather up his equipment. Aunt Nettie sat down on the couch and began to sort the magazines our burglar had tossed around.

The chief kept picking up, but he looked at me while he stowed things away. "You know, Ms. McKinney, there could be a connection to what happened at Clementine Ripley's house."

"You don't really think my aunt or I had anything to do with that?"

"I can't rule it out. Or maybe the burglar was looking for something you took away from there."

"What was I going to take? A ladle from the kitchen? A glass from the bar? That house isn't exactly full of stuff that would be easy to steal. There are no doodads on the tables, and the few paintings on the walls are too large to stick in my pocket."

He grinned that Abe Lincoln grin. "I didn't really figure that you stole anything."

"The only things I handled belonged to Herrera Catering. Glasses, linens, sodas, and mixers. Booze. Lemons and limes. And I didn't bring any of them away."

"I sure do hate coincidences."

"You mean the burglary? I agree completely. From my point of view it seems weird to be dealing with the police two days in a row. But coincidences do happen, Chief Jones."

He nodded, but he still looked skeptical.

"Besides," I said, "we still don't know that Clementine Ripley's death was anything but natural."

"Well . . ." The chief seemed to speak reluctantly.

I felt sure he knew something I didn't want to hear. "What's happened?"

"The Grand Rapids office of the state police is going to announce it at six. It seems Greg Glossop was right for once."

"He was right?"

Chief Jones nodded. "Yep. After what he said, the state lab tested the candy for cyanide."

"You don't mean—!"

"Sorry to be the one to break the news. Cyanide had been injected into all the chocolates in the little box your aunt fixed. The cause of death won't be official until the autopsy results are in, and that'll take several days. But Clementine Ripley's death is being investigated as a murder."

All of a sudden the living room was again as topsy-turvy as it had been after the burglars left. I grabbed the back of one of Aunt Nettie's antique rocking chairs to keep from turning upside down myself.

Then I looked at Aunt Nettie. Her face had crumpled like limp lettuce. "Oh, my stars," she said. "*That's* not going to be good for business."

"It certainly isn't," I said.

But all in all Aunt Nettie took the news the way she takes everything—calmly.

"You aren't surprised?"

"Maybe I don't really understand it yet, Lee. At first it seemed impossible. But when a person everybody in the world had some reason to dislike—someone like Clementine Ripley—dies under such odd circumstances . . . Well, maybe it would seem stranger than ever if she'd died of natural causes."

"Mr. Ainsley said he wouldn't have been surprised if somebody shot her," I said. "But poisoning is hard to believe. I was just sure she died of a stroke or something. This is awful."

"It's going to be bad for everybody," Chief Jones said.

"And now I guess you'll need those statements from both of us."

"You'll have to give statements, but I won't be taking them. As soon as we got the report, I called in the state police."

"Oh? Is that standard procedure?"

"It's optional." For the first time Chief Jones sounded short-tempered. "It seemed like the best idea. We'd have to use their lab anyway."

His jaw clenched a couple of times before he went on. "They're sending one of their best men—Detective Lieutenant Alec VanDam. He'll have a team, of course, in a case this high profile. He'll be in touch with you. And I guess I've done about as much as I can around here. Jerry may find a neighbor who saw something."

It took me a minute to realize that Jerry must be the patrolman, the one whose name tag read CHERRY. His name was Jerry Cherry, it seemed. I was too upset to giggle.

The chief was still talking. "Some neighbor may have seen a car, or a stranger. But there's a lot of traffic along Lake Shore Drive, and the trees hide Nettie's house."

Chief Jones went out to his car and began to put his case in the trunk. Patrolman Jerry Cherry came back and told him he hadn't had any luck with the neighbors. "I'll try the mailman," he said. "But I'm afraid he comes in the morning."

When he spoke again he lowered his voice, but I could still hear him through the open door. "Who'd you draw from the state police?"

"Alec VanDam."

"Didn't he work that holdup and shooting over at Perkins Lake?"

"Yeah, he's the one. I was sure they'd send somebody good. High-profile case like this."

"It's still a dirty deal. You woulda done just as good, Chief."

Chief Jones snorted. "It would raise too many questions," he said. He got in his car and drove away.

Dirty deal? What had Jerry Cherry meant by that?

I decided I wanted to know. So I went out on the porch, leaned against the railing, and turned on my Texas accent. "Off-cer Chairy?"

"Yes, Ms. McKinney?"

"We really 'preciate all this attention. I grew up in a small town, in north Texas, and the law enforcement officials were just as kind as you and Chief Jones have been. In fact, my daddy's garage has the contract for mainte-nance on the sheriff's cars. But then I moved to Dallas, and it was a dif'rent story in a big city! I'm shore glad to see that the small-town spirit is still alive up here in Michigan."

Cherry straightened his shoulders, just a little. "We try to serve, Ms. McKinney. Chief Jones is real firm about that."

"Chief Jones sure is an interesting man. Is he a native of Warner Pier?"

"Oh, no! He was one of the top detectives in Cincinnati. We're really lucky to have him here."

"From Cincinnati to Warner Pier? The city fathers must have offered him a lot of money!"

Cherry laughed. "He took early retirement from the Cincinnati force, and he and his wife moved up here. That was more than five years ago."

"I see."

"They'd always vacationed in the area—you know, decided they'd like living here. But Mrs. Jones died three years ago."

"That's too bad."

"Yah. It kinda left the chief at loose ends. So when the job of police chief opened, he applied. The council was smart enough to hire him."

I sat on the porch rail. "If he has a lot of experience as a detective—well, I'm a little surprised that he called in the state police to investigate the death of Clementine Ripley. Seems like he would have handled it himself."

I smiled—not flirtatiously, but in a friendly manner. And I looked at Of-ficer Cherry and waited for him to speak.

But he didn't. His jaw clenched just the way the chief's had. I didn't say anything, either.

This game of nonverbal chicken went on for about thirty seconds, I guess, though it seemed like thirty minutes.

Finally Jerry Cherry spoke. "It's up to the chief," he said. "I'd better go. You call in if anything else happens."

He got in his car and drove away, leaving me and my Texas accent flat.

"Lee," I told myself, "you're definitely losing your touch." I'd have to ask somebody else. Maybe Aunt Nettie.

But Aunt Nettie wasn't likely to know. She concentrated on TenHuis

Chocolade almost to the exclusion of everything else, and she was too kind-hearted to enjoy idle gossip.

So who did I know who would know? Well, all the city officials, the mayor . . .

"Ye gods!" I said. "How lucky! I forgot to go by and give Mike Herrera my Social Security number."

Chapter 7

Mike Herrera's office, Aunt Nettie told me, was down the block from TenHuis Chocolade, above Mike's Sidewalk Café. And, yes, Mr. Herrera did own the café.

"He's bought several Warner Pier restaurants," Aunt Nettie said. "I think he leases most of them, but Mike's and the main restaurant, Herrera's—down on the water—he operates himself."

I went down the street—past T-Shirt Alley, with silly sayings in the window; Leathers, which displayed expensive handbags and luggage; and the Old Time Antique Shop, whose window was packed with stuff Aunt Nettie and I used at home every day. I crossed the street and climbed the stairs to the office of Herrera enterprises. A middle-aged woman who identified herself as the bookkeeper gave me the proper forms to fill out so I could get paid for the few hours of work I'd done. There was no sign of Mayor Mike Herrera.

"I need to talk to Mr. Herrera," I said. "Is he here?"

"I think he's over at city hall," the bookkeeper said. "But he'll be back soon. He always checks on things before the evening dinner crowd shows up at Mike's."

Mike's was new since my high school days, and I had noticed it seemed to be packed at every meal. It wasn't quite your standard sidewalk café. Yes, it had tables on the sidewalk, inside a little railing, but it really got its name from its decor. The floors of both the outside dining area and the inside room were covered with graffiti—they looked like children had been writing on a sidewalk. I'd figured out that this was actually paint, since the waitresses ran back and forth all the time and the chalk never wore off.

The aisles between the tables were delineated by hopscotch games, and the walls were decorated with jump ropes, jacks, and other children's toys and games. There was a big black slate wall, too, where customers were invited to write their own graffiti.

Kids loved the place, obviously, but after five p.m. children were only served in one section and by ten p.m. or so, I'd noticed, Mike's turned into a date bar. It seemed as if Mr. Herrera had covered all the bases at Mike's—Aunt Nettie had even remarked that the food was pretty good, high praise from her.

When I came down the steps and looked into Mike's, it was nearly six p.m. and the place was filling up. Mike Herrera was at the back of the restaurant, headed into the kitchen. I went inside and called out. "Mr. Herrera! Can I talk to you a minute?"

He stole a glance at his watch before he motioned me to a stool at the end of the bar and stood beside me. His beaming smile contrasted with his earlier look at his watch. "Miss Lee. A pleasure."

I decided a frontal attack was going to be the best plan for a busy man. "I'm here with a nosy question," I said quietly, "but I have an excuse. I heard that cyanide was found in Clementine Ripley's chocolates, and I'm determined to stay on top of this situation because of my aunt."

Mike Herrera looked concerned. "The situation is truly shocking, but I'm sure the lovely Mrs. Nettie has nothing to do with the events."

"I'm sure of that, too, but her chocolates were apparently used as a murder weapon. So she—and I—are involved whether we like it or not."

"So what was your question?"

"I'm trying to understand why the state police have been called in when I hear that Chief Jones is himself an experienced detective. Can you explain?"

"Eet is a motter of routine," Herrera said.

Hmmm. His Spanish accent had abruptly reappeared. Did that mean my question had made him nervous?

"The choice was up to Chief Jones heemself," he said. "The officials of Warner Pier weesh to cooperate fully in the death of thees prominent woman, to make sure that all channels of investigation are fully explored. Chief Jones—indeed, all the city employees—weel work with the state detectives en any way we can."

I felt that I'd just given him a chance to practice for a press conference. But I hadn't gotten any kind of an answer.

"I'm sorry to be a pain in the neck," I said. "It's just that so much gossip goes around a small town. I'd much rather get the story from an authoritative source—such as the mayor himself—rather than relying on Glossop. I mean, relying on gossip!"

I couldn't believe I'd done that. I'd actually threatened to ask Greg Glossop, the bigmouthed pharmacist, and I had pretended the threat was a slip of the tongue. I waited for Mike Herrera's reply.

He stared at the floor for a moment, then leaned close and gave me a smile that told me I was about to receive a confidence. "I'm sure you've been told that Chief Jones and Ms. Ripley had a history."

A history? I raised my eyebrows, but I kept my mouth shut.

"In his previous job in Cincinnati, our chief was a witness in a case Ms. Ripley defended. I do not think this is a pleasant memory for the chief. I hope that as the press descends to cover Ms. Ripley's death—well, we all hope that they will not make this factor of too much importance." He shook my hand solemnly. "Now I mush check on the kitchen. Jason! Please give Ms. McKinney a drink on the house."

He turned and almost ran into the kitchen. I looked around to see my ponytailed cohort from the Ripley party grinning at me from behind the bar. "Hi, Lee," Jason said. "What can I get you?"

"Nothing, thanks. I've got to get back to work. I hope I didn't upset Mr. Herrera."

"Oh, the first reporters have arrived. That's what upset him."

"I didn't help. But I really feel I need some background, or I might put my foot wrong. Do you know what the situation was between Chief Jones and Clementine Ripley?"

"I know Mike doesn't want the reporters to figure it out, but . . ."

I waited without saying anything while Jason polished a glass. His hair and his big dark eyes made him look like an eighteenth-century pirate.

Finally he grimaced and spoke again. "There's no way to keep it a secret. But so far none of the reporters have tumbled to the fact that Chief Jones used to be Detective J. H. Jones—the guy who lost the Montgomery case for the Cincinnati Police Department."

"Oh? I have only a vague memory of the details . . ."

"He was the chief investigating officer. The only way the Ripper could keep Thomas Montgomery out of jail was to make the police look incompetent. So she did it. It ruined Hogan Jones's career." He leaned across the bar. "You didn't hear it from me."

I nodded, thanked Jason, and headed back to the chocolate shop, mulling over what he had told me. So Clementine Ripley had ruined Chief Jones's career. The guy must have felt haunted by her. First she ran him out of Cincinnati, so he retired and moved to Warner Pier. He became police chief here. Then she showed up and built a showplace weekend home.

Yikes! That alone was motive for murder. It's as if she had deliberately had it in for him.

Yes, Chief Jones definitely needed to step aside and let someone else investigate her murder. He might not want her murderer caught at all.

He would even be a suspect. After all, he'd been out at the Ripley estate before the party—he'd been going in as I left after delivering the chocolates.

And the state police's top detective had been assigned to the case. I shoved the door to the shop open. I felt sure I'd get to meet this Alec Van-Dam from the Michigan State Police—and his team—quite soon.

When I got inside, Aunt Nettie was in the workroom.

"What are you doing here?" I said.

"Some detective called the house and asked me to come in. He wants to talk to both of us."

She didn't look at all afraid. And suddenly I loved her so dearly that I could have cried. When I was an obnoxious teenager upset about my parents' divorce, she'd taken me in—given me someone who would listen, who taught me to work hard and be proud of what I did, who was always there for me. Now, twelve years later, my own marriage had fallen apart, and she had taken me in again. She was simply good through and through, and she saw only goodness in others.

The only exception to this had been Clementine Ripley. Aunt Nettie had adored Uncle Phil, and she had blamed Clementine Ripley for his death, as lots of people had known. And now a chocolate Aunt Nettie had handled and packaged might be linked to Clementine Ripley's death. Aunt Nettie might be accused of killing her.

Did she even see her own danger? She might not. She was such an innocent that she might walk right into some sort of trap, incriminate herself.

But she wasn't alone. She had me. And I was going to make sure her innocence wasn't used against her.

I gulped and got ready to face down that detective.

At least he hadn't come to take either of us away. We didn't seem to be threatened with arrest. I toyed with the idea of recommending that Aunt Nettie call her lawyer. But wouldn't that make it seem as if she was guilty? Besides, Aunt Nettie's lawyer would be some local guy who drew up wills and checked land titles. Would he be any real help in a murder investigation?

And the state police's request to see us obviously centered on the chocolate shop. If not, they would have come out to the house, or asked the two of us to meet them on their own turf. This was perfectly logical; the investigators would have to understand how the suspect chocolates had been handled—where they'd been made, stored, packaged.

Anyway, I didn't mention calling a lawyer.

Warner Pier's traffic was typical for a Saturday night, of course—awful. Half the tourists in western Michigan were circling through the business district looking for parking places, and two tour buses were in town, so the sidewalks were packed as well. It was twenty more minutes before two men in suits came in the front door and showed their badges.

Detective Lieutenant Alec VanDam looked as Dutch as his name. He had the face of a Van Gogh peasant, a plodding gait suitable for wooden clogs, and a shock of hair of such a bright gold it would have looked natural on one of those Dutch boy dolls they sell up in Holland, Michigan. He introduced his companion—his subordinate, obviously—as Detective Sergeant Larry Underwood. Underwood was younger than VanDam, maybe around thirty, with a blocky build and blunt features. He wore a buzz cut that left only an inch or so of black hair standing on top of his head. Neither of the detectives was quite as tall as I am.

"Please wait a few minutes, Ms. McKinney," VanDam said. "Then we'll go over the events of yesterday afternoon with you. Right now we're simply trying to understand what happened and the order it happened in, and we'd like to talk to Mrs. TenHuis first."

Aunt Nettie took them back to the break room, and I worked with Tracy and Stacy. They'd had to cut their dinner breaks short, but they were so excited that neither of them complained. I stood behind the counter with them while I waited for the detectives.

I was nervous about the interview, of course. I reminded myself to stand quietly and pretend to be poised—a lesson I was taught during my semi-successful career on the beauty pageant circuit. Don't twitch your hands, I'd been told. Don't fool with your hair or jewelry. Don't bounce your foot or pick at your nails.

Don't twist your tongue—that wasn't on the list, but it was the one I had the most trouble with. As I loaded boxes with chocolates and made change I tried to prepare answers for every question the detectives might ask, all the time knowing that was probably the worst thing I could do. But I was willing to look dumb—I had to be ready to fight for Aunt Nettie, even with my malapropish tongue.

I stayed in the shop, but I saw Aunt Nettie lead the detectives out of the break room. She showed them the workroom and the storage area, where racks on wheels held stacks of twenty-five trays of chocolates at a time. No doubt she described the routine of the middle-aged ladies who made the candy, the ones who had gone home at four p.m. She wheeled out a rack that held storage trays, then pulled out the tray on which the Amaretto truffles were stored. She pointed out the white chocolate that covered them and the accent stripes of milk chocolate that identified the Amaretto truffles. Then she took an Amaretto truffle from the tray, gave the detectives a rather defiant look, and ate it in two bites.

Of course, I was way ahead of the detectives in one way. They were still checking how the chocolate had been handled here at TenHuis Chocolade. I was sure those truffles had been pure, unadulterated yummy when Aunt Nettie gave them to me. If one of them had been used to poison Clementine Ripley, it had been given the cyanide treatment after I left it at the big, cold house on the point.

When my turn came, I went over the same material. I described how I had watched Aunt Nettie arrange the chocolates and dipped fruits on the silver trays that Clementine Ripley had sent us and how I had tasted an Amaretto truffle. How they'd gone into the van. How I'd left the van locked while I walked around to the house to pick up a check. How Clementine

Ripley had taken a chocolate cat, gulped it down in two bites, then instructed Marion McCoy to take the box up to her room.

I was careful to include the exchange we'd overheard between Joe Woodyard and his ex—"I want my money." Frankly, VanDam and Underwood didn't seem too interested. I guess they'd already heard about that, maybe from Joe.

Then I explained why I happened to go back that night as a waitress.

"You can ask Lindy Herrera," I said. "She suggested it."

"We'll talk to her," VanDam said. "Did you see the little box of chocolates after you went back?"

"No."

"And you stayed in the kitchen, the dining room, and the reception room?"

"Except when I went down to the office."

"You went down to the office? That room back by the garage?"

"I didn't see a garage, but there was a utility room across the hall. It's at the east end of the house."

"And why did you go back there?"

"The cat, Junker. I mean, Yonkers! Champion Yonkers. Ms. McCoy was trying to find him. She said they planned to lock him in the office. After she'd gone, he showed up out in the main party room—jumped onto the bartender from the balcony, then tried to eat a bowl of olives. I grabbed him and took him back to the office."

"How did you know where it was?"

"I figured it was the same one she'd taken me to that afternoon, so I kept going east until I found a familiar landlord. I mean, landmark! When I saw the utility room, I turned left."

"You didn't see the chocolates in the office?"

"Not then. They should have been upstairs with Clementine Ripley by then."

He didn't ask me what I did see in the office, and I wasn't about to volunteer any information. We went over the rest of the events—my walk back down the peristyle and past the kitchen and dining room, and my arrival in the main reception room just in time to see Clementine Ripley tumble over the balcony and land on the polished wooden floor.

At that point VanDam and Underwood seemed to be about to close their notebooks and leave. So I felt called upon to make a statement.

"Lieutenant VanDam," I said, "I'm sure of one thing."

"Yes, Ms. McKinney?"

"Those truffles— well, they weren't poisoned here!"

A slight smile flashed over VanDam's serious Dutch face.

I went on. "I wouldn't even have any idea of how to get hold of cyanide, and I'm sure my aunt doesn't either."

"Actually," VanDam said, "getting hold of cyanide is not a big problem in this part of Michigan. Not in the summertime."

"What do you mean?"

"Peach pits contain it."

"Peach pits!"

He nodded. "Also cherry pits. I understand the process of brewing a little isn't too hard."

"That may be true. But after meeting my aunt Nettie, you can see that she'd never—well, it's not possible for her to have any connection with any action that would harm anyone. She's—she's just good clear through."

VanDam smiled at that. "Right now we're just trying to understand how the chocolates were handled," he said. He flipped his notebook closed and stood up. Detective Underwood imitated his actions almost exactly.

"We need to find out who had an opportunity to tamper with them," VanDam said. He grinned. "Like you, Ms. McKinney."

"Me!"

"You were alone with them for quite a while," he said. Then he headed for the front of the shop, and my stomach went into a knot no Boy Scout could have tied.

I followed the detectives. I didn't know what to say or do. VanDam's comment wasn't exactly news, of course. Both Aunt Nettie and I had had access to the chocolates. In theory I could have spiked them with cyanide.

So should I maintain my innocence? Point out that I had no reason for killing Clementine Ripley? Deny that I had ready access to cyanide? Yell? Scream? Beat my breast?

I decided that a dignified silence would be best. I pretended I was Miss America taking her final trip down the runway as I escorted the two state detectives to the front door. I even offered them a sample chocolate from the front counter. They declined.

I opened the door for them. "Good-bye, Lieutenant VanDam," I said. "Good-bye, Sergeant Underling."

I had closed the door before I heard VanDam laugh and realized what I'd said. I went back to the break room ready to cut my tongue out. It seemed determined to betray me.

Aunt Nettie had taken her interrogation calmly. The detectives had been polite, she said. They'd wanted to know how things were handled in the workroom at TenHuis Chocolade and specifically how the chocolates she'd sent to Clementine Ripley were selected.

"I just told them the truth," she said. "I knew her favorites, because she always buys Amaretto truffles—I mean she always bought them. Sometimes she'd buy a whole pound of nothing but Amaretto truffles. I knew she had quite a sweet tooth, and I didn't want her to mess up the display trays before they were served. But those specific truffles were taken right from our regular stock. And I do not believe that one of my ladies had poisoned some Amaretto truffles at random, and that Clementine Ripley just happened to get them."

"I agree," I said. "That would be too hard to swallow."

She looked at me narrowly, then laughed. "Oh, Lee, you're so funny!"

Then we had a big discussion on whether she should go home. I was still nervous about the burglar.

"Handy Hans called to say the window is fixed," Aunt Nettie said firmly. "The house is as safe as it's been for the past hundred years, and I've been living there for forty of those years. I'm not leaving my home."

"That house may be inside the city limits, but it's still awfully remote."

"I have wonderful neighbors."

"I know! But you also have an acre of ground. The neighbors aren't close enough to hear you holler, and they can't see the house for all those trees."

Aunt Nettie sighed. "I guess you have a point. And if you're nervous about staying out there . . ."

"You're not staying alone!"

We never made any progress beyond that. She wasn't leaving her home, and I wasn't leaving her. I did call the nonemergency number for the Warner Pier Police Department and request a few extra patrols of our area. The dispatcher—or whomever I talked to—assured me that Chief Jones had already laid that on.

"So if you see a police car in your drive," the dispatcher said, "don't worry."

We left it at that. We were spending the night in our own beds.

Aunt Nettie left the shop around eight-thirty p.m. At eight-forty p.m. I started cleaning the big front window. At eight-forty-five p.m. a car stopped in front of the shop and a man wearing a funny mesh vest with lots of pockets got out. He leaned back inside his car and pulled out a camera.

I yanked the shade down on the window and turned to Tracy and Stacy.

"Let's close up early," I said.

I pulled the shade on the other big display window, then locked the front door. I stood by it while Tracy and Stacy finished up with the last two customers. The man with the camera came to the door and rapped, but I ignored him.

I opened the door just a slit for the customers. They had barely squeezed through when a second man draped with photographic equipment came running down the sidewalk.

"Hey!" he said. "Did the fatal chocolates come from here?"

CHOCOLATE CHAT
ORIGINS

- The first chocoholics believed that the cocoa bean was the gift of a god. The god was Quetzalcoatl, a benign deity of the sometimes blood-thirsty Aztecs. According to legend, Quetzalcoatl stole the cocoa plant from the "sons of the Sun" and gave it to the Aztecs. They made the beans of the tree into a drink seasoned with pimento, pepper and other spices. They called it tchocolatl.

- Quetzalcoatl may have done the Aztecs a favor in giving them chocolate, but their belief in him helped end their empire. When the conquistador Cortez arrived in Mexico in 1519, he came in wooden sailing ships unlike any the Aztecs had ever seen. The Aztecs thought Quetzalcoatl had returned and greeted Cortez with open arms—and gifts of chocolate. Cortez—obviously not a man who went for spicy, bitter drinks—traded the chocolate for gold, and the Aztec empire began to fade away. The Spanish took chocolate to Europe.

- The myth of chocolate is echoed in its scientific name—Theobroma Cacao—which translates as "food of the gods."

Chapter 8

Stacy and Tracy were staring at me.

"Let's clean up fast and skedaddle," I said. "And you girls may get tomorrow off. I'll call you if it looks as if we'll be open."

They were still staring, so I went on. "And you'll get tomorrow off with pay if you don't talk to those reporters outside."

That seemed to suit them, and the three of us did the final cleanup—sweeping out, scrubbing down the counter, and restocking the showcase—in record time. We ignored repeated knocks on the front door; the crowd seemed to be growing. I scooped the cash from the register and left it unbalanced, although that almost crushed my accountant's soul. I stuck the money in a bank sack and put the bank sack in my purse. Tracy and Stacy waited at the door to the alley while I turned out all the lights but the security light behind the counter. Then I made my way to the back of the shop.

Tracy's eyes were big, and her hair looked stringier than ever. "Do you think they'll be waiting in the alley?"

"I hope not," I said. "I'll go out first, and I'll take you girls home."

They both assured me this wasn't necessary, but I insisted. I didn't want them waylaid; they were just high school kids, no match for the tabloid press. I was afraid the reporters were lurking in the alley, lying in wait like lionesses at a waterhole.

Which turned out to be almost the case.

The business district of Warner Pier is quaint enough to make the back entrances hard for strangers to figure out, but the first reporters found the alley just as we reached the van. I guess it was lucky Tracy and Stacy were teenagers; the hairnet ladies would never have been agile enough to jump into the van fast enough for us to make our escape.

As it was I had to drive through a half dozen reporters and photographers. Strobe lights were flashing, and people were yelling, but I kept edging the van down the alley toward Peach Street.

"Hey! Let us tell your side!" That was one of the yells.

"Is it true your aunt's been arrested?" That was another.

"Is it true you're having an affair with Clementine Ripley's husband? Is it true you were Miss Texas?"

I tried not to even look at them, just kept moving slowly forward. When I got to the street, I whipped the van left and pressed down on the accelerator. "Look back," I said. "See if they follow us."

"There are a couple of cars," Stacy said. "But it's hard to tell just who's who."

I cut through the alley on the next block.

"One car followed us," Stacy said. "Why don't you head down Lake Shore Drive?"

"I don't want to lead them to Aunt Nettie's. Her house is hard to find, so maybe they won't find it tonight. If I go somewhere else—"

"I mean the north shore end," Stacy said, "and I can tell you how to lose them!" Tracy (stringy hair) was being real quiet, but Stacy (plump) was enjoying the whole thing. "Head for the old Root Beer Barrel," she said. "Circle around it, and there's a drive at the back, kinda hidden by bushes. The guys do it all the time."

"The Root Beer Barrel? It's still there?"

"Yes, we can get away that way."

"You're sure?"

"I guarantee it!"

I started north on the Lake Shore Drive. In that part of Warner Pier, the road runs right along the lake, and the lake side has been eaten away. The road is only about one and a half lanes wide, and there's no shoulder at all, only a guardrail. On the other side of the guardrail there's a steep drop, almost a cliff, about forty feet down to a narrow beach. When I see an article about Great Lakes erosion, I think of that spot. Years ago it used to be a stretch of road with businesses facing the lake, between Lake Shore Drive and the beach. Now the buildings have collapsed into the lake, half the road is gone, and the section is supposed to carry only local traffic.

The old Root Beer Barrel had been a landmark. The drive-in has been closed for years, since the state highway was moved, but now I saw that the giant barrel was still there. And, I noticed, there was a streetlight at the entrance to what was once the drive-in's parking lot. The lot was now a mess of broken asphalt and sand.

The car that was following us wasn't staying too close; the guy must have been hoping to follow me home and find Aunt Nettie. I drove as fast as I dared when I got near the barrel, then whipped into the drive. I cut my lights as soon as I was off the street, but I'd seen the tracks in the sand. "You're right, Stacy," I said. "Lots of cars have been using this lot."

"Yeah, the guys do doughnuts in here. Go around on the left side of the barrel, then make a sharp right."

I followed directions, coasting to slow down without hitting the brakes, since I didn't want our pursuer to see the lights. Once I was behind the barrel, I faced a solid wall of green, and the streetlight was a long way off.

"Go straight through," Stacy said. "See the tracks?"

Now I saw them. A faint, two-rut driveway led into the bushes, and I followed it. Branches and leaves hit the windshield and the sides of the van.

Magically, I came out into the clear almost immediately. And I was in the back of the parking lot of Warner Pier's one supermarket.

"I can't believe this!" I said. "I had no idea that the Superette was that close to the Lake Shore Drive."

"You can drop us here," Tracy said. "I'm supposed to call my mom for a ride anyway."

"I'll park over there where the other cars are and wait until your mom comes," I said.

Tracy and Stacy agreed to that. They went to the pay phone, then came back to the van. It was a warm night, so I rolled the windows down.

"I'm sorry y'all had such a scary ride," I said. "But I appreciate your help in getting away from that bunch."

The two of them looked at each other. Then Stacy took a deep breath and spoke. "Is it true?"

I decided I'd better be careful about what question I was answering. "Is what true, Stacy?"

"Were you really Miss Texas?"

I laughed out loud. "That one's easy. No."

"Oh." Stacy's face fell.

"Sorry if you're disappointed. I was in the Miss Texas Pageant once, along with about a million other girls, but I did not place in the top ten."

"What about Joe Woodyard?"

"I don't think he placed in the top ten either." I tried to keep the sharpness out of my voice. "When I was your age, Joe was a lifeguard at Warner Pier Beach. I knew who he was. I don't recall ever having a conversation with him. I hadn't even heard anything about him again until yesterday when I ran into him out at the Ripley house."

"You didn't date him?"

"Not when we were in high school. Not recently. Not anytime in between." And Rich's private detectives would back me up on that, I thought. Rich had had them investigate every aspect of my life.

"Oh." This time both girls looked really disappointed.

I laughed again. "Sorry if I've let y'all down. I lead a very dull life."

Tracy spoke then. "My mom says she hates to see such a smart guy throw his chances away, and my dad says Joe's turned into a gigolo."

She pronounced "gigolo" Gig-alow. Tracy was my kind of girl, stringy hair and all. I hid a laugh, but I decided I'd be better off not joining in

Warner Pier's gossip sessions during my first week back in town, even if I wasn't impressed with Mr. Woodyard.

"I guess I'll let Joe handle his own life," I said.

"He doesn't seem to know how to handle it, according to my mom," Tracy said. She dropped her voice and spoke confidingly. "He quit being a lawyer and—"

I tried to cut her off by interrupting. "What kind of car does your mom drive?"

"Ford Fiesta. Joe got all kinds of scholarships, see, and he did real well at Ann Arbor. Then he went to law school."

"Good for Joe," I said desperately. "What color is your mom's car?"

"It's red. Then he got mixed up with that Clementine Ripley, and he blew it all. That's what my dad says. He says Joe's really got a chip on his shoulder."

She paused for a breath, and I decided I was going to have to be blunt.

"Listen, Tracy, Joe has plenty of friends in Warner Pier, and I'm sure they've all been interested in what's happening in his life. But Clementine Ripley has been murdered, and you saw all those reporters that have shown up, nosing around. Now is the time that Joe's going to need all the friends he's got. And the first thing he needs from those friends is silence."

Tracy looked big-eyed. "But—"

"I mean it, Tracy. I already asked you not to talk to the reporters about my aunt and the chocolate company. Now I'm asking you not to talk about Joe Woodyard. That kind of speculation is exactly what he doesn't need right now."

"But if you're not friends with him—"

"Joe and I are not enemies," I said. "We just don't know each other."

"Then why . . . ?" Tracy sounded completely bewildered. "Then why is he here?"

"Here?"

I heard a sardonic laugh behind me, and I whirled around so fast that I nearly got a crick in my neck.

Joe Woodyard was standing right outside my window.

I could have killed the jerk. "You nearly gave me a heart attack!"

"Sorry." He didn't sound sorry.

"What are you doing here?"

"I saw that the reporters had laid siege to the chocolate shop, and I toyed with the idea of creating a diversion. But you didn't need me."

"There was only one car after us. Stacy told me how to escape."

"Actually, there were two cars. I was the second one." Joe leaned down and looked in the van window. "That swing around the old Root Beer Barrel was slick, Stacy. I drove over here the long way round. I thought you might stop in the parking lot, and I wanted to make sure everything was okay."

He was still treating me as if I were incompetent. "Thanks, but you don't have to help out," I said.

He gave me a dirty look, then turned his attention to Stacy and Tracy. I could see both of them perk up. Even with anger bubbling just beneath the surface, Joe still had the pizzazz that had made the girls at the beach stand around the lifeguard's perch drooling. Luckily, my drooling days were over.

"I appreciate you girls helping Ms. McKinney escape," he said. "Now could one of you help me out?"

"Sure." They answered in unison. He could have asked them to blast the tabloid reporters with a bazooka, and they'd have simply asked where the On switch was.

"I need a bottle of Tylenol, but the Superette drug department is the last place I want to go tonight."

Stacy laughed, and Tracy spoke. "Mr. Gossip."

"I didn't say anything," Joe said. "But if I gave you girls a ten, would you run in and buy me a bottle of Extra-Strength Tylenol Gelcaps?"

"Sure!" They were delighted. They climbed out quickly. "We'll be right back!"

"I won't be here," Joe said. "It's not smart for me to hang around with Ms. McKinney. I'll go back to my truck. The blue one over on the next row."

They scampered off across the parking lot, toward the door of the Superette. Joe turned away and looked after them.

He still sounded gruff when he spoke again. "Thanks for the kind words."

"Kind words?"

"The antigossip advice. When I walked up here."

"That was more to do with Aunt Nettie and me than with you." I gripped the steering wheel. "Tracy and Stacy are nice girls. They're just young. They don't know yet how much harm talk can do."

"Sounds like you've learned."

"I've had a few opportunities to find out." Like when your ex-husband's first wife calls and says she heard at the beauty shop that you're dating a Dallas Cowboy and she wants to know which one, and you've never even met a Dallas Cowboy in your life, much less gone out with one, and all you can think is that your ex-husband started the rumor himself.

"Anyway," Joe said, "thanks." He turned away.

Suddenly he looked incredibly lonely. Just the way he had out at the Ripley house, when he'd moved the chair to sit beside his ex-wife's body. Maybe he wasn't such a jerk as I'd thought.

"Joe," I said, "did you see the state detective? VanDam?"

"Oh, yeah. After today we're well acquainted."

"What did you think of him?"

"He's polite."

"That's one of the things I found scariest about him."

"You've got a point. But I called a law school buddy who's now in the Detroit prosecutor's office. He says VanDam is about the best Michigan has."

"I'm worried about Aunt Nettie. She simply lives for TenHuis Chocolade. She's afraid that the company will be damaged."

"That could happen."

"I'm terrified that she'll even be a suspect." I thought back to the warning I'd had from Inspector VanDam. "I guess we will all be suspects."

Joe gave a humorless laugh. "Yeah. The ex is always the prime suspect. VanDam didn't seem impressed when I told him I didn't gain a thing from Clemmie's death. In fact, we had a business deal, and now . . . Anyway, her death leaves me in deep water with the bottom of the boat stove in. And I've got nothing to bail with."

Joe and I looked at each other for a long moment. Then he turned and walked away.

A small red Ford cruised slowly through the parking lot, and in a minute Tracy and Stacy came out of the Superette and flagged it down. The car waited while they took a small sack over to Joe's blue pickup. Then they waved in my direction and left.

One responsibility out of the way, I started the van and headed home, using back streets only a little less obscure than the escape hatch behind the Root Beer Barrel. I had to cross the bridge over the Warner River, but apparently the out-of-town reporters hadn't figured out that that would be the best place to watch for a gray van with Texas tags.

I wished I could do something about those Texas tags, but I was stuck with them until Monday at least. Besides, I didn't have the money to buy Michigan car tags. For the moment I was financially dependent on Aunt Nettie.

Aunt Nettie's house was in a semirural area; in fact, it had been outside the city limits of Warner Pier until two or three years before. As I mentioned, there were a lot of bushes and trees between the house and the road. And the drive was just one lane of sand; it didn't really look like a driveway. It would be hard for the reporters to find in the dark. But I stopped on the Lake Shore Drive, where the mailbox was located, and tossed a rag over the nameplate on top of the mailbox. As a final touch, I parked the notorious minivan with Texas tags behind the garage of the next house down the road. The Baileys lived there, and Aunt Nettie had mentioned that they were out of town.

I walked along the path that led through the woods from the Baileys' house to Aunt Nettie's. Her big Buick—she insisted a big car was best for the Michigan winters—wasn't in the drive. That surprised me for a minute, but then I saw her moving in the kitchen, and I realized that she'd been cautious enough to take the unusual step of putting her car in the garage, a remote little building that during the summer was usually reserved for garbage cans and snow shovels. She had locked the back door, too, and I had to knock. She even called out, "Lee?" before she let me in.

Aunt Nettie had finished straightening up the mess the burglar left. So much had happened since the burglary—interviews with detectives, the invasion of the tabloids—that it was hard to remember we ought to be nervous about staying in a house where there had been a break-in. So we weren't.

The phone rang, but we unplugged it and rehashed the events of the day. Aunt Nettie found my wild chase around the old Root Beer Barrel quite entertaining. And she agreed, sadly, that we'd probably better plan on closing TenHuis Chocolade Sunday.

"Sundays aren't as busy as Saturdays," she said, "but I sure hate to miss a single day during the season."

We went to bed around eleven. I read until I dropped off, and I was deeply asleep at three o'clock when Aunt Nettie shook me awake.

"Lee! Wake up!" she said. "Somebody's trying to break in!"

Chapter 9

I sat up and listened. I didn't hear a thing. Maybe I didn't want to hear a thing. I listened some more. For at least thirty seconds I sat there with my ears perked up like a German shepherd, trying to convince myself that Aunt Nettie was just nervous. Heaven knows she had every reason to be.

Aunt Nettie didn't move, but she finally whispered, "He's around behind the house."

Then I heard the sound, a sort of thump. Aunt Nettie clutched my hand, but she didn't speak.

"Sounds like the back porch," I said. "Maybe it's a raccoon."

I threw back the covers, got out of bed, and stuck my feet into my slippers. The night was cool, and Aunt Nettie turns her heating system off between Memorial Day and Labor Day, so I was wearing flannel pajama pants and a T-shirt. I didn't fumble around for a robe. I tiptoed out of my room, across the hall, and into the back bedroom, the one with the window overlooking the back porch. Unfortunately the window was closed, and I was afraid opening it would make noise. I pressed my head against the glass, but the porch roof blocked most of my view.

Then I heard something again, and that something was fumbling around with some small metal trash cans Aunt Nettie keeps on the back porch as raccoon-proof storage. As I watched, a large black blob moved close to the porch rail, then again disappeared under the roof.

If that was a raccoon, it was the biggest sucker in Michigan.

I turned around and found myself nose to nose with Aunt Nettie. I jumped so high my T-shirt nearly turned into a parachute as I came down.

Luckily, I didn't scream. "You scared me," I whispered. "I thought you'd stayed in the other room. Have you called the police?"

"The phone won't work."

We'd unplugged it. Aunt Nettie had forgotten that, I decided. I crept across the hall and down the narrow stairs—there are doors at the top and the bottom so Aunt Nettie can compartmentalize the Michigan winter cold—with her close behind me. The stairs end in the corner of the living room, and I peeked around the door at the bottom before I came out. I saw nothing, but once again I heard that noise.

I walked into the kitchen as quietly as I could and found the phone cord where I'd draped it across the back of the kitchen stool. I ran my hand along the cord, feeling for the funny little plug that would fit into the bottom of the telephone. And my hand ran right up the cord to the telephone.

The phone was already plugged in.

I picked up the receiver and put it to my ear, but it was just a gesture. If that phone was plugged in, then Aunt Nettie was right. The phone wasn't working.

It was time to panic.

I was stuck in a house well out of earshot of any neighbor and surrounded by bushes and trees. There was an intruder on the back porch. He or she had disabled the telephone. And I felt responsible for my aunt—who was a perfectly capable sixty-year-old woman, although she might not be much help in a fight.

But if that black blob on the back porch got into the house—again?—fighting might be our best option.

I put my lips close to Aunt Nettie's ear. "Think of some kind of a weapon," I said.

She whispered back, "I don't own a gun."

"I know! But this house should be full of blunt instruments."

"I'll grab Grandma TenHuis's big iron skillet."

"Good! Just don't hit *me* with it. I'll go get the fireplace poker."

I tiptoed into the living room. I was feeling for the poker when I heard a crash from the kitchen, and I nearly jumped out of my T-shirt again.

Aunt Nettie spoke, sounding perfectly calm. "I dropped the skillets," she said.

There was no more point in trying to be quiet. I grabbed the poker and sent the tongs and shovel flying onto the brick hearth, then ran back toward the kitchen. "Turn on the porch light!"

I heard a terrific clamor on the back porch.

I flew to the window of the dining room, which stuck out at an angle to the main house and had a clear view of the back porch. I got there just as the porch light came on, and I looked out on a scene of complete slapstick. Aunt Nettie's porch chair was ricocheting off the railing. A hanging pot was swinging wildly, the petunias in it bouncing. Tin trash cans were rolling everywhere, and the lid of one of them flew away and crashed into the back door like a badly tossed Frisbee. Unfortunately it had covered the can filled with sunflower seed for the bird feeders, and the slick black seeds poured down the back steps like lava.

And in the middle of it all, a black figure was falling off the porch.

It had arms and legs this time, and I tried to get a good look at it. But it was still just a faceless blob, and the darn blob wouldn't hold still. It rolled around with the tin cans, got up to its knees, slipped on the birdseed and fell down again, got up once more and staggered off around the corner of the house.

I ran to the living room window, on the side of the house, parted the curtains, and looked out. All I could see was a flashlight beam, moving rapidly toward the drive.

I turned to run to the front door and look out, and I had another one of those moments of sheer terror when I bumped into Aunt Nettie. Again.

"Auntie! Make some noise!" I pushed past her and ran to switch on the front porch light and look out the window that faced the road. Aunt Nettie was right behind me. But we were too late to get any kind of look at the intruder. The black figure had disappeared into the trees, and all we could see was the bouncing beam of the flashlight. Aunt Nettie and I stood there holding the skillet and the poker and watched the light disappear when it reached the Lake Shore Drive.

"Whew!" I said. "I'm sure glad you heard that noise."

"I'm not," Aunt Nettie said. Her lips were pursed angrily. "That burglar apparently didn't want to get into the house this time. If I'd just kept quiet, maybe we could have had an uninterrupted night's sleep."

At that point our sleep had definitely been interrupted. I went upstairs, turned on the dim bedside lamp—somehow that seemed safer—and started getting dressed in black jeans, a dark sweatshirt, and an old pair of dark-colored sneakers.

Aunt Nettie came to the door. "What are you doing?"

"The phone's out. I've got to go call the police."

"No! You're not leaving this house!"

"What if he comes back?"

"Then we'll scare him off again."

"Aunt Nettie, he might bring weapons next time. Or reenactors. I mean, reinforcements."

"What if the reinforcements are already here? What if he wasn't alone? What if someone else is hidden outside?"

Well, that had already crossed my mind. But we couldn't simply sit in that house and wait until daylight. So I clenched my jaw, hoping that would keep my teeth from chattering. "I don't think that's too likely," I said. "I'll run along the path to the Baileys' house and call the police."

"The Baileys aren't home."

"Don't you have a key? Anyway, my van's parked over there. If I can't get in the house, I can drive down to the all-night station."

Then I stopped and considered Aunt Nettie. I wasn't sure I wanted to leave her alone. "Maybe you'd better come, too."

"No! Neither of us is stepping out that door."

We were still at an impasse when I tied my last sneaker string and went down the stairs. I was determined to go, and Aunt Nettie was determined that I wasn't leaving the house. The argument had almost reached the "Are not!" "Am too!" stage by the time we got to the living room.

That was when somebody knocked at the front door.

Of all the things that had happened, that one was the scariest. I do believe my heart stopped dead right inside my rib cage.

Aunt Nettie and I clutched each other.

"Mrs. TenHuis?" a deep voice said. "It's the police. Are you all right?"

We did have the sense to look out the window and check to make sure the vehicle in the drive had a light bar on top before we opened the door. Then we yanked a young blond patrolman inside so quick he almost got a knot in his nightstick.

"I saw the lights on," he said. "Is anything wrong?"

We poured out our tale, and he pulled his radio off his shoulder and told the dispatcher to send him some backup and to contact Chief Jones. Then he looked at the back porch.

"We might get some footprints," he said. "Not out here, but around at the side of the house."

"Well, when you find the guy," I said, "he's going to have bruises up and down his shins and shoes full of sunflower seeds."

"Oh, dear," Aunt Nettie said, "the birds are going to be all over the porch tomorrow morning."

She was wrong. By morning the porch was so thick with reporters and photographers that the birds couldn't get near it.

Both front and back porches were thick. We found out later that the just-out-of-journalism-school editor of the *Warner Pier Weekly Press* listened to the scanner on his way back from a party in Kalamazoo, and he apparently let out the news that two witnesses in the Ripley killing had been threatened by an intruder. He probably did it to curry favor with the big city reporters. I guess it worked for him; he left for a new job the next week, before Ten-Huis Chocolade could yank its advertising.

Thanks to his efforts, by sunup we were under siege. And I don't mean sunup as when the sun hit the house. I mean sunup as when it came up over the horizon way over there behind all those trees and bushes that were habitat for deer and turkeys and which kept Aunt Nettie's house gloomy until after eight o'clock on July mornings.

We didn't answer the door, once we saw who was out there, but it sure wasn't like a relaxing Sunday morning. And we didn't even have a working telephone. The phone company had told the police they couldn't get a repair crew out until Monday.

"Maybe we should go down to the shop," Aunt Nettie said. "We could hide in the break room."

"But how will we get there? We'd have to fight our way through."

Rescue came in a truly surprising form.

First we heard a siren coming down Lake Shore Drive. It grew louder and louder. Then it seemed to be right at the end of our drive, not moving. I peeked out around the shade on the upstairs window, and I saw the Warner Pier rescue truck edging through the crowd of press.

"Good heavens!" Aunt Nettie said. "I hope none of those reporters has had a heart attack or anything."

"I'm not as charitable as you," I said. "I wouldn't mind if the whole bunch dropped dead."

As we watched, the rescue truck drew up right in front of the front door, and Greg Glossop got out and strutted up onto the porch. He pounded on the door.

Aunt Nettie gave a deep and disgusted sigh. "Well, I can't ignore him," she said.

"I can."

But she was already on the way downstairs.

"Don't open the door," I said. I followed her.

Aunt Nettie went into her bedroom, which had a window that opened onto the porch. She moved a chair, pushed the curtain back a few inches, then opened the casement window a crack. A roar went up from the reporters, and Glossop moved over to the window.

"Chief Jones sent us to get you out," he said. His light-colored eyes were dancing with excitement, and his plump face was self-important.

"Why?"

Glossop bounced on his toes, and his round belly looked like a basketball being dribbled. "Don't you want to get away from these reporters?"

"Yes, but why does the police chief care?"

"That state detective wants to talk to you."

"Then why doesn't he come and get us himself?"

Glossop's belly jiggled again. "The chief talked him out of that. He says if they come in here with a police car it'll look like you're being arrested."

"But neither of us needs an ambulance."

"We're calling it a practice run."

"Oh."

Aunt Nettie closed the window and turned to me. "Should we go, Lee?"

"We can hardly refuse. If the state detective wants to talk to us, and if the chief doesn't want to cause more commotion . . ." I shrugged.

Aunt Nettie cracked the window again. "Give us ten minutes to get ready."

Glossop nodded, then crossed to the front door and stood there, arms folded, on guard. He didn't look quite as intimidating as Hugh, Clementine Ripley's goonlike security guard.

Aunt Nettie put on blue chambray pants and a coordinating tunic, and I put on a plaid flannel shirt over my jeans and T-shirt. Then Glossop and the other two members of his crew formed a protective arc around us and escorted us across the porch and into the back of the ambulance. We ignored the yells. "Who's sick?" "Where are you going?" "Did you poison the chocolates?" "Who tried to break in?"

Once we were inside, the driver turned on the siren and edged through the crowd and onto Lake Shore Drive. Looking out the back window, I saw reporters and photographers running for their cars, and I sighed. They were obviously going to chase us, and then everyone would know that we'd been taken in for more questioning.

But after about a block, the driver suddenly sped up, and I saw a Warner Pier police car pull out into the road behind us with lights flashing. Then another pulled out. The two of them blocked the road, and we drove off—figuratively giving the press the finger. It was a great moment.

As soon as we were around the curve and out of sight, the driver cut the siren.

"Oh, my," Aunt Nettie said. "That was fun."

Glossop preened. "The chief and I worked that maneuver out. Now we'll have you at the Ripley house in a few minutes."

"The Ripley house!" I almost yelped out the words.

"Yes, that's where they've set up a sort of command post. It's easy to control access there, you see. And there's lots of space."

"I guess so." Yes, access to Clementine Ripley's house was controlled.

"Of course, you and Nettie are going to see the top-dog detectives. They sent another team over to the police station. They're interrogating the catering staff." Glossop shrugged off the importance of the catering staff.

Huh, I thought. The catering staff was all over that house. Any of them could have poisoned those chocolates. I was somewhat comforted to learn that we weren't the only people being questioned.

"I can understand why you wouldn't want to go back to the Ripley estate," Glossop said.

"Oh, I don't mind."

"Well, I mind going! I don't even want to think about that terrible woman."

"No one seemed to like her."

"Well, I certainly didn't! She caused me a lot of problems—and only because I insisted on performing my duty." Greg Glossop reached under his seat and produced a can of Diet Coke. He took a drink, then leaned back against the side of the ambulance, looking self-righteous.

I found myself madly curious. Glossop had obviously had a run-in with Clementine Ripley, but he was such a notorious and obnoxious gossip that I didn't want to encourage him to talk—about anything. I leaned against the other side of the ambulance and closed my eyes. I'd find out some other way, I told myself.

Aunt Nettie chatted easily with the other EMT, but neither Glossop nor I had anything more to say on the way to the Ripley house. More reporters were stationed there, and I ducked instinctively when we turned into the drive. And I admit that my stomach knotted up again as the big iron gate shut behind us. It was too much like being led into jail.

The ambulance drew up in just the same spot where I had stopped to unload the chocolates two days earlier. The back doors opened, and I started to climb out.

To my surprise the person who stretched out a hand to help me step down was Duncan Ainsley.

"Mr. Ainsley!" I said. "I thought you were going back to Chicago."

"I haven't been allowed to leave. Stuck here like a coon up a tree."

"We all have to cooperate, I guess. And perhaps they like having someone with some business connection to Clementine Ripley on the scene."

"They don't need me," Ainsley said. "They have the new owner of the property here to lend authority to their investigation."

"The new owner? Oh. I wondered who Ms. Ripley's heir would be."

"Clementine may be astonished at the way things have turned out. At this very moment she may well be standin' at the Pearly Gates gapin' in surprise."

"Surprise?"

Ainsley grinned sardonically. "Yes, even the heir appears to be amazed."

"The heir?"

"It seems Clementine never got around to signing her will. Joe Woodyard gets everything."

Chapter 10

That was a shocker. Just twelve hours earlier Joe had told me he would suffer financially because of his ex-wife's death, that he faced ruin because she had promised him money for a business deal and hadn't come through before she died. Now it seemed he scooped the pot.

I wondered, wickedly, if Marion McCoy had known this all along. Was that the reason she'd been so mad at Joe after she learned that Clementine Ripley was dead? And I wondered how she was taking the news.

I didn't expect Ms. McCoy to be happy, but I was still surprised by what happened when a uniformed state trooper opened the front door of the Ripley mansion.

Marion McCoy rushed toward me, shrieking, "Get him! Get him!"

For a moment I thought she wanted us to join her attack on Joe Woodyard. Then I realized a large white-and-brown dust bunny was slithering past my shinbone.

"Stop him! Don't let him get out!"

Champion Yonkers was sneaking out the front door, headed for freedom.

Duncan Ainsley made a valiant grab. He caught Yonkers and wrestled him up. There were a loud yowl and a flurry of brown feet. Duncan cursed and dropped the cat. Blood oozed from his hand, and the cat ran under a shrub beside the flagstone steps.

Marion came to the door with an expression more lethal than poison gas. "Duncan, you fool! You know he hates men."

The bush in which Yonkers had taken refuge was a fairly bushy bush, with branches close to the ground. Marion knelt and looked under it. Then she looked at me. "You! Go around on the other side. Make sure he doesn't get out that way. You!" That was directed to Gregory Glossop. "You stand in front. Be ready to grab him. And, Duncan, you go to the cat cupboard and bring out his can of treats and his catnip mouse."

Her fury was so great that I didn't even consider not obeying. I scurried around to the other side of the bush, which looked like some sort of holly, and Greg Glossop covered the front. We had the cat surrounded, but I couldn't see that it was doing us any good. Our perimeter was full of gaps.

Duncan Ainsley gave an exasperated sigh, but he went into the house, as ordered. Marion began to coo at Champion Yonkers. "Here, Yonkers. Here, kitty. Nice kitty." It didn't sound sincere.

The forgotten person in all this was Aunt Nettie. Now she appeared at my shoulder. "Here, Lee," she said.

She handed me the Diet Coke can Greg Glossop had been drinking from in the ambulance. I stared at her in amazement. "That's Greg Glossop's," I said.

"Rattle it," Aunt Nettie said firmly.

I moved it halfheartedly, and I nearly jumped out of my skin when it made a noise.

"I put some pebbles in it," Aunt Nettie said. "Rattle it. Some cats like that."

I looked back at Champion Yonkers, huddled under his bush. "Here, Yonkers," I said. "Come and see this toy." And I rattled the can.

Miraculously, Yonkers crept toward me.

Greg Glossop moved, but Marion McCoy stopped him with an imperious gesture. Aunt Nettie knelt next to me, maybe four feet away. I rattled the can and spoke coaxingly again. "Here, Yonkers. Come and see what I've got. Come and get the can. You're such a handsome fellow."

Flattery will get them every time. Yonkers crept closer to the edge of the bush. I rolled the can back and forth, then moved it toward him, keeping it within my reach. Then I rolled it to Aunt Nettie. She rolled it back to me. We all held our breath.

And Yonkers pounced on the can. He batted it back and forth idly, not far from Aunt Nettie. She reached out and petted his head, managing to tuck a thumb under his collar. Then I slid my hand around his body, and we had him, Coke can and all.

I scooped him up. "You are a naughty cat," I said. "You scared Ms. McCoy." She was looming over me, and I handed him to her.

"Thank you," she said. She glared. The look wasn't for me or for Champion Yonkers, but for some target behind me. "He's a valuable animal, and I certainly wouldn't want to fail in my responsibilities to his new owner."

With that, Ms. McCoy turned and marched back into the house. I heard a snort—maybe it was a growl—and I turned to see Joe Woodyard approaching from the path that ran around the house. Ms. McCoy's glare had apparently been aimed at him.

Joe didn't acknowledge my presence, and I didn't speak either. I was still withholding my opinion on Mr. Woodyard. A uniformed state policeman motioned, and I followed Aunt Nettie toward the door of the Ripley mansion.

Joe Woodyard had disappeared, but Duncan Ainsley reappeared with cat toys, holding a tissue to his scratched hand. He was all attention to both Aunt Nettie and me. Chief Jones materialized—from behind the bushes, I guess—and headed off Greg Glossop, keeping him outside.

We entered through a massive door and found ourselves in a large foyer. Although the decor was as severe as that in the house's main reception room, on that day it seemed suitable. It formed a quiet background for masses of flowers and plants. At least Clementine Ripley's demise had been a windfall for the florists of Warner Pier. Probably for the florists of every town in western Michigan.

Detective Underwood met us in the foyer and motioned for Aunt Nettie and me to go into that big reception room. It, too, was full of flowers and plants, but its atmosphere was still cold. But Marion McCoy was mad enough to heat things up. She spoke sternly to Underwood.

"I'm going to have to leave the cat in here, since the detectives won't allow me to use my office, and that's the spot we ordinarily use if we have to coop him up." She put him down on the floor, and he immediately made for the stairs to the balcony. Once up them, Yonkers disappeared behind a large white ceramic pot.

Marion spoke again. "I would appreciate everyone taking care not to let him out. *Again.*"

She glared around at all of us, as if we'd conspired to let the cat reach the dangerous outdoors. For the first time I noticed that Marion was wearing what appeared to be deep mourning—calf-length black skirt, black turtle-necked T-shirt, black loafers—even opaque black stockings. Her skin looked washed out, and there were deep shadows under her eyes.

"Perhaps if we *try*, we can handle this situation with a modicum of efficiency," she said.

Underwood was plainly annoyed at her dressing down, but I could see that he was in a bad position. His superiors would obviously have adopted a policy of politeness for this group, given the intense press scrutiny the crime was getting, and apparently some representative of the state police had been responsible for the cat getting in a position to slip out the front door. But Marion McCoy wasn't in charge there; the state police were. Underwood could hardly allow her to give the orders.

I was relieved when Duncan Ainsley smoothed the situation over, speaking quietly and in his most folksy tones. "Marion, I know you feel like you've been pulled through a knothole, but you and the investigating officers will need to work together if y'all are goin' to get all your coons up one tree."

Marion McCoy laughed. It wasn't a pleasant sound. "I'm going to my suite," she said. "Duncan, I leave you in charge of the cat."

It wasn't much of a curtain line, but she exited on it.

Duncan Ainsley left, too, murmuring something about finding a Band-Aid. Underwood seated Aunt Nettie and me on the couch in front of the stern stone fireplace. Then he disappeared, and Lindy Herrera appeared.

She came from the kitchen, neatly dressed in black slacks and a white jacket. She winked at me and said, "Could I get you a cup of coffee?"

"Lindy!" I struggled up from the couch, which turned out to be just as hard to get out of as I'd anticipated it would be.

Aunt Nettie spoke to her without getting up. "What are you doing here?"

"Joe decided he needed somebody around to keep things picked up and to feed the two houseguests."

"Houseguests?"

"Ms. McCoy and Mr. Ainsley."

"Oh. Mike sent you over?"

"No, Joe called me himself. He knew we could use the money, with Tony laid off. I'll just be here from ten until four for a few days, and my mother said she could watch the kids some, if Handy Hans calls Tony to work. So I came. All I really have to do is fix lunch and then leave something that Ms. McCoy can heat up for dinner. But I've been keeping a pot of coffee on. Do you want a cup? Or a soda?"

Aunt Nettie and I both declined. Lindy went back to the kitchen, and I looked around, assessing the situation before I sank into the couch again. That was how I happened to witness the next Yonkers attack.

Chief Jones came into the room from the foyer, an entrance that required him to walk under the balcony from which Clementine Ripley had fallen. Just as he reached exactly the right spot, there was a flurry of white and brown, and the chief gave a loud yelp. Yonkers bounced off his shoulders and onto the bar—almost exactly as he had the night of the party.

It was just as funny as it had been when Yonkers gave Jason the treatment. I stood there and tried to keep a straight face.

The uniformed state policeman, however, didn't try. He hooted with laughter. "Gotcha, Chief," he said. "Now I'm not the only one."

The chief looked at me, and I belatedly tried to look sympathetic. "I'll carry an umbrella when I walk under that balcony," I said.

"Ms. McCoy says you're safe," Chief Jones said. "She says the cat only does that to men."

"I thought you had taken yourself off the case," Aunt Nettie said.

"I'm just a gofer," the chief replied. "Just coordinating between the local force and the state police. They took over my office, so I came out here to get under their feet." He went out the door onto the terrace.

I sank back into the soft leather cushions. I'd barely hit bottom when something furry brushed against my leg, and I looked down to see that I'd been joined by Champion Yonkers.

I offered him my hand. "Hi, Champ. You'd better behave yourself."

Yonkers narrowed his blue eyes, twisted his milk-chocolate snout into a sneer, then scooted under the couch, turned around, and poked his head back out between Aunt Nettie's feet and mine.

Aunt Nettie leaned over and looked at him. "He certainly looks like his picture."

"Looks like his chocolate copy, too. I was a little surprised when I saw him wandering around Friday. I thought champion cats would be raised in cages and wouldn't be allowed the run of the house."

"It's called raised underfoot," a deep voice said. "It helps what they call socialization."

I looked up and saw Joe Woodyard coming in one of the doors from the terrace. He left the door open, but pulled a sliding screen door across it.

"Are you into showing cats, too?" Aunt Nettie said.

"No. But Yonk and I got along."

"Does he jump on you, too?"

"Hasn't so far." Joe pulled one of the spindly chairs over and sat down near the fireplace. Yonkers immediately came out from under the couch and wound himself around Joe's feet, mewing and rubbing his fluffy side and tail around Joe's jeans.

"He's beautiful," Aunt Nettie said.

"Do you want him?"

"Heavens, no! I have no place for a pet. Are you looking for a home for him?"

Joe nodded. "I can't have him around the boat shop. He mostly lives at the Chicago apartment, and that'll be gone pronto."

"This place . . ."

"Will also go on the market."

"Oh. Yonkers ought to be worth a lot of money."

"I suppose so. Maybe he'd be happier with a breeder, at that." Joe reached down and scratched Yonkers under the chin. The cat arched his neck and lifted his head, indicating the exact spot he wanted to receive attention.

Joe grinned at the cat. "Yonkers would probably love having a large harem."

"I can picture him lying on a silk cushion," I said, "watching his ladyfriends do the cat equivalent of a belly dance. He'd just loll around like a Persian pasha."

"Uh-oh!" Joe reached down and covered Yonkers's ears. "Don't use the word 'Persian' around Yonkers. Birmans are not Persians, and some of the breeders are very touchy about that. It's an old controversy."

I bowed to the cat. "I do apologize, Champ. I had no idea."

Yonkers gave a sassy meow, and disappeared under the couch with a haughty flick of his chocolate-tipped tail. Aunt Nettie, Joe, and I all laughed.

Interesting. Joe had been nothing but rude to me, but he had no trouble being friendly with a cat.

Joe started to speak to Aunt Nettie, but before he had more than a few words out—"Thanks for the sandwich. It"—we heard a bang behind us.

Joe jumped to his feet. "Bad cat!" He moved toward the sound. I looked over the back of the couch and saw that Yonkers had knocked over a wastebasket that had been under a spindly little writing table. "You still have your bad habits," Joe told the cat.

He set the wastebasket upright again, but Yonkers had captured a wadded-up piece of paper and was batting it around the polished floor. Joe let him keep it.

"I guess that's his favorite trick," I said. "He knocked the office wastebasket over Friday, then batted the trash around."

I saw movement out of the corner of my eye, and Duncan Ainsley came in, walking rapidly, reappearing out of the hall where Marion McCoy had disappeared a few minutes earlier. "Joe, have you got a minute?"

"Sure," Joe said. He frowned at something behind me. I followed the frown and discovered the uniformed state policeman sitting quietly against the wall, taking in our whole conversation. "I'm waiting to see VanDam."

Ainsley took him aside and spoke quietly. However, I could hear what he said, and I'm sure the state policeman could, too. He was making a pitch, asking to keep Joe as an investment client after he assumed control of his ex-wife's estate.

Joe frowned. "It's all very much up in the air, Duncan."

"Who's the executor?"

"Apparently I am."

"Oh?"

"I was surprised Clemmie left it that way," Joe said. "Anyway, the first thing I need is a report on just what Clemmie's investments are."

"Certainly." Ainsley's voice was enthusiastic. "I'll E-mail my assistant this afternoon, and she'll have the report for you tomorrow morning."

"Let it wait, at least for a few days. I may not have time to look at it that quickly."

"It's just a matter of pressing a few buttons. We can get you a report anytime."

Just then a new voice was heard. "Mr. Woodyard!"

It was Detective Underwood. He had entered from the hall. "Please come back and talk to Lieutenant VanDam."

"That's what I've been waiting to do," Joe said. He followed Underwood.

Aunt Nettie pulled a notebook from her purse and began to write in it. I settled back on the uncomfortable couch and folded my arms. This was worse than the dentist's office. At least the dentist provided magazines. I was toying with the idea of lying down on the couch, pretending to be relaxed, when Duncan Ainsley pulled up a chair and sat down beside me.

"I wanted to talk to you," he said.

I recalled his phone call Friday night. "If it's local information, you'd be better off asking Aunt Nettie."

"No." He smiled his most winning smile. "I wanted to know more about you."

"Me? Why?"

"Humor me. Did you say you're an accountant?"

"I have a bachelor's degree in accounting."

"Where did you graduate?"

"University of Texas, Dallas. Finally."

"Finally? You went to several colleges?"

"No, I did it all there, but it took me a long time. I was what they call a nontraditional student. My parents couldn't help me, and I was determined to get through without a load of debt."

I didn't explain why I had a horror of debt. Growing up with bill collectors pounding at the door will produce that effect, and so will seeing money problems wreck your parents' marriage.

"I worked and took a few courses every semester. Then I got married, and I didn't work at all for five years, but that didn't help me get through college any faster. I still just took one or two courses a semester." I decided not to explain that either. How can you tell a stranger your husband actively obstructed your efforts to get a degree? Or that he was furious when you made the dean's list?

"So it took me a long time to graduate," I said. "Why do you ask?"

He gave me a direct look. If we'd met at a party, I'd have thought he was coming on to me. "What's your particular field of interest?"

"In accounting? I know I'm not interested in taxes. It may depend on what sort of opportunities open up."

"Then you're not wedded to the chocolate business?"

"Not permanently. Right now Aunt Nettie needs me, and I need her."

"Lee, you should have a great business career. If you ever decide to leave Warner Pier, let me know."

I could feel my jaw drop.

Ainsley laughed. "You look astonished."

I didn't answer.

"Do you have any interest in investments?" he said.

"Not in picking them."

"Good! There are too many of us trying to do that already. But you'd be great at client presentations."

"Oh, I can't do oval—I mean . . ." I stopped, formed the words in my mind, and said them slowly. "Oral presentations. I can add like crazy, and I know an asset from a debit. But I don't talk well."

Ainsley looked quizzical. "But according to this morning's *Chicago Tribune*, you've done the beauty pageant circuit, so you didn't just fall off a turnip wagon. I judged a few pageants, some years past. They require a lot of poise."

"If the reporters get around to checking my pageant scores, they'll reveal that I did okay in bathing suit and evening gown and so-so in talent. But I completely bombed the interviews." I decided it was time to change the subject. "Now your career has been really remarkable, Mr. Ainsley. Why were you drawn to investments?"

"Just like to be around money, I guess." He grinned. "You're like all the other girls. Just interested in me because I know . . ." He mentioned a famous movie actor.

"I admit I'd love to know what he's really like," I said.

For the next fifteen minutes, Duncan entertained Aunt Nettie and me. He told me the in-stuff about that actor, about a certain rock star, about a well-known author of trash novels, about a soap opera star I had idolized as a teenager. It was amusing and just slightly wicked. I enjoyed it thoroughly. At the same time, I had the feeling I was watching a well-rehearsed and carefully developed stand-up act. He'd told those stories a lot of times, and he knew just when to pause for a laugh.

But it was still a pleasant interlude, and I hadn't had many of those lately. I was almost sorry when Chief Jones came in.

"Ms. McKinney," he said, "it seems the Warner Pier Police Department has assumed the duties of your social secretary. I have a phone message for you."

"A phone message? Oh, with the phone at the house out of order . . ."

"Right. The caller couldn't get through. Since the call seemed to be of a personal nature and the dispatcher said the party was pretty concerned about you, I said I'd hand it along."

"Thank you, Chief Jones." He handed me a pink message slip. "It's a Dallas number," I told Aunt Nettie. "It must be Mom. I thought she was in the Caymans. She must have read about all this mess in the newspaper."

"You'd better call her."

Lindy showed me a telephone in the kitchen. I found my credit card and dialed the number. The phone was picked up on the first ring.

"Lee?"

It wasn't my mother. It was Rich Godfrey, my ex.

"Rich? Why are you calling?"

"Honey, I just heard about this situation up there. I'm getting on the first plane to Detroit."

"Detroit?"

"I'll rent a car and be there by this afternoon."

"Why?"

"Lee honey, you're going to need money—money for attorneys, for public relations consultants. You don't have to face this alone."

"I see."

And I did see. It was more of the stupid Lee syndrome. It works this way: A. Lee is attractive. B. Lee has a problem with saying the wrong word. So she's stupid.

Rich thought I was too stupid to handle the situation. And maybe Lieutenant VanDam thought I was stupid enough and Aunt Nettie was naive enough that one of us would incriminate herself and admit we had poisoned Clementine Ripley's chocolates.

I'd been trying to protect Aunt Nettie by taking an active interest in what was going on, but now I saw that "active" wasn't going to be good enough. I needed to move up to "aggressive."

But first I had to take care of Rich.

"Rich," I said, "if I need help, I'll call on someone who knows Lake Michigan from Lake Erie."

"Huh?"

"You said you were going to fly to Detroit. Warner Pier is on Lake Michigan and Detroit is closer to Lake Erie—a couple of hundred miles from Warner Pier. And if you show up here, I'll throw you to the tabloid press. Get out of my life! And take your money with you!"

I hung up and took two deep breaths.

Lindy laughed. "Right on!" she said.

I pumped my fist at her and headed back into the reception room.

"Aunt Nettie!"

I must have sounded different, because her eyes were wide when she swung around to look at me. "What's wrong?"

"What's wrong is that I'm tired of people pushing us around. Burglars. State police. Cops and robbers. It's time we stood up for ourselves."

Aunt Nettie smiled. "What do you suggest?"

"I suggest we ask Lieutenant VanDam to step down here and then we insist he assign his best officers to search the chocolate shop and the house. Right now!"

Chapter 11

A unt Nettie beamed at me. "Lee, that's a wonderful idea!"
But Duncan Ainsley jumped to his feet, looking horrified. "Lee!
Mrs. TenHeist! What are y'all thinking of?"

Ainsley almost squeaked out the words, including the "t" he put at the
end of Aunt Nettie's name.

"Ask any lawyer!" he said. "The authorities should get a warrant."

"What on earth for?" Aunt Nettie said.

"You can't just allow the police into your home."

"I've begged them to come twice in the last two days, thanks to our burglar," she said. "A piece of chocolate from my business contained poison. I
know it didn't get poisoned at the shop, but the police don't. So the authorities
are going to have to search the shop sometime. Besides, if somebody's put
something poisonous in my house or my shop or my car, I want to know about
it. I want the police to look in every nook and cranny. I want them to test every
bottle on the flavoring shelf, check out every bar of chocolate in the storage
room, look under every chocolate mold, behind every pot and in every pan."

I was glad she saw it the same way I did. I knew that Aunt Nettie and I
hadn't poisoned the chocolates. I felt sure none of the hairnet ladies or the
teenage counter girls had done it. And the police knew we'd had two
break-ins—or one break-in and an attempted break-in. If they found evidence in the garbage can full of birdseed on the back porch at Aunt Nettie's
house or in the plastic bin of cherry filling in the shop's storeroom or in a
shoe box in my closet, good enough. I wanted them to have it.

But Ainsley was still arguing. "Ask your lawyer," he said. "He'd be
ready to cut his suspenders and go straight up!"

Aunt Nettie waved his objections away. "Don't be silly. If our break-ins
are related to a poisoning, we need to search the whole house anyway, just
to make sure the burglar didn't leave any surprises for Lee and me. If the
state police are willing to do it for us—and to check out the shop at the same
time—well, I hope it's a complete waste of public funds, but I appreciate
their doing it."

Joe came out of the hall right then, and Ainsley appealed to him. "Joe, you're a lawyer. Tell this nice lady she shouldn't encourage a search of her premises."

"I'm not a lawyer anymore," Joe said. But he did react in a lawyerly fashion, I guess. At least he asked Aunt Nettie to explain her side before he expressed an opinion.

"Clem would have gone for the search warrant," he said. "But I don't think you need to insist on one." He turned to look back toward the hall, and I saw VanDam standing there looking at us. "After all," Joe said, "the police are fully aware that you've had a break-in at the house. It's possible that something was planted. You need to know."

"Exactly." Aunt Nettie beamed. She struggled up from the couch. "Let's go on and get started. I've got a lot of work I need to do at the shop, and I can't do it until we get this over with."

"Ahem!" I said loudly. "And I have another suggestion. Aunt Nettie and I need to stop avoiding the press."

Duncan Ainsley frowned, Joe glared, and Aunt Nettie looked dubious.

But I went on. "We need to write a statement pointing out that the reputation and the business of TenHuis Chocolade are threatened by this investigation, demanding that the police proceed as quickly as possible, and telling the world we're asking the authorities to make a complete search of our premises."

Aunt Nettie smiled. "That's an excellent idea, Lee. And we'll both wear TenHuis shirts, and we'll insist on getting the shop's logo in every photograph."

Joe laughed. "Maybe you've got something. If they don't kill you."

I ignored him. "We'll meet them on the sidewalk in front of the shop, where they can't miss the sign in the window. We'll pass out chocolates, if Lieutenant VanDam will allow it, and we'll include copies of that fact sheet on all the different varieties of chocolate."

"And a price list," Aunt Nettie said happily.

"Sure," I said. "We'll even offer to answer questions, but no matter what they ask, we'll talk about chocolate."

Even VanDam grinned at that, but Joe still looked unconvinced.

"That's a good plan," Aunt Nettie said. "Can we start the search of the premises now?"

Chief Jones, who had been a silent spectator to all this, joined the conversation at that point. "How about it, Alec? Can I ask a favor for one of my Warner Pier merchants?"

VanDam shook his head. "Well, I guess the lady is right. We do need to search the place. Might as well do it now. But when you face the press, no talk about the case, okay?"

"Of course not," Aunt Nettie said. "That's your business. It has nothing to do with TenHuis Chocolade. Can we leave now? We've got a lot of work to do."

Of course, it wasn't that simple. We couldn't get into the shop to start work until the state police crew was out. They did agree to start on the office, so that we'd be able to get in there as soon as possible. Aunt Nettie went over to the shop with Underwood, and Chief Jones took me out to the house to get Aunt Nettie's car. I still didn't want to drive that conspicuous Texas tag around town, so I left my van behind the Baileys' garage for the moment.

"Okay, Chief," I said as we drove away from the Ripley house. "Are we doing the right thing?"

"Yeah, I think so. Us coppers get real suspicious of people who insist on search warrants. Normally an innocent person reacts like your aunt; they see the necessity for the search and want to get it over with. The only time people are likely to stand on their rights is if they're involved, or if they are afraid some member of their family is involved."

"What about talking to the press?"

"That's probably a good idea, too. But my relations with the press were so bad at one time—I'm not the one to ask."

He glanced over at me. "When it comes to motive, VanDam knows I belong at the top of the list."

"I heard that you tangled with Clementine Ripley on the witness stand."

"If I'd known she was going to move to Warner Pier, I'd have retired someplace in Wisconsin."

He spoke with his usual easygoing drawl, but his hands were clutching the steering wheel tightly. As if he were strangling it.

I decided to ask one more nosy question, concealing it as well as I could. "You might have a motive, but you didn't have opportunity, did you?"

"Yes, I did. Clementine Ripley summoned me out to the house Friday afternoon. She wanted to tell me how she wanted my boys to handle the extra traffic for the benefit. We talked in that office back by the garage, and I had to wait for her for a while. And I think that box of candy was sitting on the desk the whole time. Now I'm told it had her name on it, a big hint that it was for her exclusive consumption."

So Chief Jones wasn't kidding when he said he was a suspect. Maybe that would work to Aunt Nettie's advantage.

The press had deserted the house. I grabbed a khaki skirt and a chocolate-brown shirt with a TenHuis logo from Aunt Nettie's closet and a TenHuis shirt and khaki slacks from mine, then headed back. By the time I got to the shop Aunt Nettie and I were allowed to begin working in the office, so I booted up the computer and wrote a simple news release. I never had a class in public relations, but I took several business communications courses, so I just wrote a letter and left off the salutation. It might not be slickly professional, but we wanted to look like a folksy small-town business. I also called the *Grand Rapids Press*, the Grand Rapids office of the Associated Press, and a couple of the television stations to tell them about our "press conference." I refused to answer any questions, but told them we'd have a statement at two p.m. at the shop.

While I did that, Aunt Nettie cut up a large white cardboard box and used a marker to write PRESS CONFERENCE 2 P.M. in big black letters. She wrote, HERE, in slightly smaller letters just underneath. She offered to add something about door prizes, but we decided that was a little too silly. We wanted to look like mid-America, not Hicksville.

She stuck the sign in the window, and almost immediately it got attention. A crowd gathered out front, and some people knocked at the street door, but we didn't answer, and the search team didn't either. They were using the back door to go in and out.

I was running off twenty-five copies of the statement I'd written when a member of the search team stuck her head into the office. "There's a guy in the alley who wants to see you, Mrs. TenHuis. He says he's the mayor."

"Mike Herrera?" I said.

"I'll talk to him," Aunt Nettie said. I went with her.

Herrera had switched from his black-and-white caterer outfit to navy-blue shorts and a polo shirt.

"Mike!" Aunt Nettie said. "What can I do for you?"

"Tell me what you're up to," Herrera said. "This town has gone loco. I'm having to neglect my restaurants to hang around city hall all day. That never has happened before!"

"Come in, quick," Aunt Nettie said.

We got Mike inside and took him into the office. Then Aunt Nettie gleefully explained that we were going to try negative psychology on the press. Instead of running from them, we were going to demand their attention.

Herrera shook his head sadly. "I've been answering questions from those guys all day."

"Oh, Mike! I'm sorry," Aunt Nettie said. "I've been so worried about my own problems that I didn't think about your position."

"Yah," he said. "My whole crew is being questioned, since we were on the scene. But I never saw those chocolates, and I don't think any of my people did either."

He patted his well-gelled hair. "But maybe you got the best idea about how to deal with those reporters," he said. "You could borrow the little sound system from city hall."

"Oh, Mike! That would be such a help."

Herrera grinned. "You need something to stand on, too. A platform. I'll call the park superintendent. We'll see what we can come up with."

Aunt Nettie sighed admiringly. I had no idea she could be so flirtatious. "I'd be happy to pay a rental fee."

"That won't be necessary." Herrera leaned over, and only Aunt Nettie and I heard him whisper. "If you killed her, you could submit a bill, and the city council would pay it without discussion." He closed his eyes. "That woman, she went back on her word. Made me look stupid." His eyes opened again. "I thought I was tellin' the council the truth—but she changed her mind. She made me a liar. It was a matter of honor. I hated her."

Aunt Nettie patted his hand. "I did, too," she said softly. "I thought of killing her a million times."

"Shut up!" I whispered, too, but I was emphatic. "Both of you! Yecch!"

Aunt Nettie giggled and whispered, "Oh, Lee, everybody knows neither Mike nor I would actually do anything to hurt anyone."

"You're wrong, Aunt Nettie. Not everyone knows that. We're surrounded by a whole group of people who don't know it and who could testify about your jokes."

Honestly! Sometimes I thought Aunt Nettie had chocolate for brains. But Mike Herrera should be a little more sophisticated, if he was going to be a politician.

At least he offered to bring us a sandwich from Mike's Sidewalk Café. We accepted. "Business is good down there," he said. "Humans is crazy people. They act like they doan have good sense. Act bad. And it's just curiosity."

His comment made me remember my own curiosity. "Okay, y'all," I said. "I've got my own problem with curiosity, and you can just help me figure something out."

Aunt Nettie looked politely interested, and Mike Herrera frowned. I told them about what Greg Glossop had said during the ride to the Ripley house.

"He definitely had it in for her," I said. "It was more than just a general dislike. Do either of you know anything about this?"

Mike frowned. "I haven't heard anything about that. Seems like Clementine Ripley left trouble everywhere she went." He looked at his watch. "I'll get your sandwiches."

The state police had almost finished their search by the time two p.m. came, and we were ready to face the press. Chief Jones sent Patrolman Jerry Cherry down with some crime scene tape to mark off an area for the reporters, keeping the hordes of tourists outside the area. Prime viewing space became the broad windows of the Upstairs Club, right across the street from us. If everybody who was pressed up against the screens over there bought lunch, the "Upstairs" must have had a big blip on their profit chart. Whoever lived in the apartment next door to the Upstairs must have cashed in, too. They removed their screens and rented their windows to two different TV crews.

Mike Herrera, now wearing long pants and a dignified stance, opened the event with a few remarks about the many attractions of Warner Pier as a vacation paradise and citing what a valuable asset TenHuis Chocolade was to the community. Tracy and Stacy had showed up, mainly to see what was going on, and they handed out samples of chocolate. ("It's a Bailey's Irish Cream bonbon," I heard Tracy say to one reporter. "It has a classic cream liquor interior." I made a mental note to talk to her about how to pronounce "liqueur.")

Most of the reporters were brave enough to dip into a box. The two girls also handed out the press releases. We'd stapled each release to a sheet describing all the varieties of bonbons and truffles produced and sold by TenHuis Chocolade and to a price list, including an order blank. As we'd hoped, our flagrantly commercial ploy seemed to cool the press's interest in us more than anything else had.

Aunt Nettie opened by saying, "We don't make fudge." That got a laugh; fudge is the saltwater taffy of western Michigan—on sale everywhere. Then Aunt Nettie talked about how hard she worked to make her chocolates of the highest quality, about how she and my uncle had gone to the Netherlands for a year to learn how to make chocolates, and how proud she was of her employees.

"If I find out who has damaged the reputation of my business—well, if that person has a penny left after he's convicted of murder, then he'll also face a serious lawsuit from me," she said. "My husband and I worked for thirty years to build this business, and I'm not going to sit on my hands and see it destroyed."

"When will you reopen?" some reporter on the back row asked.

"Tomorrow. Unless the state police want me to stay closed. We're cooperating in every way."

She handled the whole thing very well. She was completely natural. Completely Aunt Nettie. I was proud of her.

The reporters and photographers seemed to love her. The bulbs flashed; the tape recorders were out. I saw that this cute little old gray-haired chocolate-maker was going to be good copy.

For a few minutes I thought I was going to escape without having to say anything. But then somebody yelled my name. "Hey, Ms. McKinney! Is it true that Ripley's ex was your high school sweetheart?"

Aunt Nettie looked at me, handing the question off just like the straight man handing off the joke for a punch line.

Think, Lee, I told myself. "If you mean Joe Woodyard," I said, "the answer is a firm no. For one thing, I didn't even go to high school in Warner Pier. For another, I never exchanged two words with him until day before yesterday."

A woman reporter on the front row spoke up. "But you were here summers, working for your aunt."

"Three summers."

"Did you know Woodyard then?"

"I knew who he was, because the girls I ran around with knew him. I don't recall ever having the nerve to speak to him."

"Why would speaking to Joe Woodyard have required nerve?"

I'd gotten myself into a mess. *Don't say anything else stupid,* I told myself. I took a deep breath. "Joe was a college guy! He scared me spitless! Weren't you ever sixteen?"

Evidently she had been, because she laughed, and most of the other reporters joined in. The moment passed, and I relaxed. Too soon. The next question nearly got me.

It came from the same reporter, the woman in the front row.

"Still, I imagine you joined most of the people in Warner Pier in thinking Joe Woodyard had made a foolish marriage?"

I just stared at her. I couldn't believe what she had said.

So she spoke again. "At least, that's the gossip I've picked up around here. People don't seem to feel that he behaved very sensibly."

I saw what she was trying to do, of course. They couldn't get me to say anything nice about Joe, so this reporter had decided to settle for getting me to say something naughty about him. It was infuriating.

"That's none of my busybody," I said.

The whole front row of reporters looked confused, and I knew immediately that I'd botched up. "Business," I said. "It's none of my business."

I took Aunt Nettie's arm and we got off the little platform that the park superintendent had improvised out of forklift pallets and plywood. We went back into the shop with as much dignity as we could gather around us, considering that twenty reporters were yelling out more questions.

Aunt Nettie locked the door and smiled. "That went about as well as we could expect," she said.

"Until the end, when I tied my tongue in a knot," I said.

I became aware then that one of VanDam's technicians had walked up to us. "The lieutenant wants to see you," she said.

We followed the woman into the break room, where VanDam and Underwood were looking at something in a small paper sack. VanDam hastily put the sack down before he spoke. "Is either of you ladies diabetic?"

"No, thank heavens!" Aunt Nettie said. "That would make it difficult to handle the chocolate business."

"Does either of you use injections of any sort?"

"Drugs? Of course not!" I said.

"Injections are not necessarily illegal, Ms. McKinney. Lots of medications are injected."

"Not by me. Not by Aunt Nettie. I take nothing but vitamin capsules."

"And I take nothing but Premarin, calcium, vitamins, and the occasional Tylenol. All by mouth," Aunt Nettie said. "Why do you ask?"

VanDam lifted the paper sack. "Can either of you identify this?" He dumped a plastic bag containing a few pieces of plastic out onto the table.

I stared at the sack. Somehow its contents seemed familiar. But the memory eluded me.

"I don't know anything about them," Aunt Nettie said.

"It's a broken syringe," VanDam said. "We found it in the Dumpster out in the alley."

CHOCOLATE CHAT

TYPES

- Bitter chocolate is the simplest form of processed chocolate—basically cooking chocolate. It contains no sugar and must be from fifty percent to fifty-eight percent cocoa butter. The remaining content is chocolate liquor.

- Bittersweet chocolate contains sugar, but is not as sweet as sweet chocolate. In the United States it must be at least thirty-five percent cocoa butter.

- Sweet chocolate is similar to bittersweet, except that it contains more sugar. Since it contains more other ingredients—sugar, cocoa butter, perhaps a slight amount of milk—it contains less chocolate liquor.

- Milk chocolate contains less chocolate and more milk, sugar and flavorings. Because it contains less cocoa, only the beans with the strongest flavor are used in milk chocolate.

- Cocoa is basically chocolate liquor with almost all the cocoa butter pressed out. It then becomes a dry cake that can be made crumbly. But cocoa does usually contain some cocoa butter. Most brands contain between fourteen percent and twenty-five percent.

- White chocolate contains no chocolate liquor, but it does contain cocoa butter.

Chapter 12

"Anybody could have put that there." I spoke quickly, but my voice sounded weak. Just about as weak as my stomach felt.

VanDam nodded. "Right. That alley obviously gets a lot of use."

"So the syringe doesn't prove anything," Aunt Nettie said. "Some drug user might have walked through there and tossed it in the trash."

"Right," VanDam said. "It will have to go to the lab for testing."

I spoke again, and I tried to make my voice a little stronger. "Even if it was used to poison the truffles, the only thing that would prove is that somebody is trying to make sure my aunt and I are the prime suspects. After all, our Dumpster is plainly marked with TenHuis Chocolade."

VanDam kept his face deadpan, but Underwood looked skeptical. I could understand why. The broken syringe was circumstantial evidence, of course, and it could easily have been planted. But it was right at our back door, so it pointed to us. Though it was hard to visualize either Aunt Nettie or me being dumb enough to put the broken syringe in our own Dumpster, then demand that the state police search our business.

Any of the numerous suspects in the murder of Clementine Ripley could have gotten hold of a syringe. Greg Glossop sold them. Chief Jones probably had an evidence locker full of them. Any of the rest of us—Mike Herrera and his crew; the inmates of the Ripley house, Marion McCoy and Duncan Ainsley; Joe Woodyard; even Aunt Nettie and me—any of us could have stolen one from a diabetic friend or gone behind the counter at the Superette pharmacy or pocketed one from the cabinet in a doctor's office. This was a small town, after all.

Any one of us was smart enough to go to the library in a large city—like Grand Rapids, less than a hundred miles away—quietly take a book on poisons from the shelf, look up how to make cyanide, get hold of either peach or cherry pits and follow the recipe, fill our stolen syringe, then go to Clementine Ripley's house prepared to kill her by injecting the poison into some sort of food. The appearance of the chocolates in a box particularly set aside for her would have been—what's the word?—serendipitous.

Greg Glossop did have the edge in one regard. As a pharmacist he ought to know how to manufacture cyanide from cherry or peach pits without looking it up. He could have injected cyanide directly into Clementine Ripley's body, then also injected cyanide into the chocolates, which were still around after he got there. Hard to do, but not impossible. In fact, he might have even doctored some prescription he'd filled for her, causing her to fall ill. As an EMT he'd know he would be called in if she collapsed.

Actually, as far as I was concerned, Glossop was the leading suspect. Maybe that was simply because I didn't like him. I wasn't even sure he had a motive. But I was willing to bet that he'd had some unusual run-in with Clementine Ripley.

Who would know for sure? The answer, of course, was Marion McCoy. But how could I ask her?

Why not try plain English?

The answer was so simple that it made me shake all over. Did I have the nerve to seek out the intimidating Marion McCoy and ask her a question about Greg Glossop and Clementine Ripley?

But even more terrifying was the thought that Aunt Nettie might be a suspect in Clementine Ripley's murder. Compared to that, bearding Marion McCoy would be a snap.

I'd do it. But how could I get hold of Marion privately? If I went out to the Ripley estate, she'd probably tell the security guard to send me away. How could I get in?

If Joe Woodyard inherited, he'd actually have the say-so on who came in and out of "his" house. I could call him.

No. Joe and I hadn't had friendly relations. I didn't want to ask him for any favors. So how could I do it?

By then the search team was leaving. They were going to take a short break, the team leader told us, then head out to Aunt Nettie's house to search there. I agreed to meet them in forty-five minutes.

I was so downhearted that I didn't have much energy, but Aunt Nettie immediately went to the refrigerator and took out ten pounds of butter and two half gallons of heavy whipping cream. She paused and looked at me. "You'll be here to help me lift the copper kettle, won't you?"

"For half an hour. What are you going to make?"

"Crème de Menthe bonbons. We're nearly out. Nancy Burton came in Friday and bought six dozen."

"Who's Nancy Burton and why on earth did she need that many Crème de Menthe bonbons?"

"Nancy manages the Deer Forest B-and-B. She puts our bonbons on the pillows when she turns the beds down, so she uses several dozen a week. Usually she warns us when she runs low, but Friday she got caught short.

So we got caught short. We got the *bojkie* made yesterday, but I need to get them filled and ready to go into the enrober tomorrow."

I thought I knew what she was talking about. The *bojkie*, a Dutch word pronounced "bokkie," is the chocolate shell that holds the filling for a bonbon. The "enrober" is a key piece of equipment in making bonbons. As its name implies, the enrober coats—or "enrobes"—the filled bojkie to produce the finished bonbon.

The enrober is the reason that very good truffles can be made at home, but making good bonbons in a typical kitchen is a lot harder. Truffles are little balls of filling that are rolled by hand in melted chocolate, but bonbons are made by filling little cups molded from chocolate. The whole bonbon is then put through a sort of shower-bath of chocolate in this special machine, the enrober. Aunt Nettie explains the difference by saying truffles are made from the inside out and bonbons from the outside in.

A small chocolate shop like TenHuis Chocolade enrobes once or twice a week; the Brach's Chocolate Cherry plant probably enrobes twenty-four hours a day. Our enrober is four feet long; theirs probably covers a city block. The theory is the same, but our chocolate doesn't contain preservatives, and we think it tastes a lot better.

Aunt Nettie usually runs the enrober on Monday, which is usually her slowest day.

"Call me when you need me," I said. I went into the office and began to balance out the cash register receipts from Saturday night, finishing up the chore I'd left undone when Tracy, Stacy, and I fled the reporters. As I counted nickles, quarters, dollars, and fives, I worried about how to get through to Marion McCoy.

When I glanced through the big window that overlooked the kitchen, I could see Aunt Nettie lighting the gas fire for the big copper kettle. That kettle is a beautiful object, but it's made for use, not admiration. It has its own free-standing gas burner, about the size of a small charcoal cooker. Copper is used for the kettle because it heats more evenly, and Aunt Nettie always uses this particular kettle to make the "base"—the mix of butter, sugar, and cream that is then flavored and turned into all the different fillings for bonbons and truffles.

Aunt Nettie added sugar and lifted the kettle onto the gas burner—the kettle isn't hard to lift when it's not hot—and began to stir.

I had balanced the register and prepared my deposit, and steam was rising from the copper kettle when I suddenly knew how to get into the Ripley estate.

"Lindy," I said. "Lindy will be there until four o'clock."

I glanced at my watch. It was already three o'clock, and I couldn't leave for a few minutes—until I'd helped Aunt Nettie with the kettle.

I shoved the deposit into a drawer, locked my desk, and went out to the workroom. "How quickly will the base be ready?"

"Maybe ten minutes. Why?"

"I thought of an errand I need to get done before I meet the search team. And I need to make a phone call."

For once my accountant's methodical mind was useful. When I had used my credit card to call Rich, I had written down the number I was calling from. It was the kitchen phone in the Ripley estate, and Lindy had told me it was a separate line. I found the number deep in my purse and called it. Lindy answered.

"It's Lee. I need a favor."

"Sure."

"I need to talk to Marion McCoy. Can you tell the security guard to let me in?"

"Well . . . I guess so. I could tell him you're bringing me a pound of coffee or something."

"Great! What kind of coffee do you want?"

Lindy laughed. "I really could use some. They usually use the special blend from Valhalla Coffee and Tea. Drip grind."

"I knew it wouldn't be Folgers. Valhalla's right down the block, so it'll be easy to get some. Please don't leave until I get there."

I whipped down the block to Valhalla ("Coffee fit for the Gods"), one of Warner Pier's three specialty coffeehouses, and picked up the coffee, getting back just in time to help Aunt Nettie lift the heavy kettle onto a metal worktable.

"Please call the police station and pass the word along that I may be a little late meeting the state police," I said.

Aunt Nettie nodded. She was already in the storeroom looking for her Crème de Menthe. "Whatever you say, Lee. Oh, dear, they did move the flavorings around when they searched!"

I headed for the Ripley estate. After I identified myself as a coffee deliverer, the massive gate slid back, and I drove in. I circled the house and parked near the kitchen, in the gravel area where the catering vans had been two days before.

Lindy was looking out the kitchen door. I handed her the coffee.

"Now," she said, "what's this all about?"

"I need to talk to Marion McCoy. I hope I don't get you fired."

"Oh, this job's only going to be for two or three days anyhow. And Joe's the boss, not Marion. He won't fire me if she gets annoyed. They can't stand each other."

"Do you know where Marion is?"

"In the office back by the garage. The cops finally left, and she went right in there and started working on the computer. Mr. Ainsley was in there, too. But he went out for a walk. Listen! Why don't I make Marion a cup of tea? You can take it in to her."

Lindy said the kettle was already boiling, so I agreed. Lindy made the tea in a china pot and put it, along with a cup and saucer, sterling silver tea-spoon and little sugar bowl, on a tray.

"I hope she doesn't get so mad at me she throws the teapot," I said.

"Oh, that wouldn't be 'being responsible for the estate,' " Lindy said.

Actually, I nearly broke the teapot when Champion Yonkers decided to walk under my feet as I started out of the kitchen.

"You come over here, cat," Lindy said. "Stay out of the way. Come on. I'll give you a plastic cup to bat around on the floor."

"I'm just glad he didn't jump on me," I said. "Well, here goes."

I walked quickly down the peristyle, trying not to lose my nerve. I really don't like unpleasant scenes, but the thought of Aunt Nettie in jail gave me courage. I gulped only once before I rapped on the office door.

Marion's "Come in!" sounded exasperated. She frowned when she saw who was disturbing her. "What are you doing here?"

"I ran an errand for Lindy. She sent you some tea. But I wanted to ask you a question."

I placed the tea on the credenza behind her desk, and I went on talking before she could call the security guard.

"Did Ms. Ripley have some problem with the pharmacist at the Superette?"

"That Glossop? She didn't have the problem. He did. Did he tell you about it?"

"No. In fact, he wouldn't say much—and that's what made me feel they'd had trouble. He talks a lot about everything else. But he wouldn't say anything about her."

"He's an officious ass."

"No argument there. But was there some specific problem between them?"

"He refused to fill a perfectly legitimate prescription."

"How could he do that?"

"It was marked no refills. Normally, a druggist would be satisfied with calling the prescribing doctor for an okay. But not Glossop! He refused to re-fill it at all until Clementine had seen her doctor again. And of course, he did all this on a Saturday afternoon, so it was difficult to get hold of the doc-tor. It caused a lot of inconvenience. Clementine was planning to file a com-plaint with the State Board of Pharmacy."

Marion frowned. "Why are you asking about this?"

"My aunt and I both handled the chocolates that held the cyanide. So I feel that I must learn all I can about the whole situation."

Marion stared at me. Abruptly, without changing her expression, she began to guffaw.

Her laughter was more hysterical than hilarious. It was more frightening than if she'd shouted in anger.

Almost immediately—as if someone had been waiting for an unusual sound—the door behind me opened. The security guard, Hugh, rushed in.

"Marion!" he almost shouted. "Calm down!"

Her laughter diminished. "Oh, Hugh! This stupid girl thinks Greg Glossop killed Clementine!"

Hugh looked from Marion to me and back again. "Well, I guess he could have," he said.

"Glossop! That milksop! His tongue may be poisonous, but he's too cowardly to give anybody cyanide." Marion turned to me. "No, you little fool. You're completely on the wrong track."

She stood up and glared at me. Oddly enough, what struck me was that she was as tall as I am. When you're almost six feet tall, it's unusual to look another woman in the eye.

Hugh went around the desk and patted her shoulder. "Now, Marion, you've got to calm down," he said. "We're not through this yet. Just hang on a few more days."

Marion shoved him away. She kept glaring at me. "You idiot. Glossop didn't have anything to do with Clementine's death. Surely any fool can see that Joe Woodyard killed her."

This conversation wasn't going anyplace. Which doesn't mean that silence fell.

Marion kept raving. "I tried to tell Clementine he was no good. He was just after what he could get—connections, money, a reflection of her status. But no! He had a hold over her no friend or associate could break. She used to look at him just the way she looked at your aunt's chocolates! It was embarrassing to see her. She'd stand any humiliation from him."

"Marion, Marion!" Hugh yelled, but he couldn't stop her tongue. I didn't even try.

"She turned her back on all her friends, on the people who loved her best, the ones who did everything for her, because of Joe Woodyard! We wanted her success. But Joe—as soon as he got into her life, he started trying to change her. Take that case, Clem. Don't defend that man, Clem—he's actually guilty!" She slapped the top of the desk. "You'd think a lawyer would know that even the guilty deserve a defense.

"Then he had the nerve to walk out on her! Thought she'd come running after him, I guess." She smiled wickedly. "But that didn't work. And now he tells the state police he didn't know he inherited. That's a lie! He and Clementine talked for half an hour Friday. I'm sure—I'm positive!—she told him she hadn't signed her new will. I feel certain of it. He had to act fast or he wouldn't inherit. He's a murderer!"

She pounded on the desk again. "God! I'm going to go insane if I can't get out of this house! If I can just last till tomorrow when I can fly away forever!"

Hugh had been trying to get a word in, trying to soothe her, and now she turned on him. "And you! You're as big an idiot as this girl is. Get out! Get out of my sight!"

I looked at Hugh, and he looked at me. He came around the desk and motioned. The two of us went into the hall. He closed the door behind us. Marion was still screaming and sobbing.

"I hate to leave her alone," I said.

Hugh nodded. "I guess I'd better ask Joe to call a doctor. Or the state police. Or somebody."

We stood there. Obviously, Hugh was as reluctant to make a decision as I was. Then a door opened behind us, and I looked around. Duncan Ainsley had come in through the utility room.

"What's going on?" he said. "Who's yelling?"

Hugh, still looking worried, explained.

Duncan gave an exasperated sigh. "Marion's been a half bubble off plumb all day," he said. "I'm hoping the state police will let her go back to Chicago tomorrow."

"She seems to be counting on it," I said. "I'm so sorry I pushed her into this, this—crisis."

"Don't you feel responsible. You were just walking by when the accident happened. I think it's time she went to bed with a hypo as big as Dallas. Is there a doctor in this town?"

"There used to be. Lindy will know."

"If she doesn't, Joe will. He was upstairs in Clementine's office." He gestured. "Would you see if you can find one of them?"

I turned and ran down the peristyle, feeling panicky. Seeing a person as strong as Marion McCoy melt down was shattering. I was still running when I reached the dining room and pivoted toward the kitchen.

And I careened right into Joe Woodyard.

Chapter 13

In a life full of humiliating experiences, nothing I ever do will match that moment. Except maybe stepping on my hem and ripping the skirt off my costume during the opening number of the Miss North Dallas pageant.

I will say a head-on collision with a six-foot-tall woman seemed to startle Joe as much as colliding with him did me. At least he jumped as high as I did, and he came down yelling, "What the hell!" Behind him, Lindy gave a little yelp.

I came down dithering. "I didn't mean to cause a commotion! I'll apologize later! Is there a doctor in Warner Pier?"

Joe grabbed me by the arms. "A doctor? What's happened?"

"It's Marian McCoy! She's hysterical."

"Thank God." Joe looked relieved. "I was afraid somebody else was dead!"

"She's screaming. Hugh couldn't calm her down. Mr. Ainsley thinks we should call a doctor."

"If Duncan or Hugh can't calm her, yeah, we'd better call somebody."

"I'll go see if I can help," Lindy said. She headed back the way I'd come.

"I'll see if I can get hold of Dr. Schiller," Joe said.

"I'm an interloper here," I said. "I'll get out."

"No!" Joe's voice was as brusque as usual. "Stick around. I want to talk to you." He headed toward the reception room, and in a minute I could hear his tennis shoes thumping as he ran up the stairway to the balcony.

I didn't know what to do. I was supposed to be out at Aunt Nettie's house, letting the state police's technical team in to search the place. But after I'd been rude enough to invade a house that now apparently belonged to Joe Woodyard, it would be even ruder to run off without giving him an explanation—feeble as my explanation might be. I did not want to face him, but I'd feel like a coward if I didn't.

In desperation, I did what I've done before. I turned to Aunt Nettie. I picked up the kitchen phone and called the chocolate shop.

The phone rang four times, and then I got a recording. "Darn!" I said. I waited until the beep, then yelled, "Aunt Nettie! It's me! Lee! Please pick up the phone!"

It took a few seconds, but she did. "Lee? What's wrong?"

"What's wrong is that I'm stuck out at the Ripley house and I'm missing my date with the technical team. Is there any way you can get out there to let them in?"

"Oh, dear. I guess I shouldn't have started these Crème de Menthe bonbons. I'm spouting."

Aunt Nettie didn't mean she was blowing her top. She meant she was using a funnel to fill square, dark chocolate shells with the Crème de Menthe flavored filling she'd made earlier. She manipulates the little stick as a plug and exactly the right amount of filling comes out the end of the funnel, filling one by one the dozens of little chocolate shells—the *bojkie*—set up on a tray. The filling has to be exactly the right temperature for this to work.

"I'll just have to leave here," I said.

"No," Aunt Nettie said. "I'll call Inez Deacon. She has a key to the house."

"Mrs. Deacon! Is she still patrolling the beach?" Mrs. Deacon and I had shared some dangerous times a dozen years earlier, when I was sixteen. She was one of Aunt Nettie's closest neighbors.

Aunt Nettie laughed. "Inez doesn't miss a day at the beach. She'll be glad to get in on the excitement. What's the number there? If she's not home, I'll call back."

I waited five minutes—timing it by the kitchen clock—then called the shop again. This time Aunt Nettie picked up on the first ring. She assured me that Mrs. Deacon had readily agreed to let the search team in and to tell them that one of us would be there as soon as possible.

With that taken care of, I got a glass of water, leaned against the kitchen cabinet, and assessed my position.

My try at active detection had certainly been a fiasco. My goal had been to find out why Greg Glossop had it in for Clementine Ripley. And I'd found the answer. He'd refused to fill a prescription, and she'd been planning to report him to the State Board of Pharmacy.

Did that matter? I couldn't believe that the picky Greg Glossop wouldn't have some legalistic defense. He was so insufferably egotistical that I felt sure he'd believe he could beat a complaint, no matter who it came from.

But that issue had paled beside the importance of the other two things I'd learned. First, Marion McCoy was telling the state police—and anyone else who would listen—that Joe Woodyard killed Clementine Ripley. Second, Marion was close to the breaking point. If she hadn't already broken. I was sorry about that, but I decided it wasn't my problem.

My problem was giving some explanation to Joe Woodyard. How should I handle this? Sitting in the kitchen like a kid waiting outside the principal's office did not appeal to me. I decided I'd better take the initiative and go to him, upstairs in Clementine's office.

I marched resolutely through the dining room and reception room and mounted the stairs. When I was halfway up, Joe came out onto the balcony.

"Were you able to reach the doctor?" I said.

"It took threats, pleading, and bribery, but he agreed to make a house call. He said he'd be here in half an hour."

"I apologize—"

Joe cut me off and pointed to the door he'd come out of. "I want to talk to you. Wait in here while I go tell Duncan and Hugh the doctor's on the way."

"Joe!" He ignored me, going down the stairs past me and turning toward the peristyle.

I stood looking after him, tempted simply to leave the premises. But that would seem cowardly. Finally I went on through the door Joe had pointed to. At least I'd get to see a little more of the house.

The room I entered was obviously the office, and it looked like someone actually worked there. The desk was enormous and held nothing but a computer, giving the maximum work space. The desk chair was the kind that can be adjusted to do anything but somersaults, and the lighting was top-notch. Bookshelves lined one wall, and they were stuffed with books, not doodads or gimcracks or even art objects. A second wall held built-in filing cabinets, flanked by decorative paneling.

The walls were painted white, just like the walls in the reception area, but they weren't blank, as the walls downstairs were. At least fifteen pictures—oils, watercolors, and woodblock prints—were hung in an arrangement behind the desk. The pictures weren't ones I'd have selected, but they were distinctive and obviously reflected the taste of a real person.

I walked over beside the desk to take a closer look at them. That was when I saw that the computer was on. Joe had been working on it, or maybe playing solitaire, when Marion's crisis arose.

I couldn't resist, of course. I looked at the computer screen to see what he'd been doing.

He'd been checking Clementine Ripley's Visa bill.

That was definitely none of my business. So naturally, I couldn't stand not taking a peek. Feeling curious—and guilty about my curiosity—I sat down in the desk chair to look at the computer screen. Then something rubbed against my leg, and I jumped up again.

Champion Yonkers walked out from under the desk.

"You again? What are you up to now?"

He yowled at me, in his usual haughty manner, then went around the desk and climbed into one of the two armchairs. He leaped from there to a shelf over the filing cabinets. He settled down there and surveyed the world with such aplomb that I deduced that it was his regular spot.

"I guess you won't rat on me," I said to him, turning back to the Visa bill.

And one item caught my eye immediately.

"Cheuy's! That's in Dallas."

I leaned close to the screen. Cheuy's is not a usual name for a restaurant, and I was sure there wasn't more than one. Sure enough—the charge was marked with DALLAS. I read on down. Neiman's. Well, nobody goes to Dallas without checking out Neiman's. And Clementine Ripley had succumbed to their goods, too. In fact, she'd spent a couple of thousand there.

I was looking on down the list of items when something clicked behind me. I jumped up guiltily, sure Joe had caught me checking out his—or his ex-wife's—private business.

But there was no one there. Then a section of the wall near the filing cabinets moved, and I jumped again. I moved from behind the desk and discovered the culprit.

"Yonkers!" I said. "You scared me."

The cat was using one white paw to open a door. The paneling on each end of the bank of filing cabinets camouflaged a closet.

"You know, Yonk, I expect they don't want you in there," I said.

I hauled him out, despite his angry yowls. I closed the door and made sure that it was latched.

Just then I heard tennis shoes thumping on the stairs. I moved away from the closet and the desk and tried to look innocent when Joe came in the door.

"I apologize for coming out here without an invitation and for stirring up Ms. McCoy," I said.

"Forget it," Joe said. "She loved having a new audience for her tale of how unworthy I was to touch the hem of Clem's gown."

"She doesn't seem to be a Joe Woodyard fan, true."

"Clem relied on her for everything—and I mean everything. Marion paid the bills, balanced the checkbook, ordered the meals, took the phone calls, told Clem when to go to the doctor and when to get her hair done. My presence interfered with all that. It's natural that she didn't like me. So she thinks I killed Clem."

So Joe knew Marion thought he'd killed his ex-wife. "Did she live with you?"

"She has a private suite here, but she has her own apartment in Chicago. And she always thought I was the intruder! But that's not what I wanted to talk to you about." He gestured at the computer screen. "You've lived in Dallas, haven't you? I don't understand these."

"Oh?"

"Clem's Visa bills. Marion is refusing to turn any financial records over until she has a court order, but I accessed the account on the Web."

He motioned, and I went around the desk and sat down in the fancy chair. I looked the list over. "This looks like a standard Visa bill to me."

"I don't understand why the balance is so high. Marion always claimed that she paid it off every month."

I studied the listing of charged items. "All of these charges were made in Dallas."

"Yes. These cover a period when Clem was trying the Romero case. She was in Dallas for two weeks. That's the reason I thought you might see something in them I don't."

"Neiman's. Stanley Korshak. Pretty upscale stuff."

"Clem liked to live well."

And Joe liked the simple life—fooling around with boats and wearing work clothes. I told myself to mind my own business. Then my fingernail tapped on an interesting item.

"Dr. Rockwell Stone!"

"I guess Clem had a cold or something."

"Maybe so, but I doubt she would have gone to Dr. Rockwell Stone for the sniffles. He's one of Dallas's leading plastic surgeons."

"Plastic surgeon?" Joe's voice was incredulous. I didn't reply, just looked at the computer screen and let him take it in.

"I can't believe Clem had plastic surgery," he said.

"This could have been simply a consultation. Except . . . well, it's quite a lot of money." Yes, the figure listed would have sent my Visa to a heart surgeon.

Joe leaned over to take a closer look. "Even a high-priced Dallas plastic surgeon should give you more than an opinion for that amount of money," he said. "I can call his office tomorrow. But there's another interesting item right under that one. A cash advance."

"Why is that interesting?"

"If Clem needed money, she wrote a check."

"Well, the rest of the charges look pretty standard. I mean, they were at exclusive stores, stores where I'd expect Clementine Ripley to shop. This makeup, for example—"

"Makeup? She bought makeup?"

"Several hundred dollars' worth."

"Impossible!"

"Joe, a purchase like that isn't unusual. Those little jars and bottles cost the earth when you go to a shop like Vivienne Rose, where they blend everything personally for each customer."

"I can believe that; Clem used to pay a bunch for that kind of gunk. But she'd never have bought it in Dallas."

"Why not?"

"Because she has a close friend in Chicago who sells that stuff. A consultant. All she had to do was call, and Jane sent over a batch. Besides, she was in Dallas to work." Joe's gesture dismissed the entire bill. "Clem was all business in court. The restaurants—maybe. Even Clem had to eat, and she entertained clients and other attorneys a lot. But she'd never have stopped in the middle of a trial and gone shopping, bought new makeup, talked to a plastic surgeon. This whole thing stinks!"

"Then who did charge these things? Do you think her credit card was stolen?"

"Not exactly."

"Then what?"

"Like I say, the only person who handled Clem's credit cards was Marion McCoy."

"Oh."

Joe stared grimly at the wall for a moment. "I guess I just wanted confirmation of my feeling that there was something funny about this bill," he said. "I never trusted Marion, but she was down on me from the time Clem and I hit it off. So I never knew if I was right about her or just reacting to her open dislike of me."

"I don't understand all this."

"You don't understand how Marion could resist my charm?"

"Oh, you're charming as all get out. But how could Ms. Ripley stand this situation? I hadn't been out at this house for ten minutes on Friday when I realized everybody was at everybody else's throat. I was glad to hand over my chocolates and get away."

"I got away, too." Joe's voice was bitter.

"I'm sorry," I said. "It's none of my affair, and I should have kept my mouth shut."

Joe went on, still speaking bitterly. "Clem had her life arranged just the way she wanted it. It suited her. She thrived on all that discord. She deliberately stirred it up. Any efforts I made to make her life smooth and happy were not welcome."

He stood up. "Maybe she only married me to make Marion mad. Anyway, thanks for taking a look at this."

"What do you intend to do?"

"Call in the accountants."

"Are you going to tell the state police?"

"I hope it won't mean filing charges."

"But doesn't this give Marion a real motive for killing Ms. Ripley?"

Joe paused. "I can't believe she did it. Her problem was that she adored Clem. I can't picture her doing anything to harm her."

"She appears to have harmed her financially. Joe, I'm sure the state police have accountants. It'll be better if you tell VanDam about this yourself than to let them find it out and have to say, 'Oh, yeah. That. Well, I was hoping not to have to file charges.' "

Joe frowned. "Accusing Marion would look so stupid. Tit for tat. She's accusing me, so I'm accusing her. I'll think about it until tomorrow."

Tomorrow. There was something about the word . . . My memory clicked into gear, and I gasped.

"Rats! Joe, tomorrow may be too late!"

"I don't think VanDam is going to arrest anybody today."

"No, it was something Marion McCoy said! When she was hysterical she yelled out that she could barely wait until tomorrow so she could get out of here. Duncan Ainsley thinks she's going to go back to Chicago then. Except . . ."

"Except what?"

"She didn't say she was going to 'go' tomorrow. She said she was going to 'fly' tomorrow."

Joe and I stared at each other. "It's possible to fly to Chicago," he said.

"Sure. Lots of people drive an hour to Grand Rapids so they can sit in the airport two hours, then fly forty-five minutes to Chicago. That would take a total of three hours and forty-five minutes. I guess some people would rather do that than drive two and a half hours the other direction and get to Chicago faster."

Joe just frowned.

"It may be silly," I said, "but it sounds to me as if Marion is planning to go someplace besides Chicago."

"It doesn't sound good. Maybe I'd better call VanDam." Joe sighed. "I can see that this estate is going to be a mess. I'll have to cash in some investments if I'm going to get the money Clem owed me."

I decided not to comment on that, though I was dying to know just why Clementine Ripley owed Joe money. "If you sell the house . . ."

"It's mortgaged to the hilt. That's the way Clem ran things. On credit. The Chicago apartment is mortgaged, too. Even the apartment building we still owned jointly is mortgaged, and Clem's promise to buy me out isn't much good now."

"Oh!" I heard myself say. That must be what Joe and Clementine had been talking about Friday. I felt quite relieved, then surprised at myself. Joe's finances were no concern of mine, were they?

"Is there anything else I can do here?" I said. "I'm supposed to be out at Aunt Nettie's, meeting with the state police technical team."

"Then you'd better get going. I'm sorry I held you up."

"It's okay."

We headed for the stairs. "I'm sorry if you're having problems getting your business going," I said.

"Wooden boats are a specialized field," Joe said. "My granddad worked on them, and I always liked fooling around in the shop with him. Now I'm trying to buy six boats—one's a cruiser built in 1928—from a guy who's retiring. It's a once-in-a-lifetime chance, and it could really set me up. But even in the shape these boats are in, and they all need complete restoration, it calls for a lot of money. If I can't get my money out of the apartment house . . . Well, I told the guy I wanted them, so it's going to be embarrassing if I have to back out."

"Do you have a contract for sale?"

"Just a handshake deal. But we're talking about the world of wooden boats. There are just a couple of hundred people doing this. Contracts aren't as important as keeping your word."

We walked on down the stairs without talking. But the atmosphere had changed. For the first time I didn't feel that my presence—my mere existence—made Joe angry. Suddenly we were almost friends.

He led me to the kitchen, then stopped. "Listen," he said. "You kept trying to apologize, but I'm the one who should be saying I'm sorry."

"Why?"

"I haven't been very polite."

"You've been under a lot of stress."

"Which is a cliché excuse for rudeness."

"You seem to be the only person who really cared for Ms. Ripley and who was genuinely sorry she died."

"I don't know if I'm sorry or annoyed. I was so angry when we first split up—it's taken me two years to get my head halfway straight, to get to the point when I'd pretty well put her behind me and begun to move on. Then she's murdered! And I can't ignore it. I'm a suspect. And her heir. Even if I don't get arrested, I'm going to have to settle her estate. It's thrown me back into some kind of emotional limbo."

I didn't know what to say. I fell back on a platitude. "It's not going to be easy, but I'm sure you'll handle it."

"I hope. . . ."

He went on to the outside door, opened it, and stepped back to let me out. Or I thought he was going to let me out. I stepped forward, and he stepped sideways, and we bumped into each other again. Suddenly we were standing in the doorway, nose to nose. This time neither of us moved. We stood just there.

The moment would have passed if either one of us had reacted normally. Or maybe we did react normally.

It was a heck of a kiss.

Not that it involved a lot of action. We didn't even put our arms around each other. Just stood there in a lip lock. For a long time.

Then I heard a loud, piercing noise. A siren.

Joe and I jumped apart like a couple of teenagers when Daddy flipped the porch light on.

We both ran out into the back driveway just as an ambulance came around the corner of the house and skidded to a stop. Greg Glossop jumped out of the passenger door.

He yelled, "Where is she?"

We spoke at the same time. "Who?"

"Marion McCoy! That Hugh called and said she needed an ambulance."

"Did Dr. Schiller think she needed hospitalization?" Joe said.

"I don't know what Schiller thought! All I know is Hugh said she wasn't breathing."

Joe and I both turned and ran, with Glossop on our heels and the other EMT close behind him. We ran back through the kitchen and dining room and down the peristyle toward the office.

Hugh was standing in the hall. "Hurry! Hurry!" he said.

Glossop and his teammate rushed in. Marion was lying on the couch.

"I managed to get her up on the couch to make her a little more comfortable," Hugh said.

We all held our breath while Glossop yanked her shirt up to her armpits, then used his stethoscope. He touched the skin of her face.

"We'll try," he said, "but it looks like another cyanide death to me."

I forced myself to look away from Marion's flushed face. And when I looked away, I saw the teapot.

It was still sitting on the credenza behind Marion's desk. Right where I had put it down a half hour earlier. But the teacup Lindy had sent was now on the desk, half full of tea.

Chapter 14

For the second time in three days, someone had died after eating or drinking something I had handed her.

My first impulse was to throw myself down and kick and scream. But Joe spoke, and he sounded calm, so I decided to pretend to be calm, too.

"Are the state police on the way?" Joe said.

In response, we heard another siren.

"Hugh, Lee—everybody except the EMTs had better go into the big living room," Joe said. "Where's Duncan?"

"He went back to the guest house," Hugh said. "I can go get him."

Joe and I were a somber pair as we walked back to the main part of the house. We stood before the fireplace until Hugh and Duncan came in, almost running down the long hall toward us. The mood was not lightened when Yonkers jumped off the balcony onto Duncan Ainsley's shoulders, using him as a springboard to bounce onto the bar. Duncan lost his Texas folksiness over that; the words he said were basic Anglo-Saxon. But neither Hugh, Joe, nor I took any notice of his language, and Yonkers had the sense to make himself scarce. He jumped down behind the bar and peeked around its end.

Joe let two uniformed state police in the front door. Then he, Duncan, Hugh, and I sat in the big black-and-white reception room. The beautiful views from the banks of windows failed to soften the cold effect, and the flower arrangements made it worse. In a few minutes I glimpsed VanDam and Underwood arriving, followed almost immediately by the technical team—including a couple of the people who had searched the chocolate shop. Then Chief Jones came in. Each group went back toward the office, leaving a uniformed officer in the front hall.

We just sat there. Joe spoke once. "I'm glad I told Lindy to go home," he said. "We're going to be here all night."

But it was only half an hour later when Chief Jones came in and joined us. He sat down in one of the spindly chairs and looked at us over the top of his glasses.

"Lieutenant VanDam has allowed me to have the honor of telling all of you that you can go home."

The three of us inhaled so sharply that the air pressure in the room dropped fifty percent. Then we all talked at once.

"What about statements?" Joe said.

"Why? What's happened?" Duncan said.

"But I gave her the tea!" That was me. "And she's dead, and she looked like Clementine Ripley. . . ."

"Yes, that's true." The chief paused—I'm sure for dramatic effect—before he spoke again. "But Clementine Ripley didn't leave a suicide note."

I almost collapsed, but Joe spoke. "Did Marion confess?"

"Said something about, 'I loved Clementine. I never meant to hurt her.' Like that."

A huge load seemed to lift off my shoulders. "It was the Visa bill," I said.

The chief frowned, and Joe made a succinct report of the questions he had about Clementine Ripley's Visa bill. "I guess she knew that was going to come out," he said.

"Sounds likely," Duncan said. "Clementine must have found out that her Visa bill was crazy as a steer on locoweed. Marion would have seen disaster on the horizon, so she killed Clementine. Then she was sorry."

"It was the chocolates," I said.

The chief frowned again. "Well, Marion apparently injected cyanide into the chocolates, but—"

"No! I mean it was the charge for the chocolates. The Visa bill. Clementine Ripley ordered over two thousand dollars' worth of chocolates from us. She wanted to put it on her Visa, but Visa wouldn't accept the charge. So I called and told Marion McCoy we'd have to have a check. When I delivered the chocolates, Clementine Ripley found out that Visa had refused her charge." I gestured at Joe. "Joe was there. He heard her. She made me tell her just what had happened. Then she told Marion to give me a check, and she said something like, 'We'll discuss this later.' So it looks as if the charge for the chocolates must have tipped her off."

"That sounds likely," Chief Jones said.

We asked for details, and he told us Marion had apparently heavily sweetened the hot tea I'd carried into the office, then spiked it with cyanide. Underwood found the suicide note propped up on Marion's dresser. The envelope was marked FOR THE POLICE, and it was sitting on top of a bottle the lab was going to test as possibly containing cyanide.

The detectives believed the note had been printed out on the ink-jet printer in Marion's office, and the original message had been found saved in her computer. The message was in memo form, printed out neatly on Clementine Ripley's letterhead, signed, folded in thirds, and sealed in a white business envelope.

Anyway, an hour after Joe and I stood in the kitchen door kissing each other, the crisis about the murder of Clementine Ripley seemed to be over. I rushed back to the shop and told Aunt Nettie what had happened, of course. Then the phone began to ring.

Nancy Burton, the customer who had taken all our Crème de Menthe bonbons for her B-and-B, called and told Aunt Nettie that only that morning she'd rented her last two rooms to reporters, and within an hour of Marion McCoy's death they'd both checked out and gone back to Chicago. So we figured that the press had gotten the word. We found out later that CNN put an item on right away, being careful not actually to say that Marion had confessed.

A steady stream of cars must have been leaving town, each with a PRESS decal on the windshield, because we saw no more of the press—tabloid or otherwise—after Marion's death.

The chief did come by the shop to give us one other interesting bit of information. "You said the burglar you had last night fell off your porch, didn't you?" he said.

"Yes," Aunt Nettie said. "He fell down the steps."

"Try she, not he."

"Marion McCoy?"

"We may never figure it out for sure, but when the EMTs got that long-sleeved black thing off of her, her arms were covered with bruises. Like she'd had a fall. So VanDam had them check her legs before they took her away. They were bruised, too."

"But why did she do that?" Aunt Nettie said. "Did her note explain that?"

"Nope. We may never know the answer to that one. But I guess she did it." He ducked his head and looked like a tall, skinny elf. "Another thing—when they got that turtleneck shirt all the way off—well, they found scars. She'd had surgery." His lips twitched. "Pretty recent. A boob job."

I gasped. "So that's what she saw the plastic surgeon about in Dallas!"

"I guess so. Anyway, I've learned a lot during the past couple of days. I've never been a suspect before, and it sure gave me a new outlook on law enforcement."

"I guess you're glad it's over," Aunt Nettie said. "Has Lieutenant Van-Dam left?"

"Oh, no. He'll hang around a couple of days, or Underwood will, making sure the lab work gets done."

"Then they're still investigating?"

The chief's manner became evasive. "They have to tie up all the loose ends. Check the fingerprints. Wait for the autopsy results."

I started to ask the chief if Joe had told him or VanDam about my idea that Marion might have been about to go on the lam, to "fly" away. But the phone rang, and by the time I got it answered, the chief had left. So I didn't mention it to Aunt Nettie.

In fact, I told myself, the whole idea had probably been wrong. If Marion was planning to kill herself, she wouldn't be worrying about flying anywhere.

But one more question did cross my mind: What had Marion hoped to gain by killing Clementine Ripley? Even if Clementine were dead, somebody was going to check that Visa bill. Then I remembered that Marion had been surprised to learn Clementine had not signed her new will, the one cutting Joe out of the estate and naming someone else executor. She'd probably thought she'd be named executor herself.

But it seemed sort of fishy. And Joe had agreed with me, had seemed to think my interpretation of Marion's ravings could well be correct. When I thought about the whole thing, my relief turned to unease.

Chief Jones might have left, but we still had visitors. First Mike Herrera knocked at the street door and came in to exult over Clementine Ripley's murder turning out to involve "outsiders."

"Now Warner Pier can get back to normal," he said. "I suppose this might even improve business this season. You know, lotsa people will have read about Warner Pier in the newspapers and seen our beautiful city on the television news."

This inspired one of the few tart answers I heard from Aunt Nettie. "I certainly hope we didn't go through all this just as a tourist promotion."

Mike seemed a little embarrassed. "Oh, nice lady! I didn't mean I'm glad it happened! I just want us to make the best of what we're stuck with."

Aunt Nettie let him off the hook. "I know what you mean, Mike. But this has surely been a strain. I just hope it really is over."

As Mike went out the front door, a new caller showed up—Greg Glossop. Since we had the door open, it was impossible not to let him in.

He was enjoying the situation thoroughly. "You can't believe the silly gossip that's already started," he said. "Someone asked me if it was true that Clementine Ripley's secretary made a run for it and drove her car into a bridge abutment down by South Haven." He preened. "Luckily, I could tell her that was a complete fabrication."

We had to hash over the whole affair before he was satisfied. And the phone kept ringing. The word was spreading like the great fire of 1871, which left half of Warner Pier in ashes. All of Aunt Nettie's friends called.

The result was that I thought we'd never get rid of Greg Glossop. In fact, he was still there when I got a call. From Joe.

Luckily, I answered the telephone that time.

"Hi," Joe said. "Your line's been busy for thirty minutes."

"I know. All of Warner Pier's called up to tell us how glad they are that we're not going to be tried for murder."

"People around here are really nice, aren't they?" Joe's deadpan tones emphasized the sarcasm in his remark.

I laughed. "Oh, people are pretty much the same everywhere, I guess. You should have heard the strange questions the Texans asked when I left my ex. Are the detectives through out there?"

"No. They're still at it. Working in the office. I'm on the kitchen line. I wanted to talk to you."

"Oh?" Was he going to bring up that kiss?

He didn't say anything for a long time. I didn't say anything either. Finally, we both spoke at the same time.

"Listen . . ." I said.

"I hope . . ." Joe said.

We both shut up again, and there was another silence. Then Joe spoke.

"Back there as you were leaving . . . I was way out of line. I owe you an apology."

His comment struck me funny. "That's not very complimentary," I said.

"I don't mean I didn't enjoy it!"

I laughed, and in a few seconds, I heard a chuckle from the other end of the line.

"As long as you're not mad," Joe said.

"No, I obviously enjoyed it, too. But . . . listen, let's forget the whole thing, okay?"

"Forget it? That's a tall order."

"I mean—well, we've both had some bad experiences, and I think . . . I think both of us need to get out more!"

There was another long silence. Then Joe spoke seriously. "You don't want my class ring?"

"No, but I'd be tempted by the letter jacket."

We both laughed. It was such a relief to be able to joke. But I couldn't forget my unease about Marion's plan to fly away.

"Joe, I had one thing I wanted to talk to you about."

"I gotta go," Joe said. "VanDam's waving at me. Can I call you later, when things calm down?"

"I may call you."

We both hung up, and I looked up to see Aunt Nettie standing in the office doorway. "Lee, do you think we could go home now?"

"Did Greg Glossop leave?"

"Finally."

The phone rang again, but this time I let the answering machine catch it.

"We're not here," I said, turning off the sound. "In fact, we're no longer murder suspects, and we're going to go out on a toot to celebrate."

"And just what kind of a toot did you have in mind?"

"I have enough room left on *my* Visa card to treat us to a pizza. How does that sound?"

"Wonderful. I definitely don't want to cook."

"Come on then. There's no cloud hanging over our heads, and we're gonna howl!"

I stuffed my doubts about the details of Marion's crime under a mental rock and led Aunt Nettie out the door to the alley.

Chapter 15

Peach Street was still crowded with tourist traffic as we drove out of the alley. The most interesting thing I noticed was a black Mercedes convertible parked in front of Downtown Drugs. There was no sign of Duncan Ainsley, however.

"Is the Dock Street still the best place for pizza?" I said.

"Well, I think they have really good sauce—and plenty of it. And they've become a sort of social center, too."

"You mean the tourists discovered it?"

"No, I mean it's a center for us locals. I understand that if a couple is seen together in the Dock Street it's practically an announcement that they're going steady. And they've put in a dining room since your day."

"A dining room? Do you want to eat there?" I nudged her. "Everybody already knows we're related."

"Sure. If we can get a table."

The Dock Street Pizza Place has been a Warner Pier institution for a long time. It's the best kind of pizza place—long on spices, cheese, and toppings and short on ambiance. I was pleased to see that we still ordered by walking up to a counter and that the "dining room" consisted of a dozen tables in what had been a garage off the alley back when I went there as a teenager. And it still smelled like garlic, tomatoes, pepperoni, and hot bread.

Aunt Nettie and I snagged a table for two in a corner, and I went up to the counter and ordered a medium Italian sausage and mushroom pizza, two side salads, and two glasses of red wine from our local winery.

I took the salads and wine back to the table. I was sitting with my back to the counter, and I was so tired that I was ignoring the social side of dinner at the Dock Street. So I was surprised when Aunt Nettie looked behind me and her eyes grew wide. "That Mr. Ainsley is coming over here," she said softly.

Amazed, I turned around. Duncan Ainsley was the last person I'd have expected to see in the Dock Street. "Duncan!"

"Lee." He smiled and patted my shoulder. Then he turned to Aunt Nettie. "And Nettie TenHuis, the famous chocolatier. I sure am glad to run into y'all. May I join you?"

"Of course," Aunt Nettie said. There was no way to refuse. Plus, I was rather honored that a man as well known as Duncan Ainsley wanted to sit with us. The *Business Week* article had described him as a "bachelor who likes to be seen with a beautiful woman on his arm." That night "beautiful" hardly applied to either Aunt Nettie or me. Duncan, however, was as suave as usual. Not a hair in that beautiful head of gray was out of place.

"I thought Lindy was fixing dinner for you," I said.

"She left something to heat up, but—thank the Lord!—I was finally allowed to get out of that house," Duncan said. "So I got."

"Are you going back to Chicago tonight?"

He shook his head. "No, I'll wait and go in the morning. There's no point in fighting Sunday evening traffic. I was able to check into a B-and-B."

"How did you find the Dock Street?" Aunt Nettie asked. "I thought only us locals knew about it."

"I asked somebody where to get some good Italian food." Duncan smiled broadly. "Pizza sounded good. And the company's a lot better than out at the Ripley house."

"Is Joe the only other person there?"

"Except for the security guard. And Joe may well be a fine fellow, but I heard too much about him from Marion."

"I know you must have known her well."

"Marion and I had an odd relationship. Sometimes it was such a headache that I was sorry Clementine Ripley had become a client. Oh, I made money on the deal, but I rarely saw Clementine, and Joe refused to have anything to do with her business affairs, even before their divorce. That left all the details to Marion. And her relationship with Clementine . . ." He wiggled his eyebrows. "You'll have figured out that it was kinda peculiar." He turned to Aunt Nettie. "Will y'all be leaving Warner Pier next winter?"

"Maybe for a vacation," she said. "Why?"

"Then you don't spend the winter in Florida, the way some of the resort shopkeepers do?"

"Oh, no," Aunt Nettie said.

I spoke then. "TenHuis Chocolade is quite busy year-round. We do a lot of mail-order business."

"I had no notion."

"I think Aunt Nettie should expand, but she wants to keep a close eye on just how TenHuis chocolates are made."

"You have to watch every detail," Aunt Nettie said.

Duncan frowned. "But I've been in the shop. You're obviously not making all the chocolates yourself. Lee, do you help?"

"Nope. I keep my hands strictly out of the chocolate and into the business side. TenHuis has about thirty-five ladies who make the chocolates."

"Thirty-five! That's a much larger business than I realized, Mrs. Ten-Huis." He turned to me again. "Then you don't put on hairnets and gloves and dig into the marshmallow cream?"

I laughed at the horrified expression that the notion of marshmallow cream inspired in Aunt Nettie. "We use neither marshmallow cream nor plastic gloves," I said.

"No? I thought health department rules said food handlers had to use them."

"Not always," Aunt Nettie said, "but we have what the health department calls an alternate policy. Our employees are specially trained in hand washing and food handling, so they don't have to wear gloves." She leaned over and spoke confidingly. "McDonalds's has the same kind of deal. My ladies do wear hairnets. But it would be extremely hard to do some of the detail work we do while wearing gloves."

"I can see that you're as busy as three windmills in a tornado."

At that point the counter girl called my name, and I went up to collect our pizza. Duncan shared our sausage and mushroom until his arrived, and we had quite a companionable time, with Duncan entertaining us with more stories about his famous clients.

At the end of the meal Aunt Nettie excused herself to speak to a friend across the room. I stood up and extended my hand. "This has been most enjoyable," I said. "I hope everything is calm for a while. I don't think I can stand any more incitement—I mean, excitement!"

Duncan stood up, too. He smiled, gave me a lot of eye contact, and made shaking my hand more than a polite gesture.

"I hope you get to leave tomorrow," I said.

"I plan to be off as soon as I have breakfast. Have a nice evening, Lee, and a nice life. If you ever want to try the big city, let me know. I hate to see a young woman as personable and intelligent as you stagnating in a little town—even a cute little one."

"The big city life doesn't appeal to everyone. Look at Joe."

Duncan raised his eyebrows. "Of course, Joe may change his mind about the big city now that his situation has changed."

"You mean because big-city life is more fun with money?"

"No, I mean that he might decide to go back into law practice. Now that Clementine isn't around to pressure him to stay out of it."

I must have looked amazed, because Duncan laughed. "Hadn't you heard that particular piece of gossip? Marion was spreading it so busily that I thought it would be all over Warner Pier."

"Clementine Ripley pressured Joe to stop practicing law?"

"According to Marion, that was part of their divorce settlement."

"But how could she do that?"

"Supposedly she had the goods on him—threatened to get him disbarred. But she gave him the out of voluntarily leaving the practice of law."

I was stunned. "Then why did Clementine leave Joe as her heir? Why didn't she sign her new will?"

"Thought she'd live forever, just like the rest of us do, I guess." Duncan shrugged. "Ask your aunt about it. She may have heard something. Anyway, if you decide to leave Warner Pier for the big city, to trade in the historic farmhouse for a high-rise condo, let me know."

I tried to swallow my amazement and keep our good-bye light. "Ah, but a condo wouldn't have a Michigan basement."

"Is that what that sand-floored cellar is called? I learn something new all the time."

Duncan smiled as Aunt Nettie reappeared. He left a lavish tip on the table—not strictly necessary in a place where you get your own food from the counter—and escorted us to the old Buick, settling Aunt Nettie in the driver's seat as gallantly as if she'd been driving a Rolls. He gave me one of his business cards and even waved as we drove away.

I could barely wait to ask Aunt Nettie if she'd heard the gossip Duncan had passed along, the news that Clementine Ripley had threatened to get Joe disbarred.

"No, I hadn't heard that," she said, "and I'm sure his mother hasn't heard it either. She was furious with Joe for quitting law and did a lot of moaning about his lack of ambition. She certainly didn't act as if he was being forced to get out of the profession."

I liked Joe. I had even kissed him. But that had just been my hormones telling me he was an attractive man. It didn't give me any insight into his character.

I reminded myself that my past record on judging people wasn't too good. I had thought Rich was one of the good guys. Now I knew that I'd never marry another divorced man without finding out more about why his first marriage broke up.

We discussed the ramifications of Duncan's revelation all the way home. Once inside, we checked out the house. The state police search team had been much neater than the burglar. Mrs. Deacon had left a note saying some of the searchers left at four o'clock—that would have been when Marion's death was reported—and the others at five-thirty.

"I guess I don't need to hide the van any longer," I said. "I'll go over to the Baileys' and get it."

"Oh, dear!" Aunt Nettie frowned. "I just remembered—I forgot to stop for gas. I'd better go back to town."

"You put your feet up. I'll take the Buick and get gas."

I don't have any excuse for what I did next. In fact, I wasn't aware that I was doing it until after I'd done it. My brain apparently went into cruise control, and my subconscious handled the whole thing.

I drove straight to the Ripley estate.

I had pulled up at the security gate before I realized where I was going.

As soon as I saw where I was, I put the car in reverse and started to leave. But it was too late. The security guard was already speaking to me electronically. I knew he could see me on his closed circuit camera. I was trapped by my own subconscious. I decided to act as if I'd come on purpose.

"Lee McKinney to see Joe Woodyard."

"Is he expecting you?"

Actually, I did have some vague memory of telling Joe I wanted to talk to him again that evening. I tried to sound confident. "I believe so."

The guard decided to believe me. "Drive on around the circle," he said. The gate slid open.

Once again I headed up the long drive that led through the trees. An elaborate system of hidden lights illuminated the driveway. Why wasn't I surprised by that?

When I pulled up in front of the flagstone steps, Hugh was waiting for me. "Mr. Woodyard's down at the boathouse," he said. "You can wait for him inside."

He opened the front door, and I went into the big foyer, still packed with flowers, then walked on into the reception room. I heard a meow over my head and looked up to see Yonkers, again hiding behind the huge white ceramic pot.

"Are you going to jump on me?" I said.

"No," Yonkers said. Actually, I suppose it was more like *naow* but he certainly responded. Then he turned and trotted along the balcony to a door that opened into a lighted room I realized was the office. I was moving toward the big, soft white couch when I heard a loud clang from upstairs.

"Yonk, did you knock over the wastebasket?" I decided I'd better see what the cat was up to, since Joe was not in the house to keep an eye on him. I ran up the stairs and went along the balcony to the office.

When I looked inside, the wastebasket was still upright, and Yonkers was nowhere in sight. "Yonk! Here, kitty!" I looked behind the desk, noting that the computer was off this time, and under the chairs.

"Where did you go, you pesky cat?"

I got a clue when the paneled door moved, just as it had that afternoon. Yonkers had once more opened the closet. But this time he was inside.

I opened the door. The closet was apparently an afterthought, maybe put in just in case Clementine Ripley or some future owner ever decided to make the office room over into a bedroom. For the moment, however, it was lined with shelves and stocked with paper, boxes of paper clips, and other office necessities. All very businesslike.

Except for the filmy black nightgown that hung on a hook on the inside of the door.

CHOCOLATE CHAT
ROMANCE

- Chocolate has long been associated with romance, but it's hard to tell how much of this was based on fact and how much on marketing. When chocolate was introduced to Germany during the 1600s, for example, the sellers whispered of its value as an aphrodisiac. Ladies were urged to offer a cup to their husbands.

- The Aztec emperor Montezuma reportedly drank chocolate before visiting his harem.

- The Spanish kept chocolate a secret for nearly a hundred years, but in 1615 Princess Maria Teresa gave her fiancé, Louis XIV of France, a gift of chocolate and the secret was out.

- Casanova was quoted as saying chocolate was more useful in seduction than champagne.

- After chocolate candy was developed, luscious, creamy bonbons and truffles came to be known as a ideal romantic gift. This developed into the heart-shaped box of chocolates—the Valentine's Day gift every teenage girl longs for—and into luxury chocolates for more sophisticated lovers.

- Still, the physical effects of eating chocolate—stimulating the heart muscle, providing extra energy, and maybe even acting as a mood booster—are a lot like falling in love!

Chapter 16

A black lace nightgown?

It was the last thing I expected to find in an office closet. Two more things were hung on top of it—a lightweight sweater, the kind you might keep around in case you got cold while finishing up a report, and a man's flannel shirt. The shirt and sweater were on wooden hangers, but I could see that a fancy padded hanger held the nightgown. Its hanger was scented, too, or something in the closet was.

Yonkers seemed as interested in the gown as I was. He began to exercise his claws on the fragile skirt.

"Bad cat!" I said. I tried to lift the skirt of the gown up, out of his reach, and it slipped off its fancy satin hanger.

"Rats," I said. I wrestled the gown away from Yonkers, tossing it onto the desk. "You're going to ruin it, you naughty thing." I clapped my hands at him. "Get up on your perch and let this alone."

Yonkers went to his perch on the shelf with a sneer, making sure I understood he was doing it because he wanted to, not in response to my order. I picked the gown up, ready to hang it on the closet door again, but first I held it up to myself, admiring its beautiful lace and delicate embroidery.

This was the moment, of course, that Joe walked into the office.

We stared at each other. Then Joe spoke. "Why did you bring *that*?"

I fell back on my say-nothing habit and merely stood there. Then I caught the implication; he thought I had come out to see him, uninvited, and had brought a sexy black nightgown along.

I gasped. "I didn't bring it!"

Joe blushed.

And I got the giggles.

Joe blushed more brightly. "I guess that wasn't a cool thing to say."

I spoke again. "I didn't bring it out here. I was trying to research it. I mean, rescue! I took the gown away from Yonkers."

"Yonkers?" Joe's color was fading, but he looked confused.

"Yes. I heard a crash, and I thought Yonkers had knocked the wastebasket over. So I came upstairs to see if he was tearing things up. He'd gotten the closet door open and was inside. I had to haul him out. When I did, I saw this gown on a hanger on the back of the door, and Yonkers began to claw at it. So I took it away from him. I was just admiring it before I hung it back up."

Joe looked more confused than ever. "The thing was here?"

"Yes. It was inside that closet."

He opened the closet door and looked inside. "In here?"

"See? The hanger's still there."

Joe lifted the scented hanger down, still frowning. "What was it doing here?"

I took the hanger. "I suppose it belonged to Ms. Ripley."

"No."

"It's obviously something she got recently."

"Clem would never have worn a thing like that."

"Maybe it was a gift." I sighed. "Joe, you and Ms. Ripley had been separated for two years. She was a very attractive woman. Frankly, it's the kind of thing a guy would give his girlfriend."

Joe shook his head. "I'd be delighted to find out that Clem had a new man in her life. But if he knew her well enough to give her a sexy thing like that, he ought to have known her well enough to see that she'd never have worn it."

"Maybe she would have—if it were a special request."

"Clem never wore anything. Like that." Joe was slightly red again. "I mean—not for sleeping. Besides, she wouldn't have kept something like a nightgown out here in the office supply closet. She had a big dressing room."

I ducked my head to look at the skirt of the gown, then took hold of it and fanned it out to examine it more closely. The skirt was of sheer nylon, practically transparent. A vision of Joe drooling as I modeled it for him flashed through my mind. I thought of the flannel sleep pants and T-shirt I wore for Michigan nights, and I almost sighed.

"Well, it's beautiful, of course," I said. "Some women do wear this sort of very feminine thing just for their own pleasure. But I'd really expect it to be worn to please a husband or a lover."

"No, Clem would never have worn something like this for any reason."

"Then I don't understand. Have the police seen it?"

"Probably. They went over this section of the house pretty thoroughly."

"But they might not have seen anything unusual about it," I said.

We both stared at the filmy black gown. I reached for the hanger again. "It's a beautiful garment. You can always give it to the National Association of Former Good Girls."

As I held it up, I caught a glimpse of the label. It was a brand I'd never heard of, since I've never been a particular fan of expensive nightgowns. Rich never bought me clothes; he gave me money or jewelry. But beneath that label was another smaller label that said 10.

Size ten? The gown was a size ten? I held the straps against my shoulders and let the skirt of the gown drift down. The hem reached past the cuff of my khaki slacks.

But Clementine Ripley had been on the short side.

I mused aloud. "I wonder what size Ms. Ripley wore?"

"Twelve petite. I asked Marion the first Christmas Clem and I were married. She said the 'petite' was important. Why?"

"This gown would never have fit her. It's way too long, for one thing. It would have trailed on the floor. And for another thing, it's too small through the bodice. I don't think Ms. Ripley could have gotten into it. And if she did, it's designed to enhance the bust, to make it look larger."

"Clem would never have worn something that would have made her look bigger."

"So even if somebody gave it to her, it wouldn't have been her favorite gift."

Joe and I looked at each other for a moment. Then he spoke. "I hope somebody did care about her. Somebody besides Marion."

I hung the gown up.

"But I still can't see any reason it would be in the closet off her office," Joe said.

"Maybe she was going to return it. Exchange it."

"Or give it to the National Association of Former Good Girls."

We both smiled, and I turned around. "I don't suppose she would have given clothes to Marion McCoy. It would have fit Marion great."

Joe's jaw dropped.

"She was tall enough to wear it," I said, "and she was thin—Oh, my gosh!"

"Marion," Joe said.

"Marion," I said. "She'd bought all those clothes in Dallas. She'd had a boob job. I'm willing to bet that gown was hers. And what's the most logical reason for all that?"

"She had a boyfriend."

"But she certainly wasn't wearing any of those new clothes when I saw her Friday, Joe. Or Saturday. Or today. She looked really dowdy. Yet she'd actually stolen—stolen!—money to buy clothes. Why would she do that?"

"She didn't want anybody to know about the boyfriend."

"I think you're right. She was keeping the boyfriend a secret even from Clementine."

"Maybe especially from Clementine."

"Why?"

Joe didn't have an answer for that, and neither did I.

The conversation was at an impasse. For the first time I looked down and saw that Joe was in his stocking feet.

"My shoes were wet," he said, "so I left them outside. The sign of being raised by a mother who hated cleaning house."

"That's why I didn't hear you coming up the stairs." I shook my head. "Actually, I didn't come here to discuss black lingerie. I wanted to know if you told Lieutenant VanDam about that flying comment Marion made."

"Yes, I did. He didn't seem too impressed."

I moved toward the door. "I just wanted to know if you'd told him. I'd better get home now." Joe followed me out onto the balcony and down the stairs.

"Apparently everybody thinks that Marion's suicide solves Clementine Ripley's murder," I said.

"That seems to be the general attitude."

"You don't sound convinced."

"I'd like to be. I'd like it to be settled for once and for all."

"How about the state police? Did VanDam talk as if he considered the case closed?"

"He seems to be keeping his options open. I know he kept the mobile lab people here overnight—or in Holland maybe. I don't think they could get rooms here."

"Duncan found one. Aunt Nettie and I ran into him at the Dock Street and he said he'd checked into a B-and-B."

"Is he still around? He left here so fast I thought he was headed back to Chicago. I'm going home in an hour or so. I'm only staying out here until I can find somebody to take care of the cat for a while tomorrow."

"A cat-sitter?"

"Yeah. A breeder from Grand Rapids is going to board him for a while, but she can't pick him up until eleven. And one of the attorneys from Clem's firm called to say he thinks we can get started on the Michigan end of the estate if we appear at the Warner County Courthouse at nine. So I need a place to leave the cat."

"That's just a couple of hours. I could keep him."

"That would be asking a lot."

"I don't go to work until noon. I could go a little early and meet the breeder at the shop."

Joe made appreciative noises, and we went on down the stairs.

"You said you intend to sell the house," I said. "Will Yonkers mind finding a new home?"

"He's more at home at the Chicago apartment. The housekeeper there is the primary person who takes care of him." Joe gestured at the imposing reception room. "I've always hated this place. The weird part is that in a way Clem built this house for me."

"I'd wondered if she came here because it was your hometown, or if you met her because she came here."

"Oh, she was here first, but she used to rent a beach house—the old Lally place, on Lake Shore."

"That's right near Aunt Nettie's."

Joe nodded. "I was with Legal Aid in Detroit then, and we had a case that was a doozy. We really needed some help with it. Something that would draw some public interest. I came home for the weekend. My mom mentioned that she'd heard Clem was in town. I decided I didn't have anything to lose by approaching her. So I went out to the Lally place, talked my way past a part-time security guy—I'd never have gotten past Marion, if she'd been there. Clem and I clicked. She helped us with the case; the rest is history." He opened the front door for me.

"How did Ms. Ripley come to build the house?"

"She already owned this property. I mentioned that I'd always wanted a place on the lake where I could have a private boathouse. The next thing I knew the architects were hard at work." Joe reached for the handle of the Buick's front door. "The plans were drawn before I knew anything about it. I got to comment on the plans for the boathouse."

I saw a chance to check out the rumor Duncan had passed on. "Do you ever think about going back to practicing law?" I kept my voice real innocent as I slid into the driver's seat.

"No. I've been approached by a couple of guys I was in law school with—but, no. I guess I'm permanently soured on law. Boat owners don't argue like legal clients do." He grinned. "I'll just keep being a disappointment to my mother."

He leaned closer, and a kiss seemed possible. Then I chickened out and looked away, and the moment passed.

He watched as I drove off. Was it my imagination, or did he look lonely? For a moment I wondered if I should have offered to make him a sandwich. But no, that would have been what my Texas grandmother called forward. I decided that after that kiss and now the mix-up over the nightgown, I'd better not even invite Joe Woodyard to church to hear a sermon on chastity. I shouldn't have gone near him. I still wasn't quite sure why I had gone.

I wasn't interested in him, I told myself, ignoring the signals my innards were sending, but he sure could get the wrong idea easily. He might even get the idea I was interested in the money he inherited from his ex-wife. Worse and worse. I took a few deep breaths and thought about a cold shower.

I had to tell Aunt Nettie I'd stopped at the Ripley estate because I had to prepare her for Joe to bring the cat by the next morning. She looked at me narrowly, but she didn't make any comment except "We can't have a cat in the shop."

"He'll be in his carrying case. Maybe I can leave him in the van."

"If he's in a case, he can probably wait in the break room."

A few minutes later a car pulled past the house and into the drive. We both ran to the window and looked out to see a Warner Pier patrol car in the driveway.

"What now?" I asked.

"It's Chief Jones," Aunt Nettie said.

The chief came in the door holding out a cell phone. "It occurred to me that you two ladies were out here with no telephone," he said.

"Don't you need it?" Aunt Nettie said.

"I can let you have it for a few days. It's an extra. Used to be my wife's."

Aunt Nettie laughed. "If you'd brought it before we stopped for pizza, we could have called the dispatcher and asked her to pass the order along. Would you like a leftover slice?"

"No, but I would like a look around the house."

"We checked under all the beds after the state police left," I said.

"I know, I know," Chief Jones said. "But humor me."

I made a pot of coffee, while Aunt Nettie followed the chief around the house. They started by going into the Michigan basement. Then they came back up and went through the kitchen and into the living room. Next I could hear them chatting in the bedroom, then on the stairs and upstairs. I don't know what the chief was looking for, but he didn't yell, "Aha!" at any point during the tour.

When they were back in the living room I offered the coffee. I knew Aunt Nettie would say yes; the chief did, too, so I got out a tray, napkins, and the whole schmeer. The chief took two spoonsful of sugar, and he seemed to relish the real cream, which Aunt Nettie snitches from the shop, taking a half cup at a time out of the half-gallon cartons she buys it in. "Ah," he said. "Great stuff."

"Lee, I think there are a few Jamaican rum truffles ("The ultimate dark chocolate truffle.") in a box in the pantry." Aunt Nettie was going all out.

I put the truffles on a plate and brought them back to the living room. "Did you find anything when you looked around the house?" I asked.

"No. Not even an idea."

"An idea? Is that what you were looking for?"

"I guess so. I hate loose ends, and I just don't understand that burglar."

"Wasn't it Marion McCoy?"

"It probably was, but what was she looking for?"

"If she took it away, we may never know."

"I don't think she found anything. After the first burglary, Saturday afternoon, you and Nettie said you looked all over and couldn't find anything missing."

"Except my grocery money," Aunt Nettie said. "Lee had to put the pizza on her credit card tonight because we haven't had a chance to get to the bank."

"True." The chief sipped his coffee. "But I wondered if that wasn't just a cover-up. Because the burglar—Marion—came back that night."

"Yes," I said. "Apparently she thought we'd hidden valuables in the birdseed."

"In the birdseed?"

"Yes. That's all that was touched really. Just those tin trash cans on the back porch. The ones Aunt Nettie uses to store seed for the bird feeder."

"Tin trash cans." The chief's voice was thoughtful. "Of course, the burglar might not have known that Nettie stores her birdseed in trash cans. She might have thought that they actually contained trash."

"You mean Marion might have been looking for something she thought we might have thrown away?"

"Why else would she have gone for those trash cans?"

"Maybe she wanted to lure some birds in for Champion Yonkers to jump on. Or maybe she wanted to plant something—like that syringe we found in the Dumpster. Sorry, Chief Jones, I just don't understand. What could we have that was so unimportant to Aunt Nettie and me that we'd be likely to throw it out, but was so important to Marion that she'd break into the house once and try to break in again looking for it?"

"I don't know." He turned to Aunt Nettie. "Did she break into your car?"

"I don't think so. Saturday afternoon the car wasn't even here. Last night it was in the garage, and the garage was locked. The garage was still locked this morning, and the Buick looked just the same."

"Oh!" I said. "I wonder if the searchers found my van."

"Your van?"

"Yeah. It's been hidden at the Baileys' house since Saturday night."

The chief choked on his coffee, and after he got his breath back I realized he was laughing. "You hid your van? That's rich."

"Why? I didn't do it on purpose."

"I don't know if you fooled your burglar or not, but you sure did fool Alec VanDam. His lab team didn't search your van."

"I didn't mean to mislead them. I thought I'd be here while they were searching, but then Marion died, and I had to stay out at the Ripley house. After that, I wasn't even sure they were going to finish the search of the house anyway."

The chief put his coffee cup back on the tray and stood up. "Maybe we ought to take a look. The van is the one thing you and your aunt own that hasn't been searched by either that burglar or the state police."

We got flashlights and jackets and hiked the two hundred feet or so along the path that led through the woods to the Baileys' house. I led the way around behind the garage and unlocked the van.

"The van's probably a mess," I said, "though I try not to leave too much junk in it."

"It looks pretty good," the chief said. "You wouldn't believe the way Jerry leaves his patrol car. I get on him all the time."

He looked in the glove box and under the front seats, using his flashlight to augment the interior lights. Then he opened the van's side door and slid it back. "What's this back here?"

"It's clothes for the cleaners. I was going to take them to Al's, but I couldn't find it."

"Al's closed," the chief said. He picked the garments up. "When did you wear these?"

"Oh, the dress I wore to work the last week I was in Dallas. The coat—well, I never got around to getting it cleaned last spring. Now the slacks—those I wore out to Clementine Ripley's house the night I worked for Herrera Catering."

The chief looked through the rest of the van, but he didn't seem to find anything else very interesting.

"I will take those slacks, the ones you wore out to Warner Point," he said.

"They're my best."

"You should have them back pretty quick."

I decided just to leave the van at the Baileys' until morning. The chief saw Aunt Nettie and me into the house, scolding us because we'd left the back door open when we went over to the Baileys'. He urged us to lock all the doors and keep the 911 phone handy that night. Then he left, Aunt Nettie curled up with a PBS special, and I eventually got in the shower.

The shower felt great. I luxuriated in the hot water for a long time and put the whole nightmare of the past three days out of my mind. So I wasn't happy when I turned off the water and heard the chief's rumbling voice. Why had he come back?

I didn't hurry out. I dried off, applied some baby powder, put on my glamorous baggy flannel sleep pants, blew my hair dry—well, half dry. I could still hear the chief's voice, and I was becoming really curious about why he was there.

I slipped into my terry robe—this outfit was certainly different from the filmy black number Yonkers had found in the closet—and went out to the living room.

"I thought you left," I said.

Then I realized that Aunt Nettie and the chief weren't the only people in the living room. Alec VanDam was also there, with his pal Jack Underwood.

"What's going on?"

"Sorry to bother you, Lee," the chief said. "But those slacks . . ."

"What about them?"

"I think Alex wants to ask you about the gloves in the pocket."

"Gloves? What gloves?"

VanDam cleared his throat and reassumed direction of his investigation.

"The food-service gloves," he said. "The lab people were still in town, so they took a preliminary look at them. The gloves may have traces of cyanide on them."

Chapter 17

"Sinus?" I said. Or later I realized that was what I said. After I'd calmed down a little.

But at the moment all I realized was that VanDam was scowling harder than ever. "Cyanide," he said again. "We need to know what you handled with those gloves."

"Food-service gloves?"

"Yes. The gloves in the pocket of those slacks."

"I didn't know there were any gloves in the pocket of those slacks. I wouldn't normally put anything in that pocket. Those pants are too tight to begin with. If I put anything in the pocket, it looks like I've got a big lump on my dairy—on my behind."

"Then you're saying someone else put the gloves in your pocket?"

"Not while I had those pants on. Believe me, I'd have noticed that. But I never use food-service gloves. I don't understand where they could have come from."

"You don't use them at the shop?"

"I don't help make the chocolates at all. If it's real busy I may work in the front, putting chocolates in boxes for customers. And up there we use little tongs."

"The tongs keep the heat of your hands from melting the chocolate," Aunt Nettie said. "But I did give you a couple of pairs of gloves, Lee. You took them out to the Ripley house with you."

"I remember now. In case the trays full of chocolates shifted and had to be rearranged." I turned to VanDam. "They were in a cardboard suspender—I mean, dispenser. I gave them to the security guard when he unloaded the chocolates. But there were bunches of food-service gloves out there. Herrera Catering uses them."

VanDam gave a deep sigh. "I think we've established there were plenty of those plastic gloves available at the Ripley house the night of the murder. What we need to know is how this particular pair wound up in your pocket."

"Let me think." I sat down on the edge of Uncle Phil's old recliner. "When I got out there, Mike Herrera told me to help set up the bar. Then Marion came by looking for the cat. I kept working behind the bar. Anyway, the cat jumped onto Jason, then onto the bar and tried to eat the olives, so I grabbed him and took him back to the office. Oh!"

"You remembered something?"

"When I got to the office, Marion was in there. The cat scratched Marion. Then he ran under the desk and turned the wastebasket over. He knocked trash all around the floor. That's when Marion stepped on something that crunched. Something plastic."

VanDam and Underwood looked at each other. "Maybe the syringe," Underwood said.

"Maybe," I said. "Anyway, I bustled around picking up trash, and then Marion told me rather pointedly that I should go back to my regular duties, and she asked me to take some glasses back to the kitchen as I left. But as I was picking up the glasses, I saw this wad of plastic in one of the chairs. It was a pair of food-service gloves."

"You recognized this wad of plastic as a pair of food-service gloves?"

"Sure did. I guess a couple of the fingers were sticking out or something. I thought one of the Herrera employees had left them there. I grabbed them and stuck them in my pocket so I'd have my hands free to carry the glasses."

This story sent all three detectives into a significant silence. Meaningful looks were shooting around the room and ricocheting off the walls.

"So I guess that's how they got in my pocket," I said. "I meant to take them out and throw them away when I got back to the bar. But when I walked into the main room—well, Clementine Ripley fell off that balcony, and I never gave the gloves another thought."

More meaningful glances bounced, and VanDam finally spoke. "It keeps coming back to Marion McCoy, no matter how you look at it. She must have realized that Ms. McKinney walked off with the gloves."

"So what?" I said. "Like you said, there were bunches of gloves out there. Why not just let me take them?"

"Because Marion McCoy was the personal assistant to a defense attorney," Chief Jones said. "She'd know about scientific evidence."

"You mean the traces of cyanide on the gloves?"

"Yes. Plus, if she used the gloves to handle the cyanide, her fingerprints might be inside. That might have made her desperate enough to break into your house trying to get them back."

"The lab just started working on the gloves," VanDam said. "I might have some more questions for Ms. McKinney in the morning." He got up and led Sergeant Underwood toward the door.

"Wait a minute," I said. "Did Joe tell you about the black nightgown?"

The words "black nightgown" definitely got their attention. I told the story of how I, or rather Champion Yonkers, found the gown in the wrong closet and what Joe and I had deduced from its size and style.

"So you think it belonged to Marion McCoy," VanDam said.

"It wouldn't have been shaped anything like Ms. Ripley," I said, "but it would have fit me. And since Marion and I were much the same height and both on the skinny side . . ."

"So you think this proves she had a boyfriend."

"That, taken with the boob job and the new clothes she got in Dallas—well, it means she either had a boyfriend or was after one," I said. "Or that's the way I'd interpret it."

VanDam glared. "But why would she hide the gown in Ms. Ripley's closet?"

"I have no idea," I said. "I don't understand why Marion did a lot of things. Blaming Marion gets Aunt Nettie and me off the hook. I guess we should count ourselves lucky and shut up. But I think there are still a lot of unanswered questions here. Everyone agrees she was so devoted to Clementine Ripley that it wasn't healthy. So why did she steal from her? Why would she kill her?"

"She stole because she wanted money. She killed to avoid being sent to prison."

"Over the credit card use? I'll bet Clementine Ripley wouldn't have prosecuted."

"Why not?"

"Because it would have made her look stupid. A person like that would lose tens of thousands of dollars rather than look stupid."

VanDam stood up. "Well, that's your opinion."

"Oh, dear," Aunt Nettie said. "It's your opinion, too, isn't it?"

VanDam dropped his eyes. "We won't drop the investigation until we've exhausted all avenues of inquiry," he said. His voice was flat, and his expression sardonic.

Then he did go to the door, followed by Underwood and the chief. I sat on the edge of the recliner and thought. Did VanDam really think there was a chance Marion hadn't killed Clementine Ripley? But if she hadn't, who had? It fit so nicely.

Almost as if it had been designed that way.

Drat! Now I really did doubt it. I got up in disgust and followed Aunt Nettie as she saw the detectives out to the back porch. It had gotten chilly, and I still felt stupid about getting caught in those flannel pants and stupid about feeling stupid.

I arrived just in time to see VanDam's unmarked car pull out of the drive, followed by the one marked WARNER PIER POLICE CHIEF.

"Now, Lee," Aunt Nettie said, "you get in the house. Standing out here in your pajamas, with wet hair—you're going to catch your death."

"It is a bit chilly," I said. "But I mainly feel real unattractive. I guess it's all that talk about the black lace nightgown when I rely on flannel for Michigan summers. I don't know why Marion even brought that nightgown to Warner Pier," I said. "She didn't bring any of these other fancy new clothes she had bought."

"I guess she planned to wear it," Aunt Nettie said.

I stared at her. "Of course!" I said. "Marion brought the gown because she planned to wear it. Because she was going to see the man who gave it to her. Marion's boyfriend was someone she saw in Warner Pier."

The two of us sat down and speculated about that for a while. Who could Marion's boyfriend have been? Who did she know in Warner Pier?

"How about Mike Herrera?" Aunt Nettie said. "He and Marion had to work together a lot, because of all the entertaining Ms. Ripley did."

"Oh! Lindy said . . ." I stopped, then went on. "Don't repeat this. But Lindy said she and Tony thought he was dating someone. Tony thought she might be an Anglo."

"I guess Mike is fairly attractive," Aunt Nettie said. "Marion could have been drawn to him. Of course, the only really attractive man in Warner Pier—older man, I mean—is Hogan Jones."

"The police chief?" I was scandalized. "You think he's good-looking?"

"Not good-looking, Lee. Attractive. Good company, friendly, and masculine, without . . ." Her voice trailed off.

"You mean he's masculine without hitting you over the head with a bag of testosterone," I said.

Aunt Nettie laughed. "That sums it up. And this boyfriend has to be someone who was out at the house Friday afternoon."

"Well, I think we can eliminate Greg Glossop." Aunt Nettie and I chuckled. "Hugh was there—the security guard. So was Duncan Ainsley. But he swears he didn't even like Marion much. Besides, he shows up in *People* magazine with starlets."

"Yes," Aunt Nettie said, "I think he'd go for a more glamorous type than Marion."

"I guess so. Plus, he bad-mouthed Marion. Called her 'Ms. McPicky.' Even if they were trying to hide their relationship, I can't see him actually insulting her behind her back.

"In fact, I wouldn't want to be cross-examined about the boyfriend's existence. A sexy black nightgown isn't really firm evidence. Maybe the police can trace where it was bought and who bought it. If it was a gift, we'll find out then."

Aunt Nettie said she was going to take a shower. We said good night, and I checked the doors and windows, then went upstairs. It had been a long and eventful day.

As I climbed into bed and pulled my blanket up to my chin, I allowed myself to hope that things were going to calm down.

"Poor Marion," I murmured. "I don't want to wish you ill, but I hope you actually were guilty. So the rest of us can get on with life."

Poor Clementine, too. She and Marion had had a strange relationship. Yet they'd both seemed to be intelligent women. How did their lives, and apparently their deaths, become so intermeshed? Some weird emotional quirk in Marion had complemented an equally weird emotional quirk in Clementine.

Which sounded like a description of my marriage.

I rolled over and thumped my pillow. I did have one thing to feel satisfied about. If I'd done anything right that day, it was telling Rich where to get off. I reached for my bedtime book. The next thing I knew it was an hour later. I'd been sleeping with the light on. My book had fallen off my chest and hit the floor. Or I guess that was what woke me up.

The house was quiet. I turned off the light. The next thing I knew it was morning, and Aunt Nettie was calling up the stairs. "Lee! Lee! If Joe's bringing that cat at seven-thirty, you might want to get up!"

I poked my nose out from under the covers. "I'll be right down!"

I went downstairs and brushed my teeth, combed my hair into a ponytail and climbed into a pair of jeans and a sweatshirt. I didn't bother with makeup. I was not trying to impress Joe Woodyard, I told myself. Then I put on a little mascara. Maybe I did want to impress him a little. I tossed my flannel pants and T-shirt onto the stairs, to remind me to take them up sometime, and poured a cup of coffee. By then Aunt Nettie was going out the back door.

"If you get cold at night, there are some blankets in the closet of the other bedroom up there."

"I know. But I've had plenty of covers. Why?"

"Oh, I wondered about the afghan," she said.

"The afghan?" She kept one in the living room, draped over the back of the couch, but I hadn't used it.

"It doesn't matter," Aunt Nettie said. Then she went out the door. "Don't worry about being to the shop on time. Take care of the cat; we'll handle things until you get there."

"Taking on this cat doesn't seem like a good idea this morning," I said. "I'm bleary-eyed, and that cat's likely to be wide awake."

Aunt Nettie left. I barely had time to drink the coffee and eat a piece of toast before Joe and Champ showed up. I walked out to meet them, and Joe rolled down his window and leaned out.

"I feel like a jerk over this," he said.

"Over what?"

"Asking you to cat-sit. Taking advantage of our brief acquaintanceship."

"I'm a big girl. I could say no."

I walked around the truck and opened the passenger door. Yonkers's carrying case was in the seat next to Joe, and the cat was lashing his tail like a tiger.

"I really do appreciate your taking care of him," Joe said. "You can leave him in the cage if you want to."

"Until eleven o'clock? He'd be mad as hops, and I wouldn't blame him. Does he have a leash, some way I can let him outside? I wouldn't want him to disappear into the woods and run off with the deer."

"I brought his litter box," Joe said. "I think he'll be all right if you let him out inside. But I warn you, he loves to explore."

"I already know he can open doors."

"He hasn't learned to turn door handles. Yet."

Joe carried Champ, cage and all, into the kitchen and told me the name of the breeder and that she would be at TenHuis Chocolade at eleven o'clock.

Joe knelt and opened the door to Champ's cage. The cat walked out and looked around the kitchen regally. He gave a disdainful meow.

"Welcome," I said. "Where's your water dish, Champ?"

Joe took the dish from a sack I'd carried in, and I filled it and put it on the floor near the basement door.

"If you need to chase Yonkers down, there's a can of cat treats in the sack. He'll usually come if you rattle the can." He looked at his watch. "I'd better hit the road. I've got to stop and see if the ATM is still speaking to me before I head out."

We managed the whole conversation without looking each other in the eye. Joe got clear to his truck, then turned and came back. "A house this old—I guess you've got a Michigan basement."

"Sure do."

"You might want to keep Yonkers out of there. He'd probably think it was a big sandbox. You might be fighting the odor for quite a while."

I waved good-bye and made sure the basement door was shut. Champ was prowling around the living room, exploring behind the television set and under the coffee table. He seemed content. I gave him a toy from the sack Joe had brought, then went into the bathroom to put on makeup. I left the door open, ready to respond to any unusual noises.

As I curled an eyelash something began to gnaw at my mind. Something Joe had said. Something about the house.

Michigan basement. That was it. "I guess you've got a Michigan basement."

Well, so what? Joe grew up in Warner Pier—home of the Victorian cottage and the 1900-era West Michigan farmhouse. There were also lots of newer houses in Warner Pier, of course. But Joe himself could well have been raised in a house with a Michigan basement. No, it wasn't what Joe had said that was bothering me about the Michigan basement. It was something else. Something to do with pizza.

"Oh, my Lord!" I jumped and nearly yanked my eyelashes out. Then I whispered, "Duncan Ainsley." I stood there staring into the mirror in horror, remembering my chat with Duncan Ainsley after eating pizza the night before.

As I was leaving Dock Street, I'd made a joke about the Michigan basement, and Duncan had said something like, "Is that what those sand-floored basements are called?"

If Duncan Ainsley hadn't known what a sand-floored basement was called in Michigan, how had he known what I was talking about? How had he known that our basement had a sand floor unless he'd been in Aunt Nettie's house?

Duncan Ainsley had been our burglar. I was sure of it.

Or perhaps he'd been one of them. He must have been Marion's boyfriend, the person who bought the black lace nightgown. And he'd helped her kill Clementine Ripley and break into Aunt Nettie's house to find the food-service gloves. He'd even mentioned plastic gloves later.

I ran to the telephone, ready to share my latest deduction with somebody, anybody. Then I realized that the phone wasn't working. The repairman was due that afternoon.

The cell phone. I could use it.

But all of a sudden I didn't want to call. I didn't even want to stay at Aunt Nettie's. It simply seemed too spooky. There were too many trees, too many bushes to hide behind. And Duncan Ainsley had already found it easy to break in. I had no reason to think he would be coming back, but I wanted out of there. I wanted to be around people. I decided to load Yonkers into his carrier and go to town.

"Champ!" I yelled. "Yonkers! Here, kitty, kitty!"

I ran into the living room. No sign of him. I went back into the bedroom and checked under the bed and in the closet. I closed the bedroom door tightly so I'd be sure he wouldn't circle around me and go back in there. Then I started to search the rest of the house. I got down on the floor and looked under things. I looked in closets and behind furniture. And I called, "Here, kitty! Here, Yonkers! Com'on, Champ."

When I got to the kitchen I grabbed the can of cat treats off the cabinet and rattled them. "Here, kitty!" There was still no response. I went into the back hall. "Darn you, Champ," I said, "if you've crawled behind the washing machine . . ."

And I heard a meow.

It wasn't behind the washing machine. It was behind me. I whirled. The basement door was ajar.

"Oh, no! I thought I checked that door! Champ, if you've gone down in that basement—"

I pushed the door open and turned on the light. I tried to make my voice enticing. "Here, kitty! Here, Yonkers. I have a nice treat for you." I rattled the can.

Again I heard that meow. It was back in the corner, behind the brick pillar that held up the fireplace.

If I went back there, that darn cat might dash around the other side of the pillar and beat me to the stairs. That would be okay, I decided. He'd be easier to catch upstairs. I started after him. Champ had evidently been having a big time down in the basement. The sand floor was all churned up.

Then I noticed Aunt Nettie's afghan. It was lying in the middle of the basement, wadded up into a sort of nest.

"Darn you, Yonkers! You dragged that afghan down here. I hope you haven't ruined it." I rattled the treat can. "Nice kitty. Nice Yonkers. Come to Lee, sweetie."

Now I could see him. He was digging at something. "Well, Joe warned me," I said. "We'll have to scoop the poop. But we'll worry about that later. Come on, fellow."

"Meow!" Yonkers batted at something on the floor, behind the brick pillar. But he didn't run away from me.

"What have you got?" I leaned over to look.

And I saw the toe of a tennis shoe.

I hesitated just long enough to take a deep breath before I jumped for the stairs. But that was long enough for Duncan Ainsley to jump after me.

He caught me before I got to the top.

Chapter 18

"Lee? Lee! It's me, Duncan!"
I knew that. Duncan had his left arm around my chest and his right hand over my mouth. And he was trying to tell me who he was?

"I didn't mean to scare you." His voice was right in my ear. "I came to the kitchen door. I called out, but you didn't answer. Then I saw the cat. He pawed the basement door open and went down. I was sure you wouldn't want him there, so I went down after him."

The words were rolling off his tongue glibly, but he hadn't relaxed his grip. "I feel like a fool," he said. "I'm going to let you go now. Okay?"

The guy was unbelievable. He expected me to swallow this story?

But maybe if I hadn't already figured out that he must have been our burglar, maybe I would have bought it. I decided I'd better play along with him. I nodded my head, and he let go of me. Slowly, beginning with the hand over my mouth.

It was time for my dumb blonde from Texas act. "Oh, Duncan! You skeered me! We've had two burglaries, you know. Besides a murder. Ah was just sure the murderer had gotten in here."

He chuckled. "You're safe, honey."

I didn't like the way his eyes narrowed. I moved away, up two steps, dropping my eyes and trying to look demure. Actually I was looking to see if I could kick him where it would really hurt and shove him back down the steps. But he moved with me, staying too close for me to try it.

"Why didn't you jes' call out?" I said. Let him answer that one.

"I'd gone down after the cat on an impulse, and I knew I was going to feel stupid. I thought I'd wait until you went to another part of the house and sneak back up."

He came out into the back hall and flashed that broad, country-boy grin, then dropped his head to give me the look that had charmed millions out of his celebrity clients. "Oh, Lee, I do feel like a fool!"

He was a strong fool. The grip he'd had on me had proved that. And he wasn't letting me get far enough away from him to feel sure that he might not grab me again.

I sidled into the kitchen, and Duncan stayed right on my heels. "I'm sorry I didn't hear you. What can I do for you? I mean, why did you come by?"

He looked really blank for a moment. Then his tongue got right to work. "I had a piece of business I needed to take care of before I could leave this mornin', and I had to wait a few minutes. And I just thought I'd like to see you one more time. So I dropped in." He grinned triumphantly.

I tried to look as if I believed him. "Would you like some coffee?" I said.

"Oh, that sounds wonderful."

I reached for the pot—yes, I was picturing pouring the scalding coffee over him—but he reached around me and grabbed it before I could.

I took a mug from the cupboard over the pot. "We used up all the crook—the cream," I said. "But I can get you some milk."

"No. I take it bank." Duncan's face looked furious for just a moment. Then he forced a parody of his country-boy grin onto his face. "I take it black," he said. He filled the mug, and the two of us stood there, looking at each other. Neither of us was being successful at pretending this was a social occasion.

When Champion Yonkers came up out of the basement and walked past Duncan, tail lashing, it was a welcome distraction. "There you are," I said. I scooped the cat up and held him in front of me, like a shield, or maybe like a weapon. If Duncan came closer, would the cat claw on command? The idea was laughable, but I wasn't laughing.

Just then I heard a strange ringing noise.

"Is that a cell phone?" Duncan said.

"It is!" I'd almost forgotten the cell phone Chief Jones had left for Aunt Nettie and me.

"Shouldn't you answer it?" Duncan said.

"I don't have to."

"I think you should." He wasn't smiling now.

I put the cat down and followed the sound into the bedroom. I found the phone on Aunt Nettie's bedside table. Duncan was right behind me. As I reached for the phone, he grabbed my arm. "Don't tell anyone I'm here," he said. He didn't even try to hide the threat that time.

I picked up the phone and punched the right button. "Hello." Ainsley held his head close to mine. I knew he would be able to hear what was said.

"Lee?"

"Chief Jones?"

"Yeah. Has your aunt left?"

"Yes, she's probably at the shop by now."

"I'll call her there. But I thought you ladies might want to know about those gloves."

"Oh?"

"The lab found one fingerprint inside." He paused for dramatic effect. "It belonged to Duncan Ainsley."

I couldn't say anything. And somehow I couldn't look at Duncan.

"Yep. The state police are on their way out to that B-and-B where he's staying," the chief said. "With any luck he'll still be there."

The chief hung up.

So Duncan Ainsley had used those food-service gloves, the ones with the trace of cyanide on the outside. At this point, that was no surprise.

The surprise was that the chief had hung up so quickly I hadn't been able to give him a hint that the state police were not going to find Duncan Ainsley out at that B-and-B. And I was sure that Duncan had heard every word the chief said.

For a minute I was sure that he was going to kill me. But I decided to give the good ol' Texas girl act one last effort.

"Oh, my!" I said. "I'll call the chief back and tell him there's some mix-up. They're actually suspecting *you* in the death of Clementine Ripley. We all know Marion McCoy did it. She even confessed!"

A smile played over Duncan Ainsley's mouth, and for the first time in my life I was grateful for my dumb blonde reputation and for the twisted tongue that kept that reputation intact. I lowered my head and batted my eyes. Then I held up the phone, ready to punch it.

Ainsley, of course, snatched it away. "No, not now."

"But, Duncan, you've got to talk to the detectives, to get all this straightened out. There's obviously some mistake."

"You're right, Lee. I do have to do that. But I can't do it yet. I have to get hold of a piece of evidence first."

"Evidence?"

Ainsley nodded. I could almost see his brain churning, trying to come up with some explanation simple enough for a dumb blonde to accept.

"The police probably know about one thing," he lied. "Marion and I had a business arrangement. When I reveal the details, it will clear me completely. But Marion had the—the papers. I told her to put them in a safe place, and the id—" His voice broke off, and he gulped twice before he went on. "She put them in a bank box."

"Oh, Duncan!" I almost squealed. "Now she's dead! That means you can't get hold of them. You'll have to tell the authors—the authorities—right away. They'll have to find her key and open the box. Will they have to get a court order?"

Ainsley smiled more confidently. Apparently he did think I believed this wild tale. "Actually, we held the box jointly."

"Oh, good! Then you can get into it yourself."

"Yes, but not until the bank opens."

Suddenly I believed that Duncan was telling me the truth. "You mean it's here in the Warner Pier bank?"

"Right down the street from TenHuis Chocolade."

"Oh, my goodness."

"So I need your help, Lee."

"But what can I do?"

"Let me stay here. Just for an hour. Until the bank opens."

"Of course, Duncan." I maneuvered past him. "Let's go back in the kitchen and sit down. I bet you haven't had any breakfast."

The next hour was the strangest I've ever spent or hope to spend. Duncan followed me into the kitchen. I tried to make him believe that I was cooperating, but maybe I tried too hard. He never eased his vigilance. He never let me get more than an arm's length from him, no matter how stupidly I prattled away.

I was able to get in a few self-protective remarks. "In a practical sense," I said, giving him my dumbest smile, "your timing is good. I have to have that cat downtown at nine a.m."—I moved the time back by a couple of hours—"or the cat breeder will come out here looking for him. And that's when the bank opens." I resisted saying we could kill two birds with one stone. No sense giving him ideas. But maybe I had given him the idea that I'd be missed fairly quickly.

I glanced out at the empty driveway casually. "Where did you park your car?"

"I hid it down the road, Lee. In some bushes. Like I said, I feel like an idiot over all this, but that car's too noticeable. The cops would pick up on it the minute I drove down Dock Street. And I do need to get to that bank box before I deal with them. I'm afraid you'll have to drive. You do have a car here?"

"Oh, yes. Like you, I decided my van was too noticeable. It's hidden at the neighbor's house so the reporters can't find it."

Duncan looked relieved.

A little later I tried one more ploy. "Marion's suicide certainly left you in a mess. What kind of deal were y'all involved in?"

He didn't bother to answer that one. He just shrugged.

By the time we'd sat there, eyeing each other, for forty-five minutes, I was a nervous wreck and about to wet my pants. But I wasn't about to say I needed to use the facilities. I knew Duncan wouldn't let me go into a room with a lock on the door alone.

At quarter to nine, Duncan asked me where my car was and how long it would take to get it.

"Oh, maybe five minutes," I said. "Are you ready to go?"

"Sure 'nuff."

We both stood up, and I called out, "Here, kitty, kitty!" Then I realized that I had no idea where to find the can of cat treats, the key to catching Yonkers. I'd probably dropped them in the basement.

Miraculously, the cat came without them. He seemed to be tired of our house and ready to move on. I enticed him with a piece of deli-sliced turkey and he allowed me to pick him up. When I tried to stuff him in his carrying case, he kicked and yowled, but he went in. Neither Duncan nor I mentioned the litter box or the sack of Yonkers's belongings. I just left them in the corner of the kitchen.

In fact, I don't know why I even insisted on taking the cat. I guess it was because I'd made such a point in telling Duncan I was supposed to deliver him in town, just so he'd think someone would come looking for me if I didn't show up.

There were a lot of bushes between Aunt Nettie's house and the Baileys'. The path on the way over there, I decided, was the best place for an escape attempt.

I latched the cage and picked it up. Then I turned to Duncan. "Here," I said.

Miraculously, he took the cage.

But he didn't let me get very far away from him. He walked beside me, his hand gripping my arm, as we went out the back door and started along the path.

I had my spot in mind. It was a low place in the path, one which was nearly always damp and muddy, with dense brush on either side. When we got to that spot, I'd pretend to fall, shove against Duncan, yank my arm out of his grasp, and leap into the bushes. With the cat cage to throw him off balance— well, it might work.

I led the way, with Duncan's hand on my arm and the cat cage bumping into the back of my thighs, and pretty soon we were close to the low spot. *Relax*, I told myself. *Keep your muscles relaxed. Don't let him know you're planning something.*

The low spot was there. I stepped in it, then threw myself backward at Duncan. I squealed. Then I yanked away and jumped sideways, between two bushes. I heard Duncan swear and Yonkers shriek.

The next thing I knew I was flat on my face in the blackberry stickers.

I thrashed around, trying to get free of the brambles. Suddenly I was yanked to my feet. I was standing up, but Duncan's arm was around my neck, and a silver pistol was pointed at my right eye.

"I didn't want to show you this little gadget while you were being so nice and cooperative," Duncan said, "but you've got to believe that I'm serious as a heart attack."

Chapter 19

Well, I tried. I might have gotten away with it, if the blackberries hadn't tripped me up. I've always hated blackberries. They're so seedy.

Duncan yanked me back onto the path. "Now you get to carry the cat," he said.

I was relieved to see that Yonkers appeared to be unhurt by his rude treatment. He was glaring out the door of his carrying cage, but he wasn't yowling or acting injured. I picked up the cage, and trying to ignore Duncan's fingers digging into my arm, I again led the way toward the Baileys' house.

When we got to the garage, I felt something sharp against my side. "I've still got the gun, honey," Duncan said. "Just don't try anything."

I led the way around the garage, then unlocked the old van and slid the side door open. I put the cage on the floor of the backseat.

"Slide it over to the other side," Duncan said. "Behind the driver's seat." I obeyed.

Then Duncan opened the right-hand front door. "You can get in here." I saw that he didn't want me going around to the other side of the van.

I hesitated, and he poked me with the pistol again. "I'm determined that I'll get to that bank before the police. So I want you to understand that you have to do exactly what I tell you."

My heart seemed to be alternately racing and coming to a complete standstill. I didn't have a single doubt that Duncan Ainsley could shoot me down in a heartbeat if he took a notion.

And I also realized that no matter what I did, Duncan planned to kill me as soon as he got an opportunity. My only chance was to cooperate until we got where there were people. Then I'd just have to take the chance of being shot and make a break for it.

"So," Duncan said, "you get in, and I get in after you. Then I get into the back of the van—thanks to these bucket seats, it'll be real easy—and I'll sit on the floor. And I'll have this pistol pointed at you every minute, Lee. So you do exactly—exactly!—what I tell you to do."

We arranged ourselves, and I started the van, backed out from behind the garage, then turned onto the road. When I got to the Lake Shore Drive, I stopped. "Which way?"

"To the bank, Lee. Just like I said. And drive carefully. No sudden moves."

All the way to Dock Street I could see the pistol out of the corner of my eye. Duncan scrabbled around, doing something, but every time I glanced sideways I saw that pistol.

As I turned onto Dock Street—I guess Duncan knew where we were when he saw the two-story brick buildings go by the windows—he spoke. "You'd better park in the alley," he said. "It might look a little strange for me to climb out of the floor of the backseat in front of the bank."

It was going to look strange wherever he did it, but I wasn't pointing that out. I turned down Peach Street, then swung into the alley and parked behind TenHuis Chocolade. Duncan eased between the seats and sat down in the front passenger seat. His appearance surprised me; now he was wearing a hat and a jacket.

It took a second to realize they were mine. The khaki-colored rain jacket and billed Dallas Cowboys cap had been tossed into the third seat. Duncan had managed to put them on as we drove along. The sleeves of the jacket were a little short, but it wasn't a bad fit. And the hat hid most of his noticeable gray hair.

He showed me the pistol. Then he put it in the pocket of the jacket. "I'll be keeping my hand on this," he said. "Now let's concentrate on getting out of this van safely."

He opened the front door on the passenger side and sort of oozed out, then stood partially hidden by the van's open door. "Now you scoot over and get out on this side."

Maybe this would be my chance. I moved slowly, but I tried to get in position to kick.

I had just eased over into the passenger seat when the back door to TenHuis Chocolade swung open.

"Lee? What are you doing here?"

It was Aunt Nettie.

Instantly Duncan had his hand on my arm and was pointing the gun in his pocket toward her. He didn't need to say a word. The threat hung in the air like a balloon.

Aunt Nettie looked perplexed. "You're not due until eleven, Lee. How come you're here now?"

I tried to think fast. "Something came up. I had to come down early."

"What became of the cat?"

"I have him. I'm afraid I'll have to leave him here for a little while."

"Here?" Aunt Nettie looked horrified. "But I can't have a cat around."

"He's in his carrying case. He can just sit in the break room. I don't think the health department will throw the book at you."

Aunt Nettie looked doubtful. Then she looked at Duncan Ainsley. A hat wasn't going to keep her from recognizing him. Suddenly I remembered that Chief Jones had planned to call and tell her about the fingerprint in the glove. So she must know Duncan was involved in Clementine Ripley's death, even if she hadn't figured out that he had been our burglar.

If she said the wrong thing, Ainsley would kill her. I had to keep that from happening.

"I'm helping Duncan," I said frantically. "He's trying to get hold of the state police to straighten out a misunderstanding. If I can't put Champ in the break room, I'll have to leave him in the van."

"All right. I guess there's no help for it."

I eased over and got out the passenger side of the van, then slid the side door open, crawled in, and pulled out the cat cage. Duncan didn't speak to Aunt Nettie, or offer to lift the cage out of the van, and Aunt Nettie didn't seem to notice his lack of courtesy. We were all acting extremely oddly, but none of us wanted to mention it.

As Aunt Nettie took the cage, she squeezed my hand.

For a moment I thought she was going to yank me inside the back door. And for a moment I desperately wanted her to do that. Then Duncan poked me with the pistol in his jacket pocket, and I pulled my hand away.

"I'll be back as soon as I help Duncan," I said.

Aunt Nettie nodded. She closed the door. Duncan Ainsley and I were alone in the alley.

Of course, it wasn't exactly private, since cars and pedestrians were passing either end of the alley. But it sure felt lonely right then.

"Well done," Duncan said. "Now let's head on down to the bank."

He held my arm as we walked back toward Peach Street. Would I have a chance to get away from him when we turned out onto the street?

I abandoned that idea as soon as we were there. Warner Pier was just waking up. The half block between the alley and the bank was empty except for a teenager sweeping out Mike's Sidewalk Café, on the opposite side of the street. If I ran for it, Duncan could shoot me down at will, and maybe shoot the kid with the broom as well. I led the way to the bank.

The bank had just been open ten minutes, and there was no rush. Only one teller was on duty, and the only customer was just leaving. No one was in the manager's office. Duncan guided me over to the teller.

"I need to get into my safe-deposit box," he said.

"I'll call the branch manager," the teller said. "You can wait by her desk."

The manager—Barbara—came from the back. "Lee? What can I do for you?"

"I'm the one who needs attention," Duncan said. "Lee's just along for the ride." He poked me with the pistol, but I knew Barbara couldn't see what he was doing. "I need to access my safe-deposit box."

"Of course."

I thought of crossing my eyes, throwing up on her desk—anything to keep Duncan out of that safe-deposit box. But it went off routinely. Barbara led us back to the cage that closed off the safe-deposit boxes. Duncan, still keeping his hand clenched on my upper arm, signed in, and Barbara opened the gate. She looked surprised when Duncan shoved me in ahead of him.

"Miss McKinney should wait outside," she said.

"I need her to sign something," Duncan said. "Can't you make an exception?"

Barbara's face clouded, but she didn't argue. "I guess it's okay, since I know who it is," she said. She took a key Duncan produced and her own key, opened the box—it was one of the small ones—then locked us in.

At least Duncan let go of my arm. Since neither of us was going anyplace, he evidently didn't consider it necessary to hold me.

He flipped the box open and took out two manila envelopes. He peeked inside the top one, and I got a glimpse. Cash. For some reason I wasn't surprised.

Then he peeked inside the second. I craned my neck, and I got a glimpse of something navy blue and flat.

A passport.

All of a sudden I wanted to laugh. Duncan was ready to fly the coop. Leave the country. Go to Texas, as the old-timers used to say. And Marion McCoy had stashed his passport and the cash for the trip in a bank box that he couldn't access on the weekend.

Well, it explained why he'd sneaked into Aunt Nettie's house, then spent the night lurking in the Michigan basement, huddled in an afghan he'd snitched from the living room, afraid that the cops would pick him up before he could leave Warner Pier. But it didn't do me any particular good. I was still a prisoner.

Unless . . . I moved toward the gate. Maybe I could yell at Barbara, tell her to leave us in the cage and call the cops.

But Duncan was right behind me, his fingers pressing into my arm again. His voice came out as the sort of whisper you hang the phone up on. "Don't even think about it. I could kill both the bank people, plus you. Then me. I'm not going to jail."

He'd won another hand. I stood there while he called to Barbara, and she came and opened the gate. The box was replaced, and Duncan and I walked slowly toward the outside door of the bank.

And once we were outside, I decided, I was going to make a break for it. If only there were no innocent bystanders on the street. I breathed a silent prayer for Peach Street to be empty.

But there was somebody coming. And darned if it wasn't someone I knew. It was one of Aunt Nettie's teenage employees. Tracy? Or Stacy? I still didn't have them straight. The one with the stringy hair was passing the bank.

She seemed delighted to see me. "Hi, Lee."

"Hi." I pushed on past her. Please let her go into the bank, get off the street. But she lingered. When I looked back, I could see her standing there, staring after Duncan and me as we crossed the street.

What was I going to do?

Just as I reached the point of despair, a miracle happened. A bright blue miracle.

Joe Woodyard's pickup came around the corner of Peach and Dock, and Joe began honking madly.

Duncan clutched my arm even harder, but we both stopped in our tracks. Joe stopped right behind us, opened his door, and got out.

"Duncan! You're the guy I've got to see!"

Duncan moved his hand. I saw that he was going to pull the pistol out of his pocket.

"Look out!" I screamed the words at the same time that I shoved Duncan sideways. He lost his grip on my arm and fell into the little white railing in front of Mike's Sidewalk Café.

Joe was still standing in the door of the pickup, gaping at me. I ran to him and grabbed his hand. I screamed, "Run! He's got a gun!" Then I turned and ran toward TenHuis Chocolade, dragging Joe with me.

Joe yelled, "What's going on?"

I heard a shot, but I kept running. The TenHuis sign was less than half a block away. I dropped Joe's hand, ready to pound on the door to the shop because I knew that it was still closed.

And I heard more feet pounding behind me. I knew it was Duncan. I was shrieking, but I'm not sure words were coming out.

Now I was nearly to the door, and another miracle happened. It swung open.

Aunt Nettie was standing there, her white-blond hair forming a halo. If I ever get to heaven, I'm sure the first angel at the gate is going to look just like she did then.

I ran in the shop, with Joe right behind me, and Aunt Nettie and I slammed the door. But we weren't fast enough. Duncan hit the plate glass and knocked the door open. Aunt Nettie fell back, and he was inside.

"Give me the keys, you little idiot!" He came for me.

I ran past the showcase and through the door into the workroom. I was still screaming, and Duncan was yelling, "The keys! The keys!"

I circled the first stainless worktable, and I saw that Joe was right behind Duncan.

One of the hairnet ladies loomed up right in front of me. I dodged and went back the other way, trying to get to the break room and the back door. I couldn't get past Duncan.

But Duncan couldn't get past Joe. Since he was concentrating on me, he didn't see Joe coming up fast. Joe grabbed Duncan in a hold that reminded me Joe had been a high school wrestler.

They grappled, and I looked for something I could use to hit Duncan. The first thing I saw was a ladle in a big bowl of dark chocolate on the table. I snatched the ladle up and whacked at the struggling pair.

I hit Duncan squarely in the temple. Unfortunately, the chocolate in the ladle hit Joe squarely in the eyes. He automatically threw up a hand, and Duncan wriggled away.

But now he was running away from me. I chased him with the ladle. He turned, and again he yelled, "The keys! Give me the keys!"

I flailed the ladle again. "What keys?"

Duncan ducked. "The van!"

If I'd known where they were, I think I would have given them to him. But someplace between the van and the bank and the chase down Peach Street, I'd lost my purse. So I screamed, "They're in the van!" And I swung the ladle.

Duncan turned and ran to the break room door. He yanked it open. Then the third miracle occurred.

Champion Myanmar Chocolate Yonkers jumped.

He had somehow gotten out of his carrying case, and according to his usual habit, he'd climbed, this time to the top of the oak china cabinet. When Duncan ran in the door, he saw one of his jumping partners, and he pounced.

Duncan screamed. Yonkers jumped from his shoulders to the back of the couch. Duncan ran toward the back door again, and this time I thought he was going to make it.

It was time for the fourth miracle. A river of chocolate.

About five gallons of chocolate—warm, melted, medium brown milk chocolate—flowed past like a flash flood down a Texas creek. It caught Duncan and left him ankle-deep in a lake of chocolate.

He tried to run again. His feet went up, and his body seemed to hang in the air, parallel to the floor. Then he fell flat. His head, his feet, his butt, his shoulders—he landed like a two-by-four dropped out of a truck. Chocolate splashed everywhere.

Duncan's eyes rolled around. He made terrible gasping sounds, but he didn't move. I realized that the breath had been knocked out of him completely.

Joe appeared at my right shoulder, and Aunt Nettie appeared at my left.

She was holding an empty steel mixing bowl that had shortly before been full of chocolate.

The three of us stood there, looking down at Duncan.

And Champion Myanmar Yonkers delicately walked over and licked Duncan Ainsley's face.

CHOCOLATE CHAT
CRIME

- Counterfeiting may have been the first crime connected with chocolate. The ancient Aztecs used the beans as currency, and early on some sneaky traders learned to take the meat—the part that makes chocolate—out of its shell and replace the good stuff with dirt.

- Europeans refined this practice, adulterating chocolate with starches, shells, and occasionally brick dust. Brick dust gave the chocolate a realistic red-brown color, and the chocolate of the day was pretty gritty anyway.

- In Mexico in the late 1600s an even more serious crime was linked to chocolate, which was then used only as a drink. Young ladies fell into the habit of having their maids bring them a cup during worship services. They claimed it prevented fainting and weakness. The bishop did not approve and forbade the practice. The ladies, aghast, began to attend a different church. The bishop refused to relent—and then he died. Rumor blamed a cup of chocolate laced with poison. Scandal followed.

- Chocolate was even linked to corporate espionage in 1980 when an apprentice of a Swiss chocolate firm tried to sell trade secrets to several foreign countries.

Chapter 20

Chief Jones ran in almost immediately, and as soon as he and Jerry Cherry had hauled Duncan Ainsley away, Aunt Nettie began to explain. The chief had called her earlier, as he'd promised, to tell her that Duncan Ainsley's fingerprint had been found in the food-service glove. When she'd seen Duncan and me getting out of the van, she'd been sure that all was not as it should be.

So she called the cops. Then she sent Tracy down to the corner to see where Duncan and I were going. But Duncan had transacted his business and started back to the van—which he probably would have forced me to drive away—before the chief had time to get there.

Joe had happened on the scene almost coincidentally. When he met the lawyer from Clementine Ripley's office, the first thing the lawyer had told him was that he'd heard rumors that Duncan Ainsley's financial empire was about to go under. Joe had rushed back to look for Duncan, but he ran into the police—looking for Ainsley. So he headed for town, apparently to warn Aunt Nettie and me.

We figured that Duncan had sneaked into Aunt Nettie's house while she, Chief Jones, and I had gone to look at the van. He probably intended to search for the gloves some more, but when we came back he heard us talking. There are no secrets in that house—you can hear anything said anywhere—and he realized the authorities had the gloves. He decided to skip going back to his B-and-B and hide out in the basement. If Yonkers hadn't found him, maybe he would have come out and stolen my van. Who knows?

"Anyway," I told Aunt Nettie and Joe, "it explains why he paid a peon like me so much attention."

Joe frowned. "Lee, a guy doesn't need an excuse to pay attention to you."

"Thanks, but let's be realistic. The first time he called me—at the shop the night Clementine died—he managed to quiz me about my hours. He was figuring out when the house would be empty, so he could search for the gloves.

"Of course, he didn't find them, because I'd neglected to check my pants pockets before I headed to the cleaners."

"Marion must have decided to give the search a try that night," Aunt Nettie said, "but we caught her."

I nodded. "Then last night I saw Duncan's car down the street as Aunt Nettie and I left the shop. He just happened to run into us at the Dock Street Pizza Place—well, he must have followed us, trying to figure out if we'd found those gloves. And incidentally, to tell me that Joe left law because he was in danger of being disbarred."

"What!" Joe looked horrified. "Where'd he get that?"

"I think he wanted me to regard you with suspicion, Joe. He wanted to make sure we didn't trade too much information. But the gossip backfired, because it made me so curious I went straight out to the house to ask you about it. Though a lot of other things came up before I could work it into the conversation."

"Well, if there was a disbarment in the wings, I didn't know anything about it," Joe said.

It took the hairnet ladies most of the day to clean up the chocolate that had trapped Duncan Ainsley. But no one seemed to mind. I told Aunt Nettie it taught everyone a new use for chocolate. "Chocolate stun guns. You should put them on the order sheet."

It was a few days before we understood just what had been going on with Duncan, Marion, and Clementine, and those days were crazy. The news media—tabloid, television, and every other kind—came back to Warner Pier. Aunt Nettie and I tried another news conference, but Alec VanDam and the state police got most of the attention.

Lindy even called me with one piece of information that surprised everybody. Her uncle ran into Mike Herrera at the movies in Holland. And he was with—tah dah!—Joe Woodyard's mom. Lindy said Tony was vindicated; his dad was dating an Anglo. But Tony couldn't say much, since he and Joe were old friends.

Chief Jones came by and told us he believed Duncan had convinced Marion that whatever he was putting in the chocolates would merely make Clementine Ripley sick. "You remember how she screamed, 'Clementine can't be *dead!*' " he said. "It would have been hard to fake. I think she'd left the estate because she didn't want to be there when her boss took ill. I think she was genuinely surprised when she died."

Joe and I avoided each other like poison. The reporters were asking enough questions about why we'd both been there when Aunt Nettie felled Duncan Ainsley with a bowl of milk chocolate. I certainly didn't want to add any fuel to their speculations about our big relationship.

I had a lot of questions about that relationship myself.

Such as, did I want it to be a relationship? Did Joe want to see me? Did I want to see him? Had the circumstances in which we met ruined any chance we would have had at getting together? Can a girl from rural Texas find happiness with a boatbuilder from western Michigan?

I saw him at the Superette a couple of times, but we both shied off from speaking. I think we were afraid even to get together and explore the question.

Finally, after a week, I was balancing the cash register and Tracy and Stacy were finishing the cleanup for the night when the phone rang.

"Hi," Joe said.

"Hi."

"Nice moon tonight. You interested in a boat ride?"

"Maybe. When?"

"In about an hour."

"I guess so."

"Do you mind meeting me?"

"Meeting you? Where?"

"At the public access area down from your aunt's house. I'll pull the boat in at the creek."

"Oh."

"There's still a reporter staking out my shop, but he doesn't seem to have a boat. I think I can dodge him."

I laughed. "Okay. I'll meet you at the creek."

I went home and got a sweatshirt, since the Lake Michigan shore isn't too balmy on moonlit nights, even in late July. Then I walked down to the beach. I'd been there only a few minutes when I heard a motor and saw the lights of a boat coming from the north. The boat putt-putted along and landed at the mouth of the creek.

I hopped in without getting my feet wet. Joe was sitting at a steering wheel on the right side of a bench seat, rather like a car's front seat. The seat was upholstered in vinyl. I could see a similar seat behind us, and varnished mahogany decking glowed in the moonlight.

"This is beautiful," I said.

"It's a 1949 Chris-Craft Deluxe Runabout," Joe said. "This may be my last trip in it; I think I've got a buyer."

"I'd love to own it. How much are you asking?"

"He's offered twenty thousand five."

I laughed. "Well, don't wait for me to top that offer."

"I won't. I need the money too bad. The bank gave me an extension, but they're going to get impatient when the word gets out about what a mess Clem's estate is."

"Are you going to get anything out of it?"

"Maybe a few thousand. Which I don't plan to keep. But it'll be months before everything's straightened out."

"Had Duncan taken her for everything she had?"

"Duncan and Marion. The two of them just about cleaned her out. And the money's abroad. We may never track it down."

"It's hard to see how they did that."

"Duncan was running a classic Ponzi scheme," Joe said.

"But he was written up in all the magazines and everything," I said. "Somebody must have looked at his record."

"I think people did, at first," he said. "He probably made legitimate investments in the beginning. But after the market went nuts, he got in a hole, and he couldn't get out. So he began to pay interest to old investors with new investors' money. Apparently most of his high-profile clients were like Clementine—too busy to worry about the details."

"But Marion figured it out," I said.

"She must have. But she was mad at Clem. Apparently I'd put a permanent wedge between Clem and Marion."

"And Duncan, well, seduced her."

"I guess so. Marion had devoted her life to Clem. But Clem had married me, which made Marion feel rejected. At the same time, Duncan was worming his way into her favors. So if she figured out there was something wrong with Clem's investments, at least she was ready to give Duncan the benefit of the doubt. Eventually, she must have thrown in with him."

"But Ponzi schemes eventually collapse."

"Apparently that's what was about to happen. So Duncan and Marion were ready to leave the country. They had fake passports."

"And cash."

"Yeah. Of course, the cash in the safe-deposit box here wasn't enough to keep them going a week. There's got to be more stashed abroad. But the fiasco over ordering the chocolates tipped Clem off to Marion's thefts."

"The Visa card!"

Joe laughed. "Yeah, you did it with the check on her Visa card. I saw Clem when she heard that her Visa was maxed out. She was furious. Marion panicked, and she and Duncan poisoned the chocolates. Chief Jones may be right—Marion may not have realized the stuff they injected was deadly. What the cops haven't figured out is where they got the cyanide."

"I've wondered if Duncan didn't provide it. In fact, I've wondered if he hadn't meant the poison for Marion."

"That would make sense," Joe said. "Marion wasn't really Duncan's type. Which might be why she insisted on holding the passports and getaway cash. She was smart enough not to trust him, even though she bought a slinky black nightgown for him."

"Or he bought it for her."

"The cops traced it. It was one of those Dallas purchases. My theory, by the way, is that Marion left it in Duncan's room, and he sneaked it into the office closet. Marion would have put it in Clem's dressing room."

"Or just left it in her own room. But how could the two of them think they were going to get away with this?"

"I don't think they intended to get away with it. They just wanted to buy time—keep out of jail until Monday morning, when they could get the passports out of the bank box and split."

I stared at the lake. "It's a sad story."

"True, but I hope it's going to get happier."

Joe stretched his arm along the back of the boat's seat, and his hand found the back of my neck. I looked at him. "Joe . . ."

"Yeah?"

I didn't know what to say, so I didn't say anything. So Joe leaned over, and I could see that he was going to kiss me.

And I really wanted him to. He was leaning closer, and the thought of our bodies stretched out together was absolutely wonderful, and . . . I gathered all my strength and remembered what a rat Rich Gottrocks turned out to be. "Joe," I said.

Before I could say anything more, Joe sat back and leaned against his side of the boat. "I didn't really ask you down here to make a pass at you."

"I *think* I'm glad to hear that. Just what did you have in mind?"

"First I wanted to apologize for acting like such a jerk the first couple of times we met."

"You already did that."

"Yeah. But I finally figured out why I did it. See, when Clem and I split up, I was really mad at the world. So I just went out to the boat shop—and sulked. I hadn't looked at another woman. I hadn't wanted to."

He leaned over and took my hand. "Then I saw you standing up to that stupid Hugh, and you were beautiful and spunky, and I knew I liked you right away. But that didn't fit my picture of myself as a woman-hater. So I tried to act as if I didn't like you."

"You were quite convincing."

"Well, it only took me a couple of days to get over it!"

We both laughed. Then Joe went on. "I guess I wanted to say that I'd like to go out with you, but—well, the next couple of months are going to be a mess."

"I can see that you're going to be really busy, both with your own business and with tying up Ms. Ripley's estate."

"It's not just the time factor. It's—well, I thought I'd gotten out from Clem's shadow, and now here I am back under it." He banged his fist against the boat's side. "I like you, Lee. I like you a lot. But if Clem's hanging over us, I might not be very good company."

I considered that for a few moments before I replied. I could see his point.

"I think I understand, Joe. You feel as if you have to get uninvolved with the first woman in your life before you can think about getting involved with a second one."

"Yeah. Only . . ." He banged the side of the boat again. "Only if I sit on my duff, some other guy is going to come along and beat my time!"

I laughed. "Thanks for the compliment! But so far you have nothing to worry about."

Joe looked at me then, and he smiled. "Well, I did bring you something. Something that might convince you I'm serious, even if I'm not able to move too fast."

He turned and reached over behind us and brought out a plastic Superette sack. I caught a whiff of mothballs as he shoved the sack into my lap. Something heavy and bulky was stuffed inside.

"What is it?" I opened the sack, and the mothball smell grew. Inside was a heavy wool jacket. It was dark in color and had light leather trim on the shoulders. I held it up, and I saw the letters WPHS across the back. It was a Warner Pier High School letter jacket.

I laughed for five minutes before I could say a word. "Joe! I'm thrilled!"

Joe was laughing, too. "I went over to my mother's house and dug it out of the attic. You're the first girl ever to get my letter jacket."

We both leaned into the middle of the boat, and our lips met. It was a lingering kiss, full of promise, but a little fearful.

When we finally moved apart, I was the first one to speak. "I think you've got the right idea, Joe. We both need to move into this a little at a time. And for now, I guess I'd better get on home."

"I'll walk you up."

"Sure."

Joe jumped out of the boat, then turned around and held his hand out toward me. He laughed again when he saw that while he was stepping onto the beach I had put the jacket on.

He lifted me out of the boat, and we kissed again, standing there at the edge of the water. Then we turned and walked across the beach, holding hands in the moonlight.

TEST YOUR CANDY KNOWLEDGE

How much do you really know about the sweet facts behind this favorite?

1. How much candy do Americans consume in one year?
   A) 10 pounds
   B) 25 pounds
   C) 50 pounds
   D) 2 pounds

2. What is the biggest holiday for candy sales?
   A) Halloween
   B) Easter
   C) Valentine's Day
   D) Christmas season

3. Chocolate comes from cocoa beans. How do cocoa beans grow?
   A) On bushes
   B) On trees
   C) Underground

4. The people from which country eat the most candy?
   A) United States
   B) India
   C) Denmark
   D) Switzerland

5. What is the favorite flavor of American consumers?
   A) Strawberry
   B) Cherry
   C) Chocolate
   D) Lemon

6. Which food contains the most fat?
   A) 15 jelly beans
   B) 1 plain bagel
   C) 2 cups of cooked pasta
   D) 1 lollipop

7. Where was milk chocolate invented?
   A) United States
   B) Switzerland
   C) Canada

8. Which food is more likely to cause tooth decay?
   A) A chocolate bar
   B) A slice of bread
   C) Pretzels
   D) None of these

Turn the page for the answers. . . .

ANSWERS

1. B) Americans consume a little more than 25 pounds of confectionery per year.

2. A) Halloween is the biggest candy holiday, chalking up almost two billion dollars in sales.

3. B) Cocoa beans come from cacao trees, which grow in tropical regions of the world.

4. C) While Americans love candy, they are no competition for the Danes. The people of Denmark consume approximately 36 pounds per person per year.

5. C) Chocolate, according to an industry survey. Berry flavors came in second.

6. B) The bagel. The pasta comes in second. Neither jelly beans nor lollipops contain fat or cholesterol.

7. B) Switzerland—a man named David Peter devised a way of adding milk to create the world's first milk chocolate back in 1876.

8. D) None is more likely than the other to cause tooth decay. Whether or not you get cavities depends on several things, including how frequently you eat and how long foods and sugary drinks stay in contact with your teeth. It's most important to brush and floss every day.

Quiz brought to you by the National Confectioners Association and the Chocolate Manufacturers Association. For more information visit www.CandyUSA.org.

The
Chocolate
Bear Burglary

Chapter 1

The bear wasn't cuddly or cute. His eyes were squinty and mean, and his face was grimy. A harness—or was it a muzzle?—was around his snout, and he looked as if he resented it. In fact, he looked like he might take a bite out of anybody who tried to take a bite out of him.

"I don't care how much milk chocolate you load into that mold," I said. "That bear's never going to be a teddy."

The other bear molds looked dirty, too. The metal clamps that held the backs and fronts together were all askew, and their silver-colored metal seemed to be tarnished. All of them looked as if they needed to be soaked in soapy water and scrubbed with a brush. I wasn't impressed with the cleanliness of the dozen antique chocolate molds Aunt Nettie was arranging on the shelves of TenHuis Chocolade.

"I'd be glad to wash all these," I said.

"Wash them!" Aunt Nettie teetered on the top step of her kitchen step stool. "You don't wash them!"

"But they're dirty-looking."

"Those are chocolate stains."

"Naturally, since they're chocolate molds. But you don't let the modern-day molds sit around dirty. Wouldn't the antiques look better if they were cleaned up?"

Aunt Nettie clasped the mean-looking bear to the bib of the apron that covered her solid bosom. She looked so horrified that I could tell my suggestion was making her wavy white hair stand on end, right up through the holes in the white food-service hairnet she wore.

But she spoke patiently. "Lee, the plastic molds we use today won't rust. These antique ones are tin-plated, and they can rust. So the normal way to maintain them—back when they were in general use—was to put them away without washing them. The coating of chocolate was like oiling them. It kept them from rusting. When the old-time chocolatiers started on their next batch of chocolates—maybe a year later—then they'd wash them."

"But since we don't plan to use these, but just to display them . . ."

"No, Lee. The chocolate traces show that the molds are authentic." She held out the mold of the mean-looking bear. "This one has been washed, and it wasn't dried properly. It's rusted already. I pointed that out to Gail Hess when she brought the molds by, so she'd know we didn't do it. Washing them would be like putting a coat of acrylic on a genuine Chippendale table."

I didn't argue.

My aunt, Jeanette TenHuis, is the expert on chocolate and is the boss of TenHuis Chocolade. I'd had to be told that lots of chocolate people use the European spelling—"mould" with a "u"—for the forms they use for shaping chocolates, and reserve the American "mold" to refer to that stuff along the hem of the shower curtain. No, I'm just the bookkeeper—business manager, if you want to sound fancy. I pay the bills for the butter, cream, chocolate, and flavorings Aunt Nettie uses to make the most delicious bonbons, truffles, and molded chocolates ever placed into a human mouth, but I don't take any part in how she assembles the ingredients.

"Anyway, I think the molds will get us into the teddy bear spirit," Aunt Nettie said.

"The chamber of commerce committee ought to approve," I said. "They're going to look nice, even if they are a bit dingy."

The little retail area of TenHuis Chocolade was looking quite festive. Warner Pier, already tourism central for western Michigan in the summer, was making a special push to draw winter visitors, and the chamber of commerce had decided on "A Teddy Bear Getaway" as the theme for a late-winter promotion. The amateur theater group was putting on a production of *Teddy and His Bear*, a comic look at the hunting exploits of Teddy Roosevelt. The Warner Pier Sewing Society had costumed the high school choir as toys, and the kids were going to present a concert with "The Teddy Bears' Picnic" as a theme. The twelve blocks of the Warner Pier business district and dozens of the town's authentic Victorian houses were festooned with bear banners, and cuddly bears shinned up the pseudo-gaslights on each corner. The Warner Pier restaurants—the ones that are open off-season— were serving honey cakes and Turkey à la Teddy. There's a bed-and-breakfast on nearly every corner in Warner Pier, and the ones that were taking part in the promotion were so full of teddy bears there was hardly room for the guests. Their special Getaway rates had been advertised as far away as St. Louis and New York. The weather seemed to be cooperating, providing picturesque snow that made us look as if we were decorated with stiffly starched antimacassars, but didn't block the roads. The snowmobile rental places were gearing up, and volunteers were checking the cross-country ski trails. Even the Warner Pier bars were offering specials—bear beer and teddy tonics. The official Warner Pier greeting was a bear hug.

We were cuddly as all get out.

TenHuis Chocolade, one of the specialty shops catering to the town's wealthy visitors and part-time residents, was getting into the spirit by displaying antique chocolate molds, loaned to us by Gail Hess, who ran the antique shop across the street and who was chairman of the promotion.

"I want to have these up by the time Gail comes back," Aunt Nettie said.

I left Aunt Nettie to arrange the molds and got down on my knees to festoon swags of red velvet ribbon along the edge of the glass showcase. Since I'm close to six feet tall, I would have had to bend way over to do it standing up, but kneeling put the counter almost at eye level for me. Of course, it also meant that the glass front of the showcase reflected my face in a frightening close-up. I'm not used to seeing every strand of my Michigan Dutch blond hair—pulled back George Washington style—and every speckle in my Texas hazel eyes jump at me in such detail.

The showcase was already filled with an artfully arranged selection of TenHuis teddy bear specialties. We had a milk chocolate teddy who was much more jovial than that cranky-looking antique one, tiny teddy bears in milk or white chocolate, a twelve-inch-high teddy with a white chocolate grin and dark chocolate eyes. Interspersed among the large molded items were miniature gift boxes of gold and silver, each stuffed with yummy TenHuis truffles and bonbons and molded bears. Tins painted with teddy bears beating toy drums held larger amounts of truffles, bonbons, and bears. Best of all, I thought, were the gift certificates—beautiful parchment scrolls peeking out of backpacks worn by eight-inch chocolate teddy bears or held in the paws of cunning six-inch cubs.

There were no peppermints or hard candies here. TenHuis makes only fine, European-style chocolates—bonbons, truffles, and molded treats.

I had just put the final red velvet swag on the counter when the door opened and Gail blew in.

It wasn't really a pun. Gail Hess walked and talked so fast that a conversation with her was like standing out in a high wind. She was fiftyish, maybe twenty years older than I was, and she wore her frankly fake red hair cut short and tousled—as if it had been styled by a hurricane. She always left me feeling as if I were back in my hometown on the Texas plains, facing into one of our thirty-mile-an-hour breezes.

Gail began talking as rapidly as usual. "IsOliviahereyet?"

My Texas ears didn't understand a word she said. Aunt Nettie seemed to, though she looked surprised. "Olivia VanHorn?" she asked.

"Yes. I invited her to come by."

"I didn't even know she was back in town."

"She's clearing out her mother's house. I was afraid she would be here before me. Nettie, the molds look lovely!"

Aunt Nettie gave an antique teddy a final tweak, then climbed down from her step stool. She seemed puzzled. I wondered what was bothering her. It couldn't be the arrangement of the chocolate molds. Gail had just ad-mired them, anyway. It must be the mention of this Olivia person.

"Who is Olivia VanHorn," I said, "and why does she want to see the dis-play of molds?"

Gail looked at me. "Oh, Lee, I keep forgetting you're almost a stranger in Warner Pier. Being Nettie's niece and all. Though I will say you two don't look as if you're related."

"We're not blood relations," Aunt Nettie said. "Phil was Lee's mother's brother. Lee has the TenHuis head for business. I bless the day she agreed to help me out."

"And I bless the day she agreed to help me get out of Dallas," I said.

We both laughed. The secret, of course, is that Aunt Nettie and I just love each other. And we respect our differences. So we're able to work together all day and share a house at night without getting on each other's nerves too often.

"Phil always handled the business side, so I was lost after he died," Aunt Nettie said. "Lee's got me back on my feet."

I gritted my teeth at that one. Aunt Nettie's business was still teetering, and we had an obnoxious banker leaning over our shoulders to prove it. But I didn't want to tell the other Warner Pier merchants that, so I changed the subject. "Now, back to my question. Who is Olivia VanHorn?"

"Oh! Olivia's a Hart," Gail said.

"I thought you said her name was VanHorn?"

"It is. Her maiden name was Hart."

"The Harts have always summered here," Aunt Nettie said. "Olivia's great-grandfather was one of the original group of Chicago people who built cottages in the 1890s."

Warner Pier society has three castes—I'd found that out a dozen years earlier, when I was sixteen and worked for Aunt Nettie during summer va-cation. First, there are the "locals," divided into subcastes such as natives, newcomers, retirees, commuters, and so forth. Then there are the "tourists," who make brief visits to Warner Pier and who count only as contributors to the community's economic kitty. And then there are the "summer people," who spend the warm-weather months in cottages or houses they own in Warner Pier or along the shore of Lake Michigan. A lot of the summer people are wealthy—some are socially prominent or others even famous—and a lot of the families have been coming to the area for seventy-five or a hundred years. They are taxpayers, but rarely vote in Warner Pier. They get special treatment even though they aren't consid-ered "locals." It's a complicated system, but knowing that the Harts had "always" summered in Warner Pier assigned Olivia Hart VanHorn to her proper station in life.

"I thought she'd never be back," Aunt Nettie said.

"She hasn't been since her husband died—more than fifteen years. And I guess she won't be back again. She and her brother are putting the cottages on the market." Gail leaned close to Aunt Nettie and lowered her voice. "The gossip is that she wants the money for Hart's campaign."

It took me a second to place "Hart." Then I remembered that Hart Van-Horn was a state legislator who was being talked up as a candidate for Congress. This Olivia VanHorn must be his mother.

Aunt Nettie raised her eyebrows. "Then he's definitely running?"

"That's the way Olivia talks."

"Are they going to sell the whole compound as one piece of property?"

"I think they'd like to." Gail used both hands to muss her hair up even more. "Three year-round houses, plus the bungalow. I'm hoping to handle the estate sale."

"Good for you," Aunt Nettie said. "The contents of all the houses?"

"Yes. Of course, it's the usual story. The family's taking the good stuff. But Timothy gave me the chocolate molds on consignment."

I spoke up. "Then the antique molds belong to this Olivia VanHorn and her brother?"

"Yes. Her grandfather started out in the chocolate business—some of the molds were actually used in his original shop in Chicago. Then he invented some special machine used in making chocolate. He sold out to Hershey in 1910."

"I'm surprised that no one in the family wants to keep the molds," I said.

Before Gail could answer, the door opened again, and I knew that the woman who entered had to be Olivia Hart VanHorn. She simply had the look of a woman whose family had a "compound" on the shore of Lake Michigan, whose grandfather had sold out to Hershey in 1910, and whose son was running for Congress. Think American duchess, and you've got it.

She wasn't beautiful. But when I'm sixty, I'll settle for flawless skin, a slender figure, erect carriage, dark brown eyes, and white hair arching back from a patrician forehead. If I can have all that, I won't complain about the big hooked nose and the thin neck. They might prevent conventional beauty, but they definitely added character.

Olivia VanHorn smiled with complete graciousness and an air of command. "I hope I'm not late."

If this gal was ever late, the clock would back up and wait for her. I almost curtsied.

Instead, Gail introduced us, and Mrs. VanHorn and I shook hands. Aunt Nettie greeted her as "Olivia," and she spoke back to "Nettie." They exchanged How-are-yous and You-haven't-changed-a-bits. Olivia VanHorn was friendly, but not effusive.

Gail gestured toward the shelves behind the cash register. "What do you think of the display?" She and Aunt Nettie turned toward the molds.

Olivia VanHorn looked at the molds, too, and slowly, very slowly, the life drained out of her face.

She stood as still as death, not even breathing. Her stillness was frightening. And she was beginning to sway. I realized she was going to faint.

I grabbed a chair, one of two we keep in the shop for people who have to wait for their orders, and I scooted the chair behind Olivia VanHorn. "Here," I said. "Sit."

I don't know if Mrs. VanHorn sat or if her knees simply buckled. But she wound up in the chair.

"Head between the knees," I said.

Instead, she leaned back in the chair. "It's all right," she said. She took a deep, sobbing breath.

All this had happened in about two seconds, and Gail and Aunt Nettie had spent those seconds staring at the chocolate molds. Now they turned around, and both of them gaped at me and Olivia VanHorn.

Mrs. VanHorn was getting her color back. "I'm fine," she said.

Gail Hess began to fuss around. "Goodness, Olivia, what happened?"

"Oh, it's nothing! I have these turns. I'm sorry if I frightened everyone. They go away quickly."

She was looking much better. "My doctor assures me it's nothing serious."

"I hope not! Shall we call a doctor?"

"Oh, no! Hart drove me in. He went down to the bank to speak to George Palmer. George chairs the party for Warner County, you know, so Hart needs to keep in contact with him. But I'm fine now."

She might be fine, but the mention of George Palmer had nearly made *me* faint. George was the local bank manager and Aunt Nettie's loan officer, and I found him annoying. Plus I'd had a real friendship with his predecessor, Barbara, so every time I had to deal with George, I missed her.

Mrs. VanHorn looked at me and smiled graciously. "Your niece reacted quickly, Nettie."

The smile froze me. It was gracious as all get out, true. But the dark eyes stabbed right through me. I had punctured the dignity of a great lady by noticing that she was about to fall down in a dead faint. Embarrassed, I moved back behind the counter.

But Olivia VanHorn wasn't through. "Thank you very much for the first aid, Lee."

I had to respond. "We have lots of practice," I said. "Everybody swans over Aunt Nettie's chocolates."

I'd done it again. Gotten my tongue tangled and used the wrong word. Gail and Olivia VanHorn stared at me and even Aunt Nettie looked puzzled.

"I'll try that one again," I said. "All our customers swoon over Aunt Nettie's chocolates."

Everybody smiled, and I went on. "Sparklin' re-party ain't my fort-tay," I said. "I git my tang tongueled."

Aunt Nettie laughed, so Gail decided I'd done it on purpose that time, and she smiled. Olivia VanHorn gave a perfunctory chuckle. I gestured at the shelves. "If you're feeling better, I hope you are pleased with the display of chocolate molds."

Olivia VanHorn looked at the display and nodded. "They look wonderful, Nettie."

"I'm going to put one or two in the showcase," Aunt Nettie said. "I'd like for people to be able to see the detail, but I know they are quite valuable. I don't want anybody picking one up to look it over."

"It's a beautiful collection, Olivia," Gail said. "I was really surprised when Timothy said you wanted to sell them. I remember the lovely display your mother had in that wonderful oak china cabinet in the bungalow. And they're highly collectible."

I'd been around enough antique dealers to know how to translate "highly collectible." It meant "nice commission for me."

Olivia VanHorn nodded. "Timothy gave them to you?"

"They were with some other things he brought in on consignment. Didn't he tell you?"

"No, my idiot brother didn't tell me. I'm delighted that you're using them for your display, Nettie. But Gail, I really don't want them sold."

"Then we'll take them down immediately," Aunt Nettie said.

"No, no! They're perfect for the Teddy Bear Getaway theme. I'll pick them up after the promotion is over." Now Olivia VanHorn gave a rather stilted laugh. "After Timothy has a piece of my mind."

Gail began to apologize profusely, but Olivia brushed her words aside. "Gail, it's not your fault in any way. In fact, it's not Timothy's fault. I remember he said he was going to take a box of old kitchen things from the basement of the bungalow to an antique dealer, and I assured him it was all right. I didn't realize the molds were in the box."

Olivia VanHorn was looking much better. She stood up, and she and Aunt Nettie began to look at the individual molds. "I always remember this one, the acrobat bear wearing a fez," Mrs. VanHorn said, tapping the shelf in front of that one. "When I was a little girl, I had a book about a circus and a bear who did tricks. I always thought this was a mold of him. Actually, of course, it's a German mold."

"Oh, yes," Gail said. "An Anton Reiche. It dates from around 1929. But it's not the most valuable in the collection. I have a friend in Chicago, Celia Carmichael, who's a real expert on chocolate molds. I believe she evaluated them for your mother, Olivia. Celia is coming up this way in the next few days, and she wants to stop by and see them."

This comment made Olivia blink, and Gail hastily spoke again. "I'll be sure and tell her they're not for sale. But she'll enjoy seeing them."

The three of them continued talking about the molds, each from her own angle. Aunt Nettie looked at their historical connection to the chocolate business, Gail at their value to collectors, and Olivia VanHorn at her childhood memories.

I stood by and listened. We weren't exactly swamped with customers that day—in fact, winters are really slow for nearly all Warner Pier retail businesses. The "hairnet ladies," the women who actually make the chocolates, stay busy with mail orders and commercial accounts, but Aunt Nettie and I don't bother to keep anybody on duty at the counter in the winter. If customers walk in, one of us runs up to wait on them.

I was considering going back to the paperwork piled up on my desk when the phone rang. I answered the extension behind the counter. "TenHuis Chocolade."

"Lee? I'm glad it's you."

It was Joe Woodyard. Calling me at the office. That was strange. Joe and I were circling around a love affair, but for a lot of complicated reasons we—or maybe just Joe—didn't want to become an item for Warner Pier gossip. So Joe phoned me several times a week, but we'd agreed that he would always call me at home.

"Hi," I said.

"Lee, I just caught a kid trying to break into your house."

"What?"

"I'd have called the cops, but—" Joe stopped talking.

"But what? Joe, if someone tried to break in . . . Who is it?"

"He claims he's your son."

Chapter 2

M y son?
    I was so astonished I think I hung up without saying another word. I headed for my office. I stepped into my boots, pulled on my ski jacket, and walked past Aunt Nettie, Gail Hess, and Olivia VanHorn without speaking. I went out the street door, leaving them gaping after me. Or Aunt Nettie and Gail gaped; Olivia merely raised a well-bred eyebrow.

I drove off in my van, which had been Michiganized with the proper license plates and three fifty-pound bags of kitty litter, carried as ballast and for emergency traction.

The day was sunny and the streets fairly clear, either covered with hard-packed snow and ice or melted through to the pavement. Snow several feet deep covered the lawns and fields I passed on the way to Aunt Nettie's house on the outskirts of Warner Pier. I drove cautiously, like a Texan in snowy weather, but I didn't really pay a lot of attention to the road. I was too upset at the thought of my "son." My son the burglar.

I'd figured out who it must be.

I was glad I'd stopped for my boots as soon as I pulled into the driveway, a sand lane about a hundred yards long that connects Aunt Nettie's two-story white farmhouse—built in 1904—with Lake Shore Drive. Every town on Lake Michigan has a Lake Shore Drive, of course. Aunt Nettie and I lived on the inland side, but this time of the year we could glimpse the lake through the bare limbs of the hundreds of trees between us and the water.

I saw that the drive was blocked by Joe's truck—a blue pickup with "Vintage Boats – Stored and Restored" on the side—and by a sporty gold SUV. Even from the road I could see that it was a Lexus RX300. That figured, if I was right about who the burglar was. The Lexus was half off the road and obviously stuck. That figured, too. The kid who drove it probably thought an SUV could go anywhere; it couldn't.

Aunt Nettie hires a man who plows the drive when it needs it. (He also scrapes the snow off the porch roof, because that roof slopes so gently it can collect enough of Warner Pier's "lake effect" snow that it might collapse. I'm not in Texas anymore.) So the drive was fairly clear, but since the snow melts and refreezes on a regular basis, its surface was icy and rough. If the Lexus had stayed on the road, though, it shouldn't have gotten stuck. I parked my van behind Joe's truck, got out and began slipping and slogging toward the house. As I passed the Lexus, I noted its Texas tag. Again, just what I expected.

Joe—six feet plus, with dark hair, blue eyes, lots of brains, and skillful hands—was standing on the front porch of Aunt Nettie's house. Sitting on the porch steps, with his head down nearly to his knees, was a skinny kid in a down jacket, jeans, and tennis shoes. He wore thick glasses, and he had a gold ring in his left eyebrow. His ears were pierced, too—no, they were more than pierced. They had big eyelets in the lobes, as if he expected to tie shoelaces through them.

The kid didn't seem to have gloves or a hat. Joe wasn't wearing gloves or a hat either, but somehow he looked macho, as if the winter didn't faze him. The kid just looked cold.

Joe and I exchanged nods, but I didn't stop to talk. I went right around him, to the kid. I could have whacked him, but I tried to stay calm.

"Hi, Jeff," I said.

The kid lifted his head to glare at me, and I saw that he also had a stud in his lower lip. Then he ducked his head and studied the walk some more. He didn't speak.

"He claims he's your son," Joe said.

"He used to be," I said. "He's Jeff Godfrey. For five years he was my stepson."

Joe looked relieved, then tried to hide it. I fought an impulse to laugh. I guess finding out I had a teenaged son would have come as a shock to him.

"Y'all might as well come on in," I said.

I knocked the snow off my boots, unlocked the front door, and went inside. Joe held the storm door open, but he had to gesture before Jeff got up and preceded him into the living room.

There was a mat by the door, and Jeff and Joe had already knocked most of the snow off their feet out on the porch. I kicked my boots off and walked around in my heavy socks. Then I looked Jeff over. I hadn't seen him in two years—it had been at Christmas two years and two months earlier. His dad, Rich Godfrey, had insisted that Jeff join us on Christmas Eve, and Jeff had sulked and sneered the whole evening. Rich had finally blown up at him. It hadn't been a happy holiday.

Jeff had grown taller, of course. He was still scrawny, but he had reached his dad's height, maybe an inch shorter than I am, and he had Rich's light brown hair. But his face was thin like his mom's, and the gray eyes behind his glasses weren't like either of them. He wasn't as spotty as he had been two Christmases earlier. Between the glasses and the jewelry installed on his head, he seemed to glitter.

"Well, Jeff, have you had lunch?" I said.

Jeff finally spoke. "No, but I'm not hungry." I was having a hard time not staring at the huge holes in his earlobes, and the stud in his lip seemed to bounce around.

"I'll fix you a sandwich anyway. Joe? Ham sandwich?"

"Thanks."

Joe took his jacket off and hung it on the hall tree by the front door. He seemed watchful, and I realized he was keeping an eye on Jeff. Did he think the kid was going to go berserk?

Would Jeff be likely to go berserk? I hadn't the slightest idea. He'd been eleven when I married his dad and sixteen when I divorced him. I'd tried to be a nice stepmom, but Jeff had always avoided me like poison.

I didn't know him at all.

I turned up the furnace heat, then showed Jeff where the bathroom was; in Aunt Nettie's old house you get there by way of the kitchen and the back hall, so it's kind of tricky. Then I started making five ham sandwiches, three on white and two on rye.

Joe came into the kitchen while I assembled bread, cheese, and ham. "How did you happen to catch Jeff?" I said.

"I was headed down to Benton Harbor to look at a boat. I thought I'd take the lake road and check on how the ice is treating the beach. I saw the Lexus stuck in your drive, so I stopped. The kid was up on the porch roof, trying to get in that window."

"The one over the stairwell?" I was horrified.

"Right. He's lucky he didn't succeed and break his neck." Joe lowered his voice. "How well do you know this kid?"

I kept my voice low, too. "Not well, I'm afraid."

"I could still call the cops."

"Let me talk to him first."

But that didn't prove easy. Even after Jeff sat down at the dining room table and decided he would eat a ham sandwich and have some milk, he was determined not to give out any information.

"How'd you wind up in Michigan?" I asked.

"Got in the car and drove."

"Why?"

Jeff took a big bite, chewed and swallowed before he answered. "I wanted to see a new place."

"You turned eighteen in July." Jeff looked up sharply at that, maybe surprised that I remembered his birthday. "Did you start college this year?"

"Yeah. SMU."

Southern Methodist. In Dallas, his hometown, but a good college, not easy to get into. Jeff had been doing something right.

"Are you still working for your mom?" Jeff's mom, Dina, has an antique shop.

"I was. Saturdays. I made some deliveries, polished stuff."

"Does your mom know where you are?"

That got a quick and angry reply. "No, and I don't know where she is!" Bite, chew, swallow. Then, "I don't live at home anymore."

"You living in the dorm?"

"I was."

"Did your dad send you up here?"

That brought a gape that made the lip stud bob around. "No! He wouldn't send me anyplace!"

Jeff's reaction was genuine enough to settle that particular suspicion. Rich hadn't sent his son as a go-between of some sort. Good. Maybe Rich had quit trying to salvage his hurt pride.

"Then why did you come?"

"Not because I wanted to see *you*."

"Jeff, please don't ask me to believe that you wandered a thousand miles from home and college and just happened to get stuck in the driveway of your former stepmother."

Bite, chew, swallow. Glare. No answer.

I was getting impatient. "Come on, Jeff! Joe still thinks we should call the cops. Explain yourself."

Now Jeff pouted.

"If you did come all this way to see me, Jeff, for heaven's sake why didn't you come by the store? Why didn't you phone? Why did you try to break into the house?"

He scowled and rubbed at one of his earlobes. I fantasized about sticking my little finger through the huge hole in it.

"I thought maybe you'd loan me some money," Jeff said. "Then when I found your house, I got stuck. I was trying to get in to use the phone."

He raised his head and shot Joe an angry glance. "This guy . . ." He stopped talking, ducked his head and stared at his sandwich. "At least he had a cell phone."

Joe raised his eyebrows. "When I drove up he was halfway in that upstairs window," he said. "I could take a look at it. Has Nettie got a ladder?"

"In the garage. The key's hanging in the broom closet off the back hall." Joe stood up. "I won't be far," he said.

Jeff sullenly ate two more bites of his sandwich, but after we heard Joe go out the back door and saw him pass the dining room windows, he glared at me. "Does that guy live here?"

I swallowed a sharp answer, then tried to speak calmly. "Obviously not,

Jeff. If he lived here he'd have a key. Joe's just a friend. He's not even a frequent visitor."

"I saw him in the papers. He's the guy you were mixed up with over that
murder."

"His ex-wife was murdered, true. Neither of us had anything to do
with it."

"Dad said—"

"Quit trying to change the subject, Jeff. What are you doing here?"

"I'm broke. Like I said, I thought maybe you'd lend me some money."

"I haven't got any money to lend. Why don't you call your mom."

"I told you. I don't even know where she is."

"Then call your dad."

"He won't talk to me."

"What happened?"

Jeff squirmed and made a low, growling sound. Then he whacked his fist
on the table and yelled, "They both threw me out!"

I could see Joe whirl around and start running back toward the house.
But Jeff was back into his sullen mode, staring angrily at his plate. I got up
and went to the back door to assure Joe the situation wasn't out of control.

As I walked back to the table, I thought about what Jeff had said. I wasn't
sure I believed it.

If Jeff had had a specialty, it had been playing his parents against each
other. When I pointed this out to Rich, he got mad at me instead of at Jeff. It
was hard to believe that Rich and Dina would ever have stopped fighting
over Jeff long enough to throw him out; Jeff would have figured some way
to divide them and ruin the plan.

Jeff might well have deserved to be thrown out. He'd always been bratty,
and his ear, eyebrow, and lip jewelry would have given his dad a stroke. But
I found it hard to believe that his parents had actually tossed him. Jeff's
mother had always doted on him, and so had Rich, in his own selfish way.
Rich saw the other people in his life merely as reflections of his own success.
Dina got a big settlement when they divorced, so he could brag to his friends
about how she took him to the cleaners. For Jeff, Rich had always provided
the best private schools—best, as in most expensive—and the best bicycle
and the best summer camp and the fanciest tennis shoes. I had benefited
from Rich's largesse, too; I'd always had jewelry, a snazzy car, a fancy house.

The only thing Rich hadn't given any of us was respect and love, but he
didn't have much of that to spare.

When I walked out and left the jewelry, the car, the house, and the
clothes behind, I was trying to convince Rich I loved him, not his money.
His reaction had shown me the truth—Rich saw his money as an extension
of himself. When I rejected the one, I had rejected the other. He hadn't for-
given me.

But if Rich loved anybody, it was Jeff. It would take a lot to make him throw the kid out. I needed more details.

"What do you mean, they threw you out? How could they throw you out if you were living in the dorm?"

"Just what I said. They finally agreed on something. They didn't like my grades. They didn't like my credit card bills. They ganged up on me and said I had to get a job flipping hamburgers and make it on my own. Earn my own spending money. Buy my own gasoline. Pay my own car insurance."

Yeah, I thought, "make it on your own" from a dorm with room and board paid. I guess I was jealous. My parents hadn't been able to help me with college.

Joe came in with the ladder and went to work on the window over the stairwell. He began by putting a footstool even with the bottom step, to make a level space large enough for both legs of the ladder. Joe then climbed up the teetery ladder to close the window Jeff had opened from outside. I held the ladder and prayed, as Aunt Nettie had a month earlier when I did the same stunt so I could change the lightbulb over the stairs.

I could see how Jeff had been entrapped. He had tried to get in a window in a row that was easy to reach from the porch roof. The one Jeff had tackled had a storm window that was warped in some way and hung a little crooked. Which, I'm sure, was why Jeff had climbed from the porch railing to the roof and up to that particular window.

Since he'd never been inside the house, Jeff had no way of knowing that the handy-dandy window was over the stairwell. He'd been darn lucky that he hadn't fallen in headfirst, tumbled fifteen feet down to the wooden stairs, and broken his neck.

I shuddered at the thought of having to tell Rich and Dina that I'd come home from work and found their son dead in my house. Jeff wasn't the only one who had had a narrow escape.

Jeff finished his sandwich and milk, then voluntarily got up to go outside and help Joe with the storm window. This time he held the ladder while Joe climbed onto the porch roof. Joe whacked the wooden frame of the storm window with a hammer and got it to fit a little better. I found a pair of Uncle Phil's old boots and lent them to Jeff. He and Joe collected a couple of shovels from the garage and went down to dig out Jeff's SUV.

As soon as they left the house I called Jeff's dad, the guy I've nicknamed Rich Gottrocks. He's a big-time real estate developer in Dallas. Or maybe he just thinks he's big-time. He had acquired a receptionist with a British accent.

Miss Brit told me Rich was unavailable. And his executive assistant was unavailable, too, she said. No, she had no idea when either of them would be back. She'd be only too happy to take a message.

I left one. "Jeff is here in Warner Poor. I mean, Warner Pier. In Michigan!

Please call." I gave my name, but didn't identify myself as an ex-wife. Then I called Jeff's mom at her antique shop. I got her answering machine. Her message said the antique shop would be closed for a week, but it didn't give me a hint about where she was or why she'd closed. I left a message there, too. Next I called information and asked for a home number for each of them. Both were unlisted. Rats!

Two long-distance calls wasted. I was still standing beside the telephone trying to figure out what to do when the thing rang.

Could it be Rich? Or Dina? I snatched the phone up, hoping I could shift the responsibility for Jeff onto one of his parents.

But the phone call was from Aunt Nettie. "Are you all right?" she asked. "You ran out like something was after you."

"Just a dirty secret from my past," I said. "You may have forgotten I used to be a wicked stepmother."

"Oh, my! Rich's son called?"

I could always count on Aunt Nettie. She knew all my secrets and loved me anyway. I poured out the whole story—Jeff's unexpected arrival, his attempt to break in, the lip stud, the eyebrow ring, the earlobe eyelets, the sullen attitude, and all the danger flags he was running up in my mind.

"So I don't know what to do about him," I said. "If he's broke, I don't really want to turn him away. I tried to call both his parents, but neither of them is available. He's apparently walked out on college. But I certainly can't see giving him money, even if I had any to give."

Aunt Nettie didn't hesitate. "What he needs is a job," she said. "He can stay there at the house, and we'll put him to work packing chocolates for TenHuis Chocolade."

Chapter 3

TenHuis Chocolade couldn't afford another employee. Aunt Nettie knew this as well as I did. She and I had even cut our own salaries to help make ends meet. This was one reason I wasn't enrolled in the review course for the CPA exam.

But we could use some packing help. And I didn't see any other way to keep Jeff corralled, to try to have a little control over him. So I offered him a job.

Jeff was not enthusiastic about becoming a chocolate packer. But I made it clear that neither Aunt Nettie nor I—and certainly not Joe—was likely to come up with a loan, so he grudgingly said he'd try it. Somehow I didn't expect him to be a long-term employee.

Jeff was also unenthusiastic about staying at the Lake Shore Drive house, but he accepted Aunt Nettie's invitation. When I quizzed him, he said he was down to less than five bucks. So he didn't have much choice.

Joe left, headed for Benton Harbor, and Jeff and I unloaded the Lexus and put his things in the bedroom across the upstairs hall from mine. He had apparently left his dorm room in a hurry, because he had nothing but a change of clothes and a laptop computer. Then I drove the two of us into town; Aunt Nettie's house is inside the city limits, but in an area that's not fully developed, so we always talk about "going to town" when we mean to the Warner Pier business district. There are plenty of parking spaces in the winter. I parked on Peach Street.

"How come all the streets in this town are named for fruits?" Jeff said.

"Because it's a big fruit-growing region," I said. "But there are a couple of non-fruity streets. Dock Street. West Street. Lake Shore Drive."

"Yeah. And Orchard and Arbor."

I made a mental note of that comment. Evidently Jeff had driven around Warner Pier before he went out to the house. At least he'd read the names of the streets in the downtown business district and identified Warner Pier's main drags. In fact, he had seemed to know which street led to TenHuis Chocolade. But if he'd driven by there earlier, why hadn't he come in? His story was full of holes.

Jeff's entrance into TenHuis Chocolade was interesting. He walked straight across the shop, went behind the counter, and looked at the dirty bear mold that had distressed me earlier.

"Your aunt collects antique chocolate molds," he said. "That's a dandy."

"It's borrowed," I said.

Jeff had moved on to the mold of the acrobat teddy bear wearing a fez. "That's a really old one."

"I was told it's a Reiche, if that means anything to you."

"I don't know a lot about them, but Reiche was one of the big guys."

"Does your mother's shop handle chocolate molds?"

"Not many. But she's got a customer—a guy who runs a Dallas chocolate company—and she keeps her eye out for anything he might like."

Aunt Nettie came in, and I introduced Jeff. She greeted him with her usual beaming smile. "Jeff, we're glad to get a little help down here. Have you ever done packing or shipping?"

"Furniture. I've packed furniture. Sometimes dishes. But not chocolates, Miz TinHouse."

Jeff's Texas pronunciation of the family name made Aunt Nettie smile, though a kid born and raised in Dallas sounds much less like a hick than a person like me. I lived in a small town out on the prairie until I was sixteen, and even two years with a speech coach hasn't removed all the twang from my voice.

"It rhymes with 'ice,' Jeff," I said. "Ten-hice."

Aunt Nettie still looked amused. "Lee said it just the same way, the first summer she worked here. But don't worry about it. You can call me Nettie, or Aunt Nettie. And the first thing you need is a sample chocolate. Every TenHuis employee gets two each day."

Jeff didn't look sullen about that. He picked an Italian cherry bonbon ("Amareena cherry in syrup and white chocolate cream"), and while he didn't gush about how good it was, he looked pleased enough to suit Aunt Nettie.

"Now, come on back and I'll show you where to put your coat," she said. "We need you, because this is still our busy season. Do you know how to use a tape gun?"

Aunt Nettie took him away, and I got back to work. She wasn't kidding about this being our busy season. The summer tourist rush is busy enough. It keeps the front shop going hard, as our summer student helpers sell bonbons, truffles, and molded chocolate to the thousands of tourists and summer residents who pour into Warner Pier every year. That rush ends at Labor Day, or whenever the Chicago schools go into session.

Then things really pick up. Halloween, Christmas, Valentine's Day, Easter, and Mother's Day are big holidays for our mail-order side, with Thanksgiving, Hanukkah, New Year's, and Father's Day also bringing in business. In addition to the sixteen types of truffles and bonbons we always keep in stock, TenHuis makes fancy molded pieces and specially packaged boxes of chocolates—like the teddy bears on display in the showcase. We ship them all over the United States. Aunt Nettie has twenty women making chocolate all winter.

Our winter hours are different, however. In the summer Aunt Nettie comes in about seven thirty and leaves at midafternoon, and I come at one and stay until the shop is closed and cleaned up, around nine thirty. Between Labor Day and Memorial Day we all work nine to five, unless we're behind on orders and need to put in overtime.

And in our current financial position, I was trying to keep Aunt Nettie from supporting overtime.

I went into my office, which has big windows overlooking both the workroom and the retail shop, and called our supplier in Grand Rapids for an extra order of heavy cream. Then I checked the figures I needed when I faced our loan officer that week. I was fighting the despair that exercise always caused when the bell on the front door chimed and a customer came into the retail shop.

I jumped up and went out to the counter. "Can I help you?"

The customer looked familiar, but I didn't think I knew him. He was a distinguished-looking older gent with a beautiful head of white hair, a perky gray mustache, and a red face. Who did he remind me of?

"I've come in to apologize," he said. "I've been told that I've pulled a major boner." He leaned forward in a sort of bow, and he gave a smile that must have wowed the sorority girls forty years earlier. "I've come to sheek your forgiveness."

The "sheek" gave me a clue about his condition. Then his head bounced around like a toy clown's. Whoever he was, he'd drunk his lunch.

"I'm sure, whatever it is, it will be all right," I said. "Your apology is accepted."

"M'sister scolded me severely," he said. "According to her, I'm selling the family treasures for filthy lucre, and I embarrashed her in front of your aunt and the antique woman."

I was beginning to figure out who this must be. "Are you Mrs. Van-Horn's brother?"

"Timothy Hart, m'dear. An embarrassing limb of the Hart family tree."

"I'm Lee McKinney, Nettie TenHuis's niece." We shook hands.

He looked at the display of chocolate molds behind me. "Mama's collection looks very nice."

"My aunt arranged it. It's a lovely collection. I understand why Mrs. VanHorn wants to keep it in the family."

"I don't understand it! Olivia's spent years trying to live down that particular side of the family. They're my favorite anchestors, but she finds them a bit too earthy. She always wants to remember that Great-grampa Amos invented the Hart centrif—centrifi—centrifugal molding machine and forget that he worked as a candy butcher. He walked up and down the cars of the Illinois Central, selling candy, apples, and bananas from a basket."

I warmed to Timothy. "But that's inspiring! A real American success story. I can see y'all have a wonderful family connection with the chocolate business."

"But if Olivia values the collection so highly, why did she toss it in a box in the basement?"

"Sometimes things get put away in the wrong place."

"True. I mustn't be too hard on her. She hasn't been around for the past fifteen years. Couldn't face the Warner Pier house after Vic died there."

"Vic? Was that Mr. VanHorn?"

"Congressman VanHorn. She's spent fifteen years grooming her son to take his place. Though that ambition may elude her."

"A political career could be very rewarding, but it's always uncertain."

"That's so." Timothy Hart shook his finger at me. "That sweet Southern accent has me pouring my heart out, Miss McKinney. I'd better leave."

"Not without a sample of TenHuis chocolate."

Mr. Hart selected a Jamaican rum truffle ("The ultimate dark chocolate truffle"). "A small additional taste of the good stuff won't hurt," he said. "I'm not driving. Lost m'license years ago." Then he shook his finger at me again. "Now, don't tell m'sister I came in here. She told me an apology would make things worse."

"You haven't made things worse at all, and I've enjoyed meeting you, Mr. Hart." I waved as he went out the door. Yes, Timothy Hart was quite pleasant—for a drunk. But if he pulled this stunt very often, I could see that his relatives would get tired of it.

I sighed, looked at the clock and went back to the office. Closing time was almost here, and I hadn't gotten started on the accounts payable or reached Jeff's parents. I called Rich's office and Dina's shop again. Both still unavailable. I left new messages. I wanted them to know about Jeff as quickly as possible.

I heard the UPS man come in the back, and Jeff appeared. I saw that Aunt Nettie had found him a baseball-style cap; at least he wouldn't have to wear a hairnet.

"They sent me for the UPS paperwork," he said.

I handed him the forms. "How's it going?"

"There's a lot more to it than I thought there would be." He took the papers and rushed back.

I smiled as I went back to my computer. Maybe a few days as a peon would do Jeff some good. Every overprivileged kid needs a lesson or two before he develops respect for the skills ordinary working people have—

such as packing fragile chocolate rabbits so carefully that they can be shipped clear across the country without arriving in pieces and ruining Easter bunny sales for Neiman Marcus.

I had the bank figures done by quitting time. It was going to be close, but we weren't going to have to increase our loan. Not that my report would suit our new loan officer. He wanted us to have to refinance; then he could increase our interest.

I could hear Aunt Nettie's hairnet ladies calling out as they left through the back door. Soon Jeff came up, saying Aunt Nettie had asked him to drive home with me. She would stop at the store and get something for dinner. I told Jeff to pick out his second chocolate for the day, and he picked a Bailey's Irish Cream ("Classic cream liqueur interior"), but he said he'd take it along to eat afterward, so I gave him a small box to put it in. I sorted my paperwork into piles, and Jeff and I drove back to the house on Lake Shore Drive. It was dark when we got there, but we could still see that the yard was covered by snowmobile tracks. The crazy people who drive those things are always riding around on the lawn and cutting through all the little paths that link us with our neighbors. It annoys Aunt Nettie.

Aunt Nettie came in a half hour later with chicken breasts and tomato sauce. Jeff was subdued—or maybe just sullen—during dinner, but he asked Aunt Nettie lots of questions about making and shipping chocolates. I was glad that he gave some impression of being interested in his job. I still couldn't take my eyes off the quarter-inch holes in his earlobes. They were more eye-catching than the lip stud.

I expected Jeff would want to check his e-mail after dinner, and I steeled myself for an argument when he was told he'd have to pay for any long-distance calls, including those made to his e-mail server. But Jeff didn't suggest that. He put stuff away in his room, then I showed him how to operate the washing machine, and he washed some underwear and a sweatshirt. As I said, he hadn't brought much, though he did have a few warm clothes, including the ski jacket he'd had on that afternoon.

While his clothes were in the dryer, I sat him down at the dining room table and tried again to quiz him about why he'd left college. He muttered something about his grades.

"I can't believe you can't do college work, Jeff," I said. "You were always a good student."

"There's a lot more to life than college."

"True. Like packing chocolate."

He scowled. "Look, my dad wants me to learn to handle money, stuff like that, but he wants to make all the decisions—my major, where I live, the kind of car I drive, how I dress. I just need to try it on my own."

I might have believed him if he hadn't cut his eyes at me. I knew he was checking out how I was taking his story. Jeff had cut his eyes the same way when he was thirteen and was trying to convince me his mother rented X-rated movies for him to watch.

At ten thirty the dryer buzzed, and Jeff folded his underwear, then said he'd take a shower. He was still pouty, but he didn't make any comments about our strange bathroom.

Aunt Nettie's house was built by my great-grandfather and originally was the TenHuis family's summer cottage. My grandparents decided to live there full-time, so they winterized the house in the late 1940s, but the bathroom hasn't changed much since the family got indoor plumbing in 1915. For one thing, there's only one bathroom in the three-bedroom house. For another, we still have an old-fashioned claw-foot bathtub. Uncle Phil had changed the plumbing to allow for a shower. He hung a circular rod over the tub, and Aunt Nettie put up a shower curtain on each side. That was the shower. It wasn't exactly like the facility I knew Jeff had in his mother's house—his own bathroom with a tiled, walk-in shower. So I was surprised that Jeff didn't complain. He'd grown up in a house full of antiques; he wasn't likely to think the claw-foot tub was quaint.

As soon as I heard the shower, I knew the noise would keep Jeff from hearing anything else. I looked at the phone and again wished I could talk to Rich or Dina, but I still had no home numbers for either of them. So I called Joe Woodyard.

Several nights a week Joe called me. But Aunt Nettie's house not only has only one bathroom, it also has only one phone. And that phone is in the kitchen. So when I talk to Joe I sit on a stool by the kitchen sink. Aunt Nettie tactfully stays in the other room. I didn't want to carry on a conversation with Joe while Jeff was digging in the refrigerator for a bedtime snack or otherwise standing around with his ears hanging out. I told Joe as much.

"So you and Nettie took the kid in," he said.

"Aunt Nettie's too kindhearted not to. But there wasn't really anything else to do."

"You could send him to a motel."

"I suppose my credit card would stand it, but Jeff claims he left college because he wants to be on his own. Lending him money doesn't seem like a good thing to do, and neither does paying his rent. And I could hardly send him to the homeless shelter."

"You could send him to jail."

"No, I couldn't, Joe. That's not a realistic opinion. I mean option."

"Maybe not. But—listen, how about if he comes over here?"

"No! You don't have any room for him." Joe was living in one room at the boatyard. He had a rollaway bed, a hot plate, and a microwave.

"I've got an air mattress and a sleeping bag. I don't like him alone in the house with you and Nettie."

"Don't be silly."

"I'm not. The kid definitely tried to break into the house this morning. That's a criminal act. You admit you don't know him too well. How long has it been since you saw him?"

"A couple of years."

"Have you heard anything about him in the meantime? Like, was he president of his Sunday-school class?"

"No, I haven't heard much about him since Rich and I divorced, and I doubt he's president of his Sunday-school class, since I never heard of either of his parents taking him to church. But I'm not afraid to have him in the house."

"Well, put a chair under your doorknob."

The water stopped then, and Joe and I hung up on that slightly antagonistic note. It seemed that a lot of our conversations had been ending that way lately.

I guess I was getting tired of sitting home by the telephone. Joe kept telling me he wanted us to start dating, but we didn't seem to be getting close to that goal.

Joe was a Warner Pier native; his mother ran an insurance agency across the street from TenHuis Chocolade. I'd first known him—or known of him—twelve years earlier, when Joe was chief lifeguard at Warner Pier's Crescent Beach, and I was one of the gang of teenaged girls who stood around and admired his shoulders. Joe had been a high school hotshot—all-state wrestler, state debate champion, straight-A student, senior class president. He got a scholarship to the University of Michigan and did well there and in law school. Aunt Nettie says his mother glowed every time his name was mentioned.

But after law school Joe surprised his mother by going to work for a Legal Aid–type operation instead of the big firm she'd pictured. His mom wasn't as excited about that.

Then Joe met Clementine Ripley. *The* Clementine Ripley. One of the nation's top defense attorneys, the one the movie stars and big financiers called before they called the cops.

Ms. Ripley went to Detroit to defend one of Joe's clients pro bono. Before the trial was over, he'd fallen for her in a major way, and she had found him a pleasant diversion. Joe convinced her that they should get married, even though she was more than fifteen years older than he was.

Warner Pier says that it was doomed from the start, and Joe says he was naïve—only he uses the word "stupid." He also might not have expected the attention the marriage drew from the tabloid press: TOP WOMAN DEFENSE ATTORNEY WEDS TOYBOY LOVER IN MAY–DECEMBER ROMANCE.

That was followed by TOP WOMAN DEFENSE ATTORNEY BUILDS SHOWPLACE HOME IN TOYBOY HUSBAND'S HOMETOWN. Next, TOY-

BOY HUSBAND OF TOP WOMAN DEFENSE ATTORNEY QUITS LAW CA-
REER, DENIES PLAN TO BECOME HOUSE HUSBAND. Finally, TOP
WOMAN DEFENSE ATTORNEY SPLITS WITH TOYBOY HUSBAND. AGE
NOT FACTOR, BOTH CLAIM, with a subhead, "Ex now repairing boats."

Joe's version is that Clementine Ripley's approach to the practice of law
crystallized his disappointment in the morality of a legal career and made
becoming an honest craftsman seem a more honorable way to make a living. So he bought a boat repair shop in his hometown. Specializing in antique wooden boats, he did beautiful work, work to be proud of. But his
mother had quit glowing whenever his name came up.

Then, just when Joe had thought he'd escaped from the glare of the
media, Clementine Ripley was murdered in her "showplace home in toyboy
ex's hometown." The tabloids came back.

The crime was solved—that's how Joe and I met each other again. Then
Ms. Ripley's lawyers dropped another bombshell. They revealed that she
hadn't changed her will after her divorce from Joe. Joe inherited her entire
estate, plus he was named executor. The tabloids stuck around.

To complicate matters further, Clementine Ripley left an extremely involved estate. Joe was having to spend several days a week with accountants, attorneys, court appearances, even finding a new home for her
champion Birman cat, who now lived in Chicago with a former housekeeper. Joe swore he wasn't going to keep any of the money—and he said
there wasn't going to be much left, anyway—but it was forcing him to
spend a lot of time concentrating on his ex-wife's affairs.

Not on his own affairs. Not on my affairs. On Clementine Ripley's affairs. The woman was haunting him.

The tabloid press was haunting him, too. They seemed to have some con-
duit into Warner Pier. Any little thing Joe did popped up in the tabloids. The
previous week he had talked to the mayor, to see if the city was interested
in owning the fifteen-acre Warner Pier estate Clementine Ripley had left behind. Two days later the headlines read, TOYBOY HEIR OF FAMED AT-
TORNEY SEEKS BUYER FOR MANSION.

Our mayor, Mike Herrera, swore he hadn't told anybody but the park
commissioners. How had the tabloid found out?

Neither Joe nor I wanted to see ourselves splashed across the *National
Enquirer*—TOYBOY HEIR OF FAMED LAWYER ROMANCES TEXAS
EX–BEAUTY QUEEN WHO WAS WITNESS TO EX–WIFE'S DEATH. So I
understood why Joe and I were having a telephone romance. But I was getting tired of it.

Jeff went up to bed, and I said good night to Aunt Nettie and went up,
too. I didn't get undressed, but I wrapped up in a comforter and read by my
bedside lamp, which is rather dim. I got interested in my book, forgot Joe,
and barely heard Aunt Nettie moving around as she got ready for bed.

Then, across the hall, I heard Jeff's bed creak. His door opened, he came out, and he stopped outside my door.

Instantly, I remembered what Joe had said about putting a chair under my doorknob.

My heart jumped up to my throat. I told myself I was being crazy, but that didn't do any good. Joe's warning had created suspicions, and it was no good denying they existed. I was scared.

I lay still, not breathing, just listening. It was ludicrous. Jeff was on one side of the door, listening to me, and I was on the other, listening to him.

I didn't breathe again until I heard Jeff move on and start down the stairs.

Stupid, I told myself. Even kids have to get up to go to the bathroom now and then.

I wondered if Jeff *was* going to the bathroom. Or if he was going to Aunt Nettie's room. That gave me another stab of fear.

So I listened carefully to his progress through the house. I'd spent a lot of time in that house. I could tell who was walking where without moving anything but my ear.

Jeff crept down the steps to the living room, then turned toward the dining room. He went into the kitchen.

Good. He was going to the bathroom.

But when he got to the kitchen, he stopped. He fumbled with something that thumped. Was it the hall tree where all the winter jackets had been hung?

I heard a click. I was sure the sound was the lock of the back door.

The door opened, then shut. I heard Jeff's footsteps cross the back porch, then scrunch through the snow in the side yard, moving toward the driveway and off into the night.

CHOCOLATE CHAT

GOLDEN AGE CHOCOLATE

One of the most famous books of the Golden Age of Mysteries is *The Poisoned Chocolates Case*, by Anthony Berkeley, published in 1929. It's based on a short story Berkeley wrote, "The Avenging Chance," published a year earlier.

In both the short story and the novel a box of chocolates is mailed to a member of a London men's club, and the man is asked to sample it as part of a marketing survey. Since the recipient dislikes chocolates, he gives them to an acquaintance, who takes them home to his wife. The wife eats one and dies—poisoned. The detectives, of course, try to figure out who had it in for the man who received the chocolates and passed them on to his fellow club member. The solution, however, is that the second man knew his fellow club member did not like chocolate and arranged to be beside him when the box arrived. The wife was the intended victim all along.

All very logical—except that part about the first man disliking chocolate. That's completely unbelievable.

Chapter 4

What the heck was Jeff up to?

I quickly turned off my bedside lamp, slid out of my cocoon of comforter, and went to the window. I pulled the curtain aside and peeked out.

Could Jeff be creeping outside to smoke? Aunt Nettie didn't have ashtrays out, true, but he hadn't asked about it. The kid would have to be a confirmed nicotine addict to go outside for a cigarette in fifteen-degree weather.

Did he want to get something from his SUV? Unless he'd hidden something under the seat, I didn't think there was anything left in it to get. I'd even given him a plastic grocery bag for his trash, and he had filled it with soft-drink cups and fast-food debris that afternoon. The SUV had looked empty.

Was he going someplace? That didn't seem likely. For one thing, I'd noticed that his gas tank was close to empty. I'd planned to buy him a tank of gas the next day, but I hadn't told him that yet. Besides, if he wanted to leave, Aunt Nettie and I had made it clear we weren't going to try to stop him. There was no reason for him to sneak off in the middle of the night.

And it was the middle of the night. My watch read 1:00 a.m.

But middle of the night or no, the interior lights flashed inside Jeff's SUV; then I heard the motor start. But only his running lights came on when the Lexus began to move. He backed down the driveway slowly. This was definitely as surreptitious a trip as he could manage.

Where was he going? I had to know. Or at least try to find out. Maybe if I followed him, I'd get a clue as to why he had left Texas.

I was still dressed, so I grabbed my purse and rushed down the stairs in my stocking feet, hoping that I wasn't waking Aunt Nettie. At the back door I stepped into my boots and pulled on my jacket and cap. By the time I got outside, Jeff's taillights had turned onto Lake Shore Drive, and his headlights popped on. I ran to my van, thudding along the cleared walk and then scrambling through the snow along the drive. I pulled the no-lights stunt until I was past the house. I was still trying not to wake up Aunt Nettie, but I half expected to see her standing at her bedroom window as I went by; Aunt Nettie doesn't miss much.

Even without lights, it was easy to see where I was going. Our part of Michigan is heavily wooded, but there are only a few evergreens; nearly all the trees are bare in winter. The snow on the ground reflected what light there was, giving the night a luminous quality. I drove about a quarter of a mile before I turned on my headlights.

By then I was asking myself if I was wasting my time. Jeff had about a three-minute head start, and even one minute would give him enough time to get away from me completely. But a few factors were working in my favor. If Jeff had gone anyplace but Warner Pier, I might as well forget the chase and go home. But if he had gone into Warner Pier, it was just a small place; I could drive up and down every street in the town in fifteen minutes. Plus, his gold Lexus RX300 was really noticeable. There probably wasn't another car like it in Warner Pier in the winter. So if I spotted one, I'd know it was likely to be him even before I saw the Texas tag.

Besides, if Jeff had sneaked out because he wanted to buy something, there was only one place in Warner Pier that was open all night, the Stop and Shop out on the state highway, at West Street and North Lake Shore Drive. I didn't consider that a strong possibility. Jeff had claimed he had less than five dollars in his pocket.

So I crossed the Warner River on the Orchard Street bridge and drove up and down the streets of Warner Pier. I was all by myself; the town shuts down completely on a winter night. Streetlights made the snow glitter at every corner, and the Victorian houses looked like wedding cakes.

The Dockster, a beer joint that rocks until dawn in the summer, was shuttered for the winter. The Warner Pier Inn had closed its dining room at nine. Dock Street Pizza, where the locals hang out, had closed at ten. The Holiday Haven, one of the two motels that stay open all winter, was dark, though a dim light in the office hinted that an on-site manager would have appeared if I had banged on its doors. I saw no reason to do such a thing. There was no Lexus SUV in its parking lot.

Even the Warner Pier Police Department, which occupies a corner of City Hall, had only one light inside and a security light outside. The Warner Pier Volunteer Fire Department was locked up tight as well. The police and fire station share a dispatcher with the county, and in case of emergency, I guess the dispatcher knows who has the keys.

The only human being I saw was the guy spraying water to form a new layer of ice on the tennis courts. Warner Pier's tennis courts are flooded and turned into a skating rink every winter, and some poor schnook has to maintain them after the skaters have packed it in.

By the time I reached the intersection of West Street and North Lake Shore Drive—where the state highway enters Warner Pier—I had just about decided that Jeff had headed back to Texas on an empty gas tank. I glanced at Warner Pier's other open motel, the Lake Michigan Inn. It looked busier than the Holiday Haven had looked; one guest room had a light in the window and there were a few cars parked outside, though none of them had Texas tags.

I drove around the corner and pulled into the Stop and Shop to turn around, and there, under the lights next to the building, was Jeff's gold Lexus.

Luckily for my surveillance project, there was no sign of Jeff himself. I flipped a U-turn through the parking lot and wheeled my old van across the street. I pulled into the circular drive of Katie's Kraft Shoppe and parked close behind the shop's van. I cut my lights and watched the Stop and Shop.

So Jeff had stopped for gas. Did he have more money than he'd told me he had? Or did he have a credit card he hadn't mentioned? Or had he bought gas? He wasn't parked at a pump.

I didn't see Jeff. It crossed my mind that he might be robbing the joint. My heart jumped to my throat. His car was in plain sight, however, nosed in near the entrance door. If he'd planned to commit a crime, surely he wouldn't have been stupid enough to park that noticeable car in so obvious a spot. Maybe he had just dropped by the Stop and Shop to buy a bag of potato chips. I tried to calm down.

The inside of the store was visible through big plate-glass windows, and I scanned the shelves and aisles. It wasn't a big place, just a half dozen aisles. There was no sign of Jeff. I turned the van's motor off. I would sit there until I got cold, I decided. If he didn't show by then, I'd go home to bed.

But I had waited only about five minutes when Jeff appeared. He came into the store from the back room, waved at the clerk, and walked out the front door.

What the heck had he been doing in the back room of the Stop and Shop?

Oh, God! Were they dealing drugs there? My heart leaped back into my throat, then dropped to my toes, and began to pound like crazy. But I had no reason to think Jeff was into the drug scene, I told myself. He hadn't acted high, and his eyes looked normal, even if his earlobes didn't. Maybe he wanted to use the Stop and Shop's restroom.

Jeff started his car, backed out, and drove toward the Warner Pier business district. I waited until he was several blocks down the street, then cautiously followed him.

He didn't seem to have any idea I was there, and he seemed to know where he was going—if he was heading back to Aunt Nettie's. At least, he turned where I would have. If I were going home myself, I'd cut over to Dock Street by way of Fifth, a route that would take me past TenHuis Chocolade, near the corner of Fifth and Peach. I was once again made aware that Jeff was more familiar with the layout of Warner Pier than he should have been.

I hung back a couple of blocks as we drove. I was beginning to wonder what I was going to tell Jeff after we both parked in Aunt Nettie's driveway.

So he caught me completely by surprise when he suddenly turned off his headlights, pulled over, and parked beside the curb, right in front of Ten-Huis Chocolade. I stopped a block away, as far away from a streetlamp as I could, and turned off my headlights.

But Jeff wasn't paying any attention to me. He remained motionless inside his SUV for about a minute; then he jumped out and ran across the sidewalk. I could see him silhouetted against the dim security light we leave on behind the counter.

Now what?

I decided I'd better intervene. I drove on down the street. By this time Jeff was running back and forth in front of the store, looking up and down the street. As I pulled in beside his car, he shaded his eyes from my headlights. His glasses glittered. He seemed to be peering at me, trying to see who I was.

I opened the van's window and leaned out. "Jeff! What are you up to?"

"Lee?" His voice was a harsh whisper. "Oh, God, you're here!"

"Yes. And so are you. Why?"

He waved frantically and whispered again. "Be quiet! Call the cops! Somebody's broken into the store!"

I got out of the van. "That's silly. This is Warner Pier."

"I don't care if it's the moon! The glass is broken out of the front door! And I saw somebody moving around. Now they're in the back room. They've got a flashlight!"

The whole thing was ridiculous. Burglaries don't happen in Warner Pier, at least not in winter. I moved toward Jeff, into my headlights.

"Warner Pier has practically no crime in the wintertime," I said. "The tourists take it home with them."

I could see myself reflected in the shop window as I crossed the sidewalk. But when I moved in front of the entrance door, my reflection disappeared.

For a moment I was reminded of a funhouse mirror—now you see it, now you don't. But when I stretched out my hand toward the door, my glove went right through the glass part of the door.

"The glass is gone," I said stupidly.

Jeff whispered again. "That's what I've been trying to tell you! The glass in the door is smashed, and there was somebody moving around inside."

Right then we heard a motor start, followed by squealing tires.

"They're getting away!" Jeff ran toward the corner.

I had an awful vision of Jeff tackling burglars, ruthless and desperate burglars armed with guns and knives.

"Jeff! Stop!" I ran after him.

It was half a block to Fourth Street, and we pounded along until we got there. But when Jeff reached the streetlight at the corner he stopped abruptly. I careened into him, and we both slipped on a patch of ice. I grabbed Jeff, he grabbed me, we both grabbed the base of the streetlight. We wound up sitting on the sidewalk, but neither of us hit the ground very hard.

Jeff was still facing up Fourth Street. "There they go! And I didn't get a good look at the car."

I twisted around in time to see taillights disappearing around a corner. "He turned on Blueberry," I said. "Or I think he did. And his taillights look funny."

"The left one is out," Jeff said, "but that's not going to be a lot of help. I think it was some kind of sports car. Maybe."

We walked back to the store. "You don't have a cell phone, do you?" Jeff asked. He made it sound like a major personality flaw.

"Sorry," I said. "But I have a key to the shop."

"We shouldn't go in the front. We might destroy evidence."

"Well, I'm not going around to the alley," I said. "It's too dark and snaky back there. Besides, the burglar must have gone out the back door, it's easy to open from inside."

"How far is the police station?"

"Just a couple of blocks, but there's nobody there. We have to call the county dispatcher."

There was little glass on the sidewalk, of course, because the burglar had knocked the glass inside. We gingerly walked in.

"If the burglars came in this way," Jeff said, "they're gonna have glass in the soles of their shoes."

I turned on the lights and looked at the display shelves.

"Thank God!" I said.

"Yeah," Jeff said. "The molds are still there."

Since the moment the word "burglar" had sprung into my mind, I'd been dreading finding the Hart collection of chocolate molds gone. They were the only thing in the shop that was valuable.

I called the dispatcher, and in about ten minutes a patrol car pulled up. I was relieved to see a tall, lanky figure get out—Abraham Lincoln in a stocking cap.

"It's Chief Jones," I said.

The chief waved at me. "Just what have you been up to now, Lee?"

"I'm a victim, Chief. Or at least TenHuis Chocolade is."

The chief stepped in through the broken glass, and I introduced him to Jeff. "You two better go in the office and close the door," the chief said. "We'll hurry up out here."

"Yeah. Chocolate gets funny-looking if it freezes. I'll call Handy Hans and see if he can do something about that door."

"Have you called Nettie?"

"No. I'll do that, too."

Telling Aunt Nettie that someone had broken into her beloved shop wasn't easy, but she took it calmly.

"Nobody's hurt?"

"Not Jeff or me. I hope whoever broke in slashed their wrists on broken glass."

"Any sign of that?"

"Nope. Apparently they—he—parked around behind, but he must not have been able to open the back door from the outside. So he came around to the front, smashed the window in the door, and got in that way. But Jeff must have disturbed him right away, and the guy ran back to the break room, opened the door to the alley and got out the back."

"I'll be right down."

Aunt Nettie's big Buick showed up within fifteen minutes. By then a second patrol car had arrived and Patrolman Jerry Cherry was taking pictures. The chief had allowed Jeff and me to start cleaning up the glass, so Aunt Nettie was able to enter the shop in a more traditional manner.

Soon afterward Handy Hans—his last name is VanRiin—arrived with a sheet of plywood, which he used as a stopgap measure against the cold, and Aunt Nettie joined Jeff and me in the office.

She looked puzzled. "What I don't understand is why you two were down here in the middle of the night. And why did you come in separate cars?"

Jeff glowered and stared at the floor.

I was going to have to tell them that I had followed Jeff. "I heard Jeff leaving," I said, "and my curlicue got the best of me. I mean my curiosity! I admit it, Jeff. I wanted to know where you were going, so I followed you."

Glower and mutter. He shot a glare at me.

I felt embarrassed and angry. "If it's any consolation, you lost me, and I found you again just a few blocks before you pulled up in front of the shop." I thought Jeff looked relieved, but he didn't speak. I went on. "I feel responsible for you, Jeff. You won't tell us why you showed up here. I can't get hold of your parents. I need to know what you're up to!"

"Good question." The comment came from the door to the office, and I looked up to see Chief Jones come in. He unwrapped a mile of wool scarf from around his neck, pulled off his stocking cap, and took a chair.

"Okay. Jeff, you did good work, scaring the burglar off like that. But what the heck were you doing down here anyway?"

Jeff's lips pursed, and his brows knitted. He looked as if he were trying to decide whether he should yell or burst into tears.

But before he could do either, Aunt Nettie took over. "Chief, does Warner Pier have a curfew?"

"No, Nettie. You know it doesn't."

"Then is there any legal reason that Jeff shouldn't have been driving around in Warner Pier, even if he did it after midnight?"

"No, there isn't, Nettie. He wasn't breaking any law by merely driving around the business district. It's just a little unusual."

She turned to me. "Lee, Jeff isn't a little boy anymore, and you're not married to his father anymore. So, if he wants to drive around all night every night, he's welcome to do so."

Then she addressed the chief. "It's getting to be time for breakfast. Let's form a caravan out to the house—you and Jerry are invited. I've got a couple of pounds of sausage in the freezer, and I've got a dozen eggs. Let's go eat."

She zipped her heavy blue jacket and pulled on her own woolly cap and gloves. She shook a bulky finger at us. "And not one of you is going to ask Jeff a single question. He saved the Hart molds, and I'll be eternally grateful to him."

She sailed out the door—solid as a tugboat, but regal as an ocean liner.

When I looked at Jeff, he had tears in his eyes.

Chapter 5

Of course, Aunt Nettie was right.

Or I had convinced myself that she was by the time I had driven out to the house. My Texas grandmother would have said Jeff was simply "bowing his neck," acting like a mule fighting the harness. He wasn't going to be badgered into telling us anything. The only way we were likely to find out why he'd come to Michigan was by killing him with kindness. It was the same technique Aunt Nettie had used twelve years earlier, when she was saddled with an angry sixteen-year-old niece for the summer.

We had to let Jeff learn that he could trust us. Which made me a little ashamed that I had followed him. But not too ashamed. When I finally got hold of his mom or his dad, they were likely to have a fit because he had left college in the middle of the semester and driven to Michigan. I didn't want to quarrel with them, and they wouldn't like it if I had let him wander around western Michigan in the snow and hadn't even tried to figure out what he was up to.

And I did wonder about those tears in Jeff's eyes.

Jeff offset the tears, however, by pouting and sulking all through breakfast. By the time Aunt Nettie had fed Chief Jones, Jeff, me, and herself—Jerry Cherry hadn't joined us—it was close to six a.m. The chief insisted on helping Aunt Nettie with the dishes, and Jeff delighted us all by going to bed. I was exhausted, but too keyed up to sleep. So I put on my jacket and boots, took my flashlight and walked down the drive to get the Grand Rapids paper out of the delivery box across the road.

Getting out and walking around in the snow is another part of my campaign not to act like a Texan who'd never seen cold weather before. Actually, it can get darn cold in Texas, but it doesn't last months and months, the way it does in Michigan.

I'd just taken the newspaper out and turned to go back across the road when headlights came around the curve. I stopped to let them go by. But the headlights didn't go by. A pickup screeched to a halt, and Joe Woodyard got out.

"Are you okay?" He sounded all excited.

"Yes. Are you?"

"No, I'm pretty upset." He came around the front of the pickup.

"What are you upset about?"

"You," he said. And then he threw his arms around me.

I tipped my head back and looked at him, astonished.

So he kissed me. Thoroughly.

I enjoyed it thoroughly, too. In fact, it felt so good I had to fight an impulse to throw him in the back of the pickup and tear his clothes off, beginning with his puffy nylon jacket and working down to the long underwear I could see peeking out at his cuff. But a little voice kept nagging in the back of my head. *What brought this on?* it asked. And, *Is this a good idea?*

It was about five minutes before I could ask my questions out loud. "Wow!" I said. "I'll have to upset you more often. What's the occasion?"

"Chasing burglars! What would have happened if you caught 'em? Don't you know I couldn't make it if anything happened to you?" Then he kissed me again. For just four and a half minutes this time.

When he worked around to nibbling my neck, I was able to talk. "Nothing did happen to me," I said. "I'm enjoying this, but I don't quite understand it."

Joe moved his head back, but he didn't let me go. We were standing sternum-to-sternum and talking nose-to-nose. "You and that kid! What were you two doing waltzing around with burglars?"

"I haven't the slightest idea, when you get down to it. How'd you find out about our adventure?"

"I had coffee with Tony out at the truck stop." Tony Herrera was married to one of my friends, Lindy. Tony, who happened to be the son of Warner Pier's mayor, drove into Holland every day for his job as a machinist. He and Joe had been friends since elementary school.

Joe went on. "We ran into Jerry Cherry."

"I see that the Warner Pier grapevine is in good shape. How come Jerry realized you'd want to know about our excitement?"

"He didn't. There was a whole table of us. I tried not to seem too interested."

He had tried not to seem too interested? Suddenly I was hopping mad. I pushed myself away from Joe.

How could he act as if I mattered to him when we were alone or when we were talking on the telephone, but pretend he hardly knew me in public?

"Oh, I think you could justify some interest in a local burglary," I said. "After all, you're a Warner Pier property owner. All the Warner Pier citizens are shocked and appalled by local crime, right?"

"Sure. Everybody was interested. But—" He cocked his head. "Are you mad?"

"No. I'm furious."

"About the burglary?"

"Not exactly." I stopped talking then. It was awfully hard to tell a guy that your relationship stunk when you didn't have a relationship. I decided I'd better not try. "I suppose I'm just tired."

"Well, yeah. You've been up all night."

"That's not what I meant, but I guess it's close enough."

"Hop in, and I'll drive you up to the house."

"Better not! Chief Jones is up there. He might see you."

I guess my sarcasm finally sank in. Joe's lips tightened, but he didn't say anything.

"I'll talk to you later," I said. Then I pushed on past him, but he caught my arm.

"If you think I like this situation, you're wrong."

"If you think I like it, you're wrong, too."

We stood there, glaring at each other. Then I pulled my arm away. "I'm completely out of patience with adolescent piccalillis—I mean peccadilloes."

"Thanks! I'm really thrilled at being lumped in with that kid."

"Actually, you and Jeff are acting quite differently. He won't talk at all, and you won't do anything else."

"What do you want me to do?"

"I don't know! But it's not real complimentary if you don't even want people to know—" I broke off. "Oh, forget it! It's a dead end anyway."

I stalked across the road. Joe followed me. "I didn't come to quarrel," he said.

"Then why did you come?"

"To see you. To make sure you were all right."

"You've seen me. I'm all right."

"And I wanted to find out just what that kid—"

"That kid's name is Jeff."

"Okay! To find out just what kind of a story Jeff told about the burglary."

"Jeff had nothing to do with the burglary. I was following him. I saw him pull up in front of the shop. I saw him get out of the SUV. He did not break the window."

"Maybe not, but Jerry said he doesn't think the chief is satisfied with his story."

"I'm not satisfied with his story either. I want to know why he went into town in the first place. But I don't think he broke the window. I do think he scared the burglar off."

"Maybe so, but . . . Jerry said that the burglar apparently went off in a car with a broken taillight."

"We think so."

"Well, Brad Michaels said—"

"Who is Brad Michaels?"

"He has the gas station south of town, down at Haven Road. Right on the interstate. And he says a kid driving a gold Lexus SUV with a Texas plate stopped there around seven a.m. yesterday. He didn't buy gas, just candy bars and chips."

"Sounds like Jeff. So?"

"So Brad says there were two Texas vehicles. The other driver didn't get out, but Brad thinks they were together."

Maybe I would have reacted differently if I hadn't already been mad. But I *was* mad. Plus tired and plain old out of sorts. I didn't want any more bad news. So I tried to kill the messenger.

"I suppose that your pal Brad says the other Texas car had a taillight out," I said.

"No, he—"

"I suppose you asked him that."

"Yes, I—"

"And I suppose you made sure he told Jerry about it."

"No! He didn't mention it until Jerry had gone."

"But I suppose you urged him to tell Jerry. Or Chief Jones."

"They're gonna find out. Warner Pier is a small town."

"Well, let them! But I'm not getting involved in any more efforts to quiz Jeff. He knows I want to find out just what he's up to. He'll tell me something when he's ready. Or he'll tell Aunt Nettie. Or the chief will question him. But right now I'm cold and I'm tired and I'm going back to the house."

I walked away without looking back. This time Joe didn't follow me.

When I got back to the house I took off all my outdoor paraphernalia, then sat in the living room pretending to read the paper. I felt pretty miserable. Joe was suspicious of Jeff even without knowing the most damning part of the situation. Nobody, including Chief Jones, knew that Jeff had been aware that the molds were valuable, but I did. Should I tell Chief Jones? Like Joe said, the chief was bound to find out. I just didn't want to be the person who caused Jeff more problems, even though he was causing me a lot.

Darn Joe Woodyard anyway! Why had he reminded me of Jeff's odd behavior? And why did I care what Joe thought? I shook the newspaper angrily. How had I wound up in this dead-end relationship?

For six months I'd been patient about Joe's hang-ups over his ex-wife and about his fear of the tabloids, but right at that moment I was sick of the situation.

Oh, maybe I'd brought part of it on myself, making it clear I wouldn't sneak around to go out with him. He had to take me out in public, or I wasn't going to go at all. And I certainly wasn't going to get too cozy with a guy I wasn't officially dating. So there'd been no weekends when we both just happened to be in Chicago and staying in the same hotel, no surreptitious meetings at the boat shop, no nights in a B&B a hundred miles up the lakeshore.

Joe wasn't the only one who had survived a bad marriage; I wasn't interested in having my self-respect further flogged by a clandestine affair, an affair that would have made me feel cheap and used.

Maybe I wasn't sure what I wanted out of a new man in my life anyway. So I had only myself to blame over the crazy relationship Joe and I had fallen into, I told myself. I half resolved to end it. Or maybe I already had. After the things I'd said, maybe I'd never get another of those eleven o'clock calls from Joe. Maybe we'd never hold each other again, never kiss like that again. Maybe I'd felt that melting sensation behind my navel for the last time.

I didn't like that idea either.

When Chief Jones left, I still hadn't decided what to tell him about Jeff. I put any decision off and simply called out a good-bye.

Aunt Nettie said she was going to bed. "We'd all better sleep as long as we can," she said. "I'll call the shop and leave a message. Telling them we'll be late."

I thought I couldn't possibly sleep, but I forced myself to undress and lie down, and the next thing I knew, it was eleven a.m. I could hear Aunt Nettie in the shower downstairs, and Jeff was snoring gently across the hall. I groaned and got up. Aunt Nettie had left the house by the time I got out of the shower.

I managed to get to work by one p.m., to find Aunt Nettie going crazy. "Thank goodness you're here," she said. "I can't get any work done for answering the phone and gossiping with the neighbors."

"I guess the news about our burglar got around."

"Naturally. The Warner Pier grapevine is up and running; we don't need radio or television or newspapers in this town. But everybody wants a personal account."

"I'll try to keep them away from you."

"I've simply got to make the *bakjes* for the crème de menthe bonbons today. Hazel's working on them, but she needs to get busy on the Neiman Marcus bunnies." Aunt Nettie froze and looked out the front window. "Oh, no! It's Mike Herrera. I can't be rude to him."

"Go on back to the shop and get up to your elbows in chocolate. I'll deal with him."

I shooed her toward her *bakjes*. *Bakjes*, pronounced "bah-keys," are the shells of bonbons, the part that holds the filling. First you cast the *bakjes*, then cool them, then fill them, then run the whole thing through an enrober, a special machine that gives the bonbons a shower-bath of chocolate. After that the tops are decorated, and you've finally got a goodie ready for the customers to drool over.

Aunt Nettie had washed her hands and moved to a stainless-steel work-table by the time the door opened. I greeted the newcomer. "Mayor Mike! Did you come to check our damage?"

Mike Herrera looked puzzled. "It's just so strange," he said. He closed the smashed front door behind him, then examined the plywood that blocked it temporarily. "We just don't have burglaries in Warner Pier this time of year."

Mike Herrera is an attractive middle-aged man who owns several successful restaurants and a catering service. He was the first Hispanic to own a business in Warner Pier and the first to be elected to public office. He's the father of Joe's friend Tony and the father-in-law of my friend Lindy Herrera; in a town of twenty-five hundred, people tend to be related.

But I'm careful not to bring him up around Tony because Lindy told me her husband isn't real happy with his father since he changed his name from Miguel to Mike. Tony's reaction to the name change was to grow a thin Latin mustache and start teaching their children Spanish. The Herreras are typical of the American experience, I guess. One generation tries to assimilate; the next clings to its roots.

Mike kept looking at the damage.

"Handy Hans called the glass installers," I said, "but they can't get here until tomorrow."

We heard a crack like a pistol shot, and Mike craned his head to look into the shop. "What was that?"

"Aunt Nettie's making *bakjes*. She whams them on the worktable to get the edges right."

"Can I talk to her?"

"As long as we don't stop her work."

It was hard to refuse Mike. He knew that Aunt Nettie could make chocolates with her eyes closed. Mike followed me into the shop and greeted Aunt Nettie, commiserating with her over the break-in. Aunt Nettie kept pouring melted dark chocolate into a mold about the size of an ice-cube tray—an ice-cube tray with forty little compartments.

"I just wondered if anybody suspicious came in yesterday," Mike said.

Aunt Nettie had apparently filed Jeff in a nonsuspicious category. "I can't think of anybody," she said. "The antique molds were the only thing valuable in the shop." She turned her filled mold upside down over her work pan, and went tappity tappity tap on its edge with the flat side of her spatula while the excess chocolate drained out. She scraped the top of the mold, wielding her spatula like a conductor wields his baton. Then she flipped the mold over and slammed it onto the sheet of parchment paper that covered the worktable. Wham!

Mike jumped about a foot. Apparently he hadn't realized that making bonbons is that noisy. The *bakje* molds are polycarbonate, a tough resin, and they're hard. Whacking them onto a stainless-steel table makes a sharp crack.

"Who knew that the molds were here?" Mike said.

"Everybody who works here knew." Aunt Nettie flipped the mold upright again, then placed it behind her, on the conveyor belt that led to the cooling tunnel. "All the Hart and VanHorn family knew. How about the retail customers, Lee?"

"We had only a few retail customers yesterday afternoon," I said, "and none of them acted very interested in the molds. Except Timothy Hart."

Aunt Nettie had filled another mold with more dark chocolate. She flipped it and began the same routine.

"Maybe it was just a coincidence," Mike said. "Maybe the burglar was looking for money. Not for the molds."

Aunt Nettie frowned, sliding her spatula over the top of the mold. Then she flipped it, and before Mike could get set, she whammed it onto the table.

Mike jumped again. "Why are you doing that, Nettie?" He's a foodie, after all. Curious about cooking.

"I'm sorry to be so noisy, Mike, but whacking it that way keeps the bonbon shell thin and gives it an even edge. Plus, it gets rid of air bubbles." She moved the mold over to the cooling tunnel. A dozen other *bakje* molds were already making their five-minute trip through the tunnel's sixty-five-degree air.

Aunt Nettie took several *bakje* molds from the opposite end of the cooling tunnel. She moved to a second table, flipped the molds over and popped the little square chocolate shells out onto more parchment paper. She was already refilling one of those molds with dark chocolate, and while she worked—tappity tappity tap; swish-swish with spatula; flip mold—she talked. "You know, Mike, I don't care what the burglar was after, but I want those molds out of here. Lee is going to call Gail and ask her to come and get them. And I'm not going to ask Olivia VanHorn's permission to take them down."

Wham! She whacked the *bakje* mold onto the table, as if emphasizing her determination.

That time Mike didn't jump. "Mrs. VanHorn is just another Warner Pier absentee property owner. I don't care what she thinks. But you're still going to take part in the Teddy Bear Getaway, aren't you?" Mike Herrera is not only Warner Pier's political chief, he's our biggest tourism promoter. He'd pushed hard to make sure all the merchants took part in the special winter tourism campaign.

Aunt Nettie's magic hands kept working. "My ladies have made and hand-decorated hundreds of teddy bears. We certainly hope to sell them." She whacked another tray onto the parchment paper.

"They'll have to do double duty as decorations in the shop," I said.

I guess I sounded impatient, because Mike spoke soothingly. "Oh, chocolate teddy bears will be fine decorations! I'm sorry if I sound worried, but I am. It's just so odd—why break in here? If there's any place in town that's not likely to leave cash in the register, it's y'all." Mike is another transplanted Texan, raised near Dallas, and his accent is an interesting mix of Southern and Hispanic.

He looked at me. "And I know, Lee, that you can swear that this stepson of yours didn't break the glass. But he is driving a Texas car."

"That's hardly incriminating," I said.

"I know, I know—it's that I'm concerned about that car they found over at the Superette."

"What car?"

"Greg Glossop . . ."

I groaned. Greg Glossop operates the Superette's pharmacy and he's notorious as the biggest gossip in Warner Pier. Joe suspected Glossop was the pipeline to the tabloids.

Mike Herrera made a calming gesture. "I know, I know, Greg's not the most popular man in Warner Pier, but he doesn't miss much. He noticed a car with a Texas tag in the parking lot this morning. It had apparently been there overnight. Some kind of a small Ford, several years old. The chief says the gas tank was empty."

I immediately thought of the car seen by Joe's buddy who worked at the station out on the highway. It was likely the mayor had also heard the truck stop gossip and was thinking the same thing.

"Jeff wasn't doing anything illegal last night," Aunt Nettie said. "I'm not going to let anybody gossip about him. He kept the burglar from taking anything." She gave Mike a firm look, then whammed another mold onto the stainless-steel table for emphasis.

Mike left, still frowning, and I called Gail Hess to ask her to come and get the molds. I got her answering machine.

I left a message, then hung up, wondering where Gail was. I also wondered why she hadn't been over first thing in the morning, or even in the middle of the night. Everybody else in Warner Pier knew about our break-in.

Then I called Mercy Woodyard, Joe's mother, because she handled our insurance. I got her answering machine, too, and left another message.

And I called the two Dallas numbers for Jeff's parents. More answering machines. Was there a human being left near any telephone in the universe?

I got a packing box from the back room. I took all the antique molds down and heaped them on the counter. Then I wrapped each of them in tissue paper and packed them in the box. That made me feel better. If Gail didn't show up to take them away, I'd take them home with me that night. Or put them in the bank. Or something.

I actually got some work done in the next thirty minutes, despite a call from the obnoxious George Palmer, our banker, reminding me we had an appointment at four o'clock. I'd just assured him that I'd be there when the bell on the street door chimed. I hung up on George to go out to the counter to wait on a customer, a great-looking guy.

He seemed familiar, but how did I know him?

His face was young, but his beautiful head of dark hair was beginning to be shot with silver. It looked soft and silky. I found myself wanting to rub my cheek against the top of his head. He would have had to sit down for that, because he was at least my height. His eyes were a dark brown, with black lashes. Then I recognized him, and I knew we had never met.

"I'm Hart VanHorn," he said. "You must be Mrs. TenHuis's niece."

He was Olivia VanHorn's son. The state senator who was rumored to be running for the U.S. House. Of course he looked familiar. Not only did he have his mother's eyes, but I'd also seen him on the evening news and in the *Grand Rapids Press*. Neither medium had shown how sexy he was, however.

He smiled, giving me lots of eye contact. Aware that I was standing there gawking at him, I quickly extended my hand in shaking position. "I'm Lee McKinney."

"Oh. It's not TenHuis?" He took my hand.

"My mother was a TenHuis. My father is a Texan."

"I see. Uncle Tim said you had a charming Southern accent."

"I don't know how charming it is, but I can legally y'all." I realized I was still holding his hand. Yikes! I was about to drool on his snow boots. I dropped his hand and stepped back behind the counter. "I enjoyed meeting your uncle yesterday. He's a charmer."

Hart VanHorn grinned. "Uncle Tim is one of my favorite people. He has his problems, but ordinary human meanness was simply left out of his character."

Also sobriety. Time to change the subject. "Did you come in to see the mules? I mean the molds." Curses! My tongue was tangled up again. "I already packed them up."

"Oh? You're not going to display them?"

"After the break-in, I didn't want to take the chance."

"Mother wouldn't mind, but I understand how you must feel. I wanted to make sure that you and your aunt weren't upset by the excitement last night."

"We were just grateful that the burglars didn't take anything. Particularly the molds."

"Down at the post office I heard that your stepson scared the burglars off."

"My former stepson. Yes. He saw someone moving around in the shop as he drove by, so he stopped. Then he saw that the glass in the door was broken."

"I'd like to give him a reward."

"That's not necessary, but it's very nice of you."

"May I meet the young man?"

"Not right now. We all slept late, and Jeff isn't here yet. I'll tell him you came in."

That seemed to bring the conversation to a halt, and I expected Hart Van-Horn to smile his beautiful smile and say good-bye. But he lingered. "I also need some candy."

"That I can take care of!"

I didn't correct his terminology directly. In the chocolate business, the word "candy" means hard candy—lemon drops and jawbreakers. Our product is "chocolate."

"We have lots of chocolate," I said, "and it's all for sale. What do you need?"

"Well, the board members from a Grand Rapids shelter for battered women helped push a bill I'm sponsoring in the legislature. They worked really hard, and I'd like to give them all something in recognition. It should be versions of the same gift—you know, not singling any one person out. So, my mother suggested a box of candy for each of the twelve board members."

"Of course. I think they'd all be delighted. We have four-ounce, eight-ounce, and one-pound boxes."

"Oh, I think at least a pound."

"That would make a very nice gift. The one-pound boxes are thirty dollars. If you want tins, it's a dollar more." I always work the prices in early in the conversation. Not everybody is pleased to pay thirty dollars for a pound of chocolates—even chocolates as delicious as TenHuis's. A purchase of twelve boxes could run him three hundred sixty dollars, plus tax. That would make some people decide on a thank-you note instead.

But Hart VanHorn didn't turn a hair of that beautiful head. "Fine," he said. "And the boxes are okay. But—well, could you put one of those chocolate teddy bears in each? They're collecting teddy bears for the children who come to the shelter. And could you wrap each box a little differently? I mean, different-colored ribbon or something?"

"I'm sure I can come up with something. And for an order that size I can give you a fifteen percent discount. When do you need them?"

"Today, I'm afraid. I have to run up to Grand Rapids, and I wanted to take them along." He smiled. "Their board meets tomorrow. Is that too soon?"

"Oh, no. I have enough ready. Unless you want them individually packed?" I pulled ready-to-go boxes from a shelf against the wall and showed him the assortments inside. I demonstrated how I could substitute a molded teddy bear for four of the chocolates, and Hart VanHorn approved the plan. Then we discussed the decorations. I found ribbons in different colors—gold, silver, red, green, blue, plaid, peppermint stripe. And the boxes came in white, gold, and silver, so making each one different from the others wasn't difficult.

I gave Hart VanHorn a dozen gift cards, and he stood at the counter writing them out while I fixed up the boxes of chocolate. He didn't refer to a list, which I found awe-inspiring. I couldn't remember the names of my twelve closest relatives without looking them up. He kept writing, but it seemed that whenever I looked at him, he was looking at me. I began to feel as if I should say something.

Finally I thought of a question. "How is your congressional campaign going?"

"It may not go at all."

"Oh? The newspaper says you're the front-runner."

"I suppose I have a good chance, since the incumbent isn't running and my mother's pulling in all her chits. But I'm not sure that's how I want to spend the rest of my life." He smiled. "That's one reason we're down here without any staff. I'm trying to make up my mind."

His mother had already made hers up, judging from her comments the day before. I didn't bring that up, just smiled and kept working. And Hart kept writing. And staring at me.

As I worked I reminded myself that Hart VanHorn was a politician, so eye contact would be his standard operating procedure. Though I did remember that the *Grand Rapids Press* had identified him as one of Michigan's most eligible bachelors.

I was impressed with him. His selection of gifts was tactful—equal, but easy to tell apart. And he didn't seem embarrassed to credit his mother with the inspiration for the twelve boxes of chocolates. That was interesting, too, though I wasn't sure of its significance. Was he a mama's boy? Or simply secure enough to admit her influence? Was she making the decisions on his campaign? Or was he? How long were her apron strings?

I tied up the final box and took out a large white shopping bag with "TenHuis Chocolade" printed near the bottom in the classy sans-serif type Aunt Nettie uses in her logo.

"Anything else?" I said. "Are there any children on your shopping list?"

Hart VanHorn grinned broadly. "Do I want fries with that?"

I laughed. "Retail sales are not my specialty. But I'm trying to learn all the tricks. How about a box for your mother?"

"Your aunt gave Mother a box yesterday."

"Then how about a free sample for yourself?"

"Sure!" Very few people refuse a sample of TenHuis chocolate. Hart

VanHorn picked a double fudge bonbon ("Layers of milk and dark chocolate fudge with a dark chocolate coating") and ate it with eye-rolling relish. Then he sighed and leaned his elbows on the counter next to the cash register.

"Ms. McKinney," he said, "I know I'm being what my mother would call forward. But honestly, I'd love to get out of dinner with her and Uncle Tim one night this week. They're not going to be good company. And you would be. Would you consider going out to the Dock Street and splitting a pizza with me tomorrow?"

Chapter 6

I almost clasped my hands to my bosom and said, "Sir! This is so sudden." In spite of the eye contact and chitchat, I had not been expecting Hart VanHorn to ask me out.

Not that I don't get asked out now and then. But I've never accepted too many invitations. When I was in high school, I was a drudge. I knew I'd have to put myself through college without much help from my parents, so I always had a job, plus I was still afraid of serious relationships because of my parents' divorce. I was too cautious for either commitment or casual sex. It made for a lot of boring Saturday nights.

But during my senior year my mom and dad decided I might be less gawky and lacking in poise if I did something public, so they pushed me into the beauty-pageant circuit. That didn't help my social life. A little success there, I discovered, meant the guys I met were either awed or thought I must be easy. I never liked either kind—a date who was too scared to say anything or a date I had to fight off before he bought me a Coke.

College didn't change much. I still lived with my mom—couldn't afford a dorm or my own place—and the pageant circuit didn't add glamour, though it meant enough money to pay for a speech coach, once I learned where to buy used evening gowns.

I was still trying to get through college when I was twenty-two, and I met the guy I thought was my dream man—Jeff's father. He was old enough and successful enough not to be impressed by having a wife who had once been a loser in the Miss Texas competition. He was settled in life, I told myself. I could trust his love.

Wrong again. Rich didn't love me. He loved his idea of me—a blonde who could look good when we went out with his business associates and who was barely smart enough to punch in the phone numbers for the right caterer and the right decorator.

I was still trying to finish my accounting degree when we got married, and he encouraged me to enroll in a full class load the next semester. I overlooked the patronizing way he wrote my tuition check, but I caught on when I brought my grades home. I made the President's List, and Rich sulked for three days. Then I asked a few accountant-type questions about his business, and Rich was furious for three weeks. Because I get my tang tongueled all the time, he'd thought I was stupid. And that's what Rich had wanted me to be. When he found out there were a few brains under my natural blond hair, it ruined our marriage.

I'd wasted five years on Rich. Then I wasted nine months on Joe Woodyard. Now Hart VanHorn was standing there, smiling at me and offering to buy me a pizza at the Dock Street. A lot of emotional baggage might have flashed through my mind, but I answered him within fifteen seconds.

"That sounds wonderful," I said.

"Great! About seven?"

"Fine. But are you sure you want to make it the Dock Street?"

"Nearly everything in Warner Pier is closed this time of the year. Doesn't the Dock Street have the best food of any place that's open?"

"Oh, yes. But the Dock Street is gossip central for Warner Pier."

Hart laughed. "I don't mind. But I don't live here. If you'd rather go into Holland . . . ?"

"No, the Dock Street is fine."

"Good. Now you tell me just where to pick you up."

I described the landmarks that identified Aunt Nettie's drive. "This time of the year you can see the house easily," I said. "I'll leave the lights on in front and in back, and you may want to come around to the kitchen. That sidewalk's easier to get to, since the drive curves around to the side of the house."

"I know the house you mean," Hart said. "It's not far from our place. I'll be there."

I rang up his chocolates. While he was signing the MasterCard slip I stood there beaming because one of the most eligible bachelors in Michigan had asked me out to a highly public place. Then our boarded-up front door opened and admitted an attack of guilt.

Joe Woodyard's mother came in.

I almost ducked down behind the counter. I'm sure I did turn red and look guilty. For a mad moment I was sure she was going to accuse me of being untrue to her son.

"Hi, Lee," she said. "Sorry I wasn't in the office when you called. Of course your insurance covers your break-in—after your deductible."

"Oh!" I'd forgotten that I'd called her. "Handy Hun called the grass destroyers."

Joe's mom and Hart VanHorn both stared at me incredulously. I'd reached a new standard in scrambled language.

I spoke again, slowly and carefully. "I mean, Handy Hans called the glass installers. They'll be here tomorrow." I gestured toward Hart. "Mercy, have you met Hart VanHorn? Aunt Nettie and I were terribly relieved that the burglar didn't take Mrs. VanHorn's mold collection."

Mercy Woodyard's whole demeanor perked up. She beamed at Hart. "No, we haven't met, but I heard the speech you gave at the insurance convention last summer. On the state violence-against-women bill. It was excellent."

They shook hands. I left them chatting about women's shelters and insurance coverage for battered wives and went to tell Aunt Nettie that Mercy was there. By the time I got back, Hart was going out the door. He waved at me. "See you later," he said.

I hoped Mercy Woodyard hadn't seen the way he lifted his eyebrows. I interpreted the lift as indicating he intended to see me at a specific time. I was flooded with confusion again, and I was afraid I was blushing.

Mercy Woodyard, however, was smiling. "Now that's one politician I might be able to support," she said.

I tried to sound noncommittal. "Oh?"

Mercy laughed ruefully. "And to think Joe could have been a member of his law firm."

"Oh?"

"Oh, yes. When he quit the Detroit job and moved over here he was contacted by one of the partners. They offered him a nice deal." She shook her head. "Joe can't do anything by halves. He stuck with the boats. But Barton and VanHorn—of course, there's a whole string of partners. It would have been a good opportunity."

Then she looked at me sharply. "Maybe you could convince Joe he should go back into law, Lee."

I almost gasped. I had assumed Joe had told his mother nothing about me. Did she know about our telephone courtship? I decided to change the subject.

"You know, Mercy, there's one thing I've been wondering, and I'm sure you know. What happened to Hart VanHorn's father?"

"Vic VanHorn? I'm afraid he wasn't much of a loss."

"He was a U.S. congressman, right?"

"Yes. At least he would have been until the next election. He had become more and more irresponsible in the way he talked. I believe the technical term is 'shooting his mouth off.' Even Olivia couldn't restrain him. The voters were getting fed up."

"People around here talk about his death as if the circumstances were common knowledge. But I'm a newcomer. Did he die there at the Hart-VanHorn compound?"

"Yes. It was a freak accident. He had come down with Olivia and Hart. And I believe Timothy Hart was there, too, but he was staying in his own house. It was in the summer, and one of those wild thunderstorms rolled in off the lake. Sometime in the night Vic VanHorn apparently walked down to the lakeshore to take a look at the lake or watch the lightning. Or something. Of course, no one will ever really know why he went down there. But he got too near the bank, and it gave way."

"How awful!"

"Nobody knew he had gone out. I guess Olivia woke up early and discovered he had never come to bed. She found his body, down on the beach."

"Then he was drowned?"

Mercy frowned. "Actually, I think the fall killed him. I seem to remember that he fell about twenty feet and hit his head on something when he landed. His body had been in the water though. Luckily, it got caught on a log and didn't drift off."

"So Olivia VanHorn didn't come back to Warner Pier for fifteen years because of the sad association?"

"Apparently so." Mercy leaned over the counter and lowered her voice. "I heard—from a really reliable source—that the governor offered to appoint her to finish out Vic's term. But she refused."

"That's surprising. She seems so interested in politics."

"I guess she'd rather work behind the scenes."

Aunt Nettie came up to the counter then, and I went back to my office. But I couldn't help looking out into the shop, to see if Mercy was acting unusual in any way.

Joe's mom is a perfectly nice woman, as far as I can see. She's trim and attractive, in her fifties. She's fairly tall, but not a giant like me. She's blond, though I suspect she originally had dark hair. We blondes who don't need "touching up" tend to feel a little smug about blondes who do.

If Mercy Woodyard has a distinction, it's that she's the best-dressed woman in Warner Pier. Or perhaps I should say she's the most professionally dressed woman in Warner Pier.

Warner Pier is, after all, a resort community. Our customers are likely to appear in bathing suits and shorts, so the clerks in the shops and the tellers at the bank and the receptionists in the offices would be ill-advised to dress as if they were working on Fifth Avenue. The clerks TenHuis Chocolade hires in the summertime wear khaki shorts or slacks and chocolate-brown polo shirts. The high school principal wears a blazer and khakis. The receptionist at City Hall wears jeans, and the mayor presides at council meetings in khakis and a sweater. I used to dress up when I worked in a Dallas office, but now I consider L. L. Bean my prime fashion consultant. That day I was wearing flannel-lined jeans and a turtleneck.

So Mercy Woodyard's power suits stand out. She could walk into any Dallas bank or Chicago brokerage firm and look as if she belonged there. And while the rest of us wear ski jackets and woolly parkas in winter, she appears in well-tailored dressy coats. Her wardrobe, I suspected, was designed to set her apart as proprietor of a "professional" business.

I had no idea what Joe thought of her. Which is significant, I guess. During the past nine months, he and I had spent hours talking on the phone, discussing every subject under the sun except his mother. He'd mentioned her a few times—saying he had things stored at her house, for example, or describing a visit the two of them made to his one remaining grandparent at Thanksgiving—but he'd never mentioned anything his mother had done, repeated anything she had said, or expressed any opinion of her.

And he'd never indicated that she knew he and I had become anything more than casual acquaintances. I didn't know what to make of her earlier comment that I might influence Joe, urge him to go back into the practice of law.

I was getting out the checkbook to write up the payment on our loan when I heard Mercy Woodyard raise her voice. "I'm going to land in the middle of Gail, anyway."

"She was only trying to help the Teddy Bear Getaway promotion," Aunt Nettie said.

"She was only trying to help Hess Antiques," Mercy said. "She's wild to handle the sale of the VanHorn furnishings. That would be quite a coup for her."

"Gail runs a nice auction."

"Of course. But I'd expect the VanHorns to deal with someone a little more upscale. Allen Galleries, maybe. Or someone from Chicago or Grand Rapids. Gail shouldn't have brought those molds over here."

"I should have realized how valuable they are. A lot of chocolate people collect them, but Phil and I simply never had time for such things. I never thought about anything happening to them."

"Gail did know they were valuable, and she should have put a rider on them if she was going to display them somewhere outside her shop. I'm going to make sure this doesn't happen again." Mercy nodded firmly and left.

Aunt Nettie was frowning as she went back toward the shop. She stopped in the door of my office. "Mercy would make a powerful mother-in-law," she said.

I laughed. "Well, it looks like that's not going to be my problem."

"Oh, dear! Did you and Joe quarrel?"

"I guess so. And then—Hart VanHorn asked me to go out for a pizza. I said yes."

"Oh, my, Lee! And Jeff turns up, too. Your life is complicated."

"I'd forgotten Jeff! I'll break the date with Hart."

"Why?"

"I don't want to leave you stuck with Jeff."

"Oh, I can manage Jeff for a few hours." Aunt Nettie raised her eyebrows. "I assume a few hours is all you had in mind?"

"It certainly is. And as far as I know it's all Hart has in mind. He may be Michigan's most eligible bachelor, but he can't be that fast a worker."

"Times have changed so much that I can hardly keep up."

"Maybe so, but right at the present moment, your niece is living a celebrate—I mean celibate—life. And that situation doesn't seem likely to change. Certainly not over one date, even if it's with Hart VanHorn."

I stood up and reached for my red jacket. "And now, it's time for me to beard George the Jerk and extend our loan."

Aunt Nettie patted my hand. "I really appreciate having you to handle that, Lee. Take him a bonbon or two. He likes Mocha Pyramids."

I put two Mocha Pyramids ("Milky coffee interior in dark chocolate") and two Amaretto truffles ("Milk chocolate interior flavored with classic almond liqueur and coated with white chocolate") in a box and headed down the block to the bank. As I walked, I psyched myself up. You're the customer, I told myself. The bank needs you more than you need them. George Palmer is your servant, your flunky. Treat him like dirt.

Of course, that wasn't my actual intention. I really intended to kill him with kindness—à la chocolates—and snow him with figures. I'd already discovered that one reason George acted so snotty was that he didn't really understand numbers. His main qualification for being branch manager had apparently been marrying the daughter of one of the bank's more important board members. Despise him, I told myself. But I still felt intimidated.

When I got to the bank, however, I looked through the glass wall that kept George separated from the rest of the bank, and I discovered he had his own problems. He was having a meeting with Olivia VanHorn.

Olivia was seated in an armchair, her casual mink thrown onto George's small sofa. She looked to be completely at ease; not a hair of her thick white hair—Hart's was going to be just like it—was out of place.

George, on the other hand, looked nervous. He was smoothly handsome and sleek, with dark hair and eyes. Like Mercy Woodyard, he wore city suits—garb I felt sure was designed to make us yokels feel our yokelhood. But even his suit wasn't helping George right then; Olivia VanHorn was obviously making him feel like nobody.

In winter the Warner Pier branch bank has a very small staff that doesn't include a receptionist, so I nodded to the only other employee present, a young guy at the one open teller station, and sat down in a chair outside George's office.

I eyed George and Olivia's conversation—she talked and he listened—and I got curious about what they were talking about. So I did a wicked thing. I decided to use the ladies' room.

That may not seem wicked, but it was. Because I knew a secret about that ladies' room and why its exhaust fan was kept running all the time. The previous branch manager, my friend Barbara, had revealed it to me over lunch one day. Because of a quirk in the heating system, she whispered, every word spoken in the manager's office was broadcast through the ductwork and was plainly audible in the ladies' room. Naturally, whatever happens in the ladies' room is also audible in the manager's office.

For this reason, Barbara never used her office for confidential conversations. And she also installed a fan in the ladies' room that ran all the time, effectively covering the noise of flushing and hand washing, so these sounds wouldn't be heard in her office.

When Barbara was given a new assignment, apparently no one had told her replacement about this little quirk. George used the manager's office all the time, closing his door and assuming his conversations were private, whether the exhaust fan was on or not.

When I quizzed one of the women tellers about it, she giggled. "We *tried* to tell him," she said.

Anyway, the more I looked at George and Olivia talking, the more I was dying to know what they were saying. I left my jacket and the file folder that held my bank records in my chair and went to the ladies' room. When I entered the tiny room, the furnace was on, and its fan added to the background noise. I took the opportunity to reach up high and unplug Barbara's specially installed exhaust fan. In a minute the furnace fan went off, and the next sound I heard was the voice of Olivia Hart VanHorn.

"You can assure Bob that Hart is definitely going to run," she said.

She sounded as if she were right in the room with me. My heart pounded for a minute. It seemed impossible that she wouldn't know I was listening.

George spoke. "To be honest, Mrs. VanHorn, that's not what Hart said to me yesterday."

Olivia spoke again. "I admit that my son has a serious handicap for a political candidate. Modesty. He sometimes doubts his own abilities. But I've helped him turn this into an advantage."

"In what way?"

"Hart is never unwilling to share credit. And since the legislative process requires cooperation and . . ."

"Back-scratching?"

"Dickering. Trading favors."

I stared at the vent. Maybe I should be feeling guilty, but I wasn't. I felt curious. After all, I had accepted a date with Hart for the next night. If he and I were going to be friends, I had a right to know what others thought of him.

Sure, I did. I threw any qualms in the trash with all the used paper towels and extended my ear toward the heating vent.

George was speaking. "Bob says you're the best politician in Michigan."
I realized the Bob he and Olivia had been talking about was his father-in-
law, a well-known political and business figure in Michigan.

Olivia laughed a ladylike laugh. "Oh, I'm not sure that's right. Michigan
has a lot of expert politicians. But I have had experience in back-scratching,
as you call it."

"Why have you never run for office yourself?"

There was a pause before Olivia answered. "Perhaps I might have,
George, if I were thirty years younger. But back when I convinced Vic he
should seek office, it was still somewhat rare for women to enter the political arena. I would have had to get involved in the Equal Rights Amend-
ment, in support or opposition of pro-choice legislation. I would have been
smeared as a woman who neglected her son, her husband."

Huh, I thought. Other women ran for office then. They made their posi-
tions known on those issues. You just wanted to be a kingmaker, the power
behind the throne.

"No, I've always thought I made the right decision," Olivia said. "I've
been able to pursue my goals through my work with Vic, with the party.
And now through Hart."

"If Hart runs."

"Oh, he's going to run. Hart has a complete, perfect background for national office, beginning with Boy's State and his success in high school debate. Then there was Harvard, study abroad, a law degree *and* a graduate
degree stressing government theory. He handled the right kind of law cases,
backed the right kind of legislation, supported the right social causes."

George didn't sound convinced. "Hart has the reputation—well, I've
heard he's been seeing . . ." His voice faded away, as if he couldn't bear to
finish the thought.

Olivia laughed. "You're worried because Hart has never married. Well,
he's a perfectly normal man, and he sees lots of women. But Hart has had
no serious entanglements. No scandals are going to surface. And he's only
thirty-five. I feel certain that soon Hart will find the right woman."

Olivia sounded as if she already had the right woman picked out. And
somehow I didn't think that Hart's wife would be a blond divorcée with a
tangled tongue. Maybe I represented rebellion to Hart.

George stammered out a few unintelligible words, but Olivia kept talking. Her voice became more triumphant. "There are no skeletons in Hart's
closet. Absolutely none. Hart has the VanHorn looks and charisma and the
Hart family's drive, ambition, and brains. Hart is going to go far, George,
and if you're smart, you'll go along with him."

I was mesmerized. Then the furnace fan started again. It broke the spell
I was under. With its noise as cover, I plugged in the exhaust van again.
Then I dashed out of the restroom before George noticed the difference in

the sound of the fan and I got caught. I sank into the chair where I'd left my jacket, whipped out my loan folder, and pretended to study the papers inside.

Wow! That Olivia VanHorn was something. Her ambition for Hart took my breath away; she obviously thought the U.S. House was just a step on the ladder. But she made me sad, too. Why had she turned that ambition loose on her husband and her son? She had even refused to serve in Congress when she had the chance, if what Mercy had said was right.

Aunt Nettie had thought Mercy Woodyard might be a difficult mother-in-law. Mercy would be a piece of cake compared to Olivia VanHorn. Suddenly I wasn't so sure I wanted to go out with Hart after all. Maybe I'd be seen as a threat to his political career, and if I were, Olivia would trample me flat.

Though Hart did seem to have the gumption to stand up to her. At least he was hesitating to commit to a run for Congress, a run she'd plainly decided he was going to make, like it or not. It was going to be interesting to see who won.

But I think at that moment I knew—though it gave me a twinge of regret—that I was never going to be seriously interested in Hart VanHorn. I had my own problems.

In a few minutes I saw George helping Olivia into her mink jacket. She nodded to me regally as she left the bank, and George motioned me into his office.

I thought he might make some comment about Olivia, but he didn't. He seemed troubled, and he barely spoke. I had no need to snow him with my figures; he didn't try to talk me into refinancing at all. He merely accepted my check, and we both signed the papers for the loan extension—at the same interest rate. Then I gave him his chocolates and left.

I was back in my own office, still thinking about what I'd overheard, when the next commotion started.

The outside door to TenHuis Chocolade was opened so suddenly and with such force that it nearly flew back into one of the show windows. A figure hooded in emerald green dashed inside and slammed the door.

I stared. When the newcomer pushed her hood back, I saw that it was Gail Hess. She was panting slightly.

"Lee!" she said. "I just heard about the burglary! Is it true you and Jeff saw the burglar's car? Tell me all about it!"

CHOCOLATE CHAT

THE CULINARY KILLERS

Mysteries, emphasizing the physical world as they do, have always paid attention to food. Even Sherlock Holmes and Dr. Watson checked out the clue of the curry in "Silver Blaze." But more recently a whole field of culinary mysteries has bloomed.

And plenty of these emphasize chocolate. Just a few . . .

- Diane Mott Davidson wrote *Dying for Chocolate*, starring caterer Goldie Bear.

- Joanne Fluke's detective, baker Hannah Swenson, solved the *Chocolate Chip Cookie Murder*.

- Heaven Lee, the caterer-detective created by Lou Jane Temple, appears in *Death Is Semisweet*.

- Magdalena Yoder, the operator of a bed-and-breakfast in Pennsylvania Dutch country, was created by Tamar Myers for a series of comic mysteries. Although Magdalena has not so far starred in a book that features chocolate in the title, in *Too Many Crooks Spoil the Broth,* Magdalena's sister, Susannah, almost loses her miniature dog when the pet, who habitually rides about in Susannah's bra, falls into a pan of Chocolate Oatmeal Drops. The little dog is not injured.

Chapter 7

I stared at Gail. "Are you just hearing about our excitement?"

"I went over to Lansing last night, so I could go to a sale this morning. I just got back. Mercy Woodyard told me about it. What happened?"

"We had a break-in. The molds are safe."

"Thank God! What did they take?"

"Nothing. My former stepson—" Suddenly I realized Gail didn't know anything about Jeff. I sighed. "It's a long story. Let me start at the beginning."

I sketched out Jeff's arrival—leaving out his trying to break into our house—and ended with his interrupting the burglar.

"So the burglar might have been after the molds, Gail. That's why Aunt Nettie and I want them out of here."

Gail seemed to think deeply. "It could have been coincidence. I mean, why? Is it true you and your stepson got a look at the burglar's car?"

"It was turning onto Blueberry before I saw it."

Gail leaned over the counter, and—I swear—her eyes sparkled. "Mercy said that one of the taillights was out."

Her reaction mystified me. "Jeff said one of them was. I didn't get a good look."

"So you don't know what kind of car it was?"

"Jeff might. Guys that age are up on cars. He thought it was some kind of sports car."

Gail looked at me with those bright, excited eyes. "It's funny that the burglar came in through the front door. I'd have tried the alley, myself."

"The door back there is steel and has a dead bolt. It would be almost impossible to get through. And the window has steel mesh. The front door may be more public, but it was a lot easier to break in."

"It's just lucky your stepson saw the burglar."

"Yes. We owe Jeff a lot."

"I guess he didn't even know there was anything valuable in the shop."

I cleared my throat. "Well, uh, Jeff's mom owns an antique shop in Dallas. He did recognize the molds as collector's items. The chief . . . well, he'll have to know about that. But Jeff had no reason to break in."

Gail smiled gleefully. "Of course he didn't! It will probably be one of those unsolved crimes." The thought seemed to delight her.

Gail took the box of molds and went back to her shop, still excited. But she'd left me down in the dumps again.

Gail's questions had reminded me about Jeff. It was now after four o'-clock, and we hadn't heard a word from him.

I called the house. The phone rang eight times, and I was about to hang up when Jeff answered with a sullen, "Yeah."

"Jeff? Were you still asleep?"

"No." There was a long pause before Jeff went on. "Sorry I didn't get down to work."

"I just wanted to make sure you were okay."

"Yeah, I'm okay. I'd have come down, but that policeman showed up."

"Policeman! What policeman?"

When Jeff answered, he didn't sound quite as sullen. "Cherry? Officer Cherry? He wants me to go down to the police station, Lee."

Was I imagining the slightly plaintive quality in Jeff's voice? "Oh! I can meet you there."

Then the tough Jeff was back on the phone. "Butt out!" he said. "It's no big deal. I can handle it."

He hung up.

He hung up on me? I made my mind up to quit feeling worried about Jeff and let him take care of himself. I angrily slammed a few things around on my desk. Then I tried to call both of Jeff's parents one more time. Both were still unreachable. I even asked Rich's British receptionist for Alicia Richardson, who had kept books for his company since it was founded. Alicia knew where all the bodies were buried. But she wasn't there either. I still didn't want to tell Miss Brit about Jeff's problems.

My stomach lurched. How would Rich react if he learned his son had run away, come to Michigan, and gotten arrested for burglary? It was like a pit opening under my feet.

It was no good. I checked the time. It had been a half hour since I talked to Jeff. I was still worried about him. I decided to walk down to the Warner Pier City Hall and find out what was going on—even if Jeff didn't want me to. I wanted to know what Police Chief Hogan Jones was up to.

Chief Jones is not your typical small-town lawman. He'd spent most of his career on a big-city force and had been headed up the final steps of the promotions ladder until Clementine Ripley, prominent defense attorney and Joe Woodyard's ex-wife, turned him inside out on the witness stand. I don't know all the details, but after that Hogan Jones retired and moved to Warner Pier, where he and his wife had long spent their vacations. A year later his wife died, and Jones, maybe feeling the need for a new interest in life, had taken the job as chief of Warner Pier's police—in charge of all three patrolmen and a part-time secretary. He seemed to get along fine in Warner Pier, maybe because his retirement income wasn't dependent on city politics. He was quite willing to tell the Warner Pier merchants and city officials where to get off. Consequently, they didn't fool with him a lot.

I put on my ski jacket and hollered at Aunt Nettie to tell her where I was going, then I went out the front door.

Warner Pier's business district is incredibly picturesque. One of the town's attractions to tourists—besides great beaches, miles of marinas, and an art colony—is its Victorian ambiance. The town was founded in the 1830s, and by the 1860s and '70s was a prosperous center for growing and shipping peaches. The captains of the lake steamers and the wealthy fruit growers built classic Victorian houses along the Warner River and on the bluffs along the lake. When the artsy crowd moved in during the 1890s, they added Craftsman-style homes and cottages. Luckily, the same families owned many of these for years, and sentiment prevailed; only a few of them had been "modernized"—another word for "ruined" in the view of the historic-preservation crowd.

The Warner Pier downtown isn't all quite as authentically Victorian as Aunt Nettie's "Folk Victorian farmhouse." Some new construction did creep in during the 1950s. But today's merchants know what's good for business; genuine and faux Victorian features abound—including several blocks of fake Victorian condos that challenge the architectural imagination.

The shops along Dock Street face the river, with a strip of park separating the business district from the marinas. Dock Street is the busiest part of town in the summer, when the river is lined with yachts, near-yachts, sailboats, and fancy power boats. Now, at the end of February and with all the boats in storage or moved to southern climes, it still looked pretty.

There was even a little weak sunlight that day, and the sidewalks had been cleared. The temperature had climbed to nearly forty. I enjoyed the fresh air on my walk to City Hall, even if I wasn't happy about my errand.

City Hall is one of the authentic Victorian buildings, originally a private home. I went up the redbrick steps, across the white front porch—decorated with the approved Victorian lanterns and a few teddy bears—and in through a front door with a beveled-glass panel.

When I came in, Patricia VanTil, the tall and rawboned city clerk, jumped to her feet and almost ran to the counter. "Oh, good, you're here," she said. "I was debating with myself about calling you."

"Why?"

"Well, I wanted to be sure you knew about your stepson being down here."

I tried to act calm. "I'm sure it's just ravine. I mean routine. Jeff did stop the burglary last night. But I'll go on back to the police department and see what's going on."

I gave what I hoped was a gracious smile—it probably made me look like one of the chocolate skulls TenHuis makes for Halloween—and went past the counter and down the corridor that leads to the two or three rooms of the police department.

Jerry Cherry was out in the main room. "Hi," I said, determined to be friendly and casual. "Don't they ever let you go home?"

"Oh, I got a few hours' sleep." Jerry looked at me suspiciously. "What can I do for you?"

"I hear the chief has Jeff in for more questioning. I decided I needed to keep informed on the situation."

"He's not under arrest or anything, Lee."

"I'm glad to hear it." In fact, about half my stomach muscles relaxed at the news. "But just what is going on?"

Jerry sighed. "I'll tell the chief you're here."

He knocked on the door of the chief's office, looked inside, and spoke. I heard the rumbling voice of Hogan Jones. "Come on in here, Lee!"

I went into the office. Jeff was sitting in a chair across the desk from the chief. Only the two of them were present. I thought Jeff looked a little relieved when he saw me, but he didn't say anything. I tried not to stare at his earlobes.

"What's up?" I said.

"I needed to ask Jeff a couple of questions. Nothing serious."

"You mean I don't need to call him a lawyer?"

Chief Jones laughed. "Oh, we're a long way from that kind of thing. Jeff's a hero, right? Stopped the only burglary the Warner Pier business district has had since Labor Day."

"He certainly did."

"As a matter of fact, I didn't want to ask him about the burglary at all."

Jeff burst into speech then. "It's some car, Lee. They think I might know something about it."

"What car?"

"We found it in the parking lot at the Superette. Out of gas. The manager called and asked us to tow it."

"Why would Jeff know anything about it?"

"It has a Texas tag." Jeff sneered. "Like I know every car in Texas."

The chief chuckled. "Yeah, that's pretty silly, isn't it? But the guy who runs the station down at Haven Road—that's five miles south of Warner Pier, Jeff, on the interstate—he said a young man in a gold Lexus RX300 with a Texas tag pulled in there early yesterday and bought some chips and stuff."

"Okay," Jeff said. "That was me."

"The guy says you weren't alone, Jeff."

"He's wrong!"

"He says another car with a Texas tag pulled in at the same time. A small Ford."

"Maybe so. But I was alone."

The chief shrugged, but he didn't say anything. I couldn't think of anything to add, so I didn't say anything either.

The silence grew until Jeff finally spoke. "No shit. I was alone. I pulled in there and bought some chips and a Coke. I sat in the parking lot and counted my money. I didn't have enough for gas, so I decided that I'd have to call Lee, see if she could help me." He turned to me. "I knew where you were because of all the newspaper stories last summer."

The chief spoke again. "You didn't see the other Texas car?"

"It was still dark!"

"Had you driven all night?"

"I pulled over and slept some."

"Mighty cold for sleeping in a car."

"I left the motor running. Guess that's how I used up all my gas." His eyes had grown wide and innocent-looking, then cut at the chief, the way they did when he was lying.

The chief's voice took on a fatherly tone. "And just why did you come to Michigan, Jeff?"

Jeff's lips tightened, but his eyes stayed wide. "I'm old enough for a road trip, if I feel like one."

"Right in the middle of the semester?"

"I wasn't so excited about my classes anyway."

"And without telling your parents?"

Jeff didn't answer.

"Jeff," I said, "I've been trying to call both your parents. I know they're worried."

"No, they're not. They're not interested in me right now."

I ignored his comment. "I haven't been able to reach either of them. Do you know where they are?"

Jeff glared at me.

"How about your mom? She always acted pretty interested in you, Jeff."

"Mom?" He gave a snorting laugh. "She's got other interests."

"And how about your dad? I couldn't get along with him, true, but he's not a bad person. Does he know where you are?"

Jeff looked up, and he looked, well, curious. "Look, Lee—what the hell did you say to Dad last summer?"

I hadn't been expecting that question. "We only spoke one time since our divorce, Jeff. It wasn't a very friendly conversation."

"Did you tell him something about he was so dumb he didn't know one Great Lake from another?"

I tried to laugh it off. "It was just a wisecrack, Jeff. He called up here when I was in the middle of that mess after Clementine Ripley was killed, and he offered to help me. I guess I should have been grateful."

"Where did the Great Lakes come in?"

"He offered to fly up. I'm sure he meant well, but right at the moment I took his offer as meaning he thought I was too dumb to help myself. So when he said he'd fly into Detroit, I made some remark pointing out that Warner Pier is a lot closer to Chicago than Detroit. I told him that if I needed help I'd get it from somebody who knew Lake Michigan from Lake Erie."

Jeff laughed. "Yeah. He would have flunked fourth-grade geography."

"I wasn't being fair, Jeff, and neither are you. He simply thought of the biggest city in Michigan. Besides, Detroit isn't exactly on Lake Erie. It's just closer to Lake Erie than it is to Lake Michigan, and telling him he didn't know the difference between Lake Michigan and Lake St. Claire wouldn't have been funny. Anyway, your dad's a Texan! Admit it, all us Texans tend to think the other states in the union are tiny little places where all the cities are just a few miles apart."

Chief Jones had been enjoying this exchange thoroughly. "How about Alaska?"

"Alaska? Never heard of it," I said. "Real Texans ignore the existence of Alaska. Jeff, what does my smart-aleck exchange with your dad have to do with the current situation? Where is he? Where is your mom? I find it hard to believe that both of them left home at the same time, and neither of them told you where they were going."

Jeff sighed. "Well, they're in Mexico."

"Both of them?"

He looked up at me angrily. "Don't you get it? After you and Dad had that fight, it was like he finally admitted he could be wrong about something. I mean, if he didn't know Lake Erie from Lake Michigan?"

"Okay. But what does that have to do with his going to Mexico?"

"Everything! See, he went to see a counselor. Kind of caught on to what a jerk he'd been to you. And to Mom."

I was beginning to see the picture.

Jeff looked at me angrily. "Get it? Mom and Dad are thinking about getting married again. They're off on a trip to Mexico together!"

Chapter 8

I didn't know if I should laugh or cry. Was this the crisis that had made Jeff walk out on college and take to the road? But wasn't seeing his parents back together the dream of every child from a broken marriage? It had been mine.

On the other hand, Jeff was a real expert at playing his parents against each other. If they started speaking to each other pleasantly, it was going to mean big changes for him.

Their renewed friendship was probably related to his lack of money. If Rich was belatedly enlisting in the forces of responsible fatherhood, tightening the purse strings would be his weapon of choice. This would be quite a switch from his previous policy of using his son as a display case for conspicuous consumption.

Meanwhile, I caught Chief Jones giving me a speculative glance. He was obviously wondering where I fit into all this. The thought embarrassed me. Because I didn't fit in the situation at all. I wanted the chief to know that, though I wasn't sure just why.

"That is a surprise, Jeff," I said. "They'd been divided—I mean divorced—nearly ten years, hadn't they? I know your dad had been single for a couple of years when I met him, and we were married five years."

Jeff scowled, making his eyebrow ring wiggle. "They split up when I was nine."

"I hope it all works out for them."

"Fat chance." Jeff's voice was bitter, but he didn't expand on the theme.

I looked at the chief. "Does that explain why Jeff decided that he needed to make a change in his life, even if it meant spending February in Michigan?"

"Maybe. But it still doesn't explain the second Texas car."

The chief let the silence grow, but Jeff didn't say anything more. After a couple of minutes that seemed like an hour, Chief Jones told Jeff he could go. Jeff and I walked back to the shop. Jeff said only nine words in the two blocks: "I found the gas money. I'll pay you back."

When we came in the front door of the shop I was surprised to see that

Gail Hess was back. She not only was back, she was up on the step stool Aunt Nettie had been using the day before.

Aunt Nettie was behind the central counter, bent over and looking down. A pair of work boots was sticking out from behind the counter at an angle that showed their wearer was lying down on the floor.

"Not here," a muffled voice said. I recognized it as belonging to Joe Woodyard.

"Not here either," Gail said. Every strand of her frankly fake red hair was standing on end.

"If that doesn't beat all, I don't know what would," Aunt Nettie said.

"What in the world is going on?" I asked.

"One of the molds is missing," Aunt Nettie said.

"Missing? But I thought none of them was taken."

"Apparently one was," Gail said. "When I got them back to the shop I did an inventory. And one was missing. It's a Reiche mold, made in Germany sometime between 1912 and 1928."

"How valuable was it?" I asked.

"Oh, it's worth something. But it's not one of the rarest in the collection."

"What did it look like?"

Aunt Nettie answered. "It was that one that you thought looked so dirty, Lee. The one that was rusty."

"The mean-looking bear? The one with the muzzle?"

"Yes," Gail said. "Though I think he represented a dancing bear wearing a harness."

Joe crawled out from under the counter and stood up. "It didn't get knocked under there," he said. "Nettie, do you remember where it was displayed?"

"It was up there where Gail's looking. I thought maybe it was still there. It could have slid down. If it was lying flat, it could have been covered up some way."

"Well, it's gone." Gail got down and dusted her hands together. Maybe it was just the gesture, but she seemed quite self-satisfied. "I just wanted to be sure we hadn't simply overlooked it."

"That's crazy," I said. "Why would the burglar take just one mold?"

Gail answered. "Because you and Jeff disturbed him?"

"But why take that one? It was one of the hardest to reach."

Gail frowned. "Was the step stool out?"

"No! I'm sure it hadn't been touched," I said.

Gail gave what looked like a delighted smile. "I guess that proves our burglar was tall," she said. "I couldn't have reached it without a stool or a chair."

I couldn't get over how calm she was about one of the molds being gone. Only her hair looked excited.

"Shall I call Chief Jones?" I said.

Her eyes narrowed. "Do you think we need to report it?"

"The insurance company will want a complete police report made, if nothing else."

"I'll take care of it." Gail spoke cheerfully and smiled again. "I've got to get back to the shop now." And she waltzed out the front door.

We all stared after her. Aunt Nettie shook her head. "Sometimes I think that messy hair of Gail's grows right out of her brain and proves that there's as big a tangle inside as there is outside," she said. "I don't understand her at all."

Nettie looked at Jeff. "I hope you've showed up to work, even though it's nearly quitting time. We need you." She hustled him into the back.

And Joe and I were alone.

I felt bad about our quarrel, although I didn't feel as if I needed to apologize for my feelings and opinions. Maybe I needed to apologize for the rudeness with which I had expressed them that morning. But I didn't know that Joe's unexpected appearance at TenHuis Chocolade had anything to do with our fight. I decided not to make an immediate reference to the quarrel.

"How did you get pulled into the mold hunt?" I said.

"I just came in to buy some chocolates," he said.

"Sure." I moved behind the counter. "What kind and how many?"

"Oh, I guess a pound."

"We have a bunch of prepackaged boxes, or I can do an individual selection."

"I think that's what I need. A specially packed box. I want three-quarters of the chocolates to be that hazelnut kind coated in milk chocolate and sprinkled with nougat."

"Frangelico truffles? Sure. And what do you want for the rest?"

"Dutch caramel."

"Yum! You're a good picker. That creamy, soft, gooey caramel is great. Do you want them in a teddy bear box?"

"No, just a regular box. Regular ribbon."

I folded a cardboard box and began filling it with two layers of chocolates. Twenty-six little milk chocolate balls—the Frangelico truffles—and eight square dark chocolate bonbons—the Dutch caramels. I was dying to ask Joe who he was buying chocolates for. But I didn't. I concentrated on the chocolates.

As I worked I tried to think of some way to smooth over how Joe and I had left things that morning—without apologizing. I couldn't think of anything. Joe didn't say anything either. The shop seemed awfully silent.

I was almost relieved when the bell on the front door rang, signaling the arrival of some new person. But I was surprised when I looked up and saw who the new person was.

Timothy Hart.

Oh, gee! All of a sudden I remembered I'd agreed to go out with his nephew the next evening. I hadn't told Joe, but he was bound to find out, Warner Pier being the size it is and the Dock Street Pizza Parlor being the community center it is.

Meanwhile, I had to remember that I sold chocolates for a living, and Timothy Hart was a potential customer. He stroked his dapper gray mustache and removed his Russian-style fur hat. "Good afternoon, Ms. McKinney."

"Good afternoon, Mr. Hart. I'll be with you in a moment. I hope you're doing well today."

"Better than I was yesterday." He gave an apologetic shrug. Then he gestured toward the door, still covered with plywood. "I'm sorry to see you received some damage last night."

"We're insured. But we're afraid that the burglars were after the chocolate molds." I decided to let Gail Hess break the news that one was gone.

"Those molds! They've been a headache ever since our mother died."

"Oh?" I kept putting chocolates in Joe's box.

"First Olivia wouldn't let anybody touch them. Then she suddenly declared that the china cabinet they were in was an eyesore, and it was banished to the basement—molds and all. I don't know what finally became of that cabinet."

"Oh, really?" I stopped and checked the number of Dutch caramel bonbons I'd put in the box.

Timothy Hart kept talking. "Of course, after Vic's accident, Olivia shunned Warner Pier completely. Wouldn't come near the place."

"That's understandable." I tied a blue bow around the box of chocolates. "Here you go, Joe. Just a second, and I'll ring you up."

"Do you have a gift card?"

I took a plain gift card and a little envelope out of a rack behind the counter. "Will this do?"

"Great. Go ahead and help Mr. Hart while I write it."

I smiled at Timothy.

"I need something for a child," he said. "A chocolate toy?"

I showed him our molded cars, airplanes, and teddy bears, and he selected a ten-inch teddy with hand-detailed features. "An eight-year-old should like that, don't you think? I wanted to give one to the housecleaner's little boy. Can you send me a bill?"

"I'm sorry, Mr. Hart. We don't run noncommercial accounts." I wasn't about to give credit to a guy with a drinking problem, even if he was a member of a well-known family. "I can take a credit card."

"Oh, I think I have the money." Timothy Hart waved airily and produced a battered billfold. He found a twenty-dollar bill and handed it to me. I gave him change and he gave me a beaming smile.

He put on his furry hat and picked up the box that held his teddy bear.

"Now, you tell that nephew of mine that he's to be a perfect gentleman when he takes you out tomorrow," he said merrily. Then he left.

I could have killed him.

I turned to Joe, ready to make the explanation I'd known I had to make, but before I could speak Joe shoved a credit card at me. His face was expressionless.

I took the card and swiped it through the appropriate gadget. I swiped a few remarks through my mind at the same time, but none of them seemed suitable. Then, as I handed Joe the credit card slip, Aunt Nettie came into the store.

"Lee," she said, "did you order the extra cream?"

I turned around and assured her that I had. She said something else, but before I could respond, I heard the bell on the door. Joe had opened it.

I turned around quickly. I needed to say something. "Joe!" Then I noticed that the chocolate he had bought was still on the counter. "Joe! You're forgetting your box."

"It's okay," he said. "I'm headed for Grand Rapids. I'll call you. Sometime." The door closed behind him.

I looked down at the pound box of chocolate. Why had he bought it, then left it behind? He had tucked the little white envelope under the ribbon, and now I saw that he'd written a name on it: Lee.

Joe had bought chocolates for me.

I pulled the envelope out and opened it. "Sorry," the message inside read. "Maybe things will change soon." Joe's name was at the bottom.

I didn't know how to react. One part of me was really pleased. Joe had obviously meant the chocolates as a peace offering, and it was nice to know he wanted us to be friends. And that he knew my favorite chocolates, Frangelico and Dutch caramel. Another part of me was insulted. A gift of chocolates was just another example of his secrecy complex, and that complex was driving me crazy.

"Darn!" I said. "He could have sent me flowers." If he'd sent flowers from one of Warner Pier's florists it would have been all over town in ten minutes. For a moment I longed for a single yellow rose, delivered ostentatiously in a florist's van.

Then I opened the box of chocolates and took out a Dutch caramel.

Actually, it was nice to have a whole box of chocolates. Aunt Nettie's rule is two pieces per employee per day, and she and I are careful to stick to that, just the way we expect the other TenHuis staff members to.

I savored the Dutch caramel. Next I slowly ate a Frangelico truffle. Then I put the box in my desk. I tucked the note inside.

Aunt Nettie sent Jeff and me home at six. It was my turn to fix dinner, so I stopped and bought hamburger and buns to make sloppy joes. It used to be one of Jeff's favorites, and I figured he deserved a break.

He ate the sloppy joe appreciatively, then asked if we'd mind if he ate the leftovers later—"If I need a snack." We assured him that would be fine. The evening dragged. We built a fire, but nobody had much to say. Jeff and Aunt Nettie watched a little television, and I tried to call Joe. He wasn't home. Apparently he really had gone to Grand Rapids. I left a thank-you message on his answering machine.

At ten thirty Aunt Nettie went to bed, and Jeff said he was going up, too. When I went up at eleven, I could hear strange electronic noises from his room, and I deduced that he was playing games on his laptop. I put on a robe and went back down to the shower—our strange, old-fashioned shower that's so loud that it can be heard all through the house and keeps the person in the shower from hearing anything but running water.

When I got out of the shower and went back upstairs, I looked out the window. Jeff's car was gone.

Darn the kid! He'd sneaked out.

Well, at least he'd been smart about it, had waited until I couldn't hear him. And at least he had gas in his car. I dried my hair and went to bed. I meant to stay awake until Jeff got in, but I was too tired. I was sleeping soundly at two a.m., when Aunt Nettie shook me awake.

"Lee! Lee!"

I sat upright. "What's wrong?"

"Mercy Woodyard just called. She says there's a big commotion down at the shop. She sounded really upset."

I jumped out of bed and ran across the hall. I gave a cursory knock at Jeff's door, but I wasn't surprised when he didn't answer. I threw the door open and turned on the overhead light. The bed hadn't been slept in.

"Where's Jeff?" Aunt Nettie said.

"I don't know," I said, "but I'll be dressed in a minute."

Aunt Nettie dressed even faster than I did, and we were at the shop inside of ten minutes. Mercy had been right; there was a big commotion. As we drove down Fifth Street, I saw flashing lights in the alley and spotted a Michigan State Police car back there. When we turned onto Peach, all three of Warner Pier's patrol cars were parked facing the shop. I parked at the end of the block, and Aunt Nettie and I ran toward the lights. Joe loomed up before we got there.

"What's happened?" I said. "Another break-in?"

"No, I don't think anybody got inside."

"Then what?"

Joe gestured at the nearest patrol car, and I saw a figure huddled in the backseat.

Jeff.

I gasped and stepped toward the car, but Aunt Nettie caught my arm. She pointed toward the door of the shop.

"What's that?" she said.

In the headlights I saw a heap of something emerald green piled on the sidewalk in front of the TenHuis Chocolade window. Nestled against it was a patch of something reddish, or maybe brownish. For a moment I thought of a red squirrel. Then the brilliant green became an object I recognized, and so did the patch of red. I was seeing Gail Hess's frankly fake hair and her bright green jacket.

"Oh, no!" I said. "What's happened?"

"Gail is dead," Joe said grimly. "And Mom found Jeff standing over her body."

Chapter 9

My stomach hit my feet with a thud. What was going on? Was Jeff under arrest?

I went to the patrol car and tried to open the door to the backseat. It wouldn't open, so I opened the door to the front seat, opposite the driver.

Jerry Cherry was behind the wheel. He turned and gaped at me. "Lee!" he said. "You can't get in."

"What is Jeff doing in a police car?" I said.

"We're trying to preserve evidence," Jerry said. "And the chief wants to question him."

"Is he under arrest?"

Jerry shook his head. "No. We want some lab work on his clothes and his hands."

Jeff looked miserable. He held up his hands, and I saw that they were stained. The light inside the car wasn't good, but the stains looked like blood.

"Does he need a lawyer?"

Jeff spoke. "I haven't done anything! I don't need a lawyer!"

I stood there, half in and half out of the patrol car, dithering. In spite of what Jeff said, I thought he might well need a lawyer. But that was not a realistic thing to want in the middle of the night in Warner Pier, Michigan. The nearest lawyer was at the county seat, thirty miles away.

Unless Joe . . . I glanced at him. Joe was a lawyer, true. He wasn't practicing, although as far as I knew he was still licensed in the state of Michigan. But his mom had discovered Jeff standing over Gail Hess's body, apparently with blood on his hands. Besides, Joe had been down on Jeff ever since he arrived in town. He wasn't the right person to involve.

Hart VanHorn was also a lawyer. I doubted that his fancy law firm practiced criminal law. He might recommend someone, but I couldn't call him in the middle of the night.

No, if Jeff needed help and advice right this minute, he might have to rely on his ex-stepmother. So I'd better figure out what was going on.

"Lee," Jerry Cherry said, "either get in or get out. The chief took Jeff's jacket, and I'm trying to keep the car warm."

"I'll be back," I said to Jeff. Then I slammed the door.

Joe was standing behind me. I grabbed his arm. "Okay," I said. "What happened?"

"I haven't the slightest idea, Lee."

"How did you get involved?"

"I got back from Grand Rapids about twelve, and about one thirty Mom called me from her cell phone. She said she'd found Gail dead on the sidewalk. She sounded scared to death. I came right down. Maybe you'd better get the story from her."

He took my arm and led me across the street to Mercy's office. She unlocked the door as we approached, then locked it again as soon as we were inside. Only one dim light was on in the office, and Mercy looked pinched and scared.

I reminded myself to act sympathetic. "Mercy, what a terrible experience! What happened?"

"I'd been working late—in the back room, sorting some things. . . ." Mercy's eyes dodged away from mine. "When I started to leave, by the alley, sometime after one, I saw headlights down there by your aunt's shop. After the burglary last night, well, I thought I'd turn down and see what was going on."

I nodded. "Then what happened?"

"When I got around the corner I saw that Jeff's SUV was parked facing the shop. And I could see Jeff leaning over something on the sidewalk. When I pulled in beside his car—well, he took off running, Lee."

"He ran? Ran where?"

"Just down to the corner, I guess. He didn't have anything on his head, and I'd seen him with Nettie yesterday afternoon, so I recognized him. I put the window partway down and yelled. Then he came back, and he told me he'd just found Gail lying on the sidewalk and asked me to use my cell phone to call 911."

"Did you look at Gail?"

"After I made the call." Mercy's teeth chattered. "There wasn't much point in calling the EMTs. But they came anyway, of course."

"When I saw Jeff—there in the patrol car—he seemed to have blood on his hands."

Mercy nodded. "I saw it."

"How did Gail die?"

Mercy put a hand to her lips and shook her head. Joe put one arm around her shoulders, then answered my question. "The medical examiner hasn't looked at her yet, Lee," he said.

I snapped at him. "Don't talk like a lawyer! Did you see her?"

"Not close," Joe said. "But her head—well, her head had been bleeding. Her hair was soaked, and there was a puddle on the ground."

"Then Jeff could have gotten blood on himself if he—oh, tried to see if she was still alive."

"Sure, he could have." Joe's voice was artificially encouraging.

"Jeff said he hasn't done anything."

Mercy spoke then. "I certainly didn't see him do—" she repeated the word—"*do* anything. But, Lee, why was he down here in the middle of the night?"

That was the question, of course. It was the question Jeff had refused to answer the day before.

The three of us stood silently, looking out through the broad front window of Mercy's office. The scene was busy. Warner Pier policemen and Michigan State Police were looking for evidence up and down the street. More merchants had turned up, afraid the previous night's burglar had hit their businesses.

As we watched, Aunt Nettie came across the sidewalk. Mercy opened the door and let her in, then locked the door again behind her.

Aunt Nettie looked like the Snow Queen, with her solid body covered by a blue ski jacket and her soft white hair peeking out like fur around the edges of her blue cap.

She spoke placidly. "The door to Gail's shop is open. The heat's all getting out. Maybe I should go and close it."

"No!" Joe and I spoke together.

"Better leave it to the police," he said. "It may be a clue."

"Oh," Aunt Nettie said. "I thought the police must have opened it. But why don't they take Gail away?"

"I think they want to get some pictures first," Joe said. "Was Gail a close friend of yours?"

"Not real close. But all the Warner Pier merchants know each other." She gestured toward Jerry Cherry's patrol car. "Why do they have Jeff in there?"

"He found Gail Hess," Joe said. "He'll have to explain why he was down here."

Aunt Nettie nodded. "Two nights in a row," she said.

Why had Jeff been roaming around Warner Pier—a town with nothing open after midnight, a town where he knew no one except me and Aunt Nettie—in the middle of the night, two bitterly cold winter nights in a row?

The night before I'd been afraid he was trying to buy drugs. Now I'd be relieved if that was the reason.

"We'll just have to wait until Chief Jones talks to him," I said. "He's got to have some kind of a story. Maybe they'll let him go then."

But Jeff's story, when he finally told it, wasn't the kind that cleared him of all suspicion.

Chief Jones had asked to keep Jeff's SUV until the state police lab technicians had had time to check it over. I brought Jeff a change of clothes, and he washed up and changed. His first outfit was bagged as potential evidence.

I insisted that Aunt Nettie go home and stay home. Then I waited at the police station. Joe waited with me. He didn't seem to be worried about it starting gossip.

It was after six a.m. before the chief called me into his office and let me listen to a tape recording he'd made of his interview with Jeff.

He had simply been driving around in the middle of the night, Jeff said. He'd seen something lying on the sidewalk in front of TenHuis Chocolade, so he'd stopped to see what it was. He had realized it was a person, lying on the frozen sidewalk, so he jumped out of his car to see what he could do to help.

"But as soon as I touched her, I knew it wasn't any good," he said. "I was going to go call the police when Mrs. Woodyard drove up. She said she had a cell phone, so I got her to call."

"Why did you run when she called out to you?"

"At first I thought she was the killer! I thought he'd come back to get me! But when I got a look at her—" Jeff's voice cut off quickly.

"Then what, Jeff?" The chief's voice was silky.

"Nothing."

"You hadn't met Mrs. Woodyard, had you?"

"I'd seen her. Across the street. Mrs. TenHuis told me who she was."

"But you still ran when she called out."

"She scared me! It was the middle of the night. I'd just found a dead body."

"Okay, it made sense for you to be scared when somebody yelled at you. So, why did you come back?"

"Huh?"

"First you thought Mrs. Woodyard might be the killer, returning to get you, too. So you ran. Then you saw Mrs. Woodyard and you changed your mind and came back. Why?"

"Her coat was wrong."

"Her coat?"

"Yeah. The guy I saw earlier—" Jeff stopped abruptly.

"There was someone there earlier?"

Long silence. "Well, I drove by once, and I saw somebody outside the shop. That's why I came back to check."

"So you found Gail the second time you came by the shop?"

"Yes."

"And when was the first time, Jeff?"

"A little while earlier."

"How long is 'a little while' in Texas?"

Another long silence. "Maybe fifteen minutes."

"Then you did more than just drive around the block." No answer. "So you saw a guy there, and you were sure he wasn't Mrs. Woodyard. Were you sure it was a man?"

"No. It could have been a woman."

"Did you see the person's face?"

"No. It was just a shape. But it wasn't Mrs. Woodyard. Her coat was wrong."

"Wrong? What's wrong with her coat?"

"It's a coat—you know, long. And it's smooth. Some kind of wool. The other guy had a bushy jacket on. Shorter than Mrs. Woodyard's coat. And a bushy hat."

And that, basically, was all Chief Jones got out of Jeff. He'd been driving around Warner Pier in the middle of the night, and he'd seen somebody in front of the shop. He drove on. But about fifteen minutes later he got curious and came down to see what was going on. And he found Gail Hess dead.

"What does he mean by 'bushy'? What kind of a coat is 'bushy'?" I asked.

"He's a bit vague," Chief Jones said. "It was bulky, and it wasn't smooth. Not like Mercy's coat."

"Flannel," I said. "Mercy's coat is flannel."

"This guy's coat wasn't flannel. And it wasn't slick and bulky, like that down jacket you're wearing. It could have been a blanket-type fabric, I guess."

"Or a fake fur," I said. I steeled myself and tried a finesse. "Now you've heard Jeff's exploration—I mean, you've heard his explanation. So, can I take him home?"

" 'Fraid not, Lee. A little more information is required."

"Chief, his story makes sense."

"Yes, as far as it goes. But he doesn't have any explanation for one important thing."

"What's that?"

"The baseball bat we found poked into the snowdrift at the end of the block. Right there at the corner Jeff ran up to."

"A baseball bat?"

"Yep. We haven't tested it yet, of course, but it sure looks as if it could be the murder weapon."

"Where would Jeff get a baseball bat?"

"In Gail's shop. It's an antique, endorsed by Jackie Robinson. Quite a collector's item, I expect. Gail's assistant tells us it was part of a display of toys and sporting equipment at the back of the store. And the door to Gail's shop was standing open. We figure Gail and her killer had some kind of confrontation in her shop. She was chased across the street and killed. Or Gail might have seen someone across the street and stepped outside to hail them. Maybe she took the baseball bat as some sort of protection."

"Why did she have her jacket on?"

Chief Jones shrugged. "Who knows? She might have simply put the jacket on because the heat was turned down in the store, and she was cold."

The chief let me say good-bye to Jeff, and I assured him that I'd get him a lawyer first thing the next morning. He nodded dully. His tough exterior had worn pretty thin.

When I reached the outer office, Joe was standing there, staring at a map of Warner Pier.

"They're going to hold him," I said. I sat down in one of the plastic chairs they keep for visitors and cried.

For a minute I thought Joe was going to put his arms around me, but instead he pulled a chair around facing me. He took one of my hands.

"I've got to find him a lawyer," I said.

"I'll call Webb Bartlett in Grand Rapids just as soon as his office opens. He's good."

I felt grateful. "Tell him Jeff's dad has plenty of money. Tell him he'll pay any kind of a fee."

Joe squeezed my hand. "If I tell him that, he'll charge any kind of a fee."

"I don't care! I can't believe Jeff did this. He's just a kid!"

Joe's lips tightened. I remembered then that he'd been on the defense team for the Medichino case—a case in which two Detroit brothers admitted to killing their parents. He knew that kids can kill.

But he didn't say anything about the Medichino boys. He just pulled me to my feet. "Come over here and look at what I found," he said. He led me to a giant map of Warner Pier. "Now where did you first find Jeff last night? I mean, night before last, the night of the burglary?"

"At the Stop and Shop."

"Didn't you say his car was parked outside, but you couldn't see him inside?"

"Yes."

"And then he came out from the back of the store?"

"Right. So what?"

"Look at the map." Joe pointed to the top of the map. "Here's the Stop and Shop. And look at what's behind it, over on the next block."

"The Lake Michigan Inn. Again, so what?"

"Do you feel up to taking a ride out that way?"

"I don't think I could sleep."

I put on my jacket, and Joe and I went out to his truck. "Why are we doing this?" I asked.

"Maybe for no reason at all."

Despite its picturesque name, the Lake Michigan Inn is a fairly standard motel. It looks like the 1950s to me; cars with big tail fins would look right at home in the parking lot. That morning the parking lot was almost empty. An SUV was parked in a shed at the back of the lot, and all the rooms were dark. The only lights came from the motel's sign and from a light over the office door.

Joe parked under the office light—the winter sun was nowhere near the horizon, but the sky was growing light in the east—and we got out. Joe knocked on the office door. He knocked again. And again.

Finally the door opened and a bleary-eyed older man peered out. "Joe? What's going on?" He looked at me, then grinned slyly. "Don't tell me you want to rent a room?"

"Nope. But I've got an important question."

"It better be damn important and not hard to answer." When he spoke I saw that he didn't have his lower plate in. He motioned us inside.

"Lee, this is Tuttle Ewing," Joe said. "Tuttle, Lee McKinney."

Tuttle Ewing was a short bald guy. "How'ja do," he said. "You're Nettie Ten-Huis's niece." I nodded, and he turned back to Joe. "Wha'ja need to know?"

"Lee's stepson came to Warner Pier day before yesterday, and I wondered if he checked in here."

I almost gasped. Jeff hadn't checked in anyplace.

"Young guy? Kinda skinny? Glasses? Stud in his lip? Crazy earlobes?"

"Right. Driving a Lexus RX300 with a Texas tag."

"Yeah, he came by."

"Did you rent him a room?"

"Yeah. He paid for three nights. Off-season rate. Funny thing though. I haven't seen the SUV since."

"Is there somebody in the room?"

"I dunno. The Do Not Disturb sign has been on the door ever since he checked in. So Maria—I've only got one maid, part-time, in the winter—she and I haven't disturbed him."

Joe and I exchanged looks. "I think we'd better disturb him now," Joe said. I nodded.

"I can't let you in the room."

"Just tell us which room it is."

"Twenty-three. Out back."

Tuttle Ewing let us out, and Joe and I walked along the covered sidewalk, toward the back of the motel.

"This makes perfect sense!" I said. "Plus, it explains the second car with the Texas tag. I should have realized that Jeff wouldn't have left college and come up here alone. He had some buddy with him, and he's been sneaking into town to see him."

"You knock at the door," Joe said. "Whoever's in there, a woman will seem less threatening. I'll wait down here." He positioned himself ten or twelve feet away, flat against the wall.

I had to knock several times before I even heard a movement inside. The door still didn't open. I pictured a scared kid standing on the other side.

"Hey!" I said loudly. "Jeff's in trouble. He needs help!"

Finally, the door opened a crack and one eye looked out.

"What is it?" The voice was a whisper.

"I'm Jeff's stepmom. Jeff's in trouble. I need to talk to you."

"Did he tell you about me?"

"It's a long story, and I'm freezing out here. Let me in, okay?"

The door closed, and I heard the clicking of the chain. When the door opened again, Joe suddenly appeared beside me. He pushed the door open wide, and we both were inside.

My impression was that we had startled a bird from its nest. Something white flitted around the room.

"It's all right," I said. "We won't hurt you. We're just trying to help Jeff."

The white figure fluttered to a stop behind the bed. A high-pitched voice spoke. "What's happened? Where's Jeff? Did he tell you about me?"

The words came from a little bit of a girl. Her hair was tousled and her eyes swollen, but there was no missing one thing about her. She was a beauty.

CHOCOLATE CHAT
EYES LIKE CHOCOLATE

Although Janet Evanovich's Stephanie Plum books are not culinary crimes, they rely on food for atmosphere.

Early in the first book, when she describes Joe Morelli, one of the major series characters, we know immediately that he's a sexy guy.

"He'd grown up big and bad, with eyes like black fire one minute and melt-in-your-mouth chocolate the next," she writes.

Somehow we're not surprised a few paragraphs later, when Joe wanders into the Tasty Pastry Bakery, where the sixteen-year-old Stephanie worked, and buys—what else?—a chocolate chip cannoli. Later, "on the floor of the Tasty Pastry, behind the case filled with chocolate eclairs . . ."

Ah, that Joe, with those irresistible melt-in-your-mouth chocolate eyes. A girl doesn't have a chance.

Chapter 10

The girl was standing on the floor, of course, but she was so fluttery that she almost gave the impression she was perched on the headboard of the bed.

"Who are y'all?" she said in a chirpy little voice.

"We don't intend to hurt you," I said. "We're trying to help Jeff."

"He promised he wouldn't tell anybody I was here."

"He didn't. We figured it out. Who are you?"

The question seemed to be too hard for her to answer. She twisted her wings—I mean her hands—stood on one foot and lowered her lashes. Maybe it was just her tousled hair that made her look so birdlike, I decided. That and her size. She was tiny, with small, delicate features. She was wearing a white T-shirt, and the effect was of a cute little bird, maybe one of those Easter chickies. Then she moved, and I amended the impression. She looked like a cute little chickie with a cute little bosom.

Her short, spiky hair and the lashes against her cheeks were almost black. She had that fine-grained, pink and ivory skin that I personally would kill for. In fact, when I was sixteen and felt like a giraffe, I'd have killed to look exactly like her.

Finally the girl spoke. "I'm Tess Riley."

"You came up here with Jeff?"

"Well, sort of. Jeff met me in Chicago." She fluttered her eyelashes, then looked at us with bright black eyes. "Where is Jeff?"

I looked at Joe, wondering what I should tell her.

Joe didn't hesitate. "Jeff's in jail," he said.

"In jail!"

"Yeah. He may be charged with murder."

"Murder! Jeff would never kill anyone." Then the dark eyes grew wide. "Oh, no! He didn't!" She pressed her hands over her mouth.

"We're hoping you can alibi him," Joe said.

"Oh, yes! Anything I can do. Jeff was with me."

"Oh?" Joe said. "He was with you about eight p.m. last night?"

I drew a breath and looked at him. Joe touched my arm in what was obviously a signal for me to keep quiet.

Tess didn't hesitate. "Eight o'clock? Oh, yes! Jeff was here then."

I almost groaned. She not only looked like a bird, she apparently thought like one. Just what we needed. A dippy little cuckoo who was willing to lie for Jeff.

She was warming to her theme now. "Right. Jeff came here a little before eight, and he brought me something to eat."

She gestured, and I saw one of Aunt Nettie's refrigerator dishes on the desk. Jeff had brought her the leftover sloppy joe. Joe and I looked at each other, but neither of us spoke.

Tess went on. "We watched television, and then we went out for a drive. Then we came back here. Jeff stayed until after midnight."

"But he came before eight o'clock?" Joe said.

"Oh, yes! I'm sure he was here by then."

"That's really funny," I said. "Since at my house Jeff was helping me with the dinner dishes at eight o'clock."

"Oh!"

"Why don't we all sit down," Joe said. "Tess, are you hungry? Lee? We could go out to breakfast. Maybe we could get acquainted a little. Then Tess might trust us enough to tell the truth."

"Oh, I wouldn't lie."

"You just did," Joe said.

"You tricked me!" Tess perched on the edge of the bed and did the eyelash thing again. "When does Jeff need an alibi for?"

"I don't think we'd better tell you, Tess. If you feel sure that Jeff would never kill anyone . . ."

"Oh, I do. Jeff would never commit murder."

"In that case, all Jeff needs is the truth. He's obviously trying to keep you out of the situation. Why?"

"Because he's really a nice guy."

I was beginning to get a little impatient with Chicky Tess. "Jeff may be a nice guy," I said, "but most nice girls don't hide out in motels. Why is Jeff trying to keep you out of sight? Why didn't he just bring you out to my aunt's house?"

"He wanted to."

"Why didn't he?"

"I was afraid."

"Of us?"

"Oh, no! Not of you. Of . . . of . . ." She wasn't a very good liar. I could see the improvisation flitting around in her head. "I was afraid of . . ."

"Forget it!" Joe's voice was harsh. "We'll just call the police to come and get you."

"No! Then he'll find me!"

"Who?"

"My family! And if they find me, then . . ."

"Then what? What would happen?"

"If they find me, my dad's boss will find out, and then the police will think they know why Jeff might want to kill a guy!"

Kill a guy? That stopped me, and it seemed to stop Joe, too. Neither of us said anything, but we looked at each other.

It was beginning to sound as if Tess thought Jeff really might have killed someone. But she expected it to be a male person—a "guy." And you could call Gail Hess a lot of things, but no Texas girl would ever call her a guy.

Joe rephrased the question a couple of times, but Tess quit talking. Finally he sighed. "Look. Tess. You obviously don't know anything about the crime Jeff is suspected of committing. If you'll just talk to the police chief, then you may be able to straighten everything out. But you've got to tell the truth. You can help Jeff the most if you tell the truth."

"But I can't. . . ."

Joe went on. "Frankly, you're not a very good liar, and you'll get tripped up right away. So get dressed, and we'll take you over to the police station."

"The police station!"

"Yes. If you tell a straight story, maybe we'll get to take Jeff home."

"Yes. Come on," I said. "If you really want to help Jeff—"

"Oh, I do!"

"Then get dressed."

Joe moved toward the door. "I'll wait outside."

Tess gathered up an armful of clothes and disappeared into the bathroom. I sat down in the one chair. Obviously Joe was right not to question Tess further. She was willing to say anything, and she wasn't bright enough to tell a good lie. She'd sound coached if we talked to her too much before Chief Jones did.

I laid my head back in the chair and realized that I was tired right through to the bone. I had almost dozed off when I heard Tess give a yelp. Then I heard a sliding noise. In two leaps I was at the bathroom door.

"What's wrong?" I said.

"Nothing! Nothing!" Tess sounded like something had happened, but she didn't explain. I heard the sliding noise again. Then the door opened. Tess came out, pouting. Behind her I saw a window, the kind with clouded glass to keep people from looking in. It had been raised about an inch.

I almost laughed. The temperature in west Michigan that February morning was about fifteen. Nobody in their right mind was going to be opening a bathroom window for a little ventilation. Tess had obviously tried to open it with the idea of crawling out. I went into the bathroom and looked out through the crack. There was a storm window, of course, and the light outside was dim, but I could plainly see Joe standing about twenty feet away, with his back to the window. He'd been way ahead of me in anticipating that our birdbrained little Tess might try to flit.

Tess had put on an SMU sweatshirt and a pair of jeans that couldn't have been bigger than size three. She was wearing socks and tennis shoes.

"Why don't you pack up your stuff, Tess," I said. "You can move out to the house."

"I don't want to impose on you."

"Do you have any money?"

"Not a lot."

"Jeff says he doesn't have any either. And I can't afford motel rooms. If you don't want to contact your parents, I don't think you have a lot of choices. I assure you my aunt is perfectly respectable, and now that we know you exist, she'll worry a lot more about you being in a motel than being in her spare bedroom."

Tess didn't look convinced, but she put her few belongings into a backpack—she obviously hadn't been any more prepared for a long trip than Jeff had—and gathered makeup and toothbrush out of the bathroom. When she got to the stage of putting on her jacket, I went to the bathroom window, pushed it up, and looked out. Joe was still there. I rapped on the storm window, and he turned around. I waved, and he made a circular motion, pantomiming coming around the building. He was there by the time Tess and I got her stuff into the floor of the truck's cab.

"I told the manager you were checking out," he said.

Tess fluttered her eyelashes. "You're not really going to take me to the police chief, are you?"

"Not on an empty stomach," Joe said. "The Stop and Shop should have some fresh doughnuts by now."

Tess refused a doughnut, and she pouted all the way to the police station. She hung on to my arm, looking terrified, after we got out of the truck. She was so short I felt as if I were dragging her along.

Chief Jones was coming out as we approached the door.

"Hi, Chief," I said. "We found out why Jeff kept coming into town in the middle of the night."

"Well, well." The chief looked Tess over. "I was gonna call all the motels after I had breakfast. I figured Jeff wasn't coming in to admire the quaint Victorian decor."

Tess cast imploring looks at us, but the chief escorted her into his office and left Joe and me in the outer room. I called Aunt Nettie to tell her the latest development.

"I should have known enough about human nature to figure that out," she said. "I'll change Jeff's bed. He'll have to sleep on the cot in the little room."

"I just hope he gets out of jail," I said.

I told Joe to go home, but he said he'd stick around.

"Thanks," I said.

He shrugged.

I sat down on a plastic chair, and I guess I fell asleep, because the next thing I knew Joe tapped me on the shoulder, and I opened my eyes and saw the chief coming out of his office. He motioned for Joe and me to come in. Tess was huddled in a chair. The four of us filled up the little office.

"Now, Miss Riley, I'm going to paraphrase your story," he said. "You correct me if I'm wrong."

Tess looked at him adoringly and nodded. He smiled back. She'd found somebody who was susceptible to eyelashes. Good for her.

The story the chief told us was incomplete. Tess said she was from Tyler, Texas, and that she was a freshman at SMU. She had left her dorm room five days earlier and had driven north from Dallas. She had not really explained why she had taken a notion to do this.

When she got to Chicago, she'd seen she was going to run out of money pretty quick. So she called Jeff—"He's a good friend," she said when the chief got to that part of the story—and asked him to wire her money. Instead, Jeff got in his car and drove to Chicago to meet her. But Jeff hadn't had any money either. So early in the morning two days earlier they had headed for Michigan, apparently because Jeff thought I'd be a soft touch.

"So," I said, "you were the person in the second car with the Texas plates." I'd figured that out, of course, but I wanted to confirm it.

"Yes, I was," Tess said. She looked at the chief and fluttered her eyelashes. "Jeff said you'd towed my car."

"It's in the lot out back."

"I guess I can pick it up now."

"The gas tank is still close to empty," Chief Jones said. He continued her story.

When Tess and Jeff got to Warner Pier, Jeff rented a motel room, using almost the last of their pooled money, then went out to Aunt Nettie's house, where he was discovered by Joe before he fell in the window over the stairwell. Jeff had sneaked into town that evening and the next to see her.

"Tess says that Jeff was with her from eleven p.m. until around one thirty last night," the chief said. Tess nodded eagerly. "She was tired of being cooped up in the motel room, so they went out for a ride a little after one o'clock. After about fifteen minutes, Jeff suddenly said she had to go back to the motel, because he'd seen something he had to check up on."

"The person in front of the shop," I said.

"Maybe. But Jeff didn't tell her that. So her story substantiates Jeff's, sorta, but it's not really an alibi."

"Still, her presence in Warner Pier explains a few things," Joe said. "Now we know why Jeff was sneaking into town in the middle of the night. That fills the biggest gap in his story. Can you let him go?"

Chief Jones looked more Lincolnesque than ever. "Well, I'd like to wait until we see what the medical examiner says. And whether or not there are any fingerprints on that bat."

I started to speak, then remembered that Joe was the lawyer.

"We couldn't really expect any fingerprints when the temperatures are down in the twenties," Joe said. "Unless the murderer was too macho for mittens. And the medical examiner isn't going to be real specific about a time of death. After all, even when I got to the scene, Gail had only been dead a little while. Jeff must have stumbled across her body very soon after she died."

"I'm still going to hold on to him until I can run a couple of checks," the chief said.

Tess fluttered her eyelashes again. "What kind of checks?"

Joe spoke before the chief could. "He's probably going to see if Texas— or anyplace else—has outstanding warrants for you or Jeff. So if there's anything you want to tell us, now's the time."

Tess sighed and leaned back in her chair. "No, that's okay."

Tess asked to see Jeff, but the chief told her to come back later. Tess produced her car keys, and the chief escorted us out to the City Hall parking lot, where Tess's car occupied a corner. Joe brought Tess's backpack around from his truck, and I began to give Tess directions to Aunt Nettie's. "We'll stop at the Shell station, and I'll buy you some gas," I said.

But Tess wasn't paying any attention to me. She was staring at her car.

"What's wrong?" I said.

Tess pointed. "My taillight. How did it get broken?"

Chapter 11

I stared at the broken taillight, trying not to panic. It was the left one, like on the car Jeff and I had seen. Would Chief Jones think that Tess had been in the car that sped away after the burglary? Would he think Jeff had tried to cover up her connection with the crime?

I tried frantically to picture the car Jeff and I had seen. I simply didn't care enough about cars to remember it. My dad was an auto mechanic, so you'd think I would have been raised knowing one taillight from another, but Rich's view of cars solely as status symbols had made me lose interest in the whole subject. If a vehicle moved when I pressed the accelerator, that was all I asked.

Tess's car was an inexpensive Ford. But Jeff had said the fleeing car had been some sort of sports car. Had he recognized it as a sports car? Or had he simply been leading us astray?

Joe and Chief Jones had also been staring at the broken taillight; and it was Tess who spoke first. "I certainly hope the city of Warner Pier will pay for that light," she said. "Those things are expensive to replace, and I'll get a ticket if I drive without it."

I bent over to look more closely, and both Chief Jones and Joe knelt behind the car.

"You won't be driving it for a few days," Chief Jones said. He and Joe looked at the snow under the rear of the car.

"Maybe you could scoop the snow up and melt it down," Joe said. "See what you find."

"It had to happen here," the Chief said. "We were looking all over for broken taillights. If we'd found an abandoned car with one, we'd have noticed. Besides, if one of my guys puts a car in the lot without making a note of anything that's wrong with it, I'll have his uniform. There was nothing on the record sheet."

"What are they talking about?" Tess said to me.

"They're saying the light wasn't broken when the car was towed in."

It made sense. If the police impounded a car, they'd be responsible for its condition when it was picked up by the owner. They couldn't leave themselves open to the kind of demands that Tess had just made, that they pay for damage that occurred while the car was in their lot.

The chief stood up. "Guess I'd better ask around, find out if anybody unusual was seen in the city lot."

"But who's going to take care of getting this fixed?" Tess said. "If it was all right when it was towed in . . ."

"For the moment, we're going to keep the car, get the crime lab to look at it," the chief said. "We'll try to find out just what happened."

"I haven't got the money to repair it," Tess said. "And my dad doesn't either." Her face was all screwed up. Tess obviously didn't come from a wealthy family. Jeff would have shrugged off the damage.

"Come on, Tess," I said. "We'll worry about getting the taillight fixed after Chief Jones investigates. Right now we're heading for the house. I've got the wonderful job of trying to track down Jeff's dad."

"Oh, no! You can't call him. He mustn't find out I'm here."

I sighed. "Come on," I said.

Joe handed Tess her backpack. He grinned at me, I guess because I was the one stuck with Tess and he wasn't. "I'll call Webb Bartlett," he said. "His office ought to be open by nine."

"Who's Webb Bartlett?" Tess was still pouting.

I started shoving her toward my van, parked around the corner. "Webb Bartlett is the lawyer Joe is going to call and ask to represent Jeff. That's why I have to get hold of Jeff's dad."

"But I can't let anybody know where I am."

"Jeff needs a lawyer," I said. "His dad is going to have to pay the bill."

"But surely there's some way . . ."

"Look, Tess! Jeff may be accused of a very serious crime. I may feel sure he didn't commit it, and you may feel sure he didn't commit it. But that doesn't count. If he doesn't have the right legal representation, he may go to prison for years!"

"But I can't let anybody know where I am!"

At that I lost what temper I had left. "Oh, yes, you can! You can quit running away like a little kid. You can tell me why you and Jeff left college and came up here. You can tell me—and Chief Jones—why you were hiding out in that motel, why Jeff wouldn't tell us you were with him. Why you abandoned your car in the parking lot of a grocery store."

"No! No, I can't!"

"Okay! Don't tell us. Stand around saving your cute little butt and let Jeff be convicted of murder!"

"Murder?" Tess gave a sob, and when she spoke her voice was just a whisper. "Murder is what we were trying to avoid."

I stared at her, and she stared back, and suddenly I was cold clear through. And only part of it was because it was dawn on a winter day in Michigan.

What had Tess meant? Murder was what she and Jeff had been trying to avoid? I wasn't sure I wanted to know, but I asked her. All she did was cry.

Tess had scared me into regaining control of my temper, and I was able to talk more calmly. "Let's go out to Aunt Nettie's. Maybe she can inject a little common sense into the situation."

We walked around the corner and got into the van, and I started the motor. "I'm exhausted," I said. "Whatever you and Jeff and the Warner Pier burglar are up to, it's sure kept me from sleeping the last couple of nights."

I started to pull out from the curb, but lights flashed in my rearview mirror, and I stopped to let a car pass. It didn't pass. It stopped, blocking me. Its door opened, and the driver jumped out. "Lee!" he yelled. "Lee!" He ran around the front of the car—it was a big Lincoln—and I saw the shock of beautiful hair. It was Hart VanHorn.

I rolled my window down. "Hart?"

"I hoped that was you. I saw the Dallas Cowboys sticker on the van yesterday."

"It's me. My dad put the sticker on, so I wouldn't forget my origins. What can I do for you?"

"A reporter I know called to find out if I'd heard anything about a murder here in Warner Pier."

"Oh, it's a regular mess," I said. "And it looks like my stepson is in the middle of it—I don't mean he did it! But he found the body, and the police are holding him."

"That's what Mike Herrera said."

"Mike Herrera? How'd he get involved?"

"As the mayor of Warner Pier, he knows most things that go on around here. So I called him."

I should have figured it out without asking. Hart VanHorn was important; a state legislator and a possible candidate for Congress. That meant he would have lots of contacts. He could probably find out anything about anybody in the entire state of Michigan with one phone call.

"Mike said the victim was Gail Hess," Hart said. "That's why Mom and I came down to find out what's going on."

"I'm sorry to say I haven't given poor Gail a thought," I said. "I've been too worried about Jeff."

"Does he need a lawyer? I could call—well, nobody in my old firm handles criminal matters, but I know people who do."

"Joe Woodyard was here—his mom was the second person on the scene. Joe said he knew somebody. Webb Bartlett?"

"Webb's a good choice." A smile flickered over Hart's face. "Joe and Webb were a year behind me in law school. Joe knows a lot more about defense attorneys than I do."

Neither of us needed to go into the reasons Joe knew a lot about defense attorneys. But Hart had brought up another point.

"Did you say a reporter called you?"

"That's right. A political reporter from the *Chicago Tribune*."

"Chicago! Oh, no!"

"He's a nice guy. We've dealt with each other before. Why does that upset you?"

"Because Chicago is a long way from the *Warner Pier Gazette*. That means the reporter got a tip. And that means somebody from Warner Pier called him. Or called somebody."

"So?"

"So, somebody around here is still in contact with the reporters—maybe the tabloid reporters—who had such a great time in Warner Pier when Clementine Ripley was killed."

"Not good."

"No." I dropped my voice. "Listen, Hart, let's forget that pizza for now."

"But I'm not afraid for the press to know I have a date with an attractive—"

"That's very chivalrous, but this is not the time."

Hart looked as if he were going to argue, but before he said anything someone else spoke. "Hart? Were you able to find out anything?"

Hart moved, and for the first time I realized that his mother was in the car behind him.

"Oh! Mrs. VanHorn," I said. "It's a real mess."

She raised her well-bred eyebrows. "Is it true that Gail Hess has been killed?"

"I'm afraid so." As Olivia and I peered at each other through our car windows, Hart stood in the street between us and Tess huddled in the seat beside mine. I sketched what I knew about the situation, worked in a casual introduction of Tess, identifying her as a friend of Jeff's, and described the discovery of Gail's body.

Olivia frowned. "This is very shocking."

"It's certainly shocking for Warner Pier," I said. "Frankly, once the tourists go home, we have almost no crime. But after the wild events of last summer"—Olivia nodded to indicate that she remembered the murder of Clementine Ripley—"this could turn into another invasion of the tabloid press."

"Yes, Mother." Hart's voice sounded mocking. "It could mean a big scandal."

Olivia shot him what—in a less-refined woman—could have been a dirty look. "I didn't know Gail very well," she said. "Had she mentioned any personal situation that might be linked to this? Any quarrels? Any threats? Family problems?"

"Family problems are the most frequent cause of murder," Hart said. "That and psychological problems." He almost sounded amused.

Was I imagining the mockery in his voice? I glanced at him, but his face was bland. "Gail hadn't said anything to me," I said. "I had only seen her a few times recently, when she came over to see the display of molds and when she came to pick them up. Then, of course, she came back when she discovered that one of them was missing."

Hart spoke then. "One was missing?"

"Yes. We hadn't realized it at first."

"She called and told me about it," Olivia said. Her voice sounded a little short.

"She and Aunt Nettie searched everywhere," I said. "It was the trained bear in the harness. All we could conclude was that the burglar took it. But we don't know why—it was up on a top shelf. That was the last time I saw Gail. Maybe she did have some personal problem. She seemed to see some big significance in that particular mold being missing. And she seemed fascinated by the sports car Jeff and I saw. Her reaction was really strange. I'm trying to figure it out."

"Strange?" Hart said. "Strange in what way?"

I opened my mouth to describe Gail's triumphant behavior, but Olivia spoke. "Lee and Jeff's friend must be freezing, Hart. We should get home."

I realized that Olivia was right about the temperature. Tess's teeth were chattering. Hart said good-bye; he and his mother drove on, and I pulled out behind them, following them across the Warner River bridge and down Lake Shore Drive, since their house was maybe a quarter of a mile beyond Aunt Nettie's. The taillights of the Lincoln kept going as I turned into the drive.

I escorted Tess inside and introduced her to Aunt Nettie. Aunt Nettie had moved Jeff's things out of the extra room and changed the bed for Tess. She'd tossed Jeff's sheets and towels into the washing machine; it was quite homey to come into the old house and find it smelling of laundry soap, bacon, and coffee. Aunt Nettie was going to have Tess eating out of her hand by lunchtime.

After breakfast I did the dishes, Aunt Nettie went back to bed, and Tess took a shower. By then it was after ten o'clock, which meant it would be after nine a.m. in Dallas. Rich's office would be open. I couldn't put off that phone call any longer. This time I had to explain the entire situation to someone who knew how to get hold of Rich—in Mexico, or wherever he was. Even if it was Miss Brit.

The receptionist with the British accent answered again, and once again she assured me that Rich was unavailable, and that his personal assistant was, too. I took a deep breath, then asked for Alicia Richardson.

"Tell her it's Lee McKinney," I said.

That put a little excitement into Miss Brit's clipped tones. We might not have met, but after my repeated phone calls I was willing to bet she had found out I was Rich's ex. If he was off on a trip with his first wife, having the second one turn up—even on the telephone—was sure to put the office on its ear.

Almost immediately I heard Alicia's soft Texas voice. "Accounting."

"Alicia, it's Lee."

"Lee? Lee McKinney?"

"Right!"

Alicia actually sounded glad to hear from me. She began a flurry of questions. "Where are you, Lee? We heard you'd moved to Michigan."

"I'm fine, Alicia, and I did move to Michigan. And I want to know all about your family. But first, I've got an emergency up here, and I need to find Rich ASAP. Can you help me?"

Alicia's voice became cautious. "Well, Lee, Rich is on a trip to Mexico. And he's deliberately out of contact with the office and—"

"I know he's with Dina, Alicia. I wish them luck."

"Oh." Alicia sounded relieved.

"But Jeff is up here, and he's in bad trouble."

The conversation went on about fifteen minutes. Alicia had worked for Rich for years—she was an old hand when Rich and I got married. She knew all the dirt on him, and she almost ran his business.

"The problem is," Alicia said, "Rich promised Dina he wouldn't be calling the office three times a day, the way he usually does when he leaves town."

"Don't I know!"

Alicia laughed. "And this time he's actually sticking to it."

"He must be serious."

"I think he is, Lee. So he and Dina may be hard to find. But I'll get on the phone and start trying."

"Thanks, Alicia. In the meantime, we're hiring Jeff a lawyer up here. And I'm assuring that lawyer that he'll be paid."

"Right. Rich is still solvent." Alicia hesitated. "And you say Jeff hasn't given you any explanation of why he came to Michigan?"

It was my time to hesitate. Should I tell her about Tess?

I thought of the possibility that Miss Brit was listening in. "Jeff hasn't explained a thing," I said. It wasn't a lie. He hadn't. Joe and I had found Tess without a hint from Jeff.

I asked a couple of questions about Alicia's family, then hung up. When

I turned around, Tess was standing in the doorway that led to the back hall and the bathroom.

"You didn't tell her about me," she said.

"There didn't seem to be any need."

"Thanks." Her voice was calm, and if she blinked back tears, at least she wasn't hysterical.

"Tess, the press is going to get hold of this," I said. "Even if I don't say anything, even if Chief Jones keeps quiet, word is likely to get out. Think about calling your parents later today."

She nodded miserably and went upstairs.

I almost went up, too. But I'd had to pump myself up to call Rich's office. Now that I could go to bed, I discovered I was too wide awake to want to. I decided to walk down to get the newspaper from the delivery box at the end of the drive.

I put on my jacket and went out onto the porch, and I entered a new world. When Tess and I had come home about eight-thirty, the sun had been coming up. The day hadn't looked too promising, but it had been only partially overcast. Now it was snowing and the large flakes were being driven at an angle by the wind. The drive was rapidly being covered. It was mighty cold to a Texas girl.

I paused and looked the situation over, and I almost went back inside. Then I remembered that I was determined not to be a wimpy Texan who was afraid of a little snow, and I zipped up my bright red jacket, pulled my white knitted hat down over my ears, and started down the drive.

Earlier, one of the snowmobile jerks had been cruising around the neighborhood, but now things were silent—silent except for the occasional faint moan of the wind, and the scrunch of my boots as I walked through the fresh snow.

It was cold, true, but it was also pure, somehow. As soon as I was twenty-five or thirty feet down the drive, the house disappeared, hidden by the blowing snow. There was quite a bit of undergrowth in the patch of trees between the house and Lake Shore Drive, so the hundred feet or so that I had to walk became like a hike into the deep forest. The bare limbs of the trees lifted up into an icy fog, and the swirling eddies of snow isolated me. I might as well have been alone in the big woods. I felt that I'd left all my problems back at the house or downtown at the police station. I could have simply walked on into the woods and left the world behind. I might have been the only person left on earth.

Lake Shore Drive, which even in the winter has some traffic, was empty. I crossed to the clump of mailboxes and newspaper delivery boxes, then pulled the rolled newspaper out of the delivery tube. I took the newspaper out of its plastic sack and stuffed the sack in my pocket. Then I simply stood there, enjoying the woods and the snow, the silence, the loneliness, and the loveliness, and wishing I didn't have to return to real life.

A snowmobile's motor started, close to me. Resentfully, I turned toward the sound. And from the drive of the Baileys' summer cottage—a house I knew was empty that time of year—a purple snowmobile came barreling out onto the road.

It headed straight toward me.

Chapter 12

The next thing I knew, I was behind the row of mailboxes.

I will always half believe a guardian angel threw me there, because I have no recollection at all of jumping, sliding, or stepping aside. But suddenly I was behind the mailboxes, and the snowmobile—after almost running over my right snow boot—had gone by me and was disappearing into the blowing snow.

I was furious. I stepped into the road and shook my fist at the snowmobile's driver, a shapeless blob in a furry jacket and a helmet like a black bowling ball. "Hey! Are you nuts?" I yelled loudly, though I knew the rider couldn't hear me over the roar of the engine.

The snowmobile was just a faint outline in the gloom, but I could see it slowing down, and for a moment I thought—maybe a tad self-righteously—that the rider was coming back to apologize.

The snowmobile turned, chewing up the frozen slush alongside Lake Shore Drive with the tractor tread that pushed the thing. It swung back to face me—looking like a giant praying mantis with skis for front legs—then headed right at me again.

I jumped back behind the mailboxes. But the snowmobile had figured that one out. This time it left the road and went behind the mailboxes, heading for my hiding spot.

The driver was trying to kill me.

That realization got my adrenaline in gear. I ducked, curled myself into an egg and scooted under the mailboxes, as close as I could get to the poles that held them up. The snowmobile came right for me. It knocked one mailbox askew, but it missed me by six inches as it went by.

I huddled under the mailboxes. I had to find a better shelter than a few fence posts. I was across the road from Aunt Nettie's house, on the lake side of Lake Shore Drive. All the houses on that side were summer cottages. And in mid-February every one of them was probably locked up as tight as the bank the day after Jesse James left town. Not only were they locked, but they had heavy shutters on the windows.

I could run into the underbrush, but I wouldn't be able to run fast, and I'd risk tripping and breaking my neck. There was no help on that side of the road.

No, I had to get across Lake Shore Drive to the inland side. Aunt Nettie's house was my nearest haven.

The snowmobile had almost disappeared in the swirling snow, but I could see the purple lump turning around again. And if I could see purple, I knew that the rider could see red. I cursed the color of my vivid jacket, but I didn't dare take time to snatch it off.

The snowmobile was coming back—and this time it might simply mow those mailboxes down. I dashed across the road, toward the house. The snowmobile came roaring right after me.

Merely running up the driveway, where I'd be an easy target, was not my plan. I made it across the road six inches ahead of the snowmobile, veered into the woods, pivoted, and jumped behind a large maple tree.

The snowmobile went up Aunt Nettie's drive, then slowed and turned around, coming back. The rider was getting better at those quick turns. The machine lay in wait in the driveway, between me and the house.

For a moment I considered just staying there, clutching my maple, in a standoff situation. But there was no permanent safety in that. I had no way of knowing if the snowmobile rider had a gun, for example. The furry jacket and helmet might disguise some kind of monster; he could get off, catch me with his bare hands, and break my neck.

No, my best bet was to try to get back on the drive, where I could run. But for now I had to stay in the underbrush, where branches and logs on the snow-covered ground would keep the snowmobile from following.

I edged forward, toward a new tree, one that was closer to the drive. But I got too close to the drive, and the snowmobile moved toward me. I leaped back toward a tree, tripped over one of those hidden logs and fell flat on my face.

For a moment I thought I was dead. I rolled into a ball, pulled my arms over my head and got ready to be run over and chewed up by that snowmobile. Its roar grew louder and louder.

Then it was past me. The log that had tripped me had also saved me. I had rolled close to it, and the snowmobile had not been able to pull in near enough to run over me.

I scrambled onto my hands and knees. The house was still a long way off, but I was within a couple of steps of the drive. I got out there and started running.

It was no good. A glance over my shoulder confirmed what my ears told me. The snowmobile was coming back. A giant cedar tree was looming up on my right. Aunt Nettie hated that tree. It followed the usual habit of cedars, so its branches only had needles on the outer edges. The whole interior of the tree was bare and ugly. But right now I thought it looked beautiful. I lowered my head and dived in among the lower branches.

That saved me from the next pass of the snowmobile, but it wasn't a good place to be. I was stuck in there. It was going to be a lot harder to get out than it had been to get in. I tried to spot another tree I could hug, one closer to the house.

In the meantime, the snowmobile was turning around again. The black helmet had a reflective visor that turned the rider into an anonymous force and made the whole apparatus look more like a man-eater than ever.

I crawled out of the cedar and ran into the drive, daring the snowmobile to come toward me. It moved slightly, and I jumped behind another maple on the other side of the lane.

I was still about fifty feet from the house, with at least twenty feet of driveway before the stretch of beach grass Aunt Nettie and I called the lawn. And the snow on that lawn was deep; it would suck at my feet. The lawn might as well be quicksand.

The snowmobile had stopped, its motor still roaring, between me and the house. I jumped forward, but the engine gunned. The snowmobile seemed to be pawing the ground, like a bull waiting to run at the bullfighter. And I jumped back behind my tree like a toreador who forgot his cape.

Rats! The snowmobile was moving toward the house. As I watched, it came to the corner where the trees ended and the beach grass began. There it waited, ready for me to try to cross the cleared area.

Well, I didn't have to do that. Pretty soon Aunt Nettie, no matter how soundly she was sleeping, was going to notice all that roaring in her yard. She'd look out. She'd see what was going on. She'd call the police.

All I had to do was stay put, and the cavalry would arrive. I contemplated that possibility, and I almost began to breathe normally.

But when it came, the cavalry was going to have a hard time catching that snowmobile. Police cars can not go down the footpaths that link the houses in Aunt Nettie's neighborhood, but the snowmobile could. It could speed off into the woods and never be seen again.

Chief Jones was going to be asking me what that snowmobile had looked like. I peeked around my tree. The snow was still swirling, and my pursuer was just a dim shape. The snowmobile's purple looked dull, a sort of eggplant. I could see the skis at the front and the heavy springs that linked them to the body of the snowmobile. Now I made out the slick plastic—fiberglass?—body, the swept-back windshield. And I could see the storm trooper who was riding it. His jacket was some dark color, black or navy, and it had a lot of texture.

The motor gunned again, and the snowmobile moved forward.

It was coming in. Maybe it planned to pin me to my friendly maple. I marked another tree a few feet closer to the house and jumped for it.

I got to that tree, huddled behind it, and put my head around to look at the snowmobile. It went by so close that I could have touched the faceless creature riding it. But he missed me. As he went by I ran closer to the house, to another maple—one tree nearer to safety. I peeked around my tree and decided I had enough time for one more dash.

And that dash took me to the tree closest to the house. Not that I could see the house very well, but this big elm, maybe sixty feet high and eight feet around, was on the edge of the lawn. The lawn was covered with several feet of snow. If I cut across the lawn, I'd cut a hundred feet or more off my dash to safety. But it wasn't going to be easy running.

The snowmobile veered out onto the beach grass and swung around. Screaming wasn't going to do any good. The snowmobile's noise was deafening. I muttered under my breath. "Aunt Nettie, wake up and call those cops."

What was I going to do? Throw snowballs at the snowmobile?

I looked at my hands helplessly. And for the first time I realized they weren't empty. I was still holding a rolled-up copy of the *Grand Rapids Press*. Fat lot of good that was going to do.

I decided to feint. I'd jump out and entice the snowmobile into making another pass. Then I'd jump back behind my tree. After the snowmobile had passed me, I'd run for the back porch. I knew the back door was unlocked.

I took a deep breath and jumped out. But the snowmobile didn't bite. It stayed on the drive.

I stepped forward one more step. Then another. Had it given up?

Suddenly the engine revved, and it came at me.

I was still out from behind my tree.

I ran back toward the tree. And that deep, horrible snow pulled at my feet every step. It was like slogging through mud, through five feet of water, through a vat of chocolate.

The snowmobile was nearly on me. I wasn't going to make it. I was going to die. Desperately, I threw the rolled-up newspaper. It hit the swept-back windshield.

And the snowmobile veered, went by me, hit a tree and tipped over. It lay on its side, its front skis sticking out helplessly, its back tread churning in the air.

I stared. Then I ran for the house.

I'd been told that snowmobiles tipped over easily. But I'd also heard that they were easy to get back upright. So I didn't wait around to check on the rider.

I didn't look back. I slogged through the snow to the back walk, skidded over the new snow that was rapidly covering the flagstones, and jumped onto the porch. I didn't stop. I charged right into the kitchen, slammed the door, and locked it. Then I took two deep breaths before I ran into the back hall, which had the closest window that looked over that side of the lawn.

For a moment the blowing snow almost kept me from seeing anything. Then I saw a purple form. And a woolly jacket and bowling-ball head. The rider was pushing the snowmobile upright. As I watched he got aboard and took off across the lawn and down the drive, leaving nothing behind but a chewed-up patch of snow. In less than a minute there was nothing to see but the snow, nothing to hear but the swish of the falling flakes.

I stood there, looking out the back window, and the whole episode seemed unbelievable. Had I really run through the snow, dodging a man-eater? I stood there in that odd little back hall—part pantry, part corridor between Aunt Nettie's bedroom and the bathroom—and for a moment I actually doubted the chase had happened.

Then the door to Aunt Nettie's bedroom opened, and she looked out. She wore a blue robe, and her hair was messed up, and I was so glad to see her that tears began to trickle down my face.

"I called the police," she said firmly. "I don't know who's riding that snowmobile around here, but I'm really tired of it. I guess they think we're at work this time of the day and won't know about it. But there is a limit!"

Then she looked closely at me. "Heavens! Lee, have you been outside? And what happened to your jacket?"

The jacket looked as if I'd been rolling in the snow. Dirty snow. The cedar had ripped a sleeve. I'd tracked snow all over the kitchen floor and into the back hall. I went back to the kitchen door, the assigned spot for taking off outside clothes, and told Aunt Nettie what had happened. I tried to laugh it off. I didn't want to frighten her.

But her round face screwed up into an angry apple. "Oh, Lee!"

"I'm not hurt," I said. "It was pretty exciting. But the police will be here soon, and I'll tell them about it. Maybe they can identify the snowmobile by its tracks."

"I doubt it." Aunt Nettie looked out the kitchen window. "It's snowing harder."

She called the police again, telling the dispatcher that the snowmobile rider had not only trespassed, but had actually chased her niece.

"Please tell whoever is on duty to get right out here," she said. "Maybe they can still tell something about the snowmobile."

"Maybe they could even follow it to its lair," I said.

But it was no good. Jerry Cherry showed up within a few minutes, quickly followed by the chief. They tramped through the yard and looked at the piled-up snow along Lake Shore Drive, but when they came inside to report, the chief said the new snow made tracking the snowmobile impossible.

"I guess my messed-up jacket is the only evidence I can show you to prove the whole thing even happened," I said.

"Did you see the rider?" Chief Jones asked.

"I could tell that somebody was guiding the darn thing," I said. "But he had on a helmet. It made his head look like a bowling ball, and it had a guard over the face. It could have been anybody."

"How big did the guy look?"

"Enormous! But that may have been the jacket." I described the jacket, saying it was made of some woolly fabric. "It could have been fake fur," I said. "Or Polartec. Something with a lot of texture."

The chief frowned, and his frown made me furious.

"You'd better not say you don't believe this happened," I said.

"Well, after the burglary night before last and a killing last night . . ."

"This was more than trespassing by a snowmobile. Trying to kill me is a major crime."

"It sure is," Chief Jones said. He was drawling, pulling his words out long. "And adding it to what Jeff said . . ." He paused again.

"What Jeff said? This is one thing you can't blame on Jeff, Chief."

"But if it was the killer of Gail Hess coming back. . . ."

"That's silly! Why would the killer hang around here?"

"I don't know, Lee. But I do know that, except for the helmet, your description of the snowmobile rider is a lot like the description Jeff gave of the person he claims to have seen minutes before Gail Hess's body was found."

Chapter 13

That remark seemed to have knocked me out. The next thing I knew I was tucked into my own bed, the clock radio read 2:30 p.m., and someone was tapping at my door.

"Ms. McKinney? Lee?"

I rolled over, barely catching my head before it fell off my shoulders. "Tess? Come in."

She peered around the door, looking as if she expected to need a whip and a chair. "I'm sorry. I know you haven't been asleep long enough. But that Joe guy called."

I groaned, sat up, and discovered I was wearing my underwear and no pajamas. The jeans and sweatshirt I'd had on when the snowmobile chased me were tossed on the back of a chair. I guess I had simply pulled them off and crawled under the covers.

I held on to my head. It wouldn't do to allow it to roll under the bed. "Is Joe still on the phone?"

"No. He said not to get you up, but if you woke up to tell you that Jeff's attorney is going to be meeting with him at four p.m. Your aunt went to the chocolate shop."

"Thanks, Tess." I yawned so widely I nearly dislocated my jaw, got out of bed, and headed for the shower.

By four o'clock I'd poured hot water outside me and coffee inside me and had dragged myself—and Tess, who didn't want to stay at Aunt Nettie's alone—to the police department in time to meet Webb Bartlett before he saw Jeff. The day was still gray, but the snow had stopped, and the streets had been plowed.

Webb might have been Joe's age, but a bald spot and a paunch made him look older. His eyes were shrewd, and he didn't bluster. I liked him, and I hoped Jeff would.

Webb didn't ask me any questions before he saw Jeff, and he told Tess she'd have to wait until he and Jeff had conferred before she could go in. So Tess and I moped around the police station. The chief was out, but the part-time secretary took me into his office and quietly told me that the chief had run a check, and neither Jeff nor Tess seemed to be in trouble with the law, either in Texas or in any state between there and here. I was almost ashamed of how relieved I was to hear that.

When Webb came out, Tess went in, armed with the clean clothes, toothbrush, comb, and razor we'd brought for Jeff. The Warner Pier Police Department doesn't really have a jail, just a holding cell, which is usually empty. But I appreciated the chief's keeping Jeff there, instead of booking him into the county jail thirty miles away. I pictured Jeff in with hardened criminals and shuddered. He might have a stud in his lip, but he was just a baby.

Webb and I sat down to talk. He brushed aside my assurances that his fee would be paid. "I'll take my fee out of Joe's hide if Jeff's dad balks," he said. "Now, the police have to charge Jeff within forty-eight hours or let him go. Maybe he won't have to go before the judge at all. What do you know about the victim, this Gail Hess?"

"Not a lot. Her antique shop is across the street from TenHuis Chocolade, but—well, in the summer we were all too swamped to socialize, and during the fall I was trying to get my job figured out and didn't get around much. I didn't really get acquainted with her until this Teddy Bear Getaway campaign started."

"She was the campaign chair?"

"Right. Aunt Nettie wasn't planning to do much with the campaign, but Gail insisted that we should take part."

"Your aunt opposed the campaign?"

"No, she thought it was a good idea, but it's not really key to our business. Most of the retail merchants in Warner Pier are completely dependent on the trade of tourists and summer residents. Some of them close up after Labor Day, and the ones who stay open, naturally they'd like to increase their winter sales. But TenHuis Chocolade has built up quite a mail-order business. Our retail shop pays for itself in the summer, but it doesn't make a lot of difference to our overall profit picture. This time of year we're busy shipping Easter and Mother's Day orders. We don't care much about retail sales. The shop's only open as a sort of courtesy. Of course, that attitude shocked Gail."

"Was she a Warner Pier native?"

"I don't know, but Aunt Nettie will. We could go over to the shop and ask her."

I spoke briefly to Jeff. Then Tess, Webb, and I left the police station and walked toward the shop.

Webb took a deep breath and gestured at our surroundings. "This is marvelous! Marvelous to be able to walk anywhere in the business district. And in a beautiful little town like this. I see why Warner Pier is such a tourist attraction."

"It is really pretty," Tess said. "In the daylight." She obviously felt like she had been let out of her motel-room jail. When Jeff had been locked up, she'd been released.

Webb Bartlett was gesturing again, this time at the upper stories of the buildings along Peach Street. "What's up there?" he said.

"Mostly apartments."

"Apartments! Maybe there were witnesses to Gail Hess's killing."

I frowned. "I doubt it. Aunt Nettie has an apartment upstairs in her building, but it's only occupied when the summer workers hit town. I think that's the case for nearly all the buildings. The downtown is deserted on winter nights."

"There's the skating rink man," Tess said. "Jeff and I saw him when we went out. That would be an awful job."

I explained to Webb that the Warner Pier tennis courts are transformed into skating rinks every winter, and that one city employee had the job of maintaining them in the depths of the night. "There are people who run snowplows, too," I said. "But I don't think they would have been out last night. The snow didn't start until this morning."

"Finding a witness would be an extra added attraction," Webb said. "I guess we'd better not get our hopes up."

By then we had reached the store, and I was pleased to see that the glass in the door had been replaced. I took Webb back into the shop to meet Aunt Nettie, who was draining milk chocolate from the thirty-gallon vat where it was kept already melted. She took a work bowl full of the ambrosial stuff to a table and began to ladle it into plastic molds shaped like the back halves of teddy bears. Without stopping her work—pour a ladleful of chocolate into the mold, tip the mold this way and that to make sure the inside was properly coated, pour out the excess, weigh the mold to make sure she'd used the right amount of chocolate, then put it aside on a tray—Aunt Nettie greeted Webb. Then she asked Tess if she'd like to make a little money by taking over Jeff's job packing chocolates. When Tess agreed enthusiastically, Aunt Nettie called to Hazel, the chief hairnet lady. Hazel escorted Tess back to the packing area for her first lesson in the shipping and handling of the fragile molded chocolate.

Aunt Nettie took her tray of hollow chocolate teddy bear halves to the cooling tunnel and started the batch along the conveyor belt.

Webb was bug-eyed. "That's fascinating," he said. "But why are you making the back half of a teddy bear?"

Aunt Nettie showed him the matching molds that were the front halves of the teddy bears, plus the miniature chocolate toys—tiny cars, tops, balls, and drums—that would fit inside the two halves. "The fronts of the bears are already decorated," she said, displaying the bears' happy white chocolate grins and dark chocolate eyes. "When these backs I'm making are firm, we put the little chocolate items inside, then we glue the halves together with chocolate. They're a special item for the promotion, but Marshall Fields is taking two hundred and fifty of them."

"It must be the dickens to get those dark and light designs on there!"

"The designs are part of the mold," Aunt Nettie said kindly. "We do that first. Then, after the design is set, we pour the milk chocolate in. It's not that hard." She smiled a little smugly. The truth is that it *is* hard. But Aunt Nettie has developed her own secret technique—which I won't describe—for making the designs quickly. Or a skilled person can make them quickly. I can't.

"I'd like to buy one for my daughter."

Aunt Nettie presented Webb with a teddy bear that had already been assembled and given its special Teddy Bear Getaway wrapping. He held it like a treasure. I could see that we'd gained a customer.

I asked her about the apartments. She agreed with me that nearly all the downtown apartments were empty in the winter.

"Most of them are rented to summer workers," she said. "Just a few are occupied. Gail's, of course."

Webb looked surprised, and I'm sure I did, too. "Gail lived over her shop?" I said.

"Yes. She said she couldn't pay a mortgage on the shop and another one on a house. You know how expensive it is to rent or buy a place to live in Warner Pier."

I knew. With people building million-dollar homes in Warner Pier and leasing houses and condos for thousands and thousands of dollars each summer—well, I knew I was lucky to live with Aunt Nettie in a house that had been in the family for a hundred years. It was that or commute from someplace way back off the main road or from Holland or Grand Rapids.

But learning that Gail lived over her shop was real news.

"I'd been wondering how she happened to cross paths with the killer," I said. "I thought maybe she'd been lying in wait for the burglar and had caught him breaking in over here again."

"She wouldn't have needed to set an ambush," Aunt Nettie said. "She would have only had to look out her front window."

I walked to our show window and looked over at Gail's shop. "It's covered with crime scene tape at the moment," I said. "I guess her apartment is, too."

Webb turned to Aunt Nettie. "Was Gail a native of Warner Pier?"

"No, but she'd lived here nearly twenty years."

"Did she have any family?"

"She was single, and I never heard her mention having been married. She never talked about any family, but that doesn't prove anything. I know who might know, though. Mercy Woodyard."

"That's Joe's mom," I said to Webb. "She has an insurance office here. She insures practically all the local businesses. I'll call her and ask."

Mercy Woodyard told me she had sold Gail a small life insurance policy. Her beneficiary was a sister, Nancy Warren. "She's a teacher in Indianapolis," Mercy said. "I gave Chief Jones her name, and he contacted her. She's due in any moment. The chief doesn't want her staying in Gail's apartment, so I made her a reservation at the Inn on the Pier. It's practically the only place open this time of year."

I didn't remind her that the Lake Michigan Inn was open, too. Mercy obviously meant that the Inn on the Pier was the only picturesque place open. And it definitely looks picturesque, though in February, when it could be called the Inn on the Ice, it also looks darn cold. It sits right on the edge of the river. In the summer boaters come up the Warner River and tie up at the inn's dock, then check in as if they'd parked their Chevys outside the Holiday Inn.

"Thanks for the information, Mercy," I said. "Jeff's attorney wanted to know."

"Webb Bartlett? Is he there? Joe wanted to see him."

"I'll have Webb give him a call."

"Joe's here. I'll tell him to drop over."

I had a slanting view of Joe's mom's office—across the street and three doors down—from my desk. Joe was already coming out the door. Something about the way he held his head told me he was mad.

"What's Jeff done now?" I may have muttered the question. It was the first thought that popped into my head.

But when Joe got to the shop, he didn't display his anger to Webb. No, he gave him the old college greeting—handshake and poke in the gut—and asked him about his session with Jeff.

I was still convinced he was mad, but he got the whole Jeff session thrashed out with Webb before he turned to me. When he spoke, he sounded accusing. "What's this about somebody chasing you with a snowmobile?"

Webb's eyes popped, and he gave a surprised, "Huh?" Aunt Nettie blinked and looked from Joe to me, frowning.

"He didn't catch me," I said. "I hit the guy with a newspaper and he fell over."

"A newspaper!" Joe still sounded angry. "Why did you hit him with a newspaper?"

"I didn't happen to be carrying a two-by-four," I said. "What's the matter?"

"The matter? You could have been killed!"

"I am well aware of that, Joe. I didn't deliberately seek the experiment—the experience."

"What were you doing out in a snowstorm, battling snowmobiles with a newspaper?"

"I was proving to the people of western Michigan that Texans aren't wimps."

"Well, that's for damn sure! When people around here go hunting snowmobiles, they use rifles. But Texans go after them with newspapers! Did you roll it up like a stick? Or throw it over the guy like a blanket?"

Aunt Nettie began to laugh. Webb joined in. Then I laughed. And finally, Joe laughed, too.

"Joe," I said. "I've been trying to take a walk, just a short one, every day, so that people around here would quit telling me that Texans are afraid of cold weather. I had walked down to the road to get the newspaper, and the snowmobile roared out of somebody's driveway and chased me back to the house. It finally got so close I threw the newspaper I had in my hand at it, and that distracted the rider, and he veered off and fell over. I got to the house before he got the snowmobile upright again."

Now Webb was frowning. "Did you call the police?"

"Yes. But, as Joe says, it was snowing when it happened. The snow covered most of the tracks before the police could get there. There are snowmobiles all over Warner Pier, and, as you'd expect, the rider was wearing a helmet with a reflective faceplate and a bulky jacket. I didn't get a good look at him."

"Do the police think this was linked to the killing of Gail Hess?" Webb said.

I sighed. "Maybe. The description of the rider's jacket matches the description of the jacket on the guy Jeff says he saw last night, when Gail Hess was killed."

Joe and Webb looked at each other. It wasn't just a glance. This was a significant exchange.

"What's the problem?" I said.

"I guess Webb and I were just thinking how that would strike a prosecutor," Joe said.

"A prosecutor? It didn't seem to concern the chief."

"Yeah, but the chief knows you. That makes him more likely to believe you."

"I hope so. But are you saying a prosecutor might not believe me?"

"Well, imagine you're presenting the case to a jury," Webb said. "Jeff says he saw this mysterious figure in the woolly jacket. Nobody else saw him."

"Right, there's nobody to back up his story," Joe said.

Webb nodded. "Then somebody else sees this figure—is actually chased by him. Voilà! Another witness. But—"

I saw what was coming. "But the other witness is Jeff's stepmother, and she's committed to proving that Jeff is innocent. And any tracks in the snow or other evidence that proves she was chased by the snowmobile were covered up before anybody else saw them."

Joe and Webb both looked glum.

"Well," Aunt Nettie said. "I saw Lee when she ran into the house, and she'd better not have tracked up the kitchen floor like that just so she could tell the police a lie."

That made us all smile again, and the atmosphere lightened.

"How did you hear about the chase?" I said.

"The chief came in asking Mom if she had any kind of list of snowmobiles insured in the area."

"Apparently the chief is trying to check my story." I turned to Webb. "My story is not going to change. So I guess we might as well move on. Is there anything I can do to help Jeff?"

"You could check these buildings along here," he said. "It sounds unlikely, but there could be someone living upstairs. I'm sure the police will be checking, too, but there's no reason our side can't ask a few questions."

"Okay," I said. "I'll ask all the business owners if anybody's living upstairs."

"It's just about closing time," Joe said. "We'd probably better wait until tomorrow."

"I can try to catch some of them. I'll call them after dinner if they've already left."

Joe looked at the floor. "You're busy tonight, aren't you?"

I felt blank. Then I gasped. I'd completely forgotten my date with Hart VanHorn—the date I'd broken at dawn that morning. But Joe hadn't forgotten. That was gratifying.

"That was called off," I said. "This trouble over Jeff. Besides—well, I was afraid the tabloids were coming back."

"The tabloids!" Joe looked wary.

I told Joe, Aunt Nettie, and Webb about the call Hart had received from a Chicago reporter. "So somebody tipped him off," I said. "You were right, Joe. The tabloids are probably still with us."

Almost on cue car lights hit the shop's front window. For a panicky moment I felt as if the four of us were on display. I went to the window to pull the shade. When the car lights died, I saw Mercy Woodyard getting out of the passenger side. She circled around the car and waited for the driver, a short woman wearing a knitted cap and dark-colored jacket. They crossed the sidewalk toward the shop, and I opened the door for them.

"Hi, Lee," Mercy said. "Sorry to come in right at closing time."

"Aunt Nettie and I will be here for a while."

Mercy and her companion came in. The second woman's face was pinched; she looked like one of the dried-apple dolls Gail Hess had sometimes displayed.

Mercy seemed quite uncomfortable. "This is Nancy Warren, Lee. She's Gail Hess's sister. She arrived right after you called. She's moving her car over to the Inn on the Pier, but she wanted to see the place where the tragedy occurred."

I gasped and made gibbering sounds, but Aunt Nettie met the occasion. She took Nancy Warren's hand. "We're so sorry about Gail," she said. "We want to help you in any way we can."

Nancy Warren's dried-apple face screwed up even tighter. "Thank you," she said. "Everyone's being so kind."

Mercy gestured toward Joe. "This is my son," she said. "After I found Gail I called him, so he was one of the first people on the scene of the . . . the death."

Joe looked even more uncomfortable than his mother, but he managed to shake Nancy Warren's hand and mumble something sympathetic.

Mrs. Warren looked miserable. "It was outside here?"

"Yes," Joe said. "She was lying on the sidewalk."

He walked outside with Mrs. Warren. I got my jacket, then went out as well. They were standing silently, looking at the spot where Gail's body had been.

"Did you talk to Gail often?" I said.

Nancy Warren shook her head. "No. We'd almost lost touch. It's my fault, I guess. Anyway, we didn't talk more than a couple of times a year."

"So you hadn't talked to her recently?"

"A couple of months ago. At Christmas. She was all excited about the possibility of handling some big estate sale." Then she gestured at the sidewalk. "I thought . . . Don't the police draw a chalk outline?"

"That's only on television," Joe said. "In real life they usually take photographs."

Mrs. Warren turned to me. "Mrs. Woodyard said your stepson was found standing over her."

I tried not to sound too defensive. "Jeff says he had just driven by and saw her body on the sidewalk. He stopped to see if he could help her. The police are holding him, but we hope to get him released quickly."

"This stepson . . . ?" She stopped talking.

"He's actually an ex-stepson," I said. "My ex-husband's son. Jeff has never been in trouble before. He'd only been in town two days." I left out any reference to the earlobe eyelets.

"Then he didn't know Gail?"

"They may have met briefly, when she came by about the Teddy Bear Getaway."

"Teddy Bear Getaway?"

"Yes. Gail was chairing the Merchants' Association midwinter promotion."

"Oh!" Mrs. Warren's voice rose to a wail. "Gail wasn't handling money, was she?"

CHOCOLATE CHAT

THE SWEET AND LOW DOWN

It takes John Putnam Thatcher, the urbane banker created by Emma Lathen, to solve a case involving machinations on New York's Cocoa Exchange.

In *Sweet and Low,* published in 1974, Thatcher—senior vice president and trust officer of The Sloan, third largest bank in the world—is named a trustee of the Leonard Dreyer Trust, a charitable foundation established by the world's largest chocolate company. The Dreyer Trust is a major stockholder in the Dreyer Chocolate Company, manufacturer of the most famous chocolate bar in the world. Thatcher gets involved when one of Dreyer's cocoa buyers is murdered on the eve of a meeting of the trust and the company's chief cocoa futures trader is killed on an elevator in the Cocoa Exchange itself.

The book is typical Lathen, giving an inside look at a particular corner of the financial world, in this case the commodities market. It's a painless way to get a whiff of economics. For many mystery fans, John Putnam Thatcher—whose deductions rival Hercule Poirot's and whose witty observations are often hilarious comments on America and American business—is one of the finest detectives.

Chapter 14

That was a strange reaction. I'm sure I gaped before I replied. "Gail had a lot to say about how the promotional budget was spent. But there's a board that approves everything."

Nancy Warren seemed to be struggling to contain herself. "I'm sure it's all right," she said. She bent over, once again examining the sidewalk she'd already looked over carefully.

I thought about Jeff sitting in the Warner Pier lockup and I decided she needed to explain. Did Gail have some secret in her past? Something to do with money? Would knowing whatever it was help Jeff?

"Why did you ask that?" I said. "About handling money?"

"Oh, no reason."

"That's hard to believe, Mrs. Warren. Had Gail had trouble over finances before?"

"No. Well, it seems she was always complaining about not making enough money. . . . I mean, if she was worried about her own finances, I'm just surprised that she took on other people's money." She laughed, but it sounded forced. "You know, the shoemaker's children run barefoot."

"Is there some reason that Gail should not have been handling money?"

"Oh, no! No. Gail had a business degree. She had operated her own business since she was thirty. I'm sure it would be perfectly all right." She produced a tissue from her pocket and dabbed at her eye. "And now, I guess I'd better get over to the bed-and-breakfast."

Joe and I gave her directions, and since it's impossible to get lost in Warner Pier, we waved her off satisfied that she would get there.

As her car disappeared down the street, Joe gave a sort of grunt. "What did you think of that?"

"She makes me wonder why Gail left Indiana."

"Right. Maybe Chief Jones knows somebody in Indianapolis."

"And maybe Aunt Nettie or your mom could suggest that the Merchants' Association audit the festival accounts."

Joe and I went inside and reported our conversation with Nancy Warren to Webb, Aunt Nettie, and Mercy. Webb was noncommittal. Mercy lifted her eyebrows and admitted that Gail's insurance had nearly been cancelled a year earlier because of a late payment. Aunt Nettie clucked and assured all of us that Gail's reputation had been fine. Then she went to the phone to call the vice president of the chamber of commerce to suggest that the accounts be checked. Joe promised to call Chief Jones and ask him to check the Indiana situation.

Mercy Woodyard left, saying she'd walked out without closing up her office. Webb shook hands, asked me to thank Aunt Nettie for his chocolate teddy bear and left. Aunt Nettie was still on the phone in the office.

Joe and I were alone in the shop. There was a moment of stiff silence. Then we spoke at the same time.

I said, "I loved the chocolates." He said, "I can help you find out about the downtown apartments."

We both looked at the floor. I felt awkward, and Joe looked as if he felt awkward. Then we did our unison speech act again.

He said, "It was kind of a dumb thing to get you." I said, "I can call everybody."

We both laughed. Joe opened his mouth, but I held up my hand like a traffic signal. Then I put my elbows on the counter and leaned over. "I'll go first," I said. "It was very nice to have a box of chocolates all my own. How did you know my two favorite flavors?"

"Then they were right? I try to listen, but sometimes I forget and talk." Joe took my hand and held it gently. "Now, how about letting me help you call the downtown property owners?"

"It'll only be this block. I can do it."

"I'll be glad to help. You take the river side, and I'll take the Orchard side."

In Texas everything is north, south, east, and west, but that doesn't work in Warner Pier. Because it's laid out parallel to the Warner River, which runs southwest into Lake Michigan, you would have to say "It's a block northeast," or "I live on the west corner." So Warner Pier's directions are divided into lake, highway, river, and Orchard, as in Orchard Street. It sounds silly, but it works.

Joe gave my hand a final squeeze, and we left it that way, with me to call property owners or merchants on the river side of the street, the side where TenHuis Chocolade was located, and Joe to call those on the Orchard side, the side where his mom's office was. We didn't need a list; we knew everybody on both sides of the block. Besides, about a third of the shops weren't open in the wintertime.

Aunt Nettie called out, saying she and Tess were leaving by the back door. Joe said good-bye and went across the street to his truck, which was parked in front of his mother's office, then drove off. I picked up some paperwork to take home. I hadn't done a stroke of work that day. I left by the street door, since I'd parked in front of the shop.

The picturesque streetlights of downtown Warner Pier don't exactly shine like spotlights, so the block was fairly dark, as well as deserted. I was locking the door to the shop when I heard a banging noise.

This was followed by someone calling out, "Gail! Gail! I'm here! Let me in!"

I whirled toward the sound. Someone was standing in front of Gail Hess's antique shop—inside the crime scene tape. All I could make out was a bulky coat, but I could tell the voice belonged to a woman.

A dim light shone in Gail's window, but nothing stirred behind the curtain. Or behind any other window on the block. The streetlights puddled on the slushy snow along the curb. When the woman stopped knocking and yelling, the whole street was silent.

The woman called out again. "Gail! I'm freezing!"

Someone was trying to rouse Gail Hess, to rouse the dead.

It was spooky. A rabbit ran over my grave, making me shudder, and I fought an impulse to jump into my van and tear out of there.

But that wouldn't do. I sternly curbed my imagination, and called out, "Hello! Can I help you?"

The woman turned toward me. Now I saw an oval of white face, topped by dark hair. "I hope you can," she said. She stepped across the yellow crime scene tape and moved toward me. "Gail Hess invited me to stay with her. She knew when I was to arrive. But she's apparently not there. Has something happened? I didn't understand all this yellow tape."

Great. I was going to get to tell one of Gail's friends that she was dead. I decided I'd better not yell it out. I jaywalked across the empty street, meeting the woman near the opposite curb.

"I'm sorry," I said, "I'm afraid I have bad news."

"Bad news? Has something happened to Gail?"

We stood there in the slush, and I told her about Gail. As far as I could see in the faint light, the woman looked shocked, but she didn't burst into tears.

"Good heavens!" she said. "Do they know who did it?"

That was a trickier question. I decided to level with her. "No," I said. "They're holding my stepson as a witness, but I'm convinced he didn't have anything to do with it."

The woman lifted her eyebrows. "And you are?"

I introduced myself and pointed out TenHuis Chocolade. "Are you an old friend of Gail's?" I asked.

"Not really. My name is Celia Carmichael. I'm the author of a book on chocolate molds."

"Oh, yes. Gail mentioned that a well-known expert on antique molds was coming to take a look at the Hart collection. But she hadn't said when she expected you."

"Are the molds in her shop?"

"I suppose so."

"I'd still like to get a look at them."

"That would be up to the police." It occurred to me that Celia Carmichael might be worth questioning. She hadn't been in Warner Pier the night Gail was killed, true, but she knew a lot about chocolate molds—if that was what our burglar had been after—and she had obviously talked to Gail recently.

Celia Carmichael sighed deeply. "I suppose I might as well drive on to Chicago. There's probably no place to stay here. Gail said most of the inns and motels were closed."

"A few are open, and they're certainly not crowded. Besides, Chief Jones might want to talk to you."

The woman's eyes narrowed. "The police chief? Why would he be interested in me?"

"I expect he's interested in anybody who talked to Gail during the past few days," I said. "Come into the shop and I'll call him."

"I don't know anything about this. I barely knew Gail. I'll just drive on. I only came to see the molds."

"The molds may be involved in Gail's death."

"How could that be?"

"She had displayed some of them in our shop, and someone broke in there two nights ago. One of them was stolen."

"One was stolen? Only one?"

"My stepson apparently interrupted the burglar, and he ran out the back way."

"What would this have to do with the attack on Gail?"

"I consider it a strong possibility that the burglar came back for the rest of the molds, not knowing my aunt had insisted that Gail take them back to her shop. If Gail came out and confronted him, he might have killed her. Please wait while I call the chief."

Ms. Carmichael frowned. "It's late, and it will still take me more than three hours to get to Chicago. I'd better go on."

I was becoming more and more convinced that she should talk to the chief. "It will take you even longer if he asks you to drive back tomorrow. After I tell him you were here."

She moved toward her car. "Look, I hardly knew Gail."

"Then why were you coming to stay with her?"

"I wanted to see the molds."

"Well, apparently the molds are still there. Stick around and maybe the chief would let you in to look at them. Maybe he'd even want you to look at them. Give him an expert opinion."

"I get paid for that sort of work."

"Not if you're subpoenaed." I tried to say that confidently. I had no idea whether or not it was true. I wasn't even sure if you could subpoena a witness for questioning, or just to testify in court.

"I'll leave my card. If the chief wants to talk to me, he can call." She pulled off one of her gloves and started scrabbling through her purse.

I didn't want her to leave without talking to the chief, but I was beginning to be afraid I was going to have to wrestle her into TenHuis Chocolade like a rodeo cowboy with a steer. "This is a small town," I said. "The chief can be here within a few minutes."

She handed me a card. "I don't want to wait."

I took the card, but I decided to try one final, desperate bit of arm-twisting. "I don't understand. You say you drove all this way to see the molds, but you won't wait ten minutes to ask the chief if he'd let you see them."

"Examining them would take longer than ten minutes. I was going to combine seeing the molds with a visit to Gail."

"But you said you and Gail weren't close friends."

"We weren't! I was only coming because . . . well, because she talked me into it."

I'd hit a nerve. "Was Gail paying you for an expert opinion?"

"No."

"Then why were you coming? And coming to spend the night? If your home base is Chicago, you could drive up, spend several hours checking the molds, then drive back the same day."

Celia Carmichael stood silently for a long moment before she spoke again. "Look, apparently you knew Gail fairly well. Did she ever try to talk you into doing something you didn't want to do?"

"Well, she wanted my aunt to display the antique molds in her shop, and Aunt Nettie wasn't crazy about the idea."

"Did Gail give up?"

"No. She kept coming around. She brought the molds over. She was pushy."

"Well, that's the way she was about my coming by here. She found out I was going to a sale in Saginaw, and she became convinced I should drive back—way out of my way—and stop to see the molds. She just pushed and pushed until it was easier to come than to argue anymore."

"You seem like a fairly strong-minded person, Ms. Carmichael. It's surprising that Gail could push you around like that."

"She must have taken lessons from you! Is everybody in this town this aggressive?"

"If we need to be. Look, just walk across the street with me and wait—in our nice warm office—while I call the chief."

She glared.

I made one final push. "It will be even more annoying if I call the chief and he asks the state police to pick you up ten miles outside of town."

She gave an exasperated growl. But she walked across the street, toward TenHuis Chocolade.

I let us into the shop, then went into the office and called the police station. The dispatcher said she'd find the chief and send him over. Then I turned around and got my first good look at Ms. Carmichael.

She looked just like Gail Hess. That rabbit ran over my grave again.

Chapter 15

As soon as my shuddering had stopped I realized that my first impression wasn't really right. The resemblance between Gail and Celia Carmichael was superficial. But it was certainly startling.

Celia Carmichael was probably fifteen years older than Gail. But like Gail, her most striking characteristic was frankly fake red hair, cut short and tousled. Her features were nothing like Gail's, but the two women were much the same height. The down coat Celia wore was bright green. Gail's coat had been almost exactly like it.

I decided I'd better act like a hostess. "You must be frozen. Can I Gail you something?" I bit my lip. "I mean get you something?"

Ms. Carmichael was scowling. "I don't look like Gail," she said angrily. "She looked like me. She used to imitate everything I did."

"What's the saying? The sincerest form of flattery?"

"It may have been sincere, but it was extremely annoying. Every time I wore something to an antique event where Gail was, the next time I saw her, she'd have something like it. When I decided to become a redhead, I thought that would stop her. But, no! She got the same haircut and colored her hair exactly the same shade."

"I can see it would be embarrassing. How long had you known her?"

"Too long!" Celia Carmichael clamped her jaw shut. She sat down in one of our straight chairs, folded her arms and glared. She declined a chocolate and refused to take her coat off. She just sat there. I called Aunt Nettie to tell her I'd be home a little late. Then Celia Carmichael and I waited silently until Chief Jones came to the door.

I'd expected the chief to ask her to go down to the station, but he merely pulled up our second chair and talked to her in his casual way. I guess it worked. He did get a bit more information out of her.

I went into the office and pretended to work, but neither Chief Jones nor Celia Carmichael lowered their voices, so I could hear every word. The tale she told the chief was the same one she'd told me, and the chief responded with the same question I'd asked her.

"If you and Gail weren't friends, why did you agree to come here and spend the night with her?"

"Gail simply nagged me until I agreed to stay over. Plus, I did want to see the molds. She wanted me to advise her about selling them. They're quite famous, you know."

"No, I wasn't really aware of that."

"Oh, yes! Matilda Hart—I guess that this Olivia VanHorn is her daughter—was one of the earliest collectors of Americana. The chocolate molds were only a part of her collection. She snapped up butter tubs, pie safes, wonderful furniture—lots of real treasures—back in the thirties and forties, when most people thought that sort of thing was just junk. Some of her collection is on permanent loan to the Smithsonian."

The chief whistled, and Celia nodded firmly. "That was why the idea of Gail handling a Hart estate sale was so silly. She didn't have the contacts, the organization. The entire Hart Americana collection is going to be worth something over a million."

"But wasn't Gail talking about an auction of things here at the Hart-VanHorn summer cottages? The valuable stuff would have been at Mrs. VanHorn's permanent home."

"Perhaps that's what the VanHorns had in mind. But Gail was thinking big."

The chief mulled that over a moment. "You say she e-mailed you. Do you still have those messages?"

"I may have killed some of them, but most should still be there. My laptop's in the car. Or I could pull them off any computer with Internet access."

The chief asked if she could use my computer, and Celia logged on and pulled up her e-mail messages. She had a half dozen from Gail, and she allowed me to print all of them out for the chief. Celia was right about one thing: Gail had definitely been thinking big about the Hart-VanHorn sale.

All the messages were gushy, in typical Gail style, but the final one really outdid itself. But gush was all it contained; no facts.

"Celia!" it began.

> You will NOT believe what has happened. I'm not saying anything until it's all settled, but I've stumbled across a MAJOR OPPORTUNITY. You'd never believe how much old glass—or even plastic—can be worth. ☺ LOL!!
> Hopefully, I'll be able to TELL ALL when I see you.
> Bye-bye,
> Gail.

Celia Carmichael swore she had no idea what Gail had been talking about. "She was always full of big plans," she said. "But none of them ever came to anything. And I know nothing about glassware. If she'd stumbled across some exciting piece of glass, she wouldn't have been telling *me* about it."

"There's no indication that this had anything to do with the Harts and VanHorns," Chief Jones said.

"No. In fact, I interpreted it as meaning she'd come up with some new project, gotten some new bee in her bonnet, maybe forgotten all about the VanHorns. That's the way Gail operated."

That ended the conference. The chief told Celia she could go on to Chicago if she wanted, then mentioned the motels and a couple of B&Bs that were open. He escorted both of us outside. But I grabbed Celia for one more question before she drove off. "Do you know anything about why Gail left Indiana?"

"No!" She snapped the word out, got in her car and slammed the door. But as soon as she started the motor her window came gliding down.

"Anything I've heard about Gail and Indiana is gossip," she said. "Ask the Indiana Association of Antique Dealers for the real story. If the executive director doesn't know, she'll be able to find someone who does." Then Celia Carmichael drove off.

Chief Jones and I walked back across the street together.

"Are you sure I can't take Jeff home with me?" I said.

"Not tonight, Lee. But I've got a few more hours before I have to charge him. Maybe I won't have to." He patted my shoulder. "And I'll run down that Indiana Antique bunch first thing tomorrow."

His promise was cold comfort. I thought about it as I got into my van. Whatever had happened to Gail in Indiana, it seemed unlikely that it would have any connection with whatever had happened to her in Michigan. The chief drove away, and I left, too. I needed to get home and start calling the merchants along Peach Street, as I'd told Joe I would.

Then, when I was nearly to the end of the block, I saw the light, both literally and figuratively.

The light in this case was in a third-floor window over Mike's Sidewalk Café, at the corner of Peach Street and Fifth Avenue. And behind the lighted window I saw our mayor, Mike Herrera, in his apartment above one of the restaurants he owned. He was pulling down the window shades.

When Joe and I had divided up the block into river side and Orchard Street side, we'd ignored the cross street, less than half a block from Ten-Huis Chocolade. Some of those buildings also had apartments upstairs. In fact, two months earlier Mike Herrera had astonished his son and daughter-in-law by selling his house and moving himself into the apartment on the third floor of his building. Now one of his restaurants, the Sidewalk Café, was on the first floor, his office was on the second, and he lived on the third.

And at that moment Mike was in his apartment, just waiting for me to quiz him. I parked, jumped out of the van, ran across the sidewalk and

began ringing the bell beside the inconspicuous door marked OFFICE – HER-
RERA ENTERPRISES. I knew that door led to the apartment as well as the office,
because I'd seen Mike and Tony carrying a mattress up those stairs.

It took a few minutes, but I heard footsteps coming down the stairs. Mike
opened the door. "Lee! My Texas friend. What are you up to tonight?"

"I'm trying to help my stepson, Mike. Can I ask you a question?"

"Of course, of course!" Mike escorted me up one flight, opened the door
to his office and turned on the lights. The office was a utilitarian affair of metal
desks and filing cabinets. He waved me toward a chair that had apparently
been rescued from one of the more downscale of his four restaurants.

Mike pulled up another chair, a straight chair with a metal frame and
ripped upholstery. "What can I tell you?"

I swiftly explained that Jeff's lawyer had suggested that we question all
the people who lived in Warner Pier's downtown apartments.

Mike shook his head. "I saw nothing of the murder, Lee. My bedroom is
at the back, you see. I knew nothing about it until I was awakened by the
commotion after one thirty. Then I saw the reflections of the lights, and I got
out of bed and looked out the front windows."

I sighed. "I was afraid that would be the case. I guess that one thirty on
a winter morning in Warner Pier is a good time to do something you don't
want witnesses for. I hoped—well, we hope someone saw a car or something."

Mike's eyes widened slightly. "I didn't see a car. Not after one a.m."

For some reason he had emphasized the time. I decided to press him a
little. "Actually, Mike, Jeff says he first saw something suspicious about half
an hour earlier, a little before one a.m. He had this silly girl, Tess, with him.
He took her back to the motel where she was hiding out, then returned to
check on the shop. That's when he found Gail's body. But Jeff says there was
a prowler of some sort earlier."

"At one?" Mike shook his head. "No. I saw nothing at that time."

Mike's voice had become singsong, molding his Texas-Michigan accent
into something with a Spanish sound. I'd noticed this about Mike before;
when he got excited or upset, he reverted to the Spanish of his youth.

But what would Mike have to be upset about?

I decided not to say anything, but just to look at him expectantly, silently.
And in the silence, I heard a noise outside the office.

It was just a little creak, a shuffling sound. The back of my neck prickled
for a second. I wondered if the sound had been my imagination.

Mike began to stammer. "I, I, I . . ."

If he hadn't reacted so guiltily, I might have convinced myself that the little noise I'd heard had merely been the old building creaking. But his confusion convinced me that someone was outside the office.

Suddenly I was crazy to see who was there.

I stood up. "Well, Mike, if you didn't see anything, I might as well get out of your hair." I whirled around and in three long strides I was at the office door.

"Lee!" Mike's voice was anguished.

I didn't say a word. The door was already ajar, and I simply snatched it wide open. The light from the office fell out onto the landing and splashed up the stairs.

And, there, partway up to the third floor, stood Mercy Woodyard. Joe's mom had changed from her business suit to a beautiful golden velvet robe and embroidered slippers.

She and I stared at each other. Then Mercy smiled and shrugged. "Hello, Lee," she said.

"Hello, Mercy," I said. I was embarrassed. After all, we'd all known that Mercy Woodyard and Mike Herrera had the occasional dinner date. If their relationship had progressed to a more intimate level, it was none of my business.

I wondered if Joe knew.

"I'd come down," Mercy said, "but there are no shades on the office windows, and Mike and I still make some effort to be discreet. Maybe you and Mike better come upstairs."

Now I began to stammer. "No, no! I didn't mean to interrupt—"

"You're not interrupting anything more exciting than a drink before dinner," Mercy said. "Anyway, Mike is going to have to go to Hogan Jones with what he saw. No later than tomorrow."

I looked at Mike. He shrugged and motioned toward the stairway. We both followed Mercy up a floor.

Mike's apartment was not fancy—it featured mass-market furniture in styles and colors from around twenty years earlier—but it wasn't bad, particularly considering it belonged to a man who was largely immersed in his business affairs.

Mike waved me to a chair, gave a deep sigh and spoke. "It was around twelve forty-five," he said. "And it wasn't out on Peach Street or on Fifth Avenue. It was in the alley between Peach and Pear."

You can't see the alley between Peach and Pear from Mike's office or apartment. I started to point that out, but I thought about it again and snapped my jaw shut. The alley between Peach and Pear Streets runs behind Mercy Woodyard's office.

"It was a car," Mike said. "A small car. It was driving out the other end of the alley, onto Third Avenue."

"What kind of car? Could you see the license plate?"

"No, no, no!" Mike sounded exasperated. "I didn't get a good look at it. But . . ." He sighed. "But the left taillight was out."

That was about all I got out of Mike. He refused to guess at the make of the car. "Small. Yes, it could have been some kind of a sports car." And there had not been enough light for the color to be seen.

"It was dark," he said. "Maybe there was something wrong with it. The motor sounded funny."

Mike couldn't explain just what "funny" meant. The engine hadn't been missing or running roughly. He didn't think there had been anything wrong with the muffler.

"It just sounded different," he said.

But at least Mike had seen enough to link the mysterious car Jeff and I had seen the night of the burglary to the second crime. I'd already assumed that might be the case, but I was relieved to have some evidence.

Anyway, Mike promised to call Chief Jones the next morning. He walked me down the stairs and over to my van. As I opened the door, he spoke.

"Mercy didn't see the car," he said. "I'd like to keep her out of this."

"I won't mention seeing her," I said. "To anybody." I let him read the name Joe into that comment.

Mike nodded. "I love Warner Pier," he said. "But it sure can be . . . small." Mike was already back inside by the time I reached the corner.

I drove home. Aunt Nettie had made hot German potato salad and bratwurst—a sausage they really do right in Michigan—but none of us had much appetite. I left the dishes to her and Tess, perched at the end of the counter, and rehearsed how to tell Joe what Mike had told me without telling him his mother had been in Mike's apartment looking cozy. I had a feeling my tongue was about to twist into a knot. When I dialed Joe's number, I was almost relieved to get a busy signal.

I started phoning people who owned property in our block. If I couldn't remember who owned a particular building, Aunt Nettie could. Periodically I tried Joe again, but it was ten o'clock and both Aunt Nettie and Tess had moved into the living room before I caught Joe.

Joe said he had found that only one of the apartments on the Orchard side of the street was occupied, and the guy who lived in it hadn't been home. I described my conversation with Mike Herrera—omitting any mention of Mercy—with only one bobble. I stumbled over where Mike had seen the car, describing it as "the alley between Parch and Peer." Joe didn't laugh, but maybe that distracted him. Anyway, he didn't ask what the heck Mike Herrera had been doing in that particular alley shortly before one a.m.

The unusual sound of the motor interested him. "I wish I knew more about sports cars," he said.

"I could call my dad," I said, "but he mostly works on pickup trucks. He rarely gets a sports car in his garage."

"You don't see the real old-time sports cars much anymore," Joe said. "Not since the SUV became the macho car of choice. Actually . . ." He paused for a long moment. "Actually, that reminded me of something odd."

"What's that?"

"The most striking sports car I ever saw around Warner Pier . . . but that was fifteen years ago. I'm sure that car is long gone by now. But its motor sure did have a distinctive sound."

"What kind of car was it?"

"It was a 1968 MGB. A real classic. It used to park outside The Dockster in the summertime. Back when I was in high school."

I decided to cut off his reminiscences. "Well, like you say, that was a while back. If you haven't seen the car recently, we need to think about current cars."

"Yeah, that's probably right. It's funny though. That car belonged to Timothy Hart."

Chapter 16

Joe and I were both silent for a moment.

"That's an odd coincidence," I said. "But Timothy told me he hadn't driven in years."

"I know he lost his license. But I wonder if he sold the car around here."

"Even if he did—Joe, that's too far-fetched."

"Yeah. You're right. Though Timothy Hart—well, he's an odd duck. To-morrow I'll ask Mom if she's insured any kind of a fancy sports car for any-body. Though she probably hasn't. A car like that would probably belong to some summer person, and it would be insured somewhere else."

Joe and I hung up, but I walked into the living room still wondering about Timothy Hart. Aunt Nettie was sewing a button on one of her white cook outfits, and I sat down beside her.

"Tell me about Timothy Hart," I said.

Her eyes grew even rounder than usual. "Every family has some sort of problem," she said.

"He described himself to me as an 'embarrassing limb' on the Hart fam-ily tree."

"That about sums him up, I guess. He's never been in any trouble that I know of. Not around here."

"Does he have a profession?"

"I really don't know, Lee. I've never taken any particular interest in the Harts."

I laughed. "And one of them was a congressman. Warner Pier amazes me. There are so many rich and well-known people around here that they're almost invisible. The CEO of this company, the president of that university, the candidate for vice president—they all hang out here, and nobody even notices them! Nobody's even mentioned to me exactly where this Hart-VanHorn property is located."

"Oh, it's on our end of the shore road. That place with the big stone gates."

"With the line of Japanese lantern-type lamps? The white frame house close to the road and the Craftsman-type house back toward the bluff?"

"There are a couple of newer houses, too," Aunt Nettie said.

"Wow! I thought that was some sort of subdivision. Is it all one piece of property?"

"I believe so, but I'm not really sure. If you really want to know, you can pick me up a bottle of vitamins tomorrow."

"Vitamins?"

"The generic senior vitamins in the drug department at the Superette." Aunt Nettie nodded. "That's the cheapest place to get them."

"The Superette drug department?" I looked at Aunt Nettie narrowly. Was she scolding me? The druggist at the Superette pharmacy was notorious as the biggest gossip in Warner Pier. Aunt Nettie did not approve of him, and she generally avoided his department. A reference to pharmacist Greg Glossop—known around Warner Pier as Greg Gossip—might be her way of letting me know I'd moved from friendly interest in my neighbors over the line into nosiness.

But Aunt Nettie was smiling. "If you really need to know more about the VanHorns, you might as well take advantage of our natural resources," she said. "Go straight to information central. Greg Glossop knows everything."

So when I walked into the Superette pharmacy department the next morning, I did so with Aunt Nettie's approval.

Greg Glossop bustled out from behind his high, glassed-off area, as I had thought he would. I knew he'd expect me to trade information, to give him the lowdown on Gail's death. I'd figured out a few harmless tidbits to use as bait, and I turned them over in my mind as he approached, almost rubbing his hands together in anticipation of the gossip goodies he was about to reap.

Glossop's comb-over failed to cover his scalp, and his lashes and brows were thin and colorless. This, added to his broad face and plump body, seemed to give him an abnormal amount of skin. As he greeted me, his round belly bounced with what could be excitement.

"Good morning, Lee. How are you coping with the current emergency?"

"Trying to hang in there, Mr. Glossop." I decided to get my licks in early. "I'm entirely convinced of my stepson's innocence, and I think Chief Jones is, too. I hope Jeff will be released today."

Glossop danced on his toes. "But if the chief doesn't think he did anything, why is he holding him at all?"

"Because Jeff found Gail's body. He stopped to try to help her, and now he's being held as a witness. It doesn't always pay to be a good Samaritan."

"Tsk, tsk." Greg Glossop was the only person I knew who actually clicked his tongue that way. "Then these wild stories about your stepson breaking into the shop . . ."

"Absolutely untrue," I said. "He could have taken a key from Aunt Nettie or me if he wanted to get into the shop. Besides, Jeff knew there was nothing valuable there."

Glossop's eyes sparkled. "What about the Hart-VanHorn chocolate molds—weren't they supposed to be quite valuable?"

"They were taken back to Gail's shop after the burglary. And Jeff knew that. As far as I know, they're still over there. I hope they're returned to the VanHorns soon. Mrs. VanHorn has been very gracious. I certainly don't want to cause her more problems."

There. I'd introduced the VanHorns into the conversation. "Apparently she's had more than her share of problems in the past," I said.

"Ah, yes. The tragic death of her husband."

"Yes. And her brother seems to be a worry."

"Timothy Hart? Oh, yes. He's been in treatment several times."

"Treatment?" It didn't take much encouragement to keep Greg Glossop talking.

"Yes." Glossop lowered his voice. "Alcoholism. But he always falls off the wagon as soon as he's on his own. In recent years, I believe the family has simply given up."

"He's a pleasant person. Does he have a profession?"

"Luckily, he has a trust fund—or so I'm told. Actually, I've heard he graduated from college with high honors." Glossop leaned forward and dropped his voice even lower. "Perhaps he is a belated casualty of Vietnam. He served there with Congressman VanHorn."

"I didn't know either of them had served in Vietnam."

"The congressman had quite a record—not the Congressional Medal, but some very high honors. He and Timothy were in the same unit, or that's the story."

"So Timothy introduced his sister to her husband?"

"Oh, yes! Congressman VanHorn came from a working-class background. He went to law school on his military benefits. Of course, I gather he was always ambitious."

I didn't want to talk about Congressman VanHorn. I wanted to talk about his brother-in-law. "So the congressman had remained friends with Timothy?"

Glossop raised his eyebrows. "Drinking buddies."

"Oh!" I tried to sound startled.

Glossop nodded and winked. "Both of them were steady customers for the Superette's liquor department."

"Oh, my," I said. "Mrs. VanHorn *has* had problems." Back to Timothy, I reminded myself. Drunk or sober, Congressman VanHorn had been dead fifteen years. "Where does Timothy live in the winter?"

"He lives here year-round."

"At the Hart compound? But they're talking about selling it!"

Glossop's eyes sparkled. Apparently we'd reached the juicy bit. "Yes. I think there are three year-round houses and the summer cottage in the Hart-VanHorn compound, plus several garages, barns, and such. Timothy Hart has always lived in what they call the 'little house.' Now Olivia Van-Horn is apparently planning to sell her brother's home to finance her son's political career."

"Perhaps Mr. Hart wants to leave. It must be lonely there in the winter."

"Oh, Timothy has lots of friends. He entertains a lot." In Glossop's mouth the word "entertains" took on a sinister meaning, hinting at drunken revels. I decided to ignore his implication.

"It can't be easy to live out there. It's almost outside the city limits, and Mr. Hart told me he no longer drives."

"Did he, now?"

"That's what he said."

"I know he says he doesn't have a driver's license." Glossop chuckled.

Now we were down to what I really wanted to know. I decided it was time to be overtly nosy. "Does he drive? Even without a license?"

"I don't know that he ever leaves the property," Glossop said. "But there are fifteen or twenty acres down there, you know. Lots of drives and paths. I delivered a prescription to him last spring, and when I arrived he met me at the gate in that old sports car of his."

It was all I could do not to grab his arm and blurt out a question: Did it have a broken taillight? But even if Timothy's old car hadn't had a broken taillight last spring—nearly a year earlier—it might have one now. Besides, the last thing I wanted to do was alert Greg Gossip to the importance of what he had told me. He would spread the word all over town within minutes, and Timothy Hart's old sports car might disappear before Chief Jones could check on it.

So I did my best not to react to this news. Instead, I paid for Aunt Nettie's vitamins, discouraged Glossop from telling me a tidbit about someone I'd never heard of, told him the two pieces of news that I'd previously prepared, and left the Superette headed for the police station and ready to solve the murder of Gail Hess.

After all, we all knew Timothy Hart was an unstable character. He had given the molds to Gail for sale without telling his sister what he had done. Olivia had probably scolded him. He must have broken into TenHuis Chocolade to get them back, though I had no explanation of why he would have taken only one hard-to-reach mold unless Jeff had interrupted him from taking them all.

But Gail must have suspected Timothy. Perhaps he even tried to break into her shop and get the molds back. Timothy must have quarreled with her, lost his temper, picked up the baseball bat from the display in her shop, chased her down the street—and killed her. I felt sure I was right. I went straight to the police station.

I was rather let down when Chief Jones didn't see the situation quite the way I did.

"Now, Lee," he said, leaning back in his desk chair and stretching his long legs across the office. "Let's not let our imaginations run away from the facts."

"Has Mike Herrera been in here?"

"Yep. Mike was here early this morning. He told me about seeing some sort of sports car in the alley behind Gail's shop."

"And now we discover that Timothy VanHorn still has a sports car, or at least he still had it last spring. You've got to admit there's a possibility that he's involved."

"I'd have to see the car first."

"You're the law! Go look at it."

"I'd need permission from the property owners."

"I'd hate to give Timothy that much warning."

"It's either that or a warrant. And I think it very unlikely that any judge would issue a warrant based on a story from Greg Glossop."

I growled. Then I sat down and glared at the chief. Neither action seemed likely to change the situation. What could I do? An idea appeared in the back of my mind.

But before I could focus on it, the chief spoke. "I was going to tell you what I found out about Gail's problems in Indiana."

"What? Was she wanted?"

"Hardly. Apparently there was some discrepancy in the accounts of a big antique show she helped organize. But the Indiana antique dealers decided it would be too embarrassing to have a full investigation. Gail 'found' the missing money, and no charges were filed."

"Then she moved to Michigan. Does this tell you anything?"

The chief shrugged. "It tells me that I might not want to elect Gail treasurer of anything."

"It tells me she might have a very unusual and creative idea of right and wrong."

"True. But Gail's not a suspect. She was the victim."

I thought about that for a minute. "How about that antique dealer who showed up last night?"

"Celia Carmichael? She's still here. The lab people didn't want anybody in Gail's shop until this afternoon, and Ms. Carmichael decided to wait and take a look at the chocolate molds."

I got up. "Well, what about Jeff?"

"Webb Bartlett has already called me," the chief said. "This is the day I've got to charge him or let him go."

"Can I see him?"

"Sure. He's bored out of his skull."

Neither of us mentioned that Jeff was lucky to be sitting in the holding cell at the Warner Pier Police Department, instead of the Warner County Jail.

Jeff didn't see it that way, of course. When the chief opened his cell and waved me inside, Jeff greeted me with a glare. "I've just got to get out of here," he said. "I didn't do anything!"

I sat down next to him on the bunk. "Unfortunately, we can't prove that, Jeff. But Webb Bartlett is working on it. And so am I. Plus, I'm trying to get hold of your mom and dad."

For the first time Jeff didn't snarl at me when I mentioned his parents. He looked down and blinked. Darn! He was just a kid. He needed his mother, for heaven's sake. I wanted to hug him.

So I did. I put my arm around his shoulder in a half hug, and Jeff didn't pull away. He dropped his head and stared at his feet.

"We're all doing our best for you, Jeff. Alicia Richardson is on the job. If anybody can find your folks, she will."

Jeff nodded. One or two wet drops appeared on the floor beside his feet. In a minute, I eased off on the hug, and Jeff took his glasses off and rubbed his eyes on his sleeve. "I guess I'd really like to see my folks," he said. His voice broke on the last word.

I promised him they would be there soon. "And maybe you'll already be out of here," I said.

We exchanged good-byes, and I got up and left. It wasn't going to do Jeff any good if I began crying, too. I collected my belongings and made it out of the police station and into the city clerk's office before I bawled like a baby. Pat VanTil gave me a tissue and the same kind of hug I'd given Jeff.

In a minute I pulled myself together. "I've got to get to work. Thanks for the emotional first aid, Pat."

Pat waved her hand. "Bring me a chocolate teddy bear next time you come, and I'll let you have a whole box of Kleenex."

I took a deep breath, walked out into the crisp winter sunshine—the temperature was up to twenty-eight—and went down to the shop. On the way I made up my mind about my next step. I was on the phone before I even took my boots and jacket off.

The phone was picked up after the fourth ring. "Vintage Boats."

"Joe, I hear that there's a big boat-storage building down at the Hart-VanHorn compound."

"So?"

"What'll you bet they've got some antique wooden speedboats down there?"

Joe thought a moment before he spoke. "You want to nose around at the Hart-VanHorn place."

"Yes. Will you help me?"

"I'll be on my way in fifteen minutes."

"I'll be ready."

"You can't go," Joe said.

CHOCOLATE CHAT

CHOCOLATE AND ROMANCE

Many mainstream novels use chocolate as a symbol or a plot device. Two major novels of the 1990s, both of which also became romantic films, were *Chocolat*, by Joanne Harris, and *Like Water for Chocolate,* by Laura Esquivel. Both use elements of magic realism; in them food makes magical things happen.

In *Chocolat* a young woman and her daughter come to a small French village just as Lent begins. The young woman, Vianne Rocher, opens a shop offering the most enticing chocolates the villagers have ever seen and plans a chocolate festival for Easter Sunday—much to the annoyance of the puritanical mayor. Vianne's chocolate becomes a symbol of everything pleasurable about human life, contrasting with the narrow life espoused by the mayor.

Like Water for Chocolate tells the story of the youngest sister in a Mexican family, Tita, who is told that she can never marry—despite her great love for her sweetheart, Pedro—but must stay home to cook and take care of her mother. The water of the title refers to a method of melting chocolate, and the hot water needed becomes a metaphor for sexual excitement. The food Tita cooks changes in magical ways the lives of those who eat it.

Chapter 17

I started to argue, but Joe kept talking.

"First, Lee, you don't buy boats. Second, Warner Pier—and that includes Timothy Hart—knows about your determination to get Jeff released. There's no way anybody would believe you'd stop in the middle of that effort to go look at antique boats. Not just out of curiosity. Even Tim's pickled brain would figure out that you were up to something the minute you got out of the truck."

Joe shut up then, without mentioning that there were a couple of more reasons I shouldn't go, but I thought of them. Third, I had accepted a date with Hart VanHorn, even though the date had been cancelled. So if I casually showed up at Hart's house in the company of Joe Woodyard, it was going to look kind of funny. Rude? Brazen? I wasn't sure, but it was going to look odd.

Fourth, Joe still didn't want to be seen in public with me. That reason rankled, but since Joe was doing me a favor I wasn't in a position to argue about it.

So I breathed deeply a couple of times, but I didn't object out loud.

"Okay," I said. "As long as you understand what you're really looking for."

"A 1968 MGB with a broken taillight."

I had to be content with that. I hung up, reminding myself that Joe might not even get on the property. There was no real reason any member of the Hart-VanHorn clan should allow an unauthorized visitor.

So until noon I stared at the computer screen, pretending to work, and chewed my nails. The hands of the clock on the workroom wall had just reached the twelve when the phone rang.

It was Joe. "You want to see a movie?" he said.

"A movie?"

"A video. I took Mom's camera along when I went boat scouting."

"Where are you?"

"Mom's office. Come on over."

I picked up a couple of papers, hoping to look as if I had business with Mercy Woodyard, put on my jacket, and jaywalked across the street. Joe beckoned me into his mother's private office, then closed the door.

"Did you have any trouble getting on the property?" I said.

"No. Poor old Timothy was glad to see a friendly face." Joe took my jacket and pointed me toward a leather couch. After we'd both taken a seat, he gestured at the television set with a remote and punched the button to start the VCR. Immediately an overall view of the Hart-VanHorn compound appeared on the screen.

I'd driven past the compound dozens of times, of course. I'd walked past it on the lake side, for that matter, so I'd probably seen the Hart-VanHorn houses from the beach. If you have lakeshore property—which is worth a small fortune per square foot around Warner Pier—the normal thing to do is build a house overlooking the beach, a house with picture windows and a deck or porch designed for keeping an eye on the kids as they build sand castles, and for watching the sunset, or for simply sitting and looking at the water, the trees, and the sand. If you have enough land for garages, boat-houses, and storage sheds, those can go up near the road, where they won't obstruct the view of the water.

The Hart-VanHorn property followed this pattern. A big barnlike build-ing was near the road, and this, plus some huge trees, meant the houses were largely hidden from passersby. Also, this was the first winter I'd spent in Michigan, so I'd never seen the property with no leaves on the trees. Now, with Joe's video, I had a clearer idea of the layout.

The compound had two sets of stone gates, one where the blacktop drive went in and one where it came out, and the video showed that a snowplow had cleared the drive. The blacktop looped through the property, passing each of the four houses.

Easiest to spot was the "little house," the one Greg Glossop had said was the permanent home of Timothy Hart. It was too close to the road to have a view of the lake, and it was an L-shaped white clapboard 1890s farm-house—a smaller version of the one Aunt Nettie and I live in. It probably had a kitchen, living room, and a dining room downstairs and two bed-rooms upstairs. One room, which I was willing to bet was the living room, stuck out as a one-story wing, and the house was sure to have a Michigan basement, which has stone or concrete walls and a sand floor. It must have central heating, or Timothy wouldn't be likely to live in it year-round, but it didn't look as if it had been modernized in any other way. It was probably the first house the Hart family had built on the property. It might well have already been there when they acquired the land.

Behind it, closer to the lake, was a low bungalow of stone and shingled siding, a prime example of the Arts and Crafts style and a generation younger than the farmhouse. Its front door faced the drive, so its side was toward the lake. The video showed glimpses of a large porch on that side, a porch that was now shuttered for the winter. Beyond the porch there seemed to be a deck or a patio, and I thought I saw a chimney out there, evidence of a built-in barbecue pit. This house must be the one Greg Glossop said was not winterized. It must have been the cat's meow in the twenties and thirties.

Beside it, and squarely facing the camera, were two houses designed to present blank walls to the road. I was sure, however, that their back walls would be entirely of glass.

One house was brick and one stone, and both had nearly solid front walls—only one or two windows—centered with heavy, grandiose doors that wouldn't have been out of place on medieval castles. In fact, the front door of the stone house was approached over an ornamental bridge that crossed a miniature moat, almost like a drawbridge. The house looked as if it could have been held against an army. But both houses were huge, twice the size of the bungalow and four or five times the size of the farmhouse. They both had a 1970s look.

It was a very impressive layout.

"Wow!" I said. "Have all those houses been sitting empty for fifteen years?"

"Except for Timothy's."

"Seems as if they'd rent them out or something. Who built the stone and the brick ones?"

"I'd guess that the VanHorns built the stone one when Hart's dad began to have political ambitions. Anyway, that seems to be the one Mrs. Van-Horn and Hart are staying in. Mom says the brick house was built by Olivia VanHorn's sister, but she moved to California and quit using it a long time back. I don't know who used the bungalow. Olivia and Timothy's parents, probably."

"Are there boathouses?"

"Nothing down on the lake. There's a big storage shed near the road. See, the red barn at the left."

"The red barn? Did you get a look inside?"

"Sort of."

We continued to watch the video. Now the scene shifted. Timothy was opening his front door.

"How did you hide the camera?" I said.

"I just tucked it under my arm and left it running."

On the video Timothy was greeting Joe effusively and inviting him in. Joe answered, telling Timothy he bought and restored wooden speedboats, and that he was scouting for likely projects.

"Well, there's my dad's old boat, over in the barn," Timothy said. "I don't know if Olivia wants to sell it. It hasn't been in the water in twenty years."

"Could I take a look at it? Maybe get some pictures? Then if you and Mrs. VanHorn put it on the market later, I'll know what we're talking about."

"I'll go back to the kitchen and get the keys and my jacket."

Joe turned around while he waited, and the video camera swept around the compound. I found myself admiring the landscaping. The snow might have covered the flower beds, but it couldn't hide the hedges, the trees, the stone walls, the tennis court. It was a beautiful property.

Apparently Joe had thought so, too, because when Timothy reappeared in a heavy red Pendleton jacket, Joe commented on the compound. "The property is in top-notch shape. Do you take care of all this?"

Timothy gave a tipsy laugh. "I'm not what you'd call handy. But I'm in charge of making sure the key's in its usual hiding place when the handyman and landscapers come."

Joe followed Timothy's red jacket across the snow. They seemed to be breaking a trail around the end of the tennis court that centered the compound. In a few minutes they reached the second part of the drive—the exit, I guess you'd call it—coming out on the blacktop near the big storage building that resembled a red barn.

"This hasn't been opened this winter," Timothy said. "We may find a squirrel's nest."

"Don't Hart and Mrs. VanHorn park over here?"

"No, there's a garage in the basement of the stone house. The barn door is around at the side."

Timothy fumbled with a lock and opened a small door. The video went dark as Joe entered the building, then brightened as Timothy turned on a glaring overhead light and the camera's automatic lens adjusted. I leaned forward, eager to see what was inside the barn.

For a moment it looked like a morgue. Then I realized that everything inside was shrouded in canvas dust covers. Timothy led the way past a couple of hulking objects; one obviously was a boat, and the other might have been anything. Then he pulled the canvas back to reveal a mahogany prow.

"This was Dad's boat," he said. "It's a Chris-Craft. He was very proud of it. It was 'postwar,' if that means anything to you. He got it when he came back from World War Two."

Joe evidently laid the camera down on the lumpy item next to the Chris-Craft, because I could see him and Tim folding the cover back. "It's a beauty," Joe said. "A seventeen-footer, I think. One of the first ones made after the war."

At that point the conversation deteriorated to a discussion of boats. Joe raved about the Chris-Craft. Timothy preened. They moved away from the camera, and I couldn't hear much and got only intermittent looks at the two of them.

"The Chris-Craft is the only wooden motor boat here," Timothy said. "Of course, there's our mother's canoe."

Joe gasped. "Where is it?"

He did remember to pick up the camera then, and he swung it around the barn, which seemed to be about the size of a four-car garage.

The canoe was up in the rafters, upside down. "A bit hard to get it down, I'm afraid," Timothy said.

"No need," Joe said. He aimed his camera up at the canoe.

Then a new voice was heard on the tape. It was muffled, but I understood the words. "What are you two doing?"

Joe swung around, or at least the video camera did, and a figure appeared silhouetted in the open door. It was just a fuzzy outline for a moment, as it moved inside and closed the door. Then it became Olivia VanHorn.

She looked as much the grand dame as ever, wearing her casual mink jacket and a wool scarf—I was willing to bet it was cashmere—draped around her head. She approached the camera, smiling graciously. "Tim? What are you doing out here in the cold?"

"Just showing Joe here Dad's old boat," Tim said. "I didn't think you'd mind." Suddenly he seemed to lack confidence.

"It's a honey," Joe said. "I'm Joe Woodyard, Mrs. VanHorn. I was in law school with Hart. But now I'm restoring antique power boats."

"Oh, yes. Your mother has an insurance agency."

The social chitchat went on between Joe and Olivia VanHorn for several minutes. Neither of them made any reference to Joe's ex-wife, though Olivia obviously knew who Joe was. Joe kept his attention on the postwar Chris-Craft, enthusiastically telling Olivia and Timothy what a nice boat it was.

"If you decided to put it on the market," he said, "I'd definitely want to make an offer."

He had tucked the camera under his arm again, so I couldn't see Olivia as she replied. But her voice sounded slightly sardonic. "If you really want to make an offer, Joe, shouldn't you be telling us it isn't worth very much?"

Joe laughed. "Oh, I think you're smart enough to get an appraisal before you sell it, Mrs. VanHorn. I don't think you'd be easy to cheat. Are there other old boats around? Mr. Hart showed me the canoe."

"No, there's the ski boat, but it's less than twenty years old."

"Then it's probably fiberglass. Not my thing. However—" Joe gave a boyish chuckle "—Mr. Hart, you may not know it, but you had a piece of fiberglass that caused me to commit the sin of envy in a big way, back when I was in high school."

Timothy Hart gave a snort. "I can't believe I ever aroused envy in anyone."

"I assure you that every guy at Warner Pier High School envied you that sports car you had. An MGB with a fiberglass top."

Joe moved the camera, and now I could see Timothy's face cloud up. He looked stricken. But I couldn't tell if he was feeling sorrowful or angry.

He spoke. "The MGB. . . ." Then he stopped and glanced at his sister. "I l-l-lost the MGB. . . ."

Olivia VanHorn jumped in to smooth over an awkward situation. "Tim doesn't drive these days," she said. "In fact, Tim, I was making a grocery list, and I wondered if you wanted anything."

Joe was being dismissed. He and Timothy replaced the canvas cover on the Chris-Craft. He swung the video camera around as he was escorted out, but the chitchat became innocuous. I was barely listening as Olivia herded the two men back toward the door.

Then I saw it.

It was the lumpy thing that had been next to the Chris-Craft. Compared to the boats, it was small, maybe ten feet long and four feet high. Its canvas cover shrouded it completely—except for one corner.

Joe probably didn't see it himself, but the camera, now held down at his side, picked up the key detail.

A ski. A ski just a few feet long. And above it, a shiny purple surface.

"Joe! Stop the tape!" I shrieked the words.

"What's wrong?"

"Look! Look under that cover. It's purple!"

Joe nodded. "Yeah. I see it."

"Joe, it could be that snowmobile. The one that chased me."

Joe and I looked at the flickering video. "It's hard to believe," he said. "I can see Timothy arguing with Gail. But why would he chase you with a snowmobile?"

My heart was pounding. Suddenly I covered my eyes. "Turn it off. That snowmobile—it was horrible! I don't want to think about it."

The next thing I knew Joe had taken me in his arms. "It's okay," he said. "I'm not going to let anything hurt you."

I got a big handful of his flannel shirt, and I hung on for dear life. I didn't say anything. I buried my head in Joe's shoulder, and I just sat there and trembled.

It was wonderful to have Joe hold me, to have him act as if he cared about what I was going through. It didn't matter if he wouldn't take me out in public. I didn't care if he was mixed-up and didn't know what he wanted, even if he ran for cover every time he saw someone who looked like a tabloid reporter. His arms were so comforting that I could have sat there all day.

I don't know why I didn't cry. I think I simply didn't dare—if I'd started I wouldn't have stopped for days.

In a few minutes I sort of pulled away and said, "I guess that I've been so worried about Jeff that I just haven't reacted to being chased by that snowmobile. I can't break down yet, Joe. But I'm beginning to think this mess will never end."

He pulled me closer and kissed my forehead. "It's going to end, and it's going to end happily. And happy or unhappy, you're going to handle it."

Then he kissed me. On the mouth this time.

As I said, Joe and I had mostly had a telephone relationship. Until our necking party a few days earlier, he'd only kissed me a few times, and those kisses had been—well, exploratory.

This one was the real thing. He was kissing me, and I was kissing him, and neither of us wanted to stop. If the phone hadn't rung, I don't know what would have happened next.

But it did ring, and it distracted both of us enough that Joe relaxed his grip and quit kissing me, and I moved away slightly. So we were looking fairly decent when Joe's mom rapped on the door, then opened it and looked in.

"It's for you, Lee," she said. "It's your aunt."

I took a deep breath, thanked her, and went to the extension phone on her private desk.

"Lee!" Aunt Nettie sounded excited. "A woman called from Dallas. She said she works for Richard Godfrey Associates."

"Alicia Richardson?"

"Yes, that was the name. She said to tell you she finally got hold of Jeff's mom and dad."

"Wonderful! Where are they?"

"I don't know that, but she said to tell you they are on their way to Michigan. They're flying into Chicago this afternoon."

Chapter 18

My first reaction of relief at the prospect of handing over the responsibility for Jeff quickly turned to dread. I hadn't seen Rich in two years; I didn't want to face him when he'd just learned that his son might be accused of murder. I had a feeling that he was going to think the whole thing was my fault.

I saw only one flimsy hope. "Wouldn't it be wonderful," I said, "if this case is solved and the right person is under arrest by the time Rich and Dina get here?"

"That doesn't look likely," Joe said. "We haven't even figured out what was really behind all this, and I don't think Hogan Jones knows either."

I sat down again. "That's right, I guess. Though obviously the burglary—the one Jeff stopped Tuesday night—had something to do with those molds. After all, the molds were at TenHuis Chocolade Tuesday night and at Gail's Wednesday, when she was attacked."

I'd almost forgotten Mercy Woodyard was standing in the doorway. "I haven't figured out why anybody would want to steal those molds," she said. "They look pretty ordinary to me."

"They're worth quite a bit," I said. "And they made a nice decoration for the shop." Then I realized something. "Mercy, you were never in the shop while the molds were on display. When did you see them?"

"They're over in Gail's storeroom in a box. I looked at a few of them when I was over there this morning."

"Is the shop no longer considered a crime scene?"

Mercy shrugged. "The tape's still up out front, but the chief told Nancy Warren she could have access to her sister's property. Nancy gave me a key, so I could keep an eye on things until she gets through the funeral and gets a lawyer to settle the estate. I let Celia Carmichael in and checked the place over earlier."

I sat up straight. "Do you think the chief would mind if I took a look?"

"Apparently not. I'll get the key and take you over."

Joe went with us, and we ducked under the yellow tape and went in

Gail's front door. Going into the shop felt spooky, but there was actually nothing gruesome about the scene. The state police crime lab had taken anything gory away—if there'd been anything. After all, the chief thought Gail confronted her killer in the shop, because that's where the baseball bat had been, but he believed she was chased across the street before the deathblows were struck. Or maybe Gail saw someone at TenHuis Chocolade, decided to confront them, and took the baseball bat with her.

"The molds are in the back room," Mercy said.

Joe and I followed her through the shop, which was the junky type of antique store. Everything was jumbled together and nothing looked too valuable. In Jeff's mom's shop in Dallas only a few pieces were out, and each one was carefully displayed, often with accent lighting and carefully draped backdrops. Gail's shop was set up to make the buyer think each piece was a bargain; Dina's shop was designed to make buyers think they were getting something rare and worth the prices she charged. I guess I prefer the more carefully arranged shops; the clutter in shops like Gail's makes me feel as if I'm about to bump into something or step on something or break things in some other way.

But I got through the shop without demolishing the Depression glass, upending an urn, or tripping over a table. As Mercy entered the storage room, she pointed to a huge cardboard box. Bold letters on the side, made with a black marking pen, identified its contents: "Hart-VanHorn collection."

Inside the box, a lot of bits and pieces were tumbled together.

"What a mess," I said. "This is obviously junk from the cellar. If getting a box like this on consignment made Gail think she was going to get to run a sale for an estate like the Hart-VanHorn compound, she was the most optimistic person I ever ran into."

"This stuff may have been tossed in the box like junk," Joe said, "but apparently the molds were in the lot." He pulled a couple of the molds out of the top of the box. "Here, lay these out on that worktable, and we'll look at them."

Mercy went back to her office, and Joe handed the molds to me. They'd been wrapped in tissue paper, and I unwrapped them and laid them in rows on Gail's table. Joe heaped the other items from the box on the floor.

I examined each mold as I put it out. The bears we'd had in the shop were on top, of course. There were seated bears and standing bears and a walking bear and an acrobatic bear who wore a funny hat and was apparently about to do a cartwheel. But there was no mean-looking bear with a harness on its snout. That one was still missing.

"It was the rusty mold, too," I said. "And Gail said it wasn't the most valuable bear in the collection. That really mystifies me."

"Huh?" Joe said.

"Just thinking out loud."

Next Joe handed me other animals. There were dogs—a funny little Scottie, a dachshund, a comical bulldog. There were elephants doing tricks, elephants trumpeting, stylized elephants and realistic elephants. Then came birds—storks, ducks, even a peacock. These were followed by dozens of molds of children—Kewpie dolls, children dressed as brides and bridegrooms, a New Year's baby.

"I seem to be down to the Santas and Easter bunnies now," Joe said.

"I had no idea how extensive the collection was," I said. "I guess it nearly filled up that big box."

"There was a lot of old kitchen stuff in there, too. I guess it's worth something, because I saw similar things out in the shop as we walked through. And there are a few pieces of wood at the bottom. And some broken glass."

Joe handed the rest of the molds up to me, and I kept laying them out in rows and examining them. They were fascinating.

And they were all in perfect condition, though some had traces of chocolate, as Aunt Nettie had said they should. Even after being stuck in a basement—ever since Congressman VanHorn died, according to Timothy—there was no sign of rust on any of them.

"That's so weird," I said.

"What is?" Joe was bent over, with his head down in the box. His voice was muffled, though I heard the occasional thump, and I decided he must be digging the pieces of wood out of the bottom of the box.

"All these molds are in perfect condition," I said. "Or I think they are."

"So?"

"The one the burglar took wasn't. In perfect condition, I mean. It was rusted."

"What are they made of? Tin?"

"They're tin-plated. I think the basic metals varied, according to the time they were made. But the outer surfaces were tin."

"Tin will rust. Or a tin can will."

"Yes, but this was a valuable collection. And judging by the condition of these molds, it had been carefully preserved. But that one mold was rusted. That particular one had been treated carelessly."

"So had this. Look."

I turned around. Joe was still kneeling on the bare wooden floor of Gail's storeroom, but he had laid some bits of wood out on the floor in front of him. He had arranged them into some sort of order, but they were still just scraps of wood with hunks of broken glass sticking out here and there. In the center were two small brass knobs.

"They were doors!" I said.

"Right," Joe said. "The stuff in the bottom of the box seems to be the glass doors of a china cupboard."

I knelt beside Joe and gently touched the glass. "It was a nice piece, too. That glass was curved. I don't know too much about old furniture, but I think china cupboards with curved glass are often considered quite valuable. Lots of people want them."

"Well, somebody didn't want this one." He fingered a two-inch gouge. "I'd guess that this had been broken up with an ax."

"That's impossible! Even if you wanted to get rid of something like this, you wouldn't break it up with an ax."

Joe shrugged. "The rest of it probably is in some Hart-VanHorn basement. The doors were in a dozen pieces."

We stared at the doors. Then I stood up. "Well, I've looked at all the molds, and you've assembled the doors. And I'm more mystified than ever."

Joe began to put the pieces of wood back in the box. "I left the broken glass in the box," he said. "I wonder what Gail made of it."

"Do you think she saw it?"

"She must have, if she dug all the molds out."

"I wonder what happened to the china cupboard?"

"If you have a live-in alcoholic, Lee, anything can happen to your furniture."

"You think Timothy got drunk and broke up the furniture?"

"Something sure happened to that china cupboard. And I don't think it was hit by a car."

"I guess we could ask the chief if there's any record of a police call out there."

Joe looked at me. He didn't need to say a word.

"Okay," I said. "I admit that Olivia would let Timothy smash up the entire house before she'd call the cops."

We looked through the rest of the shop, but we saw nothing worth getting excited about. It would have taken an army of technicians to do a complete search.

A smashed china cabinet and a rusty mold. What significance could they possibly have?

I started for the door, then turned to Joe. "Has Timothy always lived at Warner Pier?"

"I don't think so, but Mom will know. Why?"

"I agree that Olivia VanHorn would never have called the cops on him. If he lived in Grand Rapids or Ann Arbor or someplace, though, and if he has a history of breaking up furniture or doing other violent things, somebody else might have called the cops about him sometime."

"You could ask the chief to check."

I went back to TenHuis Chocolade feeling let down. I finally decided it was because I liked Timothy Hart. I didn't want him to be guilty. But I felt that the VanHorn collection just had to be connected with the burglary, and hence with Gail's murder. And Timothy seemed to be the only Hart or Van-Horn unstable enough to get into such a mess. Now that his "drinking buddy," Congressman Vic VanHorn, was gone.

It was a real puzzle.

When I got to the shop, the situation there was even more depressing. Aunt Nettie and Tess were in the office, sitting in my two visitors' chairs. Tess was crying.

I hovered at the door, wondering if I should stay out, but Aunt Nettie motioned for me to come in.

"Tess is fearful about what may happen after Jeff's folks get here," she said.

"I feel so selfish," Tess said. "I know Jeff needs their help. But I'm so afraid!"

I pulled my chair around the desk, and I sat down beside Tess. Now she had Aunt Nettie on one side and me on the other. She was effectively boxed in.

"Tess, why are you so frightened of Jeff's parents?" I had a sudden thought. "Tess, you're not pregnant, are you?"

"Oh, no!" It was almost a wail. "Jeff and I don't sleep together. I mean, I've never slept with *anyone*!"

Aunt Nettie patted her hand. "It's hard for us to understand, Tess. Obviously, something very frightening happened to you in Texas. But you and Jeff don't seem to be involved in any sort of crime."

Tess shook her head vigorously.

"Your problems seem to be more serious than something like grades."
Tess nodded.

"Yet you ran away from college, and you seem terrified that someone from Texas will find you. You're even afraid of Jeff's parents, whose help he needs very much right now."

"I know. That's why I feel so guilty. But I'm so afraid they'll find me!"

"Jeff's parents?"

"No! My parents! My dad's boss."

Aunt Nettie patted again. "Why are you so frightened of your father's boss?"

"It's not him." She sobbed two more sobs, looked around the office desperately—as I said, we had her boxed in—and finally spoke. "It's my dad's boss's son!"

Tess seemed to feel that she'd explained everything that was necessary, but I was still clueless. Luckily, Aunt Nettie was beginning to get a glimmer.

"Tess," she said, "did you date your dad's boss's son?"

"Only once. Only because I thought my dad wanted me to."

Now I was beginning to get the picture, too. "He came on a little too strong, huh?"

"Oh, yes. He parked way out in the back of the Wal-Mart parking lot. It was really late. I barely got out of the car. I had to walk home."

"And then he wouldn't leave you alone."

She nodded miserably. "He kept calling. I told him I wouldn't tell his dad, but he kept calling me anyway. He kept driving past the house. I thought that when I went away to college he'd forget about it, but he didn't! He came over to Dallas and got a job. He used to cruise around the campus."

"Did he threaten you?"

Another nod. She pulled her arm out of the sweatshirt she wore and pulled up the sleeve of her T-shirt. "The marks are almost gone," she said.

True, the bruises on her upper arm were faint, but they were there. And they definitely had been made by fingers.

Aunt Nettie hugged her, and I patted her shoulder.

And another part of the picture came into focus. "You came up here to get away from this guy, right?"

Tess nodded.

"But you were afraid he'd follow you. Am I right again? Maybe even afraid he'd kill you?"

Another miserable nod.

"Tess, that morning when Joe and I came to the motel—were you afraid Jeff had killed him?"

This time she sobbed. When she could talk again, she said, "I knew it didn't make sense. But I've been scared for so long. It seemed like Jeff was the only person who would help me. If he tried to protect me . . ." Then the tears really ran.

Aunt Nettie hugged her.

"Tess, you know there are laws against this kind of thing," I said. "You could send that guy to jail."

"But my dad! His job! Wally says he can get my dad fired."

"If he does, his dad will be very sorry," I said. Maybe I spoke more firmly than I should have, but I felt that I had to calm Tess's fears. "There are laws about that, too, Tess. If this guy's dad fires your father because you won't have sex with his son, your dad could sue the pants off him. He could wind up owning his boss's business."

Tess's eyes got big. "But my dad would never sue anybody!"

"You'd be surprised what dads will do when their girls are threatened," I said. "You haven't told your parents all this, have you?"

She shook her head.

"That's the first thing you must do. Can you call them now?"

"No! I mean, both of them would be at work."

Aunt Nettie spoke gently. "You must call them tonight, Tess. I'm sure they're worried sick." She hugged Tess again. "Let them have an opportunity to back you up."

Tess still looked miserable, but she seemed calmer. After a little more re-assurance, she left the office, telling Aunt Nettie she'd go back to work as soon as she had washed her face.

"What do you think?" I said. "Does that explain why Tess has been in such a state? Why she ran away from college?"

"It certainly seems to explain it, Lee. Violence against women is such a hard problem to deal with. A lady named Rose worked here for a while. She used to come in all black-and-blue. She finally got the nerve to leave her husband, but she wound up having to move clear across the country to get away from him. Hiding out sometimes becomes the only defense." She sighed. "It's really sad."

I had tossed my jacket on a chair when I'd come in. I stood up and started to hang it up on the coat tree in the corner of the office. I heard a clunk, and looked down to see a key on the floor.

"Rats! I forgot to hand Joe the key to Gail's shop. I'll have to take it over to Mercy." I put the jacket back on and stomped out the front door, unhappy at the interruption.

As I crossed the street I noticed that Joe's truck was still sitting in front of his mom's office. When I went inside Mercy beckoned me into her private office. Joe was in there, too. He was on the telephone. He nodded, but he didn't speak into the phone. I decided he was on hold.

"I forgot to give the key back," I said. "Plus there's been a new development, though I'm not sure that it means anything."

I repeated Tess's story. Halfway through it Joe turned his back on us and began to speak into the telephone receiver.

I kept talking. "It's hard to believe that Tess would be so scared she ran away from college, instead of telling her parents and getting a lawyer."

"Tess is just a young, inexperienced girl," Mercy said. "And some women never get up the nerve to confront these situations. It can become an insurance problem—health coverage, even death benefits and liability. That's one of the reasons our state organization took it on as a project."

I edged toward the door. I didn't have time to listen to a speech. "I know it took a lot of women speaking out to begin to make a difference."

"Oh, yes! Violence against women was definitely a crime that was hidden away—along with insanity, incest, and even cancer. But it covers all segments of society from the poorest to the richest. Why, a few years back the ex-wife of the CEO of a blue-chip company wrote a book describing years of abuse by her husband. She would hide in the closet when she heard him come in from a board meeting, afraid he'd come upstairs and beat her!"

"That's terrible."

"Even today it's hard to get legislators involved. That's why we were so lucky to get the support of Hart VanHorn." She smiled. "I guess most of us fail to get interested in other people's problems unless we have some sort of vested interest."

I stared at her. "Are you saying Hart has personal experience with wife beating?"

Mercy gave a little chuckle. "He's never been married, so I don't think he's ever beaten anybody or been beaten. But he speaks very emotionally about the issue, and the episodes he describes from his years as a prosecutor . . ."

I was still staring at Mercy. Hart had a personal interest in spousal abuse. He had an alcoholic uncle. And according to Greg Glossop—who occasionally was right, darn him!—his father had been a drinking buddy to that uncle. Could Hart's father have been a wife beater?

But that was silly. Who would have the courage to abuse a woman with a personality as strong as Olivia VanHorn's? Plus, Olivia was old money. Why would she put up with a situation like that? She could walk out. Olivia was afraid of nothing.

Well, she was afraid of one thing. The conversation I'd eavesdropped on had revealed that. She was afraid of damaging Hart's political career. Had she been just a little too emphatic when she denied that there was any scandal in Hart's past?

Before I could complete the thought, Joe spoke. He had hung up the phone. "The librarian's going to fax something you might want to see."

"The librarian?"

He nodded impatiently. "Yeah, after you wondered if Timothy had ever been accused in any sort of assault—a barroom brawl or anything—I decided Webb might be able to find out."

"Jeff's lawyer?"

"Sure. Webb's one of these guys who knows everybody, and Mom said that Timothy lived in Grand Rapids before he moved down here full-time."

I was still confused. "Webb knows a librarian?"

"At the newspaper. He called down there and got me in touch with the person who's in charge of the archives. She's faxing me a story about Timothy. It seems he once punched out his brother-in-law at a Grand Rapids banquet."

Chapter 19

I was definitely interested in that, so I hung around until Mercy's fax
began to groan. A client came in, and Mercy had to go back into the front
office, but Joe and I stood over the machine, reading as a copy of a newspaper clipping slid out. It wasn't a long story, but the headline spread over
three columns:

CONGRESSMAN ATTACKED AT BANQUET;
BROTHER-IN-LAW SHOUTS THREATS

The date was only a few weeks before Vic VanHorn had died. The gist of
the story was that U.S. Representative and Mrs. VanHorn had been attending a political dinner, and Timothy Hart had been seated next to his sister.
The word "drunk" was never used, but witnesses reported that just before
the baked Alaska was served, Timothy got to his feet, went around his sister, and accosted her husband, "calling him names." At first he demanded
that VanHorn accompany him outside. When the congressman refused, he
threw a punch. Bystanders pulled Timothy away from the table and removed him from the dining room. Timothy continued to yell, but the newspaper did not quote any of his shouts. The congressman apparently had not
been seriously hurt.

"Wow," I said. "I bet Olivia was frosted."

"There's another sheet coming," Joe said.

He pulled it off the fax machine. This headline was much smaller, probably one column. It had run the day after the first story:

CONGRESSMAN
ASKS LENIENCY
FOR OLD FRIEND

That story reported that Representative VanHorn told the prosecutor
that he had not been injured and pled the case of his brother-in-law, citing
him as a Vietnam veteran. Since the congressman did not want to file
charges, the prosecutor had agreed to release Timothy Hart, "one of the
heirs to the Hart food-processing fortune."

And that was all the *Grand Rapids Press* had in its files on Timothy Hart.

"They hushed that up in a hurry," Joe said.

"I can see why," I said. "I guess Chief Jones ought to see these clippings. This definitely shows that Timothy has a history of violence."

Joe offered to take the faxes down to the police station, and I went back to the chocolate shop. I sat in my office and stared at my computer screen, feeling unhappy about the situation. In spite of his problems, Timothy Hart was a likeable old guy. I wasn't pleased with the thought of him as a killer. Of course, I liked the thought of Jeff as a killer even less. Yes, the more Timothy could be made to look like a possible killer, the more likely it would be that Chief Jones would release Jeff.

And the closeness of Timothy's attack on his brother-in-law to the death of that brother-in-law was interesting. Had Timothy still been angry the night Vic VanHorn wandered out into a heavy rainstorm and stood too close to the bank that overlooked Lake Michigan?

Chief Jones would say I was letting my imagination run away with me on that one. Olivia VanHorn would do a lot to avoid scandal, but it was hard to believe she'd cover up a fight between her husband and her brother if it made her a widow.

The whole situation made me feel miserable. I opened my desk drawer and had a Dutch caramel from the box Joe had given me. It didn't make me feel better, but it did remind me that I hadn't had lunch. I admitted to myself I wasn't getting any work done, stood up and put on my jacket, then told Aunt Nettie I was going down to the Sidewalk Café for a sandwich.

At least the weather was pleasant that day. The sun was shining, and I tried to cheer up as I walked down the block. But the thought of Jeff in the Warner Pier Police Station was like a heavy weight on my shoulders. I was sure he was innocent. But all Joe and I had been able to do was dig up another suspect. We had no real evidence against Timothy.

Then there were Gail's actions right before her death. She'd acted crazy. Why had she been so pleased when the mold turned up missing after the burglary? What had she meant when she e-mailed Celia Carmichael and told her she'd found a piece of valuable glass, "or even plastic"? Didn't she know which it was?

Darn it! Joe had gotten so close to finding out whether Timothy still had his old sports car—and checking to see if it had a broken taillight. . . .

I stopped dead in my tracks, right in front of Downtown Drugs. Old glass or maybe plastic! Could Gail have been referring to the taillight of a car? Could she have been aware that Timothy's car was still around, and that it had a broken taillight? Could she have tried to blackmail Timothy over the broken taillight?

Suddenly it became very important to find out whether that classic sports car still existed. I half turned, ready to go down the street to the police station.

And at that moment Hart VanHorn walked out of Downtown Drugs and almost bumped into me. He smiled.

"Oh!" My squeal sounded guilty to me, but I guess I sounded thrilled to Hart.

He beamed at me. "Listen, I'm still eager for us to go out sometime."

"That sounds supper, Hart." Supper? Had I said supper? "Super!" I said. "It sounds great. But right now things are in tumult. I mean turmoil."

"The police are still holding your stepson?"

"Yes. But we did find his parents. They'll be here tonight."

"Good. Then all the responsibility won't be on you."

"All the blame may be."

I was aware that I sounded glum. Hart looked sympathetic. "I wish I knew something to do to help."

I thought briefly of suggesting that he turn his uncle in for killing Gail. But I quickly faced the fact that even if Timothy was involved in Gail's death, Hart probably knew nothing about it. Timothy, even with his pickled brain, would be unlikely to confess to his nephew.

"Webb Bartlett seems to know what he's doing," I said. "And Jeff has confidence in him." It was time to change the subject. "You're bustling about today."

"I'm off again. Some vacation." Hart gestured, and I turned and saw his mother's Lincoln parked by the curb. "Mother and Uncle Tim are with me. We stopped to pick up a prescription, and I've got to talk to a guy in Grand Rapids."

I waved at Timothy Hart and Mrs. VanHorn and said good-bye to Hart. I went on toward the Sidewalk Café but I didn't go inside. When I got to the restaurant I turned and looked back. Yes, the VanHorn car was turning the corner, headed toward the highway to Grand Rapids.

I lost interest in eating lunch and formed a new goal.

Running into Hart might seem coincidental, but in a town of twenty-five hundred, coincidences like that happen all the time. You can't go to the grocery store, or to the drugstore, without running into someone you know. But this particular meeting seemed to be full of meaning.

If Hart, Olivia, and Timothy were all going to Grand Rapids—driving time at least an hour up and an hour back—then the Hart-VanHorn compound would be deserted, possibly all afternoon.

It was the ideal time for a burglary.

I took two deep breaths and made up my mind. I would break into that barn-garage where the Harts and VanHorns stored their vehicles, and I would check under every canvas cover until I made sure that a 1968 MGB wasn't there. And I'd check out the snowmobile.

I made a swift U-turn and went back to the shop. I stuck my head in, told Aunt Nettie I was going to be gone for a while, then got into my van and drove off. I tried to do it all without hesitation. I knew that if I thought the situation through, my law-abiding nature would pop back into control, and my career as a burglar would be over before it started. So as I drove to the Hart-VanHorn compound, a quarter of a mile south of Aunt Nettie's driveway, I concentrated on how to accomplish the task at hand.

First, I needed a place to hide my van. That was no problem. I decided to leave it in Aunt Nettie's driveway and walk to the Hart-VanHorn place.

I took a flashlight out of the glove compartment and went back to Lake Shore Drive. I stepped along briskly, trying to look as if I were just out for some exercise, and walked down Lake Shore Drive to the big stone arch that marked the Hart-VanHorn entrance.

The white gate was closed, but it was only designed to keep out cars. A pedestrian could climb right over, and I did.

The compound's drive had been carefully plowed, so what snow was there was hard-packed and would not show footprints. I might be determined to become a housebreaker, but I wasn't particularly eager to pay a penalty for my actions. I'd been careful to wear my gloves—slick leather ones that wouldn't leave fuzzies behind—and to cover my hair with a stocking cap I kept in the van. My red jacket was a problem, but it was too cold to leave it in the van. Anyway, the neighborhood wasn't exactly thronged with people that time of the day and that season of the year.

As I walked I decided that the simplest way to break into the barn was to first break into Timothy's house and find the key to the barn. That barn was solid metal, with metal doors and no windows. It would be much easier to break into the old farmhouse.

Timothy's walk had been neatly shoveled. I followed it to the front porch. I knocked on the door, just in case. Then I tried the handle. No luck. Timothy's brain wasn't so addled that he went off and left his door unlocked. I shrugged. But what had he said on the tape? He was responsible for leaving the key in the usual place for the handyman and landscapers.

Timothy routinely left a key outside his house. Where?

A quick look showed me that it wasn't under the mat. And the mailbox was back on the road, so that wouldn't be a good place to leave it. My grandmother had always wired an extra key to a bush outside her house, but all of Timothy's bushes were bare of leaves. I would have seen a wired-on key in a minute.

Well, there are a few advantages to being tall. I pulled off one of my gloves and felt the top of the door frame. Nothing. I wiped any fingerprints away with my balled-up glove.

Maybe the key was at the back door. I hopped over the edge of the porch into the snow and headed around the house. I did try to swish my feet around, hoping to obliterate my footprints. Timothy had old-fashioned wooden storm windows, the kind with ventilation holes along the bottom.

I tugged at a couple, but they were in solidly. I was prepared to smash one out, but I hoped it wouldn't come to that.

I tracked snow onto the back porch and tried the kitchen door. Locked. Then I reached up and felt the top of that door frame. And my fingers felt something furry.

I nearly jumped out of my skin. And as I did something flew through the air and landed on the porch floor with a kerplunk.

It was a strip of fur with a key ring attached. And that key ring held a key.

My heart began to beat faster as I used my glove to erase any fingerprints from the top of the door frame, then slid it back on. I was about to break and enter.

It was a big disappointment when the key didn't fit the back door. It was much too small. Now what? There must be dozens of locks on the four houses and assorted outbuildings of the Hart-VanHorn compound. Which one would this key open? Or did it open a door at all? It really was tiny.

I looked over the edge of the porch and saw an old-fashioned cellar door. The "slide down my cellar door" kind. By all rights it should have been covered with snow, but Timothy had apparently opened it recently and it was fairly clear. And like most of its kind from around 1900, it was kept closed by latch and a padlock.

In a split second I was off the porch and trying that little key on the padlock. It opened. I pulled open the cellar door, grabbed my flashlight out of my pocket, and was down the stairs and into the house. My career as a burglar had begun.

As I'd guessed, Timothy had a Michigan basement. Most older houses in our area, including Aunt Nettie's, have them. I flashed my light around. All I could see were boxes and heaps of the kind of stuff that accumulates in basements. The stairway was along the right-hand wall.

I went back and wrestled the cellar door shut. Then I crossed the sandy floor to the stairway, stamped my feet to remove what snow and sand I could on the bottom step, and went up to a closed door. The door opened into the kitchen. I looked around. It was a very ordinary kitchen. Judging by the red-and-white color scheme, just like my Texas grandmother's, it had probably been updated sometime in the 1950s. As I walked across the floor, I left sandy tracks. Tough. Maybe I'd have time to sweep before I left.

"I'll go back to the kitchen and get the keys." That's what Timothy had said on Joe's videotape. I was in the kitchen. So, where would Timothy Hart keep keys? In a drawer?

It took me maybe three minutes to find the keys. They were in the broom closet on a key rack made of varnished wood with little brass cup hooks screwed in a row. A child's wood-burning set had obviously been used to cut the word "Keys" into the top of the rack. The rack had such a

Boy Scout–project look about it that it summoned up a picture of Hart as a dark-haired twelve-year-old making a Christmas present for his favorite uncle.

The key rack made me feel like an interloper. But I reminded myself that Jeff had been a cute little twelve-year-old, too, and I looked at the keys.

Luckily, most of them were labeled, and I found one that said Garage and one that said Barn right away. Since I wasn't positive what Timothy called the big storage building, I took both of them. Then I went on through the house, unlocked the dead bolt on the front door, and left it unlocked. Again, I might need to get back through that door in a hurry. I left via the front porch.

I followed the path Timothy and Joe had taken that morning—it was pretty well trampled down by their traipsing back and forth—and went over to the big storage building. The Barn key fit the side door, the one Joe and Timothy had entered by. I closed the door behind me and used my flashlight to find the light switch. There before me were all those shrouded mounds I'd seen on the video.

I didn't fool around looking at wooden boats. I began nearest the door and moved from mound to mound, yanking up the canvas covers.

The first thing I found was that purple snowmobile. I pulled its cover all the way back and looked it over as well as I could. Of course, snowmobiles all look pretty much alike to me. Unless I found newsprint from the *Grand Rapids Press* on the windscreen, I wouldn't be able to tell if this was the one that chased me. But it sure did look like it.

I found the model and serial numbers and committed them to memory, one advantage of being a number person. I shuddered and pulled the canvas back over it.

Then I looked under the other covers. I found the newer boat, the one Joe had sneered at as fiberglass; the old wooden Chris-Craft; a big riding mower; a garden tractor; and a small camping trailer. And at the end of the row, exactly opposite a closed overhead door, was an empty space.

It was obviously the place where a car could have sat.

But there was no car there.

I stared at that empty space. I'd convinced myself that Timothy still owned his MGB. Greg Glossop had seen it just a year earlier.

But it wasn't there. Tears welled up in my eyes, and I stood there blinking.

Then I spoke sternly to myself. "Cry later, Lee," I said aloud. "Right now you're trespassing. Get out of here. Then you can bawl all you want."

I walked clear back to the end of the barn, making sure there were no more rooms to it. But it was just a big, empty shell. There was a loft over half of it, true, but I didn't think Timothy Hart was strong enough to toss a sports car up there. Just to be sure, or maybe just out of curiosity, I ran up the little stairway and shone the beam of my flashlight around.

Old furniture and boxes. I could see why Gail had been so eager to handle any estate sale the Hart-VanHorn clan planned. There was enough old stuff out there to stock a dozen shops the size of Gail's.

But there was no MGB. I had broken and entered for nothing.

Now to get out. I hurried back to the door and peeked out, almost afraid I'd be facing some law officer summoned by a neighbor. But there was no one in sight. I stepped outside and pulled the key out of my pocket.

And a second key dropped into the snow.

I scrabbled around until I found it. It was the key marked Garage. I locked the barn door, then stared at the second key.

"Garage." Hmmm. On the videotape Timothy had said that his sister had a garage in her house. As a matter of fact, the other house, the brick one, probably had a garage, too. Of course, it was unlikely that Timothy's car would be parked in either of his sister's garages.

But as long as I had the key, I thought I'd better look.

I trotted down the drive, toward the stone house with the little bridge leading to the porch. The drive, of course, was well cleared down that way, too, and it led around the end of the house and curved down a slope. As soon as I went around the curve, I saw a three-car garage.

The garage was under the house, in the basement, and it had two overhead doors, a double and a single. The Garage key didn't fit either of them. Perhaps the key fit a garage in the brick house instead.

I stood in the driveway and stared at the key stupidly. Then I noticed a sidewalk that led to the back of the house. It was covered with snow, but its outline was clear. I followed it, doing the foot-twisting trick I hoped would keep my boot tracks from being identified. And there, under a deck overlooking the lake, was another door, an ordinary door, not an overhead door. And the Garage key from Timothy's kitchen fit.

I went inside and groped for a switch. There was none near the door, and I had to use my flashlight to find a way to turn the overhead light on. And when it came on, I saw another of those canvas-shrouded mounds the Van-Horns were so fond of.

This one was long, but not too tall. I was afraid to lift the canvas. It seemed to be my last chance to clear Jeff.

I forced myself to grab the canvas sheet and throw it back.

And there, dirty and mud spattered, was a black sports car.

My heart nearly stopped.

I yanked the cover completely off. I walked down the side of the car, leaned over, and examined the left taillight.

It was broken.

"Yee-haw!"

I'm not a Texan for nothing. I jumped up and down. I crowed with delight. I howled like a coyote.

Jeff was going to get out of jail. Before Rich arrived!

"Yee-haw!"

I was still yelling and jumping when a motor clicked on and the double garage door began to go up.

CHOCOLATE CHAT

JUST A LITTLE BITE

Many short stories have used chocolate as a prop.

- The ultimate story focusing on chocolate may be "Of Course You Know that Chocolate Is a Vegetable," by Barbara D'Amato. Published in 1998 in *Ellery Queen's Mystery Magazine*, the story won the Agatha, Anthony, and Macavity Awards for Best Short Story in 1999. It was anthologized in *Crème de la Crime* in 2000. And what is the exotic murder weapon used in the story? I'll never tell!

- Agatha Christie wrote a story called "The Chocolate Box," published in the United States in *Hercule Poirot's Early Cases* in 1974. It's typical Christie, expertly using sleight of hand to confuse the reader. In it Hercule Poirot describes a case of political and religious intrigue that he investigated as a young detective in Belgium. And the key clue turns out to be not the chocolates, but the box they are in.

- Lee McKinney also made her debut in a short story. A look at Lee when she was sixteen and first worked at TenHuls Chocolade was the background for "The Chocolate Kidnapping Clue," published in 2001 in the anthology *And the Dying Is Easy*.

Chapter 20

I nearly wet my pants.

The dirty cheats! Less than an hour earlier, Hart had told me they were headed to Grand Rapids. They couldn't possibly have driven all the way up there and back again already.

I left the dust sheet off the sports car and the garage light on, and I ran out the door I'd come in. I made a sharp right turn and ran along under the deck. There was a little snow there, but I didn't worry about making tracks. I was making time.

My troubles began when I got to the end of the deck and came out at the other end of the house into hip-deep snow. Not only had the snow been piling up there since November, but the ground also rose steeply. I slipped and slid as if I were climbing the Matterhorn without a safety rope.

But I kept going, slogging through the snow, trying to get around the side of the house, out of sight.

Then I heard a voice. "Lee! Lee! What are you doing? It's only me. Olivia!"

Just as she yelled my feet went out from under me. I landed on my fanny and slid halfway down the slope. I could hear Olivia laughing, though she didn't sound terribly amused.

"Lee," she said. "Come here. I'm not going to hurt you."

I'd been caught. But I hadn't been caught by Timothy. Timothy, who'd already killed. It was very likely that Olivia didn't know that her brother had sneaked his car out to make clandestine trips into town to commit crimes. I'd realized that I'd have to confront her sometime. I'd planned to have Chief Jones there, but it now seemed I was going to do it alone.

I got to my feet and came back, feeling really stupid. Olivia VanHorn was her usual poised self, stunning in winter-white slacks, polished boots, and her casual mink.

"I owe you an apology," I said. "I'm trespassing."

"Now you're not. Now you have my permission to be here. Were you looking for the MGB?"

I nodded. "Yes. I've simply got to get Jeff out of jail. And that meant I had to find that car. The taillight is broken. It's going to implicate your brother."

Mrs. VanHorn's eyes widened. She made a noise that could only be described as a ladylike grunt. Her mouth twitched. Then she led the way into the garage and went to the back of the sports car. "I had suspected Timothy had taken the car out," she said. "I guess I lacked the courage to check the rear end, even after I heard the police were hunting a sports car with a broken taillight."

She leaned over and looked at the taillight closely. Then she sighed. "We might as well call the police."

"I can drive back to the station and talk to Chief Jones."

Mrs. VanHorn shook her head. "No, I have to face it. You're quite right about your stepson. We can't let that innocent young man remain under suspicion any longer. Come into the house with me, and I'll call Chief Jones."

I was amazed at how calmly she was taking the whole thing. I followed as Mrs. VanHorn went to a door in the center of the back wall, then led me up a stairway that ended in a beautifully decorated kitchen. "Take your coat off," she said. "There's a coat rack behind the door. Just let me put my boots away, and then I'll telephone the police."

She walked on through a foyer and down a carpeted hall. I was a little surprised that she didn't take her own boots off before she stepped onto the carpet. Then I realized that Olivia hadn't been running through the snow the way I had. Her boots were dry.

I found a small rug near the back door, and I stood on it, stamping the snow off my feet, trying to keep from spotting the tile. I unzipped my jacket, but I didn't take it off, though I saw a navy blue Polartec parka hanging on the rack Olivia had mentioned. I wondered if Timothy had worn it when he chased me with the snowmobile.

I was still standing there, feeling ill at ease, when Olivia VanHorn came back down the hall. I was surprised to see that she hadn't taken off her boots, or her coat either.

I was even more surprised when she pulled a pistol from behind her back.

I gave a yelp. "What's going on?"

Olivia sighed. "You're a burglar, Lee, and I'm going to shoot you."

"Shoot me!"

"Yes. Young woman, you are simply too nosy. I must protect my family."

"But Timothy—he'll get off with diminished responsibility. I can't believe you would kill to protect him!"

"Timothy? Don't be silly. Timothy wouldn't kill anyone. He passes out by nine o'clock every evening. He couldn't possibly get out in the night, meet people, do the things I had to do to protect my son."

"Your son!"

"Certainly. You can understand that—after all the trouble you've taken to protect a boy who's merely your stepson."

"Hart? You're trying to protect Hart?"

"It's imperative, I'm afraid. I really have no choice. If this story comes out, it will ruin his political career. Please step a little further into the kitchen."

I ignored her request. "Did Hart kill Gail Hess?"

"That wretched blackmailer? Of course not!"

"Then how will killing me protect Hart?"

"We won't go into that. Please, step a little further into the kitchen."

I didn't budge. "Why?"

"So it will be clear that you were an intruder, that I surprised a burglar who was actually in the house. Then it will be legal to shoot you."

I backed up a step.

"No, no!" Mrs. VanHorn spoke as if I were a backward child. "Don't move away. Come forward."

I stared at her. This situation was unbelievable. This ladylike, gracious woman was going to kill me. And she had invited me into her home so that it would look legal. It was like the advice of a cynic—if you shoot a burglar on the porch, drag him inside the house to make it look legal.

The whole thing was so absurd I was tempted to laugh. But the pistol in Olivia VanHorn's hand and the calm resolve on her face kept the situation from being funny.

I put my hand behind me and touched the doorknob. To get out I'd have to open the door and run all the way down the narrow stairway. Mrs. Van-Horn would have plenty of time to shoot me as I ran.

Or I could rush forward and try to slam into her. She'd have plenty of time to shoot me that way, too.

But either fate would be better than standing there and letting her kill me, then pass my death off as the shooting of a burglar.

Now Mrs. VanHorn's eyes narrowed. "I'm tired of waiting," she said. "Move forward!"

My fingers gripped the doorknob. Getting shot in the back would be the best way, I decided. That way she wouldn't have such an easy time passing my death off as the murder of an intruder.

I shrank back against the door.

"Very well," she said. "I'm not waiting any longer."

She raised the pistol. I turned the door handle.

And the doorbell rang.

Mrs. VanHorn and I both froze, and in the awful silence I heard Timothy Hart's voice coming from outside. "Olivia? Olivia! Someone's broken into my house! There are tracks all over the kitchen floor and the front door's unlocked! I called the police!"

Olivia's head whipped toward his voice.

I whirled, yanked the door open, and plunged down the steps to the garage.

Thumpety thumpety! My boots hit every other step. Then a louder thump drowned them out. A shot! I didn't think it had hit me. I fell down the last three steps, but I caught myself with the door handle. The door into the garage swung open, and I stumbled out and ran headlong into Hart VanHorn.

I screamed like a Texas banshee.

Hart grabbed me. He screamed, too. But the sounds he made produced words. "What's wrong? What's happened?"

At first I could only point at the door and shriek. Then I managed, "A gun! She's got a gun. She's going to kill me!"

Olivia came rushing out. She was still brandishing her pistol, and she aimed it at me.

Hart's grip on my arms tightened, and for a second I thought he was going to hold me still so his mother could shoot me. Then he slung me around.

He shoved me behind him. He put his body between me and his mother. He yelled, "No! Stop!"

Olivia looked like a madwoman. Her calm façade had completely collapsed. "Get out of the way!" she screamed.

"No!"

"She's a burglar! I'm going to shoot her!"

"No!" Hart let go of me, and I staggered against his mother's car. A shot echoed thunderously, bouncing off the garage walls.

Hart jumped toward his mother. They were both yelling. He grabbed at the pistol, and it went off again.

Blood spurted. I shrieked. Hart growled.

Olivia screamed. "I've shot you!"

The "you" was Hart. He clutched his arm and leaned against the fender of his mother's Lincoln. I realized he was still trying to stay between me and the gun.

Olivia dropped the pistol to her side and stared at him. Fear, horror, shock, and anger washed over her face.

In the sudden silence, Hart spoke quietly. "Mother, no matter how many people you kill, I'm not going to run for Congress."

Now the emotion on Olivia's face was agony, and her voice was a whisper. "Hart, Hart. I love you. I wanted to protect you."

"I know, Mother. But I can't hide behind you any longer."

"Does it all have to come out?"

"Yes. This can't go on."

Olivia sobbed. After all the screaming, the yelling, and the shots, that simple sound may have been the most soul chilling of all.

Then she turned and ran back into the house.

Behind me I heard Timothy Hart's voice. "What on earth is wrong with Olivia?"

"I'm not sure," I said. "But call an ambulance. Hart's been shot."

I heard a piercing, shrill sound. A siren. The cavalry—personified by the Warner Pier Police Department—had arrived.

I saw a box of what looked like clean rags on a shelf near the door to the kitchen stairs. I grabbed a handful. I went to Hart, helped him out of his jacket and applied pressure to his arm. Timothy was disappearing up the driveway, I assumed to direct the police car to Olivia's garage. In a few seconds I heard him speak. "Thank God you got here so fast. Olivia's gone berserk. And we need an ambulance."

Right at that moment I heard a far-off, muffled thump from inside the house. Hart closed his eyes and groaned, way down deep in his chest.

I was using both hands to hold the rags on his arm. "I'm so sorry, Hart," I said. "I'm so sorry."

It didn't seem adequate, but what else was there to say?

Faced with an armed suspect, Jerry Cherry followed procedure and called for a backup. Chief Jones and a Michigan State Police car were there within minutes. The chief and the state cop entered the VanHorn house through the garage while I sat in the patrol car, shaking. Olivia did not challenge them or answer the questions they called out to her.

They found her in the bathtub, dead, still wearing her fur coat. There was a note on the bathroom counter, which the chief let me see later. "I killed Gail Hess," it read. "She was a filthy blackmailer, and she had found out I broke into the TenHuis shop and took the mold. Fifteen years ago, I killed my husband. Hart had nothing to do with it."

As usual, word of what had happened at the Hart-VanHorn compound spread through Warner Pier rapidly. By the time I got to the police station to make a statement, Joe was on the spot. He met me with a big hug, a hug I deeply appreciated, and he didn't reproach me for breaking and entering.

We were sitting on a bench in the main room, holding hands, when Hart VanHorn and Timothy Hart came in. Hart's arm was in a sling.

Timothy gestured at Hart. "He should have stayed in the hospital."

Hart shook his head. "My arm's not that serious," he said. "I need to talk to Chief Jones, and I want to do it now."

"It's all my fault!" I didn't know the words were coming out until I'd spoken them. "I suspected Timothy of being our burglar, because I learned he'd still owned his MGB as recently as a year ago. So I—I admit it—I broke into the storage barn at the compound looking for that car. When it wasn't there, I looked in your mother's garage."

"And you found the MGB," Hart said.

"Yes. And the taillight was broken. I was desperate to get Jeff out of jail."

"I could have told you the car was there, but I didn't know about the taillight."

I decided to ignore that. "I thought your mother and Timothy had gone to Grand Rapids with you."

"No, they went only as far as Holland. I had to pick up my SUV at the dealer's there, so they dropped me off and came back. None of us went to Grand Rapids."

"You said you had to see a man in Grand Rapids."

Hart smiled gently. "I didn't deliberately mislead you, Lee, but what I said was that I needed 'to talk to a man in Grand Rapids.' I never intended to go there to talk to him. I—well, I knew Mother was up to something, though I wasn't sure just what. I wanted to talk to my psychologist about it. I called him from Holland because my cell phone works better up there."

I clutched Joe's hand, but I spoke to Hart. "Your mother caught me in the garage. First she acted quite friendly. She laughed! She invited me into the house. Then she said I was a burglar, and she was going to shoot me."

Hart dropped his head.

"I know it's hard to believe," I said. "I couldn't believe it while I was running for my life."

"Oh, I can believe it," Hart said. "Mother was very coolheaded, and she had an extremely creative way of handling the truth. She wouldn't have wanted anybody to know about that car. Any more than she wanted anybody to know I'd been seeing a psychologist."

"She didn't want people to know you'd seen a psychologist?" I was mystified. "So what? So who hasn't? That's nothing to get excited about."

"It might have meant nothing to you, maybe, but to Mom it was the kiss of death to my political career."

"Surely people are not that ignorant. . . ."

But Hart was shaking his head. "It wasn't the mere fact that I was seeing a psychologist, Lee. It was what she was afraid I might tell him."

"Oh." Suddenly I didn't want to know any more.

But it seemed I was going to, because Hart went on talking. "You see, I killed my father."

I was silent, and Joe squeezed my hand.

Timothy spoke. "But this is stupid, my boy. Nobody killed your father. He fell! It was an accident. Nobody ever suggested it was anything else. And now both you and Olivia claim to have killed Vic."

Hart smiled at his uncle. "Mother didn't kill him, Uncle Tim. She was still trying to protect me. Me and my wonderful political career. But I can't stand to lie about it anymore. I killed my father. Oh, it wasn't murder—only manslaughter, I guess. Maybe even justifiable homicide.

"Fifteen years ago—when I was twenty—my father was drunk. He threatened my mother. I punched him, trying to protect her. He fell against the china cabinet, the one that held my grandmother's collection of chocolate molds. The cabinet fell over. It landed on him, and the back of his head was smashed in.

"I was willing to call the police. At least an ambulance. But my mother wouldn't hear of it. She got a wheelbarrow from the storage barn, and the two of us threw my father's body over the bank into the lake. His death was accepted as an accident.

"The china cabinet was smashed, and it had blood on it, and one of the molds—some kind of a bear—had a lot of blood on it. I broke the cabinet up with an ax, and we burned it in the fireplace. But we couldn't burn the doors, because of the metal and the glass. Mother washed the bear mold and tossed it and the other molds into a box in the basement of the bungalow. She put some other old kitchen utensils on top, made it look like a box of junk. The collection was too well known to simply get rid of, and I'm sure she figured it would end up going to a museum or something eventually."

He patted his uncle on the shoulder. "Uncle Tim didn't know anything about it. He found the kitchen utensils and molds in the basement and gave them to Gail to sell. The molds wound up being displayed at the TenHuis shop. At first Mother thought that was okay, but then she found out some expert on chocolate molds was going to come to look at them. Apparently Mother tried to break into TenHuis Chocolade and get hold of that bear mold before the expert could want to know why it had been treated badly. Gail must have figured out that the burglar used Uncle Tim's MGB, because of the broken taillight."

Tears were running down Timothy's cheeks. "Gail had seen the MGB," he said. "I showed it to her when she picked up the molds. She knew it had a broken taillight. She may have thought that I was the burglar."

I was having trouble taking all this in. "Did your mother use the snowmobile to chase me?"

"She did have the snowmobile out yesterday," Hart said.

"Why would she chase me?"

Hart rubbed a hand over his forehead. "I know that something you said upset her, when we talked outside the police station that morning. She must have decided you knew something. Maybe that Gail had told you about the MGB and its broken taillight."

The chief came in then. The first thing he said was that Hart should get a lawyer. Then the chief instructed Jerry Cherry to let Jeff out of the holding cell, and he told me we could leave. He and Hart were still arguing about whether Hart should call a lawyer as Joe, Jeff, and I headed out into the winter dusk.

But as we stepped outside that dusk was shattered by strobe lights. I almost ran back inside. Two guys had been waiting, and I recognized them as part of the tabloid crew that had invaded Warner Pier the previous summer.

"Cool it!" Joe told them. "The story's inside the police station! Not out here."

The photographer laughed and flashed his strobe again. "That's not what George said."

"Shut up!" That came from his companion, a man with a notebook.

"You'd better get inside to talk to the chief," Joe said. "I think you're the first team on the scene, and this is going to be a big story."

"Wait a minute," I said. "Did somebody from Warner Pier call you? George? George who?"

"Never mind!" The reporter grabbed the photographer and the two of them hotfooted it into City Hall.

Jeff, Joe, and I stood looking after them. "George?" I said. "Surely he didn't mean George Palmer?"

"Surely he did," Joe said. "George is on the park commission. I thought one of the commission members had to be the tabloid source. They were the only people who knew I'd approached Mike Herrera about selling the Warner Point property to the city."

"Why didn't you say something earlier?"

"I couldn't rule out someone from the lawyer's office blabbing. I tried to give George the benefit of the doubt."

"He's so obnoxious!"

Joe shrugged. "Well, I'll tell Mike Herrera what we've deduced, and Mike will call George's father-in-law, and maybe old George will have a new job pretty quick."

"Wouldn't that be great! Maybe Barbara can come back."

Jeff's jacket was still being held as evidence, so the three of us ran the two blocks to TenHuis Chocolade for a joyful reunion with Aunt Nettie and Tess. We were all in the workroom, jumping up and down and turning cartwheels, when someone came in the front door. One of the hairnet ladies went up to the counter.

I heard a deep voice with a Texas accent. "Ah'm lookin' for Lee McKinney," it said.

Jeff's eyes suddenly were the size of dinner plates. "It's Dad," he said in a whisper.

I sighed. I had to face Rich sometime. "Bring him back to the shop," I said.

Rich came in. Dina was with him. Dina's eyes locked on only one thing. "Jeff!" she said. "You're here!"

Suddenly they were in a three-way hug. "I'm all right!" Jeff kept saying. "I'm all right."

They finally loosened their grips and turned around toward the rest of us, all three of them with tear-streaked faces. And sometime in there Jeff's lip stud had disappeared.

Jeff started talking. "Lee kept working 'til she figured out who really killed that woman. She got me out of jail."

That led to more commotion, of course. Dina had to hug me—and after a minute, Rich did, too. They had to meet Tess. They had to confirm the news Jeff had told us earlier—they had gone to Mexico in an attempt at reconciliation.

Apparently it had worked. Dina held out her left hand and proudly showed off her new wedding ring. I was surprised at its appearance. It was a simple piece of Mexican silver. No clusters of diamonds. No ruby the size of an idol's eye. It was definitely a sincere wedding ring, not one to show off to your business associates. Maybe Rich actually had changed his ways.

I hugged her. Dina had always been pretty nice to me. "I want you two to be really happy," I said. I shook Rich's hand.

Then they had to hear the whole story of our burglary and the murder of Gail Hess. Through all of this, Joe leaned against a worktable, saying nothing. It was nearly an hour later when Rich looked at his watch and said, "Are we going to be able to find a place to stay?"

I called the Inn on the Pier and was assured they had rooms available. "Good!" Rich said. "Now, I already noticed a restaurant open down the street. I'd like to take everyone to dinner."

I looked at Aunt Nettie. She looked at Tess. Aunt Nettie used her mental telepathy powers and told both of us to say no.

"I think I'd better go home, take a hot shower and get into my flannel pj's," Aunt Nettie said.

"And I think I'd better go with you," Tess said. "I have to call my parents." Aunt Nettie patted her hand and smiled.

"Lee?" Rich looked at me.

Behind me Joe stirred. "Sorry," he said. "I'm taking Lee to the Dock Street Pizza tonight."

I went over to Joe. "You're sure?"

"I'm not taking another chance on losing you, Lee."

Then he put his arms around me, right in front of God and everybody. Which included Aunt Nettie, Rich, Dina, Jeff, Tess, and three of the hairnet ladies who hadn't left yet.

But Aunt Nettie had one more comment. "Before the party breaks up," she said, "would anybody like a sample chocolate?"

Rich had an Italian cherry bonbon and immediately began talking to Aunt Nettie about boxes to give as business gifts.

Dina told him to hush and picked out a raspberry cream bonbon ("Red raspberry puree in white chocolate cream interior"). "It smells heavenly in here," she said.

Tess went for a double fudge bonbon and Jeff asked for a Jamaican rum truffle.

"Could Lee and I take ours in a little box?" Joe asked. He took a coffee truffle ("All milk chocolate, flavored with Caribbean coffee") and I chose a Frangelico one. Aunt Nettie settled for solid chocolate with bits of hazelnut.

Ten minutes later—after we'd seen the others off and I'd locked up—Joe and I went out the front door. Joe took my hand again.

"Our friendship is about to meet a new challenge," Joe said. "The big question is, do you like anchovies on your pizza?"

"No!"

"Good! Come on."

We got in Joe's truck and headed for Dock Street Pizza. Right in front of God and everybody.

The
Chocolate Frog
Frame-Up

Chapter 1

If you're going to have a fistfight in a small town—and avoid a lot of talk about it—the post office is not a good place for the battle.

And shortly before five o'clock in the afternoon—when it seems every merchant in town is dropping off the mail and lots of the tourists are buying stamps—is not a good time for it.

The fight between Joe Woodyard and Hershel Perkins erupted in the Warner Pier Post Office at 4:32 on a Monday afternoon in late June. Later I decided that it had been planned that way. And I didn't think Joe was in on the plan.

I was one of the local merchants who witnessed the fight, since I walked into the post office with a handful of outgoing statements for TenHuis Chocolade just in time to hear Joe speak.

He sounded calm. "What are you talking about, Hershel?"

Hershel Perkins did not sound calm. He was almost shouting. "It's about the old Root Beer Barrel. Don't try to act innocent!"

"The old drive-in? I'm trying to sell it."

"Yes, you money-grubbing piece of . . ."

Those were fighting words to Joe, I knew, because Joe—who happens to be my boyfriend—was in a financial hole right at the moment. It's a long story, but he needed money, even if he had to grub for it, and the sale of the dilapidated and abandoned drive-in restaurant might be the raft that kept his business afloat.

Joe raised his voice just a little when he answered. "What is your interest in this, Hershel?"

"I hear you might tear it down!"

"Tear it down? It's already fallen down."

"It's a piece of history!"

"History?" Joe sounded puzzled, as well as annoyed. "It's a bunch of boards lying in a parking lot. It's junk."

I was all the way inside the post office now, and I could see Hershel. He seemed to be puffing himself up. Not that Hershel was all that small. He was at least five nine, just a few inches shorter than I am. He was around forty, with a broad face and a wide, narrow-lipped mouth that made him look like a frog. It was a resemblance he seemed to relish—he combed his thin hair flat and always wore green shirts, flannel in winter and cotton in summer. Even his voice was a froglike croak, and he went places in a green canoe named the *Toadfrog*.

He gave an angry grunt. "Junk! You call it junk? It's vernacular architecture!"

Joe laughed.

Hershel went nuts. He rasped out incoherent phrases. Words like "typical commercial," "innovation," "rehabilitation," "social geography," and "culturally significant." None of it made sense to me—and I was willing to bet it didn't make sense to Hershel, either. Hershel is not one of the brightest bulbs shining on Warner Pier, Michigan.

Joe tried to talk over the ranting, which meant he had to raise his voice. "Hershel, I already talked to the Planning Department. The Historic District Commission has no interest in that property since the building was destroyed by an act of God."

Hershel kept up the angry bullfrog act, although hollering out "architectural ethnicity!" is not an effective way to argue.

Finally Joe did absolutely the worst thing he could have done—even worse than laughing. He turned his back on Hershel and reached for his post office box.

Hershel gave a loud roar and began to pummel Joe's shoulders with both fists.

Joe whirled around, throwing up his elbows to protect his face. Then he caught hold of Hershel's arms—first the left and then the right—and he whirled again. He pinned Hershel against the wall of post office boxes, almost the way he had pinned his opponents to the mat in the days when he was a high school wrestling champ.

Hershel finally shut up.

"Hershel," Joe said very quietly, "you can't go around hitting people. Get in your canoe and paddle home."

A couple of Warner Pier locals—one of them Hershel's brother-in-law, Frank Waterloo—appeared beside Joe. From the back of the room I heard another deep voice, this one smooth and slightly accented with Spanish. It was our mayor, Mike Herrera. "Yes, Hershel," he said, "pleeze go home. We have a forum for discussion of theese design matters. You can bring it up at the Preservation Commission. There ees no need to battle it out here. Not weeth all our summer visitors as weetnesses."

The altercation had upset Mike. I could tell by his long "E's." Mike was born in Texas, and his accent usually tends more toward a Southwestern drawl than Spanglish.

Frank Waterloo, who's a bald, hulking guy, made his voice soft and gentle as he spoke to his brother-in-law. "Let's go, Hershel," he said.

Joe let go of Hershel. Hershel eyed the ring of guys around him. I swear he flicked his tongue in and out like a frog after flies. Then he walked slowly toward the street door, ignoring Frank. After Hershel pulled the door open, he paused and looked back. "That's what you say!" he said hoarsely.

He went outside, followed by Frank, then poked his head back in for a final croak. "I'll file charges!"

And he was gone. Nervous laughter swept the post office, and a couple of guys went over to Joe and assured him they'd back him up if Hershel filed any kind of complaint.

"The guy's crazy," Trey Corbett said. "The Historic District Commission has no interest in seeing the Root Beer Barrel rebuilt." Trey is a member of the commission.

"You haven't voted yet," Joe said.

Trey ran a hand over his thin, wispy hair and adjusted his thick glasses. To me Trey looks like a middle-aged boy. He's only in his mid-thirties, but his worried expression and nerdy appearance make him look as if he ought to be older. He doesn't sport a pocket protector, but he looks as if he should.

Trey shook his head. "Besides, Hershel hit you first. You only punched him in self-defense."

"Joe didn't punch him at all," I said. "He just griped—I mean 'grabbed'! He grabbed him." No harm in getting that idea foremost in the public mind right away.

Mike Herrera said, "Joe, you handled it as well as you could. But we sure doan want any gossip right at this point, do we?"

I wondered what that meant, but I decided this wasn't a good time to ask. So I spoke to Joe. "Are you hurt?"

Joe shook his head. "I'm fine, Lee." He turned to Mike and Trey. "Let's forget it. Hershel's just a harmless crank."

"He's a crank," Trey said. "But that doesn't mean he's harmless. Some cranks wind up walking up and down the streets with an Uzi."

"I'm no mental health expert," Joe said. "See you later." He turned to me. "You going back to the shop?"

"Oh, yeah. I'm there till closing."

"I'll walk down with you."

I dumped my invoices into the proper slot while Joe closed his post office box and stuck his mail in his shirt pocket. We walked down Pear Avenue toward TenHuis Chocolade. TenHuis—it rhymes with "ice"—is where my aunt, Nettie TenHuis, makes the finest European-style luxury bonbons, truffles, and molded chocolate in the world and where I'd be on duty until after nine o'clock.

The Fourth of July, when the biggest invasion of tourists hits the beaches

of Lake Michigan, was still more than a week away, but the sidewalks of
Warner Pier were crowded, and cars, vans, and SUVs were parked bumper
to bumper. The three classes of Warner Pier society were out in force.

The first class is the tourists—people who visit Warner Pier for a day or
a week and who rent rooms in the local motels or bed-and-breakfast inns.
They were dressed in shorts or jeans with T-shirts—lots of them touting either colleges ("M Go Blue") or vacation spots ("Mackinac Island Bridge").
The tourists wander idly, admiring the Victorian ambiance of Dock Street,
giggling at the sayings on the bumper stickers in the window of the novelty
shop, licking ice-cream cones and nibbling at fudge, pointing at the antiques
("Gramma had one just like that, and *you* threw it away!"), and discussing
the prices at the Warner Winery's shop. They buy postcards or sunscreen or
T-shirts, and sometimes antiques or artwork or expensive kitchen gadgets.

The second class is the "summer people," the ones who own second
homes in Warner Pier or along the shore of Lake Michigan and who stay in
those cottages or condos for much of the summer. Summer people tend to
wear khakis and polo shirts, or other forms of "resort wear." They walk
along more briskly, headed for the furniture store, the hardware store, or the
insurance office. Lots of the summer people are from families who have
been coming to Warner Pier for generations. Lots of them are wealthy; some
are famous. They're important to the Warner Pier economy, too, since they
pay high property taxes for the privilege of living there part-time.

Joe and I represented the "locals," people who live in Warner Pier year-
round. There are only twenty-five hundred of us. The other twenty thousand (I'm overestimating, but not by much) thronging the streets were
tourists and summer people.

Locals wear every darn thing. Joe had on navy blue work pants and a
matching shirt, an outfit suitable for working in the shop where he repairs
and restores antique boats. I was wearing khaki shorts and a chocolate
brown polo shirt with "TenHuis Chocolade" embroidered above the left
boob. A few Warner Pier locals actually wear suits and ties. A very few. Most
dress more like the summer people, except for the artsy crowd. That group
goes in for flowing draperies and ripped jeans.

The throng on the street kept Joe and me from exchanging more than a
few words as we walked along. When we got within a few doors of TenHuis
Chocolade, Joe spoke. "Can I come in and talk to you for a minute?"

"Sure," I said. I opened the door and savored the aroma that met me.
Warm, sweet, comforting—pure chocolate. Also chocolate laced with cherry,
with rum, with coconut, with strawberries, with raspberries, with other delicious flavors. I never get tired of it.

The two teenagers—Tracy and Stacy—working behind the retail sales
counter seemed to be handling the half-dozen tourists who were salivating
over the display cases, so I just waved to them and led Joe into my office.

The office is a small, glass-enclosed room which overlooks both the retail shop and the workroom where the chocolates are made. The skilled women who produce the chocolates were cleaning up for the day—checking the temperatures on the electric kettles of dark, milk, and white chocolate, washing up the stainless steel bowls and spoons, putting racks of half-made bonbons in the storage room, running final trays of chocolate frogs and turtles through the cooling tunnel.

Lifelike frogs, turtles, and fish molded from chocolate were Aunt Nettie's special item for that season. The small ones—about two inches—were plain molded chocolate, but the larger ones—six or eight inches—were more elaborate. Most of the larger ones were of milk chocolate, with fins and other detailing in either dark or white chocolate. The milk chocolate turtles, with their shells decorated with white chocolate, were especially nice, and the frogs—white chocolate decorated with dark chocolate eyes, mouths, and spots—looked as if they might actually hop.

In the office Joe and I both sat down. "Any chance you could get off early tomorrow?" he asked.

"I could talk to Aunt Nettie. She's planning her big pre-tourist season cleanup project—taking the chocolate vats apart—so she may be here late. I guess Stacy could balance out the cash register."

Joe opened his mouth, but before he could say anything the bell on the street door rang, and I caught a flash of bright green from the corner of my eye. Hershel Perkins was walking in.

Joe had his back to the door, so he couldn't see him. I leaned over and spoke quietly. "Hershel just came in to scrounge his daily chocolate. Let's go back to the break room."

Joe and I both avoided looking into the shop again. We walked through the workroom and into the very pleasant break room. It's filled with homey furniture—an antique dining table and some easy chairs—and on the walls are several framed watercolors by local artists.

But right at the moment the break room was crowded. The ladies who had finished up were leaving, and that room is the passage to the back alley. They were walking through, one at a time and in groups, making a great show of not paying any attention to the business manager and her boyfriend.

Joe frowned, then spoke quietly. "I need to talk to you privately. Could you walk down to the park? I'll buy you an ice-cream cone."

"Let me tell Aunt Nettie."

Aunt Nettie was up in the shop, talking to Hershel. It was a little ritual—she was practically the only person in Warner Pier who acted glad to see him.

"Hershel, you mustn't save that too long," she was saying as I came in. "They're for eating, not looking at."

"Aunt Nettie," I said. "I'm going out for a few minutes."

Aunt Nettie turned her back to the counter. "Certainly, Lee. And I'm just getting a eight-inch frog for Hershel. It's the first one we've sold. He wants it as a mascot for his canoe."

I was astonished. Hershel Perkins came in the shop every afternoon and asked for a sample piece of chocolate. I'd never known him to *buy* anything. Particularly not an expensive molded frog. Stacy—Stacy was the plump one; Tracy had stringy hair—turned around and waggled her eyebrows at me. She was obviously astonished, too.

I smiled at Aunt Nettie. "That's great, Mr. Perkins."

Hershel just scowled.

I went back to the break room. "The roof may fall in," I said. "Hershel is actually buying something. He comes in nearly every day to cadge a sample."

"Why does Nettie let him get away with that?" Joe said.

"She says everyone who comes in the shop gets a sample, and Hershel's no different. I think she feels sorry for him."

"I feel sorry for him, too, and I don't want to argue with him again. But I've got to talk to you. Now. Come on."

I was extremely curious. We went out through the alley door and down to the Old Fashioned Ice Cream Parlor, stood in line behind a half-dozen tourists, then took our cones over a block to the Dock Street Park.

The Dock Street Park is the pride of Warner Pier. It's narrow, but it stretches along the Warner River for a mile. The riverside is lined with marinas and public mooring spots for hundreds of small craft. As usual, the river itself was crowded with boats, which can either follow the Warner River upstream or travel down the river and out into Lake Michigan.

None of the park's benches was empty, so we walked along the dock near the public mooring area. Down the way I saw a knot of people gathered around a spiffy wooden motorboat, and I recognized Joe's 1949 Chris-Craft Runabout. Its mahogany deck and sides shone as beautifully as they had the year the boat was built.

I was surprised to see it; Joe usually drives his pickup to town. If he uses a boat, he uses his 1948 Shepherd Sedan. "How come you brought the runabout in?" I said.

"A guy up at Saugatuck wants to see it," Joe said. "I'm going to take it up the lakeshore. Besides, I'm trying to show it off around the marinas. Since the sale fell through."

The boat's price tag was $20,500. Twice Joe and his banker had celebrated because they thought it had sold. Twice the sale had fallen through.

But Joe obviously didn't want to talk about boats. He stopped out of earshot of the gawkers.

"What's this about?" I asked.

Joe stared at his ice-cream cone—one scoop of French silk and one of pecan praline. "I've got a proposition for you," he said.

Then, to my astonishment, he blushed. And he began to stammer. "That was the wrong word. I mean, I've got an invitation. I mean, if you'd like to . . . Maybe we could . . ."

This was really amazing. I'm the one who stammers around, using the wrong word. Joe is the former defense attorney who could convince a jury to turn loose Attila the Hun.

He finally stumbled to a verbal stop and stared at me, apparently at a loss for words.

"What is it, Joe?" I asked.

He took a deep breath. "I did some work on a cabin cruiser for Dave Hadley—you know, at the Warner River Lodge. So—well, he's offered me an evening out at the lodge in exchange. I thought we could take the Shepherd Sedan up there for dinner. Then we could cruise farther up the river. Or out into the lake, if it's calm. I mean, if the mosquitoes aren't too bad. But—you know—we'd need to do it on a weeknight. Because—well, of how crowded the lodge is on weekends. I thought about tomorrow night. If, that is, if you could get the night off."

It wasn't the most gracefully phrased invitation I'd ever had.

Joe's ice-cream cone was dripping down his hand, and he didn't seem to notice. He flushed a slightly deeper shade. "I sound like an idiot," he said. "But I really want you to go."

He looked at me anxiously, and I wanted to laugh. Or give him a big hug. Joe obviously wanted this to be a big romantic evening, and his awkwardness made it plain that he really wanted me to go.

Didn't he know how complimentary that stumbling and stammering was? Because Joe really *was* cool. If asking me to go to the Warner River Lodge for dinner could throw him into a tizzy . . . If he could make the trip into an event, with a ride up the river . . . It meant my answer was important to him.

Which was both gratifying and surprising.

"Lick your ice cream," I said. "When do you want to leave?"

Joe grinned from ear to ear and hauled an arm back as if he was going to yell "Ycehaw!" the way us Texans do. Instead, he exuberantly threw his ice-cream cone about fifty feet out into the river. Then he used his clean hand to squeeze mine. I was sure he wanted to kiss me, but hand-holding is as big a display of affection as I'm likely to get from Joe on a public sidewalk in a public park.

Joe and I had been edging into romance for nearly a year, but it had been a slow journey, and our final destination was still unknown. We both were hauling a lot of emotional baggage, mainly connected with our former spouses, and events such as murder had thrown even more obstacles in our way. For months we hadn't done anything but talk on the phone.

Finally, late in February, Joe had invited me out in public. Since the night we'd made our official appearance at Dock Street Pizza—social center of Warner Pier, Michigan—all our friends and relations had regarded us as a couple. I was twenty-nine and Joe was thirty-three; they assumed we were ready to settle down.

But we weren't a couple yet. And there were a lot of pitfalls in the way of our becoming one.

The first was money, and that was largely my fault. I have a horror of debt which I developed by watching money problems break up my parents' marriage, and my feelings about money only grew more complicated after I married a wealthy man who thought he could buy a solution to any difficulty. Since I knew Joe didn't have a lot of money, I wouldn't let him spend much on me. Seeing him pull out a credit card to pay for dinner ruined my whole evening.

Money bothered Joe, too. By now his buddies from law school were buying big houses and taking European vacations, and he must have had moments when he regretted leaving the practice of law. Because of his legal problems involving his ex-wife—who died deep in financial doo-doo and without changing an old will which made Joe her executor—he could only work part-time on his boat business, so it wasn't growing very fast.

Plus, our living arrangements put a lot of traps in the pathway to romance. Joe lived in one room at the boat shop and cooked with a hot plate and a microwave. His décor included a roll-away bed and a worn recliner. Because of this, he didn't like to invite me over. I shared a house with my aunt. I'd asked Joe over to dinner a few times, but Aunt Nettie insisted on retiring to her bedroom, where she tried to be quiet. Joe and I sat in the living room, uncomfortably aware of her presence.

Then the tourist season hit, and I started working from noon until around ten p.m. We had a lot of problems just scheduling dates.

But the biggest pitfall may have been that we both recognized that we weren't in this for a casual fling. Maybe we were making excuses to keep each other at arm's length. Maybe the truth was that we were both scared.

Our situation was very much up in the air. Sometimes I got really impatient. Dating Joe was like reading a book when I was simply dying to know how it would end. But I couldn't turn to the back page to find out.

It had been a long, cold winter and spring. But now the weather had warmed up enough for a trip up the Warner River in Joe's favorite wooden boat. And a client had offered Joe dinner for two at a snazzy restaurant, so I wouldn't feel compelled to lecture him about wasting money. I thought I could get an evening off. No wonder the two of us stood there looking into each other's eyes and beaming more brightly than Michigan's summer sun.

Then a cloud crossed Joe's face. He yanked my hand. "Come on!" He pulled me along the dock. "Here comes Hershel."

I looked at the boats beside us. One was a bright green canoe with the words "The Toadfrog" on the prow. "Yikes! We're right beside his canoe."

Joe and I walked down the dock at a brisk pace.

"Hershel never wears a life jacket," I said. "Maybe he'll drown himself on the way home."

The remark didn't seem so funny twenty-eight hours later, when Hershel's canoe was found smashed and half submerged in the Warner River.

Chapter 2

We almost ran up the dock to the next sidewalk, then cut back through the park, toward Dock Street. Joe was still holding my hand, but he was frowning. "I don't understand what got into Hershel down at the post office," he said. "I've never had any quarrel with him."

"How have you missed? He's quarreled with everybody else."

"I avoid him. In the past whatever bee he's had in his bonnet hasn't caused our paths to cross. Until now. Because I'm not backing down on the Root Beer Barrel. I'm going to sell that property."

"But why should Hershel care?"

"Who knows why Hershel does anything? Why did he picket the Superette two years ago, wanting them to put a warning label on all products containing refined sugar?"

I had lived in Warner Pier only a year, so this was news to me. "You're kidding! And he snags chocolates from Aunt Nettie every day? What does he think sweetens them?"

"Nobody expects Hershel to make sense. Last year, as you may recall, he devoted himself to an attack on the use of gasoline-powered engines in boats."

"Hence the canoe?"

"Right. I lay low on that one. He didn't seem to realize I repair gasoline engines, so he concentrated his harassment on Green Marine. Apparently his new craze is historic preservation."

I looked back and watched Hershel paddling across the river toward the willows that hid his ramshackle house. His distinctive canoe—the only kelly green canoe on the river—wobbled, since Hershel wasn't much of a canoeist.

"I hope we've heard the last of Hershel for a while," I said.

Aunt Nettie agreed easily with my plan to take Tuesday evening off.

"You and Joe need more time together," she said. "If the girls have any questions, I'll be here. I'm planning to start cleaning the vats about four o'-clock."

"You're sure I don't need to help?"

"No! I want you to keep us solvent, not mess around with the chocolate. Go out with Joe."

So at eleven o'clock that night, I was standing in my closet doorway and trying to figure out what to wear the next evening when I went out to dinner at the Warner River Lodge, with the prospect of a boat ride afterward.

My fragrance would be simple to select—mosquito repellent would fill the bill. Formal dress would not be required; Warner Pier is a resort, after all. I decided to wear cream-colored slacks, a cotton sweater in a soft green, and a shirt printed with green fronds on a cream background. Joe had once told me that sweater made my eyes look green; he seemed to consider it a compliment. Plus, it was an outfit I could wear tennis shoes with, and rubber-soled shoes would be best in a boat.

I went to work at eight-thirty the next morning. Aunt Nettie showed at one p.m. Beginning at four, she tore up the entire workshop—the chocolate making area—as she superintended the cleaning of the chocolate vats.

TenHuis Chocolade depends on having a ready supply of melted chocolate for the bonbons, truffles, and molded chocolate we produce. So we keep a vat of each kind of chocolate ready all the time. These are TenHuis-sized vats, of course. They're nothing like the enormous vats the Hershey plant would need. But the vats still range from four to five feet tall and are a couple of feet in diameter. The smallest one—for white chocolate—holds one hundred seventy-five pounds of chocolate. The dark chocolate vat holds two hundred pounds of chocolate, and the milk chocolate vat two hundred fifty pounds.

The vats are made of stainless steel and are something like giant thermos bottles—vats within vats. The inside vat holds the chocolate, and the outer vat holds hot water. An electrical element keeps the water at an even temperature, and the water keeps the chocolate at an even temperature. The top to the inner vat opens so that solid chocolate can be dropped in, but when Aunt Nettie or one of her helpers needs to take chocolate out, they use a tap and run the melted chocolate into a pitcher or mixing bowl, just like getting water from the sink. Inside the vats are paddles which churn gently twenty-four hours a day.

Those vats are boogers to clean. All the chocolate has to be drained—which means you have pans and kettles of chocolate sitting around the shop getting solid. The paddles and other internal parts have to be scraped down, then washed by hand in hot, soapy water. The hot-water vessels have to be drained and the water replaced.

Fortunately, the job doesn't have to be done very often. Aunt Nettie insists that it be done early in the summer, before the heavy tourist season starts and before she and her crew begin producing the first Halloween items.

It was a good thing Aunt Nettie didn't need my help. I spent the day in a dreamy state, making even more verbal faux pas than usual. I handed some tourist a dark chocolate bonbon with a white dot in the center of the top and told him that I'd give him the raspberry, leaving out the word "cream" ("Raspberry Cream—Red raspberry puree in a white chocolate cream interior, coated in dark chocolate"). Then I asked Tracy to check the supply of mocha perimeters, instead of mocha pyramids ("Milky coffee interior in a dark chocolate pyramid"). The worst one was when I reached into the display case for a Midori coconut truffle, and at that moment Stacy asked me if Joe and I were going out that evening. I nodded and said, "We're rolling in coconut." This was a reference to the truffle I was picking up ("Very creamy all-white chocolate truffle, flavored with melon and rolled in coconut"), but don't ask me why the chocolate's description worked its way into my reply.

Luckily, the answer cracked both Stacy and me up—something about picturing Joe and me rolling in bushels and bushels of Angel Flake—and we laughed the rest of the afternoon. Every time we quit one of us would start again. The customers must have thought we were nuts. Coconuts.

We were still snickering when a plump brunette walked in the door. I didn't know her, but I immediately classified her as a member of the Warner Pier art colony. Something about her flowing draperies and folksy beads.

Stacy spoke to her immediately. "Hi. How's your summer going?"

"Racing by, Stacy," the brunette answered. "Racing by. But today I'm hunting my brother. I don't suppose he's been around?"

"No—unless he came in this morning." Stacy turned to me. "Did you see him?"

"I'm sorry," I said. "I don't know whom we're talking about."

"Oh!" Stacy looked astonished. "This is Mrs. Waterloo. She's my English teacher."

Thank goodness I'd said "whom." And I'd certainly misjudged her profession. But Waterloo? Was this Mrs. *Frank* Waterloo? If so, she was a sister to the cranky Hershel Perkins. I regarded her warily. Was Hershel's crankiness a family trait?

But the plump brunette was smiling in a most uncranky way. She did have thin lips and a wide mouth like Hershel's, but on her the family feature became generous and humorous. She did not resemble a frog at all.

"You're Lee McKinney, aren't you? We haven't met. I'm Patsy Waterloo." She extended a hand that was covered with rings—the handcrafted kind. "Hershel Perkins is my brother. Nettie is always terribly patient with him. I know he's not much of a customer."

"Mr. Perkins bought a big frog yesterday," Stacy said. "First one we've sold."

"But he hasn't been in today," I said.

Patsy Waterloo made a face that was half-friendly and half-dismayed—I guess you'd call it a grimace. Then she moved down to the end of the counter and cocked her head, beckoning me to join her. When I did, she spoke again, dropping her voice almost to a whisper. "You're the girl Mercy Woodyard's son has been pursuing, aren't you? Pardon me for being such a nosy bitch."

I laughed. "Nobody else in Warner Pier apologizes for being interested in their navels—I mean, their neighbors! Yes, I'm seeing Joe."

"Have you talked to him today?"

"No. Why?"

Mrs. Waterloo's grimace became more concerned than friendly. "Well, we haven't seen Hershel since last night."

"Oh, does he live with you?"

"No, he lives next door. But he usually eats dinner with us. Anyway, after that scene in the post office . . ."

Her voice seemed to fade away. She turned around, draperies swirling, and nervously walked up and down, back and forth in front of the counter. Then she leaned over, very close to me, and spoke more softly than ever. "Hershel was still talking wildly last night. About Joe. I thought he'd gone home to bed. But this morning . . . his bed hadn't been slept in."

"If you're worried, I could call Joe."

"I tried to call him, but he's not answering the phone at the boat shop."

"I'll try his cell phone."

I went into the office, and Patsy Waterloo followed me. I guess her concern was catching. I had only Joe's landline on my speed dial—he normally uses the cell phone just to call long distance—so I had to punch the numbers in. The moments until the phone began to ring seemed terribly long, and the rings seemed to be five minutes apart.

But there were only two rings before the phone was picked up. "Vintage Boats," Joe said.

"Are you OK?"

"Everything's OK if you haven't changed your mind about tonight."

"Oh, no! But . . . Patsy Waterloo is here. She wanted to talk to you." I abruptly handed Mrs. Waterloo the telephone. As I did I heard Joe's voice again. "The teacher?"

Patsy Waterloo was looking more cheerful. "Yes, sir, the teacher and sister of the village idiot. Hershel Perkins."

Now Joe's voice was just a murmur. Patsy listened a few seconds, then she spoke. "Oh, I know that's too strong a term for Hershel. His actual diagnosis is minimal brain damage caused by a birth injury. But Hershel hasn't been around bothering you, has he?"

She listened some more. "Well, I'm glad to hear it. We try to control Hershel, but he can be a problem. And you know how he roams around."

Again she told the story of her brother's wild talk during dinner the night before and of her discovery early that afternoon that he had apparently never gone to bed the night before. "We don't know where he is," she said.

Joe's voice rumbled, and Patsy Waterloo frowned. "I know, I know, Hershel is regarded as entirely harmless. And he's never done anything beyond annoying people before. That's why Frank and I were so surprised yesterday when—according to Frank—he actually hit you."

More listening. Then she shook her head. "But that's what worried us. It's so unlike Hershel to do more than simply talk wildly."

She handed the phone back to me, then sank into one of my extra chairs. "I'm back," I said to Joe.

"Are you scared to go up the river tonight?" he asked.

"It seems as if the river would be pretty safe," I said. "You haven't seen Hershel?"

"No. The phone hasn't even rung today. I'll meet you at the dock around five thirty."

Joe hung up, and I turned back to Patsy. "So Joe hasn't seen Hershel. I wonder where he could be."

Patsy had regained her cheerful air. She stood up, draperies flying. "I know I'm being silly. But Hershel . . . well, you know he's odd. Everybody in Warner Pier knows he's odd. That's one reason Frank and I came back here after Mother died. We figured that here, where people knew Hershel was odd but harmless, it would be easier to control the situation. But I can't help worrying. Especially when he roams around."

"Why does that worry you?"

"We discover him prowling around, asking nosy questions. He annoys people. You can't blame them. So I worry."

She moved toward the door, then turned back, smiling sadly. "Hershel will always be my little brother."

I tried to say a few reassuring words as I walked to the door with Patsy Waterloo. She seemed like a nice person, and her problem with Hershel made me glad I'm an only child.

There was a lull in retail customers, so I began to try to get my balance sheet caught up. In between addition and subtraction I thought about Joe, and I forgot Hershel completely.

At exactly five o'clock Aunt Nettie came up front from the workroom, carrying a big spoon covered with dark chocolate. She stood in the door of my office and looked at me accusingly. "You're off duty," she said. "Go away."

I laughed. "I guess I'm outta here," I said.

I closed out my computer, then went back to the alley and got the green and cream outfit from my van. I changed clothes and freshened my makeup in the restroom. I even took my hair out of its businesslike queue and brushed it hard, trying to make it look smooth and sexy. After all, there's no point in being half Dutch if you don't flaunt your naturally blond hair now and then.

Having made myself as beautiful as possible, I waved at Aunt Nettie, went out the back door, and walked over to the dock to meet Joe.

I was, I admit, a bit excited. Joe had planned a big evening for us. I wanted it to go off well.

When I got to the docks, Joe's personal antique boat—the Shepherd Sedan—was easy to find. Antique boats are always the center of a group of people pointing and asking questions.

A "sedan," as Joe has explained it to me, is a roofed boat. His Shepherd was manufactured in 1948 by a Canadian company. It's a twenty-two-footer, and its hull is mahogany, burnished to a lustrous brown through weeks of sanding and varnishing, more sanding and varnishing, and even more sanding and varnishing—a total of ten coats of varnish, each sanded by hand before the next one went on. Elbow grease and patience are the keys to restoring old boats, Joe says.

The Shepherd's roof mimics the shape of automobile roofs in the late 1940s. The front window is Plexiglas. The side windows are safety glass and they roll up and down, just like the windows in automobiles of the day did. The roof itself is of molded plywood, covered with canvas. The dashboard and steering gear are remarkably like an automobile of the 1940s as well.

In fact, Joe had told me the steering wheel was actually manufactured for a car.

Joe has spent hundreds of hours working on the sedan, and the result is a gorgeous boat with a mahogany hull and an off-white roof. It doesn't really have a cabin, since the back is open, but the roof makes it a great craft for either cool or sunny weather. The Shepherd Sedan may not fly over the water like a Cigarette boat, true, but it's pure class.

When I made my way through the knot of people looking the boat over, however, I saw a problem. Trey Corbett was sitting in the stern.

He was leaning forward, talking earnestly. His stance made him look nerdier and more middle-aged than ever.

When I saw him, Hershel Perkins immediately flashed through my mind—I guess because Trey had been a witness to the altercation at the post office the day before. So the sight of Trey didn't make me happy.

I stopped beside the sedan, which was parallel to the dock and a few feet below it. Joe looked up and grinned, but Trey didn't seem to realize I was there.

"You know the river so well," Trey said.

"Not as well as a lot of other people," Joe said.

"We need your help, Joe."

Joe just shook his head. He extended his hand toward me, then led me down the dock for two steps, until I was opposite the step pad, that rubberized gadget that gives you enough traction to step into the boat gracefully, instead of falling in awkwardly.

Trey finally noticed that I was coming aboard. He leaped to his feet. "Oh! Hi, Lee."

"Hi, Trey."

Joe ignored Trey while I stepped into the stern of the boat. He guided me under the roof and up to one of the two front seats.

Trey stood up, looking worried. "I hope we find Hershel soon," he said. "I really need to be working on the fireplace at the Miller house this evening. I'm giving it a faux marble look, and there's nobody around to do it the way I want. I worked on it all yesterday evening."

"Maybe he'll turn up all right," I said.

"Listen, Trey," Joe said. "Considering the altercation Hershel and I had yesterday, I really don't think I ought to get involved in any search for him. Besides, I promised Lee a nice dinner and a boat ride tonight."

"But, Joe . . ."

Joe shook his head. "No, Trey. I'm not joining any search party. But Lee and I are going up the river, since we've got reservations for dinner at the lodge. If I see a bright green canoe floating by, I'll make sure Hershel's not under it."

Chapter 3

Trey left, but he didn't look happy about it.

Joe cast off the lines that held the sedan to the dock, assuring me I didn't need to help, then sat down behind the wheel of the sedan.

"What makes Trey think Hershel's capsized?" I said.

"He and his canoe are both missing."

"Patsy Waterloo didn't mention the canoe. She just said Hershel was gone."

Joe reached over and squeezed my hand. "Forget Hershel. I am really glad to see you. If you'd backed out of this little trip—well, I think I might have done something desperate."

"Cut your suspenders and gone straight up, as my Texas grandma would have said? But why would I back out?"

"It just seems as if everything else that's happened for the past twenty-four hours has failed to turn out the way I wanted it to."

Joe started the motor and the boat began burbling. The motors of old boats are cooled by pumping water around the engine, and the design gives them a distinctive sound—a bubbling, murmuring, lush sound that lots of people find the most attractive thing about them.

We pulled away from the dock and moved gently out into the river. All of the dock area, of course, is a no-wake zone, so Joe kept the speed slow and steady. This meant the engine was not terribly noisy, and we could talk, if we yelled. I leaned over Joe's shoulder. "What went wrong?"

"Oh, last night was a fiasco. A wild goose chase."

"You were going to show somebody the runabout?"

"Yeah. Some guy called, said he had seen the runabout at the South Haven show. Said he wanted to look at it, give his wife a ride. Said he was really determined to buy it. So I chased clear up to Saugatuck in high waves and went to the house he described—and nobody was there."

"Nobody was there?"

"Not only that, the house he directed me to—one of those right on the water, with its own dock—it's empty. The neighbors said nobody's been there for two summers. And the owner's name is not the same as the man who claimed he wanted to buy the boat. It was some kind of hoax."

"That's awful! Why would anybody do a thing like that?"

"I have no idea. I was afraid I'd find the shop burned down when I got home, but everything was okay. It sure did ruin my evening. I had to beat the waves back down to Warner Pier."

Handling a small boat in fairly high waves isn't easy. You have to head into the waves, which points your prow away from the shore and means you're basically traveling sideways. Then when you go over the top of the wave, you suddenly swing the wheel toward the shore—or is it away from the shore? I don't understand the process at all, and even Joe considers it a struggle.

"I didn't get back until way after dark," Joe said.

I slid my hand onto his shoulder. "Tonight we'll just be on the river. No waves."

Joe grinned. "All we'll have to look out for is weeds, mud, and other boats."

The Warner River is about a quarter of a mile wide at Warner Pier—which is one reason it was a good place to build a pier, I guess, when Captain Hoseah Warner decided to do that a hundred and fifty years ago. Still in the no-wake zone, we traveled slowly up the river, past the house Captain Warner built in 1850—now a bed-and-breakfast inn; past the pseudo-Victorian condos which sell for a half-million each; past Hershel's funny little house, which always reminds me of the witch's cottage Hansel and Gretel found. For the first time I noticed the bigger, restored Craftsman-style house behind Hershel's. Now I realized that must be Patsy and Frank Waterloo's home.

Joe guided the boat out into the main channel and stepped up our pace. Joe's a very safe boater, but he likes to rev it up and run his boat all over the lake or the river at top speed; it's a guy thing. We sped past the entrance to Joe's boat shop, on our left, and the turrets of Gray Gables, one of Warner Pier's historic summer homes, came into view on the right. It wasn't long before the broad glass windows of the Warner River Lodge appeared around a bend. Joe cut his speed way back, and we floated gently alongside the lodge's dock. The dock attendant caught the mooring line, and we tied up. Joe cut the engine and stepped out—he makes it look easy—then held out a hand so that I could use the step pad to get out gracefully.

"We're early," he said. "We can have a drink on the terrace." He grinned. "Behind one of the umbrellas."

Two hours later we'd had drinks on the terrace and a marvelous dinner in the dining room. We came back down the stairs to the dock hand in hand. Joe helped me into the sedan, then tipped the dock attendant. The sun was still up. Once we'd cast off, Joe even gave me a quick kiss. I wanted it to last much longer, but Joe started the motor.

I turned sideways in the passenger's seat and slid my hand around the nape of Joe's neck. He patted my knee as we moved away from the dock, the motor burbling softly. The boat headed upstream. We were alone.

So it was quite a surprise when a sound like the final trump thundered over the river.

"Joe! Joe Woodyard!"

Joe whirled so fast he must have nearly given himself whiplash, and I jumped higher than I knew I could sitting down.

Downstream we saw a large white boat approaching. Its prow was crowded with spotlights, and the roof of its little cabin was loaded down with radar gear and antennas.

Joe cut the motor to trolling speed. "It's the city patrol boat," he said.

I squinted at the boat, looking into the sun. "Chief Jones is aboard."

As a community that straddles a river and abuts a lake, Warner Pier has to be prepared for law enforcement and emergencies on the water. In the tourist season, there's a full-time water policeman who enforces safety regulations on the river, and the city owns a nifty patrol boat which he uses. It's also used to rescue boaters if there's an accident and to drag the river if there's a drowning. But the chief rarely goes out in the boat, and ordinary boaters who are obeying the rules and minding their own business—as Joe and I had been—wouldn't normally be hailed by the city patrol boat.

"What do they want?" I said.

Joe didn't ask until the two boats were alongside. "What's up, Chief?" he said. "I hope you're not going to haul me into the big search for Hershel's canoe."

Chief Hogan Jones looked grim. "Nope, Joe. We're not looking for Hershel's canoe any longer. His body, maybe."

"His body!" I yelled, and Joe made a surprised exclamation.

"Yep," the chief said. "We found his canoe caught in some purple sedge near the entrance to your place, Joe."

Some police chiefs really know how to spoil a romantic mood.

Chief Jones sure spoiled Joe's. His face got nearly as dark as his hair, and his jaw clenched and unclenched more often than it had while he was eating his prime rib and steamed baby asparagus in the dining room of the Warner River Lodge.

But there was no help for it. We had to turn downstream and follow Chief Jones back to Joe's boat shop.

Vintage Boats is in an isolated spot at the end of Dock Street, barely inside the city limits of Warner Pier. The area is pretty close to rural. It's heavily wooded, like most of western Michigan, a quality which gives a Plains person like me a spooky feeling. Joe had few neighbors, and those few couldn't see his shop for the trees.

The shop itself is very ordinary, just a big metal building not too different from my dad's automotive garage in north Texas. The building is heated and well insulated, of course, since Joe works in it all year round. It even has some air conditioning, a rarity for such a shop in Michigan, because Joe sometimes has to close part of it up in the summer to keep dust out of his varnish. It has one main room, forty by eighty, with a couple of fifteen- by twenty-foot rooms at one end. One of those was the office and the other was the space Joe had made into a rudimentary apartment. The only sign of luxury in it was a fancy sound system he said was left from his bachelor days—before he made the marriage he always refers to as "stupid."

The shop is not a boat house. It's a hundred feet from the water, but Joe does have a dock on the river. A gravel drive enters the property from Dock Street, circles the building, and leads down to an area where he can launch a boat.

There are a lot of trees and bushes, but no landscaping. No grass to mow, no flower beds to weed. And there are about a dozen antique boats lined up on one side—each covered with canvas or plastic tarps. These represent a big part of Joe's money woes—he agreed to buy them before his ex-wife died and landed him in the middle of her legal and financial problems. If he can ever get back to his business full-time, the collection of antique boats has the potential to make him a lot of money. But until then, they're just so much junk he has to make a bank payment on every month.

Joe's dock is equipped with a boat lift, a sort of big cradle that can lift a boat out of the water. The lift is covered with a canvas roof. This allows Joe to keep one boat ready to go in the water all the time. Right at that moment, the boat lift held the 1949 Chris-Craft Deluxe Runabout, the boat Joe was trying to sell. He usually kept the sedan tied up on the other side of the dock. Any other boats he wanted to take for a ride had to be hauled to the river on trailers and put in the water just the way my daddy puts his bass boat in Lake Amon G. Carter, down in North Texas.

Most small boat shops, I've found out, are not on the water. In Warner Pier, they're certainly not. The waterfront property—either on the river or on the lake—is too expensive to waste on workshops; it's all occupied by apartments, marinas, B&Bs, restaurants, resorts, and high-dollar homes. Joe had been able to hang on to his property, known locally as the "old Olson shop," because it was on the outskirts of town and had not yet attracted the eye of a developer. But the time was coming when he might find it wiser to do without a private dock than to keep paying taxes on a piece of property worth more than enough to pay off the mortgage. I knew he'd sell if he got a good offer.

As the sedan neared the dock we saw that the area had become the center of the search for Hershel. A couple of skin divers were in the water, and several boats were standing by. One of Chief Jones's patrolmen, Jerry

Cherry, was on Joe's dock rigging up lights, though it was still at least an hour before sundown.

Joe idled the sedan's motor and glided up to his dock. Jerry came over and took our bow line and wove it around the mooring cleat on the dock. Joe stepped out onto the dock, leaving me behind. He was polite to Jerry, but I knew he was still mad.

"I'll open the place up, Jerry," Joe said. "You can use my electricity." He walked toward the shop.

Jerry held out a hand to me and gave me a yank as I stepped onto the dock. "Have they found anything?" I asked.

"Just the canoe."

"Where was it?"

Jerry pointed toward the channel. "Out there. Caught in some sedge. About where Maggie Mae—I mean, Meg—is."

"Maggie Mae?"

"Trey Corbett's wife. We called her Maggie Mae in high school. She's in the boat."

"Which boat are you talking about?"

"Trey's boat. The *Nutmeg*."

Jerry wandered off, and I stared toward the boat he'd indicated. It was not big, as Warner Pier boats go—maybe a twelve-footer. I'd become conscious of the length and types of boats since I began to date Joe. But Joe wouldn't have been interested in this boat because it was fiberglass. He had a sign on the door of his office that proclaims the wooden boat fan's manifesto: "If God wanted us to have fiberglass boats, He would have made fiberglass trees." No, Joe wouldn't have given Trey Corbett's boat a second glance.

However, any guy might well have given a second glance to the woman in the boat. She wasn't dressed sexy. In fact, maybe "well bred" would have been the best description. Her regal air turned the khaki shorts and navy sweatshirt she wore into basic black and pearls. She had a little-girl prettiness. Her hair was artfully streaked with blond and had been cut short by a master stylist.

The lights flashed for a moment, and I realized that Joe and Jerry Cherry had the Warner Pier Police Department's floodlights ready to be used. I looked back toward the boat shop and saw Joe and Jerry walking toward something bright green. Something that was balanced on a couple of saw horses. It had to be Hershel's canoe.

I started to join them, but I took one more look at the *Nutmeg* and saw that the boat was coming toward me. Meg Corbett called out, "Lee!"

She evidently knew me, even if I didn't remember meeting her. I stood still until she guided the boat alongside, then took the line she tossed me and wrapped it around one of the dock's piers. I expected her to get out, but instead she stood still and extended her hand toward me, apparently expecting me to shake it. Or maybe kiss it. I picked shaking.

"Hi, Lee. We haven't really met, but I'm Meg Corbett. I think you know my husband."

"Sure. Trey and I are both on the chamber's Economic Deployment—I mean, Development!—the Economic Development Committee. What can I do for you?"

Meg's face wore a strange expression. I decided she was pretending to look sympathetic. The mouth was the right shape, but her tiny little pupils gave the whole thing away.

"Actually," she said, "I was going to offer you a ride home."

"A ride home?"

"Or to your car. Or wherever you want to go."

"I wasn't planning to go anywhere."

"Well, this isn't going to be very pleasant."

I looked around the scene. I didn't stare at Joe particularly, but I thought about him. I didn't want to leave until I found out what was going on.

"I'm too curious to leave," I said. "Joe will see that I get home."

"If he's able to." Meg's voice had developed a smirk.

"What do you mean?"

"The police may want to question him."

"Why?"

"Hershel's canoe was found right outside his boat shop. They're going to wonder why he didn't report it."

"The answer to that is obvious. He must not have seen it."

Meg Corbett shook her head slowly. "It would have been impossible to miss."

I stared at her for a moment. "If he had seen Hershel's canoe, why wouldn't Joe tell the police?"

"He might have reasons. Joe has always had a secretive side." Meg's ladylike veneer was slipping rapidly. "I know that he and Hershel had a fistfight in the post office yesterday. I know that Hershel seems to have left home last night determined to see Joe again. I know that Hershel's canoe was found near Joe's dock, right where Joe takes his boats in and out."

Meg gestured vigorously, apparently forgetting she was standing up in a small boat, and the *Nutmeg* bounced from side to side. She sat down suddenly and not too gracefully in one of the upholstered seats. Then she tried to look smug. "If I were a policeman, I'd have a lot of questions for Joe Woodyard."

I resisted the temptation to reach down, grab the side of her boat, and turn it over. "But you're not a policeman," I said. "And Chief Jones knows Joe. Besides, Hershel wasn't exactly an expert canoeist. We all expected him to have an accident someday."

Meg's voice was ominous. "If this was an accident."

I decided I'd talked to Mrs. Corbett long enough. I didn't say good-bye. I walked away. If Meg wanted either to get out of her boat or to shove it back into the river, she'd have to do it without me.

I walked over to Joe and Jerry. Now I could see the gold lettering on the prow of the smashed aluminum canoe. The *Toadfrog*.

But Jerry was pointing at something quite a way back from the prow. "It's this big dent in the middle of the canoe, Joe," he said. "I hate to say this, but it looks for all the world like somebody in a power boat ran old Hershel down."

CHOCOLATE CHAT

GODS GAVE MANKIND CHOCOLATE

- The Olmec probably domesticated cocoa. Known to most twenty-first century folks as the creators of those enormous stone heads, the Olmec developed a civilization which existed from about 1500 BC to 500 BC, centered on the coast of the Gulf of Mexico, in the area where today's Mexican states of Veracruz and Tabasco are. Olmec territory was extremely fertile, and they grew a wide variety of crops—maize, beans, squash, chili peppers. Chocolate was very likely among them.

- Both the Mayas and the Aztecs had myths that the foods which mankind needed to survive were brought from beneath the surface of the earth by the gods. Cacao is listed in ancient manuscripts as being one of the foods the gods provided.

- Ancient Americans served most if not all chocolate in the form of drinks. Numerous painted pots and carvings show people pouring chocolate from a pot held at shoulder height into one on the floor, a process which produced froth.

- The Aztec and Maya had many recipes for preparing chocolate. Almost none were sweet. Chili peppers were one ingredient of such drinks. Others might have been maize, vanilla, and numerous other spices and herbs. Some of the drinks were served hot, but cold or room-temperature was more likely. Chocolate was for the elite and was rarely drunk by common folk.

Chapter 4

No wonder everyone was assuming Hershel had drowned. If something hit the canoe that hard, anybody in it would have been thrown into the water with terrific force.

At least I now understood where Meg Corbett was coming from. She obviously had seen the canoe. And she'd apparently already made her mind up about what happened to it.

Then she'd jumped to a completely mistaken conclusion.

I slid my arm inside Joe's.

"Well, Jerry, the damage shows you Joe didn't have anything to do with this," I said.

Jerry looked at me, frowning slightly, and I went on.

"If Joe ran into a camel—I mean, a canoe! If Joe ran into a canoe, he'd be in one of his boats, right?"

"Guess so."

"So that proves he didn't do it," I said.

"I don't follow you there, Lee."

"Joe's too good at herding a boat to run into one by accident," I said. "And there's nothing Hershel—or anyone else—could do that would make Joe risk putting a scratch on one of those boats on purpose. Those boats are his babies."

Jerry chuckled.

"Aw, com'on, Lee," Joe said. "You're nearly as important to me as the '49 Runabout."

Joe, Jerry, and I stood there staring at the beat-up canoe. I didn't feel as cheerful as I'd tried to act.

I knew Joe could never hurt Hershel on purpose. Even the day before, when Hershel had actually attacked him in front of witnesses, Joe had merely grabbed Hershel and pinned him against the wall of mailboxes.

As for Joe injuring Hershel in self-defense, Hershel was too ineffectual to be any real threat to Joe. Joe was bigger, smarter, stronger, and more athletic than Hershel. Unless Hershel had brought along a weapon. And if Joe had hit Hershel or otherwise done something to him because Hershel had a gun or a knife, Joe would have immediately called the police.

I completely shrugged off the possibility that Joe had run down Hershel's canoe by accident. Joe really was too good at handling a boat to do that; certainly to do that without noticing that he'd hit something. Again, if he had had an accident Joe would have called the police immediately.

Thinking Joe might be involved was silly, and I resolved not to be a party to any such speculation.

Having made up my mind, I noticed noises from behind me. Joe, Jerry, and I all turned around.

Meg hadn't shoved her boat off, she'd gotten out of it and had walked up the bank in our direction. The patrol boat was just touching its nose to the dock, and as I watched Chief Jones jumped out. He nearly overshot and went into the drink on the other side. I was so annoyed that I didn't even feel sympathetic. And Trey Corbett had appeared from someplace, maybe the patrol boat. Chief Jones recovered his balance, and he, Trey, and the ultra-gracious Meg walked toward us.

"Better not touch the canoe, Joe," the chief said.

"I'm keeping my hands to myself," Joe said. "Who found it?"

"Trey did," Meg said. She sounded proud. "He searched both sides of the river from Warner Marina to Gray Gables. You know, his family's summer place."

Actually, I hadn't known Gray Gables was Trey's family's summer place. Gray Gables was a real showplace. I knew a rich and prominent Corbett family owned it, but I hadn't associated Trey with that particular branch. Trey never acted rich or prominent; he acted like a struggling architect specializing in restoring Victorian houses. Very interesting. I filed the relationship away for future contemplation and attended to the conversation.

Joe turned to Trey. "Exactly where was the canoe?"

"Up against the sedge," Trey said. Purple sedge has a pretty flower later in the summer, but don't admire it in front of a Michigan native. It's an invasive plant—not originally part of the Michigan ecosystem—and it's pushing a lot of the native plants out of the state's wetlands and streams. It grows thickly along the Warner River. I listened as Trey carefully described the spot where he'd found the canoe.

"I couldn't have missed seeing it," Joe said. "It definitely wasn't there when I left."

Joe and Trey would have dropped the subject, I think, but Meg joined the argument. She had regained her ladylike demeanor, and she spoke firmly but with dignity. "If Trey says that's where he found it, Joe, that's where it was."

"Maybe so, Maggie Mae, but it wasn't there before five o'clock."

Meg looked down her nose at Joe, which was a hard trick since she was five five and he was six one.

Joe looked at her coldly. I guess they would have stood there glaring all evening, but Chief Jones spoke. "It could have drifted down there after Joe left," he said. "That's not the question."

Joe shifted his stare to the chief. "I guess you haven't found anybody who saw how the canoe was damaged."

"Nobody's come forward. Of course, we want to find Hershel—find out exactly what happened to him—before we jump to any conclusions."

"And I gather nobody's found any sign of him yet."

The chief sighed. "We found a life jacket. It was floating farther down the bank. A hundred yards upstream from Green Marine."

Trey spoke then. "Hershel never wore his life jacket."

"Right," Chief Jones said. "The river patrolman had spoken to him about it, but it didn't do any good."

"We need to keep looking for Hershel," Trey said.

"Oh, we'll keep at it," the chief said. "And we're calling in the state crime lab to look at his canoe."

The whole bunch of us swung to look at the *Toadfrog*.

"It does appear as if a much bigger boat hit it," Joe said.

"That's one question for the crime lab," the chief said. "This is the other one."

He pointed toward the canoe.

At the spot where the canoe was smashed in most severely, traces of red were visible.

Behind me, Meg gasped. "Blood?" she said.

"Don't be silly," I said. "If the canoe was in the water any length of time, blood would have washed off. That red has to be paint."

Like a chorus line, we all swung the other direction. And there, suspended in the boat lift beside Joe's dock, was the Chris-Craft Runabout, the boat Joe had been running up and down the river the day before, the boat he had been trying to sell, the one he had taken up the lake to Saugatuck to meet a potential buyer. It hung there, beside the dock, a foot out of the water. We could all see it clearly.

The deck and upper part of the hull were burnished mahogany. But below the waterline the boat had been painted a bright red.

We all stared at the boat for a long moment. Then I spoke angrily.

"I suggest you take a paint sample from the Runabout. That should settle the mattress."

That got everybody's attention. The chief, Meg, Trey, Jerry Cherry, even Joe—all of them quit staring at the boat and turned their attention to me. Every jaw dropped.

"Matter!" I said. "That should settle the matter."

Chief Jones chuckled, and Meg smirked, but Joe was the only one who laughed out loud. Which was unusual. He ordinarily ignores my verbal tumbles.

He put his hand on my shoulder. "I need to take care of something in the shop," he said. "Lee, come and help me. And, Chief, if you want a sample of the paint on the Runabout—help yourself. Try not to chip it too badly."

With what dignity I could recover, I followed Joe into the shop, picking my way among the overturned hulls, the wooden hoist that can lift a boat half the size of a yacht, and assorted tools, ladders, saws, cans of paint, and brooms. "What do you need me to do?" I asked.

"Stand guard."

"Stand guard? Why? What are you going to do?"

"Make a phone call. One I want to be sure isn't overheard."

Joe went into his office and picked up the phone. He put it to his ear and clicked a few buttons, then glared at the instrument.

"The darn thing isn't working," he said. "No wonder I didn't get any calls all day today."

"Patsy Waterloo said she called you several times and didn't get an answer, but I figured you'd been out. Can you use your cell phone?"

"Sure. Just stand by the door and warn me if anybody comes."

I stood in the office door, staring toward the other end of the shop. The door we'd come in was open, and I could glimpse the action outside. I could hear Joe as he made his call.

"Mike," he said. "You know that agenda item you had in mind for the breakfast meeting tomorrow? We'd better forget it for now."

Mike? Was Joe talking to Mike Herrera, the mayor of Warner Pier? Mike, who dated Joe's mom?

I continued to wonder while Joe sketched the situation at the shop, describing where Hershel's canoe had been found and telling about the damage to it:

"No, there's no sign of Hershel," Joe said. "But you can understand the situation out here. I'm suspect number one. We'd better put that possibility on hold for a few days."

He listened again. "Sure, Mike, you're right. Hershel could still turn up. But looking at that boat—well, I'll be surprised if he turns up in one piece. Anyway, the canoe was found near my dock. So if you could hold off until they figure out what happened . . ."

His voice trailed off. He listened again, then laughed harshly. "Thanks for the vote of confidence. I'll be in touch."

He pushed the OFF button on his phone.

"What was that all about?" I asked.

"Oh, a little discussion item Mike had for the city council workshop," Joe said. "Where's the directory? I need to call the phone company."

"First you'd better make sure it's not your own telephone that's sick."

"I guess you're right. I'll borrow a phone from Mom and check it."

"But what's this deal with Mike?"

"Nothing much. What I'm wondering is, did someone call the Waterloos?" Joe walked around me, then out into the shop and toward the door that led to the dock and the search for Hershel. Leaving me with my mouth open and no words coming out.

"Did someone call the Waterloos?" he'd said. I thought we could trust Chief Jones to take care of that. In any case, the Waterloos had nothing to do with why Joe had been talking to the mayor of Warner Pier.

Joe had flatly dodged my question about why he had called Mike Herrera.

I could have popped him. I was so curious that I almost ran after him and demanded to know more. Then I decided against it. After all, Joe and I still had secrets from each other. I told myself that I had no right to demand that he tell me all his business. But I sure wanted to know.

I bit my tongue and went back outdoors, where I found Joe repeating his question about the Waterloos to Chief Jones.

"I got hold of Frank, and he was going to find Patsy and bring her over," the chief said.

The Waterloos showed up five minutes later in a beat-up and rusty old Dodge sedan. Frank was at the wheel, and he skidded to a stop in Joe's gravel parking lot. Patsy—still in her flowing draperies—jumped out and ran toward Chief Jones, tripping over the gravel in her sandals.

"Oh, Hogan! Have you found him?"

"Not yet, Patsy. We'll keep looking until it gets dark."

Patsy hugged herself and shivered all over. "I just can't believe Hershel actually capsized. I worried and worried about him and that canoe. But somehow he always seemed to get home safely. Even when we found out he hadn't come home last night . . . I still felt he'd turn up all right."

Frank had joined her. "Is there any way to expand the search, Hogan? Hire divers? Charter more boats?"

"I don't think there's anything else to do, Frank," Chief Jones said. "It's going to be getting too dark to continue the search pretty soon. But the water patrol volunteers are on top of things."

"You know that Hershel had—has—plenty of money, and this would be a legitimate expense for the trust," Frank said.

"I think this is one problem that can't be helped by throwing money at it," Chief Jones said. He patted Patsy on the shoulder. "Do you have a jacket? It's getting cool."

"I'm not cold," Patsy said. "I just keep shaking."

"It's a nervous reaction," Chief Jones said. He looked around, and he seemed to remember that I was there. "Lee, maybe you could take Patsy inside."

"No! No!" Patsy said. "I want to watch."

"We could sit in your car," I said. I hoped my unwillingness to talk to Patsy didn't show in my voice. "You could watch from there."

Patsy agreed to this, and the two of us went over to the rusty old vehicle. As I climbed into the driver's side I cursed the male belief that women are better than men at dealing with emotional crises. Not that it isn't true. But I hardly knew Patsy Waterloo. I didn't think she'd want to cry on my shoulder.

I did feel sorry for Patsy. That afternoon she'd referred to Hershel as her "baby brother." Her concern had seemed completely sincere. Hershel would have been a terribly annoying relative, but Patsy had made me feel that she loved him despite his problems.

She was still shivering. I looked in the back seat and saw a sweatshirt. With my long arms I was able to reach back and pull it into the front. It was a large, hooded garment with a zipper. I handed it to Patsy. "Here," I said. "Why don't you wrap this around you like a shawl?"

"I'm not really cold."

"Maybe not, but your teeth are rattling. Wrap it around you. It'll make me feel warmer."

Patsy smiled. "I suppose these cool summer evenings seem odd to someone from Texas."

"Oh, Texas has cool evenings. It's just that they come in March, April, October, and November, not June, July, and August."

Her smile faded. "How many boats are involved in the search?"

"At least half a dozen."

"Is Joe helping?"

I didn't know how to answer that one. I didn't want to tell her Joe was suspected of causing the boating mishap that very likely had drowned her brother. "He's helping the chief," I said finally.

"I thought maybe he found the canoe."

"No. Trey Corbett found it."

"Oh? I thought—Hogan told Frank it was near Joe's dock . . ."

"I guess it drifted there. Joe left before five o'clock, and he says he's sure the canoe wasn't there at that time."

"But that would mean Hershel was upstream when the accident happened."

"I guess so."

"But how did he get there?"

"Paddled, I guess."

"But that can't be!"

"Why not?"

"It takes a strong canoeist to paddle upstream when there's this much water in the river." Patsy gave a short laugh. "Hershel is not a strong canoeist. It's a couple of miles from our dock to here. I'm not sure he could have made it this far, much less even farther upstream."

I didn't have an answer to that. We both sat silently, and it gradually occurred to me that Patsy might know why Hershel had attacked Joe—first verbally, then physically—in the post office. Had that happened only a day earlier?

I gulped, thought a few moments, and phrased my question carefully.

"Joe says he had never had any cross words with Hershel before yesterday. Do you know why Hershel was angular?"

Patsy turned to me, looking blank.

"Angry!" I said. "Do you know why Hershel was angry with Joe? Yesterday. In the post office."

"Frank didn't tell me any details, and I tried to keep Hershel from talking about it. Just what did Hershel say?"

"He yelled a bunch of stuff about the old Root Beer Barrel. I never could understand what he was mad about."

"Oh." Patsy sounded as if I'd clarified the whole argument for her. She looked out into the river, watching the boats and divers. "It doesn't matter now."

"Probably not. But did Hershel say anything to you? Did he make any complaint about Joe?"

"Nothing I believed."

"Then there was . . . ?"

Before I could finish my question, Patsy gave a squeal. She yanked at the door handle. "Look! They've found something!"

We both jumped out of the car and went down to the dock. Chief Jones, Jerry Cherry, Frank Waterloo, and Joe were standing there, all looking into the sunset. Out in the river I could see the boats forming a tight circle. The *Nutmeg*, with Trey and Meg Corbett aboard again, was part of the circle.

"What is it?" Patsy said. "Oh, Frank, have they found him?"

Frank put his arm around his wife's shoulder. "I hope not, Patsy. I hope not."

We all watched intently as a diver rolled overboard backward, as lines were tossed into the water, and as boats jockeyed around bumping into each other.

"Can you see it?" Chief Jones said.

I looked at him and realized he had an earphone plugged into his ear and was talking into a small gadget. He was in radio contact with the city boat, maybe with some of the other boats as well.

"Nuts!" he said. "False alarm."

The divers pulled something up. Even from the dock I could tell it was a log. They let it drop back into the water. Patsy Waterloo whirled around and dropped her head into her hands.

Chief Jones went over and patted her back clumsily. "I guess we'd better call it off for tonight, Patsy," he said. "It's getting too dark for the boats to accomplish anything. Maybe we'll have more luck tomorrow."

Patsy looked up, her face all screwed up. "You think he'll be floating by tomorrow!" She made the words an accusation.

The chief didn't answer; he simply walked a few feet down the dock and began to talk into his radio again. The rest of us stood silently as the patrol boat began to haul the divers aboard. Trey and Meg brought their boat over to Joe's dock.

Joe spoke. "Mrs. Waterloo . . . Patsy, I honestly did not see Hershel's canoe in the river when I left. I can't believe it was there."

Patsy wiped her eyes. "It's not your fault, Joe. Hershel was—well, not crazy, but—I could never figure out where he got his ideas. I mean, why would you deliberately knock down the Root Beer Barrel, anyway?"

Chapter 5

I heard Meg Corbett gasp, but I think I simply stared at Patsy for a full
minute. I couldn't believe what she'd said. Joe had knocked the Root Beer
Barrel down on purpose?

Joe's reaction was much like mine, I guess. He didn't change his expression until Meg gasped, and then he blinked twice. He lowered his head and
looked closely into Patsy's face. "Hershel thought I knocked down the Root
Beer Barrel?"

"I didn't believe it, Joe!"

"Where did Hershel get that idea?"

Before Patsy could answer, Trey Corbett somehow leaped onto the dock
and started talking. "Hershel had a terrific imagination," he said. "I was
often amazed at what he'd come up with."

The comment didn't seem extreme to me, but its effect on Patsy Waterloo was—well, inflammatory. She flared up as if Trey had tossed kerosene
on her and added a match. She almost shouted a reply. "Yes, Hershel had a
wonderful imagination! When he was a little boy—and later on. If it had
been encouraged. But it wasn't. He was just criticized and made the butt of
the whole town."

Trey stepped back from her attack and nearly fell off the narrow dock.
"Patsy, I'm sorry . . ."

"Oh, I don't mean you, Trey! You were one of the few who didn't make
fun of Hershel, who didn't mock him." Her eyes flashed around the group.
Was it my imagination, or did they linger on Meg?

But it was Chief Jones who drew fire next. He made the mistake of putting his mike away and turning back to our group, and Patsy pounced.

"And you!" She was yelling. "You'd think the chief of police would have
some patience with his town's eccentrics!"

"I thought I was patient for a long time," the chief said.

"You threatened Hershel with jail!"

The chief sighed. "Now, Patsy . . ."

"Don't you 'now, Patsy' me. I was the one who had to find Hershel that time. He was hiding up at the old chapel. He only goes there when he's really upset! He was scared to death!"

"I'm sorry, Patsy. But we had to keep him from turning in these crazy reports."

"I could have stopped him. All you had to do was call me!"

"I didn't know that then. You'd just come back. You were in the middle of your renovation. I didn't . . ." Chief Jones stopped talking and scowled at his shoes.

Patsy attacked again. "Didn't what? Didn't want me to know about it?"

"I didn't want to bother you," the chief said.

Frank moved in then. "Patsy . . ." And Patsy turned on him.

"It's all my fault, Frank! I talked you into coming back to Warner Pier. I thought I could handle the situation. Now we've squandered our money . . . ruined our marriage."

Frank grabbed her. I think it was supposed to look like a bear hug, but it looked more like a stranglehold from where I was standing. He crushed her face into his shoulder. "Shhh! Shhh! We're not going into that now. Just calm down, honey."

Patsy pushed him away. "I'm just so tired of it! I try to meet my family responsibilities, but it's been hard! I thought I could do what Mother asked if we kept Hershel here. I thought the trust could help both of us. But it's turned into a nightmare. Especially for you, Frank."

I stood there helplessly, watching Patsy cry. Then I felt a breath on my neck, and Joe leaned over my shoulder. He whispered. "Get Patsy inside the shop and see if you can calm her down."

I wanted to turn around and glare at him. Another case of the menfolks thinking that the womenfolks can take care of an emotional crisis. But I had to admit he had a point. When Frank had tried to act sympathetic, it only seemed to make Patsy worse. Maybe another woman could help matters. And Meg didn't seem to be ready to offer support. She was hiding behind Trey.

"Patsy," I said, "why don't you come inside with me for a minute. Joe keeps a big box of Kleenex in his office. You and I can sit in there and use it up."

I put my arm around Patsy's shoulder and aimed her at the door to the shop. She didn't move very fast, but I was able to maneuver her inside.

Once I had her sitting in Joe's office chair, with Kleenex in hand, I pulled up a straight chair and sat opposite her. I didn't say anything.

Patsy sniffed. "I'm sorry."

"You're entitled to a good cry."

"It's just been really hard."

"I can see that it has."

"Hershel bothered everybody in town."

I smiled. "He didn't bother TenHuis Chocolade. Aunt Nettie always acted happy to see him, and he never gave me any problem."

"You're lucky! Meg got the idea—I could have smacked her. But she's that type."

"I just met her tonight, but I admit she didn't make a good impression. What problem did she have with Hershel?"

"She always thinks all the men are after her. She got the idea Hershel was stalking her! It was crazy."

I didn't speak. Stalking is crazy, true, but I didn't think that was what Patsy meant.

"It was Trey he was stalking," Patsy said.

"Trey?"

"Oh, stalking is the wrong word. Hershel got hipped on a new subject. It happened all the time. When Trey was working on our renovation, Hershel would hang around. He lives on the property, after all. Trey was always nice to him."

"Trey seems like a pleasant person."

"He is. I don't know how he got mixed up with that Meg. Her name used to be Maggie Mae, you know. And Trey—well, true, his name is Charles Thomas Corbett the Third, but he was known as Chuck until he took up with her. I think it was her idea to rub everybody's nose in his family connections. But everybody knows he comes from the poor side of the Corbetts. Anyway, Trey explained some things about historic preservation to Hershel—actually treated Hershel like a grown-up. Of course, it backfired. Hershel began going over to their house."

"To Gray Gables?"

"No, to Trey and Meg's house. On Arbor Street. He was only trying to see Trey, but Meg got all excited." Patsy subsided into her Kleenex again.

I thought her outburst was over. If she had told the truth, I had a certain sympathy for Meg. I wouldn't like Hershel hanging around my house. It wasn't as if you could really be a friend to Hershel. He wasn't unintelligent, but he was so unpredictable that he wasn't any fun to talk to.

I heard a tap at the office door, and I turned around to see Joe standing there. "I brought Patsy a cup of coffee," he said.

"Oh, Joe, that was nice of you," Patsy said. "You didn't have to make coffee."

Joe grinned and came into the office. "I didn't. They had a jug of it on the patrol boat. Frank said you didn't take sugar or cream."

Patsy sipped the coffee. "I'll try to straighten up. Then Frank and I will go home."

"Before you go, I'd like to know how Hershel got the idea that I knocked down the Root Beer Barrel."

"I don't know exactly what made him think that. You know how he prowled around town."

"But the Root Beer Barrel came down during the last big snow storm. In March."

Patsy patted her eyes again. "I know. Hershel loved to walk in the snow. Especially along the lakeshore. He told me the Barrel had fallen down before I heard it anywhere else."

Joe thought a moment. "It's at least a mile from Hershel's house to the Root Beer Barrel property," he said. "Just what did he tell you he saw?"

"Hershel never made much sense. It was something about a truck. What difference does it make?"

"It would make a lot of difference to me," Joe said. "It might give me problems selling that property. We'd better tell the chief about it. Can you stand to talk to him?"

Patsy gave a weak smile. "I'll try. I need to apologize to Hogan anyway. He tried to be patient with Hershel."

We went back outside, but Joe, Frank, Patsy, and I stood around waiting while the chief finished up with the water patrolman. By the time he joined us, there was only a little sunset glow left in the western sky and Jerry Cherry's portable lamps were casting a harsh light on the dock. Meg and Trey were gone.

At Joe's insistence, Patsy repeated her story. In fact, Joe cross-examined her. Joe doesn't do his lawyer act too often, but when he does do it, I can see that he must have been good at it. He went at Patsy from six different angles.

But Patsy didn't know anything else, and Frank swore Hershel had never said anything to him about the old Root Beer Barrel.

"Why does it matter?" Patsy said. "I didn't believe it. Apparently Hershel didn't spread it around town. Why do you even care, Joe?"

Joe and the chief looked at each other. "It's the Historic District Regulations," Joe said.

"I've never heard of the city having to enforce a case," the chief said.

"Yeah, it's usually just obeyed," Joe said. "I certainly would never buck the city regs."

"Historic District Regulations?" Frank said. "I know we had to follow them when we renovated Patsy's mom's house. Trey did the design, and he advised us. We didn't have any problem."

Joe nodded. "Trey's an expert on the regulations. They aren't all that onerous, but there's a part that deals with 'demolition by neglect.' In other words, if you own a historic structure and you just let it fall down. That's not allowed. I'd have to look at the ordinance to see what the penalty would be. Then there's a section about deliberately demolishing a historic structure—a property owner couldn't get away with that. He'd have to pay fines. He might even have to restore the demolished structure in some way."

I was confused. "But why would the Historic District Regulations even apply to the old Root Beer Barrel? It didn't have any artistic or historic merit, did it? Not like—oh, say, Gray Gables. That's a real mansion."

"Right, Lee," Joe said. "Gray Gables is worth preserving because it's beautiful—at least to people who like High Victorian architecture—and because it was owned by a famous man—Trey's great-grandfather, the ambassador—and because it's a great example of the late nineteenth century summer home. But as I understand the ordinance—and I studied it pretty carefully—ordinary structures are also covered."

"You mean all that stuff Hershel said at the post office . . . ?"

"Yeah. Hershel was right. Vernacular architecture is considered worth preservation. An unusual business structure like the Root Beer Barrel would definitely be included. That's one of the main reasons that section of Lake Shore Drive hasn't been redeveloped since the road fell in."

Joe turned to Patsy. "Believe me, I did not allow the old Barrel to deteriorate on purpose."

"I didn't think you did, Joe," Patsy said. "You only became the owner last fall, right?"

"I'm not really the owner at all. The owner is Clementine's estate. I'm just the executor. The estate acquired the property as settlement for a debt. But it was of limited value, because the ordinance required that the old Root Beer Barrel be preserved. I admit I gave a loud 'hurrah' when the storm blew the thing down. But I didn't help it along."

We all stood silently, contemplating the fate of the old Root Beer Barrel. Then Chief Jones spoke. "At the time, nobody suggested that the Barrel had any help coming down. I don't know how we could figure out what happened to it now, three or four months after it happened. I'll talk to Trey and some of the other experts. But as Patsy says, it probably doesn't matter at this point."

The circling boats had left by then. Patsy and Frank drove off in their SUV, and Jerry Cherry and the chief began to load up some equipment. The trees all around were closing in on me. I moved a little closer to Joe.

He spoke to me quietly. "I guess I need to get you home."

"Do you?"

"Our romantic evening is completely shot."

"I guess so. At least we had a good dinner." I led Joe inside the shop, out of sight of the chief and Jerry Cherry. "May I have a goodnight hug?"

Joe obliged. He expanded the hug to include a kiss. And another kiss.

"I guess we don't have to take a boat ride," I said.

Another pause. "We could go by the shop," I suggested. "The break room ought to be deserted. I could make coffee."

"Well, it would make an awful nice interlude before I go to jail," Joe said. "Could I have a double fudge bonbon?"

" 'Layers of milk and dark chocolate fudge with dark chocolate coating.' You could have two."

"Yum, yum. I'll have to lock up."

"I could help you."

Joe and I went back down the dock, and he fastened the sedan in its proper place, locking its mooring chain. Chief Jones and Jerry called out good-byes, promising to be back early in the morning.

Joe followed the chief to Jerry's car. "If I'm not around, and you need to get into the shop, there's a key in a magnetic case behind the drain pipe at the corner of the building." He pointed to the corner he meant.

We waved, and the Warner Pier police car drove away. Joe and I watched as their lights disappeared behind the trees that surrounded the shop. Then we got in Joe's truck, alone at last. I moved over to the center of the truck, and Joe put his arms around me. We sat there several minutes, fully occupied with each other. The windows of the truck were rolled up. It was really dark.

Then I gasped. "Oh!"

"What's wrong?"

"I left my tote bag in the sedan."

Joe nibbled my ear. "I guess you need it."

"I guess so."

He nibbled again. "I'll get it for you."

"Thanks. I'll be waiting."

Joe fished a large, square flashlight out from under the seat of the pickup, then got out of the truck. He closed the door. I could hear his footsteps crunching over the gravel and could see the beam from his flashlight bouncing over the ground as he walked around the side of the shop. Then the light disappeared, but I could still see it reflected overhead on those scary trees. The sound of Joe's footsteps faded away, and all I could hear was the night insects.

Then a voice hissed out of the darkness. "Miss McKinney! Miss McKinney!"

Someone rapped on the passenger's side window.

Chapter 6

If I didn't wet my pants, it was because I was too busy trying to restart my heart. It had come to a dead stop. My head, however, whirled toward the sound at the speed of light.

I don't know if I whispered or shouted. "Who's there?"

"It's me. Hershel Perkins." The croaking voice was unmistakable.

"Hershel!"

Oddly enough, knowing it was Hershel outside the truck calmed my fears. Hershel was strange, but I wasn't afraid of him. I rolled the window partway down. "Hershel! We thought you were dead! Where have you been?"

"I'm hiding."

I tried to open the truck's door, but Hershel pressed against it, holding it closed. "No! Don't open the door! I don't want any light."

"Why not? You must be hurt. We need to get help for you."

"I'm not hurt as bad as some folks want me to be."

"People think Joe rammed your canoe. We've got to tell the police you're all right."

"No! I can't trust them."

"Sure you can."

"No! I saw all those people on the dock. They're out to get me!"

"The police? Your sister? Surely not."

"Oh, Patsy might be all right. But there's Frank. I don't know about him."

"Joe was there. He doesn't want to hurt you. And Trey's always been nice to you, hasn't he? They'll be relieved to find out you're all right."

"No! They may all be in it together."

"Why, Hershel? Why would anybody—anybody at all—want to hurt you?"

"I don't know why. But they do!"

Suddenly I didn't want to be alone with Hershel. This was not the harmless crank who had come into TenHuis Chocolade for a free treat every day. This was a new Hershel, one who feared other people, who might strike out, thinking he was protecting himself.

"Joe's just on the other side of the shop." My voice almost trembled. "He'll be back in a minute."

"I've got to be gone before he comes. The only person who can help me is your aunt."

"Aunt Nettie? How can she help?"

"She's the only one I can trust! Don't tell anybody else. I'll meet her at the old chapel at midnight."

"The old chapel? What old chapel?"

"She'll know where I mean. Midnight!"

Footsteps skittered over the gravel, and Hershel was gone.

Suddenly I could make a noise again. "Joe!" I threw the truck's door open and stood up with my head outside. "Joe! Come quick!"

Immediately I saw the reflection from Joe's flashlight bouncing around in the trees. I heard the *crunch, crunch, crunch* as he ran through the gravel. He yelled, "What's wrong?"

I couldn't make myself get down from the truck. For a minute I stood there, sticking my head out of the cab like a giraffe. Then I sat back down and slammed the door. Joe would be there in a second. He had his cell phone. He'd call the police. Jerry, Chief Jones—they'd be back lickity split. They'd search the woods for Hershel.

And they wouldn't find him.

It would be impossible to find Hershel in the dark in the woods around Joe's shop. Hershel could hide in those woods. He could climb a tree or lie down behind a bush. He could listen to everything the searchers did, see a lot of what they did.

And Hershel would know I hadn't obeyed his instructions not to tell anyone but Aunt Nettie. He wouldn't keep his end of the bargain and go to the old chapel—wherever that was. But meeting him there might be the simplest way to find him.

Just as Joe reached the hood of the truck I reached a decision. I couldn't tell Joe what Hershel had said. Not there, not at the boat shop, with Hershel still out in the woods. Maybe close by, listening. No, I had to get away from there, find Aunt Nettie and ask her how to handle the situation.

Joe yanked his door open. "What's wrong?"

"I'm sorry," I said. "I guess my imagination got the best of me."

"Huh?"

I spoke loudly and distinctly. "I thought I heard something. I got scared. But I guess it was just an animal."

Joe stood there, staring at me. I'm not usually the clingy type—even when I'm threatened by trees. I could tell he was mystified. But I couldn't worry about that.

"Joe, could we get out of here?"

"Sure." Joe handed me my tote bag and slid behind the steering wheel. He started the truck's motor.

"I need to get the van and head home," I said. I slid over next to the right-hand door and fastened my seat belt.

Joe turned his head toward me. In the dim light from the dash I could see that he looked more mystified than ever. And maybe angry. But I couldn't help that.

"You sure changed your mood in a hurry," he said.

Yikes! I'd forgotten that I'd offered Joe coffee and chocolate at TenHuis Chocolade. Now I was having to back out. "I'm sorry. But I've got to see Aunt Nettie."

"Your aunt?"

"It's important."

"What's wrong, Lee?"

"Nothing."

"Did I do something? Say something?"

"No! No, I've just got to pick up my van and get home to see Aunt Nettie. Let's go!"

Joe stared another moment. Then he backed the truck around and drove off, down the narrow road that led to the settled part of Warner Pier.

Once we were away from the shop, I opened my mouth, ready to tell Joe about Hershel. Then I pictured his reaction. He'd certainly never let Aunt Nettie and me meet Hershel at the old chapel without him. And if Joe was there, Hershel might not come.

And where was this old chapel? Was it the place Patsy had mentioned—the one Hershel went to when he was really frightened? It must be.

I didn't know what to do. I waffled all the way to the shop.

My silent debate was the only conversation that went on. Joe didn't say a word. He is not usually sulky, but he had a right to be mad—certainly puzzled—by my sudden about-face, building him up for a late-night tête-à-tête, then changing my mind. But I was too frantic about how to deal with Hershel to worry about him.

When we drove down Peach Street, past TenHuis Chocolade, I saw lights inside. "Oh. Aunt Nettie's still here!"

"Why would she be there so late?"

"I don't know. I hope nothing went wrong with the big kettle cleanup. Just pull up in front."

The minute the truck stopped moving I opened the door and got out. "Thanks for the ride."

"Lee!"

"I can't talk, Joe."

I started across the sidewalk, and Joe jumped out of the truck and followed me. "Lee! What came over you? Did I do something wrong?"

"No! I've just got to see Aunt Nettie."

"Why? I want to know what's going on."

"Nothing's going on!" Inside the shop, back in the workroom, I could see Aunt Nettie. She was standing beside the dark chocolate vat. On the work table behind her I could see several big stainless steel bowls.

"Lee . . ."

"Joe, I've got to go."

I yanked away and turned toward the front door of the shop, but before I could get there, a terrific bang rang out.

"Lee!" Joe jumped about six feet, grabbed me by the arms and shoved me up against the brick wall beside the door. "Get down!"

"Joe! Let me go!"

"That was a shot!"

"It was not! Aunt Nettie is breaking chocolate!"

Joe backed off slightly. "Breaking chocolate?"

"Breaking chocolate. We got stuck with some chocolate that comes in ten-pound bars. They can't go into the chocolate vats until they're broken up."

"I never heard that noise around the shop before."

"We usually get chocolate in little bits—almost granules. But our supplier substituted bars. Let me go, please."

Joe moved away, scowling.

"I'm sorry, Joe," I said. "I know I'm not behaving rationally. But I thought of something while you were getting my bag, and it's vital that I talk to Aunt Nettie about it."

This time Joe didn't argue. I went into the shop and closed and locked the door behind me. I didn't look back at him.

The aroma of warm chocolate enfolded me, and Aunt Nettie looked up. "Lee? What are you doing here?"

"Something came up. I had to see you right away."

"My goodness! I hope you and Joe didn't have a fight."

"Sort of. But that's not the important thing."

"Back when I was dating your uncle, a fight would have been the most important thing in my life." She was standing in the middle of the work-room, beside a big sheet of white paper which had been laid on the floor. As I came into the work room she picked up a white package about a foot long. She lifted it over her head, then hurled it onto the paper. *Bam!* She leaned over and picked up the package. Its contents were now obviously in pieces.

"Oh, Aunt Nettie, listen to what's happened." I poured out the story of the missing Hershel, the damaged canoe, the probability that Joe was a suspect, and, finally, Hershel's appearance at the truck's window in the dark.

Aunt Nettie stared at me, idly turning the crumpled package back and forth. Now her eyes were as round as her tummy.

I looked at my watch. "And it's nearly eleven now. Hershel emphasized that he wanted to meet you at midnight. Where is this chapel anyway? How do we get there?"

Aunt Nettie's face took on a look of complete dismay. "I can't go," she said.

I squinched my eyes closed. She must be afraid. I could hardly blame her. But I had to find Hershel and get him to turn himself in to the chief—or to somebody. It was the fastest way to prove that Joe had nothing to do with running down Hershel's canoe. And it was the fastest way I could think of to get Hershel to a hospital and to treat any injuries he might have.

Somebody had to be at the chapel at midnight. And if I had to go alone, I'd do it.

"Okay," I said. "Just tell me where this chapel is."

"I suppose he means the old Riverside Chapel. It's just about a mile from Joe's shop, and there's a hiking trail along the river. I'm sure Hershel could find it, even in the dark."

"Okay. Can you draw me a map? I'll go alone. I know it's a scary situation."

"I'm not *afraid* to go!"

"You probably should be. Hershel is really talking crazy."

"Nobody could be afraid of Hershel. It's this chocolate. I simply have to get these vats going, or we'll lose a day of work."

I took a deep breath. "How long does it take to get from here to the old chapel?"

"Maybe fifteen minutes in a car."

"Is there a road?"

"Yes. When I talked about the trail, I was thinking of Hershel. He must be on foot."

I checked my watch again. "So we have forty-five minutes before we'd have to leave."

"Yes."

"Okay," I said. "Tell me what to do, and we'll get as much done on the chocolate vats as we can. But I'm dragging you out of here at twenty to midnight. Meeting Hershel at that chapel is the quickest way to prove Joe did not run his canoe down, and I'm finding that guy and bringing him back."

Aunt Nettie smiled. "Wash your hands, and I'll tell you what to do."

I took off my green sweater and put a big bib apron on over my cream slacks and green and cream shirt. I tucked my hair into a food service hairnet. I washed my hands in approved food service fashion—even turning the water off with the paper towel so that my clean hands didn't touch the fixture. Aunt Nettie told me to get a knife and start digging chocolate out of the big bowls.

"Just put a few pieces of the chocolate back in the vats at a time," she said. "Remember, chocolate melts easily—the melting point is only ninety-two degrees. But we have to be careful not to put too many pieces in at once. That could jam up the paddles."

I eyed the pans of chocolate warily. None of them was very full, but the chocolate in them looked solid. The chocolate obviously had been out of the vat for several hours.

Aunt Nettie moved over beside the dark chocolate vat, climbed on to a kitchen step stool, and ripped open the package of chocolate she'd just shattered on the floor. She began putting the chunks into the vat.

"First, you can break up three or four more bars of dark chocolate," she said.

I whammed the ten-pound bars into the floor, then set the packages—now filled with chunks of chocolate—aside. Next I worked on the white chocolate—the smallest kettle—chipping the now-solid chocolate from the bowl on the worktable into pieces and feeding them into the vat. While I was waiting for the white chocolate to melt, I worked on the pan of milk chocolate. Aunt Nettie was concentrating on the dark chocolate.

Through all this I was frantically checking my watch, and at twenty-five to twelve I gave Aunt Nettie a five-minute warning. By twenty minutes to twelve we had all three chocolate vats going. There were a lot of dirty pots and pans in the sink, but I got Aunt Nettie into her sweater and out the back door.

She shook her head as she climbed into my van. "I don't understand why Hershel wants to see me," she said.

"He's highly suspicious of everybody—including his sister and her husband. You've always been nice to him."

Aunt Nettie sniffed. "I never thought a chocolate now and then would mean a trip to the old Riverside Chapel in the middle of the night."

"Just tell me how to get there."

"Head up Dock Street to Fifteenth."

"It's before Joe's shop, then?"

"It's farther, but you don't pass Joe's shop to get there. Turn off Dock Street on Fifteenth, then turn right at a corner with a big white house. I think the street is Elm."

"It would be a tree."

Aunt Nettie laughed. "I don't understand why you dislike trees so much, Lee."

"Some of my best friends are trees. I don't dislike them individually. It's only trees in mobs."

"You'll see whole crowds of trees before we get to the Riverside Chapel. It's way back in the woods. Lots of people think the woods up that way are beautiful."

"I'm sure they are beautiful. I can admire the patterns sunlight makes on the forest floor. Stuff like that. It's just that when you're surrounded by trees you can't see the horizon. They get you all mixed up about which way is north. And you never know what's hiding behind them."

"On the other hand," Aunt Nettie said, "if you need to hide, it's handy having a tree you could jump behind."

"Well, you know the joke about the West Texas boy who went to visit the big woods of Minnesota," I said.

"I guess not."

"When he got back, someone asked if there wasn't some mighty pretty country up there. And the Texan answered, 'I don't know. There were so many trees I didn't see a thing.' "

Aunt Nettie and I were joking about our differing feelings about trees because we were nervous. Heading out into the deep woods to meet the town crank at a ruined chapel at midnight is not my favorite activity. In fact, stated like that, it was absolutely stupid. I thought wistfully of having Joe along—a big, strong guy who knew the terrain and who was smart and who could wrestle and who had a cell phone. Right at that moment I was wishing I'd invited him to the party.

But if Joe had been there, I reminded myself, Hershel probably wouldn't show up.

"See the big white house?" Aunt Nettie said. "Turn right."

We had already been driving down a heavily wooded blacktop road, and our right turn—once we were past the big white house—took us into the real woods. The blacktop became gravel, the road narrowed, and the trees closed in. They met overhead and choked the ditches, crowding in on the road. I had to struggle to keep my teeth from chattering. Aunt Nettie's voice was soothing. "It's not more than a half mile," she said. "I haven't been up here in years."

"What is this place? This Riverside Chapel?"

"Originally, it was a boys' camp, I think. There are some cabins and some sort of pavilion that must have been the dining room. When the camp closed down, a group of the summer people started a nondenominational chapel there."

"Like the Lake Shore Chapel?"

"I think that's what it turned into. This location was so remote that the congregation found a more central site and built a real building."

"So the old chapel was just abandoned?"

"As far as I know. Oh, people used it for picnics or family reunions. But there's no plumbing—or maybe just a well."

"And it's posted," I said. I stopped the van with the headlights on a sign. "PRIVATE PROPERTY," it read. "NO TRESPASSING."

"I don't think we can let that stop us," Aunt Nettie said.

"It certainly wouldn't have stopped Hershel," I said. "According to Patsy Waterloo, he prowls everywhere—all around Warner Pier."

"I think she's right. I know I've seen him over on our road and on the beach, just trudging along. I wouldn't go so far as calling him a window peeper—but . . ."

"But he spies on people, I gather." I took a deep breath and edged the van forward. "At least the old chapel doesn't seem to have a gate."

I had spoken too soon. Around the next bend in the road a barred gate appeared. "I'll open it," Aunt Nettie said. Before I could say more than, "Aunt Nettie . . . ," she was out of the van and over to the gate. She shoved at it. It wiggled, but it didn't open. She came back.

"The gate's padlocked. We'll have to walk from here. I hope you have a flashlight."

We'd come this far; neither of us was going to balk at going the last few feet. I reached into the bin under Aunt Nettie's seat and produced a heavy flashlight—the kind my dad says every vehicle should be equipped with.

"I'll leave the van's lights on," I said. "At least we'll be able to find it on our way back."

Aunt Nettie and I climbed over the gate. The road was not graveled but was merely a sandy lane—the type with grass down the middle. The trees, of course, met overhead and were crowding into the road.

"It can't be far," I said.

"It's not. In fact—Lee, shine the flashlight up ahead."

I was terrifically relieved to see a structure less than a hundred feet away.

"We can make it," I said.

I dropped the light back onto the ground immediately in front of us, and the two of us walked up to the building. As Aunt Nettie had said, it was a rustic pavilion suitable for use for picnics or outdoor worship. The roof, which probably had holes in it, was held up by posts—four on each end, and eight down each side. There were no walls, and the floor—I could see bits of cement slab—was covered with matted leaves and other forest debris.

The place was deserted. Nobody called out to us, and I didn't see Hershel standing there waiting. Aunt Nettie stepped under the roofed area, and I used the flashlight to check my watch. "It's five till twelve," I said. "I vote that we don't wait long."

"Lee!" Aunt Nettie's voice was tight. "When you lifted the flashlight—there's something over in that corner. Shine the light over there."

She gestured, and I turned the flashlight where she directed. I saw nothing.

"Farther back," Aunt Nettie said. "It was outside the pavilion, I guess."

She clutched my arm as I inched the light farther and farther away, directing the flashlight's beam to the edge of the pavilion, then beyond. Now I saw something, too. It was a lump, huddled on the ground. I turned the light full on it.

We were looking at a bright green shirt.

Chapter 7

A unt Nettie and I clutched each other.
    "That's Hershel's shirt," I said.

"He's hurt," Aunt Nettie said. "We'd better see if we can help him." She took a step toward the heap.

"Wait!" I grabbed her arm. "Let's look around first."

"But, Lee . . ."

"Hershel can wait another minute," I said. I guess I'd already decided Hershel hadn't been hurt in some kind of accident. I felt sure he'd been attacked, and I wanted to make sure the person who had attacked him wasn't still there waiting for us to lean over Hershel and become easy targets.

I pivoted slowly, shining the flashlight's beam all around the pavilion. I saw nothing. Nothing but trees.

Aunt Nettie shook off my hand and went to Hershel. I followed her.

Hershel was on his back, with his face turned slightly away from us. He looked peaceful, lying there in a clump of ferns. His eyes were open, but the bright light from my flashlight brought no reaction from his pupils. A pool of red had spread beneath his head.

Aunt Nettie knelt and touched his wrist. "He's still warm," she said. "It's been a long time since I took first aid, but I don't think he has a pulse. I don't think we can do anything to help him."

She spoke very calmly, but I saw that her hand was trembling.

"Let's go," I said.

"I don't think we should leave Hershel here alone."

"I'm certainly not leaving you here with him. And I'm not volunteering to stay myself. We'll have to go back to town and call the police."

"It doesn't seem right."

"Oh, yes, it does!"

I pulled her to her feet, and in the process I nearly dropped the flashlight. It swung around crazily.

And, at the other end of the pavilion, the light reflected on a pair of eyes. Someone was standing there looking at us.

I nearly went into cardiac arrest for the second time that night. Then I forced myself to focus the flashlight on the eyes. And I saw Joe Woodyard leaning against one of the pavilion posts, squinting.

"What the heck are you two doing?" he said.

I've had a lot of emotional ups and downs in my twenty-nine years, but right then I felt as if I were on a roller coaster. I was so relieved it was Joe that I could have kissed him and so mad at him for scaring us that I could have killed him. My feelings ricocheted around that pavilion.

But when I spoke, I guess I sounded fairly calm. "Do you have your cell phone?"

Joe reached for his pocket. "Yeah. I'm not sure it'll work up here—the reception on this side of town is iffy. Who do you want to call?"

"The police." I turned sideways and motioned toward Hershel.

Joe gave a low whistle and walked toward us.

"He doesn't have a pulse," Aunt Nettie said. "At least, I can't find one."

Joe checked Hershel's pulse, then listened to his chest and put a wisp of grass beneath his nostrils. "I don't think CPR would do any good," he said. Then I remembered that Joe had been a lifeguard for three summers.

He pulled out his cell phone and punched in numbers. And he didn't punch in 9-1-1. He tapped in a whole string of numbers.

"Who are you calling?"

"City Hall. The dispatcher can hear the answering machine this time of night. It's quicker than getting the wrong 9-1-1. Which is easy to do from a cell phone."

That made sense. But other questions flitted through my mind. How had Joe known the number of Warner Pier's City Hall? And why did he know all this stuff about the dispatcher's routine? The questions evaporated before they could get out of my mouth. It didn't seem all that important at the moment.

Joe waited, then spoke, apparently to the answering machine. "Hey, Lorraine—are you on duty? Pick up, please. It's Joe Woodyard. We've found Hershel Perkins, and he's dead."

The dispatcher came on immediately, and Joe described exactly where we were. "I think we're still inside the Warner Pier city limits," he said. Trust a lawyer to worry about jurisdiction at a time like that. "Okay. We'll wait here." He put his phone back in his pocket.

"She said she'd get the patrol car and the chief right away," Joe said. "Just what were you two doing up here?"

"We came to meet Hershel," I said. "How did you happen upon the scene? And how did you get to the pavilion without our hearing you?"

"Tiptoed. I was following you."

"Why?"

"After the way you acted, I thought you were up to something. And I sure hope that answer satisfies Hogan Jones. Because he's also going to wonder just what I was doing up here."

Joe chivalrously offered to stay with Hershel while Aunt Nettie and I went back to the van, but we refused to leave. I explained how Hershel had come up to the truck and told me he wanted to see Aunt Nettie. Then the three of us stood there waiting. The atmosphere was cozier with three of us. It was a long five minutes before we heard a siren, and several minutes later before we saw car lights flashing among the trees.

"That'll be Tom Jordan. I'll walk down and meet him," Joe said. I knew Tom Jordan—an older guy who worked for the Warner Pier Police Department part-time during the summer tourist season. But I hadn't known who was on duty that night. I wondered how Joe had happened to know.

In a minute Tom—his gray hair glimmering in the flashlights—came toward the pavilion, with Joe leading the way. Chief Jones was close behind them. The chief wearily asked Aunt Nettie and me how we'd happened on the scene, then told us to go home. "I'll get your statements tomorrow," he said.

I pictured my van, parked on that one-lane road with its nose right up against the gate. "You'll have to let us out," I said. "I guess there are three cars behind us now."

"Just Tom and me," the chief said. "Who else did you think would be there?"

I turned to Joe. "Where did you leave the truck?"

"There's a little turnoff a couple of hundred yards back down the road," he said. "I nosed the truck in there, in case I didn't want you and Nettie to know I was here."

The chief looked at Joe closely. "You didn't come with Lee and Nettie?"

"No. Lee acted so odd—well, I figured she was up to something. So I followed them."

"But you parked back down the road?"

"Right." Joe sighed. "It doesn't look good, does it?"

I didn't get it. "What doesn't look good?"

The chief shrugged, so Joe answered the question. "Since I'm not parked behind you, I can't prove I arrived after you did," he said.

"But what difference does your time of arrival make?" I said. Then I saw the answer. "Oh!"

"Yeah," Joe said. "I could have been here ahead of you—in plenty of time to kill Hershel. First his canoe was apparently run down near my dock, then I'm on the scene when he's killed. If I were the chief, I'd have me down at the station in a flash."

I wanted to argue, but Joe shook his head. "You'd better get Nettie home," he said.

By this time the patrolman was moving the two Warner Pier PD cars, and

I couldn't really justify hanging around. So I backed down the narrow lane to the place where Joe had turned in—the patrolman walked along and showed me where it was—then I turned around and headed back to Elm Street.

We had to go to the shop, of course, because Aunt Nettie's car was parked behind it. And going behind the shop meant going inside, so that she could make sure the big electric chocolate kettles were functioning properly. I almost had to lasso her to keep her from washing the pots, pans, and bowls we'd left in the sink.

"No," I said. "You're going home. You came to work a long time ago. The morning crew can wash the dishes."

Aunt Nettie sighed. "I guess I'm getting old."

"You don't seem to be, but I'm aging fast."

We went home. We got in bed. I didn't close an eye, but morning came anyway.

At seven a.m. the phone rang. I could hear Aunt Nettie in the bathroom, so I ran downstairs and caught the call.

"Lee? It's Trey."

"Trey?" I double-checked the time. Why was Trey calling so early? Why was he calling at all? "What's up?"

"Is it true that you and Joe found Hershel's body last night up at the old chapel?"

"I'm afraid so." I didn't mention Aunt Nettie.

"So Hershel didn't drown?"

"Not unless—" I bit back a snotty remark about a wash tub. "No. It looked like a head injury, but I'm no expert. I guess you and the rest of the river patrol volunteers wasted your time looking for him in the water."

"That doesn't matter! We were home by dark. After Meg and I had a bite, I even went over to the Millers' to work on that fireplace. But I guess you and Joe kept looking for him."

"That's not exactly the way it happened, Trey."

"I'm just stunned. If Hershel had a head injury, I wouldn't have expected him to be able to get to the chapel."

"What do you mean?"

"The chapel's way up on the bluff. If he was that badly injured, I'd have expected him to be found down by the river."

I answered without thinking. "He didn't get the head injury in the boat accident!"

"What do you mean?"

I thought about it. Could Hershel have been that badly injured and still talked to me in the dark, down at the boat shop, coherently? Or as near coherently as Hershel ever talked? Could an old wound have begun bleeding or something? Could a twenty-four-hour-old injury have killed Hershel?

Trey spoke again. "What do you mean, he didn't get the head injury in the boat accident?"

"I don't know, Trey. Maybe he did. I guess I'd better shut up until the chief has taken my statue. I mean, my statement!"

"How did you and Joe think to look for Hershel up there at the pavilion?" Trey chuckled. "Or shouldn't I ask?"

"Why shouldn't you ask?"

"Well, that spot used to be known as quite the lovers' lane." Trey gave a nervous giggle. "Before they locked the gate. Anyway, that's what the locals say."

"I'd never even heard of the place before last night. So I guess I'm still just a summer visitor."

"Joe never told you about it? Seems as if he would have known. Maybe even taken somebody up there."

"I'm sure he was a normal teenager."

Trey snickered. "Well, yeah. I guess Joe has given Warner Pier plenty to talk about over the years. He's played the field. Or that's what Meg tells me. She's the local at our house." Trey snickered again. "Of course, *you* have nothing to worry about, Lee."

Something about that second snicker got to me. It changed Trey's jokes into snide remarks. If Trey could be snide, I decided, I could be snide, too.

I snickered back at him. "Have you asked *Meg* about the old chapel?"

"Meg wouldn't go there!"

"But you said she was a Warner Pier local."

The silence grew so long that I finally spoke again. "Did Meg go to school here?"

"High school."

"High school was a long time ago," I said. "For all of us. I guess I'd better get ready for wolf. Work! I mean, get ready for work."

"I'm sorry I bothered you so early." Trey hung up abruptly.

I was completely mystified. Had Trey called just to gossip about Hershel's death? I supposed that was logical enough—every coffee klatch in Warner Pier was going to be buzzing over the killing of the town crank. But somehow I didn't feel that had been the real purpose of Trey's call.

I thought he was dropping a hint about Joe. Trying to tell me Joe was seeing someone else. Or had seen someone else. But when I'd turned that tactic on him and asked him about his wife, he'd begun to sulk.

Hmmmm. Very interesting.

I made a pot of coffee, got out the toaster, and prepared to waylay Aunt Nettie at the breakfast table. Maybe she knew something about Meg's past.

By the time Aunt Nettie came out in her white pants and tunic, I'd had some caffeine and my brain didn't seem to be quite as foggy.

"Who was on the phone?" she said.

"Trey Corbett. But I can't figure out why he called."

"What did he say?"

"I'm not sure I understood what he said. But when I made a joke about Meg, it completely killed the conversation."

"Ah." Aunt Nettie gave the syllable enough nuances to fill a semester of English lit.

"What does 'ah' mean? Is there something I should know about Meg? Some deep dark secret in her past?"

"I'm sure you know all that's necessary."

"Necessary? Why should anything be necessary? I never even heard of Meg Corbett until yesterday."

"Oh?" That syllable had a lot of nuances, too.

"Aunt Nettie! If I'm about to put my foot in it up to the knee, tell me! Is there something I should know about Meg?"

"Well, back when she was in high school—back when she was Maggie Mae Vanderveer—well, she and Joe dated for a while."

I rolled my eyes. "Is that what's bothering Trey?" Then I opened my eyes wide. "She didn't leave town in scandalous circumstances?"

"Oh, no! I know Mercy wasn't very happy about Joe seeing her. Maggie Mae—Meg—well, she didn't have the best family life. But I don't like to criticize Meg. It would have been easy for a girl from her background to slide into a lax way of life. The way her mother did, if we're honest. But Meg was ambitious. She got herself through college."

"Sounds like someone I know. If Meg had had an Aunt Nettie to put her on the right path, she'd be president."

Aunt Nettie laughed. "She's nothing like you, Lee. And her family's nothing like yours. You never went hungry or were so dirty the neighbors called the welfare department."

"That happened to Meg? Hard to believe somebody so high-toned could have come from trash."

"I don't know for sure. So much of this is gossip I hear from the ladies in the shop. I try not to believe everything they say." She checked the kitchen clock. "I'll get coffee and a roll at the shop," she said. "There's a woman spending the summer in a cottage near Gray Gables. She's writing a cookbook of some sort. She has a really funny name, and Lois Corbett—that's Trey's cousin's wife—asked me to talk to her, and she's coming in this morning."

Aunt Nettie went to work then, leaving me with a lot more questions about why Trey had called.

I'd been aware that Joe existed when I was in high school just because he had been the head lifeguard at the Warner Pier Beach during the three summers I worked for Aunt Nettie and Uncle Phil. But we didn't know each other. Besides, by that time Joe wasn't in high school. He was a student at the University of Michigan. I assumed he'd had girlfriends in high school—most popular and good-looking guys did—but I didn't remember any of my friends telling me who they were. If Meg, or Maggie Mae, had been around during those summers, I hadn't known her.

By the time Joe and I met twelve years later, each of us had been married and divorced. I'd never quizzed Joe about ex-girlfriends. He'd volunteered the reasons why his marriage hadn't worked, and I'd confided my problems with my ex. Neither of us had offered to detail every romantic encounter we'd had in our past lives. Frankly, that would seem like a pretty dumb thing for either of us to do.

Besides, we weren't engaged or anything. We weren't even lovers—though that would probably come as a big surprise to the gossips of Warner Pier. Our abstinence was based more on fear than on moral qualms. We were both conscious of our past mistakes and timid about committing future ones. Maybe we were both also aware that we lived in a small town. If our romance ended in a dramatic bust-up, we were still going to be running into each other at the grocery store. There were a lot of reasons for us to be cautious, and so far we had been.

Knowing that Joe and Meg had once dated each other did give me a clue to that undertone of antagonism between them that I'd noticed the day before. It could help explain why Meg was so eager for me to see Joe as a suspect in Hershel's death and why Joe had glared at her once or twice and carefully ignored her the rest of the time. Or could that antagonism be a screen for another feeling?

Was I jealous of Meg? Should I be? By the time I got to that question I was upstairs in my bedroom, looking in the mirror. I had to admit that right at that moment I wasn't the most beautiful woman in the world. Tossing and turning most of the night will do that to you. And Meg was attractive. She had even looked good after spending an afternoon out in a boat, helping search for a drowning victim.

I went to the closet and pulled out an outfit that I thought was becoming—a brown and peach plaid skirt and a V-necked cotton sweater in the same peach. To heck with the TenHuis Chocolade uniform—that day I was going to feel good about myself. I headed for the shower.

I spent some extra time on my hair and face. I dug some sandals out of the back of the closet, sandals I hoped would make my legs look long and shapely. The plaid skirt and sweater did give my morale a boost. I ate a couple of pieces of toast and contemplated the day.

One thing the day was going to include, I realized, was giving Chief Jones a complete statement on my encounter with Hershel. I decided that I'd better call and see if he wanted me to come by at any particular time.

It seemed as if the chief had been waiting for my call.

"Chief? It's Lee McKinney. Do you want me to come in today and make a statement?"

"Yep."

"When?"

The chief gave a deep sigh. "Right away, I guess. In fact, maybe you can identify the murder weapon."

CHOCOLATE CHAT
COLUMBUS DISCOVERS CHOCOLATE

- The first European contact with chocolate was made by Christopher Columbus during his fourth voyage. On August 15, 1502, at a place called Guanaja on an island north of Honduras, Columbus captured two gigantic Mayan trading canoes. The goods in the canoes included cotton clothing, war clubs, copper pots, maize, and some special "almonds" which the Indians apparently valued highly. Columbus apparently never ate or drank any chocolate.

- The Spanish invaded Yucatan in 1517 and Mexico in 1519. At first they found the strange drink of the country repulsive. But as the Spanish began to eat native foods—and as they began to intermarry with their conquered subjects—they added chocolate to their diet. They often sweetened it with sugar, and they also developed the wooden *molinillo,* a tool which looks something like a pinecone on a stick and which is used to beat chocolate and make it frothy. This replaced the Indians' custom of pouring chocolate from vessel to vessel.

- The Spanish occupiers went back and forth to their native country frequently, of course, but the earliest written report of chocolate being taken back with them comes from 1544, when a Mayan delegation accompanied some Dominican friars on a visit to Prince Philip of Spain and presented Philip with cacao beans.

Chapter 8

I approached the Warner Pier City Hall and Police Department with dread, of course. I couldn't imagine what horrible object had been used to kill Hershel. And I couldn't imagine why Hogan Jones thought I might be able to identify it.

When I saw the weapon, I was completely mystified.

"Jerry Cherry and I were out there at daybreak," the chief said. His tall, skinny shape bent over a table in his office, and he pointed a bony finger at an object which lay there. "Jerry found this," he said.

The object was a rock about four inches around and three inches thick. A simple, rounded stone—one of the millions which vacationers stub their toes on along any beach on the shore of Lake Michigan.

"What on earth makes you think that was used to kill Hershel?" I said. "There are at least a zillion rocks like that on the beach at Warner Pier. What made this one stand out?"

"It wasn't on the beach," the chief said. He was looking tired—he'd probably been up all night—and his weariness deepened the lines in his face and made him look more like Abraham Lincoln than ever. "It was just inside the woods, about thirty-five feet from the pavilion, close to this."

He picked up a paper sack and showed me that it held a rag. It looked like an ordinary red commercial rag—the kind my dad uses to wipe up grease in his garage, and the kind Joe uses to get varnish off his hands in his boat shop. The kind an industrial laundry delivers or Home Depot sells.

"The rag was what got our attention," the chief said. "The preliminary report says there are red fabric fibers in the wound in Hershel's head. And the rock we found with it appears to match the size and shape of the wound. Wounds."

I shuddered away from a picture of Hershel being hit repeatedly. "Why did you think I could identify it?"

The chief used the eraser end of a pencil to turn the stone over. "It's got something written on it," he said.

I looked closely. I could see three letters. "J.R.W." And a date.

It took me a second to realize they were Joe's initials—Joseph Robert Woodyard. At the same time I realized there was a small hole in the top of the stone, and a second hole on the side.

I put my lips near one hole and my hand near the second and blew. Air rushed out onto my hand.

"What are you doing?" Chief Jones said.

"It's a 'lucky'!" I said. "Don't you look for lucky stones?"

"I don't even know what they are."

"They're a TenHuis family tradition. When you walk along the beach, you look at the stones, and if you find one with a hole that goes clear through it—it's a lucky. If you can't see through it, you have to prove it's a lucky stone by blowing through the hole or by pouring water through it. Then you write your initials on it and take it home. I don't know if anybody but us does it. But that's a lucky stone."

"It wasn't so lucky for Hershel. Do you have any explanation for how this particular stone could have gotten up to the old chapel?"

"I didn't take it up there. I'd never even heard of the place until last night." I sounded defensive, even to myself. I'd already thought of a place I had put a lucky stone with those initials, but I didn't want to say where.

The chief waited silently, looking at me steadily. He wasn't buying my cover-up. I decided to abandon it.

"Okay," I said. "Joe and I took the runabout up the lakeshore one of the first nice days in May. We had a picnic. It was too cold to swim or even to wade, so we walked along the beach, and I found three or four lucky stones, and Joe found one. When we got back to the shop that evening, I put my stones in the back of the van, and I laid the one he had found near the shop's downspout."

The chief nodded. "We found a gap where it looked like one of the stones was missing. The weather had made a little pocket for it."

All of a sudden I was very angry. "So you knew where it came from all along, and you wanted to trap me into saying the stone came from Joe's shop."

"I wasn't trying to trap you. I was trying not to put words in your mouth at all."

"You thought I'd lie to protect Joe."

The chief opened his mouth, but I kept talking. "Well, Chief Hogan Jones, let me tell you that I would not lie to protect Joe."

"Lee . . ."

"I wouldn't lie to protect him, because Joe doesn't need projecting. I mean, protecting! Joe would never have harmed Hershel. I completely deject—I mean, reject!—that idea."

"Calm down, Lee."

"I'm not going to calm down. I thought you were a friend of mine, a friend of Aunt Nettie's. I thought you liked Joe, too."

"I do, Lee. I like all of you. But an investigating officer has to look at all possibilities."

"But you *know* Joe. He's a decent human being! He wouldn't hurt anybody. Besides, what conceivable reason would he have had to harm Hershel?"

The chief gave a little snort. "Face it, Lee. Anybody in the vicinity of Warner Pier might have had a reason to get Hershel out of the way."

"Because he was annoying? That would be a pretty extreme reaction."

"Not because he was annoying. Because he was nosy. He wandered all around town, more or less spying on everybody."

"But he hadn't spied on Joe."

"Not until he brought up all this business about the old Root Beer Barrel being pulled down."

"But that wasn't true!"

"What if it was true, Lee? Joe's had an awful time with his ex-wife's estate. Right?"

"I've never asked all the details."

"I don't know all the details either, but I do know Joe took the Root Beer Barrel property as payment on a bad debt—a debt owed to Clementine Ripley's estate. But the property was virtually worthless."

"Lakefront property is not worthless. Not in Warner Pier."

"But the lot couldn't be redeveloped because of the Root Beer Barrel, right? The Historic District Ordinance required that the Barrel be saved. And that made the property hard to sell."

"That rule was silly. The previous owner had allowed the old Barrel to become dilapidated. Joe was planning to go to the board and ask permission to take it down."

"He might not have gotten that permission. And just at that moment the Barrel happened to blow down."

I was silent.

"A simple coincidence," Chief Jones said.

"Of course!"

"Except that Hershel said it wasn't a coincidence."

"Nobody believed Hershel! Besides, all this happened three months ago. Nobody thought anything about it when it happened. Why didn't Hershel come forward then, if he knew anything?"

The chief shook his head. "I don't understand it, Lee. And I'm not hauling Joe down to the station yet. But when Hershel's canoe is sunk and then Hershel himself is found dead—and both these things happen near Joe's boat shop—and Joe doesn't have an alibi for either event, I can't just say, 'Ol' Joe wouldn't do a dastardly deed like that,' and ignore it. I've got to look at one of the primary rules of detection—'Cui bono?' Who benefits?"

That pretty much ended our conversation. I made my statement, then agreed to come back at noon—when the chief's secretary would have it ready to sign. But I left in a huff. I was furious at the chief's suspicions of Joe.

I was also scared spitless. The chief was right. Joe had argued with Hershel. And he really was eager to sell the Root Beer Barrel property. And he did not have an alibi for either time Hershel had been attacked. The first time he'd been out in the lake on a boat. The second time he'd followed Aunt Nettie and me up to the old chapel—except as he himself had pointed out, he could have been there first.

I had to do something. But what? The whole situation was scary. Joe would never have knocked the old Root Beer Barrel down. I wasn't even sure he'd know how.

At least, I was sure I didn't know how. Who would know? Who worked with old structures and could tell me how to demolish one?

The answer, of course, was Trey Corbett. And he'd hung up on me at seven that morning after he'd implied my boyfriend might be seeing someone else and I'd countered with a similar implication about his wife.

Then Aunt Nettie had handed me the news that his wife and my boyfriend had once dated each other. What did that mean? They went out a few times? Went steady? Were queen and king of the prom?

I knew Meg didn't have Joe's letter jacket, because he'd dug it out of his mother's attic and given it to me, more or less as a joke. I'd hate to think Meg had had it earlier—but high school was a long time ago. Maybe I needed to call Trey and apologize. I mean, Trey and I were both doing business in Warner Pier. We needed to get along, right? We even served on a Chamber of Commerce committee together.

When I opened the shop door and saw the two teenagers behind the counter and the dozen hairnet ladies calmly molding chocolates in the workroom, I felt relieved and comforted. Aunt Nettie was bustling about with her usual happy expression, and the wonderful aroma of warm chocolate filled the air. I concluded that my amateurish work at refilling the chocolate vats the night before hadn't done any harm. Business seemed to be progressing as usual. Tracy was getting a Bailey's Irish Cream bonbon ("Classic cream liqueur interior") for a broad-beamed woman wearing red shorts not quite big enough for that broad beam.

It was tempting to forget poor Hershel, lying dead with rock-shaped wounds in the back of his head. And I might have tried to forget him, if I hadn't been so worried about Joe.

I helped myself to a Dutch caramel bonbon ("Creamy, European-style caramel in dark chocolate") and reminded Aunt Nettie that sometime that day she needed to make a formal statement about finding Hershel. Then I went to the telephone. I got out the Warner Pier Chamber of Commerce directory—all ten pages of it—and found Trey's number. I made a few notes about what I needed to ask him, then I called.

The phone was picked up immediately. Trey's voice said, "Hello."

"Hi, Trey," I said. "I wanted to apologize for . . ."

But Trey's voice was still speaking. "You've reached the office of C.T. Corbett Architectural Services," he said. "Please leave a message after the tone."

I had to gulp hard before I could leave a message. I'd been so psyched up about speaking to Trey that it didn't seem possible he wasn't in his office. I managed to stammer out my name and the TenHuis phone number, then hung up. His secretary must be out. If he had a secretary. Trey's operation didn't seem to be very large.

I remained uneasy. Maybe I should talk to Joe. I stared at the telephone, tapping my finger on the key that would speed dial the boat shop. Then I remembered that Joe's phone was out of order, or it had been the day before. Besides, the chief had probably kept him up all night; he was likely to be asleep.

I punched in the numbers for Joe's cell phone. If he was asleep, surely he would have turned that phone off.

He answered immediately. "Vintage Boats."

Suddenly I had nothing to say. I had no real excuse for calling Joe. I just wanted to hear his voice.

"Vintage Boats." Joe repeated his greeting. One more second and he'd decide I was a crank call and hang up.

"Joe," I said. "It's Lee."

"Are you okay? Haven't stumbled over any more bodies?"

"Not this morning." Better keep this light. "Did the chief keep you up all night?"

"Just until a little after 2 a.m. Then he and Jerry were at the shop poking around before seven. I hadn't slept much anyway. Has he already had you in for a statement?"

"Yes."

"Then you know about the stone they found."

"Yes, he made me identify the initials. Some lucky stone."

"This whole deal with the Root Beer Barrel has been unlucky."

I remembered that I'd told the chief I had never asked about the details of Joe's business dealings. That was deliberate. Money problems—too much, not too little—had been a major factor when my first marriage broke up. I guess I'd shied away from discussing money with Joe because I was afraid we'd argue about it.

But at the moment I needed to be nosy. "Exactly how did you get hold of the Root Beer Barrel, anyway?"

"A guy named Foster McGee owed Clementine money. He's a Chicago insurance executive. She got him off on a fraud charge."

Joe paused, and I prompted him. "So?"

"McGee had paid Clementine only half her fee, so he owed her money, and as you know, she owed me money. McGee owns a condo up here, and he'd been suckered into buying the Root Beer Barrel—didn't realize it wouldn't be easy to redevelop the property. The city began giving him some trouble over letting the property become dilapidated. When the interest he owed Clementine's estate got too high, he offered the estate the property as payment."

"Why did you agree to take it?"

"Because McGee is almost bankrupt and is none too honest. I knew it wouldn't be easy to do anything with the property, but if he went belly-up the estate might never get anything at all. I started preparing a petition, getting ready to ask permission to demolish the Barrel. Then a miracle happened—or so I thought. The thing blew down. I thanked my lucky stars and thought there might actually be light at the end of that particular tunnel. Especially when a real live potential buyer showed up."

"Who is this buyer?"

"A guy from Grand Rapids—somebody Frank Waterloo works with. He owns a development company up there, and he wants to expand in our direction."

"What does he want to build down here?"

"I don't know. And I don't care. He'll have to comply with the Historic District Regulations, and I don't think the city would go for a McDonald's."

I laughed. Warner Pier's economy depends on its Victorian atmosphere, so the city is extremely picky about what new structures look like. Plus, pressure from local merchants keeps the Planning Commission and City Council notoriously wary of fast food chains. "Yeah, McDonald's couldn't get in, even if they put gingerbread up and down the arches."

"True. As I said, the thing's been a headache all along."

"And now this. But Joe, after three months—they'll never be able to prove whether or not the Barrel was deliberately torn down."

"I know. And I don't think they can prove I killed Hershel either. But if they don't figure out who did do it—well, I'm sunk anyway."

"None of your friends will believe this. It's silly!"

"But it ruins my reputation."

"Your reputation? I never knew you to worry about what other people thought of you!"

Joe was silent for a moment before he spoke. "Sometimes other peoples' opinions can be pretty important."

Then he hung up.

Our conversation hadn't been reassuring. I was more confused than ever, especially by Joe's reaction. Instead of relying on his friends to believe in him, he seemed more concerned about the opinions of people who didn't know him.

"Lee." I looked up to see Aunt Nettie standing in the doorway. "Do you want to go over to the Waterloos' house with me?" she said. "I stopped by the Superette and bought a ham."

Chapter 9

Food equals sympathy. The universal belief of small town America.

"I could get some coffee and tea," I said.

Aunt Nettie beamed. "That's a good idea."

I noticed that she had changed from her white pants and tunic into light blue slacks and a matching cotton sweater. I was glad I'd happened to dress up a little, though my plaid skirt might be a little short. But Aunt Nettie seemed to think three inches above the knee was okay for a condolence call.

It was a beautiful summer day in west Michigan, which stars at producing beautiful summer days. We stopped at the grocery store—where I bought three pounds of gourmet blend coffee and a big jar of instant tea, drove across the Orchard Street bridge, then turned up Inland Avenue. Nice of the Warner Pier city planners to label the street which led away from Lake Michigan so clearly. If we'd turned the other direction, we'd have been on Lake Shore Drive, the street that eventually led to Aunt Nettie's house.

The Waterloos' drive was full of cars, of course, and since Hershel had lived next door, I wasn't surprised to see a Warner Pier PD patrol car and the Michigan State Police mobile crime lab along the curb. The chief would be searching Hershel's house.

We parked down the street and walked back past several beautiful cottages—two Gothic revivals, one folk Victorian, and a Queen Anne which was heavy on the turrets and shingles. The Waterloo house was Craftsman, the style that led up to Frank Lloyd Wright. All us Warner Pier folks know this stuff; we can tell Greek revival from colonial revival with only a brief glimpse of a roofline.

When we walked up onto the broad porch, Betty VanNoord, a math teacher at Warner Pier High, opened the front door. Behind her were two other women I recognized from the Warner Pier High School honor assembly I'd gotten roped into attending the day Stacy got a scholarship. Patsy's fellow teachers had apparently taken over hostess duty.

"Thanks for coming," Betty said. "I'll put the food in the kitchen. Patsy's out on the deck."

"We don't want to intrude," Aunt Nettie said.

"Patsy will want to see you," Betty said. "You two found Hershel."

I hadn't considered that aspect. I hoped Patsy didn't want a play-by-play description.

Another teacher led us through the house to the deck. I'd seen the deck from the river, of course. It was a beautiful addition of a twenty-first century amenity to an early twentieth century house. It was like an extended porch and overlooked a lawn which led down to the river. There was a small dock, but no boat.

Frank was leaning on the deck's rail, big and bald as ever. Nearby Patsy, dressed in a new set of artistic draperies, was sitting in a wicker chair. Both got up and greeted us with the obligatory air kisses, while we murmured useless phrases. But they seemed glad we'd come.

One of the teachers brought coffee, and Patsy asked us to describe what had happened the night before. I gave a general report, slurring over Hershel's disdain for "that bunch on the dock," a group that had included both Patsy and Frank.

"I was afraid to bring anybody except Aunt Nettie to meet Hershel," I said. "He was adequate—I mean, adamant! He was really firm. He wanted to see her and nobody else. Then he ran off into the woods, and I didn't see how anybody could find him unless he wanted to be found."

"Hershel prowled around so much. I guess he knew every foot of the riverbank, and the lakeshore, too." Patsy dabbed at her eyes with a tissue. "When you found him . . . did he look . . . was he . . . ?"

Aunt Nettie took her hand. "He looked as if he was sleeping, Patsy."

Patsy nodded, and tears ran down her face. They ran down Aunt Nettie's, too. After all, my Uncle Phil—the man she'd been married to for forty years—had been a homicide victim, too. He'd been killed by a drunk driver. I wouldn't have described Hershel as looking "as if he was sleeping." But if Aunt Nettie thought it would help Patsy to be told that he looked that way, it was fine with me.

I realized I was tearing up, too, mainly because I also missed Uncle Phil. But crying with Hershel's sister made me feel like a hypocrite. I sympathized with Patsy, but I had regarded Hershel as a pain. Pitiable, yes, but a pain. Acting as if he had been a personal loss made me feel dishonest. Finding his body had been a shock, true. But what I was really interested in was the evidence that made Joe look guilty when I was convinced he had nothing to do with Hershel's death.

I eyed Frank, still standing at the rail. Joe had said that the Grand Rapids man who wanted to buy the old Root Beer Barrel was someone Frank knew. Maybe Frank could tell me a little more about the circumstances. Under Chief Jones's rule of "Cui bono?" or "Who benefits?" that guy was a suspect. He wouldn't have wanted to buy the property if the old Barrel hadn't fallen down.

I patted my eyes with a tissue, then got up and took my coffee cup over to the rail, standing beside Frank.

I nodded toward the rustic cabin under the trees, closer to the lake than the Waterloos' house. "Is that where Hershel lived?" Yellow tape surrounded the cabin, and I could see a couple of guys bent over outside, apparently searching the ground.

"Yes. I guess we can redo it as a rental. Something."

"You've done a beautiful job on this house. How old is it?"

"Patsy's great-grandparents built it in 1919."

"It's lovely. Did you do the remodeling work yourself?"

"Oh, no. Trey Corbett was entirely in charge of our restoration project—designed the plan, found the subs, got the work done. Patsy made the final choice on the wallpaper, and I wrote the checks."

"Writing the checks is a major contribution, Frank. Projects like that get out of hand financially real fast."

"I will say that Trey paid some attention to the budget we had. I was nervous about the cost of the project, since he comes from a wealthy family and lots of those people have no idea of the value of money. We still had to scramble . . ." His voice trailed off.

I saw a way to introduce Frank's links to construction, and I jumped in. "Your construction experience must have been a big advantage."

"My what?"

"Your experience with construction."

Frank chuckled. "I have no experience with construction. I can't tell a paintbrush from a band saw. What gave you the idea I know anything about building?"

"Something Joe said. I guess I misunderstood his meddling. His meaning!"

"I think so." Frank held out his hands. "See these? Ten thumbs. I can't drive a nail. What would have given Joe the idea that I had something to do with construction?"

"Oh, he said you know the developer who's interested in buying the old Root Beer Barrel property. That you were business associates. I suppose I deduced that you knew him through construction. But you must have known him through some other connection."

"Known who?"

"I don't know his name. The man who's interested in buying the Root Beer Barrel."

"I'm supposed to know this guy?"

"That was the impression I had. When the Barrel blew down, the man heard about it, realized it would make the property easier to redevelop, and came forward with an offer. He told Joe he'd heard about the property through you."

Frank laughed. "That's small town gossip for you."

"It's not true?"

"No. I was in California visiting my mother when that big storm hit. There may have been some discussion about it around here at the time, but I didn't find out that the old Barrel had blown down for weeks. I definitely didn't tell anybody about it."

"Nobody in Grand Rapids?"

Frank shook his head. "I don't know anybody in Grand Rapids who's in construction or development. I don't know anybody there at all. We only moved here five years ago—when Patsy's mother died. All I've been able to find is a crummy job as night manager in a printing plant. I never get to put my nose out the door!"

"I guess I definitely misunderstood."

Frank frowned angrily. "We only came here because of Hershel. We thought handling the trust ourselves would be easier." He laughed harshly. "And now this!"

I heard Patsy's voice. "Frank . . ."

Frank leaned close to me. "Don't tell Patsy I was griping. We had to move to Warner Pier—and it's fine, most of the time. A nice little town. But now and then I have to blow off steam."

I nodded, and the two of us went back to Patsy. But I was confused by what Frank had told me. Joe had been definite about the prospective purchaser for the old Barrel's plot. He'd said it was someone who worked with Frank.

There was probably a simple explanation. Someone Frank knew, but whom he didn't know was in the construction or development business.

Aunt Nettie and I began to make noises about getting back to the office. But when I looked out toward the river I saw Chief Jones loping across the lawn with his disjointed gait. He carried a paper sack in his hand. He brought it up onto the porch and beckoned to Patsy, who went over to him.

Aunt Nettie and I kept edging toward the door, but I was curious. It was the same kind of sack Chief Jones had put the red rag in. I figured it was some sort of evidence.

"No!" Patsy spoke loudly. "I never saw Hershel with such a thing!"

We all swung to look at her. She looked around wildly, and her eyes settled on me. She took two steps in my direction. "Lee will know," she said.

"What is it, Patsy?" I asked.

She reached for the sack, but Chief Jones pulled it out of her reach. "We don't need to involve Lee," he said. "I can ask Joe."

But Patsy was still talking. "It's a horrible color. Where could Hershel have picked up such a thing?"

She came over and looked at me, eyeball to eyeball. "Joe couldn't do that, could he?" she said. "Even if he came over to Hershel's house, he wouldn't have killed him. Why should he kill my baby brother?"

I was still gaping when she turned and ran into the house. I turned to the chief. "Okay," I said. "Let me see it."

"Don't touch," he said. "We'll check it for fingerprints."

I put my hands behind me, leaned over slightly, and looked into the sack. I saw something a bilious, nasty green. I immediately knew what it was.

"Oh," I said, making my voice casual, but loud enough for all the teacher-hostesses to hear. "It's one of those giveaway pens Joe got to hand out at the wooden boat fictional. I mean, festival! I don't think that a pen like that is conclusive evidence that Joe was at Hershel's house. Those pens are probably all over town."

The chief nodded. "We'll find out," he said.

Aunt Nettie and I left. Despite my attempt at being casual, I was more upset than ever. Because those pens were *not* "all over town."

Joe had bought five hundred to hand out at the wooden boat festival up at Muskegon, and he had deliberately picked the most eye-catching color the novelties company offered. The pens were a perfectly ghastly shade of chartreuse. I hated the color so much I'd refused to have one on my desk. As far as I knew, Joe still had three hundred of them in a box in his desk and a half-dozen in a coffee mug beside his computer. They wrote fine and had good erasers, but the color was so horrible he couldn't even give them away.

Aunt Nettie and I said gracious good-byes and left. We arrived back at the shop to face two reports. Hazel, Aunt Nettie's chief assistant, said that Deer Forest Bed and Breakfast needed four dozen crème de menthe bon-bons ("The formal after-dinner mint") so they'd have plenty to put on their clients' pillows every night. Nancy Burton, the owner of the B&B, couldn't leave to come and get them because she was waiting for a plumber. And Tracy, who'd been on telephone duty, said that Trey Corbett had called me twice and seemed extremely eager to reach me. He said he'd call back in twenty minutes.

"Well, I can handle both those problems," I said. "First, if Hazel has the crème de menthe bonbons ready, I'll drop them by Nancy Burton's. That shouldn't take more than ten minutes. Then I'll be here when Trey calls."

At last, a couple of things I knew how to cope with.

Chapter 10

I dropped the mints off, then turned back toward downtown Warner Pier. As I turned onto West Street, I saw the pretty little cottage at the corner of MacIntosh Avenue. It might look authentically Victorian, but it hadn't been there when I was a teenager. Aunt Nettie had told me that Trey Corbett had built it to house his architectural and construction business.

Looking back, I should have kept straight on to the office and waited for Trey to call. But the impulsive side of my nature took over, and I turned into the parking lot. The SUV was there; I deduced that Trey was, too. We could talk face-to-face.

As soon as I was inside the office I began to suspect that my deduction was wrong. The outer office was empty, and I could hear Meg's voice coming from the inner office. I peeked around the corner and saw her talking on the phone. Meg frowned and waved. I mouthed, "I'll wait," and popped back into the outer office.

Darn. I didn't want to talk to Meg. I wanted to talk to Trey, and he apparently wasn't there. But I could hardly leave again without telling Meg why I'd come. I moved across the office, making sure I couldn't hear her conversation.

The office was beautifully decorated, with furniture in classic styles. No gimcracks, no curlicues, no cute Victorian. Just plain, good design. The front wall was all proper Victorian-style windows, but more of them than the Victorians would have wanted. A giant, abstract oil painting dominated the back wall. One side wall, the one farthest from the office door, was taken up by an object I call a map rack. It's actually a dozen racks, each designed to hold two large maps or drawings, back to back. The racks swing out from the wall like a book when you want to look at them, then swing back flat for storage. Rich Godfrey, my ex-husband, was a real estate developer, and he always had a couple in his office, ready to display plats for potential property buyers.

The map on the front of the rack was a detailed plat of Warner Pier. I wandered over and took a look at it. Yes, there was Peach Street, where Ten-

Huis Chocolade was located. There was the corner where my friend Lindy Herrera lived, Ninth and Cider Alley. I took a close look at North Lake Shore Drive, particularly the area around the old Root Beer Barrel neighborhood. The map didn't tell me anything I didn't already know.

I idly swung the rack to look at the map behind it. But there was nothing back to back with the plat, in the position corresponding to page two in a book. And the "page three" rack didn't hold a map. It held an elevation— an architect's drawing. I recognized it as Patsy and Frank Waterloo's house. It was a beautiful picture. Trey had drawn an idyllic home, surrounded by lush plantings and flowers, and he had tinted the whole thing with dreamy pastels. The elevation was a work of art. In the corner was a neatly lettered title, "Home of Frank and Patsy Waterloo, Warner Pier, Michigan."

I turned to the next rack and saw another elevation. This one was Trey's own office building. The drawing was just as lovely as the one of the Waterloo house. "Office Building," the label read. No details. I turned to the next rack. It was a house I had never seen, though I recognized the style— Italianate. The label read, "Home of George and Ellen VanRiin." I didn't know the VanRiins, but they lived in a beautiful house.

I turned the rack again and again, looking at a half-dozen more lovely drawings of quaint Victorian buildings. All of them were on right-hand "pages," as it were, of the rack. I was sorry when I came to the last one, a drawing of a bed-and-breakfast inn I recognized. I assumed it was the final thing in the rack, but I automatically looked behind it. To my surprise I realized there was one more elevation. This one was in the left-hand rack, back to back with the previous drawing.

This elevation was of a much larger structure than the others. I didn't recognize the building, but again the drawing was beautiful and the colors delicate. In fact, it might have been the most charming drawing of all. The building stretched out over the whole width of the paper. It had tall trees behind it. One section was like townhouses, delightful cottages with steeply pitched roofs. The other end was a three-story building with broad verandas. It looked like a period resort, a relic of some Victorian watering place. It made me long for a floor-length skirt, a pompadour, and a parasol.

I looked at the corner of the drawing to see where it was located. But there was no label, no name, no hint as to what or where it was.

I was flipping back through the drawings when Meg Corbett suddenly shoved herself between me and the map rack. She spoke angrily. "What do *you* want?"

I took a step backward, determined to be nice, even if Meg wasn't. "Meg, Trey's elevations are lovely! He should have a show of them."

"Trey is very talented. But you didn't come to see his elevations. Why did you come?"

"I wanted to talk to Trey a minute. Is he here?"

"No." Meg began turning the sections of the map rack back, one after the other. "Why did you want to see Trey?"

I almost turned and walked out. Meg was certainly not being hospitable. But I reminded myself that I was a Texan, not a damyankee, and Texans are polite. "I guess I was looking for free technical infection— I mean, information! Like collaring a doctor at a party to ask him about your athlete's foot."

"What did you want to know?"

"How to knock down the old Root Beer Barrel."

"What!" Meg gave me a sharp look, then turned more map racks, banging them back against the wall.

"Everybody keeps talking about how Hershel claimed it was knocked down on purpose," I said. "I just began to wonder how hard it would be to do that. I thought Trey would know."

"I'm sure he would." Meg turned the final map rack. "Trey's gone to Holland. I told him you called, and he said he'd return your call on his cell phone."

"He did. I missed the call. Then I was out on an errand and saw that his SUV was here, so I pulled in."

"He drove my car."

"I'm sorry I bothered you."

I turned toward the door, but Meg spoke. "Wait, Lee." When I looked at her, she had changed her mouth from huffy to happy, but her pupils were still tiny and hard. "You and I need to talk for a minute," she said.

"Sure." I decided I could match Meg hypocrisy for hypocrisy. I put on my beauty pageant smile and took the chair she waved toward.

Meg sat in an identical chair. She was wearing another summer visitor outfit—jeans with tennies and a pale blue cotton sweater over a white polo shirt. As she had the day before, she looked almost too well bred. Hard to believe she had been a child so neglected the neighbors called the welfare department.

"I'm sorry I snapped," she said. "We're all upset about poor Hershel."

Her comment confirmed my opinion of her as a real witch with a capital "B." Meg hadn't cared a whit about Hershel. I made my smile even toothier. "What can I do for you?"

"Oh, Trey told me he'd called you this morning, and he was afraid you'd misunderstood."

"Oh?"

"He said he made some reference to Joe Woodyard."

"I hadn't been up long when he called. I'm afraid I wasn't making a lot of sense." I made my smile wide enough for Miss America competition, and I decided to spike her guns. "I didn't understand—was he trying to tell me that you and Joe dated each other in high school?"

"Oh? Had Joe told you about that?" Was it my imagination, or did she look rather disappointed?

"I know about it." I didn't learn it from Joe, but I knew. "I hadn't put a lot of importance on it."

Meg's smile grew as big as mine, and her pupils grew even smaller. "That's a *good* attitude, Lee. Of course, *you* know all the little tricks to keeping a man interested."

"Tricks?"

"Those things we learn at our mother's knee. Keep 'em guessing, never let them feel overly confident about you, things like that."

So Meg thought romantic relationships were based on little tricks. I wasn't surprised, but I found her attitude annoying. I kept smiling. "I've even been known to fall back on sincerity," I said. "When you can fake that, you've got it made."

A frown briefly clouded Meg's perfect eyebrows. She didn't seem to know what to make of my comment. "Well, as long as you understand that there's been *nothing* between Joe and me since high school."

"I don't really worry about ancient history."

Meg simpered. "Well, it *is* ancient history. I didn't want you to think anything else."

"I didn't."

"Though it's gratifying to know Joe *mentioned* me."

"Joe's been around the block a couple of times since high school, Meg. You shouldn't feel too bad if he seems to have gotten over your teenage romance."

Her jaw tightened. "He was really mad when we broke up. But by the time I was a senior, I could see that Joe wasn't really my type. I've told him repeatedly, over the years, that I have no interest in him. And, of course, events have proven me right."

"What events?"

"Well, you know. His . . . lack of purpose."

Was she referring to Joe's decision to quit practicing law and open a boat shop?

Meg spoke again. "You know, there's no substitute for family background."

That comment confused me further—I didn't know anything particularly disreputable about Joe's family. His parents had been divorced, and his mother ran a successful insurance agency. His father—now deceased—had been a carpenter. His family wasn't rich or famous, but it was respectable. Unlike Meg's had been, apparently. I contented myself with raising my eyebrows at Meg.

Meg's laugh tinkled out again. "Anyway, I met Trey—and, well, I fell for him in a major way. He had all the qualities I was looking for—you know."

I began to think I did know. I was getting the picture of what Meg had been looking for in a husband. I did the eyebrow wriggling bit again. "Family background?"

Meg—well, the only word is "preened." "Trey is intelligent and trained to a profession, of course. But the Corbetts give their sons a top-notch education. There's a family trust dedicated to that purpose."

I couldn't resist a dig. "I understand perfectly, Meg. Trey probably went to prep school . . ."

"Capperfield."

"And to a 'good' college . . ."

"Hyde."

He'd been to such a good college I'd never even heard of it. I had trouble not making my smile a smirk. ". . . and he has the family fortu . . . I mean, *connections*! The connections to help him become successful." I leaned forward. "Which has always made me curious. What is Trey doing in a little place like Warner Pier?"

"I beg your pardon?"

"I mean, why isn't Trey practicing architecture in New York, in Chicago, even in Grand Rapids?"

Meg's expression hardened. "His interest is Victorian architecture—and here he's able to indulge it."

"That *is* lucky."

Meg stood up. "Trey says Warner Pier is the perfect place for him to learn Victorian building practices and design from the ground up. He's written papers on the buildings he's restored here."

"Wonderful."

"Trey's going to knock Michigan on its ear," she said. "He has big plans."

I excused myself. We both waved and smiled our hypocritical smiles as I backed out of the parking lot. I didn't understand why Meg had wanted to talk to me. Was she trying to make me jealous, with her comments about how she'd told Joe to shove off "over the years"?

When I got back to the shop, Trey had called again. This time he had left his cell phone number. I called him, and Trey answered.

"It's Lee," I said. "I'm calling to apologize if I was rude this morning."

"I'm the one who needs to apologize. I shouldn't have called so early."

Apparently Trey wasn't going to make any reference to Meg and Joe. I wasn't going to mention them either. "I needed to be up and doing. But now I have one question for you—if you have time."

"I'm driving down from Holland, Lee. I can talk. Just don't ask me a question so startling that I run off the road."

"I don't think it would startle you. How would you knock down the old Root Beer Barrel?"

There was a moment of silence. Then I heard a horn blare. Yikes! Maybe he had run off the road. "Trey? Are you all right?"

"Yes. But that *was* a startling question. I hope you're using the word 'you' as a general term for humanity, not asking how I actually did it."

I laughed. "I guess I meant it as a general term for people who know a lot about how buildings are constructed, Trey."

"But I don't know a lot about commercial properties of the 1940s. I specialize in the Victorian and Edwardian eras. And I try to keep the structures up, not knock them down."

"I know, Trey. But you were the only person I could think of that I knew well enough to ask."

"Sorry. I never looked closely at the old Root Beer Barrel. I don't know how it was constructed. It might be that a good ram with a bulldozer would have brought it down. Or it might have had to be taken apart plank by plank. Why do you want to know?"

Suddenly I didn't want to go into it. "Just nosiness, I guess. Patsy said Hershel claimed it was knocked down deliberately, and I began to wonder how hard it would be to do that."

"Don't worry, Lee. Nobody but an idiot would think that Joe would take it down."

"Thanks, Trey." This time we both said good-bye politely before we hung up.

That hadn't helped. The whole morning had been confusing. I was at a complete loss about how the rock that had killed Hershel had gotten from Joe's workshop to the old chapel. I didn't understand why Joe thought Frank Waterloo had steered a buyer for the Root Beer Barrel property in his direction and Frank denied it. I didn't understand what Meg and I had been talking about, or why Trey wouldn't at least take a guess about pulling the Root Beer Barrel down. There were a lot of unanswered questions, and I wasn't making any progress at answering them.

I fought down a mad desire for a coffee truffle ("All-milk chocolate truffle, flavored with Caribbean coffee"), went to my desk, took out a yellow legal pad, and wrote down two of the questions.

First, why did Joe think Frank had steered a property buyer his way?

Second, what was the relationship between Meg Corbett and Joe?

These were two questions I could simply call Joe and ask. I might not like the answer I got to one of them, but I could ask them. I picked up the phone.

Chapter 11

Joe answered almost immediately. I didn't hit him with Meg's implications right away. Instead I told him that Frank denied telling anybody about the Root Beer Barrel property.

"He says he didn't even know the old Barrel had blown down for a couple of months," I said.

"So what?"

"Well, I've been thinking about the Barrel, Joe. If Hershel was right, and it was deliberately wrecked, the chief has been thinking in terms of its destruction helping you sell it. But it also made it possible for this guy in Grand Rapids to buy it."

Joe was silent.

"In a property sale," I said, "both parties should benefit."

"You're right. Let's go ask him."

"Go ask him?"

"Sure. I need to pick up a boat in Grand Rapids anyway. We can stop by and see this guy."

"The buyer? Who is he?"

"His name is Tom Johnson. Sounds like an alias. But I've seen his letterhead. Johnson-Phinney Development. Can you come with me?"

"Well, I need to get some work done around here . . ."

"We could leave about three, get to Johnson's office before he closes, then pick up the boat. I'll even buy you some Mexican food."

"No way!" That was an ongoing joke between the two of us. As a Texan I refused to eat Mexican food as far north as Michigan. Which is silly, because west Michigan is full of Hispanic-Americans, but I was always sure the restaurants wouldn't serve real Tex-Mex, and I wouldn't touch it.

"German?"

I looked at the work piled up on my desk and thought about my scheduled shift, which was supposed to end at nine-thirty or ten p.m.

Joe spoke again. "Indian? Hungarian? French? Tibetan? Serbo-Croatian?"

I made up my mind. "Three o'clock? I'll be ready. And I vote for Chinese."

At noon Tracy brought me a sandwich to eat at my desk, and I worked straight through until three. Which didn't make up for the time I was taking off, but I did get a few things done. Aunt Nettie doesn't mind if I leave early, but I hate to ask for special treatment.

Joe looked neat—khakis and polo shirt—when he came to get me. I was glad I'd dressed fairly decently that day, since I hadn't had time to go home and change. I got my extra sweater from the van and we started the hour-long drive to Grand Rapids. I was grinning as we drove out of town and got on the interstate.

"You look like the proverbial cat with a mouthful of feathers," Joe said.

"It's skipping out in the middle of the day. I feel as if I'm getting away with something. But tell me what you know about this Tom Johnson."

"All I know about him is that the cashier's check he gave me as earnest money was good."

"A cashier's check is always good, Joe. When are you supposed to finalize the deal?"

"He asked for ninety days. So he's still got a month."

"He didn't tell you what he wanted to do with the property."

"Nope."

"And you didn't ask."

"Nope. I figured it wasn't any of my business. The city has rules about what can go in various zonings. The state has rules about what can go on the lakeshore. It's not my business to enforce their rules. Once that property is off my hands I have no interest in it."

"How did you meet Tom Johnson?"

"He called one day, said Frank Waterloo had mentioned the property to him, and arranged to come down to see it. He'd seen it earlier, of course."

"He told you that?"

"No, but he knew how to find it, and finding it is not that easy. Besides, if I wanted to buy a piece of property, I wouldn't approach a seller until I'd at least driven by it. Though Johnson didn't seem to know where the property lines were, so he hadn't poked around too much."

"Had anybody seen him over there?"

"I didn't ask around. But you know that neighborhood. It's practically deserted until you get to the houses two blocks away. He could have done anything over there."

"Including pulling down the old Root Beer Barrel."

"True. Nobody would have noticed anything. But I am sure he told me he'd heard about the property from Frank Waterloo." Joe reached over and patted my hand. "So, we'll ask him how he knows Frank."

The Root Beer Barrel property wasn't a spot you would simply stumble over while driving through Warner Pier. It was on North Lake Shore Drive—

across the river and a couple of miles up the lake from Aunt Nettie's house. It was located on a section of Lake Shore Drive where Lake Michigan had eaten away part of the road, leaving the structures on the inland side—well, stranded. You had to know how to get there if you wanted to find the area.

Fifty years earlier, I'd been told, that part of Lake Shore Drive had been a state highway. It was lined with motels, service stations, and restaurants. Then the lake had eroded the property on the west side of the road. Several buildings had fallen into the lake. The state highway route was moved several blocks away from the lake, and the businesses on the inland side closed because of the lack of traffic. Yet the spot was still lakefront property. It would be expensive to stabilize the bank, of course, but condos, restaurants—lots of businesses would find the property valuable.

If Tom Johnson had any kind of backing at all, he should be able to redevelop the property successfully.

"Is Johnson expecting us?" I said.

"No. I thought it would be best to surprise him."

"If he's there."

"Oh, he's there. I called. I used what we lawyers call a subterfuge to make sure he'll be there until closing time." Joe glanced over at me. "Now I'm going to ask a sexist question."

"Sexist? You usually seem to avoid that. What's the question?"

"Do you know how to flirt?"

I batted my eyelashes and crossed my knees. "Have I been too straightforward with you?"

"Not with me. I like you just the way you are."

"Then why should I flirt?"

"I've been trying to think about the best way to approach Johnson. He's the kind who isn't even ashamed of being sexist."

"And you want me to vamp him?"

"Not vamp him. I'm not thinking of anything more serious than getting him to ogle a little. I want to distract him, throw him off balance some way. Have you got a better idea?"

"I don't want to be uncooperative, Joe, but I've tried not to encourage these sexist types. How about if I slap his face?"

"That might be a little extreme. It would be embarrassing if he sued you for assault. We'll have to wing it. But if you think of a way to distract him from the business at hand, just jump in there."

Grand Rapids is a typical American city—all the retail and restaurant chains are there in shopping centers lined up along through streets that can't be told apart from similar streets in Dallas, Miami, Seattle, or, I guess, Boston. In between the shopping centers are the strip malls, and in an older strip development we found the office of Johnson-Phinney Development. It didn't look particularly prosperous.

The outer office was empty, though the reception desk was cluttered with enough debris to indicate that someone usually sat there. As the door closed behind us, a deep voice called from the inside office.

"My girl is out! I'll be there in a moment! Have a seat!"

Joe and I found chairs, and the voice continued talking, apparently on the telephone. It said things like "I'll run that by Phin, but my own feeling is negative" and "Listen, if we don't have the contract within thirty days, the deal is off."

I nudged Joe and pointed to the telephone on the reception desk. It had little plastic buttons for the different lines, and none of them was lighted.

Joe grinned and spoke softly. "He could be using a cell phone." I nodded, but I waited for Johnson with a suspicious attitude.

In a few minutes the telephone call was apparently concluded, and seconds later a big man loomed in the doorway to the inner office. My first thought was what a perfect Santa Claus he'd make. He was tubby and had plenty of white hair—lots on top of his head and even more on his chin. Then he looked at me, and the Santa illusion faded. Santa Claus doesn't leer.

His eyes bounced from me to Joe and back to me. "Helloooo. What can I do for you?"

A creep. I decided he was fair game for flirting. I lowered my head—he was shorter than I am—and looked up at him from under my lashes.

"Hi, Tom," Joe said. "Joe Woodyard. We've got a contract for sale of that lakefront property at Warner Pier."

Tom pulled his eyes back to Joe. He looked blank for a minute, then grinned broadly. "Joe! Good to see you. What brings you to Grand Rapids?" He bent over the reception desk and checked the calendar there. "I haven't gotten mixed up on the date we agreed to conclude the property sale, have I?"

"It's still a month off. I just thought I'd check in with you, see how things are going."

Johnson rubbed his hands together. "Fine, fine! Everything's on schedule!"

Joe shared something interesting that the title search had turned up, and Johnson topped his story. Through it all Johnson's eyes switched from Joe to me and back again. They kept lingering in my direction, but Joe didn't introduce me.

Finally, Johnson gave a little bow. "Now, Joe," he said. "You haven't introduced me to Mrs. Woodyard."

"My mom?" Joe blinked. "Oh, you mean Lee. I'm sorry. This is Lee McKinney, Tom. Lee is business manager for TenHuis Chocolade down at Warner Pier. She's on the Economic Development Committee for our Chamber of Commerce."

I'd been wondering just how Joe was going to explain me. I bared my teeth into my Miss Texas contestant smile.

Johnson beamed so widely I expected him to bounce his belly and give a ho-ho-ho. "How d'ya do, Ms. McKinney. Well, well, well. If you're a typical member of the Warner Pier Chamber of Commerce, I guess I'll have to join."

"We always welcome new members, Mr. Johnson." I reached for my Texas accent. "But I will admit I particularly wanted to meet you. Ever'one in Warner Pier is jus' dyin' to know what plans you have for the Root Beer Barrel prope'ty."

Johnson shook his finger at me, looking more like a lecherous Santa than ever. "Now, now, Ms. McKinney, I can't say a word until my funding is fully committed. You must let us developers have our secrets."

"Oh, c'mon, Mr. Johnson. You kin give me a hint." I pronounced it "hee-nt."

He chuckled. "No can do. Not even for a pretty girl."

"We-ell, okay. I'll just have to keep on tryin' to git the information out of Frank Waterloo."

"Who?" Johnson looked completely blank.

Joe jumped in then. "Maybe I misunderstood, Tom. I thought you said Frank Waterloo tipped you off about the availability of the property."

"Oh!" I could almost see Johnson's brain scrambling as he tried to recover. "Well, old Frank doesn't know anything about the specific deal. We just talked about Warner Pier in general."

Joe nodded. "How'd you meet Frank?"

"Damned if I remember. Ran into him at a party someplace. I don't know him well." The Santa smile grew stiff. "Anything more I can do for you two?"

Joe again assured Johnson his visit had merely been a routine call, and I promised to send him some information on the Warner Pier Chamber of Commerce. We all shook hands—he gave mine an unnecessary squeeze— and Joe and I left. Johnson stood in his office window and watched until we were in the pick-up and driving away.

"Odd to see a beard with a beard," Joe said.

"What do you mean, a beard?"

"You know, a beard. A front man."

"You think he's acting for someone else."

"It seems likely. Remember that 'Who?' He didn't have the slightest recollection of Frank Waterloo's name. That little session makes me very doubtful that the sale will be concluded."

"Oh, Joe! I hope the deal doesn't fall through."

"I'm beginning to hope it does. On second meeting, I find Charley Johnson on the unsavory side. I'm not sure I want to see him or any of his associates around my home town. Somebody else will buy that property."

"Johnson is certainly not like any developer I ever met before." I shot a glance at Joe. He knew that my past included five years of marriage to a Dallas land developer.

Joe apparently didn't have any qualms about that. "Your ex wasn't so secretive?"

"When he or one of his friends was planning a new project, it was generally hard to get them to shut up about it. Of course, there might be reasons for being secretive. Such as trying to buy up other property in the area."

"I'll ask the other property owners in the neighborhood if they've been approached. But we'd all discussed how much to ask per front foot, and my price was in line with that." Joe hit his turn signal and changed lanes. "Still in the mood for Chinese?"

I used the time it took us to reach the restaurant and get settled in a booth to prepare to bring up the second item I wanted to discuss—my odd conversations with Trey and Meg Corbett.

It was a little early for dinner, so we ordered drinks. After the waiter left, I crossed my knees and did the old-fashioned footsie bit under the table. "How was my flirting?"

"Great!" Joe grinned and used his foot to nudge me back. "Tom never knew what hit him."

"Then let's change the subject. I had a strange talk this morning."

I quickly sketched the conversations I'd had with Trey and with Meg. "It's odd, Joe. I never did figure out what Trey was up to. Was he trying to make me jealous? Was Meg? I didn't understand any of it."

Our drinks came then, and Joe stared at his for a long moment. "Did Meg make you jealous?"

"Not of her. Actually, you have a perfect right to chase any woman you please."

"You're the only woman I want to chase, Lee."

"I'm delighted to hear it. But I don't see you as the kind of guy who chases married women. You're not perfect, but you don't seem to be stupid."

Joe grinned. "I defended a few guys who shot people who were fooling around with their wives. The thought of a husband with a gun sure makes adultery unattractive."

"Do you think Trey has a gun?"

"Probably not. It might wrinkle his pocket protector." Joe stared at his glass again. "I'm not sure what to tell you about Maggie—I mean, Meg. She was Maggie Mae in high school."

"I'm not asking for high school confessions."

"That's a relief."

"We'd all be better off if we could erase our teenage years from our memories. But if you knew Meg back then, or more recently, can you figure out what her motive was in telling me all that stuff about you chasing her?"

"Just trying to make herself appear attractive, I guess. She always thought all the men were after her."

"Were they?"

"Some were. That was one thing that got her talked about. She was illegitimate, for another thing. And, well—her mother was illegitimate, too. Warner Pier can be a really small town about that sort of thing. My mom's not any more narrow-minded than most, but she really didn't like my dating Meg."

"You were popular in high school, Joe. Class president and wrestling champ. I don't see you taking out the school slut."

"Meg's reputation was nothing like that. She wasn't 'easy.' She was just a girl who lacked 'background.' Or that's what my mom thought. Meg talked wilder than she acted. I always thought she was dramatizing herself."

"A pretty normal teenage trait."

Joe contemplated his drink seriously, then looked at me. "They say a gentleman never tells, Lee. But as far as Meg went, well, I finally decided she was more of a tease than anything else. If anybody showed an interest in her, she bragged about it."

"That's—well, is 'pitiful' the right word?"

Joe shook his head. "I'm no therapist, but Meg . . . Okay, let's admit it. All us Warner Pier locals look at the summer people with at least a little bit of envy. They have more money than most of us do. They have more status in the larger world. They've *seen* the larger world, and us small-town guys haven't! Some, like Trey's family, are what passes for 'aristocratic' in America. It takes lots of us a few years to get that envy out of our systems."

I knew Joe was talking about himself and his disastrous marriage to a rich and famous summer visitor; her glamor had been one thing that attracted him to her. I'd seen the same feelings displayed by other locals. "Is that why Lindy told me not to date a summer guy if I didn't want to ruin my reputation with the Warner Pier guys?"

"Exactly! That's all based on envy. The Warner Pier guys don't think they can compete, so they bad-mouth any girl who goes out with a summer visitor. But Meg broke that taboo. And she got away with it."

"How'd she manage that?"

"She didn't give a hoot about what the local guys said. The first time she saw she could catch the eye of a summer guy—and not just as a sexual plaything—all the Warner Pier guys, including me, were history."

I sipped my drink. "This morning she indicated that Trey—or Trey's family money and connections—were exactly what she'd been looking for in life. I wonder what Trey saw in her."

"A sexy little piece, probably. I hope he wasn't disappointed." Joe lifted his glass. "Here's to Meg. May she get every damn thing she wants in life, and may she never bother us again."

"Hear, hear!" I said. "And may we never again talk about her or about Hershel Perkins or about the *Toadfrog*."

And we didn't for at least an hour and a half. We stuffed ourselves with the deluxe dinner for two—including Pupu tray. I let Joe worry about paying for it. Then we drove half an hour across Grand Rapids to a beautiful neighborhood where an executive of an office furniture manufacturing company lived. He proudly showed Joe the boat he'd bought, a twenty-foot 1955 Chris-Craft Continental. It looked to me as if it needed a lot of work. His wife made coffee, and the guy insisted on telling the whole yarn of how he'd found the boat in an old barn. Joe made admiring noises, hooked the trailer to his pickup's hitch, and told the guy he wasn't promising any particular delivery date.

"It'll take a lot of hand finishing," Joe said.

"I know, I know," the man said. "I've always dreamed of owning a boat like this. I don't want a slapdash job."

When we left it was nearly dark. By the time Joe and I had driven back across Grand Rapids and entered I-196 heading south, there was hardly any light in the western sky.

We were almost back to Warner Pier before the next excitement started.

CHOCOLATE CHAT

CACAO CASH

- Cacao was money—literally—to the Aztecs and other Mesoamerican natives. They used the beans as currency, as well as grinding them up and using them to make drinks.

- An early Spanish visitor to what is today Nicaragua reported a rabbit could be purchased for ten beans, a slave for a hundred beans, and a visit to a prostitute for eight to ten beans. Naturally, counterfeiting developed.

- The Aztecs did not weigh cacao beans but measured by counting individual beans. Approximately twenty-four thousand beans would fit in one of the backpacks carried by traders. One early Spanish reporter claimed that the warehouse of the emperor Montezuma held forty thousand such loads, or 960 million cacao beans. Most of these, of course, would have been used for paying soldiers or servants and for buying supplies for the emperor's household, but the household also drank a lot of chocolate.

- On one recorded occasion, when Montezuma was a prisoner of the Spanish, servants of the foreign invaders broke into his storehouses and spent the night making off with thousands and thousands of beans. The beans were stored, it was reported, in huge wicker bins, which were coated with clay.

Chapter 12

L ooking back, we made it easy for the guy.
   One of the disadvantages of living in a quaint and beautiful tourist town, of course, is that a lot of day-to-day items, such as gasoline and groceries, are sold at tourist prices. As Warner Pier business people, Aunt Nettie and I—and Joe, too—try to patronize other local businesses. But when gasoline is a nickel higher per gallon in Warner Pier, some of us are not eager to cough up the difference.

The Marathon station ten miles north of Warner Pier, at the Willard exit, always has gasoline eight to ten cents cheaper than the Warner Pier stations. So Warner Pier locals who've gone to Grand Rapids or Holland universally follow the habit of stopping there to buy gas on their way back into town. As long as we're there, we figure we might as well top off the tank. Besides, the restrooms are usually clean.

Joe hadn't hurried as we left Grand Rapids. First, he's not one of these immature guys who has to pass everything on the highway. Second, he tries to use as little gasoline as possible, though being forced to drive a pickup truck with enough moxie to haul a big boat means he can't worry too much about mileage. Plus, I-196 traffic is heavy day and night, weekdays and weekends.

Joe didn't even mention his plan to stop for gas. He just pulled off the Interstate at the Willard exit and hauled the boat over to an open gas pump. When I asked him if he wanted a Coke, he said, "I can get them," and I answered, "Oh, I'll do it. If you want a candy bar, you're on your own."

I got out of the truck, visited the ladies' room, then bought two one-liter bottles of soda—one Diet Coke and one regular. As I was going back out to the pickup, I noticed a big black panel truck—the kind a plumber or electrician might drive—parked off to one side. I noticed it for a silly reason. It had tinted windows, and it looked empty, but just when I happened to be looking at it, it moved. It rocked back and forth, just slightly. The motion made me wonder just what was going on inside. I grinned as I got into the pickup, and I pointed the panel truck out to Joe when he came back.

He laughed. "I guess I'll have to get my windows tinted," he said. "Turn the pickup into a love nest."

He drove out of the station and onto the entrance ramp, paused until the Interstate traffic cleared, then gunned the pickup until he was up to highway speed. He reached up to adjust his rearview mirror so that it dimmed the headlights of the vehicle behind us. "Jerk's following too close," he said.

I looked back, and I realized the vehicle behind us wasn't only too close. It was coming up really fast, too.

"You'd almost think he was trying to ram us!" I said.

"He'd better not hit that boat," Joe said grimly.

There was no one in the left-hand lane, and the vehicle moved out to pass us.

"He could be drunk," I said. "I hope he stays in his own lane while he gets by."

Joe's voice was level. "He's not staying there," he said. "He's coming over. Hang on."

Joe hit the brakes, hard. The boat began to fishtail. Joe edged over to the right, fighting to keep control of the truck and the trailer. I thought we were leaving the road—until I looked out the window. We were on a bridge. The railing was really close. We weren't going to be pulling off on that side. The guy on our left was trying to crush us against the railing.

I took a deep breath and held it. The vehicle kept coming over into our lane. Joe hit the brakes again, whipping the boat back and forth and slowing the pickup.

The speeder missed our front fender by maybe an inch, then shot ahead of us.

Joe touched his accelerator gently, and as we speeded up, the trailer we were towing straightened out.

I exhaled. "Yee-haw! That was close. Good driving!"

"The cell phone's in the glove box," Joe said. "Try to call 9-1-1. We need to report that guy."

I was staring at the vehicle that had just gone around us. It was square in the pickup's headlights and moving away rapidly. I could see that it was a black panel truck. "Is that the truck we saw back at the Willard station?"

"It looks like it. Can you read the tag number?"

"Not the letters." I was reaching into the glove box while I talked. "I think the numbers are eight, eight, four."

The black panel truck was moving away fast, already disappearing around a semi. I found the cell phone and punched in 9-1-1. I spoke as soon as I heard a voice. "We want to report a reckless driver on I-196 just south of the Willard exit. He nearly ran us off the road."

"Where?"

"I-196, maybe a mile south of Willard."

"What state is that in?"

"Michigan!"

"We're Wisconsin."

"Rats," I said. "Joe, the cell phone bounced us across the lake."

"Hang up," Joe said. "We'll call the Warner Pier dispatcher. She can call the state police. We'll try to follow that panel truck, see where the guy goes."

"Sorry," I told the phone. "We'll try a local number."

The semi ahead of us had slowed down, and Joe pulled into the left lane and passed it. He told me the number for Warner Pier City Hall. "How come you have that number memorized?" I said. He didn't answer.

I was punching in the numbers as Joe pulled up beside the semi.

"Where'd he go?" he asked.

The black panel truck had disappeared.

"He can't have been traveling that fast," I said. "He'd have to be driving the speed of light to have disappeared already."

Joe kept his speed up, passing a couple of cars, but nothing that looked remotely like the black panel truck appeared.

"Weird," he said. "I don't think we imagined it." He settled into the right-hand lane and slowed down, several car lengths ahead of the cars he had passed.

I was looking back. "Oh, no! Somebody's coming up fast in the left-hand lane."

It was a replay of the whole first episode. The headlights came rushing at us—the driver must have been hitting at least ninety. When the vehicle got beside us, I could see it was the same black panel truck. It was coming over into our lane. And once again the whole thing was happening on a bridge.

"Look out!" I said.

"Hang on!" Joe said.

Again he hit the brakes. Again the boat whipped back and forth, while Joe fought to control the pickup. Again we edged toward the shoulder and slowed.

This time I closed my eyes. When I opened them, the black panel truck was oozing in ahead of us. His tag was right out there in the headlights. Then the truck headed on up the road at warp speed, passing two cars and moving out of our line of sight.

"This time I got the letters from the tag," I said.

I finished calling the Warner Pier dispatcher and told her about the whole episode, including the license plate number. She promised to call the Michigan State Police.

"Scary," Joe said.

"How did he get behind us again? Where did he hide?"

"He must have pulled onto the shoulder, waited until we'd gone by, then taken off again. If we were out beside the semi, we wouldn't have seen him."

"Why? He can't have it in for us particularly."

"I don't know why he would, but he seems to be able to pass anybody else without trying to shove 'em off the road."

"Should we stop?"

Joe thought a minute. "Better not," he said. "We're in danger in the pickup, but if he's really after us, we might be in more serious danger if we aren't moving."

There was no exit from the Interstate before Warner Pier. We drove on. Joe stayed in the right-hand lane. He didn't pass anybody, though the two cars we'd passed now passed us. Joe drove conservatively. But his hands gripped the steering wheel as if it were the neck of the jerk in the black panel truck.

Two miles before the exit to Warner Pier there's a rest area. I've never stopped there—it's too close to home—but I'm sure it's a standard rest area, with parking for trucks and for cars, restrooms, and machines dispensing soft drinks and snacks. That's where the black panel truck ambushed us the third time.

We had just pulled past the exit from that rest area when the semi behind us began to flash its lights and honk.

"What's he doing?" Joe said.

I looked back. "Oh, God, Joe! Here comes that panel truck again!"

"He's not going to get away with it this time," Joe said. He pulled over to the left.

"Joe! There's another bridge! He can push us into the rail on either side!"

"I've got to try something or he's going to kill us."

The black truck was gaining fast. When he got within twenty-five feet of us, Joe suddenly moved right, straddling the center line. Then he hit the brakes, hard. The boat began to whip back and forth frantically.

"It's working!" I yelled. "He's dropping back."

Of course, Joe couldn't keep the boat fishtailing. He had to gain speed or lose control of the pickup. And, of course, as soon as he let up on the brakes and began to speed up, the panel truck was right on us again.

Again Joe let him get closer. Again he hit the brakes, slewing the boat trailer all over the road. Again the panel truck was forced to drop back.

Joe muttered. "That'll never work a third time."

"At least we're off that bridge," I said. "We're within a half-mile of the exit. Maybe . . ."

"No. Here he comes again!"

This time the panel truck didn't let the boat stop him. He pulled out onto the left-hand shoulder, apparently determined to come up alongside us.

I tried to keep my voice calm. "He's going out to the left," I said.

Joe fishtailed the boat again, and I felt a shock. "The boat hit him!"

"Not hard enough."

Joe pressed hard on the accelerator, and we pulled ahead. But the black truck wasn't ready to give up. He was even with the pickup's bed now, and he was so close I could see the Dodge hood ornament glittering, could see something shiny inside the cab. Maybe a pair of glasses.

"He's coming over!"

Now Joe suddenly swung the wheel right. The pickup veered across the highway, then off the highway, onto the shoulder. We were racing down the Interstate, but we weren't on the pavement. We were on the shoulder. The black truck shot by us.

Then we weren't on the shoulder any more. We were on the grass. Then we were in the bushes. Then we were heading down a slope. There were trees ahead.

"Hang on," Joe said. The pickup was slowing.

We came to a stop with the hood of the pickup about a foot from a fence post.

Behind us, the semi honked long and hard. He whizzed by.

Joe and I spoke at the same time. "Are you okay?"

Apparently we both were. We unhooked our seatbelts and met in the middle of the pickup's front seat. Neither of us said anything for a long moment. We just held each other.

"Well," I said finally, "if you get tired of repairing boats you can take up driving a race car."

"The finish line didn't go exactly the way I planned. I thought I could stop on the shoulder. But it took a lot longer to brake than I'd expected."

"I thought those trees were going to stop us."

Joe's voice was savage. "The guy better not have damaged that boat."

Joe pulled his flashlight from under the seat and got out to inspect the boat. I started to follow him out the door on the driver's side, but Joe stopped me. "Wait there. There's probably a lot of poison ivy out here, and you've got on that short skirt."

So I sat sideways, with my legs dangling out of the truck. It was a typical west Michigan June night—temperature in the mid-fifties—so I put on my extra sweater. By this time several cars had stopped, and people were coming down the slope to us. We assured them we weren't hurt. I picked up the cell phone, which had landed on the floor, punched "redial" and told the Warner Pier dispatcher what had happened. She promised to have the state police there ASAP.

Joe was dealing with the spectators, so I leaned against the door frame and tried to figure the whole thing out.

What the heck had happened? Three times a guy—or maybe a gal—in a black panel truck had tried to wreck us. The third time he or she had suc-

ceeded. Despite Joe's best efforts, we had hit the ditch. Joe's efforts, however, had meant we left the highway gradually and slowed at a suitable rate
of speed, and neither of us had been hurt. Our luck had been due, I was convinced, not simply to dumb luck, but to skill on Joe's part and to his experience in hauling boats with that particular pickup.

But why? Why had the person in the black panel truck made such a determined effort to run us off the road? We hadn't seen the truck before we
stopped for gas at the Willard exit. In fact, I was convinced I had never seen
it before in my life.

Had it been waiting for us?

That thought sent a chill up and down my spine, and I had to admit it
was possible. Anybody familiar with the customs of Warner Pier could have
predicted we'd stop at Willard on our way back from Grand Rapids. And
the truck had been sitting there, waiting. No one had been visible through
the windshield, and the side windows had been so heavily tinted we hadn't
been able to see inside them. But, I reminded myself, something had made
the truck move slightly. It could have been the driver, moving around inside
while he watched us.

Plus, the driver had apparently been familiar with that stretch of highway. At least, he'd known exactly where the bridges were, where being
pushed off the road would be most dangerous.

The whole thing was unbelievable. Someone had tried to shove us off the
road. Maybe kill us. But why on earth would anybody want to do that?

It was a relief to see flashing red, white, and blue lights on the highway.
The state police had arrived.

Once they made sure we weren't hurt, Joe began to describe what had
happened. It didn't sound any more logical when he told it than it had
when I thought it through. The state police officer, frankly, was looking
skeptical.

Just as Joe got to the end of the tale a really tall man walked down the
slope. "I lost the S.O.B." he said.

We all stared at him. The state police officer spoke. "Who are you?"

"I was in that semi right behind this guy." He gestured at Joe. "I saw
what happened. I tried to follow the jerk who shoved him off the road." He
turned to Joe. "You guys okay?"

We assured him we were, and he nodded. "It looked as if you were
pulling off slow, and there were other cars around. I figured they'd help
you, so I took off after the truck."

Then I remembered that the semi had tried to warn us the last time that
the black panel truck attacked. And he'd blasted his horn after we went off
the road.

The trucker—he must have been at least six six—said his name was Ron
Vidmar. He told us he had followed the black panel truck five miles south,

where the truck exited at Haven Road. "I lost him after that," he said. "My rig's not too good as a chase vehicle on those back roads. Lots of houses. Lots of trees and bushes."

"Yeah," Joe said. "There are plenty of summer places down there. Plenty of little roads and subdivisions. But we sure appreciate the effort. Especially since we may need a witness."

I wrote Ron Vidmar's name, address, and cell phone number down and thanked him for coming back to report. A wrecker came. I got out of the truck—refusing Joe's offer of a piggyback ride—walked up to the highway, and stood by the state police car, shivering in the night air, while first the boat and then the pickup were hauled back to the pavement. Joe looked mighty relieved when the pickup started right up.

Ron Vidmar's semi came by again—he'd had to drive back to the previous exit and swing around to get back on the Interstate going the right direction—and he gave a farewell blast of his horn. I got into the truck, and I thought we were on our way when another car with flashing lights pulled off the highway and parked on the shoulder ahead of us. The word "PO-LICE" was stenciled on its trunk.

Another tall guy got out and walked back to the pickup. Chief Hogan Jones.

"Joe," he said. "What the hell were you doing going to Grand Rapids? Suspects in a murder case are supposed to tell the investigating officer before they take off."

Chapter 13

The state police wanted us off the Interstate, of course, so Chief Jones followed us out to Joe's shop, where Joe opened the double doors at the end and backed the 1955 Chris-Craft Continental inside. He turned on all the lights.

"So why didn't you tell me you were going to Grand Rapids?" the chief asked.

"It didn't occur to me that you'd be interested," Joe said. He began looking at the side of the boat.

"Is it damaged?" I asked.

"A crack and a bad scrape." Joe ran his hand along the side. "That plank had to be replaced anyway. It didn't do anything that can't be fixed."

"Good."

That's when Chief Hogan Jones raised his voice. "You two! Pay attention to me!"

We turned toward him. "I'm sorry, Chief," Joe said. "I guess I'm not thinking too logically yet. Do you want to hear what happened?"

"First, I want to know why you went to Grand Rapids."

Joe and I looked at each other. "I guess it was my fault," I said.

"But it was my idea," Joe said. He sketched our concerns about the old Root Beer Barrel and Frank Waterloo's possible connection to Tom Johnson, who wanted to buy it. Then he told the chief about our trip.

The chief glared. "Then you didn't go to the airport?"

"Why would we go to the airport?" I asked.

Joe and I stared at the chief, and he stared back. I was still mystified, but Joe began to frown. "Who thought we were headed to the airport?" he said.

"He didn't give his name."

"Did you believe him?"

"Not enough to put out an all-points for a blue truck."

"Wait a minute," I said. "Are you saying somebody called you and said Joe and I were headed for the Grand Rapids airport?"

The chief nodded. "An anonymous call. He said Joe was on his way out of the country. Didn't mention you, Lee."

"Why would anybody say that?"

Joe leaned on the boat. "He did it to make it look as if I was fleeing the investigation."

I turned on the chief. "You couldn't believe that! It's obstreperous! I mean, preposterous!"

Joe spoke very quietly. "The chief didn't believe it, Lee. If he had, he would have had the Grand Rapids police pick us up."

The chief looked a little embarrassed. "Well, I did call TenHuis and ask for Lee. Nettie told me the two of you had gone to Grand Rapids to pick up a boat. I figured that if you were breaking for the Canadian border, you wouldn't haul a boat along."

"Certainly not on an airplane," Joe said.

I was still irate. "But who would make a call like that?"

"Apparently I have an enemy," Joe said.

"Yeah," Chief Jones said. "Any ideas on who it might be?"

Joe shook his head. "I guess I've stepped on as many toes as anybody else in my life. But I don't have any idea who would dislike me so much they'd try to frame me for murder. And, Chief, that's what's going on."

The chief nodded, and I decided to jump back into the conversation. "Yeah, and when the chief didn't send the Grand Rapids police after us, whoever this is took direct action and tried to shove us into a bridge railing. Three times!"

I belatedly remembered something about those three episodes, and I turned to the chief. "The license number! I gave the license number to the dispatcher. That'll tell us who was in the black panel truck!"

The chief shook his head. "No such luck, Lee."

"What do you mean? It was a Michigan plate. You should be able to check it."

"We were able to check it. We have a magic computer that checks license plates almost instantaneously."

"What did it say? Who owns that truck?"

The chief sighed. "It isn't that easy, Lee. The license tag number you gave the dispatcher belongs to a four-year-old Ford . . ."

"It was a Dodge!"

The chief went on. ". . . a four-year-old Ford pickup. Registered in Dearborn. Sorry, Lee. Either you got the number wrong or the driver of the panel truck faked the tag."

There didn't seem to be a lot more to say or do, so the chief left pretty soon, and Joe began closing up the shop. "Guess I'd better get you back to pick up your van," he said.

"You know," I said, "I may have figured out the real motive of the anonymous caller."

"Yeah?"

"Put your arms around me, and I'll explain it."

Joe complied with my request willingly. A few minutes later he nibbled my ear. "So? Explain."

"Explain what?"

"Explain why the anonymous caller sicced the cops on us."

"It's a part of a plot designed purely and simply to interfere with our romantic life."

"Oh, is that why all this is happening?"

"Yes. Just analyze it. Last night you planned a romantic evening for us. Right?"

"Yep. Boat ride, nice dinner. Even warned you about the possibility of mosquitoes."

"Correct. I'm sure you noticed I wore my sexiest scent of Deep Woods Off."

Joe breathed deeply on the nape of my neck. "Mmmmm."

"And what happens? We barely get dinner down, and we're called back because that dumb green canoe has turned up at the boat shop."

"You just might be right," Joe said. "Just think—later on, after we got everybody cleared out around here, I thought I had enticed you back into the romantic mood and—bingo! Hershel turns up."

"Yes. And that ruined the rest of the evening." I clenched my fists in Joe's shirt. Finding Hershel hadn't really been a joking matter.

"Then today I took up the effort again," Joe said, "luring you up to Grand Rapids. A town simply thick with motels and hotels."

I began to laugh. "Yeah! And think what would have happened if we'd checked into one of them."

"What?"

"The chief would have decided we were taking too long on our trip and called the Grand Rapids police. We would have been hauled out in the middle of our tryst and taken down to the station."

"It might have been worth it," Joe said.

He kissed me again, and this time I didn't laugh. Tears began to run. I had to stop kissing, go into Joe's office, and use one of his Kleenexes to blow my nose. I sat down behind his desk and bawled. He followed me, looking helpless, the way men do when faced with an emotional woman.

"I'm sorry," I said. "This whole thing is just . . . so . . ."

"Yeah. It's getting me down, too." Joe kissed me again, but this time his target was the top of the head. "Come on. I guess I'd better get you back to your van. And then I'm going to follow you home."

"You're the one who's got an enemy."

"Apparently. And the best way to hurt me would be to hurt you."

Aunt Nettie was in bed when I got home. Joe didn't insist on looking in all the closets and under all the beds, though he waited until I was inside. I didn't think I'd sleep, but somehow I did. Pure exhaustion, I guess.

In fact, I slept until after Aunt Nettie had left for the shop the next morning. I had barely dragged out of bed at nine-thirty, when she called the house. "What's this I hear about you and Joe having a wreck?"

"It's a long story. Neither of us was hurt. Who told you about it?"

"Trey Corbett. He came in wanting to know all the details. He apparently had a run-in with the same driver."

That was interesting. Maybe Trey had been able to identify the driver. As soon as Aunt Nettie hung up, I called Trey. I got his chatty answering machine. I left a message, then got ready for work and dashed to the shop.

The ladies in hairnets were bustling about, and Aunt Nettie was standing over her large copper kettle, the one she uses to make fillings for truffles and bonbons, the one with its own gas burner. The big white plastic pail of fondant was on the work table next to her, and as I came in she was using a broad spatula to dip out a chunk of the fondant and put it onto a scale.

"Hi, Lee," she said. "I'm sure glad to see you're not bruised all over." She eyed the scale, then added the fondant to the copper kettle, adjusted the gas flame, and began stirring.

"If I'm not black and blue, it's thanks to Joe's driving," I said. "I just wanted to assure you everything was all right before I went to the post office."

"Fine. But when you get back, I want to hear all the details."

I gave Aunt Nettie a hug and headed down the street. The two blocks to the post office and two blocks back turned into a long walk that morning. It seemed that every downtown merchant in Warner Pier had already heard about our excitement and wanted a personal report.

By the time I got back to TenHuis Chocolade, the aroma of the place had changed. When I opened the door I had the sensation that I'd fallen into a vat of syrup. I realized that Aunt Nettie was making the filling for maple truffles, "A milk chocolate truffle flavored with sweet maple." Sounds like a cliché candy—I mean, everybody makes a maple cream. But everybody doesn't make one like Aunt Nettie's.

I took a deep breath and walked back to the workroom. Maple flavoring has the strongest aroma of any flavoring Aunt Nettie uses. Somebody broke a bottle of it once, and we smelled sickeningly sweet for a week. But in the proper proportions—in Aunt Nettie's proportions—maple flavoring smells absolutely wonderful.

I smacked my lips enthusiastically. "Can I lick the dish?"

Aunt Nettie smiled. She added a ladle of warm milk chocolate to the copper kettle and stirred. "First you tell me about this wreck you and Joe had."

I told her. The whole story. I didn't gloss over what had happened. I gave up trying to keep things from Aunt Nettie a long time ago.

She didn't gloss it over, either. "I don't suppose Joe could take a trip for a while," she said. "Just get out of town and stay away from whoever is after him."

"I don't think the chief would like that. Besides, he would have to come back eventually."

"And Joe doesn't have any idea who would be so eager to get him involved in Hershel's death?"

"No. The whole thing won't be resolved until the chief catches the person who really murdered Hershel. Right now, it strikes me that the best way to do that would be to find out who was driving that black panel truck."

Aunt Nettie vigorously stirred the mixture in her copper kettle. She added the maple flavoring. "Trey said he'd call back. Maybe he saw something."

It was an hour before I heard from Trey. He came in the door, looking more nerdy than ever. He seemed scrawnier. I wondered if he was losing weight, though he didn't have any to lose. I motioned for him to come into the office.

"You okay?" I said. "Aunt Nettie said you had a run-in with the same jerk Joe and I did."

"The chief says it sounds like the same truck," Trey said. "Black Dodge Cargo Van. At least I think it was black. I'm guessing by the color of the paint down the side of my Explorer."

"It actually hit you? I didn't realize that. What happened?"

"I'd been over to Gray Gables—you know I'm the local caretaker for the family?"

I nodded. "It's a beautiful place. Do they ever have tours?"

"No, but I can show you and Joe over it. My cousins don't come down much. Anyway, last night I left there a little after ten, and I decided to head back to town on Inland Road, rather than getting on the Interstate."

"I didn't realize Gray Gables was that far from town. I've only seen it from the water."

"It's not far, but the roads over there are so twisty it's quicker to go down Haven Road, get on the Interstate, and come back that way."

"Haven Road! That's where the black panel truck got off the Interstate."

"Apparently so. I had just turned onto Inland when this black vehicle came up behind me, traveling like the proverbial bat out of hell. He went around to pass and scraped along the left-hand side of my Explorer. I'm just darn lucky I didn't have my arm out the window. I nearly ran off in the ditch. Then I blasted the horn—I'm sure everybody in the neighborhood heard me. Of course, he didn't stop."

"Did you see where he went?"

"He turned off to the left, but I couldn't see just where. Michigan Road. Lakeview. Maybe even Benson Drive."

"Are there other houses around there?"

"Oh, yes. It's a built-up neighborhood. But the lots are big."

"I wonder if anybody else saw him."

"Chief Jones was going to ask. He was also going to try to find out if anybody in that neighborhood owns a black Dodge Cargo Van with tinted windows."

"Did you get a look at the license plate?"

"I thought you and Joe got the number."

"We thought we did, too, but when they ran a check, the number we had was not the number of a Dodge panel truck."

Trey frowned. "I thought it had a couple of eights. I guess they could have been sixes. I didn't get the letters."

I gave Trey a sample chocolate—he picked a milk chocolate fish on a stick. Then I walked outside with him to see the damage to his silver SUV. An awful scrape ran down the driver's side, and the black paint showed up clearly.

"This guy must be crazy," I said.

"The chief's convinced he had it in for Joe. He thinks I just got in the way. Does Joe have any idea what he did to annoy him?"

"No."

"I don't know Joe all that well. It seemed to me he usually tries to mind his own business. I never heard of him making anybody mad. Of course, there was that Chicago man who wanted to make an offer on the Ripley place. Joe wouldn't even talk to him. I guess that guy was kind of upset."

"Someone wanted to buy the Ripley place?"

Trey got a look of little-boy guilt on his face. "Joe didn't tell you? Maybe I was wrong." He shuffled his feet uneasily. "Guess I'd better go. I'm supposed to meet a painter. I'm still working on the Miller cottage."

He left, repeating his offer of a tour of Gray Gables. I went into the office with something new to think about.

Somebody had offered to buy the Ripley place? That sounded completely screwy.

The Ripley property, also known as Warner Point, was the showplace home of Joe's ex-wife, the famous defense attorney Clementine Ripley. It included a fabulous house on a ten-acre plot which was bounded by Lake Michigan on the west and the Warner River on the south. The property was part of the estate which had become such a booger for Joe to settle. The Ripley property was worth millions, and it was costing her estate thousands in upkeep.

Clementine Ripley might have been a brilliant defense attorney—the one movie stars and politicians called when they were in trouble—but she hadn't been a good financial manager. She'd also owned a co-op apartment in Chicago, and she and Joe had owned an apartment house jointly. All of her real estate, Joe said, was heavily mortgaged. Plus, she'd trusted the wrong person with her finances, and nearly every cash asset and almost all her investments had been stolen or transferred to offshore accounts that were not in her name. She hadn't even gotten around to signing a new will after she and Joe were divorced, which was the reason he was stuck with settling up. Getting any of the stolen assets back was proving to be a legal nightmare.

And thanks to the current drop in the real estate market, Joe had told me, he didn't want to sell the Chicago real estate. The co-op apartment was rented. The apartment house made a profit, but it also kept Joe's personal savings tied up. Between them, the two pieces of property provided barely enough income to pay the taxes, insurance, mortgage payments, and maintenance on the Warner Pier estate. No one wanted to rent the Warner Point property—which might have something to do with the two murders that had occurred there, I guess. It was simply a money pit and a pain in Joe's neck financially.

If I was reading the situation right, Joe ought to be glad to sell the Ripley property. So, if he had a chance, why wouldn't he have sold it?

I could call him up and ask him, of course. But I'd been so careful to stay out of his financial affairs, I didn't quite have the nerve. If Joe wanted me to know, he would have told me.

Probably, I told myself, the offer hadn't been enough to pay off the mortgage.

For a minute I wondered just what my future with Joe was. We'd never discussed marriage. We'd never even explored those important questions like "Do you want to have kids?" and "Do you want to live in Warner Pier forever?" These things just hadn't come up. So how could I quiz him about his finances? They weren't any of my business, as things stood.

The phone rang, and I sighed and reached for it. I'd better quit brooding on company time.

That phone call was the first of many. A dozen people called that morning—Joe's mom, making sure I was all right; our neighbors, the Baileys; the chair of the chamber's Economic Development Committee; lots of others. It was a replay of my walk to the post office.

"I might as well have stayed home," I said as Aunt Nettie walked by the office door. "I can't get a thing done for the telephone."

Aunt Nettie smiled. "I'm glad you're here. If you weren't, I couldn't get a thing done for the telephone."

The morning passed. It was straight up noon when the twelfth call came. "Lee! Are you okay?"

It was Lindy Herrera, who had been a friend since we were teenagers.

"Hi, Lindy. Yes, I'm all right. Joe's all right. Even the truck's all right."

"You don't sound all right."

"I'm just tired, I guess. The phone's been ringing off the desk, and you're the first caller I actually wanted to talk to."

Lindy laughed. "Sounds as if you need to do lunch."

"Not in Warner Pier. It'll be just like taking the phone with me. Are you working today?" Lindy worked in the restaurants and catering business of her father-in-law, Warner Pier's mayor, Mike Herrera.

"Actually, I'm a lady of leisure this summer. I decided to stay home with the kids. But today they've gone to the Grand Rapids Zoo with my mom and dad. Why don't you come out here? I'll fix something."

An idea began to tickle my brain. "Isn't there a park up Inland Road, not far from Gray Gables?"

"Riverside Park. Why? Are you in the mood for a picnic?"

"Yes, I am. And maybe a drive around that neighborhood with a local guide."

"You're on. I'll fix the sandwiches."

"I'll bring chocolate."

Chapter 14

Warner Pier is, as I say, a small town. And one sign that a town is really small is that everybody is related to everybody else in some way. If they're not blood relations, they go to the same church, went to high school together, get their hair cut at the same shop. It's a mishmash of interconnected circles.

For example, back when Lindy Herrera was Lindy Bradford, she and I had worked together behind the counter at TenHuis Chocolade for three summers. At eighteen she married Tony Herrera, who had been a close friend of Joe's in high school. Tony's dad, Mike Herrera, was now Warner Pier mayor. He owned three restaurants and a catering service, and he also dated Joe's mom, Mercy Woodyard, who ran Warner Pier's largest insurance agency, with offices right across the street from TenHuis Chocolade. Interconnected circles.

The circles continue. Tony has a job as a machinist in Holland, but when he was laid off the previous summer, he worked for Joe. Lindy works for her father-in-law. Since she fills in the gaps where Mike needs help, I never know if I'll see her dishing out barbecued chicken at the Chamber of Commerce banquet or serving up French dips at Mike's Sidewalk Café, a half-block from TenHuis. Our circles intersect all the time.

Tony and Lindy have three kids. Tony works days and Lindy usually works nights. I know they have trouble making ends meet. It was the kind of life my parents had, until debt and the struggle to get by drove them apart. It was the kind of life I had been trying to avoid when I scrambled my way through college. But Lindy and Tony seemed to be coping.

I picked Lindy up at her little house at Ninth Avenue and Cider Alley. "I brought Cokes and chips," I said. "And I hope you still like strawberry truffles."

"Yum, yum!" Lindy held up a small Styrofoam cooler. "I've got turkey wraps and carrot sticks. This is quite an outing for me. No kids!"

"Your kids are darling."

"Of course they are. What would you expect? But school's barely out, and I'm already frazzled."

I tried not to think about the fact that I was twenty-nine years old and had no kids and no prospect of having any. We crossed the river on the Orchard Street bridge, then turned on Inland. We passed the Waterloos' house, which still had a driveway full of cars.

"I guess I've seen Riverside Park from the water," I said. "But the main thing I remember about it is a boat ramp."

"For years a boat ramp really was the only thing there," Lindy said. "In the last few years the city's fixed it up—playground equipment, a picnic shelter. I think the land was given by the Corbett family. Years ago."

"Does it adjoin Gray Gables?"

"It doesn't adjoin, but I think the Corbetts owned acres and acres on that side of the river originally. Now there's a whole housing addition between the park and the big house."

We pulled into the park and easily found a space to spread the old quilt I keep in the back of the van. Several boat trailers were parked in the proper places for boat trailers, but picnickers were few. Yet the park was very nice—shady, with a well-kept playground.

"Is this park a secret from tourists?" I said.

"I think they all go for the beach. I bring the kids over here sometimes. Now, how about this tour you mentioned?"

"It's just idle curiosity," I said. While I ate my turkey wrap—it had special horseradish sauce I remembered paying extra for at Mike's Sidewalk Café—I described the adventures Joe and I had had with the black panel truck. Then I added Trey's experience.

"So the truck disappeared out in this area," I said. "That doesn't mean it's still here, of course."

"It could have hidden out a while, then gotten back on the interstate or taken off by the back roads."

"Sure. So I don't want to go door-to-door or anything. That's Chief Jones's job. But I realized that I've never been over here enough to have any idea of what's here or how it's laid out."

Lindy laughed. "I think I can find my way around. Tony and I parked on every road on this side of the river."

"It'll have to be a short tour. I do need to get back to the shop."

"Okay. But now I gotta know. Has Joe proposed?"

I should have expected that, I guess. But, Lindy caught me by surprise, so I stumbled around. "We haven't been dainty—I mean, dating! We haven't been dating but four moons—I mean, months!"

"Four months! More like a year."

"We met each other a year ago, Lindy. We didn't date for a long time after that."

"Well, you ought to . . ."

"Lindy!" She stopped talking and looked at me expectantly.

"Neither Joe nor I wants to make another mistake. Don't rush us!"

I said that merely to shut Lindy up, but when I heard my own words, they convinced me. For the moment at least, I felt confident about my relationship with Joe. It was unsettled, but so what? I didn't know where it was going. That was fine. I said as much to Lindy. "It's okay."

Lindy shrugged. "Okay."

"So, what's going on with you?"

The most exciting development in Lindy's life, to my surprise, was her job.

"Mike wants me to start working for him full-time in the fall," she said. "I'll be a sort of second-in-command for the catering business."

"That sounds like a promotion."

"At least it's a raise. I'll be meeting clients, deciding on menus, stuff like that—very little cooking and serving. It won't mean as much night work, since somebody else will handle the actual events. So maybe Tony and I will get to see each other now and then."

"Sounds good."

"Mike has a sense of family, you know. He couldn't get Tony interested in the business, so he's turned to me."

She gave me a full report on each of the kids, and I told her about my mom—who's a travel agent in Dallas and is frequently off to Timbuktu or Tanzania. Then we hashed over the romance between her father-in-law and Joe's mom, a topic I don't discuss with just anyone—particularly not Joe.

After we got that settled Lindy began to stuff paper napkins and other debris into a plastic sack. "Are you ready for the tour?"

"Sure. I want to see all the romantic spots where you and Tony made out."

Driving on up Inland Road brought us into an area that had as many trees as the road up to the old chapel had. It wasn't scary in the daylight, with the sunlight making patterns on the forest floor here and there, but the trees were thick and crowded the road.

There were quite a few houses, but the woods made most of them feel secluded. "This is Riverside Addition," Lindy said. "It was a hot development when I was a kid. My mom used to wish she could afford to move over here."

"There are some beautiful homes—when you can see them."

We wandered around on several side roads, including the ones Trey had mentioned: Michigan, Lakeview, Benson Drive. They were lined with houses, but all the houses were heavily landscaped. Bushes, shrubs, and big trees were everywhere.

"This is like driving through the deep, dark woods," I said. "Only now and then a house peeks out."

"It's a lot like your aunt's neighborhood."

"I know, but her house was built a hundred years ago, when that area was rural. The houses over there 'just growed.' This neighborhood actually encouraged all these trees. None of these houses get any sun. Not a woman over here can see more than three feet out her kitchen window."

Lindy laughed. "A little further along here, the road ends at the entrance to Gray Gables. You can turn around there."

In a quarter of a mile the road curved, and I found the hood of my van up against an elaborate iron gate, closed and locked, with iron fence stretching out on either side. Beyond it, a gravel drive led into a small grove of trees. I caught a glimpse of a roof—a shingle-covered cone—high above the trees.

"Trey offered to give Joe and me a tour of this place," I said.

"You should see it," Lindy said. "The Corbetts have lent it out a few times for special events I served, but it's hard to get inside. It's fabulous. Like going back in time. All the original furnishings."

"I think I'll take a closer peek, as long as we're here."

We both got out of the van and walked up close to the gate. I craned my neck to see around the darn trees. "I can see one corner," I said. "Queen Anne modified. Gee! It matches the side you can see from the river."

Lindy laughed. "If you can identify the style of the house by seeing one corner, you've been hanging around with the artsy-fartsy crowd too much."

All I could see of the house was the tower that held up the cone-shaped roof. The bottom two floors were clapboard and the sides of the tower's top floor were shingled. It was all, of course, painted gray.

"I wonder why they put the observation tower on the inland side of the house," I said.

"It's on the lake side."

I turned around and looked behind me. "Lindy, Gray Gables is on the river, not the lake. The lake is nowhere near here."

"Look at a map, Lee. It's only about half a mile. When this house was built, or so I've been told, you could see the lake from the house."

"Unbelievable! I told you all these trees would cause problems. It would have been fabulous to be able to see the river on one side and the lake on the other. But no more. Not that this isn't a lovely spot."

Lindy took a deep breath. "And one of the loveliest things about it is the smell," she said. "Just like TenHuis Chocolade."

For a moment I thought I must smell like maple flavoring. Then I sniffed and caught the same odor Lindy had identified. "It *is* chocolate," I said. "Where do you suppose it's coming from?"

"It can't be from Gray Gables. That's too far away."

We looked around. No sign of human habitation. Except . . .

"Lindy! There's a house over there."

I pointed. Among the trees to our right I had caught sight of tell-tale evidence. A straight line, running diagonally among the tree branches. Straight lines are never found in nature.

"Oh, my gosh!" Lindy said. "There is a house. And it's real close—right behind that row of trees. But there's no drive."

I pointed to a narrow gap in the bushes. "I guess that's a path."

"But how would you get to the house in a car?"

At that moment the bushes burst asunder and a giant stepped out. "The drive comes in from that road on the right!" a voice roared. "It's wide enough for my VW!"

Lindy and I actually clutched each other. I was nearly as startled as I had been when Hershel popped up outside the window of Joe's truck. "Yikes!" I said. "Where'd you come from?"

The giant—now I realized it was a giantess—laughed. It was a deep, rolling laugh, a laugh that matched her appearance. I'm very close to six feet tall, and this woman towered over me. She must have been at least six foot three. And she was broad. I would guess her weight at well over two hundred pounds; she had a bosom like the prow of a battleship. And after the first shock of her size, her coloring was equally shocking. Her hair was a bright red, and her face was ruddy and freckled. Her eyes bugged, and they were bright blue. She was wearing blue jeans and an enormous, brilliant blue sweatshirt with the name of an Ann Arbor restaurant across the front.

"Didn't mean to startle you!" she roared. "I'm staying in the cottage for the summer! Heard a car stop! Stepped out to see what was going on!"

"We were gawking at Gray Gables," I said. "I'm sorry if we disturbed you."

The giantess laughed again. "Ho! Ho! Ho! Not at all!"

Lindy was peeking through the trees behind the woman. "Did you say you're staying out here? Isn't it awfully remote?"

"That's what I like about it!" The woman didn't seem to be able to speak at a normal sound level. Every sentence was shouted out. "Wanted to get away from people for a couple of months! Cabin's pretty ramshackle, but it has electricity! Walk to beach! Only low-rent place I could find!"

She looked at me and her expression grew even more jovial. "Hey! You work in that chocolate shop. I can tell by your shirt!"

"Yes." It was hard not to yell back at her. "I'm the business manager, Lee McKinney. Have you been in?"

"Naturally. Ms. TenHuis gave me a tour!"

"Oh, Aunt Nettie mentioned it. You're the friend of Mrs. Corbett."

"Yes! Not a close friend, but she rented the cottage to me. I loved your shop! Chocolate! That's my kind of flesh-pots!"

"Be sure you come back." I walked toward the woman, with Lindy trailing along. Our reason for being there belatedly reappeared in my tiny brain. "I suppose the police have already bothered you today."

"Police! Ho, ho, ho! Do I look like a crook?"

"Not at all. They're investigating an accident I was involved in last night." I sketched our reasons for wanting to know if the black panel truck had been seen in the area.

"Doubt he'd come up this road. Dead end!"

"Right. Unless the driver was a stranger. So you didn't hear anything?"

"Not last night. Two nights ago was the commotion!"

"I doubt that had anything to do with our accident. But what happened?"

The giantess gestured over her shoulder with a thumb. "Back in the woods! Closer to the Interstate! Hobo jungle!"

"Oh!" Lindy gasped. "I'd be terrified if I was out here alone."

The red-haired woman gave a shrug, and her whole body shook as if she'd been hit by an earthquake. "They don't bother me. I don't bother them."

"Except two nights ago," I said. "You said you heard a commotion."

"They didn't bother me! I just heard them. Thrashing around in the woods. Yelling!"

"Oh." I decided the woman knew nothing about the black panel truck. But she was sure an interesting character and apparently a TenHuis customer. "Let me give you a card," I said. "Next time you come in the shop, we'll have an extra sample for you."

I got my purse out of the van and wrote "Quarter pound box" on the back of a business card. Then I gave it to the giantess.

She read my name, then offered her hand in shaking position. "I'm Dolly Jolly!"

I remembered that Aunt Nettie had said she had a funny name. My opinion must have showed, because Ms. Jolly spoke again. "Dorothea, of course! But I've always been Dolly!"

"Like Dolley Madison. One of my heroines."

She beamed. "Love chocolate!"

"You must be baking," I said. "We smelled cookies."

"Chocolate chip. I'm writing a cookbook!"

"Then you're a real foodie. So's Lindy." I introduced them and included Lindy's job. "I'm just a bookkeeper. And I've got to get back to work."

We got in the van and started to drive away, but after I'd turned around Dolly Jolly waved us down again. She came up to my open window and spoke.

"Another fellow might have seen your panel truck! Prowls around everywhere! By here nearly every day the first week I moved in! Little guy with dark hair and a big mouth! Raspy voice! Looks like a frog!"

CHOCOLATE CHAT

CHOCOLATE—RICH AND RICHELIEU

- By the early 1600s, the Spanish royal court was drinking chocolate—probably using recipes for a hot beverage which the Spanish occupiers of Mexico had sent home.

- Chocolate requires quite a bit of processing—fermenting, drying, winnowing, grinding—so it's not surprising that working people rarely drank it, either in the New World or the Old World. It was not only expensive to buy, but expensive to prepare. Only the richest Spanish could afford it.

- Tradition has it that when the Spanish princess Anne of Austria was married to Louis XIII of France, she brought chocolate along as part of her dowry. However, Anne—she's the one whose troubles Alexandre Dumas described in *The Three Musketeers*—was only fourteen when she married and apparently never had much influence over her bridegroom. Other authorities believe that chocolate was introduced to France by the Cardinal of Lyon, who then passed its secrets on to his younger brother. Since that younger brother was Cardinal Richelieu, also a character in *The Three Musketeers* and a guy with more clout than anybody else in seventeenth century France, chocolate was soon popular.

- Another report states that nuns in a Mexican convent produced delicacies of solid chocolate quite early. And they apparently made good money selling these in Europe. The Sisters of St. Godiva?

Chapter 15

"Hershel!" Lindy and I spoke at the same time.

"That his name? Figured everybody in town would know him! He lectured me about the little cabin. Said it was a workman's cottage from the 1850s. Kind of a character!"

"We won't be asking Hershel anything," I said. "He was killed. Night before last."

I told Dolly about finding Hershel's body.

"Rotten deal!"

"It was pretty awful," I said.

"Hershel? That his name? Over here Monday! Close to dark!"

"Monday? That's the night he disappeared!"

Dolly scratched her head. "Think that was it. He walked out of the woods. I was sitting out, enjoying the twilight!"

"You ought to tell the police chief about this."

Dolly shrugged. "Don't know anything! Didn't tell me he was going to get killed!"

"I know the chief is trying to trace his movements Monday night."

I wrote the chief's name and the location of the police department on the back of another TenHuis card and gave it to her. We offered her a lift to town, but Ms. Jolly said she would call the chief for an appointment.

"Got a cell phone!" she shouted. "Won't bother to get a landline connected! Don't need the Internet! I'll take my VW to town!"

We left then. After we reached Haven Road, Lindy began to laugh. "I hope that VW's a van," she said. "That's the largest woman I've ever seen."

"Not too many people of either sex make me feel dainty," I said. "But she did. And think of her seeing Hershel the night he disappeared."

I drove a few blocks before I spoke again. "I wonder what Hershel was doing out by Gray Gables?"

"I can't imagine," Lindy said. "Trey Corbett might know."

I decided I'd had enough contact with Trey for one day, but I did plan to give Chief Jones a call instead and tip him off about Dolly Jolly. But when I got back to the office, work intervened. All afternoon I actually had to earn my salary. Customers called wanting rush orders sent out. Our sugar supplier had our bill screwed up, and I had to talk fast, dig out two months' bank statements, find copies of canceled checks, and fax the copies to them before the crisis was settled. Barbara, a close friend who's manager of the Warner Pier branch bank, dropped by—apparently making a customer call—and stayed. And stayed. And stayed.

Barbara is an attractive brunette of maybe forty. She has a business degree from Kalamazoo College. She has big dark eyes and a nose so large it dominates her face. Barbara doesn't care about her nose, and after her customers see her smile, they don't either. She's as smart as a tree full of owls, as my Texas grandma would have said, and she's got a real head for figures. She's been a valuable friend and colleague to me since I moved to Warner Pier, but that afternoon I thought she'd never leave.

Barbara had finally headed for the door when she dropped a small bombshell. "I guess Frank and Patsy Waterloo may put their divorce on hold," she said.

"Divorce! The Waterloos? I hadn't heard that."

"I heard it from one of the high school teachers. Not at the bank. Loose lips sink banks. So it's just gossip."

She left then, but she left me curious. Just what was the story on Frank and Patsy Waterloo? Why would Hershel's death affect any plans they had for a divorce one way or another?

I knew who probably knew the answer to that, but I sure hated to sink low enough to ask him. I was glad when the phone rang and distracted me. "TenHuis Chocolade."

"Lee? Hogan Jones here."

"Oh! I was thinking about calling you, but I never found time. Lindy and I ran into this woman . . ."

"Big redhead."

"Yes. Dolly Jolly. I guess she came in to make a statement."

"Right. She says she told the two of you that Hershel was out at Gray Gables the night he disappeared. Have you passed that information on to anybody?"

"No."

"Don't. Okay?"

"Whatever you say. But why not?"

I could hear the chief sigh. "She saw more than she realizes. If it gets out—she could be at risk."

"Oh!"

"I know you wouldn't want to be responsible if anything happened to her."

"Of course not! I won't say a word. Do you want me to call Lindy and tell her to keep quiet?"

"I'll do that. Don't talk about it to anybody, okay? Not Lindy. Not Joe. Not even Nettie."

I hung up feeling cowed. What could Dolly Jolly have seen? It took me twenty minutes to calm my curiosity down. Until the next time the phone rang. It was Joe.

"Did I talk to you about going out to dinner tonight?" he said.

"I don't think so."

"Well, I can't get away."

I laughed. "Gee, Joe, when you start breaking dates we hadn't even made . . ."

"Pretty much of a jerk, huh. I meant to ask you, but the telephone repairman says he'll be coming around five. I guess I'd better not plan on any particular schedule."

"How about me bringing a pizza out there?"

"Hey! That sounds like a pretty good deal."

We agreed that I'd come at my own convenience. I discussed the dinner break schedule with Stacy and Tracy, and about five-thirty I called the Dock Street Pizza Parlor and ordered. Then I decided to pick up a bag of salad at the Superette on the way. It would be cheaper than the Dock Street's salad.

Or that's what I told myself. The truth, of course, was that I was still curious about the Waterloos, and the person most likely to have wormed out the real story on them was to be found at the Superette—Greg Glossop, who ran the pharmacy there. If "Mr. Gossip" didn't know the real story—well, he'd make up something interesting.

As I'd anticipated, all I had to do was walk into the drug and beauty supply end of the Superette and look at a display of mascara. Greg Glossop bounced his little round belly right out of his glassed-in pharmacy. He trotted down the nearest aisle and greeted me. "Lee!"

"Oh, hello, Greg," I said.

"Well, young woman. You've had a nasty experience."

"Finding Hershel, you mean? It wasn't a lot of fun. Of course, we weren't really friends. It's Patsy and Frank I feel sorry for."

"Tch, tch," Greg said. "Of course, we've all felt sorry for them all along."

"Taking care of Hershel must have been an awful strain." I leaned a little closer and lowered my voice. "I even heard that they were considering divorce."

Greg Glossop nodded wisely. "I guess the whole situation was really getting Frank down. Between the responsibility for Hershel, Frank's problems finding a good job, and their money situation—it would get anybody down."

"Patsy seemed sincerely sorrowful about Hershel's death, but I could understand if it was something of a relief. Maybe that will solve one of the problems."

"It'll solve two. It's no secret that Patsy and Hershel's mom left her whole estate in trust to take care of Hershel."

"Oh, really? That's odd. But I guess she figured that Patsy and Frank could take care of themselves."

"Exactly. And Hershel couldn't. But that meant Patsy and Frank had to move back to Warner Pier, which meant that Frank had to quit his job and take one that apparently pays a lot less."

"Of course the house they inherited is worth a lot."

Greg Glossop shook his head. "They didn't inherit it. The property belongs to the trust set up to care for Hershel."

"You mean they were dependent on Hershel?"

"No, no. Just for use of the house. But the trust requires that all of Patsy's mother's money must support Hershel. Now that Hershel's gone, Patsy gets the trust."

"Did the trust pay when they renovated the house?"

"No. I hear they used the money from the sale of their California house for that—and apparently they didn't have a lot of equity. Anyway, I'm under the impression that rebuilding the house here nearly wiped them out."

He leaned closer and lowered his voice. "It's understandable if Frank got so frustrated he—well . . ."—Glossop cleared his throat—"went a little crazy. Didn't come home nights. Began to hit the bottle."

That was news. I lowered my voice. "Oh?"

"I'm merely guessing by his purchases in the liquor department. And from some of Patsy's remarks."

All of a sudden I felt as if I'd fallen in a mud hole. And I was so ashamed of myself that I probably blushed. I could barely pay Greg Glossop off with a tidbit about one of the ladies who worked at TenHuis being pregnant. She was telling everybody, so I wasn't letting any cats out of any bags. Then I sidled toward the produce aisle, and Greg Glossop had to leave me and go back to his eyric above the drug and beauty department.

I picked up my bag of salad and stood in line at the checkout stand, feeling ashamed of gossiping. But I was also looking at another possible motive for getting rid of Hershel. A motive for Patsy and Frank. Not only was Hershel an annoying and frustrating relative to have on their hands, he'd also forced them into a bad financial position and threatened their marriage. And if Frank was fooling around or drinking—I didn't consider Greg Glossop's evidence conclusive; Frank might have been taking booze home to Patsy—Hershel's spying might have inconvenienced him, as well.

Yes, Frank and Patsy were going to be a lot better off without their troublesome relative—financially and personally.

I picked up the pizza and headed for Joe's. When I got there, the telephone company's truck was parked beside the shop and the shop's doors were all open, but there was nobody around. I called out, but nobody answered.

I decided that Joe and the repairman were probably tracking down the phone problem. I took the salad and pizza and went into Joe's little cubbyhole of a bedroom-living room-dining room. He'd already set the card table with plates, forks, knives and a can of parmesan cheese, but he hadn't anticipated salad. I found a couple of bowls in the cupboard and filled them with salad.

Still no Joe. I decided that the microwave oven was the only small, enclosed space in the room—the only place where the pizza might stay warm. I had just clicked the microwave's door open when I heard a noise in the shop, and Joe came to the door.

"Hi," I said. "Dinner's just about ready."

"Will it wait? I want you to see something."

I put the pizza in the microwave, then followed Joe outside. He led me down the drive and out onto the road—actually the tag end of Dock Street, but that far from the center of town, it had turned into a gravel road.

"What are we going to see?" I asked.

"The phone man found it. I've called the police."

I stopped dead. "Not another body!"

"No! I wouldn't drag you out to see something gruesome."

I continued to follow Joe, but with some dread. A line of utility poles, of course, followed the road. Wires were over our heads, mixed in among the trees. In about a hundred feet I saw a man in the uniform of the phone company.

"I want you to show that wire to Ms. McKinney," Joe said.

Wordlessly, the phone man pointed down. A cable trailed down from above him, and the end lay near his feet.

The end. It wasn't attached to anything. The other end led up into the trees. But this end was just lying on the ground.

The phone man looked almost pleased. "It sure wasn't equipment failure," he said. "This wire was deliberately cut."

Chapter 16

Chief Jones arrived shortly. Joe and I left him taking pictures and went back to the shop to eat our salad and pizza. When I drove away a half-hour later the telephone man was up on the pole, and the chief was walking toward the shop. We waved at each other.

An hour after that the chief showed up at TenHuis Chocolade.

I was in my office, working away, when I saw him come in the street door. He paused and peered around the shop, looking more Lincolnesque than usual. Tracy and Stacy were busy with a half-dozen tourists, so I waved, and the chief came on back. He slouched down in a chair. Somehow ordinary furniture never seemed tall enough to fit Chief Jones.

"What happened to the phone line?" I asked.

"Somebody cut it."

"Somebody climbed the pole and cut it?"

"I didn't say that. I don't know exactly how the guy did it. He could have brought a ladder or climbed on top of a truck or swung from a tree like Tarzan. Me, if I wanted to cut a phone line, I'd use a pruning hook. The kind on an extended pole."

I sighed. "Not too hard to find in orchard country."

"Nope. Matter of fact, Joe's nearest neighbor has one, and he keeps it in an unlocked garage. But now I want to ask you a couple of questions."

"Sure. But I don't know a thing about that phone line except that Joe's phone wasn't working on Tuesday. And finding it was cut would seem to be yet one more factor proving that Joe is innocent. He's definitely the victim of a frame-up."

"I didn't come to talk about Joe. I want you to go over what Hershel said to you when he came up to the truck that night."

I collected my thoughts a minute, then retold the episode. Hershel, after scaring me half to death, had demanded to meet Aunt Nettie at the old chapel. He had refused my offer to get medical help. He had refused my assurances that people missed him and were looking for him. He had refused to trust anybody but Aunt Nettie.

"I don't want to hurt your feelings, Chief," I said, "but he particularly scoffed at you, Trey, Jerry Cherry, Meg, Patsy, and Frank. He said, 'I saw that bunch on the dock.' "

"Don't forget, Joe was there with us."

"I admit that. And we all know Hershel was already mad at Joe. But he was quite firm about not trusting any of you. Talked as if he suspected some sort of conspiracy."

"He didn't go into details?"

"No. I was surprised when he included Trey. Apparently they'd become buddies during the remodeling of Patsy and Frank's house."

"I think Trey had been real patient with Hershel while he was working on the Waterloos' house, but Meg didn't share his patience. Hershel started hanging out at Trey's office and at their house. Meg finally called me to complain about Hershel. Trey backed her up, of course. Hershel couldn't understand that he had to."

"He had to back up his wife, you mean?" The chief nodded, and I went on. "Patsy said Meg complained that Hershel was stalking her. But Patsy said he wasn't really interested in Meg. She thinks it was just Hershel's fascination with Trey."

"I think that was a lot of it, but we have to remember that Meg can be pretty fascinating by herself."

Was I imagining it, or was the chief giving me a sidelong look? "If you meant that for me personally," I said, "I'm aware that Joe and Meg dated each other in high school. I talked to Joe about it, and he doesn't seem to be harboring a guilty passion for her. Does all this seem to fit into Hershel's conspiracy theory?"

"I don't see how. But you're forgetting me. Apparently Hershel suspected me of conspiring against him."

"He also seemed to suspect Jerry Cherry."

The chief grimaced. "I can't find that Jerry ever had any particular contact with Hershel. Hershel may have mistrusted his uniform."

I grinned. "I trust you both, Chief."

"Thanks. But I admit I got crossways with Hershel over the way he roamed around town. A couple of times we had window-peeping complaints about him. I had to be the bad guy."

"It sounds as if Hershel wasn't as harmless as Patsy thinks."

"Oh, he just looked. And a warning would stop Hershel. If I told him, 'Don't go around the Corbetts' house again,' he might grumble, but I could feel sure he wasn't going to go over there. Patsy says I scared him after Meg complained, but Hershel didn't act scared when I talked to him."

"That's funny. Patsy said he hid. That she found him trembling all over. If you didn't scare him, what did?"

"Maybe I'd better try to find out. But now I want to ask you a different question. Who'd you tell that you were going to Grand Rapids last night?"

"Aunt Nettie."

"Who else?"

"Nobody, Chief. I was a little embarrassed about leaving early, so I didn't tell the girls on the counter I was going on a date. Aunt Nettie may have told somebody."

But when we asked Aunt Nettie, she denied mentioning it to anybody. "It just didn't arise," she said firmly. "Besides, it's nobody's business but Lee and Joe's."

Bless her heart, she'd been avoiding gossip.

The chief asked her several ways. Had she talked on the phone about it? Had Joe's mom popped in and brought it up? Had anybody come in asking for Lee and she'd said, 'Oh, she's gone to Grand Rapids'?"

Aunt Nettie denied every situation. "I didn't mention it to anybody," she said. "In fact, I went home right after Lee left. I left Hazel and the counter girls in charge. But I don't think any of them knew where Lee and Joe had gone."

"We didn't mean for our trip to be a secret," I said. "Joe may have told someone."

The chief shook his head. "He says he didn't. We know nobody called him—his landline was out of commission, and apparently you and his mom are the only two people who ever call on the cell phone. And he says his mother didn't call yesterday afternoon." He turned to me. "You see why it matters?"

I nodded. "If someone called you and said we were headed for the Grand Rapids airport . . . And if that panel truck lay in wait for us at the Willard station . . ."

"Right. Our boy had to know you were coming."

On that happy note the chief went out the door, leaving my innards all atremble. I'd already faced the possibility that somebody had deliberately tried to shove us into a bridge railing—three times. The whole situation was scary. Could that be connected with Hershel's death? I didn't see how.

But to me Hershel's murder had almost become a side issue. Whoever had killed Hershel also seemed determined to implicate Joe. That's what worried me.

Somebody had to know Joe and I were going to Grand Rapids. And nobody had known.

I suddenly realized I was partially wrong. No one had known we were going to Grand Rapids, but one person had definitely known we were there.

Tom Johnson.

Tom Johnson, who looked like Santa Claus and leered like a satyr. Tom Johnson, whom Joe had described as "a beard," a person who's acting for someone else. He had talked to us at his office and would undoubtedly have realized we were likely to eat dinner before we headed back. Tom Johnson, who had signed an option to buy the old Root Beer Barrel property.

We were right back to that lot. I didn't understand why. But I did know I wanted to talk to Joe. I was reaching for the phone when it rang.

"TenHuis Chocolade."

"Lee? It's Joe."

"I was just going to call you."

"What about?"

"The chief was in asking who I'd told we were going to Grand Rapids. I hadn't told anybody. But someone knew we were there."

"Yeah. Tom Johnson."

"Did you tell the chief that?"

"No. I admit I didn't think of him at all until a few minutes ago. When Tom called me."

"He called! What did he want?"

"He wants to finalize the deal on the Root Beer Barrel property next week."

"Whoops! I guess your suspicions were wrong, Joe. I guess ol' Tom really does want to buy the property."

"Ol' Tom or his pal, whoever that is."

"You still think he's acting for someone else?"

"Oh, yeah. But I guess that's not my concern. I'm getting the money I wanted for it. I haven't had a chance to check with the other property owners along there, to see if they've had offers."

"You could still back out."

"I'd owe him some interest on his earnest money, but I guess Clem's estate could find the bucks somewhere. I'll ask around before we close the deal. And I know a few guys in Grand Rapids. I'll try to find out if he has any connection with some other developer."

"I was wondering if he had any connection with somebody who owns a black panel truck."

"I'll leave that one up to Chief Jones. But I'd sure hate to queer the sale of that property merely because of my suspicious nature. And speaking of that property—how'd you like to go by there tonight? After you get off work."

"I won't be off until nine-thirty or ten."

"I know. The moon is just visible over the trees now. Nine-thirty or ten ought to be a good time for a boat ride."

"Well . . ."

"And the lake's supposed to be calm. Wind five miles per hour from the southwest."

I laughed. "In that case, I'll meet you at the dock."

Joe had known the prospect of a calm lake would be the final enticement. I love being out on Lake Michigan—particularly in the moonlight—but rough water gives my tummy trouble. A moonlight cruise isn't romantic if one party is leaning over the side of the boat. It's lucky Joe's love of boats emphasizes working on them and admiring them. If he wanted to go places in them all the time, he'd ditch me and my queasy innards in a hurry.

Anyway, I called home and warned Aunt Nettie that I'd be late. Joe appeared at the door of TenHuis Chocolade at 9:31 p.m. He swept the floor while I balanced the cash register and Tracy and Stacy alternately giggled and cleaned the counter and the showcases. I got my jacket and scarf out of the van, and we were all out of the shop by 9:50 p.m.

The temperature was brisk—mid-50s. But Joe was right about the moon; it was full and gorgeous. He had brought the Shepherd Sedan, and the motor gurgled soothingly as we puttered down the river channel through the no-wake zone that led clear out to the lake. The motor meant there was no conversation, but what did we need to say? We were alone. Everything was beautiful, and I don't mean just the moonlight, the lights of the houses and businesses along the shore, the ranks of boats in the marinas. Then we passed the jetty that protected the river channel as it emptied into the lake, and the water unfolded before us, stretching to the horizon to the south, to the north, and to the west. The moon had moved into the western sky, and its reflection created a path to infinity. I felt as if we could turn the boat onto that path and follow it right up into the stratosphere. We did not need a rocket ship; we had the Shepherd Sedan.

Joe didn't turn into the moon's path, of course. He turned right, swinging out beyond the sand bar that parallels the shore, and we headed north, about a quarter of a mile offshore. We passed Warner Point and the elegant mansion which was giving Joe such fits as he tried to settle his ex-wife's estate. Neither of us even pointed at it. Then we saw the trees and the houses along North Lake Shore Drive, with rolling, tree-covered dunes behind them. In the moonlight, the private stairways leading down to the beach were clearly visible, as was the one block of condominiums that had been built on the lakeshore. Far ahead, miles away, we could see the warning beacon from the lighthouse at Holland. It was all like a dream, and we both were in a sort of reverie as the boat gurgled along in the brilliant moonlight.

We weren't completely alone out there. There were other boats. Most of them were farther out. Many were big—some people would be sleeping out there, others would be fishing, there might be a party going on aboard one of the yachts. But none of them was close to us; no one seemed to be interested in us as we moved up the lake.

After the block of condominiums, the shoreline was marked by a section of trees. When we were opposite that spot, Joe cut the engine. His required running lights and his anchor lights were on, but the brilliant moonlight almost hid them. The boat swayed gently. Calm is a relative term when it comes to a giant body of water like Lake Michigan. The lake isn't like an ocean, but it's never really still. Warm water was rippling gently up from Chicago, a hundred miles away.

I gave a huge sigh. "If you could bottle the peace and quiet out here and sell it, we could retire tomorrow."

Joe chuckled. "And people think I was stupid to quit practicing law so I could fool around with boats." He pointed at the shore. "Can you see the Root Beer Barrel site?"

"What is there to see, now that it's collapsed?"

"I always find it by the old DeBoer house."

"I can't see a thing."

"Here." Joe took my hand and pulled me to my feet. We went to the back of the boat, out from under the sedan's roof. He put his arm around me, took my right hand in his and used my finger to point toward the shore. "Now do you see it?"

"Yes. If it's that tall sucker with all the turrets."

"Right. It's a huge place. Three stories high, plus attics. After that section of Lake Shore Drive went commercial—back in the 30s, I guess—they tried every kind of business in that house. Boarding house, tourist home, restaurant. The ambulance service was there for a while. It's been empty for ten years now, and it's in bad shape."

"But still on the historic list."

"All of Warner Pier is a historic district, remember."

I nodded. "I'd never even noticed the—what did you call it?"

"The DeBoer house. No relation to the diamond people. The house sits to the north of the Root Beer Barrel property, but it's back from the street and those trees you dislike so much hide it. You can't see anything of it except the roof, and you can only see that from the water." He swung my pointing finger to the south. "On the right-hand side of the Barrel is the Old English Motel."

"That I've noticed. In fact, it always seems familiar to me."

"I think there were a lot of motels built on that pattern at one time, fake English cottages, tiny motel rooms with pointed tile roofs. You've probably seen one somewhere else."

"I guess that's it. There's one very similar to it in my home town."

"Dallas?"

"My real home town. Prairie Creek, Texas. Home to cowboys for 150 years."

"You gotta take me down there some day."

I turned around and put my arms around Joe. He put his arms around me. The moment became quite romantic.

Until the spotlight hit us.

We jumped apart. The boat rocked madly, and I grabbed the roof to keep my balance.

"Dadgum!" I said. "Is one of those boats court-busting?"

"Court-busting? What's that?"

"That's what my dad calls driving up and down country roads shining a bright light into parked cars."

"I don't think that's what these people have in mind," Joe said. "They're coming right at us."

The light was growing closer, and the boat's motor was getting louder. I had the impression that it was a big boat, too, at least twice as long as the sedan. I couldn't see clearly because of the light.

I realized Joe had ducked back under the sedan's roof and slid behind the wheel. He looked back at me and yelled. "Get down!"

I ducked back under the roof and into the seat on the passenger's side. The sedan's motor burbled into life, and we began to move forward. I was dying to ask Joe if he thought we were about to be boarded by pirates, but I couldn't. The boat was too noisy. But the situation seemed ridiculous.

Joe gunned the motor, and we jumped forward. The sedan isn't the fastest boat on the lake, but it can move pretty well. And Joe moved it. We headed up the lake, parallel to the shore, at top speed.

Joe used his thumb to gesture over his shoulder. I deduced that he wanted me to keep an eye on the bigger boat.

It was easy to see. It had that spotlight aimed right at us. And the spotlight kept coming closer. It was following us.

Chapter 17

"Closer! It's closer!" I screamed the words, but I knew Joe couldn't hear me.

He seemed to understand. At least he began what I would consider evasive action. He cut the sedan's lights, all of them, even the safety lights. He swung hard left. The searchlight lost us, then found us again. He swung right. The same thing happened. The light lost us, then found us again. Then Joe repeated the maneuver—left out of the spotlight, then—after it focused on us again—right, into the dark.

All the time he was doing this, the big boat was getting closer. The sedan is a great boat, but it isn't particularly fast. I knew that eventually the larger, more powerful boat would be able to catch us. Dodging in and out of its searchlight wasn't going to be a useful escape technique in the end.

And it could well be the end. If the bigger boat hit us—I pushed the mental picture of flying debris and flying bodies out of my mind.

I crawled back to the rear seating area and lifted the seat, revealing the hatch where the life jackets were stored. Right at the moment, a life jacket seemed like a really good idea.

The boat swerved again, and I was thrown sideways. But this time Joe didn't straighten out. We kept traveling in a circle. Centrifugal force almost glued me where I'd landed, against the side of the boat. But we were out of that damn searchlight.

I struggled to get up, at least to my knees, and I finally made it. The sedan was bouncing over the waves—I was just grateful that they weren't very big waves. I looked up and saw the bigger boat going by—I could see oblong portholes, chrome railings, and a big area of smooth and shiny white fiberglass.

The sedan straightened out then, and I looked around Joe to see where we were going. There was nothing but lake ahead; the big boat was behind us. Joe had made a U-turn, and we were headed in the opposite direction, south instead of north, toward the Warner Pier channel.

I allowed myself to hope that we'd make it.

But the big boat was turning, too. Already it was broadside to us. As I realized that, Joe suddenly cut the sedan's speed drastically. The boat settled back in the water like a duck landing on a pond, and we were moving at no-wake zone speed.

"What are you doing?" I yelled. "We were getting away."

Now Joe turned the boat again, heading it directly toward the shore, which was about a quarter of a mile away. He inched along, the motor gurgling gently.

I put my lips close to his ear. "What are you doing?"

"Trying to hit the channel!"

I looked ahead. The only channel I knew of was the channel of the Warner River, the channel we'd come out of. It was marked with lights. I could see it—still far south of us.

I stayed on my knees. Maybe prayer would help. I sure didn't understand what Joe was doing.

But I understood what the big boat was doing. It was turning in circles, casting its searchlight all around, trying to find us. When it did, it was going to come at us like gangbusters. And instead of racing down the lake while we had the chance, we were moseying along. A kid with an inflated sea serpent and a good flutter kick could have passed us.

Just then the sedan shuddered, and Joe threw the motor into reverse. We inched backward. Then he changed gears again and we inched forward. We moved a few feet, then the boat shuddered again. Joe threw the motor into reverse again. We inched backward, but this time the boat shuddered and stopped moving almost immediately.

Joe turned the motor off. He turned sideways in his seat and began to pull his shoes off.

"We're aground," he said. "Shuck your shoes and your jacket. And those slacks. We're gonna have to swim for it."

"Swim! He'll run us down in the water!"

"We'll be inside the sandbar, and he'll be outside. I think it's our best chance."

I reached for the locker that held the lifejackets.

"Wed better leave the life jackets," Joe said. "Or better still . . ."

He snatched two life jackets from me, stood up, and hurled them out into the lake, away from the shore.

"Maybe those'll distract him for a minute. And if he does know how to get around the sandbar—and there is a way—they'd make us too easy to spot." He planted a quick kiss on the top of my head. "I think I remember enough about being a lifeguard that I can get us ashore."

"I can swim," I said.

"That'll be a help."

I pulled my jacket off. Then I yanked off my tennis shoes without untying the laces. I looked up to see a pair of blue boxer shorts in my face—Joe and I were undressing in close quarters and he'd just dropped his jeans.

"Keep that scarf on," Joe said. "That blond hair would be easy to spot in the water."

"I'm keeping my shirt, too. If I drown, I don't want my body to be found in nothing but a padded bra."

Joe was climbing over the side by that time, and he just stood there, with his head and shoulders visible. I peeled my khaki slacks down. "Is it that shallow?"

"We're on the sandbar. Come on!"

Right at that moment the search light hit the water about thirty feet from us, and if I had any tendency to hesitate, I lost it. I tumbled over the side like a skin diver, with my slacks still around my ankles.

The west Michigan theory is that a southwest wind brings warm but dirty water to the beaches. A north wind brings cold but clean water. Or so swimmers are told. After that night, I'll never believe that again. The wind and waves might have been moving in from the southwest, but the water was so cold that Lake Michigan might as well have been the Antarctic Ocean. My tumble over the side paralyzed me.

Joe grabbed me and got me to my feet. I gasped and regained the ability to move. We both ducked down behind the boat. I finished stepping out of my slacks.

"Ready?" Joe said.

The searchlight's beam bounced off the boat. "Ready," I said. I took a deep breath, did a surface dive, and pulled hard in the direction of the shore.

I came up about twenty-five feet away. Now my feet couldn't touch the bottom.

"Lee! Lee!" Joe's voice sounded frantic.

"Come on!" I said. "I'm heading for shore!"

I struck off, using the breast stroke with some idea of not splashing. Joe caught up with me shortly. "You said you could swim," he said. "You didn't mention diving."

After that we didn't talk a lot. We stayed close together, and once Joe suggested that I stop and float for a minute. I must have been panting. He was panting, I remember that. He turned onto his back and pulled me over, so that I was lying on my back on top of him. We both concentrated on floating and breathing easily for a few minutes. Funny how hard something like breathing can get. Swimming may be like riding a bicycle, in the sense that you never forget how, but I was way out of condition. And a quarter of a mile is several laps of an Olympic-sized pool.

About half the time we were swimming that big boat was circling around behind us, but it didn't move closer to shore, so I thought it was staying out beyond the sandbar. Once the searchlight cut the water quite close to us, and light seemed to be headed in our direction.

"Sink," Joe said.

I held my nose and sank. I stayed under as long as my lungs held out, and when I popped to the surface again the light was nowhere to be seen.

I'd stopped looking toward the shore because it seemed so far away. But finally I peeked, and this time the tree line was looming almost over my head. I put my feet down and felt the rounded stones of Lake Michigan.

"Maybe I'll walk the rest of the way," I said.

"It's gonna be mighty cold when we get out," Joe said.

The water was up to my armpits. We waded across ten feet of stones, then sand began. We came out of the water on a narrow beach about thirty feet from a creek. Trees grew up the bank, which towered above us. I would have sunk down and rested, but Joe yanked me along, toward a set of stairs that led up the bank.

"I don't want to stop while we're in the moonlight," he said. "Besides, we're going to get even colder when we quit moving."

I knew he was right, though I was about played out. We kept going, across the beach and up the stairway. When we got to the top, I did stop.

"Joe! This is somebody's backyard."

"Right. Maybe they left a beach towel on the porch."

"Maybe they'll call Aunt Nettie to come and get us."

Joe nodded.

But the house was dark, and there was no beach towel on the porch.

My teeth were chattering. "Sh-sh-should we b-b-break in?"

"I'm not sure I can manage to burgle a house barefoot and in my skivvies. Let's go around in front, see if we can spot a light somewhere. We may even know somebody in this neighborhood. Once we figure out where we are."

I checked my watch and discovered it was still running. "You'd think some of these people would want to stay up to watch the eleven o'clock news," I said. "There ought to be a light someplace."

We made our way around the house—trampling a flower bed in the process—and found ourselves out on what had to be Lake Shore Drive. Suddenly I recognized a landmark. "Joe! That big tree! The one almost out in the middle of the road. I know that tree!"

"Yeah. We're at the back of Clem's place."

"I don't suppose there's a security guard there."

"No, but I can get in."

Hand in hand, almost naked, soaking wet, and shivering in the fifty-degree temperature, we headed toward the Ripley place, the one that was giving Joe such fits as he tried to settle Clementine Ripley's estate. I'd become acutely aware that my wet T-shirt didn't cover my underwear. I wasn't willing for everybody in Warner Pier to be sure I was a natural blond, so I wrapped my scarf around my waist like a pareo, and it clung to me like a sheet of ice. But the hardest part of the deal was my feet. I kept stumbling over rocks, and I'll swear there was more gravel than blacktop on that road.

"I think I'm leaving bloody footprints," I said.

"Just keep leaving them."

We persevered, though I cast longing glances as we passed a couple of houses with lights. But Joe seemed eager for us to reach the Ripley place before we asked for help. After about five minutes of pussyfooting down the road we came to the big gate that marked the entrance to the estate.

Joe went to the key pad next to the gate. I shivered and my teeth chattered. Down the road, I saw lights reflected off the trees.

"Here comes a car," I said. "Maybe they'll help us." I stepped toward the street.

Joe grabbed my arm and pulled me back into the bushes. "Let's make sure they're not looking for us," he said.

We waited until the car had gone slowly by. I hated to see it go; it had represented help. I sighed. "I guess I probably wouldn't stop if I were driving down a lonely street and a couple of naked people jumped out of the bushes at me."

Joe didn't answer. He just pushed buttons on the key pad, and the gate to the Ripley estate slid open. Then we had another long walk up a blacktop driveway. This one was completely shaded by trees, so we had only intermittent patches of moonlight to see by. Gravel had been scattered on it, too, and had landed in the most unlikely places. My feet hurt so bad I almost forgot how cold I was.

We had to go clear around the house to reach the key pad that opened the back door. Once we were inside Joe hit the light switch, and I saw that we were in the back hall, with the kitchen beyond.

"Whew!" I found a kitchen stool, sat on it and rubbed my feet. Joe went straight to the telephone. He found the directory on a shelf under the phone, searched for a number and punched it in. "Mike? Is Mom there? It's important."

A pause. "Hi, Mom. Lee and I were out in the sedan, and we had a little excitement. We wound up having to abandon ship and swim ashore."

I heard squawking noises from the telephone.

"We're okay! We're okay! Lee's a good swimmer." Joe turned and grinned at me. "We came ashore not far from Clem's place, so we came in there. But we need clothes and shoes. Can you get something from my place and bring it out here? There's a key behind the downspout."

More squawking. Then Joe looked at me. "What size shoe do you wear?"

"Nobody's feet are as big as mine. Tell her not to worry about shoes. My feet are beyond help already."

Joe repeated what I'd said. "But hurry, Mom. Okay? I left the sedan aground, and I want to go get it."

Joe hung up, then immediately looked for another number. "Harry? Hope I didn't get you up."

I realized he was calling Harry Barnes. Harry ran a marina in Warner Pier.

Joe quickly sketched our problem—but I noticed he hadn't told either his mother or Harry how we got in this fix.

"I left the Shepherd Sedan aground," Joe said. "I want to get it off quick."

He listened, then spoke. "I was trying to hit the little channel that runs out from North Creek. But it's too narrow this year."

He paused. "Harry, you can laugh all you want later. Right now I need two favors."

Harry's voice echoed on the phone. "Yeah, yeah. I'll tell you about it later. But I need you to give me a tow. And on your way, see if that Tiara 5200 of Jack Sheldon's is docked."

He was silent. "Just see if it's in its slot! I'll meet you at the Ripley boathouse, okay?"

He hung up.

"Joe, I hadn't thought about the sedan. I do hope it's not damaged."

"It's not as likely to be damaged as it would have been if we hadn't abandoned ship." He put his arms around me. "You're not damaged. That's the main thing."

We hugged each other, but it didn't help us warm up much. Joe said the heating system had been turned off, but he found an electric heater in the pantry and plugged it in. I looked through the kitchen drawers, and all I found were some dishtowels. Joe draped one around his fanny like a sarong, and it hit me that he was feeling as naked as I was. Wet boxers are pretty revealing.

One other thing had me puzzled. "Joe," I said, "I assume you think that this boat you mentioned is the one that chased us."

"I'm not sure. It looked like a Tiara 5200, and Sheldon's the only guy who docks a boat like that in Warner Pier. It could have come up from Saugatuck or down from Holland."

"Or South Haven or Chicago or Onekama or Milwaukee or Sheboygan. But you didn't tell either your mom or Harry that it chased us."

Joe frowned. "I don't want to get held up making statements. I want to look at Sheldon's Tiara and get the sedan off the sand bar. Then I'll tell Hogan Jones what happened."

We were just beginning to get warm when a buzzer rang.

"That'll be Mom," Joe said.

He went to a control panel and spoke into it. "Yes?"

"Let us in." It was Mike Hererra's voice.

"Come around to the kitchen." Joe punched a button.

"I guess I should have known Mike would come with her," I said.

When Mike's car came around the side of the house a second car followed. And this one had lights on top.

"Damn," Joe muttered. "The chief's with them, too."

Mercy jumped right out and ran to Joe, making mother noises. Joe assured her he was all right, but his eyes didn't leave the chief's car.

Chief Jones unfolded himself and got out of his car, then walked over to us. He shook his head slowly, almost sorrowfully. "Well, Joe," he said, "I never had a heck of a lot of success with women back in my young days, but I will say I never had to run a boat aground to get one to go skinny-dipping with me."

Chapter 18

Joe's prediction came true, of course. The chief wanted to hear the whole story. Harry's boat was honking down at the Ripley place's boathouse and Joe was still wrapped in a dishtowel and arguing with the chief.

"Joe!" I said finally. "Take the chief with you!"

My suggestion apparently had merit, because the two of them ran off toward the boat. Joe carried an armful of clothes, and he had stuffed his feet into a pair of sneakers. He looked so weird that Mercy, Mike, and I stood there and laughed until after he and the chief were out of sight.

Mercy had brought me some sweatpants and a sweatshirt of Joe's. Plus, bless her heart, a pair of his white socks and some sandals.

"Not very glamorous," she said, "but they'll get you home without freezing. I didn't want to take time to go by my place and try to figure out something better."

"They look gorgeous," I said. "I doubt you own anything that would reach past my knees. Not being able to borrow clothes is one of the problems of being nearly six feet tall. On the other hand, none of my high school friends ever wanted to bolster—I mean, borrow!—they never wanted to borrow my clothes."

Mercy turned her back and spoke very casually. "I looked for some underwear for you, but I couldn't find anything."

Gee. Even my boyfriend's mother thought I might be keeping clothes at his place. I answered in what I hoped was the same casual tone. "My underpants are nearly dry, and with this sweatshirt I can go braless."

I put on the sweatpants and shirt in the powder room off the back hall. When I came out Mercy made some efforts at asking me just what had happened, and I told her, in a general way. I didn't understand everything, of course. I wouldn't have recognized the boat that chased us, for example. I could only describe it as having one of those chrome railings all around the front, the kind that look as if they're designed for people to walk around on the prow when the boat is traveling a hundred miles an hour.

"Tall," I said. "It loomed up over us. And fast. A lot faster than the sedan."

I guess I shuddered, because Mike Herrera gave me a one-armed hug. "Mercy," he said. "Let's get this young lady home."

They took me back to TenHuis Chocolade, where I picked up my van, and for the second night in a row, I was followed home by someone worried about my safety. Mike and Mercy even insisted on coming inside to make sure no one was lying in wait for me. Naturally, Aunt Nettie heard our whispers and got up, so Mike wound up searching the entire house before we could persuade him to leave. He even called the police dispatcher and, using his authority as mayor, directed her to have the patrol officer on duty drive by the house periodically. He seemed a little let down to learn that Chief Jones had already given that instruction.

He did pick up one piece of information. Jack Sheldon's Tiara 5200 had been found tied up at one of the public docks in the Dock Street Park. The night patrol officer had gotten Sheldon out of bed, and Sheldon had denied having the boat out that evening. He also admitted he kept a key to the boat on a nail in his garage. When he checked, the key was gone.

Oddly enough, Sheldon lived across the street from Frank and Patsy Waterloo. Hmmm. I wondered if that was significant, or simply another of the interconnecting circles of small town life.

Aunt Nettie was twittering, but I was so tired I couldn't make sense of what she was twittering about. I crawled up to bed and slept until eleven a.m. There's nothing like vigorous exercise to ensure a good night's sleep.

I woke up sore in every muscle—another effect of vigorous exercise. I lay in my bed, a mahogany number once occupied by my grandparents, and stared at the ceiling. As soon as I remembered the reason I hurt all over, I began to try to figure out why I'd been forced to go swimming in a cold lake and to walk down gravel-strewn roads in even colder night air, barefoot and in my underwear.

Someone had chased Joe and me in a boat—much the same way they had chased us in a truck the night before. Who? Why?

It kept coming back to the Root Beer Barrel property. Hershel had argued with Joe about it, had become so angry he actually tried to hit Joe. The next thing we knew, Hershel was dead, and somebody was trying to make it look as if Joe had killed him.

But there were intermediate steps. First, we still didn't know who the guy in the black panel truck was, and we didn't know how he had found out we were on the road back from Grand Rapids so that he could lie in wait for us. I resolved to ask the chief if he'd been able to find out if Tom Johnson had phoned anybody in Warner Pier after we left him Wednesday night.

Second, how had the creep in the boat known we were going to be out on the lake?

Now, that was a real stumper. He could have followed us, but it didn't seem likely. Following people is not all that easy in a town the size of Warner Pier—especially around Joe's shop, which was almost in a rural area. A tail would be hard to miss. He would have had to hide some place, see Joe leave in the sedan, guess that he was picking me up, steal the Sheldons' key, steal the Sheldons' boat, and beat us out into the lake.

It would have been a lot easier if he'd known where we were going and waited for us. But we'd only decided to go an hour before we left. I hadn't told anybody where we were going, and I was sure Joe hadn't either. We'd made all our plans on the telephone.

I sat up, even if it did hurt. Well, duh! The answer was as plain as a Hershey bar without almonds. Joe's phone was tapped.

I tried to jump out of bed, and every muscle rebelled. This made me slow down in my rush for the telephone, and I realized I couldn't call Joe to tell him his phone was tapped. In fact, it might be that my phone was tapped, too, so I didn't want to try his cell phone. I threw on some clothes—my own, not Joe's—and headed for the boat shop.

I was let down to see the Michigan State Police mobile crime lab van outside.

I jumped out of my van and limped into the shop. Joe met me at the office door. "Have they found the bug?" I said.

He nodded. "You figured that out, huh? Have you figured out who put it there?"

"No. Have you?"

"Nope."

"There's no way to tell by looking?"

"Today's taps don't have to use wires. They have little transmitters. You can order them on the Internet. Guy wants to check on his tap, he parks a mile away and dials it up."

"Anyway, that tap absolutely proves that somebody's been trying to frame you. Though I don't understand why he also cut the phone line."

"All I can figure out is that he wanted me to be unreachable at that specific time. So he cut the line. But once the line was repaired, he wanted to listen in."

"And then he tried to kill you."

"I'm not so sure about that, Lee. Seems as if every time somebody tries to hurt me, you're along."

I stared. "That's silly! No one would want to kill me."

"Why would they want to kill me?"

"I don't have a specific reason, but it's got to be something to do with the old Root Beer Barrel. Mixed in with hate. Malice. Envy. Avarice. One of those seven deadly sin deals."

"Why would none of those apply to you?"

I found a chair and sat down. "I'm just too darn lovable, I guess." Then I looked up at Joe. "I don't think I'm important enough for anybody to dislike that much. But I don't see why anybody would dislike you either."

Joe pulled up a second office chair and sat down beside me. He took my hand. "You are darn lovable, Lee. And you try to get along with people. I don't see why anybody would want to kill you. But all this has got to link up with Hershel's death. Is there anything you haven't told the chief about what Hershel said? When he came up to the truck?"

"No! The chief asked me about that in detail yesterday, and I went over the whole conversation. I did not hold back a thing. Besides, no one else was there to hear what Hershel had to say. If he told me who killed him—right out loud—what's the difference? The murderer has no way of knowing. Unless your pickup is bugged."

We sighed and stared for at least a full minute. Then Joe spoke. "I'm sure of one thing. The guy is working alone."

"Why?" I said.

"Because if there'd been two people in Sheldon's boat last night, we wouldn't be here now. If there'd been one guy to operate the light, and a second one to handle the boat—well, we'd never have been able to get away. They would have run us down."

That vision of shattered mahogany planks flying through the air—and Joe and me flying with them—bounced through my mind. I resolutely shoved it back into my subconscious. "He—or she—may also have been operating an unfamiliar boat," I said, "since it was stolen."

Joe nodded. "In fact, I don't think he—or she—was used to a boat that size at all. Something about the way it swerved. But I can tell you another thing. Whoever chased us gets around Warner Pier a lot."

"Why do you say that?"

"He—or she—knew about the old chapel and that Hershel hung out there. He—or she—knew where to get the keys to Sheldon's boat. He—or she—knew how to disappear down Haven Road. He knew where to find a black panel truck."

"You don't think the guy owns a black panel truck?"

Joe shook his head. "No. This baby is too smart to use his own boat or his own vehicle when he's up to no good."

"It's got to be somebody close to Hershel, Joe."

We both thought. I spoke first. "My money's on Frank."

"Why?"

I sketched what I'd learned from Barbara and from Greg Glossop.

"Hardly conclusive," Joe said. "And Frank hasn't lived in Warner Pier very long."

"Five years!"

"Has it been that long?"

"Long enough for a lot of Sunday drives. He's a neighbor to the Sheldons. And he and Patsy are sure better off without Hershel."

"To an outsider it seems that way. But Patsy doesn't seem to think so. Speaking of the Waterloos—are you going to the funeral?"

"When is it?"

"This afternoon. I guess I'd better stay away. The chief thinks Patsy might hit me with a spray of chrysanthemums."

"I'll check with Aunt Nettie and find out the proper Warner Pier etiquette."

I reached for Joe's phone, but he pushed my hand aside. "Use my cell phone."

I could feel my eyes getting round. "Is the phone still bugged?"

"The chief is considering leaving it that way. So don't say anything about it, okay?"

I didn't have time to think about that. I called Aunt Nettie and was instructed to be ready for Hershel Perkins' funeral at one p.m. "Your light blue dress will be fine," she said. "Or something similar."

"I remember," I said. "Don't wear more black than the widow. In this case, the sister."

I hung up. "Gotta go. My hair's still full of Lake Michigan ick." I started for the door, then turned back. "I didn't ask about the sedan. Was it damaged?"

"No. Harry and I got it off the sandbar before the waves pushed it around enough to do any damage. Oh, I've got your clothes." Joe brought a bundle out of his room. "At least, here are your shoes and your jacket."

"I guess we can write off my socks and khakis. Darn it! Those pants were new."

Joe looked stricken. "I'll walk that stretch of beach. Maybe they'll wash ashore."

"Never mind. I'm not sure I'd want to wear them again."

By one o'clock I had clean hair and was wearing a longish black and white print skirt, a short-sleeved white cotton sweater, and flat-heeled black pumps. Patsy and Frank had decided on a graveside service for Hershel. About twenty-five people gathered in the Warner Pier Cemetery—I recognized the corps of high school teachers, plus some people Aunt Nettie said lived up Inland Road near the Waterloos. Then there were those of us somehow connected with the investigation into Hershel's death—Trey, Meg, Aunt Nettie, me, and Chief Jones.

Trey, like the other men, wore Warner Pier dress-up—khakis and a sports shirt—but Meg hadn't followed the "less black than the widow" rule. She had on a sleeveless black linen dress and was wearing a short strand of what I was sure were real pearls. There were no chairs, and she kept shifting from foot to foot. I guessed she was trying to keep her high heels from sinking into the turf and thanked my lucky stars I'd thought to wear flats.

Patsy was in navy blue and had regained her composure since the afternoon she'd almost accused Joe of murdering her brother. The minister was mercifully generic, relying on Bible verses and standard platitudes. Which is sad in itself—I mean, when no one can dredge up any happy memories of the deceased, it's a sign of a wasted life.

Afterward, we shook hands and murmured at Patsy and Frank and a cousin who had materialized from Kalamazoo for the occasion. Then Aunt Nettie and I started for her car. We were nearly there when I heard rapid footsteps behind us. Trey called out, "Lee!"

I turned to see both Trey and Meg approaching. Meg bore down on Aunt Nettie, neatly cutting her off, and Trey took me aside. "Were you serious about seeing Gray Gables?"

"I'd love to, Trey."

"It looks as if tonight would be a good time for a tour."

"Tonight?"

"I know that's pretty short notice. But my cousins are the actual owners, you know. They'll be coming this weekend and may stay the rest of the summer."

"Trey, I can see it another time. Next fall, next year."

"No, I have to be over there tonight anyway. I want to change the lock on the kitchen door. I'd be delighted to show you and Joe around." He leaned closer. "Please don't tell anyone. My cousins don't mind me showing people like you through, but they don't want—you know, public tours."

"Fine. As soon as I get back to the shop I'll call Joe and see if he can come."

"Just leave a message on my answering machine."

I told Trey nine-thirty was the earliest time I'd be able to take a tour, and I caught up with Meg and Aunt Nettie. Meg was talking hard about the Junior League of Grand Rapids, a topic which I knew did not interest Aunt Nettie in the slightest. Unless the group voted to buy chocolate.

Meg then began to ask me about the chase on the lake; apparently word was getting around town. Aunt Nettie and I extricated ourselves as quickly as possible. I again told Trey I'd call him, then we went back to the office. As soon as I was there, I went to the phone to call Joe to pass on Trey's invitation.

But Stacy headed me off. "Joe called," she said. She looked at a note she was holding. "He said he would be tied up all afternoon and evening. He said to tell you . . ." She referred to her note. "He said, 'Tell her not to do anything risky. Tell her to keep safe.' " She looked up. "What did he mean?"

I tried to smile. "I expect he wants me to stay home, to avoid highways and lakes," I said.

"Will you do what he says?"

I could tell my reputation as a feminist was on the line. "It seems to be a reasonable request," I said, "considering the events of the past two evenings. Besides, I don't really have any particular place to go. I won't let his instructions keep me from anything I think is important."

We left it at that. I called Trey and left a message that Joe and I could not make a tour of Gray Gables that evening. I stayed in the office until nearly seven p.m.

Then I took my dinner break and went out and solved Hershel Perkins' murder.

CHOCOLATE CHAT
CHOCOLATE AND POLITICS

- Coffee, tea, and chocolate arrived in England at almost the same time, the mid-seventeenth century. Chocolate was advertised in a British newspaper as early as 1657.

- In Spain and France, chocolate had been a drink of the aristocracy, but in England it was offered to the public—along with coffee and tea—at a new institution, the coffeehouse.

- Coffee was the cheapest of the three new beverages. Chocolate cost a bit more, and tea was most expensive of all.

- The famous diarist Samuel Pepys (1633–1703) often recorded drinking chocolate, apparently at coffeehouses. This reflects the life of London at the time; coffeehouses were centers of discussion. Consequently they were also focal points for development of a new social institution—the political party. This made King Charles II uneasy, and in 1675 he ordered the coffeehouses closed. Public outcry kept the order from ever going into force.

- In line with the democratization of chocolate drinking, the English developed quicker, easier ways of preparing it. Most chocolate in seventeenth century Europe was prepared from powdered cakes. But it still had to be stirred all the time to keep it from separating. The French invented a special pot with a hole in the lid to make this easy.

Chapter 19

I didn't solve the murder on purpose. It was an accidental process that began when I stood up and realized my pantyhose were drooping.

The sagging pantyhose were uncomfortable, of course, and that discomfort made me aware that I wasn't wearing one of my five pairs of comfy khaki slacks, and being aware that I wasn't wearing one of them reminded me that the newest pair had sunk in Lake Michigan the previous evening. Then I remembered that Joe had mentioned walking up and down the beach over by the old Root Beer Barrel to see if the slacks had washed ashore.

Joe had apparently not been able to do that. But, I decided, I could. Even though the chance of the slacks washing ashore was remote.

Walking up and down the beach was not at all risky, I assured myself. I could park at the Root Beer Barrel site, cross Lake Shore Drive, climb down the bank, and walk up and down the Lake Michigan beach as far as I wanted to. Or as far as I had time to, because I needed to get back to the shop and be there until closing time.

So, shortly before seven o'clock, the time Tracy was due back from her break, I phoned Mike's Sidewalk Café and ordered a sandwich to go. I put on the jacket I keep in the office. I found a pair of flip-flop rubber sandals in the van, then slipped out of my pumps and droopy pantyhose. I even grabbed a garbage bag big enough to hold the slacks. I was thinking positively. I might actually find them.

I picked up the sandwich—roast beef on rye with a side of slaw—and drove over to the former location of the Root Beer Barrel. This would be a private beach picnic. Quite a nice dinner break, whether I found the slacks or not.

There were no handy-dandy stairs leading down to the beach opposite the Root Beer Barrel property. But I located a path—fairly well-used—and slipped and slid thirty or forty feet down the sandy hill to the beach without getting my long black and white skirt too dirty or getting sand in my sandwich. I even found a big log that had drifted ashore and made a lovely spot to sit and eat my dinner. The wind had changed, and now the waves were coming from the northwest—just the opposite of the direction they'd been coming the night before. That was good; it meant that if the slacks washed up the beach, they might then have washed back down and stayed more or less even with the location where I'd lost them. Unless they'd sunk permanently in thirty feet of water.

I finished my sandwich, stuffed the trash in the sack the food had come in, tucked it into my big garbage bag, then walked down the beach. A walk on the beach is always a wonderful experience. The sun wasn't yet low enough to blind me if I looked out at the lake, and I strolled along, stepping over the stones and through the beach grass, shaking the sand out of my sandals now and then, keeping an eye on the time, and looking for those slacks.

I admit I was surprised when I found them.

By rights they should have been at the bottom of the lake, but there they were—caught on a piece of driftwood and wafting back and forth in the waves. When I tried to pick them up, however, I nearly decided to leave them there. They were heavy with water, and I wasn't dressed to wring them out. But I wrestled them into the garbage bag and started lugging the sack back up the beach.

I dreaded the climb back up the sand dunes. That's when it was going to be hard to keep my skirt clean. I guess that's why I eyed the stairways which led up to the cottages along the lake.

Not all lakeshore cottages have stairways down to the beach. For people who can afford them, they're a very nice amenity. But they're privately owned. The beaches are public, but property owners have a right to get snotty if strangers walk up their stairs the way Joe and I had the night before. The strangers wind up, as we had, in somebody's back yard. That's trespassing. So I kept looking at the stairs, but I didn't go up any of them.

Then I recognized the stairs Joe and I had used the night before. They had a deck about halfway up that was quite distinctive. A white-haired woman dressed in white shorts and a blue T-shirt was just coming down the stairs.

I stopped and called out to her. "Hello! Are you the lady of the house?"

She nodded, narrowing her eyes slightly.

"I owe you an apology," I said. "We got a boat aground last night, out on the sand bar, and we had to swim ashore. We used your stairs to get up to the road, and I'm afraid we trampled through your flowers."

"Oh!" The woman came a few steps down. "Thanks for telling me. We thought we'd had window peepers."

"No, we didn't peep. We were mighty cold, so we did knock at the door on your deck, but nobody answered."

"What time was this?"

"Sometime after ten."

"We went to Holland to the late movie. I'm sorry we weren't here to answer the door. You must have been frozen."

"I'm sorry about the flowers." By now the woman was nearly to the bottom of the stairs, so we introduced ourselves. Her name was Carla Maples, and she said she and her husband had moved to the cottage "full-time" after he retired.

She smiled broadly when I told her I was business manager for TenHuis Chocolade. "I love that place! Especially those almond-flavored truffles. Amaretto."

" 'Milk chocolate interior coated in white chocolate.' I like those, too. And now I need to get back to work."

"Do you want to use the stairs again?"

"That would be a big help. I'm parked down by the old Root Beer Barrel property, and there aren't any stairs down there."

"It's a couple of blocks away, but we can see that area from our front yard," Mrs. Maples said. She led me up the stairs. I admired her flowers and her house and didn't say too much about why Joe and I had been swimming ashore, instead of waiting for someone to get us off the sandbar.

We skirted the house on stepping stones Joe and I had missed in the moonlight, then came out on Lake Shore Drive. Mrs. Maples gestured in the direction of the Root Beer Barrel in a genteel manner. "We used to be able to see the old Barrel through the trees in the winter. I was really surprised when it blew down."

A faint hope stirred. "You didn't see it happen, did you?"

"No. We were in Florida for the month of March, and it was gone when we got back. I've heard a rumor that the property may be redeveloped."

I decided I didn't have time to go into all the details. "I've heard that, too. I'm sure that all the neighbors around here would like to see something built there. The site is an eyesore as it is."

Mrs. Maples sighed. "It's not just that particular lot. It's that whole stretch. The old motel—that's almost overgrown now. And the DeBoer House. That's a beautiful structure, but you can't even see it now. It's too bad that something can't be done with it."

We shook hands and I made a mental note to write Mrs. Maples a thank-you note and to give her some chocolates. Then I walked on up the Lake Shore Drive toward my car. The episode didn't amount to much, but it was significant because it caused me to approach the Root Beer Barrel site from a different direction. I'd never come toward it from the south before.

I decided Stacy and Tracy could manage without me for another five minutes. I wanted to get a look at this DeBoer house everybody kept raving about.

It took me the whole five minutes to figure out how to approach it. There was a heavy bank of trees and shrubs between it and Joe's property, but I finally found a pathway from the main road, beat my way through—I should have been wearing jungle gear, not an ankle-length skirt and flip-flops—and came out of the bushes around thirty feet from a beautiful, broad veranda.

I stood there looking at that veranda, the graceful steps leading up to it, the picturesque turrets at the corners of the building. Then I swung back and peeked through the bushes in the direction of the Old English Motel. I couldn't see it because of the heavy undergrowth. But I knew it was there.

And I also knew who had killed Hershel, and I knew why.

"Oh, my stars!" I said. I turned and made what speed I could getting down that overgrown path back to the road. Then I tried to run for the van—not the easiest thing to do wearing flip-flops. I stumbled and slid, but I finally made it, dug my keys from my pocket, jumped in the van, and sped toward town.

My mind was racing madly. I had to tell Chief Jones. I had to tell Joe. I had to tell somebody.

I parked in the alley behind TenHuis Chocolade, unlocked the back door, and dashed in. Tracy and Stacy stared at me openmouthed as I rushed by them without speaking and snatched up the telephone. I hit the speed dial for Joe's number, then hung up. His phone was tapped, and he'd told me the chief wanted to leave it that way. I punched in his cell phone number. It rang and rang, then I got some electronic message box in some office someplace far away. I hung up on the electronic voice.

Chief Jones. That was the person I really needed. City Hall was closed, of course. I thumbed through the telephone book until I found his home number. But when I dialed it, he didn't answer either.

I did, however, leave a message on his answering machine. And it wasn't just "call me." I left the name of Hershel's murderer.

I wasn't through. I called the city hall number, using the trick Joe had used the night when we found Hershel's body. The answering machine picked up, and I yelled for the dispatcher. But nobody came to the phone.

Finally, I called 9-1-1 and identified myself. "It's imperative that I reach Chief Hogan Jones," I said.

"The Warner Pier police chief?"

"Yes."

"This is the Warner County Sheriff's office. The Warner Pier Police Station is not available. I can handle any emergency."

"No. I need Chief Jones."

"Chief Jones is not on duty."

"But this is about the murder of Hershel Perkins, and I must talk to him immediately."

"I don't believe he's available."

"I know you can page him. This is an emergency! Please."

"I'll try to reach him, but what sort of emergency do you have?"

I didn't answer. It was going to be terribly hard to explain.

She kept talking. "Fire? Accident? Crime? I need to know who to send."

I thought another minute, then spoke. "It's not that kind of an emergency. I'm sorry I bothered you."

I hung up. After all, what was my hurry? It wasn't as if the killer was likely to flee to Canada that night. I'd keep trying to reach Chief Jones, but the killer would still be in Warner Pier the next morning. After all, Hershel had been killed partly to protect the killer's place in the community—or so I thought. The killer wasn't going to throw it up now, not unless the killer learned that I'd tumbled to what happened.

At least, I'd believe that was the truth if I could find Joe. Where was he? Joe didn't know who the murderer was, and I believed he was meant to be a second victim. If nothing else, the killer's attempts to chase us down with a panel truck and with a stolen boat proved that.

Joe could be in deadly danger, and I didn't know how to warn him.

I halfheartedly tried to call Jerry Cherry, but I wasn't even surprised that he didn't answer his phone. Then I looked out at the shop. At least a dozen customers were standing in line. Tracy and Stacy needed a couple of extra hands. I didn't know what else to do, so I went out to help them.

As I served out Frangelico truffles ("Hazelnut interior with milk chocolate coating, sprinkled with nougat") and cute little chocolate lizards, I tried to remember what Joe had said when he had talked to Stacy. And he'd said nothing. Just that he was going to be tied up that evening. But why had he turned off his cell phone? Where was he?

As the rush began to clear, I looked across the street at Joe's mom's office. There was a light. So, as soon as the front counter was down to two groups of customers, I went into the office and called her. Maybe Joe had told her where he was going.

But she said he hadn't. "I haven't talked to him since this morning, Lee. He called and told me not to use his landline. Do you know what all that was about?"

"It's a long story." I hesitated. "Mercy, I think I've figured out who killed Hershel Perkins. And I think Joe is next on the list. I've tried every way I know to reach Chief Jones, and I can't find him either. I've simply got to find Joe and warn him. Do you have any ideas?"

I'd been counting on Mercy not to panic, and she didn't. "Actually, he could be out at the shop. If he turned the cell phone off . . . Or he might have left a note on his calendar. Something simple like that."

Or he could be lying out there in a pool of blood. Mercy's idea made sense. "I'll go see if he's there," I said.

"We'll both go. I'll pick you up." Mercy hung up.

I once again ran off and left Tracy and Stacy with the shop. By now it was nearly nine, close to closing time. I didn't give them any explanation, and they both looked amazed, but I grabbed my purse and ran out the front door, still wearing my flip-flops, long skirt, and jacket.

Mercy and I didn't talk as we drove out to Joe's shop. About halfway there I suddenly fantasized that he might have another woman out there. That would certainly be an explanation of why he was "tied up all evening." And it might explain why he'd turned off the cell phone.

I could be headed toward an end to our relationship. But I was so worried about his safety that I didn't care.

It was not yet dark. In June in southwest Michigan the sun doesn't set until after nine-thirty, another situation that amazes the Texan in me. Somehow it doesn't seem decent for the sun to stay up that late.

I felt a wave of relief when we pulled into Joe's parking area, and I saw his pickup in its usual spot. But all the doors to the shop were closed, and the place looked deserted. The sedan was not tied up at the dock. Mercy and I got out and pounded on the door. Nobody answered our summons.

We spoke to each other almost in unison. "Do you have a key?"

Then we both sighed and did our unison act again. "No."

"I'll get the one from behind the downspout," I said.

The key container was very low down and flat against the steel building. I waved the box at Mercy, then came back to the door. The key worked immediately.

It might not have been dark outside, but inside the shop was like the old Smothers Brothers song which describes falling into a vat of chocolate. Dark chocolate. The only windows are in the office and in Joe's one-room apartment, and the doors to both places were closed.

I felt for the switch beside the door. As the banks of fluorescent lights flashed on, I called out, "Joe!"

My voice reverberated around the big steel building. I went first to the office, then to Joe's apartment, opening the doors and calling out. No answer. Both rooms were empty.

When I came out of the apartment, Mercy was in the office. She pointed to the desk. "What's this about?"

On the desk was a tape recorder. It was sitting next to the telephone. A long cord went from it to a round rubber deal that was attached to the side of the phone.

I'd seen a similar setup. "It's a microphone," I said. "At one of the office jobs I had I used one of those to record reports the salesmen called in."

"A bug?"

"You could use it that way. But it's usually used to record your own calls."

Mercy reached for the tape recorder and flipped the lid open. A tape was inside. "Maybe this will tell us something," she said.

She rewound the tape, then hit the "play" button.

"Hello." Joe's voice began.

"Listen, Joe, we need to talk. You've figured out that I'm involved in this Root Beer Barrel deal, haven't you?"

"I was beginning to get that idea."

"I suppose you found my link to Tom Johnson."

"It wasn't too hard."

"I can explain all that. But I don't want to do it on the telephone. Can you meet me at Gray Gables?"

"Why there?"

"Because it will be completely private. I'm in Grand Rapids, and I won't be back until around nine. I've got to go over there this evening. We'll be able to hash the whole thing out."

"Around nine?"

"I'll leave the gate unlocked for you."

"Don't bother. I'll come in the boat."

The call ended. Mercy and I were staring at each other wide-eyed.

She spoke first. "That was Trey's voice!"

"My God!" I said. "Joe's agreed to meet the murderer all alone and on his own turf! We've got to stop him."

Chapter 20

Neither Mercy nor I is the type to stand around wringing our hands. She headed for the door, and I beat her to it. The only reason I was there first was because Mercy had whipped a cell phone out of her purse and was talking as we ran.

"Mike! Mike! Emergency!" she was saying.

She was jamming the cell phone back in the purse as we got to the door. Luckily that door had an automatic lock. We ran for her car so fast that we would have left it standing open.

"Mike can track down Chief Jones if anybody can," she said. "But he didn't pick up his cell phone. Let's head for city hall. You drive. I'll keep phoning."

"There's nobody at city hall tonight, is there? I called and got the county operator."

"The local dispatcher must have been on her dinner break."

Mercy handed me her keys, and I got behind the wheel of her car. I burned rubber getting out of there. Mercy—proving herself a real insurance woman—dug a phone book out of the back seat and began calling Mike Herrera's restaurants. He wasn't at Herrera's. He wasn't at Mike's Sidewalk Café. He wasn't at the Waterside. By the time she'd screamed "Emergency!" and her cell phone number at someone at each restaurant, we were at city hall. I skidded into a parking spot normally reserved for one of the Warner Pier patrol cars, and we both jumped out. Mercy ran to the side door and began to pound on it. I could see the dispatcher jumping to her feet inside.

"You tell her what's happened," I said. "I'm going to try something else."

I turned and ran down the street, flipping and flopping in those darn rubber beach sandals toward the alley behind TenHuis Chocolade. If Trey was at Gray Gables, I believed that I would be able to get inside.

I rushed to my van, flipped the rear door up, and scrabbled through the stuff I'd tossed in over the weeks and months. I might be determined to face down a murderer, but I didn't want to do it without a weapon of some sort. But I couldn't think of anything lethal in my van.

To my surprise, over in one corner I found a lucky stone, one of the ones I'd found in May when Joe and I picnicked. The average lucky stone, I'd guess, weighs three ounces; they're usually pretty small. But this was one of the atypical ones—a three-pound number, even bigger than the one we'd left beside Joe's shop, the one Trey had used to kill Hershel. And I found a chamois my father had given me for washing the van.

I wrapped the lucky stone in the chamois and put the improvised weapon in my purse. It seemed to be poetic justice. I was quite prepared to kill Trey Corbett with the same sort of weapon he'd used on Hershel.

I had just started the van when Aunt Nettie appeared in the back door of the shop.

"Lee!"

I punched the button that lowered the passenger-side window. "I can't talk! Got to go! Joe's in trouble!"

I backed out and drove away wondering why she'd come back to the shop. There was no way she could know about Joe being in danger. I could have used help, true, but I didn't want to involve Aunt Nettie. She's not frail; she's stronger and healthier than I am. But despite the rock, I didn't intend to use violence on Trey. I intended to use guile to distract him, to keep him from harming Joe until Mercy could get the police there. I didn't see how Aunt Nettie could fit into this plan.

I would simply go to the gate of the estate, then honk my horn to attract attention. I'd claim that I had found out that Joe was, after all, able to make the tour of Gray Gables, so I'd decided to join the two of them.

The big risk was that Trey would kill Joe as soon as he got there. I pushed that possibility into my subconscious.

My plan, like most of the ones I make, fell apart almost immediately. When I got to Gray Gables, the gate was locked, as I'd expected. But when I honked, nothing happened.

I could see that same corner of the house through the trees. But I sat there honking while the hands of my watch whirled through six minutes, and no one came to the gate. No Trey came walking or driving up the drive to the gate. Nothing. Gray Gables, for all intents, was deserted.

Well, if I couldn't get in through the gate, I'd have to do it another way. I backed up, then turned, backed, and turned. After doing this several times, I managed to get the van sideways in the drive, almost touching the gate. I'd climb on the top of the van and get over that way.

But when I opened the door and got out of the van—I'd decided to use the back seat as a ladder—a voice boomed out of bushes.

"Ms. McKinney! What in the world are you doing?"

I nearly fell flat on my flitter. Then I realized it was Dolly Jolly—all six feet three or four inches and 250 pounds of her. Well, of course. She'd heard me honking, even if Trey hadn't.

And I also realized she might tell me how to get into Gray Gables without risking my neck by tumbling over that wrought-iron gate. Dolly Jolly lived in a cottage that was almost on the grounds of Gray Gables. I couldn't believe she wouldn't have peeked inside the property. Maybe she would help me.

"Dolly! I've got to get into Gray Gables. Can you show me a back way?"

She frowned. "I think they keep the gate locked because they want to keep people out!"

"It's a matter of life and death!"

She lowered her voice to a dull roar that she probably intended as a whisper. "There's something going on over there tonight. Better stay away."

"No! That's what I'm afraid of. Oh, God, it's too long a story, but my boyfriend's been lured over there by a killer! The police are on the way, but Joe doesn't know he's in danger and I've got to warn him!"

I realized I had closed in on Dolly and I was gripping her arm. I tried to back off. "Please. It's really important."

Dolly sighed. "Well, if you've called the police . . . I guess I could go over there with you. Keep an eye on things."

"Anything! But I've got to get in."

"There's a better way than climbing over the gate." She led me through the bushes, down the path that she'd used to confront Lindy and me. The sun was nearly down to the horizon—miles away over Lake Michigan—and the woods were growing dark. I glimpsed a simple little house, but Dolly walked past it, following a path that led back toward the left. "There's a gap in the fence," she said. She was still trying to talk quietly. "Probably something to do with the hobo jungle!"

We got through a line of shrubs and came to a high, chain-link fence. Then we turned right and followed the fence. I don't know how far we went, but she suddenly grasped the woven wire and pulled it back. We'd come to the gap. I went through the fence, then pushed at the wire to keep the gap open for Dolly. Inside the fence was more undergrowth, but there was definitely a path. And after twenty or twenty-five steps, we came to a cleared area with large trees here and there. The giant house—three stories of turrets, gables, and porches—loomed between us and the river. The last rays of the sun were slicing through the trees, but the half-mile of woods between the mansion and the lake meant that we were in heavy shade. Inside the house, it would have been dark. And there were no lights in any of the windows.

I whispered. "They've simply got to be there."

"Let's go around the house," Dolly said. She really was speaking quietly now.

We turned left and circled the house. There was a sidewalk, but we stayed away from it, keeping our distance from the structure. When we rounded the end, we saw the broad lawn leading down to the river. But that side of the house was dark, too, and no doors were open. The whole area was quiet. We could hear a motorboat down on the river, but nothing any closer made a sound.

Had I been wrong? Was Joe not there? Or had Trey already attacked him? Killed him? Dumped him in the river? I shivered all over. Then I pointed. "There's a car!"

It was Trey's SUV. It was parked about a hundred yards away, close to a long wooden shed. The shed, I realized in a minute, was down by the river.

"It's by the boathouse," Dolly said.

"Of course! Joe came in his boat."

To my relief I saw that the structure she described as the boathouse had no windows on the side facing us. I began to run toward it, realizing that people inside would not be able to see me approaching unless they came outside. Dolly Jolly followed me, also running. Two big, tall women jogging down the lawn.

When we got near the boathouse, I slowed down and tiptoed. After a few more steps I could hear voices. Just a murmur, but two men were talking. I moved closer, planting my feet firmly, daring those darn sandals to make a flip or a flop.

The boathouse was an old wooden building, more of a work shed for storing boats in the winter than a place for them to be tied up. I couldn't see that any boats were around. Probably the building was open on the other side, with a dock going out into the water.

I was concentrating so hard on being quiet that a sudden thud made me jump and whirl around. It was a car door slamming, up near the road.

Dolly had turned toward it, too. I leaned close to her. "Maybe it's the cops," I said. "Can you go back and let them in?" She hesitated. "Please."

She nodded and started back up the lawn, walking fast, but obviously trying to keep quiet.

I went around the corner of the boathouse, looking for an entrance. I found a door, and I touched the handle. It moved. I was able to crack the door—just slightly. I got ready to do my act: Throw the door open and walk in demanding a tour.

Then I heard Joe's voice.

"I think I've earned a cut," he said. "I don't know why everybody in Warner Pier thinks I'm not interested in money. I am."

"You could have made a lot more practicing law than you're likely to re-pairing boats." It was Trey's voice.

"Yeah, and be stuck in an office in a suit my whole life. Having to kow-tow to the client. You don't like that. Why should I? But I don't object to making money. I like to think I'm not greedy, but I don't see why I shouldn't get in on this sweet deal you've come up with."

A cut? A deal? What was Joe talking about? I peeked through the crack, but I couldn't see anything but a bunch of junk. I saw weathered oars, rusty fishing tackle boxes, a couple of antique wooden barrels, scrap wood, tangled wire—just general trash. But there was no sign of either Joe or Trey.

I looked around the outside of the building, and I spotted a window. It was about six feet farther down the wall and rather high. But it wasn't too high for a tall woman to look through. I stood on tiptoe and looked inside. Now I could see that the shed really was a boathouse. The opposite end was open to the river, and I could even see Joe's sedan tied up just outside. I could see Joe and Trey, too. They were standing inside the door I'd been peeking through. If I had looked in the door, they definitely would have seen me.

Joe spoke again. "Anyway, Trey, I ought to thank you for pulling the Root Beer Barrel down. It needed to be done, and I wouldn't have known how to do it."

"That was easy. I just put a rope around it, borrowed a big truck, and pulled."

"How did Hershel get involved?"

Trey laughed. It wasn't a pleasant sound. "Stupid jerk! He was always prowling around."

"I guess you told him I did it."

"I didn't have to. He came to me, told me about seeing the truck over there, then seeing the Barrel go down. It mystified the poor jerk. All I had to do was point out that it was going to be a lot easier for the property owner to redevelop that lot if an Act of God got rid of the Barrel."

"But you didn't like it when he accused me—to my face—of pulling it down."

"As long as you thought it blew down—well, you were doing exactly what I needed done. If you got too curious, I didn't know what would happen."

Joe's voice became cold. "I ought to punch you until your teeth rattle, Trey. There was no need to try to kill me. And Lee!"

"Oh, those weren't serious attempts, Joe." Like heck, I thought, remembering that cold swim and that scary ride in Joe's pickup. "I just wanted to distract you."

"Well, I didn't appreciate it—whatever you had in mind. So I don't expect us to become close friends over this, Trey. But there's no reason we can't be business partners. What are you planning to do with that strip, anyway?"

"What do you mean?"

"Today I talked to the people who own the DeBoer House and the Old English Motel. Tom Johnson is dealing with them, too. That's nearly a city block long. You've obviously got bigger plans than some little restaurant or motel on the site of the Root Beer Barrel."

It took all my self-control to keep from going to the door, throwing it open, striding inside, and telling Joe just what Trey's plan was. But I didn't understand the conversation I was hearing. Joe was trying to cut himself in on the deal? He didn't mind making money? That was probably true, but he certainly hadn't talked to me like that. I didn't want to believe that Joe would go along with anything crooked, and what Trey had done—pulling down the Root Beer Barrel—was illegal. Killing Hershel was even more illegal. But now Joe was proposing to participate in whatever Trey was up to. I was more confused with each word I heard from Joe.

But it was Trey's next words that really caught me by surprise.

"We can go into the details later. And we might be able to work out some kind of a deal, but if we do, there's one perk you're not going to get. From now on, you're going to stay away from my wife."

Chapter 21

I gasped, but luckily Joe gasped even louder, hiding the noise I'd made. Then he laughed.

"Maggie Mae—I mean, Meg—is a very pretty woman. But if you think we're fooling around, you've got it all wrong."

"You dated her."

"When I was seventeen! She was sixteen. It's ancient history. I hadn't seen her again until you two moved back to Warner Pier. Then maybe we'd see each other in the checkout line at the Superette. I've never even been alone with her since we got out of high school. Fifteen years!"

"She said she slept with you."

Joe was silent a minute. "I don't know why she'd tell you that."

"Because I asked her!" Trey yelled it out.

Joe yelled his answer. "Then you're dumber than you have a right to be!"

I expected that Trey would yell back and that the argument would escalate. It didn't worry me too much; I was sure that if it came to a fight Joe could turn Trey inside out.

But that's not what happened. Instead, Trey gulped three times. I could see his Adam's apple move up and down as he swallowed his anger. Then the one eye I could see narrowed craftily and he spoke. "Maybe I overreacted. Maybe she was teasing me."

"That's got to be the answer, Trey. There's nothing between Meg and me."

Trey nodded. "But you asked about what I planned for the Lake Shore Drive site. Let me show you."

Had he brought the drawing here? To the boathouse? I watched as Trey turned and gestured toward a large table behind him. The table was covered with a sheet, which he carefully removed, folding it and laying it aside.

And there, displayed under the bare bulbs of the boathouse, was a four-foot-long model of the structure I'd seen in the drawing—the beautiful Victorian resort hotel.

It incorporated the Old English Motel in the form of a mock Victorian village, and it used the DeBoer House as the main hotel. But there were no remains of the old Root Beer Barrel in between. On the model the motel and the historic home were linked by picturesque cottages. A swimming pool and elaborate landscaping completed the model.

The old Root Beer Barrel would definitely not have fit in.

Joe whistled. "Wow! What a layout." He leaned over, concentrating on the model.

Trey leaned over, too, and to Joe it probably seemed that he was also admiring his model. But I could see his right hand. I could see it move behind the table's leg and bring out a metal bar. I caught a glimpse of the split end, and I recognized it. It was a small crowbar.

Trey did not need a small crowbar to show Joe a model of a resort hotel. He definitely had another plan for the tool. I reached into my purse and grasped my own weapon, the lucky stone wrapped in a chamois.

Trey straightened up, but I didn't wait for him to hit Joe with the crowbar. I yanked out my improvised sling—sending my purse flying—and I smashed the window I was looking through.

Then I began to yell, and I ran for the door, hoping the smash and noise would distract Trey from his attack on Joe.

I plunged through the door and into the harsh light of the boathouse.

Trey was gawking over his shoulder, looking toward the window, but Joe had already taken action. He was reaching for Trey's hand, the hand that held the crowbar.

Then—well, all hell broke loose.

A tarp in the back seat of Joe's sedan lurched as if a small earthquake had hit it. It was thrown back and Jerry Cherry popped up. The boat rocked wildly as he scrambled onto the dock.

Footsteps pounded outside the boathouse, the door I'd come in was smashed back against the wall, and a whole crowd ran in. I was so confused I could barely identify them as Mercy Woodyard, Mike Herrera, Dolly Jolly, and Aunt Nettie.

Then a loudspeaker started booming. "This is the police! Put down your weapons! Come out with your hands raised!"

The boathouse wasn't really big enough for all this activity. Especially since Joe and Trey were now having a wrestling match under the table that held the model. I danced around, trying to get a chance to use my lucky-stone sling—rather hard to do when your intended target is under a table.

Mercy was yelling, and she and Mike fell to their knees. Each of them grabbed for one of Trey's flailing feet. But the feet were flailing too hard; they couldn't catch hold of them.

Then Joe rolled on top of Trey, and the two of them hit the table leg. The table jumped and the model went flying. Trey screamed like a wounded she-bear. They rolled again, this time out from under the table. I began to swing my weapon, something like little David getting ready for Goliath, but I was afraid I'd hit Joe. So I just kept swinging it around.

Joe and Trey flipped one more time, and this time they were close to the water. I thought both of them were going to go in, right between the dock and the sedan.

And finally—finally—Jerry Cherry was able to get through the crowd and grab Trey. He and Joe wrestled Trey face down onto the dock. He couldn't move, though his feet were still flailing.

Dolly poked her head over my shoulder. "Do you want me to sit on him?" she said.

"Nah," the voice came from the darkness. "I think we can manage now."

Chief Hogan Jones and the other two members of the Warner Pier Police Force came in through a door near the open end of the boathouse.

Then all of us—Joe, Jerry, Chief Jones, Mercy, Mike, Dolly, Aunt Nettie, and me—said the same thing, in unison.

"What are you doing here?"

By the time Chief Jones and Jerry Cherry had Trey handcuffed, and Chief Jones had sent one of the patrol officers for a car to come and get him, we'd begun to sort it out. Apparently three separate groups had decided Joe needed rescuing and had taken on the job.

Aunt Nettie was the one who mystified me. "How did you get involved?" I asked her. "What were you doing at the shop? I thought you were safely home in bed."

"Stacy called me," she said. "She said you had gone tearing out of there with Mercy. She and Tracy overheard you leaving a message for Chief Jones. She thought I'd like to know."

"I don't know if I should be mad at her or at you."

"All's well, Lee. Joe's okay, and I guess Hogan got the goods on Trey Corbett."

Joe joined the conversation then. "That's what I'm afraid isn't true," he said. He unbuttoned his shirt and pulled something electronic out.

I stared, then realized what it must be. "You were wired!"

"Yeah, yeah. It's certainly reassuring to know that my nearest and dearest friends and relatives—my girlfriend, my mom—all thought I was dumb enough to have a one-on-one meeting in a secluded spot with a murderer."

"That's why you kept asking Trey to cut you in on the deal!"

"You heard that? Chief Jones and I were trying to get him to admit he killed Hershel."

"So the whole thing is on tape."

"Not that it's going to do much good." Joe looked at the chief.

Hogan Jones frowned. "We can get him for the attacks on you and Lee."

"But doesn't that prove he killed Hershel?" I said.

The chief and Joe shook their heads in unison. "Nope," Joe said. "If I were still a defense attorney, I'd have a great time with that recording. All it does is establish me as a crook."

"And now," Chief Jones said. "I'd appreciate all of you stepping outside. I have permission from Jim Corbett, the owner of this property, to search. Trey was apparently using this building for the projects he wanted to keep quiet, and there's always the possibility we will find some evidence that Hershel was here. Not that it will do much good."

Mercy spoke that time. "Why not? If you can prove Hershel was here . . ."

"It won't prove a thing," Joe said. "He probably had been here. It's established that Hershel followed Trey around. Even if the chief finds Hershel's fingerprints on every inch of this boathouse, it won't prove he was here the night he was killed."

I was feeling extremely dispirited as I turned to follow the group outside. We picked our way through all the junk carefully, but it was too late. We'd had good intentions, but we'd definitely contaminated the crime scene.

It was Mike Herrera who stumbled and kicked the trash basket over. Sawdust, hunks of plastic, paint cans, scrap wood—everything dumped out in a heap on the floor.

Mike growled and leaned down as if he were going to scoop it all back up.

"Leave it!" The chief's voice was sharp. "We'd have to go through that basket anyway."

But Aunt Nettie had already leaned over. "Oh, look," she said. "A Ten-Huis box."

And there, covered with sawdust, was a white box tied with a blue ribbon. I didn't need to see the snazzy sans serif type in the corner to recognize it. It was the kind of a box we use for a pound of chocolates. Or for a fancy molded chocolate item.

"Chief!" I almost jumped up and down. "If there's a bog in that fox it will prove Hershel was here the night he disappeared! I mean, a frog! In the box!"

"Oh, yes!" Aunt Nettie said. She looked nearly as excited as I did. "Hershel bought one of our eight-ounce white chocolate frogs the afternoon he disappeared. I packed it for him personally—in a box just like that one. It's the only one we've sold so far. If that's the frog . . ."

Chief Jones knelt and looked at the box. "Let's get some photos before we look inside," he said.

He motioned all of us non-lawmen on out the door. We stood around, talking excitedly. Through the door we'd come out, we could see flashbulbs now and then. But it was nearly ten minutes before the chief came out, carrying a brown paper sack.

"I guess I'll never get all of you to go home unless you see what was in the box," he said. He spread the top of the sack open, and held it out at arm's length. "Nettie, we'll let you peek first."

I knew what it was as soon as I saw her face, but my heart was pounding as I took the second peek.

Nestled inside the box, wrapped in tissue paper, was a big white chocolate frog with dark chocolate spots on his back.

"Yee-haw!" I said.

It's hard to do a group hug when you're jumping up and down, but we managed.

Chapter 22

There's one nice thing about hanging out with foodies. First, Aunt Nettie insisted that everybody come by TenHuis Chocolade for a talk session and some chocolate, and Mike immediately said he'd bring coffee. Nobody said no. Aunt Nettie, Mercy, Mike, Dolly Jolly, Joe, and I all met in our break room. Mike brought two party-sized Thermoses of coffee and a bottle of brandy. Nobody said no to that, either.

After Aunt Nettie had served up a plate of truffles, bonbons, and solid chocolate—but no chocolate frogs—Joe wanted to know how I figured out Trey was the bad guy, and I wanted to know how he and Chief Jones figured it out.

Joe took an Italian cherry bonbon ("Amareena cherry in syrup and white chocolate cream") and started talking. "You remember I was going to ask a few questions about Tom Johnson? I turned my pal Webb Bartlett loose on the project."

Webb Bartlett is a law school buddy of Joe's who practices in Grand Rapids. He's one of those people who knows practically everybody in the world and if he doesn't know them, he know somebody else who does.

"Webb discovered Tom had been involved with a crooked developer who had conned a Grand Rapids architect. Webb knew the architect, so he called him and found out Trey used to work for his firm. And yes, Trey had been around when the architect got involved with Tom Johnson. So Trey had known Tom. That established a link. The chief had thought all along that Trey's story about being sideswiped by that black panel truck sounded fishy. Besides, another witness you and I didn't know about . . ."—Was it my imagination, or did Dolly Jolly's natural ruddiness grow even redder?— "had seen something that involved Trey. So I was able to convince Chief Jones that Tom Johnson was probably fronting for Trey, who must be the actual buyer for the old Root Beer Barrel property."

"But why couldn't Trey simply buy the property in the regular way?"

"Because he sat on the Historic District Commission."

"That doesn't mean he can't own and develop property in Warner Pier."

"No, but it does mean he's not supposed to vote on issues he's person-ally involved in. And he wanted to vote on demolishing the old Root Beer Barrel. So he had to make it appear that he had the idea for the resort and bought the property after—*after*—the Barrel had been torn down. Plus, Trey must have had money problems. I've gathered that he's a sort of poor rela-tion to the wealthy side of the Corbett family. Buying a whole block of lake-front property would take a bundle of money. Maybe two bundles. He didn't have it."

"He'd have to have major financing to get that much money together," I said. "He couldn't do it without bringing in partners."

"I don't think Trey wanted partners. From what Webb picked up from Trey's former boss, he fired Trey because Trey's not a team player. He's the kind of architect who wants to make all the decisions on a project. He didn't want to build buildings that suited the client—the kind that architects actu-ally get paid for."

"That fits with what Frank Waterloo said about him," I said. "Trey made all the decisions on their renovation—just let Patsy make the 'final choice' on the wallpaper." Since I had the floor, I described finding the elevation showing Trey's plan for the site and how I had later recognized the site after I got a look at the DeBoer House.

"Meg nearly had a fit when she realized I'd seen the drawing," I said. "At the time I didn't understand why. I'm guessing that Trey figured out the justification—I mean, juxtaposition!—the relationship of the Old English Motel and the DeBoer House, and he saw the potential for the site to be-come a re-creation of a turn of the twentieth-century resort. But the Root Beer Barrel was 1940s commercial. It didn't fit in with his ideas."

"He'd been urging me to petition the commission for permission to take the Barrel down," Joe said. "If I had, then my guess is he would have backed the idea and voted for it. Then he would have 'discovered' the site's potential and bought it. But he was probably afraid someone was going to beat him to the property. Maybe the high winds in that last winter storm gave him the idea. I think he simply saw a chance to take a shortcut, get rid of the Barrel faster than he could legally. So he must have borrowed a heavy truck from some of his builder pals, then gone over there and pulled the old Barrel down.

"Unfortunately, Hershel saw what happened. He probably didn't see who was in the truck, but he mentioned it to Trey. Trey let him think I had done it. But I knew I hadn't. If Hershel had accused me to my face—an event that became more and more likely as Hershel kept sulking about the situation—I was going to deny it. Then I might actually quiz Hershel, might figure out someone really had pulled the Barrel down. If it got out that Trey, a member of the Historic District Commission, had illegally torn a building down—well, the fine wouldn't be much, but it would pretty well finish his business in Warner Pier."

"So Trey decided to kill Hershel," I said.

"Right." Joe reached for a Bailey's Irish Cream bonbon ("Classic cream liqueur interior"). "And let's get one thing straight. We're talking murder in the first degree here. This was no crime of impulse. Trey had to set up his own alibis. Remember how he kept telling everybody he'd been working on the fireplace at the Miller cottage, even if we didn't ask where he'd been? He had to call me, pretend to be a potential boat buyer, and send me on a wild goose chase up to Saugatuck. He had to cut my phone line, so that nobody could just happen to call me at a moment that would have been inconvenient for him. Sometime in there he stole that lucky stone he used to kill Hershel from outside the shop. I can't swear he took the shop rag from my box of rags, because they're too common. But that would have been easy to do."

"One thing really puzzles me," I said. "Did Trey first cut your phone line, then tap it? Frankly, that doesn't make a lot of sense."

"It puzzles me, too. I wonder if he didn't do it the other way around—maybe it's been tapped for a long time."

"Why?" Mercy asked.

"Apparently Trey had gotten the idea that Meg was seeing another man. I suspect that he was checking to see if she and I had revived our teenaged affair." Joe took my hand. "I'm happy to say, first, we hadn't, and second, neither Lee nor I like to talk dirty on the phone."

We all laughed, but the idea of Trey listening in on our calls was—well, nasty. I took the taste out of my mouth with a sip of brandy and a mocha pyramid.

"I wonder if he didn't even goad Hershel into attacking you at the post office," I said. "If he was already determined to frame you . . . You wouldn't have been such a ready-made suspect if it weren't for that little set-to."

"Unless Trey tells us, we'll never know the answer to that one," Joe said.

I went on. "But whose boat did he use to run the *Toadfrog* down? His boat, the *Nutmeg,* is too small. Plus, it would have left evidence."

Joe shook his head. "I always thought running down Hershel's canoe was an awfully iffy way to kill him, and I don't believe it happened that way."

"What do you think happened?"

"I've suggested to Chief Jones that the state police crime lab people look around outside at Gray Gables. If I were going to make a canoe look as if it had been hit by a bigger boat, I'd simply put it up against some sort of pole—on a tennis court, maybe, or a flagpole—tie a rope around it lengthwise and attach the rope to my pickup. Then I'd pull. Those aluminum canoes are not exactly battleships."

"That's almost exactly what he did!" We all jumped as Dolly Jolly's voice boomed out.

"Oh!" I said. "The chief told me that you saw more than you realized. Was that what you saw?"

"Didn't see him bending the canoe! Saw him dragging it up onto the lawn!" She turned to Joe. "He painted a board red and nailed it to a tree!"

"Sure! He needed paint that would match the runabout. That makes perfect sense."

Dolly Jolly cleared her throat. She helped herself to an amaretto truffle ("Milk chocolate interior flavored with almond liqueur"). "Don't want all of you to think I'm just a snoop! The owners of Gray Gables—cousins of this Trey Corbett—they asked me to look around, keep an eye on the property! Think they realized he'd been using the boathouse for some private project. One reason they rented me the old cottage!"

We all nodded wisely. It seemed logical that Trey's relatives would have been suspicious.

"Meanwhile," I said, "I guess Trey lured Hershel to Gray Gables, hit him in the head, and left him unconscious. He must have planned to throw him in the water and leave him to drown."

"Yeah," Joe said. "He'd already sent me off to Saugatuck so I wouldn't have an alibi. But Hershel must have come to and staggered off. As I understand head injuries, Hershel may not have remembered what happened to him, but he probably knew it was something bad. But this was Hershel, who wasn't always logical even when he hadn't been hit in the head. Instead of calling an ambulance or the cops or going to Ms. Jolly's house for help, he got across the river somehow. Maybe just walked across on the Haven Road bridge. He was probably headed for the old chapel."

"Which," I said, "Patsy said he regarded as a refuge."

"Right," Joe said. "He hid in the woods around the chapel, then tried to get hold of Nettie, because he trusted her."

Aunt Nettie shook her head sadly. "But Trey found him before Lee and I did."

Joe went on. "Trey knew that Hershel saw the old chapel as a hideout. He'd probably been looking for him there ever since Hershel disappeared. He might not have been too worried about him being found alive. People wouldn't believe anything Hershel said."

The party broke up not too long after that. There were ramifications afterward, of course.

First, Meg left town that night, and as far as I know has never been seen in Warner Pier again. I now believe she told Trey she'd had an affair with Joe to make her husband jealous. That would be in line with the "tricky" philosophy she told me was the best way to deal with men.

She obviously knew about Trey's plan to build the snazzy resort hotel; I've always suspected he came up with the project because Meg wanted him to make some real money. But Trey denied she was involved in the murder and the murderous attacks on Joe and me, so she got away. If the Corbett family helped her or Trey, they didn't do it publicly.

As for her relationship with Joe when they were in high school, Joe asked me if I wanted to know more, and I declined. We've never mentioned Meg again, and I don't plan to bring her up. I hope I'm not as stupid as Trey.

Dolly Jolly came by TenHuis Chocolade a few days later and asked if the apartment over Aunt Nettie's shop would be available for rent the next fall.

"I don't usually rent it in the winter," Aunt Nettie said.

"I've decided to stay in Warner Pier year round!" Dolly said. "Living over a chocolate factory sure would smell good! Hope to find a job!"

"What kind of job are you interested in?"

"Food! Food-related!"

So that situation looks interesting.

A week after Trey was arrested a house painter named John Adolph called the county sheriff to report that someone had broken into his storage building and stolen his black Dodge panel truck. He'd been on vacation and had just missed it. Why, yes, he said, he had done several painting jobs for Trey Corbett's projects, and, yes, Trey was familiar with his workshop and knew where he stored his equipment. The panel truck turned up late the next October, after the leaves began to fall, in a ravine about a mile from Gray Gables. Fake numbers had been painted on its tag, with the zeros turned into eights.

As for Frank and Patsy, they're still together. If he's drinking and staying out nights, Greg Glossop hasn't spread the word yet.

Joe says he suspected that Frank had been mishandling Hershel's trust. When the final accounting was made the judge asked some pointed questions—or so Joe heard over at the courthouse. But in the end Frank wasn't accused of any misdeeds.

But all that was later. The big discussion between Joe and me came the night Trey was arrested. I'd stayed to lock the shop up after our little chocolate-coffee-brandy gathering. Joe stayed, too, because he'd left his boat at Gray Gables, and he needed a ride home.

As Mike went out the front door, he clapped Joe on the shoulder and said, "I am relieved to have this settled. Now we'll put our discussion item back on the workshop agenda. Ten a.m. Wednesday. City Hall."

Joe just nodded, but I stopped Mike. "What are you all conspicuous about? I mean, conspiring! What are you conspiring about?"

Mike grinned happily. "Lee, you're so funny!" Then he spoke to Joe. "I guess you keep her around for laughs, right?"

"Actually," Joe said, "she never does that when we're alone." Then Mike left, and I locked the front door.

While I was locking up I realized that Joe had spoken the truth. I rarely made my verbal gaffs when he and I were by ourselves. Why was that?

I didn't try to answer my own question. I wanted to ask Joe about this "agenda item" Mike had mentioned. Joe had gone out the alley door and was standing between my van and our Dumpster.

I followed him out into the alley and locked the door. Then I demanded an explanation. "Joe, what are you and Mike up to?"

"Up to?"

"Don't act innocent. He's made several references to this mysterious 'agenda item,' and you even called him once and talked about it."

"Oh. That."

"Yes. That. What's going on?"

"Warner Pier has never had a city attorney. They just hire somebody if they need legal counsel. Now Mike's going to recommend that they put someone on retainer. Just part-time. I'm going to apply for the job. But Hershel's death put a crimp in our plans. They couldn't hire me if I was involved with a crime."

"But you said you never wanted to practice law again. You gave me all this stuff about the sanctity of craftsmanship and the morality of boat restoration."

Joe laughed. "I'm trying to have my craftsmanship and eat it, too. Warner Pier isn't exactly swamped with legal problems. I think I can read over the contracts and warn the city councillors that they're about to break the law without giving up Vintage Boats."

"I don't like that. You're already handling two full-time jobs—winding up the Ripley estate and the boat shop. Now you're going to take on another job part-time?"

"The problem with the two jobs I have now is that neither of them pays on a regular basis. The boats pay when you finish a job or when you sell a boat. The Ripley estate, as you know, doesn't pay at all, since I'm still determined not to take any money on that deal. Oh, I'm keeping track of my expenses—lunch, mileage, phone calls. But my real aim is to get the estate in good enough shape that I can give the Warner Point property to the city."

He tugged at my hand until I was facing him. "Don't tell anyone that, okay? Not even Mike. I may not be able to work it out, so I can't make a commitment."

"Did anybody ever tell you you're an awfully nice guy?"

"I'm a guy who feels guilty. The city should have had that property all along. In a way, I was responsible for Clementine's deciding to build a summer place here and snagging the property out from under Mike's nose. It's simply a matter of justice. But her estate is so far in debt I may not be able to bring it off. I've had one offer, and I may yet have to sell it. So please don't say anything."

I kissed him. He kissed me back. After a few moments of this, he spoke. Actually, he swore.

"Dammit! I went to a lot of trouble—moonlight boat rides, trips up the river for dinner—so we could have this conversation in a romantic setting. And we wind up having it leaning on a Dumpster!"

I laughed. "I don't see anything particularly romantic about your taking a third job. I barely fit into your schedule as it is."

"The point of the city job is really you."

"Why?"

"You've made me realize that I don't want to live in one room in the back of a boat shop for the rest of my life. I might even want to get married."

"Oh." I gulped.

"Or I might if I could interest the right person," Joe said.

"You probably could," I said. "But people who've made one bad decision are sometimes scared of making another."

"Are you scared?"

"I don't pull my malapropisms when we're alone. Maybe that means I feel safe. Are you scared?"

"Terrified. I'm scared of losing you." He kissed me again. "We don't have to rush into anything, but I don't want to wait forever."

"No," I said. "Not forever."

CHOCOLATE CHAT

DUTCHING LEADS TO CHOCOLATE BARS

- Dutch chocolate maker Coenraad Johannes van Houten revolutionized the drinking of chocolate. Van Houten invented what Americans call cocoa, patenting his process in 1826.

- Van Houten first used a hydraulic press to reduce the percentage of cacao fat in his product. The resulting powder was then treated with alkaline salts, a process known as "Dutching." This improves its ability to be mixed, though it does not make it dissolve more easily.

- Van Houten's new process meant the old thick beverage, which required frequent stirring, was now much easier to prepare and only needed to be stirred now and then. His process also meant that cocoa and chocolate could now be produced on a large scale. Chocolate was no longer the elite, expensive drink and food it had been.

- In 1847 the British firm of J S Fry & Sons developed a method of mixing cocoa powder, sugar, and melted cacao butter into a product that could be cast in a mold.

- The chocolate bar was born, and the taste buds of chocoholics have been grateful ever since.